THE

ANNOTATED

# UNCLE TOM'S CABIN

W. W. NORTON & COMPANY

New York   London

# THE
## ANNOTATED
## UNCLE TOM'S CABIN

EDITED WITH AN INTRODUCTION AND NOTES BY

## HENRY LOUIS GATES JR.
### AND HOLLIS ROBBINS

Photos selected by Karen C. C. Dalton and Noam Biale

# HARRIET BEECHER STOWE

For information about permission to reproduce selections from this book,
write to Permissions, W. W. Norton & Company, Inc.,
500 Fifth Avenue, New York, NY 10110

Manufacturing by The Courier Companies
Book design by JAM Design
Production manager: Andrew Marasia

Library of Congress Cataloging-in-Publication Data

Stowe, Harriet Beecher, 1811–1896.
The annotated Uncle Tom's cabin / Harriet Beecher Stowe ; edited, with an
introduction and notes by Henry Louis Gates, Jr. and Hollis Robbins.—1st ed.
p. cm.
Includes bibliographical references.

ISBN-13: 978-0-393-05946-5 (hardcover)
ISBN-10: 0-393-05946-4 (hardcover)

1. Uncle Tom (Fictitious character)—Fiction. 2. Master and servant—Fiction.
3. African Americans—Fiction. 4. Fugitive slaves—Fiction. 5. Plantation life—Fiction.
6. Southern States—Fiction. 7. Slavery—Fiction. 8. Slaves—Fiction. 9. Stowe, Harriet
Beecher, 1811–1896. Uncle Tom's cabin. I. Gates, Henry Louis. II. Robbins, Hollis, 1963–
III. Title.
PS2954.U5 2006
813'.3—dc22

2005004946

W. W. Norton & Company, Inc., 500 Fifth Avenue, New York, N.Y. 10110
www.wwnorton.com

W. W. Norton & Company Ltd., Castle House, 75/76 Wells Street, London W1T 3QT

1 2 3 4 5 6 7 8 9 0

# ACKNOWLEDGMENTS

WE WOULD LIKE to thank Michael Anderson, who first came up with the idea for this project. We would also like to thank our editor at W. W. Norton, Bob Weil, for shepherding this project with an acute sense of the importance of *Uncle Tom's Cabin* historically and politically. We thank Tom Mayer for his tireless efforts in keeping us on schedule; Mary Anne Boelscevsky for her attentive and intelligent work on the early annotations; Paula Garrett for her scholarship on the importance of Stowe's editor at the *National Era*, Grace Greenwood; Tim McCarthy for his detailed response to an early draft; Abby Wolf for research assistance; and Karen C. C. Dalton and Noam Biale for their perseverance in collecting and selecting images for the volume. We would like to thank James E. Bowley, William Gleason, Eric Griffin, Evelyn B. Higginbotham, Anne MacMaster, Werner Sollors, and John Stauffer for their invaluable insights on the complexity and importance of Stowe's novel historically and culturally.

And, as always, thank you to Joanne Kendall and Michael B. Rothman.

# CONTENTS

# INTRODUCTION

[Baldwin] has relied more and more on the abstract categories of social research and less and less on the poetic insights of the creative artists. So much so that the very characteristics of protest fiction which he once deplored in the work of Harriet Beecher Stowe and Richard Wright now seem to be his stock in trade; they are in any case the things he is now world famous for. . . . Polemics, however, are not likely to be epics. They are likely to be pamphlets, even when they are disguised as stories and plays. Thus, ironically enough, Baldwin's historical role in the civil rights struggle has also been all but indistinguishable from the one played by Harriet Beecher Stowe in the Civil War. And with some of the same exasperating confusion.

—Albert Murray, *The Omni-Americans*

I FIRST ENCOUNTERED UNCLE TOM and his cabin as a child in the late 1950s, while watching the 1932 Our Gang/Little Rascals film *Spanky*, in which the Rascals put on their production of the novel. What I remember most vividly is, of all things, not Uncle Tom but Eliza, fleeing her evil pursuers by navigating ice floes (brilliantly re-created with moving crates—it was a barn-theater production, after all), Breezy playing a stunningly, hauntingly evil Simon Legree; and either Speck or Wheezer cross-dressing as Miss Ophelia. Stymie, the sole black actor, was doomed to double as both Uncle Tom and Topsy—one of the penalties of token integration in the 1930s, I suppose. But Simon Legree will always be, for me, a bearded, nasty Breezy, played by the actor Kendall McComas.

I read *Uncle Tom's Cabin* in my eighth-grade "Prose and Poetry" course in 1964; it was still probably required reading for many school children in America then. But I would be introduced to Stowe's novel again most forcefully in the latter half of that decade through the *black* public imagination, of all places. As I came of age in the militant black 1960s, my sense of the book soon became inextricably intertwined with the negative stereotype of an "Uncle Tom," the black man all too eager to please the whites around him. Accordingly, Uncle Tom became for us the most reviled figure in American literary history. He was the embodiment of "race betrayal" and an object of scorn, a scapegoat for all of our political self-doubts. He was the repository of our deepest anxieties about how our newfound opportunities created by affirmative action would affect our relationship with all those we might be leaving behind. We talked about him as *the* model to be avoided. I doubt whether anyone who tossed that epithet around during those years had actually reread Stowe's novel, or even James Baldwin's scathing 1949 critique of the novel's sentimentality, "Everybody's Protest Novel," which he had boldly linked to Richard Wright's novel *Native Son*, the text du jour of the Black Power advocates.[1] But the label "Uncle Tom" became such a potent two-word brand of impotence that nobody really cared how far the

1. James Baldwin, "Everybody's Protest Novel" (hereafter cited as EPN), in *James Baldwin: Collected Essays*, ed. T. Morrison (New York: Library of America, 1998). First published in 1949 in *Partisan Review* 16: 578–85 and reprinted in *Notes of a Native Son* (Boston: Beacon Press, 1955).

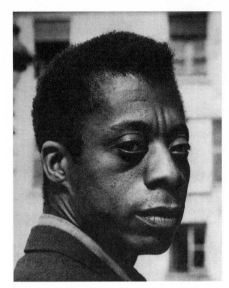

James Baldwin (1924–1987), novelist and essayist, who was elected to the National Institute of Arts and Letters, the nation's highest honor society of the arts.   Undated publicity handout photograph

public perception had traveled from the literary reality. We knew what an "Uncle Tom" was, and it was not good.

Coming to *Uncle Tom's Cabin* again in middle age, with children nearly grown and a new generation of antiwar protesters taking to the streets, I am struck by two things: the extent to which Harriet Beecher Stowe's forceful political voice is grounded in home and family and how much of the novel's sentimentality fails to mask its polymorphous sexual energy, both themes dear to James Baldwin but which, curiously, he failed to include in his litany of the book's many sins.

The fact of the novel's domesticity shouldn't really be a surprise. The title of the book refers to a home (or at least a rude shelter). Should we be surprised that we ignored the issue of house and home during a radically political time when Black Power activist Stokely Carmichael was calling NAACP Executive Director Roy Wilkins "a [expletive deleted] Uncle Tom" in 1966, or when the Student Nonviolent Coordinating Committee was asking, incredibly, in its position paper on Black Power: "Who is the real villain—Uncle Tom or Simon Legree?"[2] We had seen the enemy, and the enemy was, if not us, then at least one of us.

This was the era when—for the first time in our history—one could be read out of the race publicly for not being "black" enough. The term "Uncle Tom" became synonymous with self-loathing. For years after, everything connected with *Uncle Tom's Cabin* recalled this nightmare, our very own version of the Inquisition, the time when blacks turned on other blacks as the enemy, as the principal targets of our revolutionary fervor. Cleaning out the cabin suddenly became more urgent than dismantling the Big House.

Some forty years removed from the Black Power movement and nearly sixty years after James Baldwin denounced *Uncle Tom's Cabin* as "a very bad novel" in its "self-righteous, vir-

This image of a brooding Uncle Tom by renowned Mexican artist Miguel Covarrubias (1904–1957) underscores both his isolation from his family and the arduous burden of the labor of slavery.   From the title page of *Uncle Tom's Cabin: or, Life Among the Lowly*, Heritage Press edition, 1938

2. "Student Nonviolent Coordinating Committee Position Paper: The Basis of Black Power"; see http://www3.iath.virginia.edu.sixties/HTML_docs/Resources/Primary/Manifestos/SNCC_black_power.html.

tuous sentimentality" (EPN, p. 11), the time seems right for a reassessment both of the novel and of James Baldwin's critique, itself by now a part of the canon. From my perspective in the first decade of the twenty-first century, when the hot-button cultural and political concerns are not only race but marriage, sexual orientation, class, language, and religion, I have come to appreciate Stowe's art as far more culturally capacious—and sexually charged—perhaps than the militant 1960s discourse could acknowledge, even if it had thought to look.

Harriet Beecher Stowe (1811–1896), prolific author of more than ten novels.

Decades ago, I never would have seen that one of the most important social concerns of *Uncle Tom's Cabin*, a topic perhaps as central to the plot as race-based slavery, is marriage, of all things. Stowe's novel is thoroughly preoccupied with marriages—broken-up marriages, failed marriages, fatalistic and tired marriages; bittersweet, evergreen, surprisingly emotional marriages; hasty, postponed, "if-only" marriages; in-name-only, bitter, clinging, and doomed marriages. The great journalist and critic Edmund Wilson wrote in *Patriotic Gore* that "to expose oneself in maturity

"In the Cottonfield." A photograph by noted stage photographer Joseph Bryon of one of the many plays based on *Uncle Tom's Cabin*. © Joseph Byron, NY, circa 1900

Wood engraving by English illustrator George Cruikshank (1792–1878) of author, orator, and abolitionist Frederick Douglass (1817/18–1895). Douglass's name and image were already iconic by the time Stowe published her novel. The character of Uncle Tom might be thought of as Douglass's polar opposite. Douglass was all that Tom could never be: articulate, independent, agnostic, and free. From *The Uncle Tom's Cabin Almanack, or, Abolitionist Memento*, 1853

to *Uncle Tom's Cabin* may . . . prove a startling experience," and indeed, its "eruptive force" on the question of marriage caught me unawares.[3]

It would be easy to dismiss the topic of marriage as a kind of contrapuntal melody, a leitmotif about "the marriage bonds" that either softens or puts in stark relief the unyielding bonds of slavery, but this would be to undervalue the complexity of Stowe's rhetorical strategy. After all, a host of slave narratives, such as those by Frederick Douglass and William Wells Brown, had expounded at length on the severing of the marriage bond as a necessary and inescapable evil within the logic of slavery.[4] One need only reread the first few pages of *Uncle Tom's Cabin*, where one finds Stowe's first description of the married Eliza, her "rich, full, dark eye, with its long lashes" and "ripples of silky black hair," whose complexion "gave way on the cheek to a perceptible flush, which deepened as she saw the gaze of the strange man fixed upon her in bold and undisguised admiration" (p. 8), to understand the danger. Lydia Maria Child's 1867 novel *A Romance of the Republic* continued the literary engagement with raging sexuality and marriage several years later.

Stowe uses the metonym of the cabin—Tom's doomed marital home—to remove the question of slavery from the male discourse of Jeffersonian individualism, which had not had much success in ending slavery by 1852, and to resituate it squarely in the heart of the family circle. By depicting Uncle Tom and George Harris not as perfect men but as perfect *husbands*—and, while doing so, implicitly provoking her female readers to ask if their own husbands embodied the ideal of Christian decency— Stowe probably managed to unsettle tens of thousands of marriages that had not had, and would never have, any *direct* connection to slavery. As historian Amy Dru Stanley notes, "No abolitionist argument

Undated photograph of an aging but fiery Frederick Douglass.

3. Edmund Wilson, "Harriet Beecher Stowe," in *Patriotic Gore: Studies in the Literature of the American Civil War* (New York: Oxford Univ. Press, 1962), pp. 4–5.

4. See Frederick Douglass's *Autobiographies*: *Narrative of the Life of Frederick Douglass, an American Slave; My Bondage and Freedom; Life and Times of Frederick Douglass* and William Wells Brown's *Clotel; or The President's Daughter.*

proved more compelling than that testifying to the conflict between slavery and domesticity, as demonstrated by Harriet Beecher Stowe's best-selling 1852 melodrama *Uncle Tom's Cabin*."[5]

I hadn't thought of it this way in my teens and early twenties. In 1978, I wrote my dissertation at the University of Cambridge on the discourse of individuality, reason, race, and writing in the seventeenth and eighteenth centuries. I focused on that part of the history of race conflict that was played out on the printed (or written) page. The rational-humanistic beliefs of the great Enlightenment thinkers would be the seeds of slavery's undoing, even if their own discourse could not always escape the wellspring of racist assumptions endemic to that time. I would like to think that a truly rational, intellectually honest human being could not help but oppose slavery, though part of me understood that the issue is far more complex than that, especially given slavery's history in black Africa, and even black-on-black slavery in the antebellum South. This aside, what other reason could there be to oppose slavery besides the obvious rational and ethical grounds? What did marriage possibly have to do with it?

Stowe's great claim was that men might embrace antislavery politics because their wives expected

Postcard titled " 'Uncle Tom.' An Old-Fashioned Southern Negro." This Uncle Tom is curiously reminiscent of a black Santa Claus; yet, his beard and staff are meant to connote a Moses figure.   Originally printed by the Asheville Post Card Co., Asheville, NC

better of them. Judging by the public's unprecedented, overwhelming response to the novel, she was surely on to something. What choice did men have if American women wanted their lovers to be as passionate and ambitious as George Harris, as loyal and uncomplaining as Senator Bird, as pious and brawny as John Van Trompe ("a great, tall bristling Orson of a fellow, full six feet and some inches in his stockings"), and as moral and steadfast as dear old Uncle Tom? Historian Ann Douglas, in her influential 1977 study *The Feminization of American Culture*, makes just this critique. In Douglas's view, Stowe's drippingly sentimental novel mocks and proclaims the author's "own problems as a woman, a writer, and a religious believer" by "triumphantly" displaying "the scene of man abject under feminine rule."[6]

Douglas's important question seems to be whether any abject man—particularly a man as physically powerful as Uncle Tom—can be a "real man." Baldwin writes that Tom "has been robbed of his humanity and divested of his sex" (EPN, p. 14). Scholar Jane Tompkins argues that Stowe "relocates

5. Amy Dru Stanley, "Home Life and the Morality of the Market," in *The Market Revolution in America*, ed. M. Stokes and S. Conway (Charlottesville: University of Virginia Press, 1996), p. 88.

6. Ann Douglass, *The Feminization of American Culture* (London: Papermac, 1996), p. 244.

Image of Uncle Tom from a 1943 Classics Illustrated Comic. This depiction of a muscular and virile Uncle Tom suggests his latent sexual prowess. He could easily be a superhero dressed incognito: Uncle Tom as Super Tom.   From Classics Illustrated Classic Comic Book no. 15, *Uncle Tom's Cabin*, 1943

the center of power in American life" to the kitchen, which means "that the new society will not be controlled by men but by women."[7] Perhaps. But it seems a much more complicated matter than this to Stowe, and to her novel. Moreover, it seems that the most important room in the novel is not the kitchen but the bedroom.

Let us begin with Uncle Tom's marital status, a subject that has long intrigued Stowe scholars. In the early part of the story, on the Shelby plantation, Uncle Tom's relationship with Aunt Chloe is implied but never explicitly stated. The reader is meant to understand that Tom and Chloe are married and have three children, but they never speak about their passion for each other. Stowe represents Tom as a devoted—even doting—father, but not as a lover. This is how Stowe describes their bedroom:

> In one corner of it stood a bed, covered neatly with a snowy spread; . . . and made, so far as possible, sacred from the marauding inroads and desecrations of little folks. In fact, that corner was the *drawing-room* of the establishment. In the other corner was a bed of much humbler pretensions, and evidently designed for *use*. (p. 27)

The "snowy spread" that covers the public bed is meant to signify the neatness and cleanliness of these exceptional slaves, refuting the stereotype of their lack of respectability.

Conception between Tom and Chloe could well be as immaculate as the bedspread. For these two there is none of the sexual chemistry that obtains between the other married couples: the nearly white George and Eliza, Senator and Mrs. Bird, and the blushing Quaker newlyweds. This lack is perhaps meant to signify the perilous and legally fragile nature of slave "marriage." But one no doubt unintended effect of this striking absence is to suggest that pure black slaves like Tom and Chloe are not capable of sublime feelings, reinforcing stereotypes of their privileging of the physical and quotidian over the metaphysical, as it were. The "sublime mystery" in the cabin is Chloe's corn cake recipe.

The problem with Uncle Tom and Chloe's sexuality is that it is depicted, if that is the right word, in the passive voice, as it were. Whereas the sexuality

7. Jane P. Tompkins, "Sentimental Power: *Uncle Tom's Cabin* and the Politics of Literary History," in *Sensational Designs: The Cultural Work of American Fiction, 1790–1860* (New York: Oxford Univ. Press, 1985), p. 145.

of Eliza and George is a burning, active passion—one even sanctioned, extraordinarily, by an elaborate wedding ceremony hosted by their mistress in the Big House—Tom and Chloe's is a highly mediated passion, somnolent almost, buried deep under Aunt Chloe's apron and Tom's gray, balding head. In fact, so at odds are their sobriquets of "Uncle" and "Aunt" with the young ages of their children that trying to imagine Tom and Chloe making love is a bit like being forced to imagine your parents (or worse, your grandparents) procreating with abandon in the dark recesses of the cabin. Just where did those babies of Chloe's come from? Given her physical description and social status among the neighbors, we can't help but think of her as old and venerable—which, given the youth of her children, evokes the image of a black Sarah, conceiving in her old age.

Stowe works hard to ensure that Tom leaves his cabin a man free from domestic bonds. Her text renders Tom's sexuality in such an ambivalent manner, chaining Tom's potency, I believe, to enable an entirely safe level of intimacy between Tom and Eva that would have been scandalous otherwise. The fact of the matter—which, curiously enough, has not escaped the attention of generations of the novel's illustrators—is that Tom leaves his home and almost immediately becomes involved with a young blonde.

It never occurred to me to think of the novel this way until the early 1980s, I must confess, when I visited Randolph Simpson's collection of "Sambo Art" in Branford, Connecticut, now housed at the Wadsworth Atheneum in Hartford. Among the thousands of images, two leapt out at me: a postcard from the early 1900s of a lynching in Texas, and another one, from the 1940s, of a lithe black man in white sailor pants and a blue and white striped navy shirt, carrying a scantily clad, nubile blonde white woman, dripping wet, out of the water. She has swooned; he is leering. The card's caption? "Uncle Tom's Cabin."

Had I missed something in the novel? Was my middle-school edition expurgated? Had I neglected to find the deeper meaning inherent in this literary work's formal and rhetorical strategies, as we had been taught to do in eighth-grade English class? What is worse, had my hero, James Baldwin, himself missed the subtext of dripping sexuality in the novel's portrayal of Tom and Eva's first embrace, when he, "broad-chested, strong-armed . . . caught her in his arms, and, swimming with her to the boat-side, handed her up" (pp. 157–58)?

Tom and Little Eva "meet cute," as they say in Hollywood. He is poor, she is rich; after he saves her life on the cruise ship, she brings him home with

Poster of Uncle Tom. This Tom, benign and paternalistic, is old and stooped, yet still required to weed the cotton field.  Created by A. S. Seer's Union Square Print, NY; copyrighted by A. S. Seer, May 1886

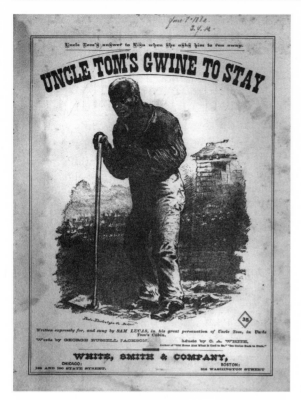

"Uncle Tom's Gwine to Stay," a cover image from one of the many musical scores written in response to Stowe's novel. Here, Tom, while stooped, retains remnants of a once-powerful physique. This anonymous image echoes the poster on the previous page.   From White, Smith & Company Publishers, 1881

her; they spend long, halcyon days together, holding hands and walking; she becomes sick and dies, and he is cast out when the only remaining person who could protect him dies as well. Moreover, in the 1933 Walt Disney cartoon short of *Uncle Tom's Cabin*, "Mickey's Mellerdrammer," Mickey plays Uncle Tom and Minnie plays Little Eva. Even I find this shocking! How did this film get past the censors? Talk about suspending disbelief. Mickey and Minnie are, as they say, an item, and unmistakably so.

Stowe all but dares the reader to see something untoward in the obsessive closeness of Uncle Tom and Little Eva. While their relationship is most certainly not sexual, it is undoubtedly— and remarkably—physical: Tom and Eva touch, kiss, hold hands, hold each other closely. It is an unfolding flaunting of the taboo of "amalgamation," of cross-racial sexual intimacy. Judging from the popular and scandalous images of Tom with nubile white women and girls that have outlived the book's canonical status in the classroom, Mrs. Stowe was not entirely successful in her attempt to neuter Tom.

So what are we to make of the fact that so many popular, nontraditional riffs, comic responses, and artistic renditions of the story focus on the implicit sexual tension between Little Eva and Big Tom? What are we to make of the fact that so many of these salacious artistic representations are vulgar and racist?

I raise these questions not to offend Stowe's admirers or to strain credulity, but to suggest that the way that the novel lives in the public imagination can be a function of what lies just barely beneath its blatantly sentimental surface. There is a reason why the term "Uncle Tom" became an insult during the era of Black Power; it had as much to do with Tom's unintelligible sexuality as with his alleged servility before his white owners. Baldwin described Uncle Tom as "black, wooly-haired, illiterate; and . . . phenomenally forbearing" (EPN, p. 14), by which Baldwin means to suggest that Tom is unduly passive, unduly "unmanly." But Tom also demonstrates a remarkable degree of sexual forbearance. He is a man surrounded by women—surrounded by temptation—throughout the novel. Literary critic Hortense Spillers even suggests that Stowe situates Tom and Eva in the Garden of Eden, adding quickly that Eva is a "temptress" and Tom is "castrated."[8] For scores of others, Uncle Tom is a Christ figure—a man similarly tempted by the flesh—a portrayal rendered even more powerfully when contrasted with Tom's oft-mentioned remarkable physique. Tom is a "hunk," but one doomed to remain in potential only.

Baldwin reveals his epistemological prejudices when he says that the "illiterate" Tom has lost both his humanity and his sex, as if those two elements of his character are somehow inextricably intertwined with his literacy, as if sexuality has something to do with the ability to read and write, reason's visible sign. The Black Power discourse of the 1960s was wholly informed (ironically enough) by the discourse of Enlightenment philosophy. The Enlightenment's notion of individual power eschews what can be seen of the body; rather, it turns on the potential of the individual's expression of the self, and the relation between expression and assertion, or action. On philosophical grounds, Baldwin's critical desire for Uncle Tom to *do* more than he does echoes the words of the great James Weldon Johnson in 1927: "I am coming to believe," Johnson wrote to novelist and critic Carl Van Vechten, "that nothing can go farther to destroy race prejudice than the recognition of the Negro as a creator and contributor to American civilization."[9] Uncle Tom, as a character, *forbears* impressively, but he does not create. Tom is spoken for: He is an object in his own narrative, not a speaking subject. He is the symbol of the Negro's capacity for religion, not art, not science. Like Richard Wright's Bigger Thomas, he is articulated; he does not articulate; like Bigger Thomas, he does not speak his own tale; an omniscient white narrator does. For Baldwin, Bigger Thomas—thought by 1960s Black Militants to be the "blackest" literary character of all—is merely a contemporary version of Uncle Tom, Uncle Tom on Chicago's South Side, Uncle Tom in the ghetto.

Still, Baldwin himself seems to have acknowledged that something dark and secret exists beneath the surface level of expression in Stowe's novel: "Sentimentality, the ostentatious parading of excessive and spurious emotion, is the mark of dishonesty, the inability to feel; the wet eyes of the sentimentalist betray his aversion to experience, his fear of life, his arid heart; and it is always, therefore, the signal of secret and violent inhumanity, the mask of cruelty" (EPN, p. 12). Sentimentality is masking something, he says, but what? Baldwin doesn't say. And yet we have a clue in *Nobody Knows My Name*: "one can only face in others what one can face in oneself."[10] Remove Bigger's mask of inarticulate anger and blind violence and there resides Uncle Tom. Remove Uncle Tom's mask and what is left? To Baldwin, not

8. Hortense J. Spillers, "Changing the Letter: The Yokes, the Jokes of Discourse, or Mrs. Stowe, Mr. Reed," in Harriet Beecher Stowe, *Uncle Tom's Cabin*, Norton Critical Edition, ed. E. Ammons (New York: W. W. Norton, 1994), p. 554.

9. James Weldon Johnson letter to Carl Van Vechten, cited in Henry Louis Gates Jr., "Negroes Old, Negroes New: On Afro-American Modernism," *ADE Bulletin* 064 (1980): 34–36.

10. James Baldwin, *Nobody Knows My Name*, in *James Baldwin: Collected Essays*, ed. T. Morrison (New York: Library of America, 1998), p. 136.

much. Forbearance, at least Tom's sort, erases the self, precludes selfhood, just as slavery sought to do. For Baldwin, this is Uncle Tom's greatest crime.

It seems clear from Baldwin's writings that his distaste of sentimentality had everything to do with the perception that sentiment undermined what it meant to be a desiring being, a rational being, and ultimately for Baldwin and I think Stowe, a *sexual* being, all salient aspects of one's full humanity. Sentiment focuses on a person's *exterior*, but art privileges the *interior*, the soul, the seat of desire. Sentimentality doesn't deny the existence of those things; it merely keeps them at a safe, highly mediated, protected distance. In nineteenth-century antebellum America, sentimentalism was the only mode Stowe could employ to write about sex—especially interracial sex— and that's what she did, wittingly or not.

To put it bluntly: Stowe's sentimental form enabled her story's sexual content. The number of such images that proliferated after the publication of *Uncle Tom's Cabin* demonstrates the public recognition that a universe of sex lay submerged beneath the surface of her novel. (A 1937 Merrie Melodies cartoon, "Uncle Tom's Bungalow," opens with an animated Little Eva pulling up her dress and showing off her lacy panties.) The vulgar, racist, sexualized images of black men—thick lipped, lascivious—groping at white women were a visceral response to what racists recognized to be the subver-

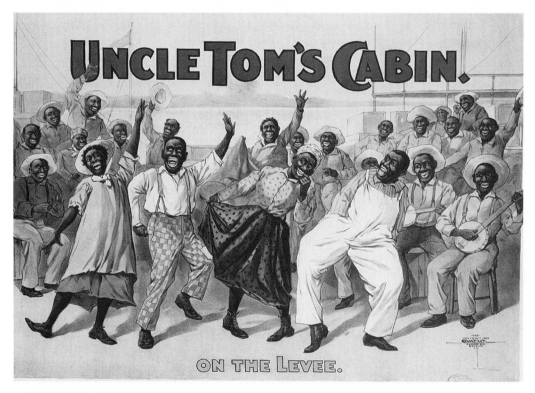

Poster: "*Uncle Tom's Cabin*. On the Levee." Images such as this were meant to underscore stereotypes of black as minstrels or "sambos," so popular in the latter half of the nineteenth century.   Courier Lithograph Co., 1899

sive message concealed not only in the proximity of the cabin and the Big House but also in the intimacy between Eva and Tom. Amalgamation was about sex. Race mingling was about sex. Abolition was about sex, because slavery, in part, was about unbridled, unregulated sex, always potentially available in the relation between master and slave.

Sentimentality masks sexuality by focusing attention on the outside of the body—tears, sighs, blushes—such that the body itself recedes from focus. Sentimentalism is concerned with the space between a body and the eyes watching it. Still, the body is always present, along with its potential for consummation. After all, the picture of Uncle Tom's strong arms around Little Eva's little white waist is the central image of the entire middle section of the book. While sentimentality attempted to function to mask or repress sexuality, it also inadvertently functioned to draw attention to it.

The great British statesman Edmund Burke's 1757 aesthetic theory of the sublime and the beautiful would put sex in the category of the sublime and sentiment in the category of the beautiful.[11] If Uncle Tom were more primitive, his potential sexuality would be more obvious. If he were more articulate, it would be unmistakable. But because he is both civilized and terse, his sexuality flies under the radar. Consider Stowe's description of Uncle Tom, America's prototypical black noble savage:

> He was a large, broad-chested, powerfully-made man, of a full glossy black, and a face whose truly African features were characterized by an expression of grave and steady good sense, united with much kindliness and benevolence. There was something about his whole air self-respecting and dignified, yet united with a confiding and humble simplicity. (p. 27)

And compare it with Aphra Behn's seventeenth-century noble savage, the title character in *Oroonoko, or the Royal Slave*:

> He was pretty tall, but of a shape the most exact that can be fancied; the most famous statuary could not form the figure of a man more admirably turn'd from head to foot. His face was not that brown rusty black which most of that nation are, but a perfect ebony, or polished jet. His eyes were the most awful that could be seen, and very piercing; the white of them being like snow, as were his teeth. His nose was rising and Roman, instead of African and flat. . . . The whole proportion and air of his face was so noble, and exactly formed, that, bating his colour, there could be nothing in nature more beautiful, agreeable and handsome. There was no one grace wanting, that bears the standard of true beauty.[12]

11. Edmund Burke, *A Philosophical Enquiry into the Origin of Our Ideas of the Sublime and Beautiful,* ed. A. Phillips (Oxford: Oxford Univ. Press, 1990).

12. Aphra Behn, *Oroonoko, The Rover and Other Works*, Penguin Classics, ed. J. Todd (New York: Penguin Books, 1992), pp. 80–81.

Behn's Oroonoko was a noble, utterly masculine individual, and as readers of the novel recall, very sexual. What Tom was like under covers in the cabin, well, only the Shadow knows.

Baldwin's concern about Stowe's depiction of skin color echoes an earlier philosophical stance that blackness is an ambiguous, if not pejorative, sign of an essence. In Enlightenment discourse—which included, in a minor key, the "noble black African," and embraced characterizations such as Behn's— the capacity to *possess* beauty is a metaphor for the black African's capacity to *create* beauty. Baldwin is hugely critical of the way Stowe writes about blacks. First, he notes that two of the novel's three leading black characters (George and Eliza) are so light in color they are almost white. His implicit critique is that, for Stowe, their creative abilities—George's inventions, Eliza's sublime flight to freedom—are a function of their "whiteness," their "white blood."

Baldwin further argues that because of Tom's blackness, Stowe needs to describe him as completely purified in his soul, somewhat like William Blake's "Little Black Boy," whose white soul masks the blackness of his skin. We see a similar gesture later in Harriet Wilson's *Our Nig*, when the "kind-hearted African," Jim, asks Mag: "which would you rather have, a black heart in a white skin, or a white heart in a black one?"[13] This is a rhetorical maneuver designed to attract reluctant recruits to the antislavery cause. In the case of Uncle Tom, this purification of soul is the height of forbearance; it stands in stark contrast to Oroonoko's eloquence and celebrated capacity for manly rebellion. Baldwin's implicit critique is that because of Uncle Tom's passivity, combined with his unadulterated blackness, Stowe is offering an implicitly racist representation of an African-American protagonist in fiction, one that domesticates native black resistance and the capacity to rebel.

And yet Baldwin, while acknowledging that Uncle Tom's triumph "is metaphysical, unearthly," notes that this triumph requires the "mortification of the flesh," and necessitates that Stowe must cover Tom's "intimidating nakedness" (EPN, p. 14). We must shut out the traditional depiction of Uncle Tom as a bespectacled old man to follow the argument. Baldwin proposes that Tom's true literary descendant, Bigger Thomas, is "flesh of his flesh" (EPN, p. 18). There is a whole lot of talk of flesh here, as an illustrated version of Baldwin's essay would make abundantly clear.

Baldwin's point, made perhaps with too many revealing reservations, is that when a black man *makes himself* in spite of white constraints, only then can we see what kind of man he truly is. But, as Baldwin would put it later, in his essay "Freaks and the American Ideal of Manhood," "Each of us, helplessly and forever, contains the other—male in female, female in male, white in black, and black in white. We are part of each other."[14] Still, for Baldwin,

13. Harriet E. Wilson, *Our Nig; or Sketches from the Life of a Free Black Slave* (New York: Vintage Books, 2002), p. 12.

14. James Baldwin, "Freaks and the American Ideal of Manhood," in *James Baldwin: Collected Essays*, ed. T. Morrison (New York: Library of America, 1998), p. 828.

truly embedding himself within the Other is something that Uncle Tom cannot do. He can only reflect white fantasies of the depth of sacrifice necessary to save the soul.

Nowhere in the novel is this stirring idea embodied more clearly than at the end when Uncle Tom lies dying (in young George Shelby's arms, as the silent-film versions usually have it)[15] and pronounces, " 'Pears like I loves 'em all! I loves every creatur' everywhar!—it's nothing *but* love!" Moments later, "the sudden flush of strength which the joy of meeting his young master had infused into the dying man gave way. . . . he closed his eyes; and that mysterious and sublime change passed over his face" (pp. 439–40). This is a same-sex, interracial *Pieta* with the dying man experiencing "le petit mort"; Baldwin seems to have missed it.

Depictions of sexuality can be found in almost every chapter of Stowe's novel, not only in the accounts of sexual humiliation of slave women but also lurking within and near the story's sentimental treatment of marriage and family life. Overwhelmingly sentimental passages such as the following may mask this sexual energy, but not completely:

> As the boat stopped, a black woman came running wildly up the plank, darted into the crowd, flew up to where the slave gang sat, and threw her arms round that unfortunate piece of merchandise before enumerated—"John, aged thirty," and with sobs and tears bemoaned him as her husband.
>
> But what needs tell the story, told too oft,—everyday told,—of heart-strings rent and broken,—the weak broken and torn for the profit and convenience of the strong! (p. 133)

The presence of sexual energy is perhaps even more obvious when Stowe describes the reunion of Eliza and George Harris in the Quaker household:

> "To-night!" Eliza repeated, "to-night!" The words lost all meaning to her; her head was dreamy and confused; all was mist for a moment. . . .
>
> She dreamed of a beautiful country,—a land, it seemed to her, of rest,—green shores, pleasant islands, and beautifully glittering water; and there, in a house which kind voices told her was a home, she saw her boy playing, a free and happy child. She heard her husband's footsteps; she felt him coming nearer; his arms were around her, his tears falling on her face, and she awoke! (pp. 148–49)

None of this was lost on the readers of the era. The language of Stowe's contemporary reviewers often echoed the submerged discourse of arousal: "It is a live book, and it talks to its readers as if it were alive. It first awakens their attention, arrests their thoughts, touches their sympathies, rouses

---

15. See Stephen Railton's excellent website, "*Uncle Tom's Cabin* and American Culture," for film clips: www.iath.virginia.edu/utc/.

their curiosity, and creates such an interest in the story it is telling, that they cannot let it drop until the whole story is told."[16]

In her own married life, Stowe was exceptionally concerned about sex and sexuality, as her biographers have noted, most particularly Joan D. Hedrick. Hedrick's brilliant and masterful *Harriet Beecher Stowe: A Life* examines the letters that the middle-aged Stowes wrote to one another during 1846–1848, after ten years of marriage and seven children.[17] It has been "almost 18 months since I have had a wife to sleep with me. It is enough to kill a man," Calvin lamented to Harriet in 1846, when she was at a spa for her health. But he wanted her to rest so that she would be healthy enough for sexual activity: "I should suffer still more from your presence, unless you can be in a better condition than you have been for a year past. It is now a full year since your last miscarriage, and you well know what has been the state of things both in regard to yourself & me ever since" (*HBS*, p. 180).

One of the struggles that Harriet and Calvin faced, as did other religious married couples in the nineteenth century, was how to have a happy sex life without adding to their domestic burdens—that is, how to keep from having more children. Typically for the era, Harriet's health had declined after marriage, Hedrick notes, with pregnancies, confinements, the drudgery of household management, poor nutrition, lack of exercise, and a drastically circumscribed routine sapping her physical and sexual energy (*HBS*, pp. 110–21). Yet sex was a central part of their marriage, especially for Calvin, as his letters indicate. Because they apparently enjoyed physical intimacy, however, Harriet often took long trips to relatives, to spas, or abroad. "Of their first fifteen years of marriage, Harriet and Calvin spent approximately half apart, for they found sexual abstinence more likely to succeed under these circumstances. It was the only method they used to limit their family" (*HBS*, p. 117). Nine months after Harriet returned from her long visit to the Brattleboro water cure, her sixth child was born.

One doesn't need to know anything about Stowe's marital life to recognize that there are two distinct marital categories in *Uncle Tom's Cabin*: intimate and not. The Shelbys are certainly not. Uncle Tom's first owner, Mr. Shelby, is characterized by impotence. He takes great comfort and pleasure in oral satisfactions—at every moment of stress, he puts something in his mouth: wine, fruit, a cigar, coffee, breakfast, and lunch.

Eliza's husband, George Harris, by contrast, is virile. Although only young Harry has lived past infancy, Eliza has borne three children, and she and George are physically affectionate with each other. In the Quaker settlement, Ruth Steadman, with her blooming face, "plump little chest," with knitting in her lap as well as a bouncing baby, is evidently intimate with her husband. Senator and Mrs. Bird are also intimate (he makes the long jour-

16. Charles F. Briggs, "Uncle Tomitudes," in *Critical Essays on Harriet Beecher Stowe*, ed. E. Ammons (Boston: G. K. Hall, 1980), p. 39.

17. Joan D. Hedrick, *Harriet Beecher Stowe: A Life* (hereafter cited as *HBS*) (New York: Oxford Univ. Press, 1994).

ney home just for one evening with her); Augustine St. Clare and his sickly wife most definitely are not.

Again, we return to the question of Tom, or Tom and Chloe. In terms of intimacy, there is no "Tom and Chloe." But there is a "Tom and George." When Tom leaves his cabin and wife, he carries a token of love and affection underneath his clothes: a gift from Master George Shelby, a coin on a string, which George ties with his own hands around Tom's neck. (The same scene will appear in James Weldon Johnson's *The Autobiography of an Ex-Colored Man*, but it is the mulatto hero's father who gives him the coin.) Stowe insists that we understand the emotional tie that binds the two men: "over his heart there seemed to be a warm spot, where those young hands had placed that precious dollar. Tom put up his hand, and held it close to his heart" (p. 111). No such warmth is emitted from the clothes that Aunt Chloe so carefully ironed and pressed for Tom's journey. Uncle Tom wants to write to her to tell her he is well, but he does not seem to want desperately to come home to her, or to bring her to a new home.

So not only is there a Tom and Master George, there is a Tom and Eva, then a Tom and Cassy, and then a Tom and George once more. These close physical relationships, along with the pairings of Ophelia and Topsy and St. Clare and Adolphus, can only really be described as queer. By "queer relationships" I don't mean merely same-sex relationships—neither do I mean necessarily *sexual* relationships—but pairings in which the sexual energy seems either so repressed or so dispersed as to be difficult to comprehend.

I should add that Harriet Beecher and Calvin Stowe were no strangers to the discourse of same-sex intimacy. While Harriet was off at her "Water Cure" spa, Hedrick notes, Calvin himself enjoyed intimate relations with male friends. "When I get desperate, & cannot stand it any longer, I get dear, good kind hearted Br[other] Stagg to come and sleep with me, and he puts his arms round me & hugs me to my hearts' content," he wrote (*HBS*, p. 180). A Mr. Farber, whose marriage had been put off, apparently fell in love with Calvin, and Calvin wrote to Harriet that "he kisses and kisses upon my rough old face, as if I were a most beautiful young lady instead of a musty old man. The Lord sent him here to be my comfort. . . . He will have me sleep him once in a while, and he says, *that is almost as good as being married*— the dear little innocent ignorant soul" (*HBS*, p. 181).

It is not really that surprising to learn that the Stowes had an active sex life. Many married couples obviously did, even in the nineteenth century! And yet the idea of a sexual Stowe seems unthinkable to most readers and critics. Jane Tompkins, for example, focuses on Stowe's conservatism and "reliance on established patterns of living and traditional beliefs," and argues that Stowe rests her case "on the saving power of Christian love and on the sanctity of motherhood and the family" ("Sentimental Power," p. 145), as if motherhood doesn't at some point require sex.

Baldwin was silent on the issue of motherhood in the context of *Uncle Tom's Cabin*. He was silent on the question of a sexual Stowe, presuming at the beginning of his essay that Miss Ophelia, the virginal New England sister, was the author's fictional double. Is this the same "dead New England woman" locked in a timeless battle with a "contemporary Negro novelist" that Baldwin describes at the end of his essay, thrusting and counterthrusting "within this web of lust and fury" (EPN p. 18)?

The most obvious reason for *Uncle Tom*'s disappearance in the college classroom was not sex but the utter disdain of the Tom character by the black community. Yet in the late 1960s, Baldwin bashing, for much the same reason, was a rite of initiation, as I noted years ago. Black Panther Eldridge Cleaver famously sneered that Baldwin's work expressed "the most shameful, fanatical, fawning sycophantic love of the whites that one can find in any black American writer of note in our time."[18] Baldwin might savage Stowe, but in the end, he too was a toady to the whites, as far as the Black Militants were concerned.

In this curiously fanciful image, Eva, Topsy, and a kneeling Tom pay homage to their creator, none other than Harriet Beecher Stowe herself.

James Baldwin strove vigorously to assert that *Uncle Tom's Cabin* was not great literature and that Stowe was not a great artist. "She was not so much a novelist as an impassioned pamphleteer; her book was not intended to do anything more than prove that slavery was wrong; was, in fact, perfectly horrible. This makes materials for a pamphlet but it is hardly enough for a novel; and the only question left to ask is why we are bound still within the same constriction." Baldwin criticized the fundamental assumptions underlying Stowe's righteous tone: "black, white, the devil, the next world." Her novel's characters "spurned and were terrified of the darkness, striving mightily for the light" (EPN, p. 11). But isn't this sort of Manichean simplicity all too frequently the central flaw of such Baldwin plays as *The Amen Corner* and *Blues for Mister Charlie*, and such novels as *Another Country* and *Tell Me How Long the Train's Been Gone*, with their stereotypical depictions of unidimensional characters, black and white—novels in which characters seem to exist as set pieces for ideological diatribes rather than nuanced explorations of their full humanity?

The paradox of James Baldwin's career as a writer is that he wrote essays with all of the lyricism and subtlety of a great novelist; when it came time to write the novels, however, he approached his craft, especially in his later years, as an essayist—a didactic, often heavy-handed essayist at that, and not the subtle master of the form that Baldwin-the-essayist, at his best, could be. Even in his early small masterpiece, *Giovanni's Room*, his most successfully crafted and fully realized novel, Stowe-like melodrama occasionally intrudes upon Giovanni's monologue, as in the following passage:

18. Eldridge Cleaver, *Soul on Ice* (New York: Dell Publishing, 1999), p. 124.

> I was thinking, when I told Hella that I had loved her, of those days before anything awful, irrevocable, had happened to me, when an affair was nothing more than an affair. Now, from this night, this coming morning, no matter how many beds I find myself in between now and my final bed, I shall never be able to have any more of those boyish, zestful affairs—which are, really, when one thinks of it, a kind of higher, or, anyway, more pretentious masturbation. People are too various to be treated so lightly. I am too various to be trusted. If this were not so I would not be alone in this house tonight. Hella would not be on the high seas. And Giovanni would not be about to perish, sometime between this night and this morning, on the guillotine.[19]

Melodrama is a form of drama rendered over the top. Its use implies a writer's deepest mistrust of the instincts or intelligence of the reader. Melodramatic eruptions often flag a writer's incapacity or unwillingness to show or to dramatize; instead, she or he tells us that this is the way it is, the way that we should feel about the novel's action, or about a character's, well, character, in extremis. Showing takes longer than telling, and melodrama is telling with a bullhorn. Bad writing within a good novel, even a novel as finely rendered to this point in the narrative as *Giovanni's Room*, can also reflect an author's inability to resolve a problem of storytelling, her or his exhaustion in the face of a certain difficulty in technique, at which point the author resorts to bad habits, to a reservoir of tics. Imagine, if you can, someone actually saying the words quoted above to another person, or even thinking them to himself! Not only is the language of this paragraph pretentious and more than a little pompous, but its forced crescendo abandons all caution, plunging us deeply into melodrama.

Melodrama depends unduly on coincidence, on the most unlikely encounters between protagonists and antagonists, from which our hero only just escapes. To this propensity of Stowe's Baldwin also succumbs, forcing, for example, an accidental meeting among Giovanni, the protagonist's girlfriend, Hella, and their friend Jacques:

> We were passing a book-store and she stopped. "Can we go in for just a minute?" she asked. "There's a book I'd like to get. Quite," she added, as we entered the shop, "a trivial book."
>
> I watched her with amusement as she went over to speak to the woman who ran the shop. I wandered idly over to the farthest book shelf, where a man stood, his back to me, leafing through a magazine. As I stood beside him, he closed the magazine and put it down, and turned. We recognized each other at once. It was Jacques. (p. 324)

Similarly, Baldwin enables Hella miraculously to find David, in one of the hundreds of bars in Nice, after he has left her, abruptly, in their home miles away:

19. James Baldwin, *Giovanni's Room*, in *James Baldwin: Early Novels and Stories*, ed. T. Morrison (New York: Library of America, 1998), p. 223.

> I roamed all the bars of that glittering town and at the end of the first night, blind with alcohol and grim with lust, I climbed the stairs of a dark hotel, in company with a sailor. It turned out, late the next day, that the sailor's leave was not yet ended and that the sailor had friends. We spent the next day together, and the next. On the final night of the sailor's leave, we stood drinking together in a crowded bar. We faced the mirror, I was very drunk. I was almost penniless. In the mirror, suddenly, I saw Hella's face. I thought for a moment that I had gone mad, and I turned. She looked very tired and drab and small. . . . (p. 354)

By the time Baldwin wrote his most carelessly crafted novels, *Tell Me How Long the Train's Been Gone* and *Just Above My Head*, coincidence and melodrama had all too often become the norm. As a novelist, Baldwin, in his worst moments, had allowed himself to become what, at the beginning of his career, he most loathed—Harriet Beecher Stowe.

Baldwin was dead-on when he took aim at *Native Son*: Dramatizing the drama of race in the American novel is, inevitably, an extended riff on *Uncle Tom's Cabin*. The danger that lurks in rendering such a fraught subject is the tendency toward melodrama, deeply inscribed in *Uncle Tom's Cabin*'s very structure. *Uncle Tom's Cabin* is the ur-text in the fictional depiction of Americans across the color line. It is also the ur-text of American melodrama. This penchant for melodrama, Baldwin rightly argued, is at the heart of the narrative structure of even a novel as "black" as *Native Son*. What Baldwin did not see, or could not escape, was this trap of melodrama in his own novels about race, indeed in all of his novels except for *Giovanni's Room*, which, of course, includes no black characters.

It is not that Baldwin could not write as artfully about "race" as he did about sexuality; indeed, his use of black expressive cultural forms—the blues, jazz, and above all else, black sacred music and the sermon—remains astonishingly powerful and effective, even today. But when Baldwin tried to step outside the seemingly sealed universe of black cultural forms to straddle the color line, more often than not he found himself in the grip of Stowian melodrama, as in the following example from *Another County*:

> He laughed again. He remembered, suddenly, his days in boot camp in the South and felt again the shoe of a white officer against his mouth. He was in his uniform, on the ground, against the red, dusty clay. Some of his colored buddies were holding him, were shouting in his ear, helping him to rise. The white officer, with a curse, had vanished, had gone forever beyond the reach of vengeance. His face was full of clay and tears and blood; he spat red blood into the red dust.
>
> The elevator came and the doors opened. He took her arm as they entered and held it close against his chest. "I think you're a real sweet girl."[20]

20. James Baldwin, *Another Country*, in *James Baldwin: Early Novels and Stories*, ed. T. Morrison (New York: Library of America, 1998), p. 375.

See that white girl, feel that boot! The problem here is not that this sort of racist madness could not have happened: The problem is that the probability of it happening was quite small. After all, how many black soldiers could actually have been physically abused by white officers in boot camp even in the South of the 1930s and 1940s? It's no accident that Rufus's friend—the nameless entertainer at whose party he meets Leona, his soon-to-be lover— repeatedly calls her "Little Eva": four times, incredibly, over the course of two pages. Uncle Tom was very much on Baldwin's mind, the silent second text lurking in his narrative subconscious. When Rufus takes Leona, Rufus is exacting Uncle Tom's revenge. Stowe's revenge, however, was to yield a legacy of melodrama and coincidence to the novel of race relations, which even a writer of James Baldwin's stature found difficult to escape.

Why would James Baldwin, one of the twentieth century's greatest essayists—and himself a sort of neoabolitionist—speak so harshly against the power of the polemic, the power of words, and yes, even literature, to persuade? I think it is because Baldwin was talking about himself as a novelist speaking to his own deepest fears that as a novelist, he was guilty of exactly the same thing he disdained in Stowe. Ann Douglas notes that "*Uncle Tom's Cabin* is a great book, not because it is a great novel, but because it is a great revival sermon, aimed directly at the conversion of its hearers" (*Feminization*, p. 245). What are Baldwin's works but revival sermons, aimed just as directly at the conversion of his readers?

In a very real sense, Baldwin was projecting onto Stowe his own anxieties

Shirley Temple in *Dimples* (1936), playing "Eva" in a stage production. Remarkably, the "black" characters are white actors in blackface.

about his failures as a novelist, his inability to extricate himself from senti-mentality. When Baldwin looked in the mirror of his literary antecedents, what he saw, to his horror, was Harriet Beecher Stowe in blackface. Although it pains me to say it, James Baldwin, in many ways, is Harriet Beecher Stowe's most legitimate twentieth-century literary heir.

# HARRIET BEECHER STOWE

## and "The Man That Was a Thing"

ON MAY 8, 1851, the *National Era*, an antislavery weekly newspaper based in Washington, D.C., carried the following advertisement:

Week after next we propose to commence in the *Era*, the publication of a new story by Mrs. H. B. Stowe, the title of which will be, "UNCLE TOM'S CABIN, OR THE MAN THAT WAS A THING." It will probably be of the length of the Tale by Mrs. Southworth, entitled *Retribution*.

Mrs. Stowe is one of the most gifted and popular of American writers. We announce her story in advance, that none of our subscribers, may lose the beginning of it, and that those who desire to read the production as it may appear in successive numbers of the *Era,* may send us their names in season.

Although Harriet Beecher Stowe, who had already established herself as an accomplished essayist and storyteller, certainly had a devoted following in 1851, to call her "one of the most gifted and popular of American writers" was a bit of an overstatement. Indeed, a best-selling novel by the far more famous and beloved writer E. D. E. N. (Emma Dorothy Eliza Nevitte) Southworth serves as a point of reference for Stowe's tale. The *Era*'s editor, Dr. Gamaliel Bailey, might be forgiven, however, for exaggerating Stowe's fame: He accurately perceived not only the worth of the novel but also that Stowe had enough literary skill to interweave political philosophy, moral outrage, comedy, and tragedy into a complex extended narrative about slavery in America. Indeed, Stowe had high literary ambitions, for she modeled her work after that of such great novelists as Walter Scott, Charles Dickens, and Charlotte Brontë.

Bailey, who had known Stowe since the late 1830s, accurately guessed that *Uncle Tom's Cabin* would touch a nerve and thereby attract hundreds—perhaps thousands—of new readers outraged by the passage of the Fugitive Slave Act of 1850. But who could have known that Harriet Beecher Stowe's novel would galvanize the country's opposition to slavery, become a global pop-culture phenomenon (generating a century-long trade in Uncle Tom, Topsy, and Eva kitsch), and would, to some minds, spark a civil war? Looking at the tranquil photographs of this demure woman, one cannot help but wonder: What possessed her to produce this strange, startling, and audacious work?

Certainly Stowe's upbringing had something to do with her rebellious voice and literary ambition. Harriet Elizabeth Beecher was born in Litchfield, Connecticut, on June 14, 1811, the seventh of nine children of Roxana Foote Beecher and her husband, Lyman Beecher, a prominent Congregational minister. Roxana Beecher died of consumption when Harriet was only five years old, leaving the family under the sole leadership of Lyman, whose severe and restrictive views on who would go to heaven Harriet militated against in much of her writing. Lyman Beecher remarried in 1817, and he and his new wife, Harriet Porter, quickly bore four more children.

A sensitive and impressionable child, young Harriet suffered from bouts of depression throughout her adolescence; in 1824, a melancholy Harriet moved to Hartford, where her older sister Catharine had recently opened the Hartford Female Seminary. There Harriet flourished as a student, reading logic, philosophy, history, math, geography, and Latin— the fruits of which are apparent in her remarkably erudite novels. She also stood out among her peers as a brilliant essayist and a leader in deciding how the school should be run. Harriet exemplified the nineteenth-century reforming spirit.

In 1832, when Harriet was twenty-one, the Beecher clan, including Catharine, Harriet, their sister Isabella, and brothers George, Henry, and James, moved to Cincinnati, Ohio, where Lyman had been appointed president of Lane Theological Seminary. Ohio was a leading abolitionist state, and Cincinnati would become a vital city on the Underground Railroad. There, Catharine and Harriet joined the Semi-Colon Club, a literary society whose members included Salmon P. Chase, later Lincoln's treasury secretary and chief justice of the Supreme Court, and James Hall, editor of the *Western Monthly Magazine*. Harriet wrote stories, satirical poems, and mock-heroic sketches; in 1834 she won a prize for her first published short story—really just a character sketch— entitled "Uncle Lot," which appeared in the *Western Monthly*. Little in these early pieces suggests that their author had the ability to transform the complexion of the American novel. But Semi-Colon Club meetings were an important outlet for Harriet's creativity; moreover, she met quiet fellow member Calvin E. Stowe, a professor and widower. The two married in 1836 and eventually had seven children.

Wood engraving by George Cruikshank of a slave family being pursued by bloodhounds. The caption quotes escaped slave William Craft (1824/28–1900) rebutting an article by Charles Dickens that Craft believed was too mild about the terrors of slavery. Craft asserts that he has "frequently seen the bloodhounds on the chase of slaves, and have seen the poor trembling victims." (William and his wife, Ellen Craft, published *A Thousand Miles for Freedom* in 1860.) From *The Uncle Tom's Cabin Almanack, or, Abolitionist Memento*, 1853

During the first years of their marriage, struggling under the burdens of domesticity and child-rearing, Harriet still found time to write. This was partly out of necessity. Professor Stowe's salary was small, and Harriet's occasional pieces for local periodicals and journals brought extra money into the household. From 1838 throughout the 1840s, as issues dealing with slavery and expansion came to seize the American consciousness, Harriet contributed stories to the prestigious *Godey's Lady's Book*. In 1843 she published her first short-story collection, *The Mayflower; or Sketches of Scenes and Characters Among the Descendants of the Pilgrims*, primarily a collection of work produced for the Semi-Colon Club.

But geography was destiny, to a great extent. Cincinnati, situated on the opposite (northern) shore of the Ohio River from the slave state of Kentucky, was an important juncture for fleeing slaves. For those slaves, crossing the Ohio River was akin to crossing the Jordon into the Promised Land; not all Ohioans, however, welcomed the comparison. And although the Beecher family had been interested in abolitionist causes since the 1820s, they were hardly radicals; their position was primarily philosophical. The leading abolitionist, William Lloyd Garrison had been a member of Lyman Beecher's congregation since 1829 and knew him personally, but they were not close. After moving to Ohio, however, Harriet witnessed slave families being sold apart and couples torn asunder, and she read accounts of physical brutality in local papers. In Cincinnati in the 1830s, it was impossible for one's position on slavery to remain purely academic. Yet Lyman Beecher tried to hold more of a middle ground, squelching the radical activism of one-time Lane Seminary student Theodore Weld (later author of the 1839 *American Slavery as It Is*: *Testimony of a Thousand Witnesses*), who staged public debates on "immediate abolition," as opposed to gradual emancipation, which remained a more moderate position.

Wood engraving of a slave being captured under the Fugitive Slave Law, by the prolific engraver W. Measom, "after George Cruikshank." Note the caption: "torn from his home, from his business, from the wife of his bosom, and the children of his love." From *The Uncle Tom's Cabin Almanack, or, Abolitionist Memento*, 1853

In the summer of 1836, the year she was married, Harriet was drawn into the growing fray when a mob attacked James G. Birney's abolitionist paper the *Philanthropist* and dumped the paper's presses into the Ohio River. Birney had known Lyman Beecher since their days in Boston and had promoted Harriet's early literary endeavors. Still reluctant to voice her opinions publicly, Harriet wrote a scathing letter to the *Cincinnati Journal* (edited during this period by her brother Henry Ward Beecher) under a pseudonym. But Catharine Beecher voiced her opposition under her own name, writing her 1837 *Essay on Slavery and Abolitionism with Reference to the Duty of American Females*. Another brother, Edward Beecher, came out publicly as a

A matronly Harriet Beecher Stowe is surrounded by depictions of scenes from her novel. These images of black "representative Americans" stand in stark contrast to the inherent nobility of images of black authors and abolitionists such as Frederick Douglass, who was cast as the "most representative colored man" of his generation.  From *Uncle Tom's Cabin; or, Life Among the Lowly,* Art Memorial Edition, 1897

leader of the Illinois Anti-Slavery Society after the murder of antislavery newspaper editor Elijah P. Lovejoy. And in 1838, Henry Ward Beecher, more radicalized than his father, began passing the plate after his services to buy freedom for fugitive slaves. Events then hit closer to home: In 1839, Harriet learned that a "colored girl" that she had hired to help with domestic chores was in fact a fugitive slave whose master had come to Cincinnati to look for her. Calvin Stowe quietly delivered her to an Underground Railroad station to send her out of reach of her pursuers. And yet Harriet was still silent.

The 1840s were for Stowe years of childbearing, domestic struggles, and limited literary output. In 1849 she and her husband suffered a loss all too common in nineteenth-century life when, in July, their eighteen-month-old son Charley died of cholera. Harriet remained grief stricken through the following year as the Stowes moved to Maine, where Calvin began teaching at Bowdoin College. In the midst of these personal upheavals, however, Stowe found herself increasingly capable of moral outrage as newspapers and politicians around the nation debated the Fugitive Slave Act in the anxious summer of 1850.

This poster—entitled "Read and Ponder"—was a tool in the abolitionist movement. Proponents of abolition were repulsed by this law, and protested against it bitterly.

The Fugitive Slave Act, part of a group of laws referred to as the Compromise of 1850, was passed into law on September 18, 1850. Crafted by Senators Henry Clay of Kentucky, Daniel Webster of Massachusetts, John Calhoun of South Carolina, and Stephen Douglas of Illinois, the Compromise hoped to solve the problem of maintaining the balance of free and slave states as the United States expanded to include California and other territories. The Compromise stated that the territories of New Mexico, Nevada, Arizona, and Utah would be organized without mention of slavery for the time being; that slavery but not slave trade would be permitted in Washington, D.C.; and that, to balance the fact that California would be admitted as a free state, a Fugitive Slave Act would require citizens throughout the land to assist in the recovery of fugitive slaves. The bill furthermore denied a fugitive's right to a jury trial and increased the number of federal officials responsible for enforcing the law. In short, that law not only allowed the recapture of fugitive slaves living in free Northern states but also put those who harbored them in criminal

jeopardy. Not surprisingly, its passage sent former slaves who had been reset-
tled for years in the Northeast fleeing to Canada.

No previous law had ever created the kind of anger that the Fugitive Slave
Act produced in the North. Among white Americans, it ignited passions
never previously seen. Stowe's personal outrage over the Fugitive Slave Act
is apparent in both the timing of *Uncle Tom's Cabin* and its searing depictions of moral cowardice. But it is impossible to separate her anger over the
law from her grief over the loss of her beloved son Charley. Put another way,
if the Fugitive Slave Law was a political impetus for writing *Uncle Tom's
Cabin*, Stowe's sorrow over losing a child was her personal motivation. Biol-
ogy and experience are destiny too; Stowe poured her heart into her wrenching descriptions of slave families severed from each other. As Harriet wrote
to children's book author Eliza Cabot Follen on December 16, 1852:

> I have been the mother of seven children, the most
> beautiful and most loved of whom lies buried near
> my Cincinnati residence. It was at his dying bed
> and at his grave that I learned what a poor slave
> mother may feel when her child is torn away from
> her. In those depths of sorrow which seemed to me
> immeasurable, it was my only prayer to God that
> such anguish might not be suffered in vain. There
> were circumstances about his death of such pecu-
> liar bitterness, of what seemed almost cruel suffer-
> ing that I felt I could never be consoled for it unless
> this crushing of my own heart might enable me to
> work out some great good to others.
>
> I allude to this here because I have often felt that
> much that is in that book had its root in the awful
> scenes and bitter sorrow of that summer. It has left
> now, I trust, no trace on my mind except a deep com-
> passion for the sorrowful, especially for mothers
> who are separated from their children.[1]

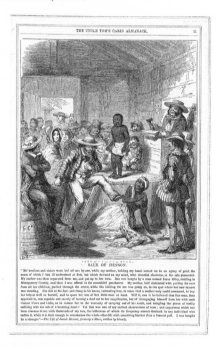

Wood engraving by George
Cruikshank of the sale of Josiah
Henson (1789–1883), who published his
autobiography, *The Life of Josiah
Henson*, in 1849. Stowe drew on
Henson's life story for her novel, as she
acknowledges in *A Key to Uncle Tom's
Cabin*. Henson advertised himself as
the real "Uncle Tom." From *The Uncle
Tom's Cabin Almanack, or, Abolitionist
Memento,* 1853

By 1851, the personal and the political were per-
manently aligned in Stowe's mind when *National
Era* editor Gamaliel Bailey asked her to keep sending material to his antislavery weekly. The fact that
Stowe decided to contribute far more steadily to the
*Era*, largely forsaking *Godey's Lady's Book*, which
focused on more traditional women's issues,
reflected a growing awareness among women that
their political voices could be heard through writ-

1. Harriet Beecher Stowe, [Letter to the Abolitionist Eliza Cabot Follen], in Harriet
Beecher Stowe, *Uncle Tom's Cabin*, Norton Critical Edition, ed. E. Ammons (New
York: W. W. Norton, 1994), p. 413.

"The Auction Scene." A photograph of one of the numerous stage versions of *Uncle Tom's Cabin*.    © Joseph Byron, NY, circa 1900

ing, especially since they were still denied the right to vote. The *Era* already had four of Stowe's stories (including a piece on the Fugitive Slave Act in the summer of 1850), but Bailey wanted more. On March 9, 1851, Stowe sent him a brief summary of the novel already in progress, on the chance he might be interested. Indeed, he was. This would be a longer literary work than she had yet attempted, but Stowe was confident that she could sustain her readers' interest week after week for nearly a year. Publication was immediately arranged, and the first two chapters of *Uncle Tom's Cabin* filled most of the front page of the June 2 edition. The novel was a journalistic coup for the newspaper and would become a runaway best seller for Stowe.

In 1851, the *National Era* had had a small but influential band of readers who paid two dollars per year for subscriptions. The paper, which reported not only political news and regional events but also cultural and international stories, saw its popularity soar as Northern indignation over passage of the Fugitive Slave Act grew. During the previous year, Grace Greenwood (Sara Jane Clarke Lippincott), a recognized social critic affiliated with *Godey's Lady's Book*, had also become a regular contributor to the *National Era*. In the increasingly politicized world of the 1850s, Greenwood, like Stowe, was much more at home in the *Era* than in the pages of *Godey's*. The fact that Stowe chose to publish her novel in the *Era* speaks both to her sense of the novel's political importance and to her sense of the story as well suited to serialization. In the spring of 1851, Greenwood edited the initial drafts of *Uncle Tom's Cabin*. In total, forty-three chapters of the serialized novel were published in the *National Era*, for which Stowe was paid a total of three hundred dollars.

Far beyond the readership of the *Era*, the novel's power immediately began spreading by word of mouth. Even as the tale was unfolding, popular writers and thinkers responded, endorsing or challenging the characterizations,

The front page of the *National Era* featuring chapter 1 of *Uncle Tom's Cabin*.

plot, and political philosophy. In the October 2, 1851, *National Era,* Greenwood, traveling in the American West at the time, reported on how the story was being received:

Wherever I went among the friends of the "Era," I found "Uncle Tom's Cabin" a theme for admiring remark—everywhere I saw it read with pleasant smiles and gushes of irrepressible tears. Mrs. Stowe is winning, not alone "golden opinions," but love and gratitude, and a hearty reverence, by this incomparable story. Its style, its spirit, its construction, scope, and purpose, are alike admirable. Since it has been in course of publication, I have felt that I should not be missed if I stood aside and listened with the rest—like a chorus-singer looking out from the side-scenes, while the Prima Donna stands in front, and with her one surpassing voice reaches and satisfies all hearts.

Months before the serialization was complete, Stowe began negotiations with John Punchard Jewett to publish a bound version of the novel. In October 1851, in the serialization's fifth month, John P. Jewett & Co. announced the upcoming two-volume edition. In a wise commercial move, Stowe delayed serializing the final chapters in the *National Era* so that purchasers of the bound edition could be rewarded with an advance version of Uncle Tom's fate. Jewett's edition appeared on March 20, 1852.[2]

As *Uncle Tom's Cabin* became widely available in bound form, the number of public comments about it grew exponentially. America's foremost abolitionist, William Lloyd Garrison, responded to the novel with mixed reviews. In a letter to the *Liberator* published March 26, 1852, Garrison praised its author: "Mrs. Stowe has displayed rare descriptive powers, a familiar acquaintance with slavery under its best and worst phases, uncommon moral and philosophical acumen, great facility of thought and expression, feelings and emotions of the strongest character." He further credited the novel's potential antislavery influence, saying "the effect of such a work . . . to awaken the strongest compassion for the oppressed and the utmost abhorrence of the system which grinds them to the dust cannot be estimated: it must be prodigious, and therefore eminently serviceable in the tremendous conflict now waged for the immediate and entire suppression of slavery on the American soil." Garrison challenged Stowe's portrayal of Tom turning the other cheek, however, questioning whether Stowe proposed such "Christlikeness" for all human beings or just for blacks: "We are curious to know

2. See Paula Garrett, "*Legacy* Profile: Grace Greenwood (Sara Jane Lippincott), 1823–1904," *Legacy* 14, no. 2 (1997): 137–53.

whether Mrs. Stowe is a believer in the duty of non-resistance for the white man, under all possible outrage and peril, as well as for the black man; whether she is for self-defense on her part, or that of her husband or friends or country, in case of malignant assault, or whether she impartially disarms all mankind in the name of Christ, be the danger or suffering what it may."

Bailey's review of the novel in the April 22, 1852, issue of the *National Era* was primarily an encomium, calling *Uncle Tom's Cabin* "this beautiful new evangel of freedom." Bailey further noted that "the work . . . gives evidence of greater power, of deeper and more various resources, than any other novel of the time" and turned to biblical language to frame his final accolade for Stowe's tale: "So great and good a thing has Mrs. Stowe here accomplished for humanity, for freedom, for God, that we cannot refrain from applying to her sacred words, and exclaiming, 'Blessed art thou among women!' "[3] Bailey added that the bound edition was for sale at the newspaper's office, thus reinforcing his paper's relationship with Stowe.

More serious reviews—and heated debate—appeared in print as well. In a letter to *Frederick Douglass' Paper* on May 20, 1852, well-known scholar and intellectual William G. Allen, one of three African-American professors at New York Central College, responded to particular lines and scenes from the novel:

> I have one regret, with regard to the book, and that is, that the chapter favoring colonization was ever written. I do not, however, apprehend so much harm from it, as some others seem to anticipate. Many of the bad features of that chapter, are somewhat modified by the admission, on the 302d page, of the right of the colored people to meet and mingle in this country—to rise by their individual worth, and without distinction of caste or color; and that they have not only the rights of common men here, but more than these, the rights of an injured race for reparation; and still further, that those who deny this right to rise without distinction of caste or color, and in particular to rise here, are false to their own professed principles of human equality.

In addition to arguments about colonization, responses to *Uncle Tom's Cabin* provoked disputes about Tom's peaceful acceptance, about George's self-possession, about Topsy's originality, and about whether slavery and Southerners were really as horrible as Stowe had described. Indeed, before the novel had been in print an entire year, it had already sparked debate among those thousands of Americans who had previously paid little attention to the peculiar institution. Moreover, the debate about unpaid labor was linked to similar struggles around the world, as the *National Era* itself noted in an editorial on November 18, 1852, after the novel was published in London:

> The sales of this work in Great Britain are incredible, and it seems to have given a new impulse there to the discussion of the question of Slavery. Our pro-slavery patriots complain of this: "What right have the Eng-

---

3. Gamaliel Bailey, "Literary Notices," *National Era*, Apr. 22, 1852.

lish to discuss or even consider the subject of Slavery?" The answer is easy: It is a question of Humanity; it concerns, not one country, but all countries, not one race, but mankind; not a single right, or one class of rights, but all rights. If Slavery be a legitimate institution here, it is legitimate in Cuba, in Brazil, in India, in Africa. If it be honest and decent in the South for one man to use for his own profit, work for his own benefit, and without wages, another man, it is honest and decent to do the same thing at the North, in England, in France, in Austria, in Russia.

Such debates fueled further sales of the book as well. According to Charles Dudley Warner's "The Story of *Uncle Tom's Cabin*," published almost fifty years later in the *Atlantic Monthly*, "three thousand copies were sold the first day, within a few days ten thousand copies had gone, on the 1st of April a second edition went to press, and thereafter eight presses running day and night were barely able to keep pace with the demand for it. Within a year three hundred thousand copies were sold."[4] Success fed on itself, and the recommendation of fans and supporters created an unprecedented momentum of sales. The sheer number of sales, in fact, made headlines. On May 13, 1852, the *Independent* ran the following notice:

> We are informed by Messrs. Jewett & Company . . . that they are now printing the Fiftieth thousand copies, making One Hundred thousand volumes issued in eight weeks! This is without precedent in the history of book publishing in this country. The demand continues without abatement. Our readers can judge of the labor of producing so great a number of books in so short a time when informed that it has taken 3000 reams of medium paper, weighing 30 lbs. to the read—90,000 lbs. of paper; and that three or four of Adam's power presses have been kept running at the most rapid rate, day and night, stopping only on the Sabbath; and that from 125–200 bookbinders have been constantly at work in binding. Weight of books when bound about 110,000 lbs. or 55 tons.

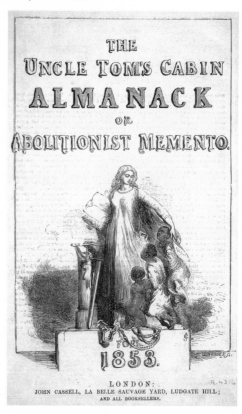

Cover of one of many collections published to capitalize on the success of *Uncle Tom's Cabin*. Slave children surround the figure of Liberty. The image of crouching slaves being freed by a standing white man or woman was a motif of abolitionist iconography. This seventy-page *Abolitionist Memento* is designed for use as a calendar and features reports, essays, drawings, news, and fiction about slavery in America. From *The Uncle Tom's Cabin Almanack, or, Abolitionist Memento,* 1853

4. Charles Dudley Warner, "The Story of *Uncle Tom's Cabin*," in *Critical Essays on Harriet Beecher Stowe,* ed. E. Ammons (Boston: G. K. Hall, 1980), pp. 64–65.

The *New York Times*, then in its infancy, ran a notice on the following day, May 14, 1852:

> Harriet Beecher Stowe, wife of Professor Stowe, of Bowdoin College, and the author of "Uncle Tom's Cabin," has received $4,000, as her share of the sales already made of that work. She receives 10 cents on each copy sold, and a Bangor paper says she has been offered $10,000 for the copyright of the book.

Less than a month later, on June 24, 1852, *Frederick Douglass' Paper* reported that "the 80,000th copy of *Uncle Tom's Cabin* will be published, 70,000 already have been sold." By July 12, 1852, the *New York Times*, emphasizing the commercial as opposed to the social power of the work, published news from the *Boston Traveller* that "Mrs. H. B. Stowe received, a day or two since, from her publishers, Messrs. Jewett & Co., the sum of ten thousand three hundred dollars, as her copyright premium on three months' sales of "Uncle Tom's Cabin." The paper recognized the significance of this figure: "We believe that this is the largest sum of money ever received by any author, either American or European, from the actual sales of a single work in so short a period of time." John P. Jewett & Co. followed its initial publication with a one-volume illustrated edition at the end of 1852. Hammatt Billings, who had done the handful of illustrations for the original publication, completed for this edition 117 illustrations (several of which are reproduced in this book). Editions were published annually throughout the remainder of the century. On July 8, 1852, the *Independent* ran a notice that Clarke and Co. of London would publish the first British edition. This notice also indicated that a "yet cheaper edition is announced, in order to facilitate the circulation among all classes. It is to be issued in 24 weekly numbers, at one penny."

With the tidal wave of popularity inevitably came criticism. In 1853, under increasingly vocal pressure from Southerners to "prove" that there was some basis of truth to *Uncle Tom's Cabin*, Stowe published *A Key to Uncle Tom's Cabin*, which featured "Original Facts and Documents, upon which the story is founded, Together with Corroborative Statements Verifying the Truth of the Work." The *Key* was a success before it was published, with Jewett reportedly receiving nearly sixty thousand advance orders. *Frederick Douglass' Paper* reported on April 22, 1853, prior to publication of the *Key*, that it "is very evident that Uncle Tom without a key has opened the door for the general discussion of slavery as a condition of society, in its comparison with the state of things at the North and in England. . . . The effect of the key will be to unlock every cabin, and open the gates of every plantation for a free and full investigation."

Although the unprecedented success of *Uncle Tom's Cabin* has never been challenged, the novel's literary merits have long been debated. As the twentieth century opened, the concept of literature underwent a transformation; it moved from the parlor into the academy, a change that would have dramatic effects on women's writing and, in turn, on Stowe's reputation. The conventional scholarly assessment of the literary merit of *Uncle Tom's Cabin* has, in fact, never really varied since its publication: The novel is a great literary spectacle but deeply flawed as literature. Just after its publication, French novelist George Sand concluded that "the truest [eulogy] that one can make of the book is to love its very faults. . . . These defects exist only in relation to the conventional rules of art, which never have been and never will be absolute. If its judges, possessed with the love of what they call 'artistic work,' find unskillful treatment in the book, look well at them to see if their eyes are dry when they are reading this or that chapter."[5]

Novelist and editor Charles F. Briggs, in an 1853 essay titled "Uncle Tomitudes," acknowledged that although there are not "any of the delicacies of language which impart so great a charm to the writings of Irving and Hawthorne, nor any descriptions of scenery . . . of Cooper, nor . . . the . . . sensuousness of *Typee* Melville . . . there are broader, deeper, higher and holier sympathies than can be found in our other romances; finer delineations of character, a wider scope of observation, a more purely American spirit, and a more vigorous narrative faculty."[6] As the great literary critic Alfred Kazin put it, "The familiar objection to the novel is that Uncle Tom is too good, too simple, just as the slave traders are too beastly, Simon Legree too awful, Eva too saintly, Topsy too cute. It can be maintained that the only complex character in the book is Augustine St. Clare, who disdains the slave system that enables him to live with so much beauty and in supreme comfort."[7]

The critical assessment of Stowe's depiction of slavery and Southern cruelty has likewise stayed within narrow bounds: Most do not think that her representations are entirely realistic. George F. Holmes's scathing review in the *Southern Literary Messenger* in 1852 claimed that Stowe "traduced the slaveholding society of the United States, and we desire to be understood as acting entirely on the defensive, when we proceed to expose the miserable misrepresentations of her story." Moreover, Holmes argued that the " 'property interest' at which the authoress sneers so frequently in 'Uncle Tom's Cabin,' is quite sufficient to ensure for the negro a kindness and attention, which the day-laborer in New England might in vain endeavor to win from his employer."[8] Kazin brilliantly observes that Holmes's claims that "the book was not so much untrue as unreal . . . [a] 'tissue of moral absolutes that if taken as a political philosophy could only lead to anarchy' . . . of course was Edmund Burke's protest against the French Revolution" (*God and the American Writer*, p. 77).

5. George Sand, "Review of *Uncle Tom's Cabin*," in *Critical Essays on Harriet Beecher Stowe*, ed. E. Ammons (Boston: G. K. Hall, 1980), p. 3.

6. Charles F. Briggs, "Uncle Tomitudes," in *Critical Essays on Harriet Beecher Stowe*, ed. E. Ammons (Boston: G. K. Hall, 1980), p. 40.

7. Alfred Kazin, *God and the American Writer* (New York: Alfred A. Knopf, 1997), p. 83.

8. George. F. Holmes, [Review of *Uncle Tom's Cabin*], in Harriet Beecher Stowe, *Uncle Tom's Cabin*, Norton Critical Edition, ed. E. Ammons (New York: W. W. Norton, 1994), pp. 469, 475.

Charles Dickens, in an 1852 letter to Stowe, commented that he had read the book with the "deepest interest and sympathy" and admired "the generous feeling" and its "admirable power." He criticized Stowe, however, for "seeking to prove too much." "I doubt there being any warrant for making out the African race to be a great race, or for supposing the future destinies of the world to lie in that direction: and I think this extreme championship likely to repel some useful sympathy and support."[9] In the same vein, the anonymous 1852 *Times* (London) reviewer remarked that, "[Stowe] should surely have contented herself with proving the infamy of the slave system, and not been tempted to establish the superiority of the African nature over that of the Anglo-Saxon."[10] George Eliot, in her 1856 review of Stowe's *Dred: A tale of the Great Dismal Swamp*, offered a more practical criticism, suggesting that Stowe should have portrayed "the negro character in its less amiable phases. . . . She alludes to demoralization among the slaves, but she does not depict it; and yet why should she shrink from this, since she does not shrink from giving us a full-length portrait of a Legree or a Tom Gordon?"[11]

Harriet Beecher Stowe and her brother Henry Ward Beecher (1813–1887) appear to be anchoring—and are anchored by—their father, the resolute clergyman Lyman Beecher (1775–1863).

Nearly one hundred years after the book's first publication, George Orwell best summarized its dilemma: "Perhaps the supreme example of the 'good bad' book is *Uncle Tom's Cabin*. It is an unintentionally ludicrous book, full of preposterous melodramatic incidents; it is also deeply moving and essentially true; it is hard to say which quality outweighs the other. But *Uncle Tom's Cabin*, after all, is trying to be serious and to deal with the real world. . . . And by the same token I would back *Uncle Tom's Cabin* to outlive the complete works of Virginia Woolf or George Moore, though I know of no strictly literary test which would show where the superiority lies."[12]

9. Charles Dickens, "Letter to Harriet Beecher Stowe," in *Literary Sourcebook on Harriet Beecher Stowe's* Uncle Tom's Cabin, a Routledge Literary Sourcebook, ed. D. Rosenthal (London: Routledge, 2003), p. 33.

10. Anonymous, [Review of *Uncle Tom's Cabin*], in Harriet Beecher Stowe, *Uncle Tom's Cabin*, Norton Critical Edition, ed. E. Ammons (New York, W. W. Norton, 1994), p. 479.

11. George Eliot, "Review of *Dred: A Tale of the Great Dismal Swamp*," in *Critical Essays on Harriet Beecher Stowe*, ed. E. Ammons (Boston: G. K. Hall, 1980), p. 44.

12. George Orwell, "Good Bad Books," in *The Collected Essays, Journalism, and Letters of George Orwell*, vol. 4, ed. S. Orwell and I. Angus (New York: Harcourt, Brace & World, 1968), p. 21.

Regardless of the reviews, Harriet Beecher Stowe's novel was the most successful commercial novel of the nineteenth century. The first edition—some five thousand copies—sold in four days. In a year it sold more than three hundred thousand in the United States and more than two million in the rest of the world. The literary critic Van Wyck Brooks observed in 1936 that "three Paris newspapers published it at once, and Uncle Tom's Cabins rose all over Europe, as restaurants, creameries and bazaars. It appeared in thirty-seven languages, and three times over in Welsh, into which Scott and Dickens had never been translated; and it sent Heine back to his Bible and made such an impression on Tolstoy in Russia that, when he came to write *What is Art?*, he took it as an example of the highest type."[13] Stowe's novel famously sold more copies than any other book except the Bible.

Abraham Lincoln reportedly said to Harriet Beecher Stowe when she visited the White House in 1862, "So you're the little woman who wrote the book that started this great war"!

Mathew Brady's first portrait of Abraham Lincoln (1809–1864), taken on February 27, 1860. This is a gaunt, beardless, but determined Lincoln.

*Uncle Tom's Cabin* has indeed been one of the great publishing successes in American history. To ignore its romantic, yet realistic, language would be to deny the fact that many of its most avid readers were women, and that Stowe inherently knew that one path toward political and social power was through women's hearts and emotions. To a great extent, another measure of the book's success was Stowe's humor. She leavened her spiritual bread with circuses. Appreciation of the silliness, slapstick, and comic wordplay is a large part of this novel's life in the public imagination, as film versions such as the Little Rascals', the (still shocking!) Minnie and Mickey Mouse short, the hilarious animated film *Uncle Tom's Cabana*, and the pop-culture

Sheet music from the 1923 Duncan Sisters' musical *Topsy and Eva*. A study in contrasts, Topsy appears to embody the demonic while Eva suggests angelic purity and refinement. Irving Berlin, Inc.

13. Van Wyck Brooks, *The Flowering of New England, 1815–1865* (New York: E. P. Dutton, 1936), p. 420.

collectibles attest. The slapstick serves to mask the sexual aspects of the story, certainly, but perhaps more importantly, it has helped sell thousands of books. Perhaps the ultimate sign of popularity was the immediate appearance of dozens of takeoffs. According to poet and critic Sterling A. Brown's *The Negro in American Fiction,* nearly fourteen pro-slavery novels appeared just after Stowe's, many of which riffed on the title, such as Mary Henderson Eastman's *Aunt Phillis's Cabin, or, Southern Life As It Is* (1852); W. L. G. Smith's *Uncle Tom's Cabin As It Is* (1852); Carolyn E. Rush's *The North and South, or Slavery and Its Contrasts* (1852); and John W. Page's *Uncle Robin, In His Cabin in Virginia, and Tom without One in Boston* (1853). There were positive riffs too. Several of the early American editions of Anna Sewell's wildly popular *Black Beauty* (1877) were subtitled *The "Uncle Tom's Cabin" of the Horse.*[14]

Nonetheless, as Edmund Wilson noted, the popularity of *Uncle Tom's Cabin* declined slowly but steadily after the Civil War; until the Modern Library Series reprinted it in 1948, is was only available secondhand. Why did people stop reading *Uncle*

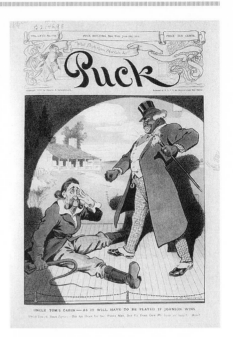

Simon Legree and Uncle Tom, in a dramatic role reversal. Tom says to Simon: "Did ah heah yo' say, White Man, dat yo' done own *me*, body an' soul? Huh?" Circa 1910.

*Tom's Cabin*? There are many theories circulating as to its eclipse. "It is often assumed in the United States that Uncle Tom was a mere propaganda novel which disappeared when it had accomplished its purpose and did not, on its merits, deserve to live," Wilson wrote. "Yet it continued to be read in Europe, and, up to the great Revolution, at any rate, it was a popular book in Russia."[15] Perhaps the most popular Cold War treatment of Stowe's novel was as a ballet production ("Small House of Uncle Thomas") in the 1951 Rogers and Hammerstein stage musical "The King and I," as well as the 1956 film version. This famous play-within-a-play gets everything wrong—Eliza never belonged to Simon Legree, and he did not drown in pursuit of her—and yet

An idealized Eliza, indistinguishable from a white woman, narrowly escaping horrendously ferocious bloodhounds. Strobridge Lithographing Co., Cincinnati, OH, 1881

14. See Peter Stoneley, "Sentimental Masculinities: *Uncle Tom's Cabin* and *Black Beauty,*" *Nineteenth Century Literature* 54 (1999): 53–72.

15. Edmund Wilson, *Patriotic Gore: Studies in the Literature of the American Civil War* (New York: Oxford Univ. Press, 1962), pp. 4–5.

"Uncle Tom's Cabin," 1898. A cakewalk was a strutting dance performed in minstrel shows. Visual renditions of *Uncle Tom's Cabin,* such as this one, mimicked and perpetuated black stereotypes from minstrelsy throughout the nineteenth century.

it somehow remains true to Stowe's original story.

Nearly twenty-five years ago Elaine Showalter wrote that the reason that *Uncle Tom's Cabin* was not taught for so long in the college classroom "has less to do with the qualities of the book itself, with its alleged sentimentality, or its enormous and shameful popularity, or its deliberate intent to change things rather than beautifully represent them, than with the fact that it is an anomaly in a period where the literary canon is exceptionally narrow and strong." That is, Stowe was a woman, and "the major figures of the miraculous half-decade 1850 to 1855 are announced to be white, male, and five in number: Emerson, Thoreau, Whitman, Hawthorne, and Melville."[16] D. H. Lawrence, Showalter notes, completely ignores *Uncle Tom's Cabin* in his *Studies in Classic American Literature.*

And yet, as Alfred Kazin notes, serious readers have never stopped reading *Uncle Tom's Cabin.* "The mature Henry James found the book too coarse, as one would expect. But in *A Small Boy and Others,* reminiscences of his early life in New York, he described with relish how: 'one lived and moved at the time, with great intensity, in Mrs. Stowe's novel . . . nothing in the guise of a written book, therefore, a book printed, published, sold, bought, and 'noticed,' probably ever reached its mark, the mark of exciting interest, without having at least groped for that goal . . .' " (*God and the American Writer,* p. 81).

This poster for a silent-film version of *Uncle Tom's Cabin* evokes sculptor Thomas Ball's famous Emancipation Memorial, which was dedicated in 1876.

As Stowe biographer Joan D. Hedrick writes, "[Stowe's] decline resulted from the removal of literature from the parlor to institutions to which women had limited access: men's clubs, high-culture journals, and prestigious universities. As literature became professionalized, the voice of the novelist became depersonalized and the standards of art became matters for aesthetic consideration rather than political passion. . . . As the standards for judging lit-

16. Elaine Showalter, "Responsibilities and Realities: A Curriculum for the Eighties," *ADE Bulletin* 070 (1981): 17–21.

A rustic, bespectacled Eliza is depicted in this pre-Prohibition political cartoon.

erature changed and the voice of the novelist became more formal and distanced, Stowe's writing was judged to be amateur, unprofessional, and 'bad art.' "[17]

Although the popularity of *Uncle Tom's Cabin* decreased in the last half of the twentieth century, Stowe's novel remains widely read and referenced. Despite continued criticism of the work on political, aesthetic, or regional grounds, the novel has remained a best seller in the United States and abroad and has been translated into more than sixty languages. Although Stowe received compensation for her copyright in the United States, nineteenth-century copyright laws could not ensure payment for copies published in other countries. Of the millions of copies of her novel published globally, Stowe received almost nothing. Indeed, in 1870 international copyright expert James Parton estimated that Stowe lost more than two hundred thousand dollars from the lack of copy-

Secretary of State Condoleezza Rice as Eliza. Stowe's novel remains a potent source for black caricature even in the twenty-first century.   © Elliott Banfield, *New York Sun*, January 21, 2005

17. Joan D. Hedrick, *Harriet Beecher Stowe: A Life* (New York: Oxford Univ. Press, 1994), p. ix.

right laws. By 1878 there were at least thirty-eight editions of the entire novel and eight abridgements, not to mention the literally countless dramatizations, musicals, songs, figurines, cartoons, and, eventually, film versions. Today, more than a hundred and fifty years after the original publication of *Uncle Tom's Cabin*, more than six hundred editions have been published in English and in translation (including seventeen in Hebrew). Currently, there are some one hundred and fifty editions in print worldwide.

# THE
# ANNOTATED

## UNCLE TOM'S CABIN

# UNCLE TOM'S CABIN;

OR,

# LIFE AMONG THE LOWLY.

BY

HARRIET BEECHER STOWE.

VOL. I.

BOSTON:
JOHN P. JEWETT & COMPANY.
CLEVELAND, OHIO:
JEWETT, PROCTOR & WORTHINGTON.
1852.

# VOLUME I[1]

## CHAPTER 1

## *In Which the Reader Is Introduced to a Man of Humanity*

Late in the afternoon of a chilly day in February, two gentlemen were sitting alone over their wine, in a well-furnished dining parlor, in the town of P——, in Kentucky. There were no servants present, and the gentlemen, with chairs closely approaching, seemed to be discussing some subject with great earnestness.

For convenience sake, we have said, hitherto, two *gentlemen*.[2] One of the parties, however, when critically examined, did not seem, strictly speaking, to come under the species. He was a short, thick-set man, with coarse, commonplace features, and that swaggering air of pretension which marks a low man who is trying to elbow his way upward in the world. He was much over-dressed, in a gaudy vest of many colors, a blue neckerchief, bedropped gayly with yellow spots, and arranged with a flaunting tie, quite in keeping with the general air of the man. His hands, large and coarse, were plentifully bedecked with rings; and he wore a heavy gold watch-chain, with a bundle of seals of portentous size, and a great variety of colors, attached to it,—which, in the ardor of conversation, he was in the habit of flourishing and jingling with evident satisfaction. His conversation was in free and easy defiance of Murray's Grammar,[3] and was garnished at convenient intervals with various profane expressions, which not even the desire to be graphic in our account shall induce us to transcribe.[4]

His companion, Mr. Shelby, had the appearance of a

1 The subtitle of Stowe's novel varied. English versions that appeared in 1852 included "*or, Slave Life in America*" (T. Nelson & Sons) and "*A Tale of Life Among the Lowly*" (George Routledge and Co.) as well as two illustrated editions with the subtitles "*or, Negro Life in the Slave States of America*" (Clarke & Company) and "*or, The History of a Christian Slave*" (Partridge and Oakey). The Partridge and Oakey publication was the first illustrated English edition. "*The History of a Christian Slave*" echoes the subtitle of Frederick Douglass's 1845 *Narrative of the Life of Frederick Douglass, An American Slave*. Indeed, each of these subtitles constructs a cultural oxymoron by yoking the terms "Christian" and "Slave" or "American" and "Slave" together.

2 Stowe begins signaling almost immediately that one of her primary concerns in the novel is the flexibility of language. She says she has used the word "gentlemen" for convenience sake. For whose convenience, we might ask: The reader's? Her own? Those who believe in white superiority? Stowe lets us know in the next sentence that she is indeed tweaking "scientific" racists: She calls the category of gentlemen a "species."

3 *English Grammar* by Lindley Murray (1745–1826), authoritative American grammarian.

4 Undermining the argument that women should be protected from the world, Stowe slyly explains that having been privy to indelicate words and behavior has not affected her sense of propriety. She has seen crude and coarse things but remains a lady.

5 It is not difficult to decipher Stowe's point: Poor Mr. Shelby has put the enjoyment of his lifestyle between his eye and the light. Stowe thus explains Mr. Shelby's compromised principles in his decision to sell Tom.

6 Given Tom's abilities, perhaps Tom should have had more control over Mr. Shelby's money and property.

"Is he a negro trader?" The illustrator here captures perfectly the Shelbys' appreciation of the finer things in life. Note Mrs. Shelby's concern for her hair, the graceful curve of the candelabra, her bureau, and Mr. Shelby's lamp. What luxury! No wonder we find Mr. Shelby in debt.   From *Altemus' Young People's Library: Uncle Tom's Cabin; or, Life Among the Lowly*, 1900

gentleman; and the arrangements of the house, and the general air of the housekeeping, indicated easy, and even opulent circumstances.[5] As we before stated, the two were in the midst of an earnest conversation.

"That is the way I should arrange the matter," said Mr. Shelby.

"I can't make trade that way—I positively can't, Mr. Shelby," said the other, holding up a glass of wine between his eye and the light.

"Why, the fact is, Haley, Tom is an uncommon fellow; he is certainly worth that sum anywhere,—steady, honest, capable, manages my whole farm like a clock."

"You mean honest, as niggers go," said Haley, helping himself to a glass of brandy.

"No; I mean, really, Tom is a good, steady, sensible, pious fellow. He got religion at a camp-meeting, four years ago; and I believe he really *did* get it. I've trusted him, since then, with everything I have,—money, house, horses,—and let him come and go round the country; and I always found him true and square in everything."[6]

"Some folks don't believe there is pious niggers, Shelby,"

said Haley, with a candid flourish of his hand, "but *I do*. I had a fellow, now, in this yer last lot I took to Orleans—'t was as good as a meetin, now, really, to hear that critter pray; and he was quite gentle and quiet like. He fetched me a good sum, too, for I bought him cheap of a man that was 'bliged to sell out; so I realized six hundred on him. Yes, I consider religion a valeyable thing in a nigger, when it's the genuine article, and no mistake."

"Well, Tom's got the real article, if ever a fellow had," rejoined the other. "Why, last fall, I let him go to Cincinnati alone, to do business for me, and bring home five hundred dollars. 'Tom,' says I to him, 'I trust you, because I think you're a Christian—I know you wouldn't cheat.' Tom comes back, sure enough; I knew he would. Some low fellows, they say, said to him—'Tom, why don't you make tracks for Canada?' 'Ah, master trusted me, and I couldn't,'—they told me about it. I am sorry to part with Tom, I must say. You ought to let him cover the whole balance of the debt; and you would, Haley, if you had any conscience."

"Well, I've got just as much conscience as any man in business can afford to keep,—just a little, you know, to swear by, as 't were," said the trader, jocularly; "and, then, I'm ready to do anything in reason to 'blige friends; but this yer, you see, is a leetle too hard on a fellow—a leetle too hard." The trader sighed contemplatively, and poured out some more brandy.

"Well, then, Haley, how will you trade?" said Mr. Shelby, after an uneasy interval of silence.

"Well, haven't you a boy or gal that you could throw in with Tom?"

"Hum!—none that I could well spare; to tell the truth, it's only hard necessity makes me willing to sell at all. I don't like parting with any of my hands, that's a fact."

Here the door opened, and a small quadroon[7] boy, between four and five years of age, entered the room. There was something in his appearance remarkably beautiful and engaging. His black hair, fine as floss silk, hung in glossy curls about his round, dimpled face, while a pair of large dark eyes, full of fire and softness, looked out from beneath the rich, long lashes, as he peered curiously into the apartment. A gay robe of scarlet and yellow plaid, carefully made and neatly fitted, set off to advantage the dark and rich style of his beauty; and a certain comic air of assurance, blended with bashfulness, showed that he had been not unused to being petted and noticed by his master.

7 *The American Heritage Dictionary of the English Language* defines a quadroon as a person "having one-quarter black ancestry," derived from the Spanish *cuerterón*. Mulatto (a person with one black parent and one white parent, derived from the Spanish term for mule), quadroon, and octoroon (a person with one-eighth black ancestry) were first used in the Spanish colonies' rigid race-classification systems. These terms were adopted in the Southern colonies and had important legal significance. Beginning in the mid-seventeenth-century, in a departure from the English tradition (and to the great economic benefit of slaveholders who sired children with slaves), any child of a slave mother was legally defined as a slave under the law. In the later eighteenth century, states further expanded the definition: A 1785 Virginia statute (copied by many other slave states) legally defined a "negro" person (and therefore a slave) as a person with a black parent or grandparent. Other states counted even smaller proportions as determining blackness. As a result, many people appearing white were slaves. The popular abolitionist writer Lydia Maria Child's 1842 short story "The Quadroons" first created the literary type of the tragic figure of a slave who looks white. Stowe followed this tradition in *Uncle Tom's Cabin* by choosing light-colored blacks as all of her major characters except, notably, Tom. The legal importance of the distinction continued well into the twentieth century, after the 1896 case of the octoroon Homer Plessy, which legally sanctioned segregation (*Plessy v Ferguson*, 163 US 537 [1896]).

8 The term "Jim Crow" had two meanings in Stowe's time. The literal meaning refered to a song-and-dance act. In 1828, a white blackface entertainer named Thomas D. Rice developed an act based on his observation of the dance of a Louisville slave owned by a Mr. Crow. Called "Jump Jim Crow," the act was widely popular in both the United States and Great Britain. Drawing on African-American song and dance, "Jim Crow" is considered an early example of white exploitation of African-American culture. The second meaning of "Jim Crow" was its use from the 1830s onward as a description for the practice of Northern railroad companies to require separate sections for their African-American riders, "Jim Crow sections." "Jim Crow" would expand its use as an adjective at the turn of the century to designate a wide group of segregation laws in the post–Reconstruction South.

9 According to the *Oxford English Dictionary* (*OED*), "grotesque" could mean "to caricature, travesty" in the nineteenth century. This meaning seems borne out by Harry's dance actions as well as the fact that the child is introduced as a miniature "Jim Crow" and not identified as "Harry" until his mother, Eliza, appears.

10 Despite his clowning, it is evident that the boy is quite familiar with hymns and sermons.

"Hulloa, Jim Crow!"**8** said Mr. Shelby, whistling, and snapping a bunch of raisins towards him, "pick that up, now!"

The child scampered, with all his little strength, after the prize, while his master laughed.

"Come here, Jim Crow," said he. The child came up, and the master patted the curly head, and chucked him under the chin.

"Now, Jim, show this gentleman how you can dance and sing." The boy commenced one of those wild, grotesque**9** songs common among the negroes, in a rich, clear voice, accompanying his singing with many comic evolutions of the hands, feet, and whole body, all in perfect time to the music.

"Bravo!" said Haley, throwing him a quarter of an orange.

"Now, Jim, walk like old Uncle Cudjoe, when he has the rheumatism," said his master.

Instantly the flexible limbs of the child assumed the appearance of deformity and distortion, as, with his back humped up, and his master's stick in his hand, he hobbled about the room, his childish face drawn into a doleful pucker, and spitting from right to left, in imitation of an old man.

Both gentlemen laughed uproariously.

"Now, Jim," said his master, "show us how old Elder Robbins leads the psalm." The boy drew his chubby face down to a formidable length, and commenced toning a psalm tune through his nose, with imperturbable gravity.**10**

"Hurrah! bravo! what a young 'un!" said Haley; "that chap's a case, I'll promise. Tell you what," said he, suddenly clapping his hand on Mr. Shelby's shoulder, "fling in that chap, and I'll settle the business—I will. Come, now, if that ain't doing the thing up about the rightest!"

At this moment, the door was pushed gently open, and a young quadroon woman, apparently about twenty-five, entered the room.

There needed only a glance from the child to her, to identify her as its mother. There was the same rich, full, dark eye, with its long lashes; the same ripples of silky black hair. The brown of her complexion gave way on the cheek to a perceptible flush, which deepened as she saw the gaze of the strange man fixed upon her in bold and undisguised admiration. Her dress was of the neatest possible fit, and set off to advantage her finely moulded shape;—a delicately formed hand and a trim foot and ankle were items of appearance that did not escape the quick eye of the trader, well used to run up at a glance the points of a fine female article.[11]

"Well, Eliza?" said her master, as she stopped and looked hesitatingly at him.

"I was looking for Harry, please, sir;" and the boy bounded toward her, showing his spoils, which he had gathered in the skirt of his robe.

"Well, take him away, then," said Mr. Shelby; and hastily she withdrew, carrying the child on her arm.

"By Jupiter," said the trader, turning to him in admiration, "there's an article,[12] now! You might make your fortune on that ar gal in Orleans, any day. I've seen over a thousand, in my day, paid down for gals not a bit handsomer."

"I don't want to make my fortune on her," said Mr. Shelby, dryly; and, seeking to turn the conversation, he uncorked a bottle of fresh wine, and asked his companion's opinion of it.

"Capital, sir,—first chop!" said the trader; then turning, and slapping his hand familiarly on Shelby's shoulder, he added—

"Come, how will you trade about the gal?—what shall I say for her—what'll you take?"

"Mr. Haley, she is not to be sold," said Shelby. "My wife would not part with her for her weight in gold."

"Ay, ay! women always say such things, cause they ha'nt no sort of calculation. Just show 'em how many watches, feathers, and trinkets, one's weight in gold would buy, and that alters the case, *I* reckon."[13]

"I tell you, Haley, this must not be spoken of; I say no, and I mean no," said Shelby, decidedly.

"Well, you'll let me have the boy, though," said the trader; "you must own I've come down pretty handsomely for him."

"What on earth can you want with the child?" said Shelby.

"Why, I've got a friend that's going into this yer branch of the business—wants to buy up handsome boys to raise for the market. Fancy articles entirely—sell for waiters, and so on, to rich 'uns, that can pay for handsome 'uns. It sets off one of yer great places—a real handsome boy to open door, wait, and tend. They fetch a good sum; and this little devil is such a comical, musical concern, he's just the article."

"I would rather not sell him," said Mr. Shelby, thoughtfully; "the fact is, sir, I'm a humane man, and I hate to take the boy from his mother, sir."

11 As Stowe's readers would have immediately recognized, Eliza's delicate neatness puts her squarely in the tradition of the poor but genteel Victorian heroine, be it Jane Eyre or Little Nell.

12 The term "article" was used to describe religion (the "genuine article" earlier); now it denotes a person. As scholar Gillian Brown writes, "When people themselves are 'articles' subject to 'mercantile dealings,' when 'the souls and bodies of men' are 'equivalent to money,' " there is no distinction between the personal and the economic ("Getting in the Kitchen with Dinah: Domestic Politics in *Uncle Tom's Cabin*").

13 This paragraph is deftly designed to raise the hackles of women readers—especially mothers.

**14** Slave trader Haley voices a common racist thought of the times, that slaves did not possess the capacity to feel. Nineteenth-century sentimentalist thought held that every human being, born a tabula rasa (blank slate), learned to have feelings and to empathize within the family. Thus, Stowe can portray the destruction of the family under slavery as preventing the full humanity of the slaves.

**15** Stowe's comment that Haley might be a second Wilberforce draws its irony from the fact that British statesman William Wilberforce (1759–1833) was a staunch opponent of slavery. Chief spokesman for abolition in the House of Commons, Wilberforce was instrumental in the passage of legislation in 1807 prohibiting the slave trade in Great Britain. One of the founders of the Anti-Slavery Society in 1823, Wilberforce, who deeply influenced the American abolitionist leader William Lloyd Garrison, died in 1833, shortly before the passage of the Emancipation Bill.

**16** As this entire scene indicates, Mr. Shelby likes his gastronomical pleasures.

"O, you do?—La! yes—something of that ar natur. I understand, perfectly. It is mighty onpleasant getting on with women, sometimes. I al'ays hates these yer screachin', screamin' times. They are *mighty* onpleasant; but, as I manages business, I generally avoids 'em, sir. Now, what if you get the girl off for a day, or a week, or so; then the thing's done quietly,—all over before she comes home. Your wife might get her some ear-rings, or a new gown, or some such truck, to make up with her."

"I'm afraid not."

"Lor bless ye, yes! These critters an't like white folks, you know; they gets over things,[14] only manage right. Now, they say," said Haley, assuming a candid and confidential air, "that this kind o' trade is hardening to the feelings; but I never found it so. Fact is, I never could do things up the way some fellers manage the business. I've seen 'em as would pull a woman's child out of her arms, and set him up to sell, and she screechin' like mad all the time;—very bad policy—damages the article—makes 'em quite unfit for service sometimes. I knew a real handsome gal once, in Orleans, as was entirely ruined by this sort o' handling. The fellow that was trading for her didn't want her baby; and she was one of your real high sort, when her blood was up. I tell you, she squeezed up her child in her arms, and talked, and went on real awful. It kinder makes my blood run cold to think on't; and when they carried off the child, and locked her up, she jest went ravin' mad, and died in a week. Clear waste, sir, of a thousand dollars, just for want of management,—there's where 't is. It's always best to do the humane thing, sir; that's been *my* experience." And the trader leaned back in his chair, and folded his arm, with an air of virtuous decision, apparently considering himself a second Wilberforce.[15]

The subject appeared to interest the gentleman deeply; for while Mr. Shelby was thoughtfully peeling an orange, Haley broke out afresh, with becoming diffidence, but as if actually driven by the force of truth to say a few words more.[16]

"It don't look well, now, for a feller to be praisin' himself; but I say it jest because it's the truth. I believe I'm reckoned to bring in about the finest droves of niggers that is brought in,—at least, I've been told so; if I have once, I reckon I have a hundred times,—all in good case,—fat and likely, and I lose as few as any man in the business. And I lays it all to my management, sir; and humanity, sir, I may say, is the great pillar of *my* management."

Mr. Shelby did not know what to say, and so he said, "Indeed!"

"Now, I've been laughed at for my notions, sir, and I've been talked to. They an't pop'lar, and they an't common; but I stuck to 'em, sir; I've stuck to 'em, and realized well on 'em; yes, sir, they have paid their passage, I may say," and the trader laughed at his joke.

There was something so piquant and original in these elucidations of humanity, that Mr. Shelby could not help laughing in company. Perhaps you laugh too, dear reader; but you know humanity comes out in a variety of strange forms now-a-days, and there is no end to the odd things that humane people will say and do.

Mr. Shelby's laugh encouraged the trader to proceed.

"It's strange now, but I never could beat this into people's heads. Now, there was Tom Loker,[17] my old partner, down in Natchez; he was a clever fellow, Tom was, only the very devil with niggers,—on principle 't was, you see, for a better hearted feller never broke bread; 't was his *system*, sir. I used to talk to Tom. 'Why, Tom,' I used to say, 'when your gals takes on and cry, what's the use o' crackin on 'em over the head, and knockin' on 'em round? It's ridiculous,' says I, 'and don't do no sort o' good. Why, I don't see no harm in their cryin',' says I; 'it's natur,' says I, 'and if natur can't blow off one way, it will another. Besides, Tom,' says I, 'it jest spiles your gals; they get sickly, and down in the mouth; and sometimes they gets ugly,—particular yallow gals do,—and it's the devil and all gettin' on 'em broke in. Now,' says I, 'why can't you kinder coax 'em up, and speak 'em fair? Depend on it, Tom, a little humanity, thrown in along, goes a heap further than all your jawin' and crackin'; and it pays better,' says I, 'depend on 't.' But Tom couldn't get the hang on 't; and he spiled so many for me, that I had to break off with him, though he was a good-hearted fellow, and as fair a business hand as is goin'."

"And do you find your ways of managing do the business better than Tom's?" said Mr. Shelby.

"Why, yes, sir, I may say so. You see, when I any ways can, I takes a leetle care about the onpleasant parts like selling young uns and that,—get the gals out of the way—out of sight, out of mind, you know,—and when it's clean done, and can't be helped, they naturally gets used to it. 'Tan't, you know, as if it was white folks, that's brought up in the way of 'spectin' to keep their children and wives, and all that. Niggers, you know, that's fetched up properly,

17 The doubling of names in *Uncle Tom's Cabin* is both unsettling and meaningful. Stowe asks her readers to recognize that external markers such as name, race, or dress do not define a man—only his inner characteristics matter.

**18** Haley continues to be the spokesman for the racist view of slaves as subhuman, possessing none of the human feelings—whether sorrow or joy, hope or despair. See also note 14 above.

**19** If the North was freedom and the South slavery, the farther south the slave went, the crueler the treatment. In abolitionist literature, being "sold South" constituted a death sentence. Border states such as Kentucky were often portrayed as practicing a "gentler" form of slavery.

**20** In *Slave Religion*, scholar Albert J. Raboteau describes "possession" as common to many African spiritual practices: "In states of ecstatic trance, described by anthropologists of religion as 'spirit possession,' the [devotees] dance out in mime the character of a god, becoming for a time the god's mouthpiece." Slaves were able to maintain such rituals. Raboteau claims, for example, that "the 'holy dance' of the shout may very well have been a two-way bridge connecting the core of West African religions—possession by the gods—to the core of evangelical Protestantism—experience of conversion."

**21** Shelby and Haley may actually be eating nuts, since they have been drinking brandy and wine, eating raisins and oranges (which they give Harry for his performance). The metaphorical meaning is clear from the context, however: The two men thought over their options silently for a while.

**22** A paraphrase of 2 Kings 8:13: "Is thy servant a dog, that he should do this great thing?"

ha'n't no kind of 'spectations of no kind; so all these things comes easier."[18]

"I'm afraid mine are not properly brought up, then," said Mr. Shelby.

"S'pose not; you Kentucky folks spile your niggers.[19] You mean well by 'em, but 'tan't no real kindness, arter all. Now, a nigger, you see, what's got to be hacked and tumbled round the world, and sold to Tom, and Dick, and the Lord knows who, 'tan't no kindness to be givin' on him notions and expectations, and bringin' on him up too well, for the rough and tumble comes all the harder on him arter. Now, I venture to say, your niggers would be quite chop-fallen in a place where some of your plantation niggers would be singing and whooping like all possessed.[20] Every man, you know, Mr. Shelby, naturally thinks well of his own ways; and I think I treat niggers just about as well as it's ever worth while to treat 'em."

"It's a happy thing to be satisfied," said Mr. Shelby, with a slight shrug, and some perceptible feelings of a disagreeable nature.

"Well," said Haley, after they had both silently picked their nuts for a season,[21] "what do you say?"

"I'll think the matter over, and talk with my wife," said Mr. Shelby. "Meantime, Haley, if you want the matter carried on in the quiet way you speak of, you'd best not let your business in this neighborhood be known. It will get out among my boys, and it will not be a particularly quiet business getting away any of my fellows, if they know it, I'll promise you."

"O! certainly, by all means, mum! of course. But I'll tell you, I'm in a devil of a hurry, and shall want to know, as soon as possible, what I may depend on," said he, rising and putting on his overcoat.

"Well, call up this evening, between six and seven, and you shall have my answer," said Mr. Shelby, and the trader bowed himself out of the apartment.

"I'd like to have been able to kick the fellow down the steps," said he to himself, as he saw the door fairly closed, "with his impudent assurance; but he knows how much he has me at advantage. If anybody had ever said to me that I should sell Tom down south to one of those rascally traders, I should have said, 'Is thy servant a dog, that he should do this thing?'[22] And now it must come, for aught I see. And Eliza's child, too! I know that I shall have some fuss with wife about that; and, for that matter, about Tom, too. So much for being in debt,—heigho! The fellow sees his advantage, and means to push it."

Perhaps the mildest form of the system of slavery is to be seen in the State of Kentucky. The general prevalence of agricultural pursuits of a quiet and gradual nature, not requiring those periodic seasons of hurry and pressure that are called for in the business of more southern districts, makes the task of the negro a more healthful and reasonable one; while the master, content with a more gradual style of acquisition, has not those temptations to hardheartedness which always overcome frail human nature when the prospect of sudden and rapid gain is weighed in the balance, with no heavier counterpoise than the interests of the helpless and unprotected.

Whoever visits some estates there, and witnesses the goodhumored indulgence of some masters and mistresses, and the affectionate loyalty of some slaves, might be tempted to dream the oft-fabled poetic legend of a patriarchal institution,[23] and all that; but over and above the scene there broods a portentous shadow—the shadow of *law*. So long as the law considers all these human beings, with beating hearts and living affections, only as so many *things* belonging to a master,[24]—so long as the failure, or misfortune, or imprudence, or death of the kindest owner, may cause them any day to exchange a life of kind protection and indulgence for one of hopeless misery and toil,— so long it is impossible to make anything beautiful or desirable in the best regulated administration of slavery.

Mr. Shelby was a fair average kind of man, good-natured and kindly, and disposed to easy indulgence of those around him, and there had never been a lack of anything which might contribute to the physical comfort of the negroes on his estate. He had, however, speculated largely and quite loosely; had involved himself deeply, and his notes to a large amount had come into the hands of Haley; and this small piece of information is the key to the preceding conversation.[25]

Now, it had so happened that, in approaching the door, Eliza had caught enough of the conversation to know that a trader was making offers to her master for somebody.

She would gladly have stopped at the door to listen, as she came out; but her mistress just then calling, she was obliged to hasten away.

Still she thought she heard the trader make an offer for her boy;—could she be mistaken? Her heart swelled and throbbed, and she involuntarily strained him so tight that the little fellow looked up into her face in astonishment.

"Eliza, girl, what ails you to-day?" said her mistress, when Eliza had upset the wash-pitcher, knocked down the

23 The *OED* glosses "peculiar institution" as "a cant phrase in U.S. for negro slavery." Stowe's translation of the phrase from "peculiar" to "patriarchal" seems directly aimed at putting the responsibility for slavery on men.

24 In chapter 8 of his 1845 *Narrative*, Frederick Douglass, who had escaped slavery in 1838, conveys his first real sense of his stature as a thing in his description of the valuation of property after the unexpected death of his master, Captain Anthony: "We were all ranked together at the valuation. Men and women, old and young, married and single, were ranked with horses, sheep, and swine. There were horses and men, cattle and women, pigs and children, all holding the same rank in the scale of being, and were all subjected to the same narrow examination."

25 Stowe signals that Shelby is as much a "type" as an actual character. His physical comforts have blinded him to the evils of slavery. Compare Shelby to Uncle Tom, who is rarely shown eating or drinking.

**26** Although silk is a common material for dresses, Stowe is suggesting that Mrs. Shelby is likewise not above enjoying fine things.

work-stand, and finally was abstractedly offering her mistress a long night-gown in place of the silk dress she had ordered her to bring from the wardrobe.**26**

Eliza started. "O, missis!" she said, raising her eyes; then, bursting into tears, she sat down in a chair, and began sobbing.

"Why, Eliza, child! what ails you?" said her mistress.

"O! missis, missis," said Eliza, "there's been a trader talking with master in the parlor! I heard him."

"Well, silly child, suppose there has."

"O, missis, *do* you suppose mas'r would sell my Harry?" And the poor creature threw herself into a chair, and sobbed convulsively.

"Sell him! No, you foolish girl! You know your master never deals with those southern traders, and never means to sell any of his servants, as long as they behave well. Why, you silly child, who do you think would want to buy your Harry? Do you think all the world are set on him as you are, you goosie? Come, cheer up, and hook my dress. There now, put my back hair up in that pretty braid you learnt the other day, and don't go listening at doors any more."

"Well, but, missis, *you* never would give your consent—to—to—"

"Nonsense, child! to be sure, I shouldn't. What do you talk so for? I would as soon have one of my own children sold. But really, Eliza, you are getting altogether too proud of that little fellow. A man can't put his nose into the door, but you think he must be coming to buy him."

Reassured by her mistress' confident tone, Eliza proceeded nimbly and adroitly with her toilet, laughing at her own fears, as she proceeded.

Mrs. Shelby was a woman of a high class, both intellectually and morally. To that natural magnanimity and generosity of mind which one often marks as characteristic of the women of Kentucky, she added high moral and religious sensibility and principle, carried out with great energy and ability into practical results. Her husband, who made no professions to any particular religious character, nevertheless reverenced and respected the consistency of hers, and stood, perhaps, a little in awe of her opinion. Certain it was that he gave her unlimited scope in all her benevolent efforts for the comfort, instruction, and improvement of her servants, though he never took any decided part in them himself. In fact, if not exactly a believer in the doctrine of the efficiency of the extra good works of saints, he really seemed somehow or other to fancy that his wife had piety and benevolence enough for two—to indulge a shadowy expectation of getting into heaven through her superabundance of qualities to which he made no particular pretension.

The heaviest load on his mind, after his conversation with the trader, lay in the foreseen necessity of breaking to his wife the arrangement contemplated,—meeting the importunities and opposition which he knew he should have reason to encounter.

Mrs. Shelby, being entirely ignorant of her husband's embarrassments, and knowing only the general kindliness of his temper, had been quite sincere in the entire incredulity with which she had met Eliza's suspicions. In fact, she dismissed the matter from her mind, without a second thought; and being occupied in preparations for an evening visit, it passed out of her thoughts entirely.[27]

27 The moral here: A woman with as many virtues as Mrs. Shelby ought not to be entirely ignorant of her husband's embarrassment. A better wife ought to have a better sense of household economy.

# CHAPTER 2

## *The Mother*[1]

1 "The Mother" of the chapter title is of course Eliza. Beyond her characterization as a virtuous and proper Victorian heroine, Eliza is a mother who will suffer physically to save her boy.

2 Here we see Stowe injecting firsthand knowledge into her tale. Eliza's beauty must be believed: The author saw her with her own eyes. This sort of self-authorization was common in nineteenth-century novels. Stowe takes her readers by the hand and assures them that her tale is "true."

3 Notice Stowe's overt fastidiousness here: There is no way to state delicately that slave women—young, old, pretty, or ugly—were routinely sexually abused by not only their white owners but also by fellow slaves (see chapter 32, p. 364). By pretending to be tactful, Stowe is ensuring that the dangers of rape will not be lost on her readers. By the next year, with the publication of William Wells Brown's *Clotel; or The President's Daughter* (and certainly by 1867, with the publication of Harriet Jacobs's *Incidents in the Life of a Slave Girl*), readers could read accounts of somewhat more consensual relationships between slave women and white men, but in 1852, in a text written by a white woman, this was startling.

Eliza had been brought up by her mistress, from girlhood, as a petted and indulged favorite.

The traveller in the south must often have remarked that peculiar air of refinement, that softness of voice and manner, which seems in many cases to be a particular gift to the quadroon and mulatto women. These natural graces in the quadroon are often united with beauty of the most dazzling kind, and in almost every case with a personal appearance pre-possessing and agreeable. Eliza, such as we have described her, is not a fancy sketch, but taken from remembrance, as we saw her, years ago, in Kentucky.[2] Safe under the protecting care of her mistress, Eliza had reached maturity without those temptations which make beauty so fatal an inheritance to a slave.[3] She had been married to a bright and talented young mulatto man, who was a slave on a neighboring estate, and bore the name of George Harris.

This young man had been hired out by his master to work in a bagging factory, where his adroitness and ingenuity caused him to be considered the first hand in the place. He had invented a machine for the cleaning of the hemp, which, considering the education and circumstances of the inventor, displayed quite as much mechanical genius as Whitney's cotton-gin.[4]

He was possessed of a handsome person and pleasing manners, and was a general favorite in the factory. Nevertheless, as this young man was in the eye of the law not a man, but a thing, all these superior qualifications were subject to the control of a vulgar, narrow-minded, tyrannical master.[5] This same gentleman, having heard of the fame of George's invention, took a ride over to the factory, to see what this intelligent chattel had been about. He was received with great enthusiasm by the employer, who congratulated him on possessing so valuable a slave.

He was waited upon over the factory, shown the machinery by George, who, in high spirits, talked so fluently, held himself so erect, looked so handsome and manly, that his master began to feel an uneasy consciousness of inferiority. What business had his slave to be marching round the country, inventing machines, and holding up his head among gentlemen? He'd soon put a stop to it. He'd take him back, and put him to hoeing and digging, and "see if he'd step about so smart." Accordingly, the manufacturer and all hands concerned were astounded when he suddenly demanded George's wages, and announced his intention of taking him home.

"But, Mr. Harris," remonstrated the manufacturer, "isn't this rather sudden?"[6]

"What if it is?—isn't the man *mine*?"

"We would be willing, sir, to increase the rate of compensation."

"No object at all, sir. I don't need to hire any of my hands out, unless I've a mind to."

"But, sir, he seems peculiarly adapted to this business."

"Dare say he may be; never was much adapted to anything that I set him about, I'll be bound."

"But only think of his inventing this machine," interposed one of the workmen, rather unluckily.

"O yes!—a machine for saving work, is it? He'd invent that, I'll be bound; let a nigger alone for that, any time.[7] They are all labor-saving machines themselves, every one of 'em.[8] No, he shall tramp!"

George had stood like one transfixed, at hearing his doom thus suddenly pronounced by a power that he knew was irresistible. He folded his arms, tightly pressed in his lips, but a whole volcano of bitter feelings burned in his bosom, and sent streams of fire through his veins. He breathed short, and his large dark eyes flashed like live coals; and he might have broken out into some dangerous ebullition,[9] had not the kindly manufacturer touched him on the arm, and said, in a low tone,

"Give way, George; go with him for the present. We'll try to help you, yet."

The tyrant observed the whisper, and conjectured its

4 A machine of this description was really the invention of a young colored man in Kentucky. [Stowe's note]

5 The legal status of slaves was fraught from the beginning of the United States. Although considered property to be counted as items in an estate and to be returned to the rightful owners in case of escape to the free states, slaves, as part of the Constitution, were also counted, for tax and representation purposes, as three-fifths persons. This formulation benefited the Southern states, which gained representation in Congress. These elected representatives, however, were not obliged to ask this group for their vote.

6 Once again, Stowe depicts white characters (particularly slaveholders) arguing with other white slaveholding characters. This tactic is a constant reminder that slavery provokes more battles between and among slaveholders than between slaveholders and abolitionists.

7 A common racist stereotype of the time considered the black man inherently lazy.

8 The *Manifesto of the Communist Party*, calling on workers of the world to unite, was published in 1848 by Karl Marx and Friedrich Engels. There is no evidence that Stowe would have read anything by Marx, but American newspapers and journals of the era (including abolitionist publications such as the *National Era* and the *North Star*) featured stories about the working class, wage labor, exploitation, and communism throughout the 1840s and 1850s.

9 I.e., a state of agitation, literally "boiling."

**10** Based on Frederick Douglass, Stowe's description of George—"that the man could not become a thing"—echoes Douglass's own famous formulation at a dramatic moment in his *Narrative*: "You have seen how a man was made a slave; you shall see how a slave was made a man" (chapter 10).

**11** Although slave marriage did not have any legal status at this time, unions were made, often in a ceremony of "jumping the broom." In appealing to her audience of white Christian women, Stowe does not neglect the more common experience of married slaves: that they and their children were often sold away from each other.

**12** Eliza's loss of two children in infancy would have even further solidified the kinship with nineteenth-century women. Infant mortality rates for the nineteenth century were staggering. Scholars Erna Olafson Hellerstein, Leslie Parker Hume, and Karen M. Offen observe in *Victorian Women* that "no account of nineteenth-century motherhood could be complete without mentioning the death of babies and young children. Death stalked the nursery, and such infectious diseases as diptheria and infant diarrhea could strike at any time." The female readers in Stowe's audience would have experienced the death of children on a "tragically common" basis.

import though he could not hear what was said; and he inwardly strengthened himself in his determination to keep the power he possessed over his victim.

George was taken home, and put to the meanest drudgery of the farm. He had been able to repress every disrespectful word; but the flashing eye, the gloomy and troubled brow, were part of a natural language that could not be repressed,—indubitable signs, which showed too plainly that the man could not become a thing.[10]

It was during the happy period of his employment in the factory that George had seen and married his wife.[11] During that period,—being much trusted and favored by his employer,—he had free liberty to come and go at discretion. The marriage was highly approved of by Mrs. Shelby, who, with a little womanly complacency in match-making, felt pleased to unite her handsome favorite with one of her own class who seemed in every way suited to her; and so they were married in her mistress' great parlor, and her mistress herself adorned the bride's beautiful hair with orange-blossoms, and threw over it the bridal veil, which certainly could scarce have rested on a fairer head; and there was no lack of white gloves, and cake and wine,—of admiring guests to praise the bride's beauty, and her mistress' indulgence and liberality. For a year or two Eliza saw her husband frequently, and there was nothing to interrupt their happiness, except the loss of two infant children, to whom she was passionately attached, and whom she mourned with a grief so intense as to call for gentle remonstrance from her mistress, who sought, with maternal anxiety, to direct her naturally passionate feelings within the bounds of reason and religion.[12]

After the birth of little Harry, however, she had gradually become tranquillized and settled; and every bleeding tie and throbbing nerve, once more entwined with that little life, seemed to become sound and healthful, and Eliza was a happy woman up to the time that her husband was rudely torn from his kind employer, and brought under the iron sway of his legal owner.

The manufacturer, true to his word, visited Mr. Harris a week or two after George had been taken away, when, as he hoped, the heat of the occasion had passed away, and tried every possible inducement to lead him to restore him to his former employment.

"You needn't trouble yourself to talk any longer," said he, doggedly; "I know my own business, sir."

"I did not presume to interfere with it, sir. I only

thought that you might think it for your interest to let your man to us on the terms proposed."

"O, I understand the matter well enough. I saw your winking and whispering, the day I took him out of the factory; but you don't come it over me that way. It's a free country, sir; the man's *mine,* and I do what I please with him,—that's it!"[13]

And so fell George's last hope;—nothing before him but a life of toil and drudgery, rendered more bitter by every little smarting vexation and indignity which tyrannical ingenuity could devise.

A very humane jurist once said, The worst use you can put a man to is to hang him. No; there is another use that a man can be put to that is WORSE!

13 Stowe's satire is not always subtle. But here, the overt contradiction is funny as well as ludicrous.

## CHAPTER 3

### *The Husband and Father*[1]

1 If Eliza is designed to be a perfect mother, George Harris is the perfect husband and father—from the female reader's perspective. He is sympathetic, articulate, sensitive, passionate, sensual, and absolutely faithful. What female reader wouldn't want a husband like George?

Mrs. Shelby had gone on her visit, and Eliza stood in the verandah, rather dejectedly looking after the retreating carriage, when a hand was laid on her shoulder. She turned, and a bright smile lighted up her fine eyes.

"George, is it you? How you frightened me! Well; I am so glad you's come! Missis is gone to spend the afternoon; so come into my little room, and we'll have the time all to ourselves."

Saying this, she drew him into a neat little apartment opening on the verandah, where she generally sat at her sewing, within call of her mistress.

"How glad I am!—why don't you smile?—and look at Harry—how he grows." The boy stood shyly regarding his father through his curls, holding close to the skirts of his mother's dress. "Isn't he beautiful?" said Eliza, lifting his long curls and kissing him.

"I wish he'd never been born!" said George, bitterly. "I wish I'd never been born myself!"

Surprised and frightened, Eliza sat down, leaned her head on her husband's shoulder, and burst into tears.

"There now, Eliza, it's too bad for me to make you feel so, poor girl!" said he, fondly; "it's too bad. O, how I wish you never had seen me—you might have been happy!"

"George! George! how can you talk so? What dreadful thing has happened, or is going to happen? I'm sure we've been very happy, till lately."

"So we have, dear," said George. Then drawing his child

on his knee, he gazed intently on his glorious dark eyes, and passed his hands through his long curls.

"Just like you, Eliza; and you are the handsomest woman I ever saw, and the best one I ever wish to see; but, oh, I wish I'd never seen you, nor you me!"

"O, George, how can you!"

"Yes, Eliza, it's all misery, misery, misery! My life is bitter as wormwood;[2] the very life is burning out of me. I'm a poor, miserable, forlorn drudge; I shall only drag you down with me, that's all. What's the use of our trying to do anything, trying to know anything, trying to be anything? What's the use of living? I wish I was dead!"[3]

"O, now, dear George, that is really wicked! I know how you feel about losing your place in the factory, and you have a hard master; but pray be patient, and perhaps something—"

"Patient!" said he, interrupting her; "haven't I been patient? Did I say a word when he came and took me away, for no earthly reason, from the place where everybody was kind to me? I'd paid him truly every cent of my earnings,—and they all say I worked well."

"Well, it *is* dreadful," said Eliza; "but, after all, he is your master, you know."

"My master! and who made him my master? That's what I think of—what right has he to me? I'm a man as much as he is. I'm a better man than he is. I know more about business than he does; I am a better manager than he is; I can read better than he can; I can write a better hand,—and I've learned it all myself, and no thanks to him,—I've learned it in spite of him;[4] and now what right has he to make a dray-horse of me?—to take me from things I can do, and do better than he can, and put me to work that any horse can do? He tries to do it; he says he'll bring me down and humble me, and he puts me to just the hardest, meanest and dirtiest work, on purpose!"

"O, George! George! you frighten me! Why, I never heard you talk so; I'm afraid you'll do something dreadful. I don't wonder at your feelings, at all; but oh, do be careful—do, do—for my sake—for Harry's!"

"I have been careful, and I have been patient, but it's growing worse and worse; flesh and blood can't bear it any longer;—every chance he can get to insult and torment me, he takes. I thought I could do my work well, and keep on quiet, and have some time to read and learn out of work hours; but the more he sees I can do, the more he loads on. He says that though I don't say anything, he sees I've got the devil in me, and he means to bring it out; and

2 Wormwood is a plant bitter in taste and an emblem of bitterness and vexation.

3 George is even more well spoken than Eliza. He almost never speaks in dialect, and he is comfortable using biblical metaphors such as "bitter as wormwood." Continuing his role as a fantasy husband, George is attentive even when upset. As their conversation continues, notice how he repeats the last word that Eliza says when he responds to her pleas.

4 Literacy in the eighteenth- and nineteenth-century United States was considered a crucial component of a full adult life. It was also prohibited for slaves. According to William Goodell's *The American Slave Code in Theory and Practice: Its Distinctive Features Shown by Its Statutes, Judicial Decisions, and Illustrative Facts*, South Carolina had laws dating from 1740 that prohibited the teaching of slaves (under penalty of one-hundred-pound fines). Georgia, Virginia, and North Carolina had similar statutes. The penalty for teaching slaves to read in Louisiana was a year's imprisonment. Several states strengthened laws against teaching slaves to read and write after the bloody Nat Turner slave rebellion of 1831. As James Olney, an expert on the autobiographical genre, observed in his groundbreaking essay " 'I Was Born': Slave Narratives, Their Status as Autobiography and as Literature," every male slave narrative had a scene featuring the narrator's road to literacy. George's complaints to Eliza about the obstacles to his becoming literate are typical. His claims to read and write *better* than his master give us a sense of his indominitable spirit.

**5** This is the third Tom we have heard about in the story.

**6** Noted abolitionist David Walker, in his 1829 *Appeal*, posed a similar question: "Have we any other Master than Jesus Christ alone? Is he not their Master as well as ours?—What right then have we to obey and call any other Master but Himself?" (Article I). In his 1843 *Address to the Slaves of the United States of America*, Henry Highland Garnet, another prominent abolitionist, wrote, "God will not receive slavery, nor ignorance, nor any other state of mind, for love and obedience to Him. Your condition does not absolve you from your moral obligation." The admonition that God is the only Master continued as a major theme in abolitionist literature through the 1850s.

**7** Eliza voices the effect of the misuse of biblical text by pro-slavery preachers when she says, "I always thought that I must obey my master and mistress, or I couldn't be a Christian." In the appendix to his 1845 *Narrative*, Frederick Douglass explains his own stance on religion. Applying his views only to "the *slaveholding religion* of the U.S.," Douglass writes that he hates "the corrupt, slaveholding, women-whipping, cradle-plundering, partial and hypocritical Christianity of this land."

one of these days it will come out in a way that he won't like, or I'm mistaken!"

"O dear! what shall we do?" said Eliza, mournfully.

"It was only yesterday," said George, "as I was busy loading stones into a cart, that young Mas'r Tom**5** stood there, slashing his whip so near the horse that the creature was frightened. I asked him to stop, as pleasant as I could,—he just kept right on. I begged him again, and then he turned on me, and began striking me. I held his hand, and then he screamed and kicked and ran to his father, and told him that I was fighting him. He came in a rage, and said he'd teach me who was my master; and he tied me to a tree, and cut switches for young master, and told him that he might whip me till he was tired;—and he did do it! If I don't make him remember it, some time!" and the brow of the young man grew dark, and his eyes burned with an expression that made his young wife tremble. "Who made this man my master?**6** That's what I want to know!" he said.

"Well," said Eliza, mournfully, "I always thought that I must obey my master and mistress, or I couldn't be a Christian."**7**

"There is some sense in it, in your case; they have brought you up like a child, fed you, clothed you, indulged you, and taught you, so that you have a good education; that is some reason why they should claim you. But I have been kicked and cuffed and sworn at, and at the best only let alone; and what do I owe? I've paid for all my keeping a hundred times over. I *won't* bear it. No, I *won't!*" he said, clenching his hand with a fierce frown.

Eliza trembled, and was silent. She had never seen her husband in this mood before; and her gentle system of ethics seemed to bend like a reed in the surges of such passions.

"You know poor little Carlo, that you gave me," added George; "the creature has been about all the comfort that I've had. He has slept with me nights, and followed me around days, and kind o' looked at me as if he understood how I felt. Well, the other day I was just feeding him with a few old scraps I picked up by the kitchen door, and Mas'r came along, and said I was feeding him up at his expense, and that he couldn't afford to have every nigger keeping his dog, and ordered me to tie a stone to his neck and throw him in the pond."

"O, George, you didn't do it!"

"Do it? not I!—but he did. Mas'r and Tom pelted the poor drowning creature with stones. Poor thing! he looked at me so mournful, as if he wondered why I didn't save him. I had to take a flogging because I wouldn't do it myself. I don't care. Mas'r will find out that I'm one that whipping won't tame. My day will come yet, if he don't look out."

"What are you going to do? O, George, don't do anything wicked; if you only trust in God, and try to do right, he'll deliver you."

"I an't a Christian like you, Eliza; my heart's full of bitterness; I can't trust in God. Why does he let things be so?"

"O, George, we must have faith. Mistress says that when all things go wrong to us, we must believe that God is doing the very best."

"That's easy to say for people that are sitting on their sofas and riding in their carriages; but let 'em be where I am, I guess it would come some harder. I wish I could be good; but my heart burns, and can't be reconciled, anyhow. You couldn't, in my place,—you can't now, if I tell you all I've got to say. You don't know the whole yet."

"What can be coming now?"

"Well, lately Mas'r has been saying that he was a fool to let me marry off the place; that he hates Mr. Shelby and all his tribe, because they are proud, and hold their heads up above him, and that I've got proud notions from you; and he says he won't let me come here any more, and that I shall take a wife and settle down on his place. At first he only scolded and grumbled these things; but yesterday he told me that I should take Mina for a wife, and settle down in a cabin with her, or he would sell me down river."[8]

"Why—but you were married to *me,* by the minister, as much as if you'd been a white man!" said Eliza, simply.

"Don't you know a slave can't be married? There is no law in this country for that; I can't hold you for my wife, if he chooses to part us. That's why I wish I'd never seen you,—why I wish I'd never been born; it would have been better for us both,—it would have been better for this poor child if he had never been born. All this may happen to him yet!"

"O, but master is so kind!"

"Yes, but who knows?—he may die—and then he may be sold to nobody knows who. What pleasure is it that he is handsome, and smart, and bright? I tell you, Eliza, that a sword will pierce through your soul for every good and pleasant thing your child is or has; it will make him worth too much for you to keep!"

The words smote heavily on Eliza's heart; the vision of the trader came before her eyes, and, as if some one had

8 What a rare and wonderful specimen of husband! George Harris complains to Eliza that his cruel master is going to make him sleep with another woman. Stowe's female readers must have nodded appreciatively.

**9** Every reader then and now recognizes this foundational American sentiment.

**10** Notice that the discord between George's master and the Shelbys does not involve abolition. Stowe worked to depict Southerners as an argumentative people.

struck her a deadly blow, she turned pale and gasped for breath. She looked nervously out on the verandah, where the boy, tired of the grave conversation, had retired, and where he was riding triumphantly up and down on Mr. Shelby's walking-stick. She would have spoken to tell her husband her fears, but checked herself.

"No, no,—he has enough to bear, poor fellow!" she thought. "No, I won't tell him; besides, it an't true; Missis never deceives us."

"So, Eliza, my girl," said the husband, mournfully, "bear up, now; and good-by, for I'm going."

"Going, George! Going where?"

"To Canada," said he, straightening himself up; "and when I'm there, I'll buy you; that's all the hope that's left us. You have a kind master, that won't refuse to sell you. I'll buy you and the boy;—God helping me, I will!"

"O, dreadful! if you should be taken?"

"I won't be taken, Eliza; I'll *die* first! I'll be free, or I'll die!"**9**

"You won't kill yourself!"

"No need of that. They will kill me, fast enough; they never will get me down the river alive!"

"O, George, for my sake, do be careful! Don't do anything wicked; don't lay hands on yourself, or anybody else! You are tempted too much—too much; but don't—go you must—but go carefully, prudently; pray God to help you."

"Well, then, Eliza, hear my plan. Mas'r took it into his head to send me right by here, with a note to Mr. Symmes, that lives a mile past. I believe he expected I should come here to tell you what I have. It would please him, if he thought it would aggravate 'Shelby's folks,' as he calls 'em.**10** I'm going home quite resigned, you understand, as if all was over. I've got some preparations made,—and there are those that will help me; and, in the course of a week or so, I shall be among the missing, some day. Pray for me, Eliza; perhaps the good Lord will hear *you*."

"O, pray yourself, George, and go trusting in him; then you won't do anything wicked."

"Well, now, *good-by,*" said George, holding Eliza's hands, and gazing into her eyes, without moving. They stood silent; then there were last words, and sobs, and bitter weeping,—such parting as those may make whose hope to meet again is as the spider's web,—and the husband and wife were parted.

# CHAPTER 4

## *An Evening in Uncle Tom's Cabin*[1]

The cabin of Uncle Tom was a small log building, close adjoining to "the house," as the negro *par excellence* designates his master's dwelling. In front it had a neat garden-patch, where, every summer, strawberries, raspberries, and a variety of fruits and vegetables, flourished under careful tending. The whole front of it was covered by a large scarlet bignonia and a native multiflora rose, which, entwisting and interlacing, left scarce a vestige of the rough logs to be seen. Here, also, in summer, various brilliant annuals, such as marigolds, petunias, four-o'clocks, found an indulgent corner in which to unfold their splendors, and were the delight and pride of Aunt Chloe's heart.[2]

Let us enter the dwelling. The evening meal at the house is over, and Aunt Chloe, who presided over its preparation as head cook, has left to inferior officers in the kitchen the business of clearing away and washing dishes, and come out into her own snug territories, to "get her ole man's supper;" therefore, doubt not that it is her you see by the fire, presiding with anxious interest over certain frizzling items in a stew-pan, and anon with grave consideration lifting the cover of a bake-kettle, from whence steam forth indubitable intimations of "something good." A round, black, shining face is hers, so glossy as to suggest the idea that she might have been washed over with white of eggs, like one of her own tea rusks. Her whole plump countenance beams with satisfaction and

1 After hearing of Tom Loker and Mas'r Tom (George Harris's master), we are finally getting around to meeting the most important Tom, Uncle Tom. First, however, we must read about his cabin.

2 The designations "Uncle" and "Aunt"— and the fact that both Tom and Chloe live in the same cabin—make clear that they are married, but Stowe does not describe them as close in the same way that Eliza and George are. Of the many illustrations and images of Aunt Chloe that have circulated, none depicts Aunt Chloe as anything but a "mammy" figure.

3 More evidence that the Shelbys have enjoyed the finer things in life on a large scale. Chloe is "head cook" and therefore complicit to a certain extent in the excesses that have led to the Shelby's insolvency. From the very first, Stowe is careful not to show Tom enjoying earthly delights.

Cover of the first edition of *Uncle Tom's Cabin* (John P. Jewett & Co., 1852); the engraving is by renowned American architect and artist Hammatt Billings (1818–1874). Here we see Aunt Chloe at the door with three children. Uncle Tom, arriving from the left, is dressed more like a house servant than a field hand.

contentment from under her well-starched checked turban, bearing on it, however, if we must confess it, a little of that tinge of self-consciousness which becomes the first cook of the neighborhood, as Aunt Chloe was universally held and acknowledged to be.[3]

A cook she certainly was, in the very bone and centre of her soul. Not a chicken or turkey or duck in the barn-yard but looked grave when they saw her approaching, and seemed evidently to be reflecting on their latter end; and certain it was that she was always meditating on trussing, stuffing and roasting, to a degree that was calculated to inspire terror in any reflecting fowl living. Her corn-cake, in all its varieties of hoe-cake, dodgers, muffins, and other species too numerous to mention, was a sublime mystery to all less practised compounders; and she would shake her fat sides with honest pride and merriment, as she would narrate the fruitless efforts that one and another of her compeers had made to attain to her elevation.

The arrival of company at the house, the arranging of dinners and suppers "in style," awoke all the energies of her soul; and no sight was more welcome to her than a pile of travelling trunks launched on the verandah, for then she foresaw fresh efforts and fresh triumphs.

Just at present, however, Aunt Chloe is looking into the

bake-pan; in which congenial operation we shall leave her till we finish our picture of the cottage.[4]

In one corner of it stood a bed, covered neatly with a snowy spread; and by the side of it was a piece of carpeting, of some considerable size. On this piece of carpeting Aunt Chloe took her stand, as being decidedly in the upper walks of life; and it and the bed by which it lay, and the whole corner, in fact, were treated with distinguished consideration, and made, so far as possible, sacred from the marauding inroads and desecrations of little folks. In fact, that corner was the *drawing-room* of the establishment. In the other corner was a bed of much humbler pretensions, and evidently designed for *use*. The wall over the fireplace was adorned with some very brilliant scriptural prints, and a portrait of General Washington, drawn and colored in a manner which would certainly have astonished that hero, if ever he had happened to meet with its like.[5]

On a rough bench in the corner, a couple of woolly-headed boys,[6] with glistening black eyes and fat shining cheeks, were busy in superintending the first walking operations of the baby, which, as is usually the case, consisted in getting up on its feet, balancing a moment, and then tumbling down,—each successive failure being violently cheered, as something decidedly clever.[7]

A table, somewhat rheumatic in its limbs, was drawn out in front of the fire, and covered with a cloth, displaying cups and saucers of a decidedly brilliant pattern, with other symptoms of an approaching meal. At this table was seated Uncle Tom, Mr. Shelby's best hand, who, as he is to be the hero of our story, we must daguerreotype for our readers. He was a large, broad-chested, powerfully-made man, of a full glossy black, and a face whose truly African features were characterized by an expression of grave and steady good sense, united with much kindliness and benevolence. There was something about his whole air self-respecting and dignified, yet united with a confiding and humble simplicity.[8]

He was very busily intent at this moment on a slate lying before him, on which he was carefully and slowly endeavoring to accomplish a copy of some letters, in which operation he was overlooked by young Mas'r George,[9] a smart, bright boy of thirteen, who appeared fully to realize the dignity of his position as instructor.

"Not that way, Uncle Tom,—not that way," said he, briskly, as Uncle Tom laboriously brought up the tail of his *g* the wrong side out; "that makes a *q,* you see."

4 The move from "cabin" to "cottage" is particularly important in 1850, after the publication of Andrew Jackson Downing's *The Architecture of Country Houses*. As American literature scholar William Gleason has written, the term "cottage" had come to denote "respectable, even desirable rural housing" ("'I Dwell Now in a Neat Little Cottage': Architecture, Race, and Desire in *The Bondwoman's Narrative*").

5 Stowe's description of such domestic attentions as the starched turban, the snowy white bedspread, and the corner "drawing-room" speak to Aunt Chloe's performance of the womanly task of making a home out of her family's dwelling. Chloe is clean and virtuous; the purity of the cabin stands in contrast to the sexuality apparent elsewhere in the novel. Note also the "colored" George Washington.

6 A stereotypical description of black hair as "wool" suggests the racist tendency to find nonhuman parallels to the physical characteristics of slaves. The children's "glistening black eyes and fat shining cheeks" are clearly inherited from Chloe, with her "round, black, shining face" and "plump countenance." This jolly mammy and her jolly children in the snug cabin ought to be the central image of Stowe's novel, as the title and the cover image of the first edition proclaim. And yet these characters exert no pull on the public imagination the way such characters as Topsy, Eva, and Simon Legree do. Most later editions of the novel feature Tom and Eva on the cover. Of all the songs and plays and sequels and rebuttals and spin-offs to *Uncle Tom's Cabin* we have encountered, only one explores the question of Chloe and Tom's children— Richard Wright's 1938 collection of novellas, *Uncle Tom's Children*—and this only ironically. Wright never mentions Stowe in these pages, assuming that his readers will know to whom the title (and the book's epigraph) refers.

7 Three children share the cabin with Tom and Chloe. They have always seemed to be somewhat too young to be Tom and Chloe's (who appear as a middle-aged married couple).

8 "Humble simplicity" is not a common characteristic in the Shelby household, even in a cabin described as full of cooking and sur-

rounded by a riot of flowers. But Tom is humble, simple, African, and dignified. Uncle Tom takes on the stature of a black "noble savage" here. The noble savage—whether Native American or African—became an important cultural figure, celebrated in the midst of his destruction. One of the earliest literary examples of the black noble savage is found in the 1688 British novel *Oroonoko, or the Royal Slave*, written by Aphra Behn and considered the first sympathetic literary treatment of Africans. Now Tom is cast as a Holy Man.

9 George Shelby is the second George in the novel (not including General Washington).

10 George, like his father, is always talking about food.

11 Brown is a lovely color, in case the reader has missed Stowe's point.

12 Use of the appellation "nigger" in slave-to-slave conversation contrasts sharply with the demeaning racist term "nigger," used by Haley in chapter 1. Harriet Beecher Stowe's depiction of dialogue among the slave characters is very contemporary sounding and surprisingly accurate—almost anthropological. See William Wells Brown's 1847 *Narrative of William W. Brown*.

"La sakes, now, does it?" said Uncle Tom, looking with a respectful, admiring air, as his young teacher flourishingly scrawled *q*'s and *g*'s innumerable for his edification; and then, taking the pencil in his big, heavy fingers, he patiently re-commenced.

"How easy white folks al'us does things!" said Aunt Chloe, pausing while she was greasing a griddle with a scrap of bacon on her fork, and regarding young Master George with pride. "The way he can write, now! and read, too! and then to come out here evenings and read his lessons to us,—it's mighty interestin'!"

"But, Aunt Chloe, I'm getting mighty hungry," said George. "Isn't that cake in the skillet almost done?"10

"Mose done, Mas'r George," said Aunt Chloe, lifting the lid and peeping in,—"browning beautiful—a real lovely brown.11 Ah! let me alone for dat. Missis let Sally try to make some cake, t'other day, jes to *larn* her, she said. 'O, go way, Missis,' says I; 'it really hurts my feelin's, now, to see good vittles spiled dat ar way! Cake ris all to one side—no shape at all; no more than my shoe;—go way!'"

And with this final expression of contempt for Sally's greenness, Aunt Chloe whipped the cover off the bake-kettle, and disclosed to view a neatly-baked pound-cake, of which no city confectioner need to have been ashamed. This being evidently the central point of the entertainment, Aunt Chloe began now to bustle about earnestly in the supper department.

"Here you, Mose and Pete! get out de way, you niggers!12 Get away, Polly, honey,—mammy'll give her baby somefin, by and by. Now, Mas'r George, you jest take off dem books, and set down now with my old man, and I'll take up de sausages, and have de first griddle full of cakes on your plates in less dan no time."

"They wanted me to come to supper in the house," said George; "but I knew what was what too well for that, Aunt Chloe."

"So you did—so you did, honey," said Aunt Chloe, heaping the smoking batter-cakes on his plate; "you know'd your old aunty'd keep the best for you. O, let you alone for dat! Go way!" And, with that, aunty gave George a nudge with her finger, designed to be immensely facetious, and turned again to her griddle with great briskness.

"Now for the cake," said Mas'r George, when the activity of the griddle department had somewhat subsided; and, with that, the youngster flourished a large knife over the article in question.

"La bless you, Mas'r George!" said Aunt Chloe, with

earnestness, catching his arm, "you wouldn't be for cuttin' it wid dat ar great heavy knife! Smash all down—spile all de pretty rise of it. Here, I've got a thin old knife, I keeps sharp a purpose. Dar now, see! comes apart light as a feather! Now eat away—you won't get anything to beat dat ar."

"Tom Lincon[13] says," said George, speaking with his mouth full, "that their Jinny is a better cook than you."

"Dem Lincons an't much count, no way!" said Aunt Chloe, contemptuously; "I mean, set along side *our* folks. They's 'spectable folks enough in a kinder plain way; but, as to gettin' up anything in style, they don't begin to have a notion on't. Set Mas'r Lincon, now, alongside Mas'r Shelby! Good Lor! and Missis Lincon,—can she kinder sweep it into a room like my missis,—so kinder splendid, yer know! O, go way! don't tell me nothin' of dem Lincons!"—and Aunt Chloe tossed her head as one who hoped she did know something of the world.

"Well, though, I've heard you say," said George, "that Jinny was a pretty fair cook."

"So I did," said Aunt Chloe,—"I may say dat. Good, plain, common cookin', Jinny'll do;—make a good pone o' bread,—bile her taters *far*,—her corn cakes isn't extra, not extra now, Jinny's corn cakes isn't, but then they's far,—but, Lor, come to de higher branches,[14] and what *can* she do? Why, she makes pies—sartin she does; but what kinder crust? Can she make your real flecky paste, as melts in your mouth, and lies all up like a puff? Now, I went over thar when Miss Mary was gwine to be married, and Jinny she jest showed me de weddin' pies. Jinny and I is good friends, ye know. I never said nothin'; but go long, Mas'r George! Why, I shouldn't sleep a wink for a week, if I had a batch of pies like dem ar. Why, dey wan't no 'count 't all."

"I suppose Jinny thought they were ever so nice," said George.

"Thought so!—didn't she? Thar she was, showing 'em, as innocent—ye see, it's jest here, Jinny *don't know*. Lor, the family an't nothing! She can't be spected to know! Ta'nt no fault o' hern. Ah, Mas'r George, you doesn't know half your privileges in yer family and bringin' up!" Here Aunt Chloe sighed, and rolled up her eyes with emotion.

"I'm sure, Aunt Chloe, I understand all my pie and pudding privileges," said George. "Ask Tom Lincon if I don't crow over him, every time I meet him."

Aunt Chloe sat back in her chair, and indulged in a hearty guffaw of laughter, at this witticism of young

13 The neighbor Tom Lincoln is the fourth Tom in the novel.

14 Uncle Tom's simplicity in all things stands in contrast to Chloe's love of the "higher branches" of cuisine.

"Uncle Tom at Home." Wood engraving by Jackson, "after George Cruikshank." Apparently, according to the engravers, the slaves' favorite dance was the jig. Master George appears to be clapping and keeping time.

Mas'r's, laughing till the tears rolled down her black, shining cheeks, and varying the exercise with playfully slapping and poking Mas'r Georgey, and telling him to go way, and that he was a case—that he was fit to kill her, and that he sartin would kill her, one of these days; and, between each of these sanguinary predictions, going off into a laugh, each longer and stronger than the other, till George really began to think that he was a very dangerously witty fellow, and that it became him to be careful how he talked "as funny as he could."

"And so ye telled Tom, did ye? O, Lor! what young uns will be up ter! Ye crowed over Tom? O, Lor! Mas'r George, if ye wouldn't make a hornbug laugh!"

"Yes," said George, "I says to him, 'Tom, you ought to see some of Aunt Chloe's pies; they're the right sort,' says I."

"Pity, now, Tom couldn't," said Aunt Chloe, on whose benevolent heart the idea of Tom's benighted condition seemed to make a strong impression. "Ye oughter just ask him here to dinner, some o' these times, Mas'r George," she added; "it would look quite pretty of ye. Ye know, Mas'r George, ye oughtenter feel 'bove nobody, on 'count yer privileges, 'cause all our privileges is gi'n to us; we ought al'ays to 'member that," said Aunt Chloe, looking quite serious.

"Well, I mean to ask Tom here, some day next week," said George; "and you do your prettiest, Aunt Chloe, and we'll make him stare. Won't we make him eat so he won't get over it for a fortnight?"

"Yes, yes—sartin," said Aunt Chloe, delighted; "you'll see. Lor! to think of some of our dinners! Yer mind dat ar great chicken pie I made when we guv de dinner to General Knox?**15** I and Missis, we come pretty near quarrelling about dat ar crust. What does get into ladies sometimes, I don't know; but, sometimes, when a body has de heaviest kind o' 'sponsibility on 'em, as ye may say, and is all kinder *seris* and taken up, dey takes dat ar time to be hangin' round and kinder interferin'! Now, Missis, she wanted me to do dis way, and she wanted me to do dat way; and, finally, I got kinder sarcy, and, says I, 'Now, Missis, do jist look at dem beautiful white hands o' yourn, with long fingers, and all a sparkling with rings, like my white lilies when de dew's on 'em; and look at my great black stumpin hands. Now, don't ye think dat de Lord must have meant *me* to make de pie-crust, and you to stay in de parlor?'**16** Dar! I was jist so sarcy, Mas'r George."

"And what did mother say?" said George.

"Say?—why, she kinder larfed in her eyes—dem great handsome eyes o' hern; and, says she, 'Well, Aunt Chloe, I think you are about in the right on 't,' says she; and she went off in de parlor. She oughter cracked me over de head for bein' so sarcy; but dar's whar 't is—I can't do nothin' with ladies in de kitchen!"

"Well, you made out well with that dinner,—I remember everybody said so," said George.

"Didn't I? And wan't I behind de dinin'-room door dat bery day? and didn't I see de General pass his plate three times for some more dat bery pie?—and, says he, 'You must have an uncommon cook, Mrs. Shelby.' Lor! I was fit to split myself.

"And de Gineral, he knows what cookin' is," said Aunt Chloe, drawing herself up with an air. "Bery nice man, de Gineral! He comes of one of de bery *fustest* families in Old Virginny! He knows what's what, now, as well as I do—de Gineral. Ye see, there's *pints* in all pies, Mas'r George; but tan't everybody knows what they is, or orter be. But the Gineral, he knows; I knew by his 'marks he made. Yes, he knows what de pints is!"

By this time, Master George had arrived at that pass to which even a boy can come (under uncommon circum-

**15** Most likely, "General Knox" is a generic name, used to designate the guests that frequent the Shelby household. General Henry Knox (1750–1806) was the Boston-born first U.S. secretary of war. Stowe hammers the point home that the Shelbys give lots of dinners.

**16** Here Aunt Chloe reaffirms the idea that women belong in the home but adds racist reasoning—that white women should be "in de parlor," whereas black women belong in the kitchen.

**17** I.e., "Stop your mischief and behave!"

stances,) when he really could not eat another morsel and, therefore, he was at leisure to notice the pile of woolly heads and glistening eyes which were regarding their operations hungrily from the opposite corner.

"Here, you Mose, Pete," he said, breaking off liberal bits, and throwing it at them; "you want some, don't you? Come, Aunt Chloe, bake them some cakes."

And George and Tom moved to a comfortable seat in the chimney-corner, while Aunt Chloe, after baking a goodly pile of cakes, took her baby on her lap, and began alternately filling its mouth and her own, and distributing to Mose and Pete, who seemed rather to prefer eating theirs as they rolled about on the floor under the table, tickling each other, and occasionally pulling the baby's toes.

"O! go long, will ye?"**17** said the mother, giving now and then a kick, in a kind of general way, under the table, when the movement became too obstreperous. "Can't ye be decent when white folks comes to see ye? Stop dat ar, now, will ye? Better mind yerselves, or I'll take ye down a button-hole lower, when Mas'r George is gone!"

What meaning was couched under this terrible threat, it is difficult to say; but certain it is that its awful indistinctness seemed to produce very little impression on the young sinners addressed.

"La, now!" said Uncle Tom, "they are so full of tickle all the while, they can't behave theirselves."

Here the boys emerged from under the table, and, with hands and faces well plastered with molasses, began a vigorous kissing of the baby.

"Get along wid ye!" said the mother, pushing away their woolly heads. "Ye'll all stick together, and never get clar, if ye do dat fashion. Go long to de spring and wash yerselves!" she said, seconding her exhortations by a slap, which resounded very formidably, but which seemed only to knock out so much more laugh from the young ones, as they tumbled precipitately over each other out of doors, where they fairly screamed with merriment.

"Did ye ever see such aggravating young uns?" said Aunt Chloe, rather complacently, as, producing an old towel, kept for such emergencies, she poured a little water out of the cracked tea-pot on it, and began rubbing off the molasses from the baby's face and hands; and, having polished her till she shone, she set her down in Tom's lap, while she busied herself in clearing away supper. The baby employed the intervals in pulling Tom's nose, scratching his face, and burying her fat hands in his woolly hair, which last operation seemed to afford her special content.[18]

"Aint she a peart young un?" said Tom, holding her from him to take a full-length view; then, getting up, he set her on his broad shoulder, and began capering and dancing[19] with her, while Mas'r George snapped at her with his pocket-handkerchief, and Mose and Pete, now returned again, roared after her like bears, till Aunt Chloe declared that they "fairly took her head off"[20] with their noise. As, according to her own statement, this surgical operation[21] was a matter of daily occurrence in the cabin, the declaration no whit abated the merriment, till every one had roared and tumbled and danced themselves down to a state of composure.

"Well, now, I hopes you're done," said Aunt Chloe, who had been busy in pulling out a rude box of a trundle-bed; "and now, you Mose and you Pete, get into thar; for we's goin' to have the meetin'."

"O mother, we don't wanter. We wants to sit up to meetin',—meetin's is so curis. We likes 'em."

"La, Aunt Chloe, shove it under, and let 'em sit up," said Mas'r George, decisively, giving a push to the rude machine.

Aunt Chloe, having thus saved appearances, seemed highly delighted to push the thing under, saying, as she did so, "Well, mebbe 't will do 'em some good."

The house now resolved itself into a committee of the whole, to consider the accommodations and arrangements for the meeting.[22]

"What we's to do for cheers, now, I declar I don't know," said Aunt Chloe. As the meeting had been held at Uncle Tom's, weekly, for an indefinite length of time, without any more "cheers," there seemed some encouragement to hope that a way would be discovered at present.

"Old Uncle Peter sung both de legs out of dat oldest cheer, last week," suggested Mose.

"You go long! I'll boun' you pulled 'em out; some o' your shines," said Aunt Chloe.

"Well, it'll stand, if it only keeps jam up agin de wall!" said Mose.

"Den Uncle Peter mus'n't sit in it, cause he al'ays hitches when he gets a singing. He hitched pretty nigh across de room, t' other night," said Pete.

"Good Lor! get him in it, then," said Mose, "and den he'd begin, 'Come saints and sinners, hear me tell,' and den down he'd go,"—and Mose imitated precisely the nasal

18 Nineteenth-century thought held that the sexes occupied separate spheres: Men held sway in the public sphere, women ruled the domestic sphere. Throughout her novel, Stowe concentrates on family scenes as places of female power. Here we see the affection shared by mother and children. Note that, even though a slave, Uncle Tom shows typical male unease with his own children.

19 I.e., leaping and dancing.

20 A figurative expression, meaning "almost made her deaf."

21 Stowe underlines the violence of her earlier figurative expression by calling the event a "surgical operation." Such noise and mischief were a "daily occurrence."

22 Because souls without access to salvation were in jeopardy of damnation, slaveowners (either willingly or under duress) often allowed their slaves to participate in Bible readings and religious services. According to Albert J. Raboteau in *Slave Religion*, by the end of the eighteenth century black Methodists and Baptists numbered more than 30,000; in the wake of the early nineteenth-century Great Awakening revival movement, the numbers grew exponentially. Meetings such as the one Stowe describes here were common, often led by a black preacher or a recognized leader.

**23** In this description of the meeting, Stowe again moves away from racial designation to universal language ("old gray-headed patriarch of eighty" as well as fifteen-year-old "girl and lad").

**24** Yet more evidence that frugality is not a characteristic of the Shelby household.

tones of the old man, tumbling on the floor, to illustrate the supposed catastrophe.

"Come now, be decent, can't ye?" said Aunt Chloe; "an't yer shamed?"

Mas'r George, however, joined the offender in the laugh, and declared decidedly that Mose was a "buster." So the maternal admonition seemed rather to fail of effect.

"Well, ole man," said Aunt Chloe, "you'll have to tote in them ar bar'ls."

"Mother's bar'ls is like dat ar widder's, Mas'r George was reading 'bout, in de good book,—dey never fails," said Mose, aside to Pete.

"I'm sure one on 'em caved in last week," said Pete, "and let 'em all down in de middle of de singin'; dat ar was failin', warnt it?"

During this aside between Mose and Pete, two empty casks had been rolled into the cabin, and being secured from rolling, by stones on each side, boards were laid across them, which arrangement, together with the turning down of certain tubs and pails, and the disposing of the rickety chairs, at last completed the preparation.

"Mas'r George is such a beautiful reader, now, I know he'll stay to read for us," said Aunt Chloe; " 'pears like 't will be so much more interestin'."

George very readily consented, for your boy is always ready for anything that makes him of importance.

The room was soon filled with a motley assemblage, from the old gray-headed patriarch of eighty, to the young girl and lad of fifteen.**23** A little harmless gossip ensued on various themes, such as where old Aunt Sally got her new red headkerchief, and how "Missis was a going to give Lizzy that spotted muslin gown, when she'd got her new berage made up;" and how Mas'r Shelby was thinking of buying a new sorrel colt, that was going to prove an addition to the glories of the place.**24** A few of the worshippers belonged to families hard by, who had got permission to attend, and who brought in various choice scraps of information, about the sayings and doings at the house and on the place, which circulated as freely as the same sort of small change does in higher circles.

After a while the singing commenced, to the evident delight of all present. Not even all the disadvantage of nasal intonation could prevent the effect of the naturally fine voices, in airs at once wild and spirited. The words were sometimes the well-known and common hymns sung in the churches about, and sometimes of a wilder, more indefinite character, picked up at camp-meetings.

The chorus of one of them, which ran as follows, was sung with great energy and unction:

*"Die on the field of battle,*
*Die on the field of battle,*
*Glory in my soul."*

Another special favorite had oft repeated the words—

*"O, I'm going to glory,—won't you come along with me?*
*Don't you see the angels beck'ning, and a calling me*
    *away?*
*Don't you see the golden city and the everlasting day?"*

There were others, which made incessant mention of "Jordan's banks," and "Canaan's fields," and the "New Jerusalem;" for the negro mind, impassioned and imaginative, always attaches itself to hymns and expressions of a vivid and pictorial nature;[25] and, as they sung, some laughed, and some cried, and some clapped hands, or shook hands rejoicingly with each other, as if they had fairly gained the other side of the river.

Various exhortations, or relations of experience, followed, and inter-mingled with the singing. One old gray-headed woman, long past work, but much revered as a sort of chronicle of the past, rose, and leaning on her staff, said—

"Well, chil'en! Well, I'm mighty glad to hear ye all and see ye all once more, 'cause I don't know when I'll be gone to glory; but I've done got ready, chil'en; 'pears like I'd got my little bundle all tied up, and my bonnet on, jest a waitin' for the stage to come along and take me home; sometimes, in the night, I think I hear the wheels a rattlin', and I'm lookin' out all the time; now, you jest be ready too, for I tell ye all, chil'en," she said, striking her staff hard on the floor, "dat ar *glory* is a mighty thing! It's a mighty thing, chil'en,—you don'no nothing about it,—it's *wonderful*." And the old creature sat down, with streaming tears, as wholly overcome, while the whole circle struck up—

*"O Canaan, bright Canaan,*
*I'm bound for the land of Canaan."*[26]

Mas'r George, by request, read the last chapters of Revelation, often interrupted by such exclamations as "The *sakes* now!" "Only hear that!" "Jest think on't!" "Is all that a comin' sure enough?"

A praying Tom, depicted by Miguel Covarrubias. This image captures the combination of piety and strength that Stowe hoped her readers to see in Tom. From *Uncle Tom's Cabin: or, Life Among the Lowly,* Heritage Press edition, 1938

25 A racist view saw "the negro mind" as particularly childlike, incapable of higher reasoning and drawn, like a child, to stories and pictures.

26 The slaves found particular solace in the book of Exodus and its story of captivity in a foreign land and of promised deliverance. As critic Sterling A. Brown has observed, "Fairly easy allegories identified Egypt-land with the South, Pharoah with the masters, the Israelites with themselves and Moses with their leader" ("Negro Folk Expression"). Many spirituals expanded on church hymns, shaping them to fit the lives of slaves and to sustain them throughout the week, not simply on Sunday. "God's A-Gonna Trouble the Water," "Go Down, Moses," and "Didn't My Lord Deliver Daniel?" are just a few titles. Thus, to "cross the river"—the Jordan or the Ohio—means to reach the land of promise.

**27** "Morale" here means sense of morals. Stowe describes Uncle Tom as moral, experienced, and educated ("a greater breadth and cultivation of mind") but only in comparison with his less fortunate companions. Tom is only "a sort of" minister with a "simple" "child-like" style of prayer. Tom seems, however, to take on the spirit. See chapter 1, note 20, on possession.

**28** In other words, Tom's prayers go straight up to heaven. Stowe may have in mind *Hamlet* 3.3.97–98, where guilty King Claudius tries to pray: "My words fly up, my thoughts remain below; / Words without thoughts never to heaven go."

**29** Again, Uncle Tom is described in this paragraph as liking simple things. His simplicity in prayer risks being lost in the "abundance of the responses," however. Stowe observes here the movement between individual and group that is the call and response pattern of African-American sermon, song, and literature, considered a bridge between African and African-American cultures.

We begin this chapter with the description of the physical Uncle Tom: his home, his wife, her food, his children. We end it with the spiritual Uncle Tom who all but disappears in his fervent prayers.

George, who was a bright boy, and well trained in religious things by his mother, finding himself an object of general admiration, threw in expositions of his own, from time to time, with a commendable seriousness and gravity, for which he was admired by the young and blessed by the old; and it was agreed, on all hands, that "a minister couldn't lay it off better than he did;" that " 'twas reely 'mazin'!"

Uncle Tom was a sort of patriarch in religious matters, in the neighborhood. Having, naturally, an organization in which the *morale*[27] was strongly predominant, together with a greater breadth and cultivation of mind than obtained among his companions, he was looked up to with great respect, as a sort of minister among them; and the simple, hearty, sincere style of his exhortations might have edified even better educated persons. But it was in prayer that he especially excelled. Nothing could exceed the touching simplicity, the child-like earnestness, of his prayer, enriched with the language of Scripture, which seemed so entirely to have wrought itself into his being, as to have become a part of himself, and to drop from his lips unconsciously; in the language of a pious old negro, he "prayed right up."[28] And so much did his prayer always work on the devotional feelings of his audiences, that there seemed often a danger that it would be lost altogether in the abundance of the responses which broke out everywhere around him.[29]

"Prayer-meeting in Uncle Tom's Cabin," by George Cruikshank. The cabin appears roomier than it is described: large enough to fit twenty-one people comfortably. The image evokes a Nativity scene; later, Stowe will depict Tom as a Christ-like figure.   From the first British edition of *Uncle Tom's Cabin* (John Cassell, 1852)

While this scene was passing in the cabin of the man, one quite otherwise passed in the halls of the master.

The trader and Mr. Shelby were seated together in the dining room afore-named, at a table covered with papers and writing utensils.

Mr. Shelby was busy in counting some bundles of bills, which, as they were counted, he pushed over to the trader, who counted them likewise.

"All fair," said the trader; "and now for signing these yer."

Mr. Shelby hastily drew the bills of sale towards him, and signed them, like a man that hurries over some disagreeable business, and then pushed them over with the money. Haley produced, from a well-worn valise, a parchment, which, after looking over it a moment, he handed to Mr. Shelby, who took it with a gesture of suppressed eagerness.

"Wal, now, the thing's *done*!" said the trader, getting up.

"It's *done*!" said Mr. Shelby, in a musing tone; and, fetching a long breath, he repeated, "*It's done!*"

"Yer don't seem to feel much pleased with it, 'pears to me," said the trader.

"Haley," said Mr. Shelby, "I hope you'll remember that you promised, on your honor, you wouldn't sell Tom, without knowing what sort of hands he's going into."

"Why, you've just done it, sir," said the trader.

"Circumstances, you well know, *obliged* me," said Shelby, haughtily.

"Wal, you know, they may 'blige *me*, too," said the trader. "Howsomever, I'll do the very best I can in gettin' Tom a good berth; as to my treatin' on him bad, you needn't be a grain afeard. If there's anything that I thank the Lord for, it is that I'm never noways cruel."

After the expositions which the trader had previously given of his humane principles, Mr. Shelby did not feel particularly reassured by these declarations; but, as they were the best comfort the case admitted of, he allowed the trader to depart in silence, and betook himself to a solitary cigar.[30]

30 True to form, in a difficult situation Mr. Shelby responds by putting something in his mouth.

## CHAPTER 5

*Showing the Feelings of Living Property on Changing Owners*[1]

1 Notice the humor in this chapter title. Stowe plays with contested and significant terms regarding slaves—"feeling" and "living" versus "property" and "owners."

2 Notice the detail with which Stowe describes the married life of Mr. and Mrs. Shelby. Again, this is in sharp distinction to the portrayal of Uncle Tom and Aunt Chloe's marriage.

Mr. and Mrs. Shelby had retired to their apartment for the night. He was lounging in a large easy-chair, looking over some letters that had come in the afternoon mail, and she was standing before her mirror, brushing out the complicated braids and curls in which Eliza had arranged her hair; for, noticing her pale cheeks and haggard eyes, she had excused her attendance that night, and ordered her to bed.[2] The employment, naturally enough, suggested her conversation with the girl in the morning; and, turning to her husband, she said, carelessly,

"By the by, Arthur, who was that low-bred fellow that you lugged in to our dinner-table to-day?"

"Haley is his name," said Shelby, turning himself rather uneasily in his chair, and continuing with his eyes fixed on a letter.

"Haley! Who is he, and what may be his business here, pray?"

"Well, he's a man that I transacted some business with, last time I was at Natchez," said Mr. Shelby.

"And he presumed on it to make himself quite at home, and call and dine here, ay?"

"Why, I invited him; I had some accounts with him," said Shelby.

"Is he a negro-trader?" said Mrs. Shelby, noticing a certain embarrassment in her husband's manner.

"Why, my dear, what put that into your head?" said Shelby, looking up.

"Nothing,—only Eliza came in here, after dinner, in a great worry, crying and taking on, and said you were talking with a trader, and that she heard him make an offer for her boy—the ridiculous little goose!"

"She did, hey?" said Mr. Shelby, returning to his paper, which he seemed for a few moments quite intent upon, not perceiving that he was holding it bottom upwards.

"It will have to come out," said he, mentally; "as well now as ever."

"I told Eliza," said Mrs. Shelby, as she continued brushing her hair, "that she was a little fool for her pains, and that you never had anything to do with that sort of persons. Of course, I knew you never meant to sell any of our people,—least of all, to such a fellow."[3]

"Well, Emily," said her husband, "so I have always felt and said; but the fact is that my business lies so that I cannot get on without. I shall have to sell some of my hands."

"To that creature? Impossible! Mr. Shelby, you cannot be serious."

"I'm sorry to say that I am," said Mr. Shelby. "I've agreed to sell Tom."

"What! our Tom?—that good, faithful creature!—been your faithful servant from a boy! O, Mr. Shelby!—and you have promised him his freedom, too,—you and I have spoken to him a hundred times of it. Well I can believe anything now,—I can believe *now* that you could sell little Harry, poor Eliza's only child!" said Mrs. Shelby, in a tone between grief and indignation.

"Well, since you must know all, it is so. I have agreed to sell Tom and Harry both; and I don't know why I am to be rated, as if I were a monster, for doing what every one does every day."

"But why, of all others, choose these?" said Mrs. Shelby. "Why sell them, of all on the place, if you must sell at all?"

"Because they will bring the highest sum of any,—that's why. I could choose another, if you say so. The fellow made me a high bid on Eliza, if that would suit you any better," said Mr. Shelby.

"The wretch!" said Mrs. Shelby, vehemently.

"Well, I didn't listen to it, a moment,—out of regard to your feelings, I wouldn't;—so give me some credit."

"My dear," said Mrs. Shelby, recollecting herself, "forgive me. I have been hasty. I was surprised, and entirely unprepared for this;—but surely you will allow me to intercede for these poor creatures. Tom is a noble-hearted, faithful fellow, if he is black.[4] I do believe, Mr. Shelby, that if he were put to it, he would lay down his life for you."

3 Mrs. Shelby clearly understands the sexual nature of Haley's offer.

4 Read "if he is black" as "even though he is black." Mrs. Shelby reflects the racist thought of the times in that she observes Tom's noble-heartedness and loyalty but finds them surprising traits in a black man. Such oppositions are typical in literature, as in "black *but* comely."

39

**5** This is a beautiful speech, but we are to understand Mrs. Shelby's naïveté on the subject of Shelby's finances through her use of the phrases "pecuniary sacrifice" and "just to save a little money."

**6** I.e., articles used in arranging hair, dressing, etc.

"I know it,—I dare say;—but what's the use of all this?—I can't help myself."

"Why not make a pecuniary sacrifice? I'm willing to bear my part of the inconvenience. O, Mr. Shelby, I have tried—tried most faithfully, as a Christian woman should—to do my duty to these poor, simple, dependent creatures. I have cared for them, instructed them, watched over them, and known all their little cares and joys, for years; and how can I ever hold up my head again among them, if, for the sake of a little paltry gain, we sell such a faithful, excellent, confiding creature as poor Tom, and tear from him in a moment all we have taught him to love and value? I have taught them the duties of the family, of parent and child, and husband and wife; and how can I bear to have this open acknowledgment that we care for no tie, no duty, no relation, however sacred, compared with money? I have talked with Eliza about her boy—her duty to him as a Christian mother, to watch over him, pray for him, and bring him up in a Christian way; and now what can I say, if you tear him away, and sell him, soul and body, to a profane, unprincipled man, just to save a little money? I have told her that one soul is worth more than all the money in the world; and how will she believe me when she sees us turn round and sell her child?—sell him, perhaps, to certain ruin of body and soul!"**5**

"I'm sorry you feel so about it, Emily,—indeed I am," said Mr. Shelby; "and I respect your feelings, too, though I don't pretend to share them to their full extent; but I tell you now, solemnly, it's of no use—I can't help myself. I didn't mean to tell you this, Emily; but, in plain words, there is no choice between selling these two and selling everything. Either they must go, or *all* must. Haley has come into possession of a mortgage, which, if I don't clear off with him directly, will take everything before it. I've raked, and scraped, and borrowed, and all but begged,—and the price of these two was needed to make up the balance, and I had to give them up. Haley fancied the child; he agreed to settle the matter that way, and no other. I was in his power, and *had* to do it. If you feel so to have them sold, would it be any better to have *all* sold?"

Mrs. Shelby stood like one stricken. Finally, turning to her toilet,**6** she rested her face in her hands, and gave a sort of groan.

"This is God's curse on slavery!—a bitter, bitter, most accursed thing!—a curse to the master and a curse to the slave! I was a fool to think I could make anything good out of such a deadly evil. It is a sin to hold a slave under laws like ours,—I always felt it was,—I always thought so when I was a girl,—I thought so still more after I joined the church; but I thought I could gild it over,—I thought, by kindness, and care, and instruction, I could make the condition of mine better than freedom—fool that I was!"[7]

"Why, wife, you are getting to be an abolitionist, quite."

"Abolitionist! if they knew all I know about slavery they *might* talk! We don't need them to tell us; you know I never thought that slavery was right—never felt willing to own slaves."

"Well, therein you differ from many wise and pious men," said Mr. Shelby. "You remember Mr. B.'s sermon, the other Sunday?"

"I don't want to hear such sermons; I never wish to hear Mr. B. in our church again. Ministers can't help the evil, perhaps,—can't cure it, any more than we can,—but defend it!—it always went against my common sense. And I think you didn't think much of that sermon, either."

"Well," said Shelby, "I must say these ministers sometimes carry matters further than we poor sinners would exactly dare to do. We men of the world must wink pretty hard at various things, and get used to a deal that isn't the exact thing. But we don't quite fancy, when women and ministers come out broad and square, and go beyond us in matters of either modesty or morals, that's a fact. But now, my dear, I trust you see the necessity of the thing, and you see that I have done the very best that circumstances would allow."

"O yes, yes!" said Mrs. Shelby, hurriedly and abstractedly fingering her gold watch,—"I haven't any jewelry of any amount," she added, thoughtfully; "but would not this watch do something?—it was an expensive one, when it was bought. If I could only at least save Eliza's child, I would sacrifice anything I have."[8]

"I'm sorry, very sorry, Emily," said Mr. Shelby, "I'm sorry this takes hold of you so; but it will do no good. The fact is, Emily, the thing's done; the bills of sale are already signed, and in Haley's hands; and you must be thankful it is no worse. That man has had it in his power to ruin us all,—and now he is fairly off. If you knew the man as I do, you'd think that we had had a narrow escape."

"Is he so hard, then?"

"Why, not a cruel man, exactly, but a man of leather,—a man alive to nothing but trade and profit,—cool, and unhesitating, and unrelenting, as death and the grave. He'd sell his own mother at a good per centage—not wishing the old woman any harm, either."

7 The sinfulness of slaveholding was a theme echoed throughout African-American and abolitionist literature. Henry Highland Garnet exhorted slaves in his 1843 *Address to the Slaves of the United States of America*, "Tell them [your owners] in language which they cannot misunderstand of the exceeding sinfulness of slavery, and of a future judgment, and of the righteous retributions of an indignant God." However, pro-slavery Christians countered with their own biblical justifications of slavery, as Stowe will dramatize in chapter 16 (p. 192). The traditional scriptural authority is based on Gen. 9:20–27 (Noah's curse on Ham, after seeing Noah naked: "a servant of servants shall he be unto his brethren") and Lev. 25:44–45 ("Your male and female slaves are to come from the nations around you; from them you may buy slaves. You may also buy some of the temporary residents living among you and members of their clans born in your country, and they will become your property").

8 Again, Mrs. Shelby gives a pretty speech, but it is meant to seem out of place. Shouldn't she be lamenting her ignorance of the financial realities rather than putting the blame on the institution of slavery? Yes, slavery is an evil institution, but Stowe would like the reader to recognize Mrs. Shelby's blindness to the fact that she has been enjoying the labor of others (recall the complicated braids and curls, painstakingly worked by Eliza). Her antislavery pronouncements are less important than this blindness.

**9** If we were in doubt before about Mr. Shelby's weakness and cowardice, Stowe puts an end to it. Perhaps Mr. Shelby is more of a gentleman than Haley, but he is equally to blame for Tom's plight.

**10** Mrs. Shelby vaguely echoes two biblical verses. The first (Num. 22:28–30) is that in which an ass beaten by his master, Balaam, is given voice by an angel to ask "What have I done to you that you beat me three times?" The second allusion is to Christ's words at the Crucifixion: "And Jesus said, Father, forgive them, for they do not know what they are doing" (Luke 23:34). Stowe suggests that what the Shelbys have done is perhaps lived too much beyond their means.

**11** Eliza has turned her room into the kind of domestic space Stowe's women readers would recognize. The importance of literacy in such a home is attested to by her "little case of books."

**12** Stowe adds this charming description of Eliza's "quiet, neat apartment" to compensate for her decidedly unladylike behavior in spying on her master and mistress. Stowe shows her skill here: In order to capture the hearts of female readers, Eliza must be a Victorian heroine as well as a slave. Stowe succeeds.

"And this wretch owns that good, faithful Tom, and Eliza's child!"

"Well, my dear, the fact is that this goes rather hard with me; it's a thing I hate to think of. Haley wants to drive matters, and take possession to-morrow. I'm going to get out my horse bright and early, and be off. I can't see Tom, that's a fact; and you had better arrange a drive somewhere, and carry Eliza off. Let the thing be done when she is out of sight."[9]

"No, no," said Mrs. Shelby; "I'll be in no sense accomplice or help in this cruel business. I'll go and see poor old Tom, God help him, in his distress! They shall see, at any rate, that their mistress can feel for and with them. As to Eliza, I dare not think about it. The Lord forgive us! What have we done, that this cruel necessity should come on us?"[10]

There was one listener to this conversation whom Mr. and Mrs. Shelby little suspected.

Communicating with their apartment was a large closet, opening by a door into the outer passage. When Mrs. Shelby had dismissed Eliza for the night, her feverish and excited mind had suggested the idea of this closet; and she had hidden herself there, and, with her ear pressed close against the crack of the door, had lost not a word of the conversation.

When the voices died into silence, she rose and crept stealthily away. Pale, shivering, with rigid features and compressed lips, she looked an entirely altered being from the soft and timid creature she had been hitherto. She moved cautiously along the entry, paused one moment at her mistress' door, and raised her hands in mute appeal to Heaven, and then turned and glided into her own room. It was a quiet, neat apartment, on the same floor with her mistress. There was the pleasant sunny window, where she had often sat singing at her sewing; there a little case of books, and various little fancy articles, ranged by them, the gifts of Christmas holidays; there was her simple wardrobe in the closet and in the drawers:—here was, in short, her home; and, on the whole, a happy one it had been to her.[11] But there, on the bed, lay her slumbering boy, his long curls falling negligently around his unconscious face, his rosy mouth half open, his little fat hands thrown out over the bedclothes, and a smile spread like a sunbeam over his whole face.[12]

"Poor boy! poor fellow!" said Eliza; "they have sold you! but your mother will save you yet!"

No tear dropped over that pillow; in such straits as

these, the heart has no tears to give,—it drops only blood, bleeding itself away in silence. She took a piece of paper and a pencil, and wrote, hastily,

"O, Missis! dear Missis! don't think me ungrateful,—don't think hard of me, any way,—I heard all you and master said to-night. I am going to try to save my boy—you will not blame me! God bless and reward you for all your kindness!"

Hastily folding and directing this, she went to a drawer and made up a little package of clothing for her boy, which she tied with a handkerchief firmly round her waist; and, so fond is a mother's remembrance, that, even in the terrors of that hour, she did not forget to put in the little package one or two of his favorite toys, reserving a gayly painted parrot to amuse him, when she should be called on to awaken him. It was some trouble to arouse the little sleeper; but, after some effort, he sat up, and was playing with his bird, while his mother was putting on her bonnet and shawl.

"Where are you going, mother?" said he, as she drew near the bed, with his little coat and cap.

His mother drew near, and looked so earnestly into his eyes, that he at once divined that something unusual was the matter.

"Hush, Harry," she said; "musn't speak loud, or they will hear us. A wicked man was coming to take little Harry away from his mother, and carry him 'way off in the dark; but mother won't let him—she's going to put on her little boy's cap and coat, and run off with him, so the ugly man can't catch him."

Saying these words, she had tied and buttoned on the child's simple outfit, and, taking him in her arms, she whispered to him to be very still; and, opening a door in her room which led into the outer verandah, she glided noiselessly out.

It was a sparkling, frosty, star-light night, and the mother wrapped the shawl close round her child, as, perfectly quiet with vague terror,[13] he clung round her neck.

Old Bruno, a great Newfoundland, who slept at the end of the porch, rose, with a low growl, as she came near. She gently spoke his name, and the animal, an old pet and playmate of hers, instantly, wagging his tail, prepared to follow her, though apparently revolving much, in his simple dog's head, what such an indiscreet midnight promenade might mean. Some dim ideas of imprudence or impropriety in the measure seemed to embarrass him considerably; for he often stopped, as Eliza glided forward,

13 Harry can sense his mother's fear but only in a childish ("vague") way.

**14** This strange excursion into the mind of an old dog is meant to suggest that he has never seen Eliza—or anyone else in the Shelby household—make improper nightly promenades toward the slave quarters.

**15** Stowe's description of the couple as "he and his worthy helpmeet" echoes the traditional Christian view of marriage, the origin of woman as, from Gen. 2:18, "an help meet for [Adam]."

**16** Again, nobody is up late in the Shelby household except for proper reasons, such as a late-running religious meeting.

**17** The use of "old man" here is not derogatory but rather Chloe's term of endearment for her "old man."

Eliza tells Aunt Chloe and Uncle Tom that she is running away. Eliza, a mulatto, and her child appear white, as in Stowe's text. Tom and Aunt Chloe appear strong and muscular, yet unsexed. From the first edition of *Uncle Tom's Cabin* (John P. Jewett & Co., 1852), illustrated by Hammatt Billings

and looked wistfully, first at her and then at the house, and then, as if reassured by reflection, he pattered along after her again.**14** A few minutes brought them to the window of Uncle Tom's cottage, and Eliza, stopping, tapped lightly on the window-pane.

The prayer-meeting at Uncle Tom's had, in the order of hymn-singing, been protracted to a very late hour; and, as Uncle Tom had indulged himself in a few lengthy solos afterwards, the consequence was, that, although it was now between twelve and one o'clock, he and his worthy helpmeet**15** were not yet asleep.

"Good Lord! what's that?" said Aunt Chloe, starting up and hastily drawing the curtain.**16** "My sakes alive, if it an't Lizy! Get on your clothes, old man,**17** quick!—there's old Bruno, too, a pawin' round; what on airth! I'm gwine to open the door."

And, suiting the action to the word, the door flew open, and the light of the tallow candle, which Tom had hastily lighted, fell on the haggard face and dark, wild eyes of the fugitive.

"Lord bless you!—I'm skeered to look at ye, Lizy! Are ye tuck sick, or what's come over ye?"

"I'm running away—Uncle Tom and Aunt Chloe—carrying off my child—Master sold him!"

"Sold him?" echoed both, lifting up their hands in dismay.

"Yes, sold him!" said Eliza, firmly; "I crept into the closet by Mistress' door to-night, and I heard Master tell Missis that he had sold my Harry, and you, Uncle Tom, both, to a trader; and that he was going off this morning on his horse, and that the man was to take possession to-day." Tom had stood, during this speech, with his hands raised, and his eyes dilated, like a man in a dream. Slowly and gradually, as its meaning came over him, he collapsed, rather than seated himself, on his old chair, and sunk his head down upon his knees.

"The good Lord have pity on us!" said Aunt Chloe. "O! it don't seem as if it was true! What has he done, that Mas'r should sell *him?*"

"He hasn't done anything,—it isn't for that. Master don't want to sell; and Missis—she's always good. I heard her plead and beg for us; but he told her 'twas no use; that he was in this man's debt, and that this man had got the power over him;[18] and that if he didn't pay him off clear, it would end in his having to sell the place and all the people, and move off. Yes, I heard him say there was no choice between selling these two and selling all, the man was driving him so hard. Master said he was sorry; but oh, Missis—you ought to have heard her talk! If she an't a Christian and an angel, there never was one. I'm a wicked girl to leave her so; but, then, I can't help it. She said, herself, one soul was worth more than the world; and this boy has a soul, and if I let him be carried off, who knows what'll become of it? It must be right: but, if it an't right, the Lord forgive me, for I can't help doing it!"

"Well, old man!"[19] said Aunt Chloe, "why don't you go, too? Will you wait to be toted down river, where they kill niggers with hard work and starving? I'd a heap rather die than go there, any day! There's time for ye,—be off with Lizy,—you've got a pass to come and go any time. Come, bustle up, and I'll get your things together."

Tom slowly raised his head, and looked sorrowfully but quietly around, and said,

"No, no—I an't going. Let Eliza go—it's her right! I wouldn't be the one to say no—'t an't in *natur* for her to stay; but you heard what she said! If I must be sold, or all the people on the place, and everything go to rack, why, let me be sold. I s'pose I can b'ar it as well as any on 'em,"[20] he added, while something like a sob and a sigh shook his broad, rough chest convulsively. "Mas'r always found me on the spot—he always will. I never have broke trust, nor used my pass no ways contrary to my word, and I never will. It's better for me alone to go, than to break up the place and sell all. Mas'r an't to blame, Chloe, and he'll take care of you and the poor—"[21]

Here he turned to the rough trundle-bed full of little woolly heads, and broke fairly down. He leaned over the back of the chair, and covered his face with his large hands. Sobs, heavy, hoarse and loud, shook the chair, and great tears fell through his fingers on the floor: just such tears, sir, as you dropped into the coffin where lay your first-born son; such tears, woman, as you shed when you heard the cries of your dying babe. For, sir, he was a man,—and you are but another man. And, woman, though

18 Haley has "the power over" Shelby because Shelby owes him money. The nineteenth-century man valued self-government, but Shelby's debt reduces him to be governed by another. Stowe's point here—as with Augustine St. Clare later—is that slavery's perpetuation in America is as much a result of moral weakness as it is of evil.

19 Again, contrast Chloe's gently affectionate term, "old man," with Eliza's passionate leave-taking of George Harris.

20 Stowe's portrayal of Uncle Tom's pride of service ("Mas'r always found me on the spot—he always will") is as uncomfortable to read today as it was when I was young. The sentiment is more easily stomached when one imagines "Mas'r" to be the Lord, but not when reading "Mas'r" as the weak, orally fixated Shelby. One can see how foot soldiers of the Civil Rights movement striving for social and political equality would have chafed at Uncle Tom's obsequiousness.

21 Notice Tom's halting speech: He breaks off before he can call them his children. Stowe's depiction of Tom's emotional rectitude paradoxically allows readers not to care deeply for the fate of these children in losing their father.

This is one of the few illustrations of Tom's grief at being sold away from his children. To his right, Eliza tells Chloe she is running away. *From Altemus' Young People's Library: Uncle Tom's Cabin; or, Life Among the Lowly,* 1900

**22** In this paragraph, notice the rhetoric of direct address and universal terms Stowe uses throughout her novel to create a bridge between the lives of the slave and of the reader. The reader is asked to consider Tom's leave-taking as an event that all experience with "just such tears" and "but one sorrow." Although not Stowe's exclusive strategy, the direct address sets the commonalities of human beings against the racist insistence that slaves are subhuman.

**23** Gliding away noiselessly is another favorite trick of Victorian heroines; Stowe would like to leave us with this image for the time being.

dressed in silk and jewels, you are but a woman, and, in life's great straits and mighty griefs, ye feel but one sorrow![22]

"And now," said Eliza, as she stood in the door, "I saw my husband only this afternoon, and I little knew then what was to come. They have pushed him to the very last standing-place, and he told me, to-day, that he was going to run away. Do try, if you can, to get word to him. Tell him how I went, and why I went; and tell him I'm going to try and find Canada. You must give my love to him, and tell him, if I never see him again,"—she turned away, and stood with her back to them for a moment, and then added, in a husky voice, "tell him to be as good as he can, and try and meet me in the kingdom of heaven."

"Call Bruno in there," she added. "Shut the door on him, poor beast! He mustn't go with me!"

A few last words and tears, a few simple adieus and blessings, and, clasping her wondering and affrighted child in her arms, she glided noiselessly away.[23]

# CHAPTER 6

## *Discovery*[1]

Mr. and Mrs. Shelby, after their protracted discussion of the night before, did not readily sink to repose, and, in consequence, slept somewhat later than usual, the ensuing morning.

"I wonder what keeps Eliza," said Mrs. Shelby, after giving her bell repeated pulls, to no purpose.

Mr. Shelby was standing before his dressing-glass, sharpening his razor; and just then the door opened, and a colored boy entered, with his shaving-water.[2]

"Andy," said his mistress, "step to Eliza's door, and tell her I have rung for her three times. Poor thing!" she added, to herself, with a sigh.

Andy soon returned, with eyes very wide in astonishment.

"Lor, Missis! Lizy's drawers is all open, and her things all lying every which way; and I believe she's just done clared out!"[3]

The truth flashed upon Mr. Shelby and his wife at the same moment. He exclaimed,

"Then she suspected it, and she's off!"

"The Lord be thanked!" said Mrs. Shelby. "I trust she is."

"Wife, you talk like a fool! Really, it will be something pretty awkward for me, if she is. Haley saw that I hesitated about selling this child, and he'll think I connived at it, to get him out of the way. It touches my honor!" And Mr. Shelby left the room hastily.

1 Many things are discovered in this chapter. Stowe would like us to wonder to which one the title refers.

2 Shaving in 1850s America involved a bowl of warmed shaving-water, a soft bristle brush to create and apply soapy lather, and a straight-edge razor, stropped to sharpness. Often, in households such as Shelby's, one of the house slaves would shave his master. The horrific possibilities of a slave with a keen razor at his master's throat would be exploited a few years after Stowe's novel, in Herman Melville's 1856 tale *Benito Cereno*. It is unclear how many black male slaves were allowed to shave their own beards.

3 House slaves in 1850 would typically have been allowed to acquire a number of personal articles: clothes, linens, shoes, some toiletries, and perhaps a small box in which to keep these items. Literate house slaves may have had books and writing implements. Field slaves and workers who lived in slave quarters would have possessed cooking implements, some clothes, and perhaps some tools. The question of whether slaves "owned" their possessions in any legal sense probably varied from state to state. Eliza, we are led to understand, has more than the usual stock of "things."

4 A good example of Stowe's subtle humor is her employment of the Dickensian idiom of generality: "There was great running and ejaculating, and opening and shutting of doors." Writers of the era tended to use participles ironically to suggest conventionality in situations that were either bizarre or, in this case, dire.

5 Stowe's unwitting use of terms such as "little black Jake" and, in the next paragraph, of "woolly-headed" and her comparison of Mandy to "a black cat" and a snake ("coiled up among the jugs") certainly reflect the racism of the time, but they also may have had political significance. The snake was an early emblem of liberty ("Don't tread on me"), and black cats were then, as now, considered powerful. Frederick Douglass was fond of alluding to an old story of the boy who told his family that there were a thousand cats fighting in the cellar when, upon inspection, "it turned out to be the family cat and another black cat." The point is that the intensity of a battle is often mistakenly thought to be a function of the number of individuals joined in battle.

6 These "woolly-headed" imps are racialized but sympathetic figures. The reader is made aware that they are voicing the reader's laughter at Haley's predicament.

7 Haley's dialect is as unconventional as the imps'. Stowe employs many tools to ensure her readers' distaste. Haley's speech prefigures that of Simon Legree, who will appear much later in the novel.

Then was great running and ejaculating, and opening and shutting of doors, and appearances of faces in all shades of color in different places, for about a quarter of an hour.[4] One person only, who might have shed some light on the matter, was entirely silent, and that was the head cook, Aunt Chloe. Silently, and with a heavy cloud settled down over her once joyous face, she proceeded making out her breakfast biscuits, as if she heard and saw nothing of the excitement around her.

Very soon, about a dozen young imps were roosting, like so many crows, on the verandah railings, each one determined to be the first one to apprize the strange Mas'r of his ill luck.

"He'll be rael mad, I'll be bound," said Andy.

"*Won't* he swar!" said little black Jake.[5]

"Yes, for he *does* swar," said woolly-headed[6] Mandy. "I hearn him yesterday, at dinner. I hearn all about it then, 'cause I got into the closet where Missis keeps the great jugs, and I hearn every word." And Mandy, who had never in her life thought of the meaning of a word she had heard, more than a black cat, now took airs of superior wisdom, and strutted about, forgetting to state that, though actually coiled up among the jugs at the time specified, she had been fast asleep all the time.

When, at last, Haley appeared, booted and spurred, he was saluted with the bad tidings on every hand. The young imps on the verandah were not disappointed in their hope of hearing him "swar," which he did with a fluency and fervency which delighted them all amazingly, as they ducked and dodged hither and thither, to be out of the reach of his riding-whip; and, all whooping off together, they tumbled, in a pile of immeasurable giggle, on the withered turf under the verandah, where they kicked up their heels and shouted to their full satisfaction.

"If I had the little devils!" muttered Haley, between his teeth.

"But you ha'nt got 'em, though!" said Andy, with a triumphant flourish, and making a string of indescribable mouths at the unfortunate trader's back, when he was fairly beyond hearing.

"I say now, Shelby, this yer's a most extro'rnary business!" said Haley, as he abruptly entered the parlor. "It seems that gal's off, with her young un."[7]

"Mr. Haley, Mrs. Shelby is present," said Mr. Shelby.

"I beg pardon, ma'am," said Haley, bowing slightly, with a still lowering brow; "but still I say, as I said before, this yer's a sing'lar report. Is it true, sir?"

"Sir," said Mr. Shelby, "if you wish to communicate with me, you must observe something of the decorum of a gentleman.[8] Andy, take Mr. Haley's hat and riding-whip. Take a seat, sir. Yes, sir; I regret to say that the young woman, excited by overhearing, or having reported to her, something of this business, has taken her child in the night, and made off."

"I did expect fair dealing in this matter, I confess," said Haley.

"Well, sir," said Mr. Shelby, turning sharply round upon him, "what am I to understand by that remark? If any man calls my honor in question, I have but one answer for him."

The trader cowered at this, and in a somewhat lower tone said that "it was plaguy hard on a fellow, that had made a fair bargain, to be gulled that way."

"Mr. Haley," said Mr. Shelby, "if I did not think you had some cause for disappointment, I should not have borne from you the rude and unceremonious style of your entrance into my parlor this morning. I say thus much, however, since appearances call for it, that I shall allow of no insinuations cast upon me, as if I were at all partner to any unfairness in this matter. Moreover, I shall feel bound to give you every assistance, in the use of horses, servants, &c., in the recovery of your property. So, in short, Haley," said he, suddenly dropping from the tone of dignified coolness to his ordinary one of easy frankness, "the best way for you is to keep good-natured and eat some breakfast, and we will then see what is to be done."[9]

Mrs. Shelby now rose, and said her engagements would prevent her being at the breakfast-table that morning; and, deputing a very respectable mulatto woman to attend to the gentlemen's coffee at the side-board, she left the room.

"Old lady[10] don't like your humble servant, over and above," said Haley, with an uneasy effort to be very familiar.

"I am not accustomed to hear my wife spoken of with such freedom," said Mr. Shelby, dryly.

"Beg pardon; of course, only a joke, you know," said Haley, forcing a laugh.

"Some jokes are less agreeable than others," rejoined Shelby.

"Devilish free, now I've signed those papers, cuss him!" muttered Haley to himself; "quite grand, since yesterday!"

Never did fall of any prime minister at court occasion wider surges of sensation than the report of Tom's fate among his compeers on the place. It was the topic in every

8 Haley's use of vernacular increases during this difficult conversation, whereas Mr. Shelby's tone becomes much more formal and studied. Mr. Shelby behaves like an English gentleman.

9 Once again, Mr. Shelby's typical reaction to events is to eat.

10 A disrespectful term, equivalent to "the Mrs." Contrast Haley's "old lady" with Chloe's "old man."

11 The *OED* credits Stowe with introducing the poetic phrase "son of ebony," denoting black skin, to the English language. In 1854, prominent British writer Henry Gardiner Adams published *God's Image in Ebony: Being a Series of Biographical Sketches, Facts, Anecdotes, etc., Demonstrative of the Mental Powers and Intellectual Capacities of the Negro Race* and dedicated it to Stowe, "as a tribute of admiration for her genius, and of that pure philanthropy, which has impelled her to devote her powers and energies to the cause of the oppressed and downtrodden negro."

12 Sam's imitation of the speech and gestures of a self-important white speaker includes a malapropism (misuse of words). The actual proverb is "It's an ill wind that blows nobody good."

13 Sam's comment that once one man's down, another can be up reflects the strict system of rewards parceled out by slaveholders. Booker T. Washington, in his 1901 autobiography, *Up From Slavery*, offered the metaphor of crabs in a barrel to lament how all too often members of the race would not let others climb up and over, but would pull back into the pot anyone who made an effort to escape.

14 To "cut stick" is to "make off" (*The New Shorter Oxford English Dictounary*). Literally, Eliza has taken off, run away. However, Andy's use of two equivalent expressions (to make off and to clear out) is not simply a repetition; it is an intensification, highlighting the dramatic nature of Eliza's departure.

15 The conversation between Andy and Sam makes liberal use of "nigger" as a fraternal term, almost synonymous with "brother." Thus, Sam's claim below that "He's de nigger" should be read as "I'm the man." Contrast this with Haley's use of the pejorative term "nigger." Again, Stowe is uncannily accurate in her depiction of playful conversation between these two male slaves.

mouth, everywhere; and nothing was done in the house or in the field, but to discuss its probable results. Eliza's flight—an unprecedented event on the place—was also a great accessory in stimulating the general excitement.

Black Sam, as he was commonly called, from his being about three shades blacker than any other son of ebony[11] on the place, was revolving the matter profoundly in all its phases and bearings, with a comprehensiveness of vision and a strict look-out to his own personal well-being, that would have done credit to any white patriot in Washington.

"It's an ill wind dat blows nowhar,—dat ar a fact," said Sam, sententiously, giving an additional hoist to his pantaloons, and adroitly substituting a long nail in place of a missing suspender-button, with which effort of mechanical genius he seemed highly delighted.[12]

"Yes, it's an ill wind blows nowhar," he repeated. "Now, dar, Tom's down—wal, course der's room for some nigger to be up—and why not dis nigger?—dat's de idee. Tom, a ridin' round de country—boots blacked—pass in his pocket—all grand as Cuffee—who but he? Now, why shouldn't Sam?—dat's what I want to know."[13]

"Halloo, Sam—O Sam! Mas'r wants you to cotch Bill and Jerry," said Andy, cutting short Sam's soliloquy.

"High! what's afoot now, young un?"

"Why, you don't know, I s'pose, that Lizy's cut stick, and clared out,[14] with her young un?"

"You teach your granny!" said Sam, with infinite contempt; "knowed it a heap sight sooner than you did; this nigger an't so green, now!"[15]

"Well, anyhow, Mas'r wants Bill and Jerry geared right up; and you and I's to go with Mas'r Haley, to look arter her."

"Good, now! dat's de time o' day!" said Sam. "It's Sam dat's called for in dese yer times. He's de nigger. See if I don't cotch her, now; Mas'r'll see what Sam can do!"

"Ah! but, Sam," said Andy, "you'd better think twice; for Missis don't want her cotched, and she'll be in yer wool."

"High!" said Sam, opening his eyes. "How you know dat?"

"Heard her say so, my own self, dis blessed mornin', when I bring in Mas'r's shaving-water. She sent me to see why Lizy didn't come to dress her; and when I told her she was off, she jest ris up, and ses she, 'The Lord be praised;' and Mas'r, he seemed rael mad, and ses he, 'Wife, you talk like a fool.' But Lor! she'll bring him to! I knows well enough how that'll be,—it's allers best to stand Missis' side the fence, now I tell yer."

Black Sam, upon this, scratched his woolly pate, which, if it did not contain very profound wisdom, still contained a great deal of a particular species much in demand among politicians of all complexions and countries, and vulgarly denominated "knowing which side the bread is buttered;" so, stopping with grave consideration, he again gave a hitch to his pantaloons, which was his regularly organized method of assisting his mental perplexities.[16]

"Der an't no sayin'—never—'bout no kind o' thing in *dis* yer world," he said, at last.

Sam spoke like a philosopher, emphasizing *this*—as if he had had a large experience in different sorts of worlds, and therefore had come to his conclusions advisedly.

"Now, sartin I'd a said that Missis would a scoured the varsal world after Lizy," added Sam, thoughtfully.

"So she would," said Andy; "but can't ye see through a ladder,[17] ye black nigger? Missis don't want dis yer Mas'r Haley to get Lizy's boy; dat's de go!"

"High!"[18] said Sam, with an indescribable intonation, known only to those who have heard it among the negroes.

"And I'll tell yer more'n all," said Andy; "I specs you'd better be making tracks for dem hosses,—mighty sudden, too,—for I hearn Missis 'quirin' arter yer,—so you've stood foolin' long enough."

Sam, upon this, began to bestir himself in real earnest, and after a while appeared, bearing down gloriously towards the house, with Bill and Jerry in a full canter, and adroitly throwing himself off before they had any idea of stopping, he brought them up alongside of the horse-post like a tornado. Haley's horse, which was a skittish young colt, winced, and bounced, and pulled hard at his halter.

"Ho, ho!" said Sam, "skeery, ar ye?" and his black visage lighted up with a curious, mischievous gleam. "I'll fix ye now!" said he.

There was a large beech-tree overshadowing the place, and the small, sharp, triangular beech-nuts lay scattered thickly on the ground. With one of these in his fingers, Sam approached the colt, stroked and patted, and seemed apparently busy in soothing his agitation. On pretence of adjusting the saddle, he adroitly slipped under it the sharp little nut, in such a manner that the least weight brought upon the saddle would annoy the nervous sensibilities of the animal, without leaving any perceptible graze or wound.

"Dar!" he said, rolling his eyes with an approving grin; "me fix 'em!"

16 Sam lampoons the typical politician's stance, hoisting his pants as he prepares to pontificate. Stowe puts the rhetoric of science to good comic use here—"particular species," "complexions," "organized method," and "mental perplexities."

17 I.e., see something obvious (*Shorter Oxford*).

18 This is the third of three exclamations of "High!" by Sam. The *Shorter Oxford* gives the expression "In full *hey* or *high jingo!*" as "a conjurer's call for, or an exclamation of surprise at, the appearance of something"— comparable in the latter case to "By God!" or "By golly!" Given the context, both meanings seem evoked by Sam's "High!" The "indescribable intonation" in this instance and his subsequent "fixing" of Haley's skittish colt with a sharp nut under the saddle seem in keeping with the work of a conjurer.

**19** Stowe delays her narrative with this bit of comedy, giving the reader a sense of the impatience and anxiety that Haley and the Shelbys feel.

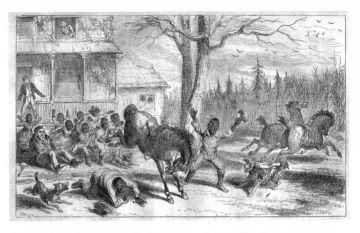

Sam and Andy scatter the horses to delay Eliza's capture. Woodcut, circa 1900, by C. W. Willis, "after George Cruikshank." Given the care taken in depicting the horses and dogs, the images of Sam, Andy, and the other slaves remain caricatures. From *Uncle Tom's Cabin*, John Cassell, London, 1852

At this moment Mrs. Shelby appeared on the balcony, beckoning to him. Sam approached with as good a determination to pay court as did ever suitor after a vacant place at St. James' or Washington.**19**

"Why have you been loitering so, Sam? I sent Andy to tell you to hurry."

"Lord bless you, Missis!" said Sam, "horses won't be cotched all in a mimit; they'd done clared out way down to the south pasture, and the Lord knows whar!"

"Sam, how often must I tell you not to say 'Lord bless you, and the Lord knows,' and such things? It's wicked."

"O, Lord bless my soul! I done forgot, Missis! I won't say nothing of de sort no more."

"Why, Sam, you just *have* said it again."

"Did I? O, Lord! I mean—I didn't go fur to say it."

"You must be *careful,* Sam."

"Just let me get my breath, Missis, and I'll start fair. I'll be berry careful."

"Well, Sam, you are to go with Mr. Haley, to show him the road, and help him. Be careful of the horses, Sam; you know Jerry was a little lame last week; *don't ride them too fast.*"

Mrs. Shelby spoke the last words with a low voice, and strong emphasis.

"Let dis child alone for dat!" said Sam, rolling up his eyes with a volume of meaning. "Lord knows! High! Didn't say dat!" said he, suddenly catching his breath, with a ludicrous flourish of apprehension, which made his mistress laugh, spite of herself. "Yes, Missis, I'll look out for de hosses!"

"Now, Andy," said Sam, returning to his stand under the beech-trees, "you see I wouldn't be 'tall surprised if dat ar gen'lman's crittur should gib a fling, by and by, when he comes to be a gettin' up. You know, Andy, critturs *will* do such things;" and therewith Sam poked Andy in the side, in a highly suggestive manner.

"High!"[20] said Andy, with an air of instant appreciation.

"Yes, you see, Andy, Missis wants to make time,—dat ar's clar to der most or'nary 'bserver. I jis make a little for her. Now, you see, get all dese yer hosses loose, caperin' permiscus[21] round dis yer lot and down to de wood dar, and I spec Mas'r won't be off in a hurry."

Andy grinned.

"Yer see," said Sam, "yer see, Andy, if any such thing should happen as that Mas'r Haley's horse *should* begin to act contrary, and cut up, you and I jist lets go of our'n to help him, and *we'll help him*—oh yes!" And Sam and Andy laid their heads back on their shoulders, and broke into a low, immoderate laugh, snapping their fingers and flourishing their heels with exquisite delight.

At this instant, Haley appeared on the verandah. Somewhat mollified by certain[22] cups of very good coffee, he came out smiling and talking, in tolerably restored humor. Sam and Andy, clawing for certain fragmentary palm-leaves, which they were in the habit of considering as hats, flew to the horse-posts, to be ready to "help Mas'r."

Sam's palm-leaf had been ingeniously disentangled from all pretensions to braid, as respects its brim; and the slivers starting apart, and standing upright, gave it a blazing air of freedom and defiance, quite equal to that of any Fejee chief;[23] while the whole brim of Andy's being departed bodily, he rapped the crown on his head with a dexterous thump, and looked about well pleased, as if to say, "Who says I haven't got a hat?"

"Well, boys," said Haley, "look alive now; we must lose no time."

"Not a bit of him, Mas'r!" said Sam, putting Haley's rein in his hand, and holding his stirrup, while Andy was untying the other two horses.

The instant Haley touched the saddle, the mettlesome creature bounded from the earth with a sudden spring, that threw his master sprawling, some feet off, on the soft, dry turf. Sam, with frantic ejaculations, made a dive at the reins, but only succeeded in brushing the blazing palm-

20 See note 18 above.

21 I.e., leaping all around (promiscuously).

22 "Certain" in these instances conveys to the reader that there is no need to go into detail. How many cups and which kind of palm leaves are immaterial to the actions of the household to delay Haley. But of course the Shelbys only drink very good coffee, Stowe reminds us.

23 I.e., a Fiji chief. Comprising more than 300 islands and islets (many uninhabited), Fiji was sighted in 1643 by the Dutch explorer Abel Janszoon Tasman. In 1840, a U.S. team made the first comprehensive description of the islands. The phrase "Fejee cannibal" or "Fejee savage" was commonly used in the mid-ninteenth century to denote a person (or culture) even more backward than the South.

24 "Coeur De Lion" ("heart of the lion") refers to Richard I, king of England (1188–1199), called the Lionhearted. He was legendary for his participation in the failed Third Crusade (1191), in which he executed 2,700 Muslims, and for his truce with Saladin, which left Jerusalem in his hands. Sam mimics such knightly exploits to comic effect.

25 Stowe's portrayal of Sam and Andy's clowning and Mrs. Shelby's treatment of them as children is a bit uncomfortable for the modern reader, but it serves several purposes. First, the comedy provides a dramatic contrast to the horror of the situation, and second, Stowe's humor softens the didactic message of the novel. Sam and Andy's clowning is a traditional part of the slave narrative genre.

26 In a chapter concerning runaways, Stowe brings the temptation of freedom even to Haley's colt.

leaf afore-named into the horse's eyes, which by no means tended to allay the confusion of his nerves. So, with great vehemence, he overturned Sam, and, giving two or three contemptuous snorts, flourished his heels vigorously in the air, and was soon prancing away towards the lower end of the lawn, followed by Bill and Jerry, whom Andy had not failed to let loose, according to contract, speeding them off with various direful ejaculations. And now ensued a miscellaneous scene of confusion. Sam and Andy ran and shouted,—dogs barked here and there,—and Mike, Mose, Mandy, Fanny, and all the smaller specimens on the place, both male and female, raced, clapped hands, whooped, and shouted, with outrageous officiousness and untiring zeal.

Haley's horse, which was a white one, and very fleet and spirited, appeared to enter into the spirit of the scene with great gusto; and having for his coursing ground a lawn of nearly half a mile in extent, gently sloping down on every side into indefinite woodland, he appeared to take infinite delight in seeing how near he could allow his pursuers to approach him, and then, when within a hand's breadth, whisk off with a start and a snort, like a mischievous beast as he was, and career far down into some alley of the wood-lot. Nothing was further from Sam's mind than to have any one of the troop taken until such season as should seem to him most befitting,—and the exertions that he made were certainly most heroic. Like the sword of Coeur De Lion,[24] which always blazed in the front and thickest of the battle, Sam's palm-leaf was to be seen everywhere when there was the least danger that a horse could be caught;—there he would bear down full tilt, shouting, "Now for it! cotch him! cotch him!" in a way that would set everything to indiscriminate rout in a moment.

Haley ran up and down, and cursed and swore and stamped miscellaneously. Mr. Shelby in vain tried to shout directions from the balcony, and Mrs. Shelby from her chamber window alternately laughed and wondered,—not without some inkling of what lay at the bottom of all this confusion.[25]

At last, about twelve o'clock, Sam appeared triumphant, mounted on Jerry, with Haley's horse by his side, reeking with sweat, but with flashing eyes and dilated nostrils, showing that the spirit of freedom had not yet entirely subsided.[26]

"He's cotched!" he exclaimed, triumphantly. "If't hadn't been for me, they might a bust theirselves, all on 'em; but I cotched him!"

"You!" growled Haley, in no amiable mood. "If it hadn't been for you, this never would have happened."

"Lord bless us, Mas'r," said Sam, in a tone of the deepest concern, "and me that has been racin' and chasin' till the swet jest pours off me!"

"Well, well!" said Haley, "you've lost me near three hours, with your cursed nonsense. Now let's be off, and have no more fooling."

"Why, Mas'r," said Sam, in a deprecating tone, "I believe you mean to kill us all clar, horses and all. Here we are all just ready to drop down, and the critters all in a reek of sweat. Why, Mas'r won't think of startin' on now till arter dinner.[27] Mas'r's hoss wants rubben down; see how he splashed hisself; and Jerry limps too; don't think Missis would be willin' to have us start dis yer way, no how. Lord bless you, Mas'r, we can ketch up, if we do stop. Lizy never was no great of a walker."

Mrs. Shelby, who, greatly to her amusement, had overheard this conversation from the verandah, now resolved to do her part. She came forward, and, courteously expressing her concern for Haley's accident, pressed him to stay to dinner, saying that the cook should bring it on the table immediately.

Thus, all things considered, Haley, with rather an equivocal grace, proceeded to the parlor, while Sam, rolling his eyes after him with unutterable meaning, proceeded gravely with the horses to the stable-yard.

"Did yer see him, Andy? *did* yer see him?" said Sam, when he had got fairly beyond the shelter of the barn, and fastened the horse to a post. "O, Lor, if it warn't as good as a meetin', now, to see him a dancin' and kickin' and swarin' at us. Didn't I hear him? Swar away, ole fellow (says I to myself); will yer have yer hoss now, or wait till you cotch him? (says I). Lor, Andy, I think I can see him now." And Sam and Andy leaned up against the barn, and laughed to their hearts' content.

"Yer oughter seen how mad he looked, when I brought the hoss up. Lord, he'd a killed me, if he durs' to; and there I was a standin' as innercent and as humble."

"Lor, I seed you," said Andy; "ant you an old hoss, Sam?"

"Rather specks I am," said Sam; "did yer see Missis up stars at the winder? I seed her laughin'."

"I'm sure, I was racin' so, I didn't see nothing," said Andy.

"Well, yer see," said Sam, proceeding gravely to wash down Haley's pony, "I'se 'quired what yer may call a habit

27 Sam is evidently very familiar with Mr. Shelby's interest in dining on schedule.

28 Read as "observation." Sam's malapropism and high-toned language ("faculty," "cultivation") create a comic effect that disguises the serious advice he gives to the younger Andy, that house slaves should make use of their position to watch the whites carefully in order to have forewarning of events (i.e., to "see which way the wind [blows]").

29 Sam's use of "cultivation" is in keeping with the nineteenth-century American belief in perfectionism that fueled many reform and education movements. Thus, each person has talents (faculties) that can be improved (cultivated).

o' *bobservation*,[28] Andy. It's a very 'portant habit, Andy; and I commend yer to be cultivatin' it, now yer young. Hist up that hind foot, Andy. Yer see, Andy, it's *bobservation* makes all de difference in niggers. Didn't I see which way the wind blew dis yer mornin'? Didn't I see what Missis wanted, though she never let on? Dat ar's bobservation, Andy. I 'spects it's what you may call a faculty. Faculties is different in different peoples, but cultivation[29] of 'em goes a great way."

"I guess if I hadn't helped your bobservation dis mornin', yer wouldn't have seen your way so smart," said Andy.

"Andy," said Sam, "you's a promisin' child, der an't no manner o' doubt. I thinks lots of yer, Andy; and I don't feel no ways ashamed to take idees from you. We oughtenter overlook nobody, Andy, cause the smartest on us gets tripped up sometimes. And so, Andy, let's go up to the house now. I'll be boun' Missis'll give us an uncommon good bite, dis yer time."

# CHAPTER 7

## *The Mother's Struggle*[1]

It is impossible to conceive of a human creature more wholly desolate and forlorn than Eliza, when she turned her footsteps from Uncle Tom's cabin.

Her husband's suffering and dangers, and the danger of her child, all blended in her mind, with a confused and stunning sense of the risk she was running, in leaving the only home[2] she had ever known, and cutting loose from the protection of a friend whom she loved and revered. Then there was the parting from every familiar object,— the place where she had grown up, the trees under which she had played, the groves where she had walked many an evening in happier days, by the side of her young husband,—everything, as it lay in the clear, frosty starlight, seemed to speak reproachfully to her, and ask her whither could she go from a home like that?[3]

But stronger than all was maternal love, wrought into a paroxysm of frenzy by the near approach of a fearful danger. Her boy was old enough to have walked by her side, and, in an indifferent case, she would only have led him by the hand; but now the bare thought of putting him out of her arms made her shudder, and she strained him to her bosom with a convulsive grasp, as she went rapidly forward.

The frosty ground creaked beneath her feet, and she trembled at the sound; every quaking leaf and fluttering shadow sent the blood backward to her heart, and quickened her footsteps. She wondered within herself at the strength that seemed to be come upon her; for she felt the

1 This is a chapter title to tug at every female reader's heartstrings.

2 Stowe's success in depicting Eliza's departure as heartbreaking requires that we see Eliza's place of residence with the Shelbys as a "home." Indeed this is the only home that Eliza has known, but Stowe seems unconcerned that some readers might see Eliza's flight as unfortunate rather than inevitable.

3 In her 1852 "Review of *Uncle Tom's Cabin*," French novelist George Sand wrote that Stowe had "the genius of goodness, not that of the man of letters, but of the saint." Yet the delicate description of Eliza's nighttime flight belies Sand's faint praise of Stowe's literary talents.

4 Stowe perhaps doesn't really need to assault the reader with these questions, but she uses this heavy-handed rhetoric to chastise us for laughing at the antics that closed the last chapter. Stowe wants to ensure that we have sobered up, that our mood is properly somber, and in this she is successful.

5 Stowe employs the rhetoric of both the supernatural and science here. While Eliza will protect Harry from the literal "bogeyman," Haley, with "a spirit . . . no part of her," the touch of the sleeping boy strengthens "in electric streams" her flesh, nerve, and sinews.

6 "T——" is an example of a long-standing literary convention of indicating places and people by only a first letter. The author's seeming discretion imparts an air of authenticity while keeping information from the reader.

weight of her boy as if it had been a feather, and every flutter of fear seemed to increase the supernatural power that bore her on, while from her pale lips burst forth, in frequent ejaculations, the prayer to a Friend above—"Lord, help! Lord, save me!"

If it were *your* Harry, mother, or your Willie, that were going to be torn from you by a brutal trader, to-morrow morning,—if you had seen the man, and heard that the papers were signed and delivered, and you had only from twelve o'clock till morning to make good your escape,—how fast could *you* walk? How many miles could you make in those few brief hours, with the darling at your bosom,—the little sleepy head on your shoulder,—the small, soft arms trustingly holding on to your neck?[4]

For the child slept. At first, the novelty and alarm kept him waking; but his mother so hurriedly repressed every breath or sound, and so assured him that if he were only still she would certainly save him, that he clung quietly round her neck, only asking, as he found himself sinking to sleep,

"Mother, I don't need to keep awake, do I?"

"No, my darling; sleep, if you want to."

"But, mother, if I do get asleep, you won't let him get me?"

"No! so may God help me!" said his mother, with a paler cheek, and a brighter light in her large dark eyes.

"You're *sure*, an't you, mother?"

"Yes, *sure*!" said the mother, in a voice that startled herself; for it seemed to her to come from a spirit within, that was no part of her; and the boy dropped his little weary head on her shoulder, and was soon asleep. How the touch of those warm arms, the gentle breathings that came in her neck, seemed to add fire and spirit to her movements! It seemed to her as if strength poured into her in electric streams, from every gentle touch and movement of the sleeping, confiding child. Sublime is the dominion of the mind over the body, that, for a time, can make flesh and nerve impregnable, and string the sinews like steel, so that the weak become so mighty.[5]

The boundaries of the farm, the grove, the wood-lot, passed by her dizzily, as she walked on; and still she went, leaving one familiar object after another, slacking not, pausing not, till reddening daylight found her many a long mile from all traces of any familiar objects upon the open highway.

She had often been, with her mistress, to visit some connections, in the little village of T——,[6] not far from the

Ohio river, and knew the road well. To go thither, to escape across the Ohio river, were the first hurried outlines of her plan of escape; beyond that, she could only hope in God.

When horses and vehicles began to move along the highway, with that alert perception peculiar to a state of excitement, and which seems to be a sort of inspiration, she became aware that her headlong pace and distracted air might bring on her remark and suspicion. She therefore put the boy on the ground, and, adjusting her dress and bonnet, she walked on at as rapid a pace as she thought consistent with the preservation of appearances. In her little bundle she had provided a store of cakes and apples, which she used as expedients for quickening the speed of the child, rolling the apple some yards before them, when the boy would run with all his might after it; and this ruse, often repeated, carried them over many a half-mile.

After a while, they came to a thick patch of woodland, through which murmured a clear brook. As the child complained of hunger and thirst, she climbed over the fence with him; and, sitting down behind a large rock which concealed them from the road, she gave him a breakfast out of her little package. The boy wondered and grieved that she could not eat; and when, putting his arms round her neck, he tried to wedge some of his cake into her mouth, it seemed to her that the rising in her throat would choke her.

"No, no, Harry darling! mother can't eat till you are safe! We must go on—on—till we come to the river!" And she hurried again into the road, and again constrained herself to walk regularly and composedly forward.

She was many miles past any neighborhood where she was personally known. If she should chance to meet any who knew her, she reflected that the well-known kindness of the family would be of itself a blind to suspicion, as making it an unlikely supposition that she could be a fugitive. As she was also so white as not to be known as of colored lineage, without a critical survey, and her child was white also, it was much easier for her to pass on unsuspected.[7]

On this presumption, she stopped at noon at a neat farmhouse, to rest herself, and buy some dinner for her child and self;[8] for, as the danger decreased with the distance, the supernatural tension of the nervous system lessened, and she found herself both weary and hungry.

The good woman, kindly and gossiping, seemed rather pleased than otherwise with having somebody come in to

7 Because of elaborate racial designations that defined as "negro" any person having a black grandparent, many slaves appeared white, a fact that allowed a light-skinned runaway slave to pass as a white person in escape. See chapter 1, note 7, for an extended description of the era's racial categories.

8 At outlying farmhouses, wanderers could expect to find food for sale (or theft). Such scenes of feeding and sheltering strangers were common in nineteenth-century literature. Moreover, Stowe's Christian readers were apt to remember the story of Lot hosting angels in disguise and thereby saving his family from the destruction of Sodom and Gomorrah (Gen. 19:1–25).

9 Eliza means, of course, dangerously ill.

talk with; and accepted, without examination, Eliza's statement, that she "was going on a little piece, to spend a week with her friends,"—all which she hoped in her heart might prove strictly true.

An hour before sunset, she entered the village of T——, by the Ohio river, weary and foot-sore, but still strong in heart. Her first glance was at the river, which lay, like Jordan, between her and the Canaan of liberty on the other side.

It was now early spring, and the river was swollen and turbulent; great cakes of floating ice were swinging heavily to and fro in the turbid waters. Owing to the peculiar form of the shore on the Kentucky side, the land bending far out into the water, the ice had been lodged and detained in great quantities, and the narrow channel which swept round the bend was full of ice, piled one cake over another, thus forming a temporary barrier to the descending ice, which lodged, and formed a great, undulating raft, filling up the whole river, and extending almost to the Kentucky shore.

Eliza stood, for a moment, contemplating this unfavorable aspect of things, which she saw at once must prevent the usual ferry-boat from running, and then turned into a small public house on the bank, to make a few inquiries.

The hostess, who was busy in various fizzing and stewing operations over the fire, preparatory to the evening meal, stopped, with a fork in her hand, as Eliza's sweet and plaintive voice arrested her.

"What is it?" she said.

"Isn't there any ferry or boat, that takes people over to B——, now?" she said.

"No, indeed!" said the woman; "the boats has stopped running."

Eliza's look of dismay and disappointment struck the woman, and she said, inquiringly,

"May be you're wanting to get over?—anybody sick? Ye seem mighty anxious?"

"I've got a child that's very dangerous,"9 said Eliza. "I never heard of it till last night, and I've walked quite a piece to-day, in hopes to get to the ferry."

"Well, now, that's onlucky," said the woman, whose motherly sympathies were much aroused; "I'm re'lly consarned for ye. Solomon!" she called, from the window, towards a small back building. A man, in leather apron and very dirty hands, appeared at the door.

"I say, Sol," said the woman, "is that ar man going to tote them bar'ls over to-night?"

"He said he should try, if 't was any way prudent," said the man.

"There's a man a piece down here, that's going over with some truck[10] this evening, if he durs'to; he'll be in here to supper to-night, so you'd better set down and wait. That's a sweet little fellow," added the woman, offering him a cake.

But the child, wholly exhausted, cried with weariness.

"Poor fellow! he isn't used to walking, and I've hurried him on so," said Eliza.

"Well, take him into this room," said the woman, opening into a small bed-room, where stood a comfortable bed. Eliza laid the weary boy upon it, and held his hands in hers till he was fast asleep. For her there was no rest. As a fire in her bones, the thought of the pursuer urged her on; and she gazed with longing eyes on the sullen, surging waters that lay between her and liberty.

Here we must take our leave of her for the present, to follow the course of her pursuers.[11]

Though Mrs. Shelby had promised that the dinner should be hurried on table, yet it was soon seen, as the thing has often been seen before, that it required more than one to make a bargain.[12] So, although the order was fairly given out in Haley's hearing, and carried to Aunt Chloe by at least half a dozen juvenile messengers, that dignitary only gave certain very gruff snorts, and tosses of her head, and went on with every operation in an unusually leisurely and circumstantial manner.

For some singular reason, an impression seemed to reign among the servants generally that Missis would not be particularly disobliged by delay; and it was wonderful what a number of counter accidents occurred constantly, to retard the course of things. One luckless wight[13] contrived to upset the gravy; and then gravy had to be got up *de novo*,[14] with due care and formality, Aunt Chloe watching and stirring with dogged precision, answering shortly, to all suggestions of haste, that she "warn't a going to have raw gravy on the table, to help nobody's catchings."[15] One tumbled down with the water, and had to go to the spring for more; and another precipitated the butter into the path of events; and there was from time to time giggling news brought into the kitchen that "Mas'r Haley was mighty oneasy, and that he couldn't sit in his cheer[16] no ways, but was a walkin' and stalkin' to the winders[17] and through the porch."

"Sarves him right!" said Aunt Chloe, indignantly. "He'll

10 I.e., odds and ends for sale.

11 Notice Stowe's confident control over her narrative: What better way to carry out a difficult jump backward in time in the middle of a dramatic chase than to simply announce that this is her plan? Stowe interrupts her description of Eliza's dramatic escape with an explicit change of scene to the captors. She keeps Eliza's flight at fever pitch by closing it to her reader's view, as she changes the mood as well to the seriocomic delaying tactics of the Shelby slaves.

12 Stowe calls attention to the cooperation needed by using the word "bargain" instead of "decision."

13 I.e., person.

14 I.e., from the beginning (all over again).

15 Here, the class distinction between the Shelbys and Haley serves a dramatic purpose: to delay the pursuit of Eliza. Chloe's perfectionism also comes in handy.

16 I.e., "chair."

17 I.e., "windows."

**18** Notice how Chloe refers to God as a "master." Abolitionist rhetoric mined this word to remind Christian audiences that the Master of everyone is God. Slavery was portrayed as not simply un-American but, most importantly, unchristian.

**19** Revelation (sometimes called the Apocalypse of Saint John the Apostle), the final book of the New Testament, which relates John's vision of the final judgment. The reference is to the verses on the breaking of the fifth of the seven seals: "And when he opened the fifth seal, I saw under the altar the souls of those who had been slain for the word of God, and for the witness that they bore. And they cried with a loud voice, saying, 'How long O Lord (holy and true), dost thou refrain from judging and from avenging our blood on those who dwell on the earth?'" (Rev. 6:9–10). Slave narratives made ample use of biblical text and imagery, especially of the books of Exodus and Isaiah, but as the nineteenth century wore on, abolitionist literature drew on New Testament references aimed at calling to task the white Christians in their audiences. In *Uncle Tom's Cabin*, Stowe puts apocalyptic references to use in her sentimentalist strategy to evoke fear of untimely end (whether of individual lives or of the world itself) in her Christian readers.

**20** Curiously, Stowe portrays Chloe shedding tears for the tearing apart of husband and wife generally, but not specifically for the wrenching apart of Tom and his family.

get wus nor oneasy, one of these days, if he don't mend his ways. *His* master'll[18] be sending for him, and then see how he'll look!"

"He'll go to torment, and no mistake," said little Jake.

"He desarves it!" said Aunt Chloe, grimly; "he's broke a many, many, many hearts,—I tell ye all!" she said, stopping, with a fork uplifted in her hands; "it's like what Mas'r George reads in Ravelations,—souls a callin' under the altar! and a callin' on the Lord for vengeance on sich!—and by and by the Lord he'll hear 'em—so he will!"[19]

Aunt Chloe, who was much revered in the kitchen, was listened to with open mouth; and, the dinner being now fairly sent in, the whole kitchen was at leisure to gossip with her, and to listen to her remarks.

"Sich 'll be burnt up forever, and no mistake; won't ther?" said Andy.

"I'd be glad to see it, I'll be boun," said little Jake.

"Chil'en!" said a voice, that made them all start. It was Uncle Tom, who had come in, and stood listening to the conversation at the door.

"Chil'en!" he said, "I'm afeard you don't know what ye're sayin'. Forever is a *dre'ful* word, chil'en; it's awful to think on 't. You oughtenter wish that ar to any human crittur."

"We wouldn't to anybody but the soul-drivers," said Andy; "nobody can help wishing it to them, they's so awful wicked."

"Don't natur herself kinder cry out on em?" said Aunt Chloe. "Don't dey tear der suckin' baby right off his mother's breast, and sell him, and der little children as is crying and holding on by her clothes,—don't dey pull 'em off and sells em? Don't dey tear wife and husband apart?" said Aunt Chloe, beginning to cry,[20] "when it's jest takin' the very life on 'em?—and all the while does they feel one bit,—don't dey drink and smoke, and take it oncommon easy? Lor, if the devil don't get them, what's he good for?" And Aunt Chloe covered her face with her checked apron, and began to sob in good earnest.

"Pray for them that 'spitefully use you, the good book says," says Tom.

"Pray for 'em!" said Aunt Chloe; "Lor, it's too tough! I can't pray for 'em."

"It's natur, Chloe, and natur's strong," said Tom, "but the Lord's grace is stronger; besides, you oughter think what an awful state a poor crittur's soul's in that'll do them ar things,—you oughter thank God that you an't *like* him,

Chloe. I'm sure I'd rather be sold, ten thousand times over, than to have all that ar poor crittur's got to answer for."**21**

"So'd I, a heap," said Jake. "Lor, *shouldn't* we cotch it, Andy?"

Andy shrugged his shoulders, and gave an acquiescent whistle.

"I'm glad Mas'r didn't go off this morning, as he looked to," said Tom; "that ar hurt me more than sellin', it did. Mebbe it might have been natural for him, but 't would have come desp't hard on me, as has known him from a baby; but I've seen Mas'r, and I begin ter feel sort o' reconciled to the Lord's will now. Mas'r couldn't help hisself; he did right, but I'm feared things will be kinder goin' to rack, when I'm gone. Mas'r can't be spected to be a pryin' round everywhar, as I've done, a keepin' up all the ends. The boys all means well, but they's powerful car'less. That ar troubles me."

The bell here rang, and Tom was summoned to the parlor.

"Tom," said his master, kindly, "I want you to notice that I give this gentleman bonds to forfeit a thousand dollars if you are not on the spot when he wants you; he's going to-day to look after his other business, and you can have the day to yourself. Go anywhere you like, boy."**22**

"Thank you, Mas'r," said Tom.

"And mind yerself," said the trader, "and don't come it over your master with any o' yer nigger tricks; for I'll take every cent out of him, if you an't thar. If he'd hear to me, he wouldn't trust any on ye—slippery as eels!"

"Mas'r," said Tom,—and he stood very straight,—"I was jist eight years old when ole Missis put you into my arms, and you wasn't a year old. 'Thar,' says she, 'Tom, that's to be *your* young Mas'r; take good care on him,' says she. And now I jist ask you, Mas'r, have I ever broke word to you, or gone contrary to you, 'specially since I was a Christian?'"

Mr. Shelby was fairly overcome, and the tears rose to his eyes.

"My good boy," said he, "the Lord knows you say but the truth; and if I was able to help it, all the world shouldn't buy you."

"And sure as I am a Christian woman," said Mrs. Shelby, "you shall be redeemed as soon as I can any way bring together means. Sir," she said to Haley, "take good account of who you sell him to, and let me know."

"Lor, yes, for that matter," said the trader, "I may bring him up in a year, not much the wuss for wear, and trade him back."

**21** This is the first declaration of Tom's religious principles. He makes many in the course of the novel; all follow this simple but powerful "sound bite" form. Tom's eye is on heavenly rather than earthly rewards. But Tom's principles appeal to less religious readers also—his consistency inspires admiration.

**22** Shelby's seeming generosity in giving Tom a day off is undercut by his use of the demeaning term "boy" for a man who has elsewhere been described as a patriarch.

23 I.e., a bit drunk.

24 Once again, Stowe depicts Sam and Andy's clowning for specific purposes, in this case to poke fun at Haley. The narrator has deemed him not a gentleman and the Shelbys have indicated their displeasure at his vulgarity, but only Sam and Andy can engage him directly and get the better of him.

"I'll trade with you then, and make it for your advantage," said Mrs. Shelby.

"Of course," said the trader, "all's equal with me; li'ves trade 'em up as down, so I does a good business. All I want is a livin', you know, ma'am; that's all any on us wants, I s'pose."

Mr. and Mrs. Shelby both felt annoyed and degraded by the familiar impudence of the trader, and yet both saw the absolute necessity of putting a constraint on their feelings. The more hopelessly sordid and insensible he appeared, the greater became Mrs. Shelby's dread of his succeeding in recapturing Eliza and her child, and of course the greater her motive for detaining him by every female artifice. She therefore graciously smiled, assented, chatted familiarly, and did all she could to make time pass imperceptibly.

At two o'clock Sam and Andy brought the horses up to the posts, apparently greatly refreshed and invigorated by the scamper of the morning.

Sam was there new oiled from dinner,23 with an abundance of zealous and ready officiousness. As Haley approached, he was boasting, in flourishing style, to Andy, of the evident and eminent success of the operation, now that he had "farly come to it."

"Your master, I s'pose, don't keep no dogs," said Haley, thoughtfully, as he prepared to mount.

"Heaps on 'em," said Sam, triumphantly; "thar's Bruno—he's a roarer! and, besides that, 'bout every nigger of us keeps a pup of some natur or uther."24

"Poh!" said Haley,—and he said something else, too, with regard to the said dogs, at which Sam muttered,

"I don't see no use cussin' on 'em, no way."

"But your master don't keep no dogs (I pretty much know he don't) for trackin' out niggers."

Sam knew exactly what he meant, but he kept on a look of earnest and desperate simplicity.

"Our dogs all smells round considable sharp. I spect they's the kind, though they han't never had no practice. They's far dogs, though, at most anything, if you'd get 'em started. Here, Bruno," he called, whistling to the lumbering Newfoundland, who came pitching tumultuously toward them.

"You go hang!" said Haley, getting up. "Come, tumble up now."

Sam tumbled up accordingly, dexterously contriving to tickle Andy as he did so, which occasioned Andy to split out into a laugh, greatly to Haley's indignation, who made a cut at him with his riding-whip.

"I's 'stonished at yer, Andy," said Sam, with awful gravity. "This yer's a seris bisness, Andy. Yer mustn't be a makin' game. This yer an't no way to help Mas'r."

"I shall take the straight road to the river," said Haley, decidedly, after they had come to the boundaries of the estate. "I know the way of all of 'em,—they makes tracks for the underground."[25]

"Sartin," said Sam, "dat's de idee. Mas'r Haley hits de thing right in de middle. Now, der's two roads to de river,—de dirt road and der pike,—which Mas'r mean to take?"

Andy looked up innocently at Sam, surprised at hearing this new geographical fact, but instantly confirmed what he said, by a vehement reiteration.

"Cause," said Sam, "I'd rather be 'clined to 'magine that Lizy'd take de dirt road, bein' it's the least travelled."

Haley, notwithstanding that he was a very old bird, and naturally inclined to be suspicious of chaff, was rather brought up by this view of the case.

"If yer warn't both on yer such cussed liars, now!" he said, contemplatively, as he pondered a moment.

The pensive, reflective tone in which this was spoken appeared to amuse Andy prodigiously, and he drew a little behind, and shook so as apparently to run a great risk of falling off his horse, while Sam's face was immovably composed into the most doleful gravity.

"Course," said Sam, "Mas'r can do as he'd ruther; go de straight road, if Mas'r thinks best,—it's all one to us. Now, when I study 'pon it, I think de straight road do best, *deridedly*."

"She would naturally go a lonesome way," said Haley, thinking aloud, and not minding Sam's remark.

"Dar an't no sayin'," said Sam; "gals is pecular; they never does nothin' ye thinks they will; mose gen'lly the contrar. Gals is nat'lly made contrary; and so, if you thinks they've gone one road, it is sartin you'd better go t' other, and then you'll be sure to find 'em. Now, my private 'pinion is, Lizy took der dirt road; so I think we'd better take de straight one."

This profound generic view of the female sex did not seem to dispose Haley particularly to the straight road; and he announced decidedly that he should go the other, and asked Sam when they should come to it.

"A little piece ahead," said Sam, giving a wink to Andy

25 A network of former slaves and antislavery Northerners, the Underground Railroad was begun in the 1780s with Quaker support and reached its height in the 1830s. Cities in border states—Cincinnati, Ohio, and Wilmington, Delaware, for example—were points where fugitive slaves were met and conducted to Canada via Great Lakes ports such as Detroit, Sandusky, Erie, and Buffalo.

with the eye which was on Andy's side of the head; and he added, gravely, "but I've studded on de matter, and I'm quite clar we ought not to go dat ar way. I nebber been over it no way. It's despit lonesome, and we might lose our way,—whar we'd come to, de Lord only knows."

"Nevertheless," said Haley, "I shall go that way."

"Now I think on 't, I think I hearn 'em tell that dat ar road was all fenced up and down by der creek, and thar, an't it, Andy?"

Andy wasn't certain; he'd only "hearn tell" about that road, but never been over it. In short, he was strictly non-committal.

Haley, accustomed to strike the balance of probabilities between lies of greater or lesser magnitude, thought that it lay in favor of the dirt road aforesaid. The mention of the thing he thought he perceived was involuntary on Sam's part at first, and his confused attempts to dissuade him he set down to a desperate lying on second thoughts, as being unwilling to implicate Eliza.

When, therefore, Sam indicated the road, Haley plunged briskly into it, followed by Sam and Andy.

Now, the road, in fact, was an old one, that had formerly been a thoroughfare to the river, but abandoned for many years after the laying of the new pike. It was open for about an hour's ride, and after that it was cut across by various farms and fences. Sam knew this fact perfectly well,—indeed, the road had been so long closed up, that Andy had never heard of it. He therefore rode along with an air of dutiful submission, only groaning and vociferating occasionally that 't was "desp't rough, and bad for Jerry's foot."

"Now, I jest give yer warning," said Haley, "I know yer; yer won't get me to turn off this yer road, with all yer fussin'—so you shet up!"

"Mas'r will go his own way!" said Sam, with rueful submission, at the same time winking most portentously to Andy, whose delight was now very near the explosive point.

Sam was in wonderful spirits,—professed to keep a very brisk look-out,—at one time exclaiming that he saw "a gal's bonnet" on the top of some distant eminence, or calling to Andy "if that thar wasn't 'Lizy' down in the hollow;" always making these exclamations in some rough or craggy part of the road, where the sudden quickening of speed was a special inconvenience to all parties concerned, and thus keeping Haley in a state of constant commotion.

After riding about an hour in this way, the whole party made a precipitate and tumultuous descent into a barnyard belonging to a large farming establishment. Not a soul was in sight, all the hands being employed in the fields; but, as the barn stood conspicuously and plainly square across the road, it was evident that their journey in that direction had reached a decided finale.

"Wan't dat ar what I telled Mas'r?" said Sam, with an air of injured innocence. "How does strange gentleman spect to know more about a country dan de natives born and raised?"

"You rascal!" said Haley, "you knew all about this."

"Didn't I tell yer I *know'd,* and yer wouldn't believe me? I telled Mas'r 't was all shet up, and fenced up, and I didn't spect we could get through,—Andy heard me."[26]

It was all too true to be disputed, and the unlucky man had to pocket his wrath with the best grace he was able, and all three faced to the right about, and took up their line of march for the highway.

In consequence of all the various delays, it was about three-quarters of an hour after Eliza had laid her child to sleep in the village tavern that the party came riding into the same place. Eliza was standing by the window, looking out in another direction, when Sam's quick eye caught a glimpse of her. Haley and Andy were two yards behind. At this crisis, Sam contrived to have his hat blown off, and uttered a loud and characteristic ejaculation, which startled her at once; she drew suddenly back; the whole train swept by the window, round to the front door.

A thousand lives seemed to be concentrated in that one moment to Eliza.[27] Her room opened by a side door to the river. She caught her child, and sprang down the steps towards it. The trader caught a full glimpse of her, just as she was disappearing down the bank; and throwing himself from his horse, and calling loudly on Sam and Andy, he was after her like a hound after a deer. In that dizzy moment her feet to her scarce seemed to touch the ground, and a moment brought her to the water's edge. Right on behind they came; and, nerved with strength such as God gives only to the desperate, with one wild cry and flying leap, she vaulted sheer over the turbid current by the shore, on to the raft of ice beyond. It was a desperate leap—impossible to anything but madness and despair; and Haley, Sam, and Andy, instinctively cried out, and lifted up their hands, as she did it.

The huge green fragment of ice on which she alighted pitched and creaked as her weight came on it, but she

26 Most critics do not give Stowe enough credit for her humor. This carefully structured scene is a masterpiece of comic timing.

27 In 1913, in his autobiography *A Small Boy and Others*, Henry James called the success of *Uncle Tom's Cabin* an inexplicable accident—nothing in its content would explain its impact:

> Appreciation and judgment, the whole impression, were thus an effect for which there had been no process–any process so related having in other cases *had* to be at some point or other critical; nothing in the guise of a written book, therefore, a book printed, published, sold, brought and "noticed," probably ever reached its mark, the mark of exciting interest, without having at least groped for that goal *as* a book or by the exposure of some literary side. . . . *Uncle Tom*, instead of making even one of the cheap short cuts through the medium in which books breathe, even as fishes in water went

"She leaped to another and still another cake." This Eliza is alone on the ice: Haley, Sam, and Andy are nowhere in sight. Hers is a solitary struggle. The artist aims more for mood than for realism; the river and ice floes are too vaguely depicted to give a sense of her actual danger.
From *Altemus' Young People's Library: Uncle Tom's Cabin; or, Life Among the Lowly,* 1900

gaily roundabout it altogether, as if a fish, a wonderful "leaping" fish, had simply flown through the air.

James's description evokes Stowe's upcoming description of Eliza's leaping flight over the ice.

28 The most famous scene in the novel, Eliza's escape draws its dramatic force from an actual incident in Cincinnati, Ohio, reported widely in the newspapers. In nineteenth-century America, where womanhood's highest value was motherhood, the story of a mother crossing the ice-choked river with her baby to gain freedom hit a cultural nerve and was taken up by several writers including Stowe. In December 1853, for example, Frances E. W. Harper's poem "Eliza Harris" appeared in the *Liberator* and *Frederick Douglass' Paper*. A famous six-minute 1944 cartoon version (*Mighty Mouse: Eliza on Ice*) portrays a very dark Eliza crossing on ice that pours out of a riverside slot machine when she puts a nickel in and wins the jackpot. Stowe's launching of the scene with the phrase "a thousand lives seemed to be concentrated in that one moment" seems to foreshadow the moment's renown.

Miguel Covarrubias's modernist lithograph of Eliza, employing a silhouette motif. From *Uncle Tom's Cabin: or, Life Among the Lowly*, Heritage Press edition, 1938

staid there not a moment. With wild cries and desperate energy she leaped to another and still another cake;—stumbling—leaping—slipping—springing upwards again! Her shoes are gone—her stockings cut from her feet—while blood marked every step; but she saw nothing, felt nothing, till dimly, as in a dream, she saw the Ohio side, and a man helping her up the bank.**28**

"Yer a brave gal, now, whoever ye ar!" said the man, with an oath.

Eliza recognized the voice and face of a man who owned a farm not far from her old home.

"O, Mr. Symmes!—save me—do save me—do hide me!" said Eliza.

"Why, what's this?" said the man. "Why, if 'tan't Shelby's gal!"

"My child!—this boy!—he'd sold him! There is his Mas'r," said she, pointing to the Kentucky shore. "O, Mr. Symmes, you've got a little boy!"

"So I have," said the man, as he roughly, but kindly, drew her up the steep bank. "Besides, you're a right brave gal. I like grit, wherever I see it."

When they had gained the top of the bank, the man paused.

"I'd be glad to do something for ye," said he; "but then there's nowhar I could take ye. The best I can do is to tell ye to go *thar*," said he, pointing to a large white house which stood by itself, off the main street of the village. "Go thar; they're kind folks. Thar's no kind o' danger but they'll help you,—they're up to all that sort o' thing."

"The Lord bless you!" said Eliza, earnestly.

"No 'casion, no 'casion in the world," said the man. "What I've done's of no 'count."

"And, oh, surely, sir, you won't tell any one!"

"Go to thunder, gal! What do you take a feller for? In course not," said the man. "Come, now, go along like a likely, sensible gal, as you are. You've arnt your liberty,

Miguel Covarrubias literalizes the symbol of a slave mother and child repressed by the hand of slavery. From *Uncle Tom's Cabin: or, Life Among the Lowly*, Heritage Press edition, 1938

This Eliza looks vaguely Mediterranean. It is difficult to imagine that she is a fleeing slave. From *Uncle Tom's Cabin*, James Nisbet & Co., Ltd., London, n.d.

and you shall have it, for all me."

The woman folded her child to her bosom, and walked firmly and swiftly away. The man stood and looked after her.

"Shelby, now, mebbe won't think this yer the most neighborly thing in the world; but what's a feller to do? If he catches one of my gals in the same fix, he's welcome to pay back. Somehow I never could see no kind o' critter a strivin' and pantin', and trying to clar theirselves, with the dogs arter 'em, and go agin 'em. Besides, I don't see no kind of 'casion for me to be hunter and catcher for other folks, neither."

So spoke this poor, heathenish Kentuckian, who had not been instructed in his constitutional relations, and consequently was betrayed into acting in a sort of Christianized manner, which, if he had been better situated and more enlightened, he would not have been left to do.[29]

Haley had stood a perfectly amazed spectator of the scene, till Eliza had disappeared up the bank, when he turned a blank, inquiring look on Sam and Andy.

"That ar was a tolable fair stroke of business," said Sam.

"The gal's got seven devils in her, I believe!" said Haley. "How like a wildcat she jumped!"

"Wal, now," said Sam, scratching his head, "I hope Mas'r'll 'scuse us tryin' dat ar road. Don't think I feel spry enough for dat ar, no way!" and Sam gave a hoarse chuckle.

"*You* laugh!" said the trader, with a growl.

"Lord bless you, Mas'r, I couldn't help it, now," said Sam, giving way to the long pent-up delight of his soul. "She looked so curi's, a leapin' and springin'—ice a crackin'—and only to hear her,—plump! ker chunk! ker splash! Spring! Lord! how she goes it!" and Sam and Andy laughed till the tears rolled down their cheeks.

"I'll make ye laugh t'other side yer mouths!" said the trader, laying about their heads with his riding-whip.

Both ducked, and ran shouting up the bank, and were on their horses before he was up.

**29** This characterizing of Eliza's rescuer as a "poor, heathenish Kentuckian" is jarring and rings false. Sarcasm rarely works when it comes from Stowe's narrator (as opposed to one of her characters). But Stowe needs a transition from the dramatic scene of Eliza's escape back to Haley, and, incredibly, she succeeds.

Poster, circa 1890, by A. S. Seer's Union Square Print, NY. This Eliza conforms to a stereotype of a gypsy.

"Good-evening, Mas'r!" said Sam, with much gravity. "I berry much spect Missis be anxious 'bout Jerry. Mas'r Haley won't want us no longer. Missis wouldn't hear of our ridin' the critters over Lizy's bridge to-night;" and, with a facetious poke into Andy's ribs, he started off, followed by the latter, at full speed,—their shouts of laughter coming faintly on the wind.

A romantic depiction of Eliza and Harry fleeing in the night.   From *Onkel Toms Hütte, oder Negerleben in den Sklavenstaaten von Nordamerika*. Konstanz. Christlicher Buch- und Kunstverlag, Carl Hirsch A. G.

# CHAPTER 8

## *Eliza's Escape*[1]

Eliza made her desperate retreat across the river just in the dusk of twilight. The gray mist of evening, rising slowly from the river, enveloped her as she disappeared up the bank, and the swollen current and floundering masses of ice presented a hopeless barrier between her and her pursuer. Haley therefore slowly and discontentedly returned to the little tavern, to ponder further what was to be done. The woman opened to him the door of a little parlor, covered with a rag carpet, where stood a table with a very shining black oil-cloth, sundry lank, high-backed wood chairs, with some plaster images in resplendent colors on the mantel-shelf, above a very dimly-smoking grate; a long hard-wood settle extended its uneasy length by the chimney, and here Haley sat him down to meditate on the instability of human hopes and happiness in general.

"What did I want with the little cuss, now," he said to himself, "that I should have got myself treed like a coon, as I am, this yer way?" and Haley relieved himself by repeating over a not very select litany of imprecations on himself, which, though there was the best possible reason to consider them as true, we shall, as a matter of taste, omit.

He was startled by the loud and dissonant voice of a man who was apparently dismounting at the door. He hurried to the window.

"By the land! if this yer an't the nearest, now, to what

1 The chapter title raises a question: Hasn't Eliza already escaped? Not entirely, Stowe suggests. Since the passage of the Fugitive Slave Law, it is against the law to harbor fugitive slaves in free states. Eliza and Harry will need to cross the border into Canada before they are truly safe.

2 Note Tom Loker's physical similarity to Uncle Tom, who is described in chapter 4 as "a large, broad-chested, powerfully-made man." But there the similarity ends.

3 "Mousing" fits well the catlike description of Loker's companion Marks and evokes the game of cat and mouse, in which the hunter cat toys with his prey (the mouse) before killing it.

I've heard folks call Providence," said Haley. "I do b'lieve that ar's Tom Loker."

Haley hastened out. Standing by the bar, in the corner of the room, was a brawny, muscular man, full six feet in height, and broad in proportion. He was dressed in a coat of buffalo-skin, made with the hair outward, which gave him a shaggy and fierce appearance, perfectly in keeping with the whole air of his physiognomy. In the head and face every organ and lineament expressive of brutal and unhesitating violence was in a state of the highest possible development. Indeed, could our readers fancy a bull-dog come unto man's estate, and walking about in a hat and coat, they would have no unapt idea of the general style and effect of his physique.[2] He was accompanied by a travelling companion, in many respects an exact contrast to himself. He was short and slender, lithe and cat-like in his motions, and had a peering, mousing[3] expression about his keen black eyes, with which every feature of his face seemed sharpened into sympathy; his thin, long nose, ran out as if it was eager to bore into the nature of things in general; his sleek, thin, black hair was stuck eagerly forward, and all his motions and evolutions expressed a dry, cautious acuteness. The great big man poured out a big tumbler half full of raw spirits, and gulped it down without a word. The little man stood tiptoe, and putting his head first to one side and then to the other, and snuffing considerably in the directions of the various bottles, ordered at last a mint julep, in a thin and quivering voice, and with an air of great circumspection. When poured out, he took it and looked at it with a sharp, complacent air, like a man who thinks he has done about the right thing, and hit the nail on the head, and proceeded to dispose of it in short and well-advised sips.

"Wal, now, who'd a thought this yer luck 'ad come to me? Why, Loker, how are ye?" said Haley, coming forward, and extending his hand to the big man.

"The devil!" was the civil reply. "What brought you here, Haley?"

The mousing man, who bore the name of Marks, instantly stopped his sipping, and, poking his head forward, looked shrewdly on the new acquaintance, as a cat sometimes looks at a moving dry leaf, or some other possible object of pursuit.

"I say, Tom, this yer's the luckiest thing in the world. I'm in a devil of a hobble, and you must help me out."

"Ugh? aw! like enough!" grunted his complacent acquaintance. "A body may be pretty sure of that, when *you're* glad to see 'em; something to be made off of 'em. What's the blow now?"

"You've got a friend here?" said Haley, looking doubtfully at Marks; "partner, perhaps?"

"Yes, I have. Here, Marks! here's that ar feller that I was in with in Natchez."

"Shall be pleased with his acquaintance," said Marks, thrusting out a long, thin hand, like a raven's claw. "Mr. Haley, I believe?"

"The same, sir," said Haley. "And now, gentlemen, seein' as we've met so happily, I think I'll stand up to a small matter of a treat in this here parlor. So, now, old coon,"[4] said he to the man at the bar, "get us hot water, and sugar, and cigars, and plenty of the *real stuff,* and we'll have a blow-out."

Behold, then, the candles lighted, the fire stimulated to the burning point in the grate, and our three worthies seated round a table, well spread with all the accessories to good fellowship enumerated before.[5]

Haley began a pathetic recital of his peculiar troubles. Loker shut up his mouth, and listened to him with gruff and surly attention. Marks, who was anxiously and with much fidgeting compounding a tumbler of punch to his own peculiar taste, occasionally looked up from his employment, and, poking his sharp nose and chin almost into Haley's face, gave the most earnest heed to the whole narrative. The conclusion of it appeared to amuse him extremely, for he shook his shoulders and sides in silence, and perked up his thin lips with an air of great internal enjoyment.

"So, then, ye'r fairly sewed up, an't ye?" he said; "he! he! he! It's neatly done, too."

"This yer young-un business makes lots of trouble in the trade," said Haley, dolefully.

"If we could get a breed of gals that didn't care, now, for their young uns," said Marks; "tell ye, I think 't would be 'bout the greatest mod'rn improvement I knows on,"—and Marks patronized his joke by a quiet introductory sniggle.

"Jes so," said Haley; "I never couldn't see into it; young uns is heaps of trouble to 'em; one would think, now, they'd be glad to get clar on 'em; but they arn't. And the more trouble a young un is, and the more good for nothing, as a gen'l thing, the tighter they sticks to 'em."

"Wal, Mr. Haley," said Marks, "jest pass the hot water. Yes, sir; you say jest what I feel and all'us have. Now, I bought a gal once, when I was in the trade,—a tight, likely wench she was, too, and quite considerable smart,—and

4 An abbreviation of "raccoon." The word "coon" was used in the nineteenth century to denote a black person; sometime in the twentieth century the term became thought of as pejorative.

5 If the reader hasn't guessed by now, enjoyment of food, drink, and cigars is not something for which Stowe has much sympathy. Nonetheless, she paints a believable picture of barroom conviviality.

**6** I.e., oddly funny.

**7** These two anecdotes are heavy-handed but impossible to forget. What Stowe sacrifices in delicacy she makes up for in descriptive power.

**8** I.e., as silent as fish.

**9** Marks makes a pun here of two meanings of "woolly." The first is the racist term used to described blacks as "woolly-headed"; the second is its meaning as "barbarous."

In this Miguel Covarrubias lithograph, top-hatted men check a slave woman's teeth, as they would do a horse. The drama of the image is contained in the child's terrified eyes. From *Uncle Tom's Cabin: or, Life Among the Lowly*, Heritage Press edition, 1938

she had a young un that was mis'able sickly; it had a crooked back, or something or other; and I jest gin't away to a man that thought he'd take his chance raising on 't, being it didn't cost nothin';—never thought, yer know, of the gal's takin' on about it,—but, Lord, yer oughter seen how she went on. Why, re'lly, she did seem to me to valley the child more 'cause '*t was* sickly and cross, and plagued her; and she warn't making b'lieve, neither,—cried about it, she did, and lopped round, as if she'd lost every friend she had. It re'lly was droll**6** to think on 't. Lord, there an't no end to women's notions."

"Wal, jest so with me," said Haley. "Last summer, down on Red river, I got a gal traded off on me, with a likely lookin' child enough, and his eyes looked as bright as yourn; but, come to look, I found him stone blind. Fact—he was stone blind. Wal, ye see, I thought there warn't no harm in my jest passing him along, and not sayin' nothin'; and I'd got him nicely swapped off for a keg o' whiskey; but come to get him away from the gal, she was jest like a tiger. So 't was before we started, and I hadn't got my gang chained up; so what should she do but ups on a cotton-bale, like a cat, ketches a knife from one of the deck hands, and, I tell ye, she made all fly for a minit, till she saw 'twan't no use; and she jest turns round, and pitches head first, young un and all, into the river,—went down plump, and never ris."**7**

"Bah!" said Tom Loker, who had listened to these stories with ill-repressed disgust,—"shif'less, both on ye! *my* gals don't cut up no such shines, I tell ye!"

"Indeed! how do you help it?" said Marks, briskly.

"Help it? why, I buys a gal, and if she's got a young un to be sold, I jest walks up and puts my fist to her face, and says, 'Look here, now, if you give me one word out of your head, I'll smash yer face in. I won't hear one word—not the beginning of a word.' I says to 'em, 'This yer young un's mine, and not yourn, and you've no kind o' business with it. I'm going to sell it, first chance; mind, you don't cut up none o' yer shines about it, or I'll make ye wish ye'd never been born.' I tell ye, they sees it an't no play, when I gets hold. I makes 'em as whist as fishes;**8** and if one on 'em begins and gives a yelp, why,—" and Mr. Loker brought down his fist with a thump that fully explained the hiatus.

"That ar's what ye may call *emphasis*," said Marks poking Haley in the side, and going into another small giggle. "An't Tom peculiar? he! he! he! I say, Tom, I s'pect you make 'em *understand,* for all niggers' heads is woolly.**9**

They don't never have no doubt o' your meaning, Tom. If you an't the devil, Tom, you's his twin brother, I'll say that for ye!"

Tom received the compliment with becoming modesty, and began to look as affable as was consistent, as John Bunyan says,[10] "with his doggish nature."

Haley, who had been imbibing very freely of the staple of the evening, began to feel a sensible elevation and enlargement of his moral faculties,—a phenomenon not unusual with gentlemen of a serious and reflective turn, under similar circumstances.

"Wal, now, Tom," he said, "ye re'lly is too bad, as I al'ays have told ye; ye know, Tom, you and I used to talk over these yer matters down in Natchez, and I used to prove to ye that we made full as much, and was as well off for this yer world, by treatin' on 'em well, besides keepin' a better chance for comin' in the kingdom at last, when wust comes to wust, and thar an't nothing else left to get, ye know."

"Boh!" said Tom, *"don't* I know?—don't make me too sick with any yer stuff,—my stomach is a leetle riled now;" and Tom drank half a glass of raw brandy.

"I say," said Haley, and leaning back in his chair and gesturing impressively, "I'll say this now, I al'ays meant to drive my trade so as to make money on 't, *fust and foremost,* as much as any man; but, then, trade an't everything, and money an't everything, 'cause we's all got souls. I don't care, now, who hears me say it,—and I think a cussed sight on it,—so I may as well come out with it. I b'lieve in religion, and one of these days, when I've got matters tight and snug, I calculates to tend to my soul and them ar matters; and so what's the use of doin' any more wickedness than's re'lly necessary?—it don't seem to me it's 't all prudent."

"Tend to yer soul!" repeated Tom, contemptuously; "take a bright look-out to find a soul in you,—save yourself any care on that score. If the devil sifts you through a hair sieve, he won't find one."[11]

"Why, Tom, you're cross," said Haley; "why can't ye take it pleasant, now, when a feller's talking for your good?"

"Stop that ar jaw o' yourn, there," said Tom, gruffly. "I can stand most any talk o' yourn, but your pious talk,—that kills me right up. After all, what's the odds between me and you? 'Tan't that you care one bit more, or have a bit more feelin',—it's clean, sheer, dog meanness, wanting to cheat the devil and save your own skin; don't I see through it? And your 'gettin' religion,' as you call it, arter

Wood engraving illustrating one of Haley's stories of maternal desperation, by W. Measom, "after George Cruikshank." The artist pays an odd amount of attention to the curves on the knife and the mother's body.   From *Uncle Tom's Cabin*, John Cassell, London, 1852

10 John Bunyan (1628–1688), English preacher and author of the dream allegory *The Pilgrim's Progress: from This World to That Which Is to Come* (1678). The book was widely translated and popular, a standard for every Christian's bookshelf. Bunyan's text had wider readership in the North, where it resonated with abolitionists. Massachusetts Senator Charles Sumner's speech before the Senate on his motion to repeal the Fugitive Slave Law on August 26, 1852, quoted Bunyan's text:

By the Supreme Law, which commands me to do no injustice; by the comprehensive Christian Law of Brotherhood; by the Constitution which I have sworn to support; I AM BOUND TO DISOBEY THIS ACT. Never, in any capacity, can I render voluntary aid in its execution. Pains and penalties I will endure; but this great wrong I will not do. "I cannot obey; but I can suffer," was the exclamation of the author of *Pilgrim's Progress,* when imprisoned for disobedience to an earthly statute. Better be the victim than the instrument of wrong.—Better be even the poor slave, returned to bondage, than the unhappy Commissioners.

**11** Tom Loker could not be more unlike Uncle Tom in his religious principles. And yet Tom Loker agrees with Uncle Tom in one respect: Haley has run up a bill with the devil and will have to pay.

**12** To lead a sinful life but convert at the end (even on one's deathbed) and thus to rob the devil of your soul.

**13** Harry is called by the racist term "monkey," a reminder of the scene in which he was introduced as the dancing, singing "Jim Crow" in Shelby's parlor.

**14** I.e., my specialty.

**15** Short for New Orleans. Sexual relations between whites and blacks were common and to a large extent formalized in this cosmopolitan city. Under the system of "placage," mixed-race, light-skinned "femmes de colour" placed themselves in the care of white protectors. In the romantic versions, white Creole men chose their beautiful and demure mistresses (whom they could not marry) at the Quadroon Balls. But it was not all magnolias and moonlight: Often, light-skinned women were sold to work as prostitutes and sexual slaves.

**16** I.e., pull it off or fool people.

**17** Tom Loker, like Uncle Tom, cannot lie.

all, is too p'isin mean for any crittur;—run up a bill with the devil all your life, and then sneak out when pay time comes!**12** Boh!"

"Come, come, gentlemen, I say; this isn't business," said Marks. "There's different ways, you know, of looking at all subjects. Mr. Haley is a very nice man, no doubt, and has his own conscience; and, Tom, you have your ways, and very good ones, too, Tom; but quarrelling, you know, won't answer no kind of purpose. Let's go to business. Now, Mr. Haley, what is it?—you want us to undertake to catch this yer gal?"

"The gal's no matter of mine,—she's Shelby's; it's only the boy. I was a fool for buying the monkey!"**13**

"You're generally a fool!" said Tom, gruffly.

"Come, now, Loker, none of your huffs," said Marks, licking his lips; "you see, Mr. Haley's a puttin' us in a way of a good job, I reckon; just hold still,—these yer arrangements is my forte.**14** This yer gal, Mr. Haley, how is she? what is she?"

"Wal! white and handsome—well brought up. I'd a gin Shelby eight hundred or a thousand, and then made well on her."

"White and handsome—well brought up!" said Marks, his sharp eyes, nose and mouth, all alive with enterprise. "Look here, now, Loker, a beautiful opening. We'll do a business here on our own account;—we does the catchin'; the boy, of course, goes to Mr. Haley,—we takes the gal to Orleans**15** to speculate on. An't it beautiful?"

Tom, whose great heavy mouth had stood ajar during this communication, now suddenly snapped it together, as a big dog closes on a piece of meat, and seemed to be digesting the idea at his leisure.

"Ye see," said Marks to Haley, stirring his punch as he did so, "ye see, we has justices convenient at all p'ints along shore, that does up any little jobs in our line quite reasonable. Tom, he does the knockin' down and that ar; and I come in all dressed up—shining boots—everything first chop, when the swearin' 's to be done. You oughter see, now," said Marks, in a glow of professional pride, "how I can tone it off.**16** One day, I'm Mr. Twickem, from New Orleans; 'nother day, I'm just come from my plantation on Pearl river, where I works seven hundred niggers; then, again, I come out a distant relation of Henry Clay, or some old cock in Kentuck. Talents is different, you know. Now, Tom's a roarer when there's any thumping or fighting to be done; but at lying he an't good, Tom an't,—ye see it don't come natural to him;**17** but, Lord, if thar's a feller in the country that can swear to anything and everything, and put in all the circumstances and flourishes with a longer face, and carry't through better'n I can, why, I'd like to see him, that's all! I b'lieve my heart, I could get along and snake through, even if justices were more particular than they is. Sometimes I rather wish they was more particular; 't would be a heap more relishin' if they was,—more fun, yer know."

Tom Loker, who, as we have made it appear, was a man of slow thoughts and movements, here interrupted Marks by bringing his heavy fist down on the table, so as to make all ring again. "*It'll do!*" he said.

"Lord bless ye, Tom, ye needn't break all the glasses!" said Marks; "save your fist for time o' need."

"But, gentlemen, an't I to come in for a share of the profits?" said Haley.

"An't it enough we catch the boy for ye?" said Loker. "What do ye want?"[18]

"Wal," said Haley, "if I gives you the job, it's worth something,—say ten per cent, on the profits, expenses paid."

"Now," said Loker, with a tremendous oath, and striking the table with his heavy fist, "don't I know *you,* Dan Haley? Don't you think to come it over me! Suppose Marks and I have taken up the catchin' trade, jest to 'commodate gentlemen like you, and get nothin' for ourselves?—Not by a long chalk! we'll have the gal out and out, and you keep quiet, or, ye see, we'll have both,—what's to hinder? Han't you show'd us the game? It's as free to us as you, I hope. If you or Shelby wants to chase us, look where the partridges was last year;[19] if you find them or us, you're quite welcome."

"O, wal, certainly, jest let it go at that," said Haley, alarmed; "you catch the boy for the job;—you allers did trade *far* with me, Tom, and was up to yer word."

"Ye know that," said Tom; "I don't pretend none of your snivelling ways, but I won't lie in my 'counts with the devil himself. What I ses I'll do, I will do,—you know *that,* Dan Haley."

"Jes so, jes so,—I said so, Tom," said Haley; "and if you'd only promise to have the boy for me in a week, at any point you'll name, that's all I want."

"But it an't all I want, by a long jump," said Tom. "Ye don't think I did business with you, down in Natchez, for nothing, Haley; I've learned to hold an eel, when I catch him. You've got to fork over fifty dollars, flat down, or this child don't start a peg. I know yer."

18 Note that once again Stowe portrays pro-slavery whites as arguing among themselves.

19 Partridges are small birds hunted for sport and sustenance. As in the earlier image of cat and mouse, slave-catching is once again a game—this time of bird-hunting. Loker refers to his and Marks's expertise as slave-catchers when he speaks to Haley.

**20** With simple asides such as this one, Stowe paints a picture of widespread acknowledgement of marriage between slaves.

"Why, when you have a job in hand that may bring a clean profit of somewhere about a thousand or sixteen hundred, why, Tom, you're onreasonable," said Haley.

"Yes, and hasn't we business booked for five weeks to come,—all we can do? And suppose we leaves all, and goes to bushwhacking round arter yer young un, and finally doesn't catch the gal,—and gals allers is the devil *to* catch,—what's then? would you pay us a cent—would you? I think I see you a doin' it—ugh! No, no; flap down your fifty. If we get the job, and it pays, I'll hand it back; if we don't, it's for our trouble,—that's *far,* an't it, Marks?"

"Certainly, certainly," said Marks, with a conciliatory tone; "it's only a retaining fee, you see,—he! he! he!—we lawyers, you know. Wal, we must all keep good-natured,—keep easy, yer know. Tom'll have the boy for yer, anywhere ye'll name; won't ye, Tom?"

"If I find the young un, I'll bring him on to Cincinnati, and leave him at Granny Belcher's, on the landing," said Loker.

Marks had got from his pocket a greasy pocket-book, and taking a long paper from thence, he sat down, and fixing his keen black eyes on it, began mumbling over its contents: "Barnes—Shelby County—boy Jim, three hundred dollars for him, dead or alive.

"Edwards—Dick and Lucy—man and wife, six hundred dollars; wench Polly and two children—six hundred for her or her head.**20**

"I'm jest a runnin' over our business, to see if we can take up this yer handily. Loker," he said, after a pause, "we must set Adams and Springer on the track of these yer; they've been booked some time."

"They'll charge too much," said Tom.

"I'll manage that ar; they's young in the business, and must spect to work cheap," said Marks, as he continued to read. "Ther's three on 'em easy cases, 'cause all you've got to do is to shoot 'em, or swear they is shot; they couldn't, of course, charge much for that. Them other cases," he said, folding the paper, "will bear puttin' off a spell. So now let's come to the particulars. Now, Mr. Haley, you saw this yer gal when she landed?"

"To be sure,—plain as I see you."

"And a man helpin' on her up the bank?" said Loker.

"To be sure, I did."

"Most likely," said Marks, "she's took in somewhere but where, 's a question. Tom, what do you say?"

"We must cross the river to-night, no mistake," said Tom.

"But there's no boat about," said Marks. "The ice is running awfully, Tom; an't it dangerous?"

"Don'no nothing 'bout that,—only it's got to be done," said Tom, decidedly.

"Dear me," said Marks, fidgeting, "it'll be—I say," he said, walking to the window, "it's dark as a wolf's mouth, and, Tom—"

"The long and short is, you're scared, Marks; but I can't help that,—you've got to go. Suppose you want to lie by a day or two, till the gal's been carried on the underground line up to Sandusky or so,[21] before you start."

"O, no; I an't a grain afraid," said Marks, "only—"

"Only what?" said Tom.

"Well, about the boat. Yer see there an't any boat."

"I heard the woman say there was one coming along this evening, and that a man was going to cross over in it. Neck or nothin, we must go with him," said Tom.

"I s'pose you've got good dogs," said Haley.

"First rate," said Marks. "But what's the use? you han't got nothin' o' hers to smell on."

"Yes, I have," said Haley, triumphantly. "Here's her shawl she left on the bed in her hurry; she left her bonnet, too."[22]

"That ar's lucky," said Loker; "fork over."

"Though the dogs might damage the gal, if they come on her unawars," said Haley.

"That ar's a consideration," said Marks. "Our dogs tore a feller half to pieces, once, down in Mobile, 'fore we could get 'em off."

"Well, ye see, for this sort that's to be sold for their looks, that ar won't answer, ye see," said Haley.

"I do see," said Marks. "Besides, if she's got took in, 'tan't no go, neither. Dogs is no 'count in these yer up states[23] where these critters gets carried; of course, ye can't get on their track. They only does down in plantations, where niggers, when they runs, has to do their own running, and don't get no help."

"Well," said Loker, who had just stepped out to the bar to make some inquiries, "they say the man's come with the boat; so, Marks—"

That worthy cast a rueful look at the comfortable quarters he was leaving, but slowly rose to obey. After exchanging a few words of further arrangement, Haley, with visible reluctance, handed over the fifty dollars to Tom, and the worthy trio separated for the night.

If any of our refined and Christian readers object to the society into which this scene introduces them,[24] let us beg

21 See chapter 7, note 25. Sandusky, Ohio, was a lake port and a terminal on the Underground Railroad that transported fugitive slaves to Canada.

22 By including such small details as a shawl and bonnet, Stowe reminds us that Eliza is to be considered a gentlewoman.

23 I.e., the Northern states. Bloodhounds lose a tracking scent when the trail reaches water—an important fact to the slave-catcher, since most fugitive slaves crossed a river into a border free state. The Missouri Compromise of 1850 had strengthened the 1793 Fugitive Slave Act, making it a crime for Northerners to aid and abet fugitive slaves.

24 Note the sly shift to an inanimate subject here as part of Stowe's rhetoric of discretion. The scene is intruding itself on the reader; Stowe shrugs that it is out of her authorial control. She is merely telling a story.

25 With this single word, Stowe shifts her narrative tone to match the linguistic capering of Sam and Andy.

26 The land of Canaan refers to the land west of the Jordan River. In African-American literature, Canaan was another name for the North and freedom—often, as in Eliza's case, across the Ohio River.

27 Sam seems to distance himself from his perhaps impolitic use of the term "Jordan" in conversation with a white slaveholder. Mrs. Shelby's response, "what *do* you mean," seems to refer both to the news of Eliza's escape and the description of the Ohio River as the Jordan.

28 "Am not I a woman?" In 1851, at the Women's Rights Conference in Akron, Ohio, the fugitive slave Sojourner Truth delivered her famous feminist speech "Ar'n't I a Woman?" Stowe clearly intends to show Mrs. Shelby's familiarity with the speech as she paraphrases words from it. Her exclamation, "My God! lay not this sin to our charge," shows, however, that she includes her husband in the sin. The relationship between the Abolitionist and the Women's Rights movements was complicated from the beginning. Although Frederick Douglass and other men were active supporters of Women's Rights in the 1850s, many women were bitter that more men did not join the fight for women's suffrage after Emancipation (1864). Amendment XV, under which the right to vote could not be denied "on account of race, color, or previous condition of servitude," was ratified on February 3, 1870. Amendment XIX, stating that the right to vote could not be denied because of sex, was ratified on August 18, 1920.

them to begin and conquer their prejudices in time. The catching business, we beg to remind them, is rising to the dignity of a lawful and patriotic profession. If all the broad land between the Mississippi and the Pacific becomes one great market for bodies and souls, and human property retains the locomotive tendencies of this nineteenth century, the trader and catcher may yet be among our aristocracy.

While this scene was going on at the tavern, Sam and Andy, in a state of high felicitation,[25] pursued their way home.

Sam was in the highest possible feather, and expressed his exultation by all sorts of supernatural howls and ejaculations, by divers odd motions and contortions of his whole system. Sometimes he would sit backward, with his face to the horse's tail and sides, and then, with a whoop and a somerset, come right side up in his place again, and, drawing on a grave face, begin to lecture Andy in high-sounding tones for laughing and playing the fool. Anon, slapping his sides with his arms, he would burst forth in peals of laughter, that made the old woods ring as they passed. With all these evolutions, he contrived to keep the horses up to the top of their speed, until, between ten and eleven, their heels resounded on the gravel at the end of the balcony. Mrs. Shelby flew to the railings.

"Is that you, Sam? Where are they?"

"Mas'r Haley's a-restin' at the tavern; he's dreffful fatigued, Missis."

"And Eliza, Sam?"

"Wal, she's clar 'cross Jordan. As a body may say, in the land o' Canaan."[26]

"Why, Sam, what *do* you mean?" said Mrs. Shelby, breathless, and almost faint, as the possible meaning of these words came over her.

"Wal, Missis, de Lord he persarves his own. Lizy's done gone over the river into 'Hio, as 'markably as if de Lord took her over in a charrit of fire and two hosses."[27]

Sam's vein of piety was always uncommonly fervent in his mistress' presence; and he made great capital of scriptural figures and images.

"Come up here, Sam," said Mr. Shelby, who had followed on to the verandah, "and tell your mistress what she wants. Come, come, Emily," said he, passing his arm round her, "you are cold and all in a shiver; you allow yourself to feel too much."

"Feel too much! Am not I a woman,—a mother?[28] Are

we not both responsible to God for this poor girl? My God! lay not this sin to our charge."

"What sin, Emily? You see yourself that we have only done what we were obliged to."

"There's an awful feeling of guilt about it, though," said Mrs. Shelby. "I can't reason it away."

"Here, Andy, you nigger, be alive!" called Sam, under the verandah; "take these yer hosses to der barn; don't ye hear Mas'r a callin'?" and Sam soon appeared, palm-leaf in hand, at the parlor door.

"Now, Sam, tell us distinctly how the matter was," said Mr. Shelby. "Where is Eliza, if you know?"

"Wal, Mas'r, I saw her, with my own eyes, a crossin' on the floatin' ice. She crossed most 'markably; it wasn't no less nor a miracle; and I saw a man help her up the 'Hio side, and then she was lost in the dusk."

"Sam, I think this rather apocryphal,—this miracle. Crossing on floating ice isn't so easily done," said Mr. Shelby.

"Easy! couldn't nobody a done it, without de Lord. Why, now," said Sam, "'t was jist dis yer way. Mas'r Haley, and me, and Andy, we comes up to de little tavern by the river, and I rides a leetle ahead,—(I's so zealous to be a cotchin' Lizy, that I couldn't hold in, no way),—and when I comes by the tavern winder, sure enough there she was, right in plain sight, and dey diggin' on behind. Wal, I loses off my hat, and sings out nuff to raise the dead. Course Lizy she hars, and she dodges back, when Mas'r Haley he goes past the door; and then, I tell ye, she clared out de side door; she went down de river bank;—Mas'r Haley he seed her, and yelled out, and him, and me, and Andy, we took arter. Down she come to the river, and thar was the current running ten feet wide by the shore, and over t' other side ice a sawin' and a jiggling up and down, kinder as 't were a great island.[29] We come right behind her, and I thought my soul he'd got her sure enough,—when she gin sich a screech as I never hearn, and thar she was, clar over t' other side the current, on the ice, and then on she went, a screeching and a jumpin',—the ice went crack! c'wallop! cracking! chunk! and she a boundin' like a buck! Lord, the spring that ar gal's got in her an't common, I'm o' 'pinion."

Mrs. Shelby sat perfectly silent, pale with excitement, while Sam told his story.

"God be praised, she isn't dead!" she said; "but where is the poor child now?"

"De Lord will pervide," said Sam, rolling up his eyes piously. "As I've been a sayin', dis yer's a providence and

29 The ice scene is so harrowing that Stowe gives us this second description of it.

**30** Stowe's narrator voices a common racist belief that blacks are children.

**31** There is no way to completely explain away the narrator's ugly tone here. Yes, Stowe is ventriloquizing the benevolent slaveholder perspective here, but one gets the sense that the sentiments are to an extent shared by Stowe.

**32** Even though Chloe and Tom are married, Mrs. Shelby seems to have little concern for Chloe's state of mind on Tom's last day with her.

no mistake, as Missis has allers been a instructin' on us. Thar's allers instruments ris up to do de Lord's will. Now, if't hadn't been for me to-day, she'd a been took a dozen times. Warn't it I started off de hosses, dis yer mornin', and kept 'em chasin' till nigh dinner time? And didn't I car Mas'r Haley nigh five miles out of de road, dis evening, or else he'd a come up with Lizy as easy as a dog arter a coon. These yer's all providences."

"They are a kind of providences that you'll have to be pretty sparing of, Master Sam. I allow no such practices with gentlemen on my place," said Mr. Shelby, with as much sternness as he could command, under the circumstances.

Now, there is no more use in making believe be angry with a negro than with a child;[30] both instinctively see the true state of the case, through all attempts to affect the contrary;[31] and Sam was in no wise disheartened by this rebuke, though he assumed an air of doleful gravity, and stood with the corners of his mouth lowered in most penitential style.

"Mas'r's quite right,—quite; it was ugly on me,—there's no disputin' that ar; and of course Mas'r and Missis wouldn't encourage no such works. I'm sensible of dat ar; but a poor nigger like me's 'mazin' tempted to act ugly sometimes, when fellers will cut up such shines as dat ar Mas'r Haley; he an't no gen'l'man no way; anybody's been raised as I've been can't help a seein' dat ar."

"Well, Sam," said Mrs. Shelby, "as you appear to have a proper sense of your errors, you may go now and tell Aunt Chloe she may get you some of that cold ham that was left of dinner to-day.[32] You and Andy must be hungry."

"Missis is a heap too good for us," said Sam, making his bow with alacrity, and departing.

It will be perceived, as has been before intimated, that Master Sam had a native talent that might, undoubtedly, have raised him to eminence in political life,—a talent of making capital out of everything that turned up, to be invested for his own especial praise and glory; and having done up his piety and humility, as he trusted, to the satisfaction of the parlor, he clapped his palm-leaf on his head, with a sort of rakish, free-and-easy air, and proceeded to the dominions of Aunt Chloe, with the intention of flourishing largely in the kitchen.

"I'll speechify these yer niggers," said Sam to himself, "now I've got a chance. Lord, I'll reel it off to make 'em stare!"

It must be observed that one of Sam's especial delights

had been to ride in attendance on his master to all kinds of political gatherings, where, roosted on some rail fence, or perched aloft in some tree, he would sit watching the orators, with the greatest apparent gusto, and then, descending among the various brethren of his own color, assembled on the same errand, he would edify and delight them with the most ludicrous burlesques and imitations, all delivered with the most imperturbable earnestness and solemnity; and though the auditors immediately about him were generally of his own color, it not unfrequently happened that they were fringed pretty deeply with those of a fairer complexion, who listened, laughing and winking, to Sam's great self-congratulation. In fact, Sam considered oratory as his vocation, and never let slip an opportunity of magnifying his office.

Now, between Sam and Aunt Chloe there had existed, from ancient times, a sort of chronic feud, or rather a decided coolness; but, as Sam was meditating something in the provision department, as the necessary and obvious foundation of his operations, he determined, on the present occasion, to be eminently conciliatory; for he well knew that although "Missis' orders" would undoubtedly be followed to the letter, yet he should gain a considerable deal by enlisting the spirit also. He therefore appeared before Aunt Chloe with a touchingly subdued, resigned expression, like one who has suffered immeasurable hardships in behalf of a persecuted fellow-creature,—enlarged upon the fact that Missis had directed him to come to Aunt Chloe for whatever might be wanting to make up the balance in his solids and fluids,—and thus unequivocally acknowledged her right and supremacy in the cooking department, and all thereto pertaining.[33]

The thing took accordingly. No poor, simple, virtuous body was ever cajoled by the attentions of an electioneering politician with more ease than Aunt Chloe was won over by Master Sam's suavities; and if he had been the prodigal son himself, he could not have been overwhelmed with more maternal bountifulness; and he soon found himself seated, happy and glorious, over a large tin pan, containing a sort of *olla podrida*[34] of all that had appeared on the table for two or three days past. Savory morsels of ham, golden blocks of corn-cake, fragments of pie of every conceivable mathematical figure, chicken wings, gizzards, and drumsticks, all appeared in picturesque confusion; and Sam, as monarch of all he surveyed, sat with his palm-leaf cocked rejoicingly to one side, and patronizing Andy at his right hand.

[33] Lurking below the satirical tone is a sense of Chloe's professionalism and love of work.

[34] Spanish: literally "rotten pot," meaning a dish containing a variety of ingredients.

**35** Italian: "lovers of fine arts," also "dabblers."

**36** In puffing himself up as a hero, Sam nevertheless voices a truth: Despite the competition, there exists solidarity among slaves, especially on the same plantation.

**37** A malapropism, possibly for "colligate," a term in logic meaning to "connect isolated facts together" (*Shorter Oxford*).

**38** I.e., consistent.

The kitchen was full of all his compeers, who had hurried and crowded in, from the various cabins, to hear the termination of the day's exploits. Now was Sam's hour of glory. The story of the day was rehearsed, with all kinds of ornament and varnishing which might be necessary to heighten its effect; for Sam, like some of our fashionable dilettanti,[35] never allowed a story to lose any of its gilding by passing through his hands. Roars of laughter attended the narration, and were taken up and prolonged by all the smaller fry, who were lying, in any quantity, about on the floor, or perched in every corner. In the height of the uproar and laughter, Sam, however, preserved an immovable gravity, only from time to time rolling his eyes up, and giving his auditors divers inexpressibly droll glances, without departing from the sententious elevation of his oratory.

"Yer see, fellow-countrymen," said Sam, elevating a turkey's leg, with energy, "yer see, now, what dis yer chile's up ter, for fendin' yer all,—yes, all on yer. For him as tries to get one o' our people, is as good as tryin' to get all; yer see the principle's de same,—dat ar's clar. And any one o' these yer drivers that comes smelling round arter any our people, why, he's got *me* in his way; *I'm* the feller he's got to set in with,—I'm the feller for yer all to come to, bredren,—I'll stand up for yer rights,—I'll fend 'em to the last breath!"[36]

"Why, but Sam, yer told me, only this mornin', that you'd help this yer Mas'r to cotch Lizy; seems to me yer talk don't hang together," said Andy.

"I tell you now, Andy," said Sam, with awful superiority, "don't yer be a talkin' 'bout what yer don't know nothin' on; boys like you, Andy, means well, but they can't be spected to collusitate[37] the great principles of action."

Andy looked rebuked, particularly by the hard word collusitate, which most of the youngerly members of the company seemed to consider as a settler in the case, while Sam proceeded.

"Dat ar was *conscience,* Andy; when I thought of gwine arter Lizy, I railly spected Mas'r was sot dat way. When I found Missis was sot the contrar, dat ar was conscience *more yet,*—cause fellers allers gets more by stickin' to Missis' side,—so yer see I's persistent[38] either way, and sticks up to conscience, and holds on to principles. Yes, *principles,*" said Sam, giving an enthusiastic toss to a chicken's neck,—"what's principles good for, if we isn't persistent, I wanter know? Thar, Andy, you may have dat ar bone,—'tan't picked quite clean."

Sam's audience hanging on his words with open mouth, he could not but proceed.

"Dis yer matter 'bout persistence, feller-niggers," said Sam, with the air of one entering into an abstruse subject, "dis yer 'sistency 's a thing what ant seed into very clar, by most anybody. Now, yer see, when a feller stands up for a thing one day and night, de contrar de next, folks ses (and nat'rally enough dey ses), why he an't persistent,—hand me dat ar bit o' corn-cake, Andy. But let's look inter it. I hope the gen'lmen and der fair sex will scuse my usin' an or'nary sort o' 'parison. Here! I'm a tryin' to get top o' der hay. Wal, I puts up my larder dis yer side; 'tan't no go;—den, cause I don't try dere no more, but puts my larder right de contrar side, an't I persistent? I'm persistent in wantin' to get up which ary side my larder is; don't you see, all on yer?"

"It's the only thing ye ever was persistent in, Lord knows!" muttered Aunt Chloe, who was getting rather restive; the merriment of the evening being to her somewhat after the Scripture comparison,—like "vinegar upon nitre."[39]

"Yes, indeed!" said Sam, rising, full of supper and glory, for a closing effort. "Yes, my feller-citizens and ladies of de other sex in general, I has principles,—I'm proud to 'oon 'em,—they's perquisite to dese yer times, and ter *all* times. I has principles, and I sticks to 'em like forty,—jest anything that I thinks is principle, I goes in to 't;—I wouldn't mind if dey burnt me 'live,—I'd walk right up to de stake, I would, and say, here I comes to shed my last blood fur my principles, fur my country, fur der gen'l interests of s'ciety."

"Well," said Aunt Chloe, "one o' yer principles will have to be to get to bed some time to-night, and not be a keepin' everybody up till mornin'; now, every one of you young uns that don't want to be cracked, had better be scase, mighty sudden."

"Niggers! all on yer," said Sam, waving his palm-leaf with benignity, "I give yer my blessin'; go to bed now, and be good boys."

And, with this pathetic benediction, the assembly dispersed.

39 I.e., salt on a wound (very painful).

# CHAPTER 9

## In Which It Appears That a Senator Is But a Man[1]

1 This is Stowe's most powerful and political chapter title. In separating the human being from the political position, Stowe is making the case that the senator has to juggle two sets of vows: those he made to his wife and those he made to uphold his office. Stowe uses the ironic "but a man" to indicate that she thinks the marriage vows are more important.

2 The senator's young son Tom is now the fifth character to share this name!

3 Like George Harris, Senator Bird is a fantasy husband. What more could a man want than a comfortable evening at home in the bosom of his family? As in nearly every marriage depicted in the novel, the Birds are quick to articulate their deep love for each other. Nonetheless, Stowe shows their marriage troubled by disagreements over slavery.

The light of the cheerful fire shone on the rug and carpet of a cosey parlor, and glittered on the sides of the tea-cups and well-brightened tea-pot, as Senator Bird was drawing off his boots, preparatory to inserting his feet in a pair of new handsome slippers, which his wife had been working for him while away on his senatorial tour. Mrs. Bird, looking the very picture of delight, was superintending the arrangements of the table, ever and anon mingling admonitory remarks to a number of frolicsome juveniles, who were effervescing in all those modes of untold gambol and mischief that have astonished mothers ever since the flood.

"Tom,[2] let the door-knob alone,—there's a man! Mary! Mary! don't pull the cat's tail,—poor pussy! Jim, you mustn't climb on that table,—no, no!—you don't know, my dear, what a surprise it is to us all, to see you here to-night!" said she, at last, when she found a space to say something to her husband.

"Yes, yes, I thought I'd just make a run down, spend the night, and have a little comfort at home. I'm tired to death, and my head aches!"

Mrs. Bird cast a glance at a camphor-bottle, which stood in the half-open closet, and appeared to meditate an approach to it, but her husband interposed.

"No, no, Mary, no doctoring! a cup of your good hot tea, and some of our good home living, is what I want. It's a tiresome business, this legislating!"[3]

And the senator smiled, as if he rather liked the idea of considering himself a sacrifice to his country.

"Well," said his wife, after the business of the tea-table was getting rather slack, "and what have they been doing in the Senate?"[4]

Now, it was a very unusual thing for gentle little Mrs. Bird ever to trouble her head with what was going on in the house of the state, very wisely considering that she had enough to do to mind her own. Mr. Bird, therefore, opened his eyes in surprise, and said,

"Not very much of importance."

"Well; but is it true that they have been passing a law forbidding people to give meat and drink to those poor colored folks that come along?[5] I heard they were talking of some such law, but I didn't think any Christian legislature would pass it!"

"Why, Mary, you are getting to be a politician, all at once."

"No, nonsense! I wouldn't give a fip for all your politics, generally, but I think this is something downright cruel and unchristian. I hope, my dear, no such law has been passed."

"There has been a law passed forbidding people to help off the slaves that come over from Kentucky, my dear; so much of that thing has been done by these reckless Abolitionists, that our brethren in Kentucky are very strongly excited, and it seems necessary, and no more than Christian and kind, that something should be done by our state to quiet the excitement."

"And what is the law? It don't forbid us to shelter these poor creatures a night, does it, and to give 'em something comfortable to eat, and a few old clothes, and send them quietly about their business?"

"Why, yes, my dear; that would be aiding and abetting, you know."

Mrs. Bird was a timid, blushing little woman, of about four feet in height, and with mild blue eyes, and a peach-blow complexion, and the gentlest, sweetest voice in the world;—as for courage, a moderate-sized cock-turkey had been known to put her to rout at the very first gobble, and a stout house-dog, of moderate capacity, would bring her into subjection merely by a show of his teeth. Her husband and children were her entire world, and in these she ruled more by entreaty and persuasion than by command or argument. There was only one thing that was capable of arousing her, and that provocation came in on the side of her unusually gentle and sympathetic nature;—anything

4 Southern critic George Holmes accused Stowe in 1852 of violating scripture by belonging to a "school of Woman's Rights" that would "place women on a footing of political equality with man" (Review of *Uncle Tom's Cabin*).

5 Again, the Fugitive Slave Act made it illegal to aid and abet a runaway slave. Stowe deliberately situates her novel at a time when Northerners—and Northern politicians—can no longer ignore their collusion in slavery.

in the shape of cruelty would throw her into a passion, which was the more alarming and inexplicable in proportion to the general softness of her nature. Generally the most indulgent and easy to be entreated of all mothers, still her boys had a very reverent remembrance of a most vehement chastisement she once bestowed on them, because she found them leagued with several graceless boys of the neighborhood, stoning a defenceless kitten.

"I'll tell you what," Master Bill used to say, "I was scared that time. Mother came at me so that I thought she was crazy, and I was whipped and tumbled off to bed, without any supper, before I could get over wondering what had come about; and, after that, I heard mother crying outside the door, which made me feel worse than all the rest. I'll tell you what," he'd say, "we boys never stoned another kitten!"

On the present occasion, Mrs. Bird rose quickly, with very red cheeks, which quite improved her general appearance, and walked up to her husband, with quite a resolute air, and said, in a determined tone,

"Now, John, I want to know if you think such a law as that is right and Christian?"

"You won't shoot me, now, Mary, if I say I do!"

"I never could have thought it of you, John; you didn't vote for it?"

"Even so, my fair politician."

"You ought to be ashamed, John! Poor, homeless, houseless creatures! It's a shameful, wicked, abominable law, and I'll break it, for one, the first time I get a chance; and I hope I *shall* have a chance, I do! Things have got to a pretty pass, if a woman can't give a warm supper and a bed to poor, starving creatures, just because they are slaves, and have been abused and oppressed all their lives, poor things!"

"But, Mary, just listen to me. Your feelings are all quite right, dear, and interesting, and I love you for them; but, then, dear, we mustn't suffer our feelings to run away with our judgment; you must consider it's not a matter of private feeling,—there are great public interests involved,—there is such a state of public agitation rising, that we must put aside our private feelings."

"Now, John, I don't know anything about politics, but I can read my Bible; and there I see that I must feed the hungry, clothe the naked, and comfort the desolate; and that Bible I mean to follow."

"But in cases where your doing so would involve a great public evil—"

"Obeying God never brings on public evils. I know it can't. It's always safest, all round, to *do as He* bids us."

"Now, listen to me, Mary, and I can state to you a very clear argument, to show—"

"O, nonsense, John! you can talk all night, but you wouldn't do it. I put it to you, John,—would *you* now turn away a poor, shivering, hungry creature from your door, because he was a runaway? *Would* you, now?"

Now, if the truth must be told, our senator had the misfortune to be a man who had a particularly humane and accessible nature, and turning away anybody that was in trouble never had been his forte; and what was worse for him in this particular pinch of the argument was, that his wife knew it, and, of course, was making an assault on rather an indefensible point. So he had recourse to the usual means of gaining time for such cases made and provided; he said "ahem," and coughed several times, took out his pocket-handkerchief, and began to wipe his glasses. Mrs. Bird, seeing the defenceless condition of the enemy's territory, had no more conscience than to push her advantage.

"I should like to see you doing that, John—I really should! Turning a woman out of doors in a snow-storm, for instance; or, may be you'd take her up and put her in jail, wouldn't you? You would make a great hand at that!"

"Of course, it would be a very painful duty," began Mr. Bird, in a moderate tone.

"Duty, John! don't use that word! You know it isn't a duty—it can't be a duty! If folks want to keep their slaves from running away, let 'em treat 'em well,—that's my doctrine. If I had slaves (as I hope I never shall have), I'd risk their wanting to run away from me, or you either, John. I tell you folks don't run away when they are happy; and when they do run, poor creatures! they suffer enough with cold and hunger and fear, without everybody's turning against them; and, law or no law, I never will, so help me God!"

"Mary! Mary! My dear, let me reason with you."

"I hate reasoning, John,—especially reasoning on such subjects. There's a way you political folks have of coming round and round a plain right thing; and you don't believe in it yourselves, when it comes to practice. I know *you* well enough, John. You don't believe it's right any more than I do; and you wouldn't do it any sooner than I."

At this critical juncture, old Cudjoe, the black man-of-all-work,[6] put his head in at the door, and wished "Missis would come into the kitchen;" and our senator, tolerably relieved, looked after his little wife with a whimsical mix-

6 The appearance of a black "man-of-all-work" at the end of Mrs. Bird's speech is startling. True to her domestic ideology, Stowe goes on to portray Cudjoe as happily married.

**7** Another instance of racist thought: Eliza's face is black *but* comely.

Eliza fainting in Senator Bird's kitchen. Wood engraving, late 1800s, by Dalziel, "after George Cruikshank." Eliza's features are so white that she could be mistaken for any of Dickens's wan heroines in distress.

ture of amusement and vexation, and, seating himself in the arm-chair, began to read the papers.

After a moment, his wife's voice was heard at the door, in a quick, earnest tone,—"John! John! I do wish you'd come here, a moment."

He laid down his paper, and went into the kitchen, and started, quite amazed at the sight that presented itself:— A young and slender woman, with garments torn and frozen, with one shoe gone, and the stocking torn away from the cut and bleeding foot, was laid back in a deadly swoon upon two chairs. There was the impress of the despised race on her face, yet none could help feeling its mournful and pathetic beauty,**7** while its stony sharpness, its cold, fixed, deathly aspect, struck a solemn chill over him. He drew his breath short, and stood in silence. His wife, and their only colored domestic, old Aunt Dinah, were busily engaged in restorative measures; while old Cudjoe had got the boy on his knee, and was busy pulling off his shoes and stockings, and chafing his little cold feet.

"Sure, now, if she an't a sight to behold!" said old Dinah, compassionately; " 'pears like 'twas the heat that made her faint. She was tol'able peart when she cum in, and asked if she couldn't warm herself here a spell; and I was just a askin' her where she cum from, and she fainted right down. Never done much hard work, guess, by the looks of her hands."

"Poor creature!" said Mrs. Bird, compassionately, as the woman slowly unclosed her large, dark eyes, and looked vacantly at her. Suddenly an expression of agony crossed her face, and she sprang up, saying, "O, my Harry! Have they got him?"

The boy, at this, jumped from Cudjoe's knee, and, running to her side, put up his arms. "O, he's here! he's here!" she exclaimed.

"O, ma'am!" said she, wildly, to Mrs. Bird, "do protect us! don't let them get him!"

"Nobody shall hurt you here, poor woman," said Mrs. Bird, encouragingly. "You are safe; don't be afraid."

"God bless you!" said the woman, covering her face and sobbing; while the little boy, seeing her crying, tried to get into her lap.

With many gentle and womanly offices, which none

knew better how to render than Mrs. Bird, the poor woman was, in time, rendered more calm. A temporary bed was provided for her on the settle, near the fire; and, after a short time, she fell into a heavy slumber, with the child, who seemed no less weary, soundly sleeping on her arm; for the mother resisted, with nervous anxiety, the kindest attempts to take him from her; and, even in sleep, her arm encircled him with an unrelaxing clasp, as if she could not even then be beguiled of her vigilant hold.

Mr. and Mrs. Bird had gone back to the parlor, where, strange as it may appear, no reference was made, on either side, to the preceding conversation; but Mrs. Bird busied herself with her knitting-work, and Mr. Bird pretended to be reading the paper.

"I wonder who and what she is!" said Mr. Bird, at last, as he laid it down.

"When she wakes up and feels a little rested, we will see," said Mrs. Bird.

"I say, wife!" said Mr. Bird, after musing in silence over his newspaper.

"Well, dear!"

"She couldn't wear one of your gowns, could she, by any letting down, or such matter? She seems to be rather larger than you are."

A quite perceptible smile glimmered on Mrs. Bird's face, as she answered, "We'll see."

Another pause, and Mr. Bird again broke out,

"I say, wife!"

"Well! What now?"

"Why, there's that old bombazin cloak,[8] that you keep on purpose to put over me when I take my afternoon's nap; you might as well give her that,—she needs clothes."

At this instant, Dinah looked in to say that the woman was awake, and wanted to see Missis.

Mr. and Mrs. Bird went into the kitchen, followed by the two eldest boys, the smaller fry having, by this time, been safely disposed of in bed.

The woman was now sitting up on the settle, by the fire. She was looking steadily into the blaze, with a calm, heartbroken expression, very different from her former agitated wildness.

"Did you want me?" said Mrs. Bird, in gentle tones. "I hope you feel better now, poor woman!"

A long-drawn, shivering sigh was the only answer; but she lifted her dark eyes, and fixed them on her with such a forlorn and imploring expression, that the tears came into the little woman's eyes.

8 The *Shorter Oxford* glosses "bombazine" as a twilled dress material often worsted with silk or cotton and used at the time in mourning clothes. It is significant that Senator Bird suggests giving Eliza both the "bombazin cloak" and, later in the chapter, his dead son's clothes; moving on from this loss is easier for him than for his wife. Thus Stowe again—but subtly—shows another difference between men and women.

"You needn't be afraid of anything; we are friends here, poor woman! Tell me where you came from, and what you want," said she.

"I came from Kentucky," said the woman.

"When?" said Mr. Bird, taking up the interrogatory.

"To-night."

"How did you come?"

"I crossed on the ice."

"Crossed on the ice!" said every one present.

"Yes," said the woman, slowly, "I did. God helping me, I crossed on the ice; for they were behind me—right behind—and there was no other way!"

"Law, Missis," said Cudjoe, "the ice is all in broken-up blocks, a swinging and a tetering up and down in the water!"

"I know it was—I know it!" said she, wildly; "but I did it! I wouldn't have thought I could,—I didn't think I should get over, but I didn't care! I could but die, if I didn't. The Lord helped me; nobody knows how much the Lord can help 'em, till they try," said the woman, with a flashing eye.

"Were you a slave?" said Mr. Bird.

"Yes, sir; I belonged to a man in Kentucky."

"Was he unkind to you?"

"No, sir; he was a good master."

"And was your mistress unkind to you?"

"No, sir—no! my mistress was always good to me."

"What could induce you to leave a good home, then, and run away, and go through such dangers?"

The woman looked up at Mrs. Bird, with a keen, scrutinizing glance, and it did not escape her that she was dressed in deep mourning.

"Ma'am," she said, suddenly, "have you ever lost a child?"

The question was unexpected, and it was a thrust on a new wound; for it was only a month since a darling child of the family had been laid in the grave.

Mr. Bird turned around and walked to the window, and Mrs. Bird burst into tears; but, recovering her voice, she said,

"Why do you ask that? I have lost a little one."

"Then you will feel for me. I have lost two, one after another,—left 'em buried there when I came away; and I had only this one left. I never slept a night without him; he was all I had. He was my comfort and pride, day and night; and, ma'am, they were going to take him away from me,—to *sell* him,—sell him down south, ma'am, to go all alone,—a baby that had never been away from his mother in his life! I couldn't stand it, ma'am. I knew I never should be good for anything, if they did; and when I knew the papers were signed, and he was sold, I took him and came off in the night; and they chased me,—the man that bought him, and some of Mas'r's folks,—and they were coming down right behind me, and I heard 'em. I jumped right on to the ice; and how I got across, I don't know,—but, first I knew, a man was helping me up the bank."

The woman did not sob nor weep. She had gone to a place where tears are dry; but every one around her was, in some way characteristic of themselves, showing signs of hearty sympathy.

The two little boys, after a desperate rummaging in their pockets, in search of those pocket-handkerchiefs which mothers know are never to be found there, had thrown themselves disconsolately into the skirts of their mother's gown, where they were sobbing, and wiping their eyes and noses, to their hearts' content;—Mrs. Bird had her face fairly hidden in her pocket-handkerchief; and old Dinah, with tears streaming down her black, honest face, was ejaculating, "Lord have mercy on us!" with all the fervor of a camp-meeting;—while old Cudjoe, rubbing his eyes very hard with his cuffs, and making a most uncommon variety of wry faces, occasionally responded in the same key, with great fervor. Our senator was a statesman, and of course could not be expected to cry, like other mortals; and so he turned his back to the company, and looked out of the window, and seemed particularly busy in clearing his throat and wiping his spectacle-glasses, occasionally blowing his nose in a manner that was calculated to excite suspicion, had any one been in a state to observe critically.

"How came you to tell me you had a kind master?" he suddenly exclaimed, gulping down very resolutely some kind of rising in his throat, and turning suddenly round upon the woman.

"Because he *was* a kind master; I'll say that of him, any way;—and my mistress was kind; but they couldn't help themselves. They were owing money; and there was some way, I can't tell how, that a man had a hold on them, and they were obliged to give him his will. I listened, and heard him telling mistress that, and she begging and pleading for me,—and he told her he couldn't help himself, and that the papers were all drawn;—and then it was I took him and left my home, and came away. I knew 'twas no use of my trying to live, if they did it; for 't 'pears like this child is all I have."

**9** The phrasing of the question suggests that Mrs. Bird sees marriage as the norm.

"Have you no husband?"**9**

"Yes, but he belongs to another man. His master is real hard to him, and won't let him come to see me, hardly ever; and he's grown harder and harder upon us, and he threatens to sell him down south;—it's like I'll never see *him* again!"

The quiet tone in which the woman pronounced these words might have led a superficial observer to think that she was entirely apathetic; but there was a calm, settled depth of anguish in her large, dark eye, that spoke of something far otherwise.

"And where do you mean to go, my poor woman?" said Mrs. Bird.

"To Canada, if I only knew where that was. Is it very far off, is Canada?" said she, looking up, with a simple, confiding air, to Mrs. Bird's face.

"Poor thing!" said Mrs. Bird, involuntarily.

"Is't a very great way off, think?" said the woman, earnestly.

"Much further than you think, poor child!" said Mrs. Bird; "but we will try to think what can be done for you. Here, Dinah, make her up a bed in your own room, close by the kitchen, and I'll think what to do for her in the morning. Meanwhile, never fear, poor woman; put your trust in God; he will protect you."

Mrs. Bird and her husband reëntered the parlor. She sat down in her little rocking-chair before the fire, swaying thoughtfully to and fro. Mr. Bird strode up and down the room, grumbling to himself, "Pish! pshaw! confounded awkward business!" At length, striding up to his wife, he said,

"I say, wife, she'll have to get away from here, this very night. That fellow will be down on the scent bright and early to-morrow morning; if 'twas only the woman, she could lie quiet till it was over; but that little chap can't be kept still by a troop of horse and foot, I'll warrant me; he'll bring it all out, popping his head out of some window or door. A pretty kettle of fish it would be for me, too, to be caught with them both here, just now! No; they'll have to be got off to-night."

"To-night! How is it possible?—where to?"

"Well, I know pretty well where to," said the senator, beginning to put on his boots, with a reflective air; and, stopping when his leg was half in, he embraced his knee with both hands, and seemed to go off in deep meditation.

"It's a confounded awkward, ugly business," said he, at

last, beginning to tug at his boot-straps again, "and that's a fact!" After one boot was fairly on, the senator sat with the other in his hand, profoundly studying the figure of the carpet.**10** "It will have to be done, though, for aught I see,—hang it all!" and he drew the other boot anxiously on, and looked out of the window.

Now, little Mrs. Bird was a discreet woman,—a woman who never in her life said, "I told you so!" and, on the present occasion, though pretty well aware of the shape her husband's meditations were taking, she very prudently forbore to meddle with them, only sat very quietly in her chair, and looked quite ready to hear her liege lord's intentions, when he should think proper to utter them.

"You see," he said, "there's my old client, Van Trompe, has come over from Kentucky, and set all his slaves free; and he has bought a place seven miles up the creek, here, back in the woods, where nobody goes, unless they go on purpose; and it's a place that isn't found in a hurry. There she'd be safe enough; but the plague of the thing is, nobody could drive a carriage there to-night, but *me*."

"Why not? Cudjoe is an excellent driver."

"Ay, ay, but here it is. The creek has to be crossed twice; and the second crossing is quite dangerous, unless one knows it as I do. I have crossed it a hundred times on horseback, and know exactly the turns to take. And so, you see, there's no help for it. Cudjoe must put in the horses, as quietly as may be, about twelve o'clock, and I'll take her over; and then, to give color to the matter, he must carry me on to the next tavern, to take the stage for Columbus, that comes by about three or four, and so it will look as if I had had the carriage only for that. I shall get into business bright and early in the morning. But I'm thinking I shall feel rather cheap there, after all that's been said and done; but, hang it, I can't help it!"

"Your heart is better than your head, in this case, John," said the wife, laying her little white hand on his. "Could I ever have loved you, had I not known you better than you know yourself?" And the little woman looked so handsome, with the tears sparkling in her eyes,**11** that the senator thought he must be a decidedly clever fellow, to get such a pretty creature into such a passionate admiration of him; and so, what could he do but walk off soberly, to see about the carriage. At the door, however, he stopped a moment, and then coming back, he said, with some hesitation,

"Mary, I don't know how you'd feel about it, but there's

10 Senator Bird looks intently downward, as though at the design of the carpet, as he decides what to do.

11 This scene calls attention to Mrs. Bird's smallness and whiteness. It also portrays her as a child, an important sentimental strategy just before the scene of "the opening again of a little grave."

**12** Stowe has carefully separated this narrative voice from the one that described the testosterone-rich atmosphere of a Kentucky tavern.

that drawer full of things—of—of—poor little Henry's." So saying, he turned quickly on his heel, and shut the door after him.

His wife opened the little bed-room door adjoining her room, and, taking the candle, set it down on the top of a bureau there; then from a small recess she took a key, and put it thoughtfully in the lock of a drawer, and made a sudden pause, while two boys, who, boy like, had followed close on her heels, stood looking, with silent, significant glances, at their mother.[12] And oh! mother that reads this, has there never been in your house a drawer, or a closet, the opening of which has been to you like the opening again of a little grave? Ah! happy mother that you are, if it has not been so.

Mrs. Bird slowly opened the drawer. There were little coats of many a form and pattern, piles of aprons, and rows of small stockings; and even a pair of little shoes, worn and rubbed at the toes, were peeping from the folds of a paper. There was a toy horse and wagon, a top, a ball,—memorials gathered with many a tear and many a heart-break! She sat down by the drawer, and, leaning her head on her hands over it, wept till the tears fell through her fingers into the drawer; then suddenly raising her head, she began, with nervous haste, selecting the plainest and most substantial articles, and gathering them into a bundle.

"Mamma," said one of the boys, gently touching her arm, "are you going to give away *those* things?"

"My dear boys," she said, softly and earnestly, "if our dear, loving little Henry looks down from heaven, he would be glad to have us do this. I could not find it in my heart to give them away to any common person—to anybody that was happy; but I give them to a mother more heart-broken and sorrowful than I am; and I hope God will send his blessings with them!"

There are in this world blessed souls, whose sorrows all spring up into joys for others; whose earthly hopes, laid in the grave with many tears, are the seed from which spring healing flowers and balm for the desolate and the distressed. Among such was the delicate woman who sits there by the lamp, dropping slow tears, while she prepares the memorials of her own lost one for the outcast wanderer.

After a while, Mrs. Bird opened a wardrobe, and, taking from thence a plain, serviceable dress or two, she sat down busily to her work-table, and, with needle, scissors, and thimble, at hand, quietly commenced the "letting down" process which her husband had recommended, and continued busily at it till the old clock in the corner struck twelve, and she heard the low rattling of wheels at the door.

"Mary," said her husband, coming in, with his overcoat in his hand, "you must wake her up now; we must be off."

Mrs. Bird hastily deposited the various articles she had collected in a small plain trunk, and locking it, desired her husband to see it in the carriage, and then proceeded to call the woman. Soon, arrayed in a cloak, bonnet, and shawl, that had belonged to her benefactress, she appeared at the door with her child in her arms. Mr. Bird hurried her into the carriage, and Mrs. Bird pressed on after her to the carriage steps. Eliza leaned out of the carriage, and put out her hand,—a hand as soft and beautiful as was given in return. She fixed her large, dark eyes, full of earnest meaning, on Mrs. Bird's face, and seemed going to speak. Her lips moved,—she tried once or twice, but there was no sound,—and pointing upward, with a look never to be forgotten, she fell back in the seat, and covered her face. The door was shut, and the carriage drove on.

What a situation, now, for a patriotic senator, that had been all the week before spurring up the legislature of his native state to pass more stringent resolutions against escaping fugitives, their harborers and abettors!

Our good senator in his native state had not been exceeded by any of his brethren at Washington, in the sort of eloquence which has won for them immortal renown! How sublimely he had sat with his hands in his pockets, and scouted all sentimental weakness of those who would put the welfare of a few miserable fugitives before great state interests!

He was as bold as a lion about it, and "mightily convinced" not only himself, but everybody that heard him;—but then his idea of a fugitive was only an idea of the letters that spell the word,—or, at the most, the image of a little newspaper picture of a man with a stick and bundle, with "Ran away from the subscriber" under it.[13] The magic of the real presence of distress,—the imploring human eye, the frail, trembling human hand, the despairing appeal of helpless agony,—these he had never tried. He had never thought that a fugitive might be a hapless mother, a defenceless child,—like that one which was now wearing his lost boy's little well-known cap; and so, as our poor senator was not stone or steel,—as he was a man, and a downright noblehearted one, too,—he was, as everybody must see, in a sad case for his patriotism. And you need

13 It can be argued that perhaps Stowe doesn't need to hammer the point home—we understand that Senator Bird has argued one thing in theory but now is doing something else in practice—but here Stowe's hyperbolic bluster elicits sympathy for the senator. Although all humans are prone to hypocrisy, the reader understands that Senator Bird's hypocrisy is relatively mild. As Stowe portrays elsewhere, it would be worse to say noble words in public that are contradicted by evil deeds in private.

14 This description serves little real purpose (save to support Senator Bird's contention that the trip is arduous and treacherous), but it pleased Stowe greatly to write.

not exult over him, good brother of the Southern States; for we have some inklings that many of you, under similar circumstances, would not do much better. We have reason to know, in Kentucky, as in Mississippi, are noble and generous hearts, to whom never was tale of suffering told in vain. Ah, good brother! is it fair for you to expect of us services which your own brave, honorable heart would not allow you to render, were you in our place?

Be that as it may, if our good senator was a political sinner, he was in a fair way to expiate it by his night's penance. There had been a long continuous period of rainy weather, and the soft, rich earth of Ohio, as every one knows, is admirably suited to the manufacture of mud,—and the road was an Ohio railroad of the good old times.

"And pray, what sort of a road may that be?" says some eastern traveller, who has been accustomed to connect no ideas with a railroad, but those of smoothness or speed.

Know, then, innocent eastern friend, that in benighted regions of the west, where the mud is of unfathomable and sublime depth, roads are made of round rough logs, arranged transversely side by side, and coated over in their pristine freshness with earth, turf, and whatsoever may come to hand, and then the rejoicing native calleth it a road, and straightway essayeth to ride thereupon. In process of time, the rains wash off all the turf and grass aforesaid, move the logs hither and thither, in picturesque positions, up, down and crosswise, with divers chasms and ruts of black mud intervening.

Over such a road as this our senator went stumbling along, making moral reflections as continuously as under the circumstances could be expected,[14]—the carriage proceeding along much as follows,—bump! bump! bump! slush! down in the mud!—the senator, woman and child, reversing their positions so suddenly as to come, without any very accurate adjustment, against the windows of the down-hill side. Carriage sticks fast, while Cudjoe on the outside is heard making a great muster among the horses. After various ineffectual pullings and twitchings, just as the senator is losing all patience, the carriage suddenly rights itself with a bounce,—two front wheels go down into another abyss, and senator, woman, and child, all tumble promiscuously on to the front seat,—senator's hat is jammed over his eyes and nose quite unceremoniously, and he considers himself fairly extinguished;—child cries, and Cudjoe on the outside delivers animated addresses to

the horses, who are kicking, and floundering, and straining, under repeated cracks of the whip. Carriage springs
up, with another bounce,—down go the hind wheels,—
senator, woman, and child, fly over on to the back seat, his
elbows encountering her bonnet, and both her feet being
jammed into his hat, which flies off in the concussion.
After a few moments the "slough" is passed, and the
horses stop, panting;—the senator finds his hat, the
woman straightens her bonnet and hushes her child, and
they brace themselves firmly for what is yet to come.

For a while only the continuous bump! bump! intermin-
gled, just by way of variety, with divers side plunges and
compound shakes; and they begin to flatter themselves
that they are not so badly off, after all. At last, with a
square plunge, which puts all on to their feet and then
down into their seats with incredible quickness, the carriage stops,—and, after much outside commotion, Cudjoe
appears at the door.

"Please, sir, it's powerful bad spot, this yer. I don't know
how we's to get clar out. I'm a thinkin' we'll have to be a
gettin' rails."

The senator despairingly steps out, picking gingerly for
some firm foothold; down goes one foot an immeasurable
depth,—he tries to pull it up, loses his balance, and tumbles over into the mud, and is fished out, in a very despairing condition, by Cudjoe.

But we forbear, out of sympathy to our readers' bones.
Western travellers, who have beguiled the midnight hour
in the interesting process of pulling down rail fences, to
pry their carriages out of mud holes, will have a respectful and mournful sympathy with our unfortunate hero. We
beg them to drop a silent tear, and pass on.

It was full late in the night when the carriage emerged,
dripping and bespattered, out of the creek, and stood at
the door of a large farmhouse.

It took no inconsiderable perseverance to arouse the
inmates; but at last the respectable proprietor appeared,
and undid the door. He was a great, tall, bristling Orson
of a fellow, full six feet and some inches in his stockings,
and arrayed in a red flannel hunting-shirt. A very heavy
*mat* of sandy hair, in a decidedly tousled condition, and a
beard of some days' growth, gave the worthy man an
appearance, to say the least, not particularly prepossess-
ing. He stood for a few minutes holding the candle aloft,
and blinking on our travellers with a dismal and mystified
expression that was truly ludicrous. It cost some effort of

**15** John Van Trompe is, in other words, a gentle giant. But what a man! I'm sure many of Stowe's female readers swooned with delight at the image.

**16** Sentimentalism held that the feelings common to humanity were formed during childhood, within the family. This belief recognized the horrors of bringing up white families and of breaking up slave families under slavery. African-American and abolitionist literature focused on the terrible effects of slavery for both slave and master. The latter strategy worked to highlight that the brutality, lust, and greed inherent in the system threatened the moral health of whites. Frederick Douglass wrote in his *Narrative*, for example, of the change in Mrs. Auld as she came under the influence of slavery: "When I went there, she was a pious, warm, and tender-hearted woman. . . . Slavery soon proved its ability to divest her of these heavenly qualities. Under its influence, the tender heart became stone, and the lamblike disposition gave way to one of tiger-like fierceness" (chapter 7).

**17** Stowe ensures that we won't think anything untoward about Van Trompe's household, and also ensures that we understand that Eliza, though tired, is not bedraggled—she is still our beautiful, Victorian heroine.

our senator to induce him to comprehend the case fully; and while he is doing his best at that, we shall give him a little introduction to our readers.

Honest old John Van Trompe was once quite a considerable land-holder and slave-owner in the State of Kentucky. Having "nothing of the bear about him but the skin," [15] and being gifted by nature with a great, honest, just heart, quite equal to his gigantic frame, he had been for some years witnessing with repressed uneasiness the workings of a system equally bad for oppressor and oppressed. At last, one day, John's great heart had swelled altogether too big to wear his bonds any longer; so he just took his pocket-book out of his desk, and went over into Ohio, and bought a quarter of a township of good, rich land, made out free papers for all his people,—men, women, and children,—packed them up in wagons, and sent them off to settle down; and then honest John turned his face up the creek, and sat quietly down on a snug, retired farm, to enjoy his conscience and his reflections. [16]

"Are you the man that will shelter a poor woman and child from slave-catchers?" said the senator, explicitly.

"I rather think I am," said honest John, with some considerable emphasis.

"I thought so," said the senator.

"If there's anybody comes," said the good man, stretching his tall, muscular form upward, "why here I'm ready for him: and I've got seven sons, each six foot high, and they'll be ready for 'em. Give our respects to 'em," said John; "tell 'em it's no matter how soon they call,—make no kinder difference to us," said John, running his fingers through the shock of hair that thatched his head, and bursting out into a great laugh.

Weary, jaded, and spiritless, Eliza dragged herself up to the door, with her child lying in a heavy sleep on her arm. The rough man held the candle to her face, and uttering a kind of compassionate grunt, opened the door of a small bedroom adjoining to the large kitchen where they were standing, and motioned her to go in. He took down a candle, and lighting it, set it upon the table, and then addressed himself to Eliza.

"Now, I say, gal, you needn't be a bit afeard, let who will come here. I'm up to all that sort o' thing," said he, pointing to two or three goodly rifles over the mantel-piece; "and most people that know me know that 't wouldn't be healthy to try to get anybody out o' my house when I'm agin it. So *now* you jist go to sleep now, as quiet as if yer mother was a rockin' ye," said he, as he shut the door. [17]

"Why, this is an uncommon handsome un," he said to the senator. "Ah, well; handsome uns has the greatest cause to run, sometimes, if they has any kind o' feelin, such as decent women should. I know all about that."

The senator, in a few words, briefly explained Eliza's history.

"O! ou! aw! now, I want to know?" said the good man, pitifully; "sho! now sho! That's natur now, poor crittur! hunted down now like a deer,—hunted down, jest for havin' natural feelin's, and doin' what no kind o' mother could help a doin! I tell ye what, these yer things make me come the nighest to swearin', now, o' most anything," said honest John, as he wiped his eyes with the back of a great, freckled, yellow hand. "I tell yer what, stranger, it was years and years before I'd jine the church, 'cause the ministers round in our parts used to preach that the Bible went in for these ere cuttings up,—and I couldn't be up to 'em with their Greek and Hebrew, and so I took up agin 'em, Bible and all. I never jined the church till I found a minister that was up to 'em all in Greek and all that, and he said right the contrary; and then I took right hold, and jined the church,—I did now, fact," said John, who had been all this time uncorking some very frisky bottled cider, which at this juncture he presented.

"Ye'd better jest put up here, now, till daylight," said he, heartily, "and I'll call up the old woman, and have a bed got ready for you in no time."

"Thank you, my good friend," said the senator, "I must be along, to take the night stage for Columbus."

"Ah! well, then, if you must, I'll go a piece with you, and show you a cross road that will take you there better than the road you came on. That road's mighty bad."

John equipped himself, and, with a lantern in hand, was soon seen guiding the senator's carriage towards a road that ran down in a hollow, back of his dwelling. When they parted, the senator put into his hand a ten-dollar bill.

"It's for her," he said, briefly.[18]

"Ay, ay," said John, with equal conciseness.

They shook hands, and parted.

18 Stowe shows money changing hands between men for completely different reasons.

# CHAPTER 10

## *The Property Is Carried Off*[1]

1 Stowe's terseness is witty. She assumes we will understand that "the property" is Tom and that "carried off" refers to his being taken away by Haley. The rhetorical term for this kind of understatement is "litotes."

2 Another racist observation—"a peculiar characteristic of his unhappy race"—is that slaves, like children or women, had tender hearts. This gentleness (in contrast to the manly spirit of George Harris) is a crucial part of the "Uncle Tom" stereotype.

3 This is the first time that the children are marked as Tom's.

4 This phrase is striking in its change of the last word. The expression is "lift up your voice and sing." James Weldon Johnson wrote his famous song "Lift Every Voice and Sing" in 1900.

The February morning looked gray and drizzling through the window of Uncle Tom's cabin. It looked on downcast faces, the images of mournful hearts. The little table stood out before the fire, covered with an ironing-cloth; a coarse but clean shirt or two, fresh from the iron, hung on the back of a chair by the fire, and Aunt Chloe had another spread out before her on the table. Carefully she rubbed and ironed every fold and every hem, with the most scrupulous exactness, every now and then raising her hand to her face to wipe off the tears that were coursing down her cheeks.

Tom sat by, with his Testament open on his knee, and his head leaning upon his hand;—but neither spoke. It was yet early, and the children lay all asleep together in their little rude trundle-bed.

Tom, who had, to the full, the gentle, domestic heart, which, woe for them! has been a peculiar characteristic of his unhappy race,[2] got up and walked silently to look at his children.[3]

"It's the last time," he said.

Aunt Chloe did not answer, only rubbed away over and over on the coarse shirt, already as smooth as hands could make it; and finally setting her iron suddenly down with a despairing plunge, she sat down to the table, and "lifted up her voice and wept."[4]

"S'pose we must be resigned; but oh Lord! how ken I? If I know'd anything whar you 's goin', or how they'd sarve you! Missis says she'll try and 'deem ye, in a year or two; but Lor! nobody never comes up that goes down thar! They kills 'em! I've hearn 'em tell how dey works 'em up on dem ar plantations."

"There'll be the same God there, Chloe, that there is here."

"Well," said Aunt Chloe, "s'pose dere will; but de Lord lets drefful things happen, sometimes. I don't seem to get no comfort dat way."

"I'm in the Lord's hands," said Tom; "nothin' can go no furder than he lets it;—and thar's *one* thing I can thank him for. It's *me* that's sold and going down, and not you nur the chil'en. Here you're safe;—what comes will come only on me; and the Lord, he'll help me,—I know he will."

Ah, brave, manly heart,—smothering thine own sorrow, to comfort thy beloved ones! Tom spoke with a thick utterance, and with a bitter choking in his throat,—but he spoke brave and strong.

"Let's think on our marcies!" he added, tremulously, as if he was quite sure he needed to think on them very hard indeed.

"Marcies!" said Aunt Chloe; "don't see no marcy in 't! 'tan't right! tan't right it should be so! Mas'r never ought ter left it so that ye *could* be took for his debts. Ye've arnt him all he gets for ye, twice over. He owed ye yer freedom, and ought ter gin 't to yer years ago. Mebbe he can't help himself now, but I feel it's wrong. Nothing can't beat that ar out o' me. Sich a faithful crittur as ye've been,—and allers sot his business 'fore yer own every way,—and reckoned on him more than yer own wife and chil'en![5] Them as sells heart's love and heart's blood, to get out thar scrapes, de Lord'll be up to 'em!"

"Chloe! now, if ye love me, ye won't talk so, when perhaps jest the last time we'll ever have together! And I'll tell ye, Chloe, it goes agin me to hear one word agin Mas'r. Wan't he put in my arms a baby?—it's natur I should think a heap of him. And he couldn't be spected to think so much of poor Tom. Mas'rs is used to havin' all these yer things done for 'em, and nat'lly they don't think so much on 't. They can't be spected to, no way. Set him 'longside of other Mas'rs—who's had the treatment and the livin' I've had? And he never would have let this yer come on me, if he could have seed it aforehand. I know he wouldn't."

"Wal, any way, thar's wrong about it *somewhar*," said Aunt Chloe, in whom a stubborn sense of justice was a predominant trait; "I can't jest make out whar 't is, but thar's wrong somewhar, I'm *clar* o' that."[6]

5 Chloe's anger reveals her assumption that by putting his master's interests before those of himself and his family, Tom would be rewarded. Her assumption is not shared by Tom, however; he continues to understand things from his master's viewpoint. Such self-lessness is a component of the stereotype "Uncle Tom." We also see that Tom has directed his protective fatherly feelings toward his master, who was "put in [his] arms a baby."

6 I.e., I'm sure of it.

7 Tom preaches to Chloe from Matt. 6:25–26: "Therefore I say to you, do not be anxious for your life, what you shall eat; nor yet for your body, what you shall put on. Is not the life a greater thing than the food, and the body than the clothing? Look at the birds of the air: they do not sow, or reap, or gather into barns; yet your heavenly Father feeds them. Are you not of much more value than they?" Chloe may not put her trust in God enough to neglect giving her husband food and clothing in the next scene, however.

8 This is another of the uglier passages.

9 Stowe quotes from Hamlet's famous "To be, or not to be" speech, in *Hamlet,* act 3, scene 1. The full sentence is:

who would fardels bear,
To grunt and sweat under a weary life,
But that the dread of something after death,
The undiscover'd country from whose bourn
No traveller returns, puzzles the will
And makes us rather bear those ills we have
Than fly to others that we know not of?

"Fardels" are burdens. Stowe's use of Shakespeare's lines in this context is fascinating: Had she always seen an analogy to the condition of slaves in this monologue?

10 Racist reasoning needed to twist and turn to reconcile a belief in the peculiar characteristic of gentleness with the obvious instances of "heroic courage" shown by runaway slaves.

11 It is unclear whether we are to see Mrs. Shelby's gesture as kind or stingy.

"Yer ought ter look up to the Lord above—he's above all—thar don't a sparrow fall without him."7

"It don't seem to comfort me, but I spect it orter," said Aunt Chloe. "But dar's no use talkin'; I'll jes wet up de corn-cake, and get ye one good breakfast, 'cause nobody knows when you'll get another."

In order to appreciate the sufferings of the negroes sold south, it must be remembered that all the instinctive affections of that race are peculiarly strong.8 Their local attachments are very abiding. They are not naturally daring and enterprising, but home-loving and affectionate. Add to this all the terrors with which ignorance invests the unknown, and add to this, again, that selling to the south is set before the negro from childhood as the last severity of punishment. The threat that terrifies more than whipping or torture of any kind is the threat of being sent down river. We have ourselves heard this feeling expressed by them, and seen the unaffected horror with which they will sit in their gossiping hours, and tell frightful stories of that "down river," which to them is

"That undiscovered country, from whose bourn
No traveller returns."9

A missionary among the fugitives in Canada told us that many of the fugitives confessed themselves to have escaped from comparatively kind masters, and that they were induced to brave the perils of escape, in almost every case, by the desperate horror with which they regarded being sold south,—a doom which was hanging either over themselves or their husbands, their wives or children. This nerves the African, naturally patient, timid and unenterprising, with heroic courage, and leads him to suffer hunger, cold, pain, the perils of the wilderness, and the more dread penalties of re-capture.10

The simple morning meal now smoked on the table, for Mrs. Shelby had excused Aunt Chloe's attendance at the great house that morning.11 The poor soul had expended all her little energies on this farewell feast,—had killed and dressed her choicest chicken, and prepared her corn-cake with scrupulous exactness, just to her husband's taste, and brought out certain mysterious jars on the mantel-piece, some preserves that were never produced except on extreme occasions.

"Lor, Pete," said Mose, triumphantly, "han't we got a buster of a breakfast!" at the same time catching at a fragment of the chicken.

Aunt Chloe gave him a sudden box on the ear. "Thar now! crowing over the last breakfast yer poor daddy's gwine to have to home!"

"O, Chloe!" said Tom, gently.

"Wal, I can't help it," said Aunt Chloe, hiding her face in her apron; "I's so tossed about, it makes me act ugly."

The boys stood quite still, looking first at their father and then at their mother, while the baby, climbing up her clothes, began an imperious, commanding cry.

"Thar!" said Aunt Chloe, wiping her eyes and taking up the baby; "now I's done, I hope,—now do eat something. This yer's my nicest chicken. Thar, boys, ye shall have some, poor critturs! Yer mammy's been cross to yer."

The boys needed no second invitation, and went in with great zeal for the eatables; and it was well they did so, as otherwise there would have been very little performed to any purpose by the party.

"Now," said Aunt Chloe, bustling about after breakfast, "I must put up yer clothes. Jest like as not, he'll take 'em all away. I know thar ways—mean as dirt, they is! Wal, now, yer flannels for rhumatis is in this corner; so be car-ful, 'cause there won't nobody make ye no more. Then here's yer old shirts, and these yer is new ones. I toed off these yer stockings last night, and put de ball in 'em to mend with. But Lor! who'll ever mend for ye?" and Aunt Chloe, again overcome, laid her head on the box side, and sobbed. "To think on 't! no crittur to do for ye, sick or well! I don't railly think I ought ter be good now!"**12**

The boys, having eaten everything there was on the breakfast-table, began now to take some thought of the case; and, seeing their mother crying, and their father looking very sad, began to whimper and put their hands to their eyes. Uncle Tom had the baby on his knee, and was letting her enjoy herself to the utmost extent, scratching his face and pulling his hair, and occasionally breaking out into clamorous explosions of delight, evidently aris-ing out of her own internal reflections.

"Ay, crow away, poor crittur!" said Aunt Chloe; "ye'll have to come to it, too! ye'll live to see yer husband sold, or mebbe be sold yerself; and these yer boys, they's to be sold, I s'pose, too, jest like as not, when dey gets good for somethin'; an't no use in niggers havin' nothin'!"**13**

Here one of the boys called out, "Thar's Missis a-comin' in!"

"She can't do no good; what's she coming for?" said Aunt Chloe.

Mrs. Shelby entered. Aunt Chloe set a chair for her in a

12 In her anger, Chloe nevertheless reminds the readers that they are seeing the last sup-per before a family (daddy, mammy, boys, and baby) is torn asunder. Notice how Stowe por-trays their last moments much more coolly than in the breakup of other families. Chloe's allusion to Tom's "rhumatis" serves to fur-ther undermine his sexuality, though else-where in the novel he seems far from geriatric.

13 Chloe emphasizes her despair by using not only the term "niggers" but a triple nega-tive ("an't," "no use," "nothin' ") as well.

14 Here we have a scene repeated in slave narratives and abolitionist literature: a family of slaves facing separation. Stowe will force such scenes upon her readers again and again in this long novel.

manner decidedly gruff and crusty. She did not seem to notice either the action or the manner. She looked pale and anxious.

"Tom," she said, "I come to—" and stopping suddenly, and regarding the silent group, she sat down in the chair, and, covering her face with her handkerchief, began to sob.

"Lor, now, Missis, don't—don't!" said Aunt Chloe, bursting out in her turn; and for a few moments they all wept in company. And in those tears they all shed together, the high and the lowly, melted away all the heart-burnings and anger of the oppressed. O, ye who visit the distressed, do ye know that everything your money can buy, given with a cold, averted face, is not worth one honest tear shed in real sympathy?

"My good fellow," said Mrs. Shelby, "I can't give you anything to do you any good. If I give you money, it will only be taken from you. But I tell you solemnly, and before God, that I will keep trace of you, and bring you back as soon as I can command the money;—and, till then, trust in God!"

Here the boys called out that Mas'r Haley was coming, and then an unceremonious kick pushed open the door. Haley stood there in very ill humor, having ridden hard the night before, and being not at all pacified by his ill success in re-capturing his prey.

"Come," said he, "ye nigger, ye'r ready? Servant, ma'am!" said he, taking off his hat, as he saw Mrs. Shelby.

Aunt Chloe shut and corded the box, and, getting up, looked gruffly on the trader, her tears seeming suddenly turned to sparks of fire.

Tom rose up meekly, to follow his new master, and raised up his heavy box on his shoulder. His wife took the baby in her arms to go with him to the wagon, and the children, still crying, trailed on behind.14

Mrs. Shelby, walking up to the trader, detained him for a few moments, talking with him in an earnest manner; and while she was thus talking, the whole family party proceeded to a wagon, that stood ready harnessed at the door. A crowd of all the old and young hands on the place stood gathered around it, to bid farewell to their old associate. Tom had been looked up to, both as a head servant and a Christian teacher,

Tableau of Tom's farewell, by Eckman. Haley stands center stage, a mournful but well-dressed Tom stands with Chloe and their children on the left. Mrs. Shelby peers over the balcony. An unidentified slave mother, also distraught, stands to the right. Tom is the tallest and most powerful male in the picture. From *Uncle Tom's Cabin, Young Folks Edition*, M. A. Donohue & Co., circa 1900

by all the place, and there was much honest sympathy and grief about him, particularly among the women.

"Why, Chloe, you bar it better 'n we do!" said one of the women, who had been weeping freely, noticing the gloomy calmness with which Aunt Chloe stood by the wagon.

"Is done *my* tears!" she said, looking grimly at the trader, who was coming up. "I does not feel to cry 'fore dat ar old limb, no how!"

"Get in!" said Haley to Tom, as he strode through the crowd of servants, who looked at him with lowering brows.

Tom got in, and Haley, drawing out from under the wagon seat a heavy pair of shackles, made them fast around each ankle.

A smothered groan of indignation ran through the whole circle, and Mrs. Shelby spoke from the verandah,—

"Mr. Haley, I assure you that precaution is entirely unnecessary."

"Do'n know, ma'am; I've lost one five hundred dollars from this yer place, and I can't afford to run no more risks."

"What else could she spect on him?" said Aunt Chloe, indignantly, while the two boys, who now seemed to comprehend at once their father's destiny, clung to her gown, sobbing and groaning vehemently.

"I'm sorry," said Tom, "that Mas'r George happened to be away."

George had gone to spend two or three days with a companion on a neighboring estate, and having departed early in the morning, before Tom's misfortune had been made public, had left without hearing of it.

"Give my love to Mas'r George," he said, earnestly.[15]

Haley whipped up the horse, and, with a steady, mournful look, fixed to the last on the old place, Tom was whirled away.

Mr. Shelby at this time was not at home. He had sold Tom under the spur of a driving necessity, to get out of the power of a man whom he dreaded,—and his first feeling, after the consummation of the bargain, had been that of relief. But his wife's expostulations awoke his half-slumbering regrets; and Tom's manly disinterestedness increased the unpleasantness of his feelings. It was in vain that he said to himself that he had a *right* to do it,— that everybody did it,—and that some did it without even the excuse of necessity;—he could not satisfy his own feelings; and that he might not witness the unpleasant scenes of the consummation, he had gone on a short business

15 We have always found it strange that Tom's love is directed not at his wife or children but at his young master.

**16** The blacksmith seems more concerned about Tom's family breakup than Mrs. Shelby.

tour up the country, hoping that all would be over before he returned.

Tom and Haley rattled on along the dusty road, whirling past every old familiar spot, until the bounds of the estate were fairly passed, and they found themselves out on the open pike. After they had ridden about a mile, Haley suddenly drew up at the door of a blacksmith's shop, when, taking out with him a pair of handcuffs, he stepped into the shop, to have a little alteration in them.

"These yer's a little too small for his build," said Haley, showing the fetters, and pointing out to Tom.

"Lor! now, if thar an't Shelby's Tom. He han't sold him, now?" said the smith.

"Yes, he has," said Haley.

"Now, ye don't! well, reely," said the smith, "who'd a thought it! Why, ye needn't go to fetterin' him up this yer way. He's the faithfullest, best crittur—"

"Yes, yes," said Haley; "but your good fellers are just the critturs to want ter run off. Them stupid ones, as doesn't care whar they go, and shifless, drunken ones, as don't care for nothin', they'll stick by, and like as not be rather pleased to be toted round; but these yer prime fellers, they hates it like sin. No way but to fetter 'em; got legs,—they'll use 'em,—no mistake."

"Well," said the smith, feeling among his tools, "them plantations down thar, stranger, an't jest the place a Kentuck nigger wants to go to; they dies thar tol'able fast, don't they?"

"Wal, yes, tol'able fast, ther dying is; what with the 'climating and one thing and another, they dies so as to keep the market up pretty brisk," said Haley.

"Wal, now, a feller can't help thinkin' it's a mighty pity to have a nice, quiet, likely feller, as good un as Tom is, go down to be fairly ground up on one of them ar sugar plantations."

"Wal, he's got a fa'r chance. I promised to do well by him. I'll get him in house-servant in some good old family, and then, if he stands the fever and 'climating, he'll have a berth good as any nigger ought ter ask for."

"He leaves his wife and chil'en up here, s'pose?"**16**

"Yes; but he'll get another thar. Lord, thar's women enough everywhar," said Haley.

Tom was sitting very mournfully on the outside of the shop while this conversation was going on. Suddenly he heard the quick, short click of a horse's hoof behind him; and, before he could fairly awake from his surprise, young Master George sprang into the wagon, threw his arms tumultuously round his neck, and was sobbing and scolding with energy.

"I declare, it's real mean! I don't care what they say, any of 'em! It's a nasty, mean shame! If I was a man,[17] they shouldn't do it,—they should not, *so!*" said George, with a kind of subdued howl.

"O! Mas'r George! this does me good!" said Tom. "I couldn't bar to go off without seein' ye! It does me real good, ye can't tell!" Here Tom made some movement of his feet, and George's eye fell on the fetters.

"What a shame!" he exclaimed, lifting his hands. "I'll knock that old fellow down—I will!"

"No you won't, Mas'r George; and you must not talk so loud. It won't help me any, to anger him."

"Well, I won't, then, for your sake; but only to think of it—isn't it a shame? They never sent for me, nor sent me any word, and, if it hadn't been for Tom Lincon, I shouldn't have heard it. I tell you, I blew 'em up well, all of 'em, at home!"

"That ar wasn't right, I'm 'feard, Mas'r George."

"Can't help it! I say it's a shame! Look here, Uncle Tom," said he, turning his back to the shop, and speaking in a mysterious tone, "*I've brought you my dollar!*"

"O! I couldn't think o' takin' on 't, Mas'r George, no ways in the world!" said Tom, quite moved.

"But you *shall* take it!" said George; "look here—I told Aunt Chloe I'd do it, and she advised me just to make a hole in it, and put a string through, so you could hang it round your neck, and keep it out of sight; else this mean scamp would take it away. I tell ye, Tom, I want to blow him up! it would do me good!"

"No, don't, Mas'r George, for it won't do *me* any good."

"Well, I won't, for your sake," said George, busily tying his dollar round Tom's neck; "but there, now, button your coat tight over it, and keep it, and remember, every time you see it, that I'll come down after you, and bring you back. Aunt Chloe and I have been talking about it. I told her not to fear; I'll see to it, and I'll tease father's life out, if he don't do it."

"O! Mas'r George, ye mustn't talk so 'bout yer father!"

"Lor, Uncle Tom, I don't mean anything bad."

"And now, Mas'r George," said Tom, "ye must be a good boy; 'member how many hearts is sot on ye. Al'ays keep close to yer mother. Don't be gettin' into any of them foolish ways boys has of gettin' too big to mind their mothers. Tell ye what, Mas'r George, the Lord gives good many things twice over; but he don't give ye a mother but once.

17 George is not a man in that he has not yet reached his majority, age twenty-one.

George Shelby gives his dollar to Uncle Tom. From *Uncle Tom's Cabin*, James Nisbet & Co., Ltd., London, n.d.

**18** Tom's voice, "tender as a woman's," as well as his recognition of George's potential mark him as simultaneously feminine and preternaturally powerful. Stowe plants the seeds of thinking of Tom as a Christ figure. George promises to return when the time is right to save Tom, but we already understand that it is George and the Shelbys and the whole weak-but-perhaps-well-meaning South that needs saving.

**19** After Stowe has developed Haley as a despicable man, she allows him to give voice to the necessary and stinging indictment of Master George: High or low, seller or buyer, any participation in slavery is evil.

Ye'll never see sich another woman, Mas'r George, if ye live to be a hundred years old. So, now, you hold on to her, and grow up, and be a comfort to her, thar's my own good boy,—you will now, won't ye?"

"Yes, I will, Uncle Tom," said George, seriously.

"And be careful of yer speaking, Mas'r George. Young boys, when they comes to your age, is wilful, sometimes—it's natur they should be. But real gentlemen, such as I hopes you'll be, never lets fall no words that isn't 'spectful to thar parents. Ye an't 'fended, Mas'r George?"

"No, indeed, Uncle Tom; you always did give me good advice."

"I's older, ye know," said Tom, stroking the boy's fine, curly head with his large, strong hand, but speaking in a voice as tender as a woman's,[18] "and I sees all that's bound up in you. O, Mas'r George, you has everything,—l'arnin', privileges, readin', writin',—and you'll grow up to be a great, learned, good man, and all the people on the place and your mother and father'll be so proud on ye! Be a good Mas'r, like yer father; and be a Christian, like yer mother. 'Member yer Creator in the days o' yer youth, Mas'r George."

"I'll be *real* good, Uncle Tom, I tell you," said George. "I'm going to be a *first-rater*; and don't you be discouraged. I'll have you back to the place, yet. As I told Aunt Chloe this morning, I'll build your house all over, and you shall have a room for a parlor with a carpet on it, when I'm a man. O, you'll have good times yet!"

Haley now came to the door, with the handcuffs in his hands.

"Look here, now, Mister," said George, with an air of great superiority, as he got out, "I shall let father and mother know how you treat Uncle Tom!"

"You're welcome," said the trader.

"I should think you'd be ashamed to spend all your life buying men and women, and chaining them, like cattle! I should think you'd feel mean!" said George.

"So long as your grand folks wants to buy men and women, I'm as good as they is," said Haley; " 'tan't any meaner sellin' on 'em, than 't is buyin'!"[19]

"I'll never do either, when I'm a man," said George; "I'm ashamed, this day, that I'm a Kentuckian. I always was proud of it before;" and George sat very straight on his horse, and looked round with an air, as if he expected the state would be impressed with his opinion.

"Well, good-by, Uncle Tom; keep a stiff upper lip," said George.

"Good-by, Mas'r George," said Tom, looking fondly and admiringly at him. "God Almighty bless you! Ah! Kentucky han't got many like you!" he said, in the fulness of his heart, as the frank, boyish face was lost to his view. Away he went, and Tom looked, till the clatter of his horse's heels died away, the last sound or sight of his home. But over his heart there seemed to be a warm spot, where those young hands had placed that precious dollar. Tom put up his hand, and held it close to his heart.

"Now, I tell ye what, Tom," said Haley, as he came up to the wagon, and threw in the hand-cuffs, "I mean to start fa'r with ye, as I gen'ally do with my niggers; and I'll tell ye now, to begin with, you treat me fa'r, and I'll treat you fa'r; I an't never hard on my niggers. Calculates to do the best for 'em I can. Now, ye see, you'd better jest settle down comfortable, and not be tryin' no tricks; because nigger's tricks of all sorts I'm up to, and it's no use. If niggers is quiet, and don't try to get off, they has good times with me; and if they don't, why, it's thar fault, and not mine."

Tom assured Haley that he had no present intentions of running off. In fact, the exhortation seemed rather a superfluous one to a man with a great pair of iron fetters on his feet. But Mr. Haley had got in the habit of commencing his relations with his stock with little exhortations of this nature, calculated, as he deemed, to inspire cheerfulness and confidence, and prevent the necessity of any unpleasant scenes.

And here, for the present, we take our leave of Tom, to pursue the fortunes of other characters in our story.

# CHAPTER 11

## In Which Property Gets into an Improper State of Mind[1]

1 Stowe's title here is perhaps more satiric than ironic. "Property" last referred to Uncle Tom; now it refers to George Harris, who is decidedly more "improper" than Tom.

2 Like Stowe's broad and metaphorical use of the word "species" in chapter 1 to describe "gentlemen," here the term "race" is used satirically to describe people from Kentucky.

3 Stowe continues her satire with her use of "sublimely" and, in the next paragraph, the archaic "mine host." This is a humorous set piece.

It was late in a drizzly afternoon that a traveller alighted at the door of a small country hotel, in the village of N——, in Kentucky. In the bar-room he found assembled quite a miscellaneous company, whom stress of weather had driven to harbor, and the place presented the usual scenery of such reunions. Great, tall, raw-boned Kentuckians, attired in hunting-shirts, and trailing their loose joints over a vast extent of territory, with the easy lounge peculiar to the race,[2]—rifles stacked away in the corner, shot-pouches, game-bags, hunting-dogs, and little negroes, all rolled together in the corners,—were the characteristic features in the picture. At each end of the fireplace sat a long-legged gentleman, with his chair tipped back, his hat on his head, and the heels of his muddy boots reposing sublimely[3] on the mantel-piece,—a position, we will inform our readers, decidedly favorable to the turn of reflection incident to western taverns, where travellers exhibit a decided preference for this particular mode of elevating their understandings.

Mine host, who stood behind the bar, like most of his countrymen, was great of stature, good-natured, and loose-jointed, with an enormous shock of hair on his head, and a great tall hat on the top of that.

In fact, everybody in the room bore on his head this characteristic emblem of man's sovereignty; whether it were felt hat, palm-leaf, greasy beaver, or fine new chapeau, there it reposed with true republican independence.

In truth, it appeared to be the characteristic mark of every individual. Some wore them tipped rakishly to one side—these were your men of humor, jolly, free-and-easy dogs; some had them jammed independently down over their noses—these were your hard characters, thorough men, who, when they wore their hats, *wanted* to wear them, and to wear them just as they had a mind to; there were those who had them set far over back—wide-awake men, who wanted a clear prospect; while careless men, who did not know, or care, how their hats sat, had them shaking about in all directions. The various hats, in fact, were quite a Shakespearean study.[4]

Divers negroes, in very free-and-easy pantaloons, and with no redundancy in the shirt line, were scuttling about, hither and thither, without bringing to pass any very particular results, except expressing a generic willingness to turn over everything in creation generally for the benefit of Mas'r and his guests. Add to this picture a jolly, crackling, rollicking fire, going rejoicingly up a great wide chimney,—the outer door and every window being set wide open, and the calico window-curtain flopping and snapping in a good stiff breeze of damp raw air,—and you have an idea of the jollities of a Kentucky tavern.[5]

Your Kentuckian of the present day is a good illustration of the doctrine of transmitted instincts and peculiarities.[6] His fathers were mighty hunters,—men who lived in the woods, and slept under the free, open heavens, with the stars to hold their candles; and their descendant to this day always acts as if the house were his camp,—wears his hat at all hours, tumbles himself about, and puts his heels on the tops of chairs or mantel-pieces, just as his father rolled on the green sward, and put his upon trees and logs,—keeps all the windows and doors open, winter and summer, that he may get air enough for his great lungs,—calls everybody "stranger," with nonchalant bonhomie, and is altogether the frankest, easiest, most jovial creature living.

Into such an assembly of the free and easy our traveller entered. He was a short, thick-set man, carefully dressed, with a round, good-natured countenance, and something rather fussy and particular in his appearance. He was very careful of his valise and umbrella, bringing them in with his own hands, and resisting, pertinaciously, all offers from the various servants to relieve him of them. He looked round the bar-room with rather an anxious air, and, retreating with his valuables to the warmest corner, disposed them under his chair, sat down, and looked

4 The "Shakesperean study" seems to allude to at least two scenes: *Much Ado About Nothing* (act 1, scene 1: "He wears his faith but as the fashion of his hat") and *The Life of Henry the Fifth* (act 4, scene 7, where Fluellen has a leek in his cap and Williams has a glove in his).

5 It is important for the tale's veracity that Stowe gets the tone right in these scenes. We must believe that she is familiar with life in yet another Kentucky tavern. She is so adept at it that one is tempted to forget that the author of this scene is a well-bred Christian mother.

6 Stowe's tongue-in-cheek rhetoric continues. Here she uses the rhetoric of science, specifically that of early genetics (heredity). "Transmitted" means "inherited." Note that Stowe is referring not to inherited traits in the individual but in the Kentuckian as a species.

**7** Remarkably, we immediately dislike this fastidious newcomer, even though he behaves much like Stowe probably would have behaved had she been offered some chaw.

Miguel Covarrubias juxtaposes George Harris's injured hand and the runaway slave notice to emphasize that each such notice corresponds to an individual act of heroism and desperation.  From *Uncle Tom's Cabin: or, Life Among the Lowly*, Heritage Press edition, 1938

rather apprehensively up at the worthy whose heels illustrated the end of the mantel-piece, who was spitting from right to left, with a courage and energy rather alarming to gentlemen of weak nerves and particular habits.

"I say, stranger, how are ye?" said the aforesaid gentleman, firing an honorary salute of tobacco-juice in the direction of the new arrival.

"Well, I reckon," was the reply of the other, as he dodged, with some alarm, the threatening honor.

"Any news?" said the respondent, taking out a strip of tobacco and a large hunting-knife from his pocket.

"Not that I know of," said the man.

"Chaw?" said the first speaker, handing the old gentleman a bit of his tobacco, with a decidedly brotherly air.

"No, thank ye—it don't agree with me," said the little man, edging off.**7**

"Don't, eh?" said the other, easily, and stowing away the morsel in his own mouth, in order to keep up the supply of tobacco-juice, for the general benefit of society.

The old gentleman uniformly gave a little start whenever his long-sided brother fired in his direction; and this being observed by his companion, he very good-naturedly turned his artillery to another quarter, and proceeded to storm one of the fire-irons with a degree of military talent fully sufficient to take a city.

"What's that?" said the old gentleman, observing some of the company formed in a group around a large handbill.

"Nigger advertised!" said one of the company, briefly.

Mr. Wilson, for that was the old gentleman's name, rose up, and, after carefully adjusting his valise and umbrella, proceeded deliberately to take out his spectacles and fix them on his nose; and, this operation being performed, read as follows:

> "Ran away from the subscriber, my mulatto boy, George. Said George six feet in height, a very light mulatto, brown curly hair; is very intelligent, speaks handsomely, can read and write; will probably try to pass for a white man; is deeply scarred on his back and shoulders; has been branded in his right hand with the letter H.
>
> "I will give four hundred dollars for him alive, and the same sum for satisfactory proof that he has been killed."

The old gentleman read this advertisement from end to end, in a low voice, as if he were studying it.

The long-legged veteran, who had been besieging the fire-iron, as before related, now took down his cumbrous length, and rearing aloft his tall form, walked up to the advertisement, and very deliberately spit a full discharge of tobacco-juice on it.

"There's my mind upon that!" said he, briefly, and sat down again.

"Why, now, stranger, what's that for?" said mine host.

"I'd do it all the same to the writer of that ar paper, if he was here," said the long man, coolly resuming his old employment of cutting tobacco. "Any man that owns a boy like that, and can't find any better way o' treating on him, *deserves* to lose him. Such papers as these is a shame to Kentucky; that's my mind right out, if anybody wants to know!"

"Well, now, that's a fact," said mine host, as he made an entry in his book.

"I've got a gang of boys, sir," said the long man, resuming his attack on the fire-irons, "and I jest tells 'em—'Boys,' says I,—'*run* now! dig! put! jest when ye want to! I never shall come to look after you!' That's the way I keep mine. Let 'em know they are free to run any time, and it jest breaks up their wanting to. More 'n all, I've got free papers for 'em all recorded, in case I gets keeled up any o' these times, and they knows it; and I tell ye, stranger, there an't a fellow in our parts gets more out of his niggers than I do. Why, my boys have been to Cincinnati, with five hundred dollars' worth of colts, and brought me back the money, all straight, time and agin. It stands to reason they should. Treat 'em like dogs, and you'll have dogs' works and dogs' actions. Treat 'em like men, and you'll have men's works." And the honest drover, in his warmth, endorsed this moral sentiment by firing a perfect *feu de joie*[8] at the fireplace.

"I think you're altogether right, friend," said Mr. Wilson; "and this boy described here *is* a fine fellow—no mistake about that. He worked for me some half-dozen years in my bagging factory, and he was my best hand, sir. He is an ingenious fellow, too: he invented a machine for the cleaning of hemp—a really valuable affair; it's gone into use in several factories. His master holds the patent of it."

"I'll warrant ye," said the drover, "holds it and makes money out of it, and then turns round and brands the boy in his right hand. If I had a fair chance, I'd mark him, I reckon, so that he'd carry it *one* while."

"These yer knowin' boys is allers aggravatin' and sarcy," said a coarse-looking fellow, from the other side of the

8 Another instance of Stowe's tone in this chapter; it is French for "a rifle salute at a public ceremony" (*Shorter Oxford*).

**9** The Kentuckian starts from the unusual premise that slaves are men whom only brutality can transform into beasts.

**10** Selling slaves "down river," i.e., to the sugar plantations of the Deep South, where few survived the climate and work conditions.

room; "that's why they gets cut up and marked so. If they behaved themselves, they wouldn't."

"That is to say, the Lord made 'em men, and it's a hard squeeze getting 'em down into beasts," said the drover, dryly.**9**

"Bright niggers isn't no kind of 'vantage to their masters," continued the other, well intrenched, in a coarse, unconscious obtuseness, from the contempt of his opponent; "what's the use o' talents and them things, if you can't get the use of 'em yourself? Why, all the use they make on 't is to get round you. I've had one or two of these fellers, and I jest sold 'em down river.**10** I knew I'd got to lose 'em, first or last, if I didn't."

"Better send orders up to the Lord, to make you a set, and leave out their souls entirely," said the drover.

Here the conversation was interrupted by the approach of a small one-horse buggy to the inn. It had a genteel appearance, and a well-dressed, gentlemanly man sat on the seat, with a colored servant driving.

The whole party examined the new comer with the interest with which a set of loafers in a rainy day usually examine every new comer. He was very tall, with a dark, Spanish complexion, fine, expressive black eyes, and close-curling hair, also of a glossy blackness. His well-formed aquiline nose, straight thin lips, and the admirable contour of his finely-formed limbs, impressed the whole company instantly with the idea of something uncommon. He walked easily in among the company, and with a nod indicated to his waiter where to place his trunk, bowed to the company, and, with his hat in his hand, walked up leisurely to the bar, and gave in his name as Henry Butler, Oaklands, Shelby County. Turning, with an indifferent air, he sauntered up to the advertisement, and read it over.

"Jim," he said to his man, "seems to me we met a boy something like this, up at Bernan's, didn't we?"

"Yes, Mas'r," said Jim, "only I an't sure about the hand."

"Well, I didn't look, of course," said the stranger, with a careless yawn. Then, walking up to the landlord, he desired him to furnish him with a private apartment, as he had some writing to do immediately.

The landlord was all obsequious, and a relay of about seven negroes, old and young, male and female, little and big, were soon whizzing about, like a covey of partridges, bustling, hurrying, treading on each other's toes, and tumbling over each other, in their zeal to get Mas'r's room ready, while he seated himself easily on a chair in the middle of the room, and entered into conversation with the man who sat next to him.

The manufacturer, Mr. Wilson, from the time of the entrance of the stranger, had regarded him with an air of disturbed and uneasy curiosity. He seemed to himself to have met and been acquainted with him somewhere, but he could not recollect. Every few moments, when the man spoke, or moved, or smiled, he would start and fix his eyes on him, and then suddenly withdraw them, as the bright, dark eyes met his with such unconcerned coolness. At last, a sudden recollection seemed to flash upon him, for he stared at the stranger with such an air of blank amazement and alarm, that he walked up to him.

"Mr. Wilson, I think," said he, in a tone of recognition, and extending his hand. "I beg your pardon, I didn't recollect you before. I see you remember me,—Mr. Butler, of Oaklands, Shelby County."

"Ye—yes—yes, sir," said Mr. Wilson, like one speaking in a dream.

Just then a negro boy entered, and announced that Mas'r's room was ready.

"Jim, see to the trunks," said the gentleman, negligently; then addressing himself to Mr. Wilson, he added— "I should like to have a few moments' conversation with you on business, in my room, if you please."

Mr. Wilson followed him, as one who walks in his sleep; and they proceeded to a large upper chamber, where a new-made fire was crackling, and various servants flying about, putting finishing touches to the arrangements.

When all was done, and the servants departed, the young man deliberately locked the door, and putting the key in his pocket, faced about, and folding his arms on his bosom, looked Mr. Wilson full in the face.

"George!" said Mr. Wilson.

"Yes, George," said the young man.

"I couldn't have thought it!"

"I am pretty well disguised, I fancy," said the young man, with a smile. "A little walnut bark has made my yellow skin a genteel brown, and I've dyed my hair black; so you see I don't answer to the advertisement at all."

"O, George! but this is a dangerous game you are playing. I could not have advised you to it."[11]

"I can do it on my own responsibility," said George, with the same proud smile.

We remark, *en passant*, that George was, by his father's side, of white descent. His mother was one of those unfortunates of her race, marked out by personal beauty to be

11 Wilson's fastidiousness takes on an air of cowardice here. Stowe would like us to understand that even though Wilson is a decent enough man, he hasn't exhibited any moral courage.

**12** Stowe blurs the line between heredity and inheritance through use of monetary terms such as "compensated."

**13** Another phrase from Bunyan's *The Pilgrim's Progress* (see chapter 8, note 10).

**14** Wilson alludes to Philemon as well as to Gen. 16:9 ("The angel bade the pregnant Hagar return to her mistress Sarah, even though Sarah had dealt harshly with her"). Stowe mentions the scriptural Hagar here, but we will meet a real live Hagar (with a son) in the next chapter.

**15** Stowe's allusion to the story of Philemon and his slave, Onesimus, is subtle and savvy in the mouth of George's kind but limited former employer. Wilson reveals his incomplete knowledge of the story, suggesting that Paul sent the runaway Onesimus back to his master simply because Onesimus was a slave. In fact, Paul writes that the newly converted Onesimus might return to his owner "no longer a slave but more than a slave, a beloved brother" (Philem. 16).

the slave of the passions of her possessor, and the mother of children who may never know a father. From one of the proudest families in Kentucky he had inherited a set of fine European features, and a high, indomitable spirit. From his mother he had received only a slight mulatto tinge, amply compensated[12] by its accompanying rich, dark eye. A slight change in the tint of the skin and the color of his hair had metamorphosed him into the Spanish-looking fellow he then appeared; and as gracefulness of movement and gentlemanly manners had always been perfectly natural to him, he found no difficulty in playing the bold part he had adopted—that of a gentleman travelling with his domestic.

Mr. Wilson, a good-natured but extremely fidgety and cautious old gentleman, ambled up and down the room, appearing, as John Bunyan hath it, "much tumbled up and down in his mind,"[13] and divided between his wish to help George, and a certain confused notion of maintaining law and order: so, as he shambled about, he delivered himself as follows:

"Well, George, I s'pose you're running away—leaving your lawful master, George—(I don't wonder at it)—at the same time, I'm sorry, George,—yes, decidedly—I think I must say that, George—it's my duty to tell you so."

"Why are you sorry, sir?" said George, calmly.

"Why, to see you, as it were, setting yourself in opposition to the laws of your country."

"*My* country!" said George, with a strong and bitter emphasis; "what country have I, but the grave,—and I wish to God that I was laid there!"

"Why, George, no—no—it won't do; this way of talking is wicked—unscriptural. George, you've got a hard master—in fact, he is—well he conducts himself reprehensibly—I can't pretend to defend him. But you know how the angel commanded Hagar to return to her mistress, and submit herself under her hand;[14] and the apostle sent back Onesimus to his master."[15]

"Don't quote Bible at me that way, Mr. Wilson," said George, with a flashing eye, "don't! for my wife is a Christian, and I mean to be, if ever I get to where I can; but to quote Bible to a fellow in my circumstances, is enough to make him give it up altogether. I appeal to God Almighty;—I'm willing to go with the case to Him, and ask Him if I do wrong to seek my freedom."

"These feelings are quite natural, George," said the good-natured man, blowing his nose. "Yes they're natural, but it is my duty not to encourage 'em in you. Yes, my boy,

I'm sorry for you, now; it's a bad case—very bad; but the apostle says, 'Let every one abide in the condition in which he is called.' We must all submit to the indications of Providence, George,—don't you see?"

George stood with his head drawn back, his arms folded tightly over his broad breast, and a bitter smile curling his lips.

"I wonder, Mr. Wilson, if the Indians should come and take you a prisoner away from your wife and children, and want to keep you all your life hoeing corn for them, if you'd think it your duty to abide in the condition in which you were called. I rather think that you'd think the first stray horse you could find an indication of Providence—shouldn't you?"

The little old gentleman[16] stared with both eyes at this illustration of the case; but, though not much of a reasoner, he had the sense in which some logicians on this particular subject do not excel,—that of saying nothing, where nothing could be said. So, as he stood carefully stroking his umbrella, and folding and patting down all the creases in it, he proceeded on with his exhortations in a general way.

"You see, George, you know, now, I always have stood your friend; and whatever I've said, I've said for your good. Now, here, it seems to me, you're running an awful risk. You can't hope to carry it out. If you're taken, it will be worse with you than ever; they'll only abuse you, and half kill you, and sell you down river."

"Mr. Wilson, I know all this," said George. "I *do* run a risk, but—" he threw open his overcoat, and showed two pistols and a bowie-knife. "There!" he said, "I'm ready for 'em! Down south I never *will* go. No! if it comes to that, I can earn myself at least six feet of free soil,—the first and last I shall ever own in Kentucky!"

"Why, George, this state of mind is awful; it's getting really desperate, George. I'm concerned. Going to break the laws of your country!"

"My country again! Mr. Wilson, *you* have a country; but what country have *I*, or any one like me, born of slave mothers? What laws are there for us? We don't make them,—we don't consent to them,—we have nothing to do with them; all they do for us is to crush us, and keep us down. Haven't I heard your Fourth-of-July speeches?[17] Don't you tell us all, once a year, that governments derive their just power from the consent of the governed? Can't a fellow *think,* that hears such things? Can't he put this and that together, and see what it comes to?"

16 Recall that the phrase "old gentleman" also refers to Satan.

17 One such Fourth of July speech, delivered by Frederick Douglass on July 5, 1852, expressed similar sentiments: "I am not included within the pale of this glorious anniversary! Your high independence only reveals the immeasurable distance between us. The blessings in which you, this day, rejoice, are not enjoyed in common. The rich inheritance of justice, liberty, prosperity and independence, bequeathed by your fathers, is shared by you, not by me" ("What to the Slave Is the Fourth of July?"). See also William Wells Brown's 1847 "Lecture Delivered Before the Female Anti-Slavery Society of Salem," in *The Selected Writings of William Wells Brown*, ed. Hollis Robbins and Paula Garrett (New York: Oxford University Press, 2006).

18 George's question echoes Mrs. Shelby's "Am not I a woman?" (see chapter 8, note 28). But once again, Stowe seems to make allusions to Shakespeare. Compare this passage with Shylock's speech in *The Merchant of Venice* 3.1.53–59:

> I am a Jew. Hath
> not a Jew eyes? Hath not a Jew hands, organs,
> dimensions, senses, affections, passions; fed with
> the same food, hurt with the same weapons, subject
> to the same diseases, heal'd by the same means,
> warm'd and cool'd by the same winter and summer as
> a Christian is?

"Persecuted Virtue." Wood engraving by George Cruikshank. This is not an illustration of an event in the novel but of George Harris's memory. The caption quotes the text: "She was whipped, sir, for wanting to live a decent Christian life." This image is triply shocking: The victim is a woman, we can see the hint of her breast, and she could be mistaken for white. Visually, she is not only a female slave; she is every woman.  From *Uncle Tom's Cabin*, John Cassell, London, 1852

Mr. Wilson's mind was one of those that may not unaptly be represented by a bale of cotton,—downy, soft, benevolently fuzzy and confused. He really pitied George with all his heart, and had a sort of dim and cloudy perception of the style of feeling that agitated him; but he deemed it his duty to go on talking *good* to him, with infinite pertinacity.

"George, this is bad. I must tell you, you know, as a friend, you'd better not be meddling with such notions; they are bad, George, very bad, for boys in your condition,—very;" and Mr. Wilson sat down to a table, and began nervously chewing the handle of his umbrella.

"See here, now, Mr. Wilson," said George, coming up and sitting himself determinately down in front of him; "look at me, now. Don't I sit before you, every way, just as much a man as you are?[18] Look at my face,—look at my hands,—look at my body," and the young man drew himself up proudly; "why am I *not* a man, as much as anybody? Well, Mr. Wilson, hear what I can tell you. I had a father—one of your Kentucky gentlemen—who didn't think enough of me to keep me from being sold with his dogs and horses, to satisfy the estate, when he died. I saw my mother put up at sheriff's sale, with her seven children. They were sold before her eyes, one by one, all to different masters; and I was the youngest. She came and kneeled down before old Mas'r, and begged him to buy her with me, that she might have at least one child with her; and he kicked her away with his heavy boot. I saw him do it; and the last that I heard was her moans and screams, when I was tied to his horse's neck, to be carried off to his place."

"Well, then?"

"My master traded with one of the men, and bought my oldest sister. She was a pious, good girl,—a member of the Baptist church,—and as handsome as my poor mother had been. She was well brought up, and had good manners. At first, I was glad she was bought, for I had one friend near me. I was soon sorry for it. Sir, I have stood at the door and heard her whipped, when it seemed as if every blow cut into my naked heart, and I couldn't do anything to help her; and she was whipped, sir, for wanting to live a decent Christian life, such as your laws give no slave girl a right to live; and at last I saw her chained with a trader's gang, to be sent to market in Orleans,—sent there for nothing else but that,—and that's the last I know of her. Well, I grew up,—long years and years,—no father, no mother, no sister, not a living soul that cared for me more than a dog; nothing but whipping, scolding, starving. Why, sir, I've been so hungry that I have been glad to take the bones they threw to their dogs; and yet, when I was a little fellow, and laid awake whole nights and cried, it wasn't the hunger, it wasn't the whipping, I cried for. No, sir; it was for *my mother* and *my sisters*,—it was because I hadn't a friend to love me on earth. I never knew what peace or comfort was. I never had a kind word spoken to me till I came to work in your factory. Mr. Wilson, you treated me well; you encouraged me to do well, and to learn to read and write, and to try to make something of myself; and God knows how grateful I am for it. Then, sir, I found my wife; you've seen her,—you know how beautiful she is. When I found she loved me, when I married her, I scarcely could believe I was alive, I was so happy; and, sir, she is as good as she is beautiful. But now what? Why, now comes my master, takes me right away from my work, and my friends, and all I like, and grinds me down into the very dirt! And why? Because, he says, I forgot who I was; he says, to teach me that I am only a nigger! After all, and last of all, he comes between me and my wife, and says I shall give her up, and live with another woman. And all this your laws give him power to do, in spite of God or man. Mr. Wilson, look at it![19] There isn't *one* of all these things, that have broken the hearts of my mother and my sister, and my wife and myself, but your laws allow, and give every man power to do, in Kentucky, and none can say to him nay! Do you call these the laws of *my* country? Sir, I haven't any country, any more than I have any father. But I'm going to have one. I don't want anything of *your* country, except to be let alone,—to go peaceably out of it; and when I get to Canada, where the laws will own me and protect me, *that* shall be my country, and its laws I will obey. But if any man tries to stop me, let him take care, for I am desperate. I'll fight for my liberty to the last breath I breathe. You say your fathers did it; if it was right for them, it is right for me!"

This speech, delivered partly while sitting at the table, and partly walking up and down the room,—delivered with tears, and flashing eyes, and despairing gestures,—was altogether too much for the good-natured old body to whom it was addressed, who had pulled out a great yellow silk pocket-handkerchief, and was mopping up his face with great energy.

"Blast 'em all!" he suddenly broke out. "Haven't I always said so—the infernal old cusses! I hope I an't swearing, now. Well! go ahead, George, go ahead; but be careful, my boy; don't shoot anybody, George, unless—

19 George's words call to mind the caution at the end of the marriage ceremony: "What God has joined, let no man put asunder."

well—you'd *better* not shoot, I reckon; at least, I wouldn't *hit* anybody, you know. Where is your wife, George?" he added, as he nervously rose, and began walking the room.

"Gone, sir, gone, with her child in her arms, the Lord only knows where;—gone after the north star; and when we ever meet, or whether we meet at all in this world, no creature can tell."

"Is it possible! astonishing! from such a kind family?"

"Kind families get in debt, and the laws of *our* country allow them to sell the child out of its mother's bosom to pay its master's debts," said George, bitterly.

"Well, well," said the honest old man, fumbling in his pocket. "I s'pose, perhaps, I an't following my judgment,—hang it, I *won't* follow my judgment!" he added, suddenly; "so here, George," and, taking out a roll of bills from his pocket-book, he offered them to George.

"No, my kind, good sir!" said George, "you've done a great deal for me, and this might get you into trouble. I have money enough, I hope, to take me as far as I need it."

"No; but you must, George. Money is a great help everywhere;—can't have too much, if you get it honestly. Take it,—*do* take it, *now*,—do, my boy!"

"On condition, sir, that I may repay it at some future time, I will," said George, taking up the money.

"And now, George, how long are you going to travel in this way?—not long or far, I hope. It's well carried on, but too bold. And this black fellow,—who is he?"

"A true fellow, who went to Canada more than a year ago. He heard, after he got there, that his master was so angry at him for going off that he had whipped his poor old mother; and he has come all the way back to comfort her, and get a chance to get her away."

"Has he got her?"

"Not yet; he has been hanging about the place, and found no chance yet. Meanwhile, he is going with me as far as Ohio, to put me among friends that helped him, and then he will come back after her."

"Dangerous, very dangerous!" said the old man.

George drew himself up, and smiled disdainfully.

The old gentleman eyed him from head to foot, with a sort of innocent wonder.

"George, something has brought you out wonderfully. You hold up your head, and speak and move like another man," said Mr. Wilson.

"Because I'm a *freeman*!" said George, proudly. "Yes, sir; I've said Mas'r for the last time to any man. *I'm free*!"

"Take care! You are not sure,—you may be taken."

"All men are free and equal *in the grave*, if it comes to that, Mr. Wilson," said George.

"I'm perfectly dumb-foundered with your boldness!" said Mr. Wilson,—"to come right here to the nearest tavern!"

"Mr. Wilson, it is *so* bold, and this tavern is so near, that they will never think of it; they will look for me on ahead, and you yourself wouldn't know me. Jim's master don't live in this county; he isn't known in these parts. Besides, he is given up; nobody is looking after him, and nobody will take me up from the advertisement, I think."

"But the mark in your hand?"

George drew off his glove, and showed a newly-healed scar in his hand.

"That is a parting proof of Mr. Harris' regard," he said, scornfully. "A fortnight ago, he took it into his head to give it to me, because he said he believed I should try to get away one of these days. Looks interesting, doesn't it?" he said, drawing his glove on again.

"I declare, my very blood runs cold when I think of it,— your condition and your risks!" said Mr. Wilson.

"Mine has run cold a good many years, Mr. Wilson; at present, it's about up to the boiling point," said George.

"Well, my good sir," continued George, after a few moments' silence, "I saw you knew me; I thought I'd just have this talk with you, lest your surprised looks should bring me out. I leave early to-morrow morning, before day-light, by to-morrow night I hope to sleep safe in Ohio. I shall travel by daylight, stop at the best hotels, go to the dinner-tables with the lords of the land. So, good-by, sir; if you hear that I'm taken, you may know that I'm dead!"

George stood up like a rock, and put out his hand with the air of a prince. The friendly little old man shook it heartily, and after a little shower of caution, he took his umbrella, and fumbled his way out of the room.

George stood thoughtfully looking at the door, as the old man closed it. A thought seemed to flash across his mind. He hastily stepped to it, and opening it, said,

"Mr. Wilson, one word more."

The old gentleman entered again, and George, as before, locked the door, and then stood for a few moments looking on the floor, irresolutely. At last, raising his head with a sudden effort—

"Mr. Wilson, you have shown yourself a Christian in your treatment of me,—I want to ask one last deed of Christian kindness of you."

"Well, George."

**20** Stowe's Christian readers would consider George's doubt about God, as does Mr. Wilson, as a troubling sign of despair which puts his soul in jeopardy. Yet another horror of slavery!

"Well, sir,—what you said was true. I *am* running a dreadful risk. There isn't, on earth, a living soul to care if I die," he added, drawing his breath hard, and speaking with a great effort,—"I shall be kicked out and buried like a dog, and nobody'll think of it a day after,—*only my poor wife*! Poor soul! she'll mourn and grieve; and if you'd only contrive, Mr. Wilson, to send this little pin to her. She gave it to me for a Christmas present, poor child! Give it to her, and tell her I loved her to the last. Will you? *Will* you?" he added, earnestly.

"Yes, certainly—poor fellow!" said the old gentleman, taking the pin, with watery eyes, and a melancholy quiver in his voice.

"Tell her one thing," said George; "it's my last wish, if she *can* get to Canada, to go there. No matter how kind her mistress is,—no matter how much she loves her home; beg her not to go back,—for slavery always ends in misery. Tell her to bring up our boy a free man, and then he won't suffer as I have. Tell her this, Mr. Wilson, will you?"

"Yes, George, I'll tell her; but I trust you won't die; take heart,—you're a brave fellow. Trust in the Lord, George. I wish in my heart you were safe through, though,—that's what I do."

"*Is* there a God to trust in?" said George, in such a tone of bitter despair as arrested the old gentleman's words. "O, I've seen things all my life that have made me feel that there can't be a God. You Christians don't know how these things look to us. There's a God for you, but is there any for us?"**20**

"O, now, don't—don't, my boy!" said the old man, almost sobbing as he spoke; "don't feel so! There is—there is; clouds and darkness are around about him, but righteousness and judgment are the habitation of his throne. There's a *God*, George,—believe it; trust in Him, and I'm sure He'll help you. Everything will be set right,—if not in this life, in another."

The real piety and benevolence of the simple old man invested him with a temporary dignity and authority, as he spoke. George stopped his distracted walk up and down the room, stood thoughtfully a moment, and then said, quietly,

"Thank you for saying that, my good friend; I'll *think of that*."

# CHAPTER 12

## Select Incident of Lawful Trade[1]

"In Ramah there was a voice heard,—weeping, and
lamentation, and great mourning; Rachel weeping
for her children, and would not be comforted."

—MATT. 2:18

Mr. Haley and Tom jogged onward in their wagon,
each, for a time, absorbed in his own reflections. Now, the
reflections of two men sitting side by side are a curious
thing,—seated on the same seat, having the same eyes,
ears, hands and organs of all sorts, and having pass before
their eyes the same objects,—it is wonderful what a variety we shall find in these same reflections!

As, for example, Mr. Haley: he thought first of Tom's
length, and breadth, and height, and what he would sell
for, if he was kept fat and in good case till he got him into
market. He thought of how he should make out his gang;
he thought of the respective market value of certain sup-
posititious men and women and children who were to
compose it, and other kindred topics of the business; then
he thought of himself, and how humane he was, that
whereas other men chained their "niggers"[2] hand and foot
both, he only put fetters on the feet, and left Tom the use
of his hands, as long as he behaved well; and he sighed to
think how ungrateful human nature was, so that there
was even room to doubt whether Tom appreciated his mer-
cies. He had been taken in so by "niggers" whom he had

1 We aren't sure exactly what Stowe means
by this chapter title right away. After reading
the chapter, we recognize another of Stowe's
ironic understatements. The verse from Matt.
2:18 evokes the ship *Rachel* from Herman
Melville's *Moby-Dick* (1851).

2 The quotes Stowe places around "niggers"
in Haley's reverie show the distinctions
Haley draws between himself and other slave
traders who treat their property like "niggers." Readers might remember his scoffing
at such fine distinctions in his earlier conversation with George Shelby about the reputed
differences between sellers and buyers in the
slave trade.

3 We can have no doubt about the heart-wrenching scene that is to follow. Note that Stowe has given us yet another Tom—this is the sixth one—and this one is a full Thomas. So far we have Tom Loker, Mas'r Tom (George's master), Uncle Tom, Tom Lincon, Tom Bird, and now Thomas Flint.

favored; but still he was astonished to consider how good-natured he yet remained!

As to Tom, he was thinking over some words of an unfashionable old book, which kept running through his head again and again, as follows: "We have here no continuing city, but we seek one to come; wherefore God himself is not ashamed to be called our God; for he hath prepared for us a city." These words of an ancient volume, got up principally by "ignorant and unlearned men," have, through all time, kept up, somehow, a strange sort of power over the minds of poor, simple fellows, like Tom. They stir up the soul from its depths, and rouse, as with trumpet call, courage, energy, and enthusiasm, where before was only the blackness of despair.

Mr. Haley pulled out of his pocket sundry newspapers, and began looking over their advertisements, with absorbed interest. He was not a remarkably fluent reader, and was in the habit of reading in a sort of recitative half-aloud, by way of calling in his ears to verify the deductions of his eyes. In this tone he slowly recited the following paragraph:

"EXECUTOR'S SALE,—NEGROES!—Agreeably to order of court, will be sold, on Tuesday, February 20, before the Court-house door, in the town of Washington, Kentucky, the following negroes: Hagar, aged 60; John, aged 30; Ben, aged 21; Saul, aged 25; Albert, aged 14. Sold for the benefit of the creditors and heirs of the estate of Jesse Blutchford, Esq.

SAMUEL MORRIS,
THOMAS FLINT,
*Executors.*"3

"This yer I must look at," said he to Tom, for want of somebody else to talk to.

"Ye see, I'm going to get up a prime gang to take down with ye, Tom; it'll make it sociable and pleasant like,—good company will, ye know. We must drive right to Washington first and foremost, and then I'll clap you into jail, while I does the business."

Tom received this agreeable intelligence quite meekly; simply wondering, in his own heart, how many of these doomed men had wives and children, and whether they would feel as he did about leaving them. It is to be confessed, too, that the naïve, off-hand information that he was to be thrown into jail by no means produced an agreeable impression on a poor fellow who had always prided himself on a strictly honest and upright course of life. Yes, Tom, we must confess it, was rather proud of his honesty, poor fellow,—not having very much else to be proud of;—if he had belonged to some of the higher walks of society, he, perhaps, would never have been reduced to such straits. However, the day wore on, and the evening saw Haley and Tom comfortably accommodated in Washington,-the one in a tavern, and the other in a jail.

About eleven o'clock the next day, a mixed throng was gathered around the court-house steps,—smoking, chewing, spitting, swearing, and conversing, according to their respective tastes and turns,—waiting for the auction to commence. The men and women to be sold sat in a group apart, talking in a low tone to each other. The woman who had been advertised by the name of Hagar was a regular African in feature and figure. She might have been sixty, but was older than that by hard work and disease, was partially blind, and somewhat crippled with rheumatism. By her side stood her only remaining son, Albert, a bright-looking little fellow of fourteen years. The boy was the only survivor of a large family, who had been successively sold away from her to a southern market. The mother held on to him with both her shaking hands, and eyed with intense trepidation every one who walked up to examine him.

"Don't be feard, Aunt Hagar," said the oldest of the men, "I spoke to Mas'r Thomas 'bout it, and he thought he might manage to sell you in a lot both together."

"Dey needn't call me worn out yet," said she, lifting her shaking hands. "I can cook yet, and scrub, and scour,— I'm wuth a buying, if I do come cheap;—tell em dat ar,— you *tell* em," she added, earnestly.

Haley here forced his way into the group, walked up to the old man, pulled his mouth open and looked in, felt of his teeth, made him stand and straighten himself, bend his back, and perform various evolutions to show his muscles; and then passed on to the next, and put him through the same trial.[4] Walking up last to the boy, he felt of his arms, straightened his hands, and looked at his fingers, and made him jump, to show his agility.

4 We didn't really need more evidence of Haley's hard-heartedness, but Stowe has provided it anyway.

Illustration by Hammatt Billings of a slave sale, featuring Aunt Hagar and her fourteen-year-old son Albert. (See note 14 on page 118.) The standing white gentlemen tower over the "lawful" property. The caricature of Aunt Hagar is particularly unflattering.   From *Uncle Tom's Cabin*, John P. Jewett & Co., 1852

"He an't gwine to be sold widout me!" said the old woman, with passionate eagerness; "he and I goes in a lot together; I's rail strong yet, Mas'r, and can do heaps o' work,—heaps on it, Mas'r."

"On plantation?" said Haley, with a contemptuous glance. "Likely story!" and, as if satisfied with his examination, he walked out and looked, and stood with his hands in his pocket, his cigar in his mouth, and his hat cocked on one side, ready for action.

Woodcut by A. J. M., "after George Cruikshank." This illustration offers a different view of the separation of Aunt Hagar and her son from the image on page 127; this one provokes more sympathy. The numerous images of this scene speak to the cultural importance of the allusion to the biblical Hagar, cast out with her child in Gen. 16 and 21.   From *Uncle Tom's Cabin*, John Cassell, London, 1852

"What think of 'em?" said a man who had been following Haley's examination, as if to make up his own mind from it.

"Wal," said Haley, spitting, "I shall put in, I think, for the youngerly ones and the boy."

"They want to sell the boy and the old woman together," said the man.

"Find it a tight pull;—why, she's an old rack o' bones,—not worth her salt."

"You wouldn't, then?" said the man.

"Anybody'd be a fool 't would. She's half blind, crooked with rheumatis, and foolish to boot."

"Some buys up these yer old critturs, and ses there's a sight more wear in 'em than a body'd think," said the man, reflectively.

"No go, 't all," said Haley; "wouldn't take her for a present,—fact,—I've *seen*, now."

"Wal, 'tis kinder pity, now, not to buy her with her son,—her heart seems so sot on him,—s'pose they fling her in cheap."

"Them that's got money to spend that ar way, it's all well enough. I shall bid off on that ar boy for a plantation-hand;—wouldn't be bothered with her, no way,—not if they'd give her to me," said Haley.

"She'll take on desp't," said the man.

"Nat'lly, she will," said the trader, coolly.

The conversation was here interrupted by a busy hum in the audience; and the auctioneer, a short, bustling, important fellow, elbowed his way into the crowd. The old woman drew in her breath, and caught instinctively at her son.

"Keep close to yer mammy, Albert,—close,—dey'll put us up togedder," she said.

"O, mammy, I'm feared they won't," said the boy.

"Dey must, child; I can't live, no ways, if they don't," said the old creature, vehemently.

The stentorian tones of the auctioneer, calling out to clear the way, now announced that the sale was about to commence. A place was cleared, and the bidding began. The different men on the list were soon knocked off at prices which showed a pretty brisk demand in the market; two of them fell to Haley.

"Come, now, young un," said the auctioneer, giving the boy a touch with his hammer, "be up and show your springs, now."

"Put us two up togedder, togedder,—do please, Mas'r," said the old woman, holding fast to her boy.

"Be off," said the man, gruffly, pushing her hands away; "you come last. Now, darkey, spring;" and, with the word, he pushed the boy toward the block, while a deep, heavy groan rose behind him. The boy paused, and looked back; but there was no time to stay, and, dashing the tears from his large, bright eyes, he was up in a moment.

His fine figure, alert limbs, and bright face, raised an instant competition, and half a dozen bids simultaneously met the ear of the auctioneer. Anxious, half-frightened, he looked from side to side, as he heard the clatter of contending bids,—now here, now there,—till the hammer fell. Haley had got him. He was pushed from the block toward his new master, but stopped one moment, and looked back, when his poor old mother, trembling in every limb, held out her shaking hands toward him.

"Buy me too, Mas'r, for de dear Lord's sake!—buy me,— I shall die if you don't!"

"You'll die if I do, that's the kink of it," said Haley,— "no!" And he turned on his heel.

The bidding for the poor old creature was summary. The man who had addressed Haley, and who seemed not destitute of compassion, bought her for a trifle, and the spectators began to disperse.

The poor victims of the sale, who had been brought up in one place together for years, gathered round the despairing old mother, whose agony was pitiful to see.

"Couldn't dey leave me one? Mas'r allers said I should have one,—he did," she repeated over and over, in heartbroken tones.

"Trust in the Lord, Aunt Hagar," said the oldest of the men, sorrowfully.

"What good will it do?" said she, sobbing passionately.

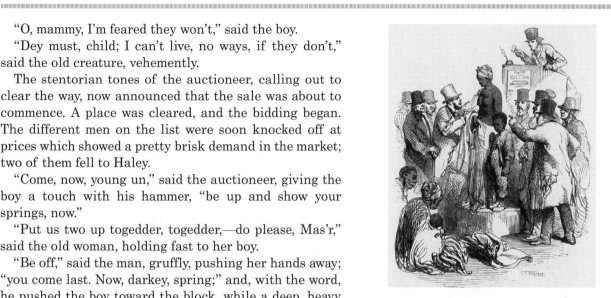

Woodcut by Thomas Williams of the slave market. Unlike Stowe's Aunt Hagar, who is in her sixties, this slave is clearly younger and nubile, revealing the lascivious underside of the slave trade. The lone black man in the image bows his head in shame.

Scene of Aunt Hagar and her son at the slave auction. The tableau is strikingly and bizarrely evocative of Georges Seurat's *A Sunday Afternoon on the Island of La Grande Jatte* (1884–86). Painted by Wm. Taylor, after a print by William Jay Baker, 1852

"Mother, mother,—don't! don't!" said the boy. "They say you's got a good master."

"I don't care,—I don't care. O, Albert! oh, my boy! you's my last baby. Lord, how ken I?"

"Come, take her off, can't some of ye?" said Haley, dryly; "don't do no good for her to go on that ar way."

The old men of the company, partly by persuasion and partly by force, loosed the poor creature's last despairing hold, and, as they led her off to her new master's wagon, strove to comfort her.

"Now!" said Haley, pushing his three purchases together, and producing a bundle of handcuffs, which he proceeded to put on their wrists; and fastening each handcuff to a long chain, he drove them before him to the jail.

A few days saw Haley, with his possessions, safely deposited on one of the Ohio boats. It was the commencement of his gang, to be augmented, as the boat moved on, by various other merchandise of the same kind, which he, or his agent, had stored for him in various points along shore.

The La Belle Rivière, as brave and beautiful a boat as ever walked the waters of her namesake river, was floating gayly down the stream, under a brilliant sky, the stripes and stars of free America waving and fluttering over head; the guards crowded with well-dressed ladies and gentlemen walking and enjoying the delightful day. All was full of life, buoyant and rejoicing;—all but Haley's gang, who were stored, with other freight, on the lower deck, and who, somehow, did not seem to appreciate their various privileges, as they sat in a knot, talking to each other in low tones.

"Boys," said Haley, coming up, briskly, "I hope you keep up good heart, and are cheerful. Now, no sulks, ye see; keep stiff upper lip, boys; do well by me, and I'll do well by you."

The boys addressed responded the invariable "Yes, Mas'r," for ages the watchword of poor Africa;[5] but it's to be owned they did not look particularly cheerful; they had their various little prejudices in favor of wives, mothers, sisters, and children, seen for the last time,—and though "they that wasted them required of them mirth,"[6] it was not instantly forthcoming.

"I've got a wife," spoke out the article enumerated as "John, aged thirty," and he laid his chained hand on Tom's knee,—"and she don't know a word about this, poor girl!"[7]

"Where does she live?" said Tom.

"In a tavern a piece down here," said John; "I wish, now, I *could* see her once more in this world," he added.

Poor John! It *was* rather natural; and the tears that fell, as he spoke, came as naturally as if he had been a white man.[8] Tom drew a long breath from a sore heart, and tried, in his poor way, to comfort him.

And over head, in the cabin, sat fathers and mothers, husbands and wives; and merry, dancing children moved round among them, like so many little butterflies,[9] and everything was going on quite easy and comfortable.

"O, mamma," said a boy, who had just come up from below, "there's a negro trader on board, and he's brought four or five slaves down there." "Poor creatures!" said the mother, in a tone between grief and indignation.

"What's that?" said another lady.

"Some poor slaves below," said the mother.

"And they've got chains on," said the boy.

"What a shame to our country that such sights are to be seen!" said another lady.

"O, there's a great deal to be said on both sides of the subject," said a genteel woman, who sat at her state-room door sewing, while her little girl and boy were playing round her. "I've been south, and I must say I think the negroes are better off than they would be to be free."

"In some respects, some of them are well off, I grant,"

5  "Poor Africa" means not the continent but rather African Americans under slavery; for centuries slaves have been taught to reply "Yes, Mas'r."

6  Psalm 137:1–4:

> By the rivers of Babylon, there we sat down, yea, we wept, when we remembered Zion.
> We hanged our harps upon the willows in the midst thereof.
> For there they that had carried us away captive required of us a song; and they that
> wasted us required of us mirth, saying, sing us one of the songs of Zion.
> How shall we sing the Lord's song in a strange land?

7  Once again, Stowe indicates that strong, emotional marital bonds exist in slavery. Uncle Tom, however, does not refer to his wife.

8  It may seem odd for present-day readers that coming to tears naturally was a characteristic of white men, but the nineteenth century saw such display of emotion as a mark of deep and manly feeling.

9  Anyone who knows anything about children knows that groups of them are not at all like so many little butterflies, but Stowe's sentimental point is that evil behavior is learned—it doesn't come naturally. Whether one agrees or not, note how consistently and imaginatively she makes the point.

**10** This mother will clothe her children in her misguided opinions, just as she clothes them in her well-trimmed baby garments.

**11** This "genteel woman" voices not only her class prejudice but the racist belief that blacks constitute a separate species. Stowe means us to understand the woman as misguided because she refuses to "reason from our feelings"—exactly the task Stowe has set her women readers.

**12** Yet again, we see Southerners arguing among themselves about slavery—not a Northerner or an abolitionist to be seen. Don't you see? Stowe seems to be saying; Southerners are *not* happy.

**13** The allusion is to Gen. 9:21–27. Noah gets drunk, and while he is passed out, his youngest son, Ham, sees him naked. Noah wakes and curses Ham, saying that Ham will be a servant of servants unto his brother. This passage in Genesis was often cited as a scriptural justification for slavery.

said the lady to whose remark she had answered. "The most dreadful part of slavery, to my mind, is its outrages on the feelings and affections,—the separating of families, for example."

"That *is* a bad thing, certainly," said the other lady, holding up a baby's dress she had just completed, and looking intently on its trimmings;**10** "but then, I fancy, it don't occur often."

"O, it does," said the first lady, eagerly; "I've lived many years in Kentucky and Virginia both, and I've seen enough to make any one's heart sick. Suppose, ma'am, your two children, there, should be taken from you, and sold?"

"We can't reason from our feelings to those of this class of persons," said the other lady, sorting out some worsteds on her lap.**11**

"Indeed, ma'am, you can know nothing of them, if you say so," answered the first lady, warmly. "I was born and brought up among them. I know they *do* feel, just as keenly,—even more so, perhaps,—as we do."

The lady said "Indeed!" yawned, and looked out the cabin window, and finally repeated, for a finale, the remark with which she had begun,— "After all, I think they are better off than they would be to be free."

"It's undoubtedly the intention of Providence that the African race should be servants,—kept in a low condition," said a grave-looking gentleman in black, a clergyman, seated by the cabin door.**12** " 'Cursed be Canaan; a servant of servants shall he be,' the scripture says."**13**

"I say, stranger, is that ar what that text means?" said a tall man, standing by.

"Undoubtedly. It pleased Providence, for some inscrutable reason, to doom the race to bondage, ages ago; and we must not set up our opinion against that."

"Well, then, we'll all go ahead and buy up niggers," said the man, "if that's the way of Providence,—won't we, Squire?" said he, turning to Haley, who had been standing, with his hands in his pockets, by the stove, and intently listening to the conversation.

"Yes," continued the tall man, "we must all be resigned to the decrees of Providence. Niggers must be sold, and trucked round, and kept under; it's what they's made for. 'Pears like this yer view's quite refreshing, an't it, stranger?" said he to Haley.

"I never thought on 't," said Haley. "I couldn't have said as much, myself; I ha'nt no larning. I took up the trade just to make a living; if 't an't right, I calculated to 'pent on 't in time, *ye* know."

"And now you'll save yerself the trouble, won't ye?" said the tall man. "See what 't is, now, to know scripture. If ye'd only studied yer Bible, like this yer good man, ye might have know'd it before, and saved ye a heap o' trouble. Ye could jist have said, 'Cussed be'—what's his name?—'and 't would all have come right.'" And the stranger, who was no other than the honest drover whom we introduced to our readers in the Kentucky tavern, sat down, and began smoking, with a curious smile on his long, dry face.

A tall, slender young man,[14] with a face expressive of great feeling and intelligence, here broke in, and repeated the words, "'All things whatsoever ye would that men should do unto you, do ye even so unto them.' I suppose," he added, "*that* is scripture, as much as 'Cursed be Canaan.'"

"Wal, it seems quite *as* plain a text, stranger," said John the drover, "to poor fellows like us, now;" and John smoked on like a volcano.

The young man paused, looked as if he was going to say more, when suddenly the boat stopped, and the company made the usual steamboat rush, to see where they were landing.

"Both them ar chaps parsons?" said John to one of the men, as they were going out.

The man nodded.

As the boat stopped, a black woman came running wildly up the plank, darted into the crowd, flew up to where the slave gang sat, and threw her arms round that unfortunate piece of merchandise before enumerated—"John, aged thirty," and with sobs and tears bemoaned him as her husband.[15]

But what needs tell the story, told too oft,—every day told,—of heart-strings rent and broken,—the weak broken and torn for the profit and convenience of the strong! It needs not to be told;—every day is telling it,—telling it, too, in the ear of One who is not deaf, though he be long silent.[16]

The young man who had spoken for the cause of humanity and God before stood with folded arms, looking on this scene. He turned, and Haley was standing at his side. "My friend," he said, speaking with thick utterance, "how can you, how dare you, carry on a trade like this? Look at those poor creatures! Here I am, rejoicing in my heart that I am going home to my wife and child; and the same bell

14 Just by the words "tall, slender" we know that this man will be more good than bad. Stowe adheres to the traditional dictates of Victorian heroic physical attributes: thin is better than fat, tall is better than short, neat is better than slovenly, quiet is better than loud, pale (typically) is better than dark, etc.

15 The black woman is John's wife, of course, but Stowe introduces her only after we have identified her race and watched her wild running, darting, and flying—mimicking the objectification of John as "merchandise." Only her sobs and tears are allowed to speak her claim to John. The scene is meant as emblematic, as Stowe makes clear: "But what needs tell the story, told too oft. . . ."

16 Another transitional moment of lament.

**17** Once again, the problem that tugs at the heartstrings is the separation of man and wife.

**18** I.e., a specific medicine or remedy (*Shorter Oxford*).

**19** Even though slaves often had little choice in the quality or cut of their attire, Stowe always signals personal virtue with the neatness or, in this case, respectability of clothing. Once again, this slave woman is married.

which is a signal to carry me onward towards them will part this poor man and his wife forever. Depend upon it, God will bring you into judgment for this."**17**

The trader turned away in silence.

"I say, now," said the drover, touching his elbow, "there's differences in parsons, an't there? 'Cussed be Canaan' don't seem to go down with this 'un, does it?"

Haley gave an uneasy growl.

"And that ar an't the worse on 't," said John; "mabbe it won't go down with the Lord, neither, when ye come to settle with Him, one o' these days, as all on us must, I reckon."

Haley walked reflectively to the other end of the boat.

"If I make pretty handsomely on one or two next gangs," he thought, "I reckon I'll stop off this yer; it's really getting dangerous." And he took out his pocket-book, and began adding over his accounts,—a process which many gentlemen besides Mr. Haley have found a specific**18** for an uneasy conscience.

The boat swept proudly away from the shore, and all went on merrily, as before. Men talked, and loafed, and read, and smoked. Women sewed, and children played, and the boat passed on her way.

One day, when she lay to for a while at a small town in Kentucky, Haley went up into the place on a little matter of business.

Tom, whose fetters did not prevent his taking a moderate circuit, had drawn near the side of the boat, and stood listlessly gazing over the railings. After a time, he saw the trader returning, with an alert step, in company with a colored woman, bearing in her arms a young child. She was dressed quite respectably,**19** and a colored man followed her, bringing along a small trunk. The woman came cheerfully onward, talking, as she came, with the man who bore her trunk, and so passed up the plank into the boat. The bell rung, the steamer whizzed, the engine groaned and coughed, and away swept the boat down the river.

The woman walked forward among the boxes and bales of the lower deck, and, sitting down, busied herself with chirruping to her baby.

Haley made a turn or two about the boat, and then, coming up, seated himself near her, and began saying something to her in an indifferent undertone.

Tom soon noticed a heavy cloud passing over the woman's brow; and that she answered rapidly, and with great vehemence.

"I don't believe it,—I won't believe it!" he heard her say. "You're jist a foolin with me."

"If you won't believe it, look here!" said the man, drawing out a paper; "this yer's the bill of sale, and there's your master's name to it; and I paid down good solid cash for it, too, I can tell you,—so, now!"

"I don't believe Mas'r would cheat me so; it can't be true!" said the woman, with increasing agitation.

"You can ask any of these men here, that can read writing. Here!" he said, to a man that was passing by, "jist read this yer, won't you! This yer gal won't believe me, when I tell her what 't is."

"Why, it's a bill of sale, signed by John Fosdick," said the man, "making over to you the girl Lucy and her child. It's all straight enough, for aught I see."

The woman's passionate exclamations collected a crowd around her, and the trader briefly explained to them the cause of the agitation.

"He told me that I was going down to Louisville, to hire out as cook to the same tavern where my husband works,—that's what Mas'r told me, his own self; and I can't believe he'd lie to me," said the woman.

"But he has sold you, my poor woman, there's no doubt about it," said a good-natured looking man, who had been examining the papers; "he has done it, and no mistake."

"Then it's no account talking," said the woman, suddenly growing quite calm; and, clasping her child tighter in her arms, she sat down on her box, turned her back round, and gazed listlessly into the river.

"Going to take it easy, after all!" said the trader. "Gal's got grit, I see."

The woman looked calm, as the boat went on; and a beautiful soft summer breeze passed like a compassionate spirit over her head,—the gentle breeze, that never inquires whether the brow is dusky or fair that it fans. And she saw sunshine sparkling on the water, in golden ripples, and heard gay voices, full of ease and pleasure, talking around her everywhere; but her heart lay as if a great stone had fallen on it. Her baby raised himself up against her, and stroked her cheeks with his little hands; and, springing up and down, crowing and chatting, seemed determined to arouse her. She strained him suddenly and tightly in her arms, and slowly one tear after another fell on his wondering, unconscious face; and gradually she seemed, and little by little, to grow calmer, and busied herself with tending and nursing him.

The child, a boy of ten months, was uncommonly large

and strong of his age, and very vigorous in his limbs. Never, for a moment, still, he kept his mother constantly busy in holding him, and guarding his springing activity.

"That's a fine chap!" said a man, suddenly stopping opposite to him, with his hands in his pockets. "How old is he?"

"Ten months and a half," said the mother.

The man whistled to the boy, and offered him part of a stick of candy, which he eagerly grabbed at, and very soon had it in a baby's general depository, to wit, his mouth.

"Rum fellow!" said the man. "Knows what's what!" and he whistled, and walked on. When he had got to the other side of the boat, he came across Haley, who was smoking on top of a pile of boxes.

The stranger produced a match, and lighted a cigar, saying, as he did so,

"Decentish kind o' wench you've got round there, stranger."

"Why, I reckon she *is* tol'able fair," said Haley, blowing the smoke out of his mouth.

"Taking her down south?" said the man.

Haley nodded, and smoked on.

"Plantation hand?" said the man.

"Wal," said Haley, "I'm fillin' out an order for a plantation, and I think I shall put her in. They told me she was a good cook; and they can use her for that, or set her at the cotton-picking. She's got the right fingers for that; I looked at 'em. Sell well, either way;" and Haley resumed his cigar.

"They won't want the young 'un on a plantation," said the man.

"I shall sell him, first chance I find," said Haley, lighting another cigar.

"S'pose you'd be selling him tol'able cheap," said the stranger, mounting the pile of boxes, and sitting down comfortably.

"Don't know 'bout that," said Haley; "he's a pretty smart young 'un,—straight, fat, strong; flesh as hard as a brick!"

"Very true, but then there's all the bother and expense of raisin'."

"Nonsense!" said Haley; "they is raised as easy as any kind of critter there is going; they an't a bit more trouble than pups. This yer chap will be running all round, in a month."

"I've got a good place for raisin', and I thought of takin' in a little more stock," said the man. "One cook lost a young 'un last week,—got drowned in a wash-tub, while she was a hangin' out clothes,—and I reckon it would be well enough to set her to raisin' this yer."

Haley and the stranger smoked a while in silence, neither seeming willing to broach the test question of the interview. At last the man resumed:

"You wouldn't think of wantin' more than ten dollars for that ar chap, seeing you *must* get him off yer hand, any how?"

Haley shook his head, and spit impressively.

"That won't do, no ways," he said, and began his smoking again.

"Well, stranger, what will you take?"

"Well, now," said Haley, "I *could* raise that ar chap myself, or get him raised; he's oncommon likely and healthy, and he'd fetch a hundred dollars, six months hence; and, in a year or two, he'd bring two hundred, if I had him in the right spot;—so I shan't take a cent less nor fifty for him now."

"O, stranger! that's rediculous, altogether," said the man.

"Fact!" said Haley, with a decisive nod of his head.

"I'll give thirty for him," said the stranger, "but not a cent more."

"Now, I'll tell ye what I will do," said Haley, spitting again, with renewed decision. "I'll split the difference, and say forty-five; and that's the most I will do."

"Well, agreed!" said the man, after an interval.

"Done!" said Haley. "Where do you land?"

"At Louisville," said the man.

"Louisville," said Haley. "Very fair, we get there about dusk. Chap will be asleep,—all fair,—get him off quietly, and no screaming,—happens beautiful,—I like to do everything quietly,—I hates all kind of agitation and fluster." And so, after a transfer of certain bills had passed from the man's pocket-book to the trader's, he resumed his cigar.

It was a bright, tranquil evening when the boat stopped at the wharf at Louisville. The woman had been sitting with her baby in her arms, now wrapped in a heavy sleep. When she heard the name of the place called out, she hastily laid the child down in a little cradle formed by the hollow among the boxes, first carefully spreading under it her cloak; and then she sprung to the side of the boat, in hopes that, among the various hotel-waiters who thronged the wharf, she might see her husband. In this hope, she pressed forward to the front rails, and, stretching far over them, strained her eyes intently on the moving heads on the shore, and the crowd pressed in between her and the child.

"Now's your time," said Haley, taking the sleeping child up, and handing him to the stranger. "Don't wake him up, and set him to crying, now; it would make a devil of a fuss with the gal." The man took the bundle carefully, and was soon lost in the crowd that went up the wharf.

When the boat, creaking, and groaning, and puffing, had loosed from the wharf, and was beginning slowly to strain herself along, the woman returned to her old seat. The trader was sitting there,—the child was gone!

"Why, why,—where?" she began, in bewildered surprise.

"Lucy," said the trader, "your child's gone; you may as well know it first as last. You see, I know'd you couldn't take him down south; and I got a chance to sell him to a first-rate family, that'll raise him better than you can."

The trader had arrived at that stage of Christian and political perfection which has been recommended by some preachers and politicians of the north, lately, in which he had completely overcome every humane weakness and prejudice. His heart was exactly where yours, sir, and mine could be brought, with proper effort and cultivation. The wild look of anguish and utter despair that the woman cast on him might have disturbed one less practised; but he was used to it. He had seen that same look hundreds of times. You can get used to such things, too, my friend; and it is the great object of recent efforts to make our whole northern community used to them, for the glory of the Union. So the trader only regarded the mortal anguish which he saw working in those dark features, those clenched hands, and suffocating breathings, as necessary incidents of the trade, and merely calculated whether she was going to scream, and get up a commotion on the boat; for, like other supporters of our peculiar institution, he decidedly disliked agitation.

But the woman did not scream. The shot had passed too straight and direct through the heart, for cry or tear.

Dizzily she sat down. Her slack hands fell lifeless by her side. Her eyes looked straight forward, but she saw nothing. All the noise and hum of the boat, the groaning of the machinery, mingled dreamily to her bewildered ear; and the poor, dumb-stricken heart had neither cry nor tear to show for its utter misery. She was quite calm.

The trader, who, considering his advantages, was almost as humane as some of our politicians, seemed to feel called on to administer such consolation as the case admitted of.

"I know this yer comes kinder hard, at first, Lucy," said he; "but such a smart, sensible gal as you are, won't give way to it. You see it's *necessary,* and can't be helped!"

"O! don't, Mas'r, don't!" said the woman, with a voice like one that is smothering.

"You're a smart wench, Lucy," he persisted; "I mean to do well by ye, and get ye a nice place down river; and you'll soon get another husband,—such a likely gal as you—"

"O! Mas'r, if you *only* won't talk to me now," said the woman, in a voice of such quick and living anguish that the trader felt that there was something at present in the case beyond his style of operation. He got up, and the woman turned away, and buried her head in her cloak.

The trader walked up and down for a time, and occasionally stopped and looked at her.

"Takes it hard, rather," he soliloquized, "but quiet, tho';—let her sweat a while; she'll come right, by and by!"

Tom had watched the whole transaction from first to last, and had a perfect understanding of its results. To him, it looked like something unutterably horrible and cruel, because, poor, ignorant black soul! he had not learned to generalize, and to take enlarged views. If he had only been instructed by certain ministers of Christianity,[20] he might have thought better of it, and seen in it an every-day incident of a lawful trade; a trade which is the vital support of an institution which some American divines tell us has no evils but such as are inseparable from any other relations in social and domestic life. But Tom, as we see, being a poor, ignorant fellow, whose reading had been confined entirely to the New Testament, could not comfort and solace himself with views like these. His very soul bled within him for what seemed to him the *wrongs* of the poor suffering thing that lay like a crushed reed on the boxes; the feeling, living, bleeding, yet immortal *thing,* which American state law coolly classes with the bundles, and bales, and boxes, among which she is lying.

Tom drew near, and tried to say something; but she only groaned. Honestly, and with tears running down his own cheeks, he spoke of a heart of love in the skies, of a pitying Jesus, and an eternal home; but the ear was deaf with anguish, and the palsied heart could not feel.

Night came on,—night calm, unmoved, and glorious, shining down with her innumerable and solemn angel

20 Dr. Joel Parker of Philadelphia [Stowe's note]. Well-known Presbyterian clergyman (1799–1873) and a friend of the Beecher family. Mrs. Stowe tried to have this note removed from the stereotype-plate of the first edition after Parker sued her, but she failed.

eyes, twinkling, beautiful, but silent. There was no speech nor language, no pitying voice nor helping hand, from that distant sky. One after another, the voices of business or pleasure died away; all on the boat were sleeping, and the ripples at the prow were plainly heard. Tom stretched himself out on a box, and there, as he lay, he heard, ever and anon, a smothered sob or cry from the prostrate creature,—"O! what shall I do? O Lord! O good Lord, do help me!" and so, ever and anon, until the murmur died away in silence.

At midnight, Tom waked, with a sudden start. Something black passed quickly by him to the side of the boat, and he heard a splash in the water. No one else saw or heard anything. He raised his head,—the woman's place was vacant! He got up, and sought about him in vain. The poor bleeding heart was still, at last, and the river rippled and dimpled just as brightly as if it had not closed above it.

Patience! patience! ye whose hearts swell indignant at wrongs like these. Not one throb of anguish, not one tear of the oppressed, is forgotten by the Man of Sorrows, the Lord of Glory. In his patient, generous bosom he bears the anguish of a world. Bear thou, like him, in patience, and labor in love; for sure as he is God, "the year of his redeemed *shall* come."

The trader waked up bright and early, and came out to see to his live stock. It was now his turn to look about in perplexity.

"Where alive is that gal?" he said to Tom.

Tom, who had learned the wisdom of keeping counsel, did not feel called on to state his observations and suspicions, but said he did not know.

"She surely couldn't have got off in the night at any of the landings, for I was awake, and on the look-out, whenever the boat stopped. I never trust these yer things to other folks."

This speech was addressed to Tom quite confidentially, as if it was something that would be specially interesting to him. Tom made no answer.

The trader searched the boat from stem to stern, among boxes, bales and barrels, around the machinery, by the chimneys, in vain.

"Now, I say, Tom, be fair about this yer," he said, when, after a fruitless search, he came where Tom was standing. "You know something about it, now. Don't tell me,—I know you do. I saw the gal stretched out here about ten o'clock, and ag'in at twelve, and ag'in between one and two; and then at four she was gone, and you was sleeping

"The Poor Bleeding Heart." Wood engraving by T. Williams, "after George Cruikshank." Her heart grieving after Haley sells her ten-month-old child, this mother throws herself in the water to drown. The engraver emphasizes the slave's sensuality.   From *Uncle Tom's Cabin*, John Cassell, London, 1852

right there all the time. Now, you know something,—you can't help it."

"Well, Mas'r," said Tom, "towards morning something brushed by me, and I kinder half woke; and then I hearn a great splash, and then I clare woke up, and the gal was gone. That's all I know on 't."

The trader was not shocked nor amazed; because, as we said before, he was used to a great many things that you are not used to. Even the awful presence of Death struck no solemn chill upon him. He had seen Death many times,—met him in the way of trade, and got acquainted with him,—and he only thought of him as a hard customer, that embarrassed his property operations very unfairly; and so he only swore that the gal was a baggage, and that he was devilish unlucky, and that, if things went on in this way, he should not make a cent on the trip. In short, he seemed to consider himself an ill-used man, decidedly; but there was no help for it, as the woman had escaped into a state which *never will* give up a fugitive,— not even at the demand of the whole glorious Union. The trader, therefore, sat discontentedly down, with his little account-book, and put down the missing body and soul under the head of *losses*!

"He's a shocking creature, isn't he,—this trader? so unfeeling! It's dreadful, really!"[21]

"O, but nobody thinks anything of these traders! They are universally despised,—never received into any decent society."

But who, sir, makes the trader? Who is most to blame? The enlightened, cultivated, intelligent man, who supports the system of which the trader is the inevitable result, or the poor trader himself? You make the public sentiment that calls for his trade, that debauches and depraves him, till he feels no shame in it; and in what are you better than he?

Are you educated and he ignorant, you high and he low, you refined and he coarse, you talented and he simple?

In the day of a future Judgment, these very considerations may make it more tolerable for him than for you.

In concluding these little incidents of lawful trade, we must beg the world not to think that American legislators are entirely destitute of humanity, as might, perhaps, be unfairly inferred from the great efforts made in our national body to protect and perpetuate this species of traffic.

Who does not know how our great men are outdoing themselves, in declaiming against the *foreign* slave-trade.

21 Stowe finds it unnecessary to populate these two views with characters. They serve only as a bridge to her subsequent direct address to readers.

**22** Thomas Clarkson (1760–1846) and William Wilberforce (1759–1833), English philanthropists and antislavery agitators who worked to pass the Emancipation Bill in Parliament in 1833. Clarkson and Wilberforce were beacons to the American Abolitionist movement.

There are a perfect host of Clarksons and Wilberforces[22] risen up among us on that subject, most edifying to hear and behold. Trading negroes from Africa, dear reader, is so horrid! It is not to be thought of! But trading them from Kentucky,—that's quite another thing!

# CHAPTER 13

## *The Quaker Settlement*[1]

Aquiet scene now rises before us. A large, roomy, neatly-painted kitchen, its yellow floor glossy and smooth, and without a particle of dust; a neat, well-blacked cooking-stove; rows of shining tin, suggestive of unmentionable good things to the appetite; glossy green wood chairs, old and firm; a small flag-bottomed rocking-chair, with a patch-work cushion in it, neatly contrived out of small pieces of different colored woollen goods, and a larger sized one, motherly and old, whose wide arms breathed hospitable invitation, seconded by the solicitation of its feather cushions,—a real comfortable, persuasive old chair, and worth, in the way of honest, homely enjoyment, a dozen of your plush or brochetelle drawing-room gentry; and in the chair, gently swaying back and forward, her eyes bent on some fine sewing, sat our old friend Eliza. Yes, there she is, paler[2] and thinner than in her Kentucky home, with a world of quiet sorrow lying under the shadow of her long eyelashes, and marking the outline of her gentle mouth! It was plain to see how old and firm the girlish heart was grown under the discipline of heavy sorrow; and when, anon, her large dark eye was raised to follow the gambols of her little Harry, who was sporting, like some tropical butterfly, hither and thither over the floor, she showed a depth of firmness and steady resolve that was never there in her earlier and happier days.

By her side sat a woman with a bright tin pan in her lap, into which she was carefully sorting some dried peaches.

1 The Quakers, or Society of Friends, were among the first religious groups to actively protest the institution of slavery in America. Quakers believe in an Inner Light shared by all persons, regardless of race or sex. Prominent Quaker abolitionists included Lucretia Mott, the poet John Greenleaf Whittier, and Thomas Garret of Delaware (Stowe's model for Simeon Halliday).

2 A "pale" Victorian heroine.

**3** Clearly Stowe is pandering to her older female readership here.

**4** Stowe's inclusion of adjectives such as "white" and "rosy" seems designed to separate Rachel, and on the next page Ruth, from Eliza even in the midst of this lovely, cozy domestic scene.

She might be fifty-five or sixty; but hers was one of those faces that time seems to touch only to brighten and adorn.[3] The snowy lisse crape cap, made after the strait Quaker pattern,—the plain white muslin handkerchief, lying in placid folds across her bosom,—the drab shawl and dress,—showed at once the community to which she belonged. Her face was round and rosy, with a healthful downy softness, suggestive of a ripe peach. Her hair, partially silvered by age, was parted smoothly back from a high placid forehead, on which time had written no inscription, except peace on earth, good will to men, and beneath shone a large pair of clear, honest, loving brown eyes; you only needed to look straight into them, to feel that you saw to the bottom of a heart as good and true as ever throbbed in woman's bosom.[4] So much has been said and sung of beautiful young girls, why don't somebody wake up to the beauty of old women? If any want to get up an inspiration under this head, we refer them to our good friend Rachel Halliday, just as she sits there in her little rocking-chair. It had a turn for quacking and squeaking,—that chair had,—either from having taken cold in early life, or from some asthmatic affection, or perhaps from nervous derangement; but, as she gently swung backward and forward, the chair kept up a kind of subdued "creechy crawchy," that would have been intolerable in any other chair. But old Simeon Halliday often declared it was as good as any music to him, and the children all avowed that they wouldn't miss of hearing mother's chair for anything in the world. For why? for twenty years or more, nothing but loving words and gentle moralities, and motherly loving kindness, had come from that chair;—head-aches and heart-aches innumerable had been cured there,—difficulties spiritual and temporal solved there,—all by one good, loving woman, God bless her!

"And so thee still thinks of going to Canada, Eliza?" she said, as she was quietly looking over her peaches.

"Yes, ma'am," said Eliza, firmly. "I must go onward. I dare not stop."

"And what'll thee do, when thee gets there? Thee must think about that, my daughter."

"My daughter" came naturally from the lips of Rachel Halliday; for hers was just the face and form that made "mother" seem the most natural word in the world.

Eliza's hands trembled, and some tears fell on her fine work; but she answered, firmly,

"I shall do—anything I can find. I hope I can find something."

"Emeline [*sic*] Sold."
Color lithograph by
Louisa Corbaux,
1852.
© British Museum

"Eva and Topsy. "
Color lithograph by
Louisa Corbaux, 1852.
© British Museum

"Topsy at Her Tricks." Color lithograph by Louisa Corbaux, 1852.
© British Museum

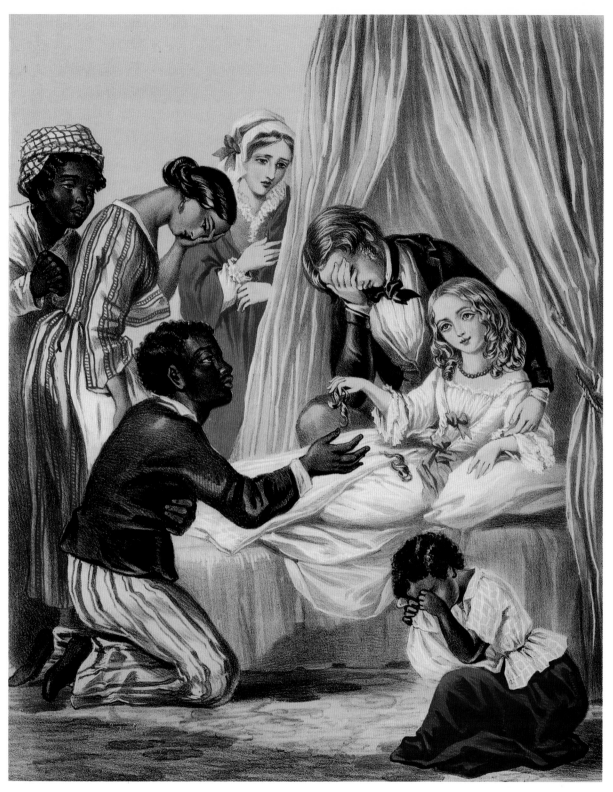

"Eva's Farewell." Color lithograph by Louisa Corbaux, 1852.
© British Museum

Tom walking into the sunset with Eva in his arms. From Classics Illustrated Classic Comic Book no. 15, *Uncle Tom's Cabin,* 1943. © First Classics Inc. All rights reserved. By permission of Jack Lake Productions Inc.

Al W. Martin's mammoth production of *Uncle Tom's Cabin.*
Cincinnati, U.S. Printing Co., circa 1898. Courtesy of the Library of Congress

Simon Legree. From Classics Illustrated Classic Comic Book no. 15,
*Uncle Tom's Cabin,* 1943.

Cassy tending Tom. From Classics
Illustrated Classic Comic Book no. 15,
*Uncle Tom's Cabin*, 1943.
© First Classics Inc. All rights reserved.
By permission of Jack Lake Productions Inc.

Tom as a superhero. From Classics
Illustrated Classic Comic Book no. 15,
*Uncle Tom's Cabin*.
© First Classics Inc. All rights reserved.
By permission of Jack Lake Productions Inc.

Marie St. Clare. From Classics
Illustrated Classic Comic Book
no. 15, *Uncle Tom's Cabin*, 1943.
© First Classics Inc. All rights reserved. By
permission of Jack Lake Productions Inc.

"Condoleezza Rice Crossing the Ice."
© Elliott Banfield, *New York Sun*, January 21, 2005

Poster: "*Uncle Tom's Cabin.* On the Levee."
Courier Lithograph Co., 1899

"Thee knows thee can stay here, as long as thee pleases," said Rachel.

"O, thank you," said Eliza, "but"—she pointed to Harry—"I can't sleep nights; I can't rest. Last night I dreamed I saw that man coming into the yard," she said, shuddering.

"Poor child!" said Rachel, wiping her eyes; "but thee mustn't feel so. The Lord hath ordered it so that never hath a fugitive been stolen from our village. I trust thine will not be the first."

The door here opened, and a little short, round, pincushiony woman stood at the door, with a cheery, blooming face, like a ripe apple. She was dressed, like Rachel, in sober gray, with the muslin folded neatly across her round, plump little chest.

"Ruth Stedman," said Rachel, coming joyfully forward; "how is thee, Ruth?" she said, heartily taking both her hands.

"Nicely," said Ruth, taking off her little drab bonnet, and dusting it with her handkerchief, displaying, as she did so, a round little head, on which the Quaker cap sat with a sort of jaunty air, despite all the stroking and patting of the small fat hands, which were busily applied to arranging it. Certain stray locks of decidedly curly hair, too, had escaped here and there, and had to be coaxed and cajoled into their place again; and then the new comer, who might have been five-and-twenty, turned from the small looking-glass, before which she had been making these arrangements, and looked well pleased,—as most people who looked at her might have been,—for she was decidedly a wholesome, whole-hearted, chirruping little woman, as ever gladdened man's heart withal.

"Ruth, this friend is Eliza Harris; and this is the little boy I told thee of."

"I am glad to see thee, Eliza,—very," said Ruth, shaking hands, as if Eliza were an old friend she had long been expecting; "and this is thy dear boy,—I brought a cake for him," she said, holding out a little heart to the boy, who came up, gazing through his curls, and accepted it shyly.

"Where's thy baby, Ruth?" said Rachel.

"O, he's coming; but thy Mary caught him as I came in, and ran off with him to the barn, to show him to the children."

At this moment, the door opened, and Mary, an honest, rosy-looking girl, with large brown eyes, like her mother's, came in with the baby.[5]

"Ah! ha!" said Rachel, coming up, and taking the great,

5 This whole scene is a bit of a fantasy.

white, fat fellow in her arms; "how good he looks, and how he does grow!"

"To be sure, he does," said little bustling Ruth as she took the child, and began taking off a little blue silk hood, and various layers and wrappers of outer garments; and having given a twitch here, and a pull there, and variously adjusted and arranged him, and kissed him heartily, she set him on the floor to collect his thoughts. Baby seemed quite used to this mode of proceeding, for he put his thumb in his mouth (as if it were quite a thing of course), and seemed soon absorbed in his own reflections, while the mother seated herself, and taking out a long stocking of mixed blue and white yarn, began to knit with briskness.

"Mary, thee'd better fill the kettle, hadn't thee?" gently suggested the mother.

Mary took the kettle to the well, and soon reappearing, placed it over the stove, where it was soon purring and steaming, a sort of censer of hospitality and good cheer. The peaches, moreover, in obedience to a few gentle whispers from Rachel, were soon deposited, by the same hand, in a stew-pan over the fire.

Rachel now took down a snowy moulding-board, and, tying on an apron, proceeded quietly to making up some biscuits, first saying to Mary,—"Mary, hadn't thee better tell John to get a chicken ready?" and Mary disappeared accordingly.

"And how is Abigail Peters?" said Rachel, as she went on with her biscuits.

"O, she's better," said Ruth; "I was in, this morning; made the bed, tidied up the house. Leah Hills went in, this afternoon, and baked bread and pies enough to last some days and I engaged to go back to get her up, this evening."

"I will go in to-morrow, and do any cleaning there may be, and look over the mending," said Rachel. "Ah! that is well," said Ruth. "I've heard," she added, "that Hannah Stanwood is sick. John was up there, last night,—I must go there to-morrow."

"John can come in here to his meals, if thee needs to stay all day," suggested Rachel.

"Thank thee, Rachel; will see, to-morrow; but, here comes Simeon."

Simeon Halliday, a tall, straight, muscular man, in drab coat and pantaloons, and broad-brimmed hat, now entered.

"How is thee, Ruth?" he said, warmly, as he spread his broad open hand for her little fat palm; "and how is John?"

"O! John is well, and all the rest of our folks," said Ruth, cheerily.

"Any news, father?" said Rachel, as she was putting her biscuits into the oven.

"Peter Stebbins told me that they should be along to-night, with *friends*," said Simeon, significantly, as he was washing his hands at a neat sink, in a little back porch.

"Indeed!" said Rachel, looking thoughtfully, and glancing at Eliza.

"Did thee say thy name was Harris?" said Simeon to Eliza, as he reentered.

Rachel glanced quickly at her husband, as Eliza tremulously answered "yes;" her fears, ever uppermost, suggesting that possibly there might be advertisements out for her.

"Mother!" said Simeon, standing in the porch, and calling Rachel out.

"What does thee want, father?" said Rachel, rubbing her floury hands, as she went into the porch.

"This child's husband is in the settlement, and will be here to-night," said Simeon.

"Now, thee doesn't say that, father?" said Rachel, all her face radiant with joy.

"It's really true. Peter was down yesterday, with the wagon, to the other stand, and there he found an old woman and two men; and one said his name was George Harris; and, from what he told of his history, I am certain who he is. He is a bright, likely fellow, too."

"Shall we tell her now?" said Simeon.

"Let's tell Ruth," said Rachel. "Here, Ruth,—come here."

Ruth laid down her knitting-work, and was in the back porch in a moment.

"Ruth, what does thee think?" said Rachel. "Father says Eliza's husband is in the last company, and will be here to-night."

A burst of joy from the little Quakeress interrupted the speech. She gave such a bound from the floor, as she clapped her little hands, that two stray curls fell from under her Quaker cap, and lay brightly on her white neckerchief.

"Hush thee, dear!" said Rachel, gently; "hush, Ruth! Tell us, shall we tell her now?"

"Now! to be sure,—this very minute. Why, now, suppose 'twas my John, how should I feel? Do tell her, right off."

"Thee uses thyself only to learn how to love thy neighbor, Ruth," said Simeon, looking, with a beaming face, on Ruth.

6 "To-night!" Eliza repeated, "to-night!" Stowe's description of George and Eliza's marital passion stands in stark contrast to Tom and Chloe's.

7 In the Quaker house, it takes several people to do the work that Aunt Chloe was shown doing single-handedly in the Shelby household.

"To be sure. Isn't it what we are made for? If I didn't love John and the baby, I should not know how to feel for her. Come, now, do tell her,—do!" and she laid her hands persuasively on Rachel's arm. "Take her into thy bed-room, there, and let me fry the chicken while thee does it."

Rachel came out into the kitchen, where Eliza was sewing, and opening the door of a small bed-room, said, gently, "Come in here with me, my daughter; I have news to tell thee."

The blood flushed in Eliza's pale face; she rose, trembling with nervous anxiety, and looked towards her boy.

"No, no," said little Ruth, darting up, and seizing her hands. "Never thee fear; it's good news, Eliza,—go in, go in!" And she gently pushed her to the door, which closed after her; and then, turning round, she caught little Harry in her arms, and began kissing him.

"Thee'll see thy father, little one. Does thee know it? Thy father is coming," she said, over and over again, as the boy looked wonderingly at her.

Meanwhile, within the door, another scene was going on. Rachel Halliday drew Eliza toward her, and said, "The Lord hath had mercy on thee, daughter; thy husband hath escaped from the house of bondage."

The blood flushed to Eliza's cheek in a sudden glow, and went back to her heart with as sudden a rush. She sat down, pale and faint.

"Have courage, child," said Rachel, laying her hand on her head. "He is among friends, who will bring him here to-night."

"To-night!" Eliza repeated, "to-night!" The words lost all meaning to her; her head was dreamy and confused; all was mist for a moment.[6]

When she awoke, she found herself snugly tucked up on the bed, with a blanket over her, and little Ruth rubbing her hands with camphor. She opened her eyes in a state of dreamy, delicious languor, such as one has who has long been bearing a heavy load, and now feels it gone, and would rest. The tension of the nerves, which had never ceased a moment since the first hour of her flight, had given way, and a strange feeling of security and rest came over her; and, as she lay, with her large, dark eyes open, she followed, as in a quiet dream, the motions of those about her.[7] She saw the door open into the other room; saw the supper-table, with its snowy cloth; heard the dreamy murmur of the singing tea-kettle, saw Ruth tripping backward and forward, with plates of cake and saucers of preserves, and ever and anon stopping to put a cake into Harry's hand, or pat his head, or twine his long curls round her snowy fingers. She saw the ample, motherly form of Rachel, as she ever and anon came to the bedside, and smoothed and arranged something about the bed-clothes, and gave a tuck here and there, by way of expressing her good-will; and was conscious of a kind of sunshine beaming down upon her from her large, clear, brown eyes. She saw Ruth's husband come in,—saw her fly up to him, and commence whispering very earnestly, ever and anon, with impressive gesture, pointing her little finger toward the room. She saw her, with the baby in her arms, sitting down to tea; she saw them all at table, and little Harry in a high chair, under the shadow of Rachel's ample wing; there were low murmurs of talk, gentle tinkling of tea-spoons, and musical clatter of cups and saucers, and all mingled in a delightful dream of rest; and Eliza slept, as she had not slept before, since the fearful midnight hour when she had taken her child and fled through the frosty star-light.

She dreamed of a beautiful country,—a land, it seemed to her, of rest,—green shores, pleasant islands, and beautifully glittering water; and there, in a house which kind voices told her was a home, she saw her boy playing, a free and happy child. She heard her husband's footsteps; she felt him coming nearer; his arms were around her, his tears falling on her face, and she awoke! It was no dream. The daylight had long faded; her child lay calmly sleeping by her side; a candle was burning dimly on the stand, and her husband was sobbing by her pillow.

The next morning was a cheerful one at the Quaker house. "Mother" was up betimes, and surrounded by busy girls and boys, whom we had scarce time to introduce to our readers yesterday, and who all moved obediently to Rachel's gentle "Thee had better," or more gentle "Hadn't thee better?" in the work of getting breakfast; for a breakfast in the luxurious valleys of Indiana is a thing complicated and multiform, and, like picking up the rose-leaves and trimming the bushes in Paradise, asking other hands than those of the original mother. While, therefore, John ran to the spring for fresh water, and Simeon the second sifted meal for corn-cakes, and Mary ground coffee, Rachel moved gently and quietly about, making biscuits, cutting up chicken, and diffusing a sort of sunny radiance over the whole proceeding generally. If there was any danger of friction or collision from the ill-regulated zeal of so

8 Venus, the Roman goddess of love, was also known in the Greek tradition as Aphrodite. The cestus (girdle) of Aphrodite plays a crucial role in Western civilization. In the beauty contest among the goddesses to be judged by Paris, Aphrodite unclasped her girdle (belt), opened her tunic, and promised Paris the most beautiful woman on earth should he choose Aphrodite as the winner. Aphrodite won; Paris got Helen of Troy, and thus began the Trojan War (*New Larousse Encyclopedia of Mythology*). Aphrodite's cestus is, above all, a symbol of female power; thus, Rachel's cestus is a symbol of female dominion, but translated into the power of nineteenth-century American women. That Rachel is a Quaker is crucial; Quakers allowed women to speak publicly at a time they were denied both pulpit and podium.

many young operators, her gentle "Come! come!" or "I wouldn't, now," was quite sufficient to allay the difficulty. Bards have written of the cestus of Venus,[8] that turned the heads of all the world in successive generations. We had rather, for our part, have the cestus of Rachel Halliday, that kept heads from being turned, and made everything go on harmoniously. We think it is more suited to our modern days, decidedly.

While all other preparations were going on, Simeon the elder stood in his shirt-sleeves before a little looking-glass in the corner, engaged in the anti-patriarchal operation of shaving. Everything went on so sociably, so quietly, so harmoniously, in the great kitchen,—it seemed so pleasant to every one to do just what they were doing, there was such an atmosphere of mutual confidence and good fellowship everywhere,—even the knives and forks had a social clatter as they went on to the table; and the chicken and ham had a cheerful and joyous fizzle in the pan, as if they rather enjoyed being cooked than otherwise;—and when George and Eliza and little Harry came out, they met such a hearty, rejoicing welcome, no wonder it seemed to them like a dream.

At last, they were all seated at breakfast, while Mary stood at the stove, baking griddle-cakes, which, as they gained the true exact golden-brown tint of perfection, were transferred quite handily to the table.

Rachel never looked so truly and benignly happy as at the head of her table. There was so much motherliness and full-heartedness even in the way she passed a plate of cakes or poured a cup of coffee, that it seemed to put a spirit into the food and drink she offered.

It was the first time that ever George had sat down on equal terms at any white man's table; and he sat down, at first, with some constraint and awkwardness; but they all exhaled and went off like fog, in the genial morning rays of this simple, overflowing kindness.

This, indeed, was a home,—*home*,—a word that George had never yet known a meaning for; and a belief in God, and trust in his providence, began to encircle his heart, as, with a golden cloud of protection and confidence, dark, misanthropic, pining, atheistic doubts, and fierce despair, melted away before the light of a living Gospel, breathed in living faces, preached by a thousand unconscious acts of love and good will, which, like the cup of cold water given in the name of a disciple, shall never lose their reward.

"Father, what if thee should get found out again?" said Simeon second, as he buttered his cake.

"I should pay my fine," said Simeon, quietly.

"But what if they put thee in prison?"

"Couldn't thee and mother manage the farm?" said Simeon, smiling.

"Mother can do almost everything," said the boy. "But isn't it a shame to make such laws?"

"Thee mustn't speak evil of thy rulers, Simeon," said his father, gravely. "The Lord only gives us our worldly goods that we may do justice and mercy; if our rulers require a price of us for it, we must deliver it up."

"Well, I hate those old slaveholders!" said the boy, who felt as unchristian as became any modern reformer.

"I am surprised at thee, son," said Simeon; "thy mother never taught thee so. I would do even the same for the slaveholder as for the slave, if the Lord brought him to my door in affliction."

Simeon second blushed scarlet; but his mother only smiled, and said, "Simeon is my good boy; he will grow older, by and by, and then he will be like his father."

"I hope, my good sir, that you are not exposed to any difficulty on our account," said George, anxiously.[9]

"Fear nothing, George, for therefore are we sent into the world. If we would not meet trouble for a good cause, we were not worthy of our name."

"But, for *me*," said George, "I could not bear it."

"Fear not, then, friend George; it is not for thee, but for God and man, we do it," said Simeon. "And now thou must lie by quietly this day, and to-night, at ten o'clock, Phineas Fletcher will carry thee onward to the next stand,—thee and the rest of thy company. The pursuers are hard after thee; we must not delay."

"If that is the case, why wait till evening?" said George.

"Thou art safe here by daylight, for every one in the settlement is a Friend, and all are watching. It has been found safer to travel by night."

9 George's "my good sir" matches the attention to language of the Quakers' "thee" and "thou." The conversation between Simeon and his son reminds George (and Stowe's readers) that Quakers practice civil disobedience, paying whatever "price" necessary, whether fines or imprisonment. (The weighing of the competing needs of conscience and law would inform the Civil Rights movement of the 1960s.)

## CHAPTER 14

### *Evangeline*[1]

1 "Evangeline" has the same root and meaning as "evangelist": one who brings redemption (*Shorter Oxford*). It contains as well the word "angel." Both of these meanings are evoked by Stowe's little angel, Eva St. Clare (pronounced "Sinclair").

2 In *The Nachez: An Indian Tale* (1827) by François-René, Vicomte de Chateaubriand (1768–1848).

*"A young star! which shone
O'er life—too sweet an image for such glass!
A lovely being, scarcely formed or moulded;
A rose with all its sweetest leaves yet folded."*

The Mississippi! How, as by an enchanted wand, have its scenes been changed, since Chateaubriand wrote his prose-poetic description of it, as a river of mighty, unbroken solitudes, rolling amid undreamed wonders of vegetable and animal existence.[2]

But, as in an hour, this river of dreams and wild romance has emerged to a reality scarcely less visionary and splendid. What other river of the world bears on its bosom to the ocean the wealth and enterprise of such another country?—a country whose products embrace all between the tropics and the poles! Those turbid waters, hurrying, foaming, tearing along, an apt resemblance of that headlong tide of business which is poured along its wave by a race more vehement and energetic than any the old world ever saw. Ah! would that they did not also bear along a more fearful freight,—the tears of the oppressed, the sighs of the helpless, the bitter prayers of poor, ignorant hearts to an unknown God—unknown, unseen and silent, but who will yet "come out of his place to save all the poor of the earth!"

The slanting light of the setting sun quivers on the sea-like expanse of the river; the shivery canes, and the tall, dark cypress, hung with wreaths of dark, funereal moss, glow in the golden ray, as the heavily-laden steamboat marches onward.

Piled with cotton-bales, from many a plantation, up over deck and sides, till she seems in the distance a square, massive block of gray, she moves heavily onward to the nearing mart. We must look some time among its crowded decks before we shall find again our humble friend Tom. High on the upper deck, in a little nook among the everywhere predominant cotton-bales, at last we may find him.

Partly from confidence inspired by Mr. Shelby's representations, and partly from the remarkably inoffensive and quiet character of the man, Tom had insensibly won his way far into the confidence even of such a man as Haley.

At first he had watched him narrowly through the day, and never allowed him to sleep at night unfettered; but the uncomplaining patience and apparent contentment of Tom's manner led him gradually to discontinue these restraints, and for some time Tom had enjoyed a sort of parole of honor, being permitted to come and go freely where he pleased on the boat.

Ever quiet and obliging, and more than ready to lend a hand in every emergency which occurred among the workmen below, he had won the good opinion of all the hands, and spent many hours in helping them with as hearty a good will as ever he worked on a Kentucky farm.

When there seemed to be nothing for him to do, he would climb to a nook among the cotton-bales of the upper deck, and busy himself in studying over his Bible,—and it is there we see him now.

For a hundred or more miles above New Orleans, the river is higher than the surrounding country, and rolls its tremendous volume between massive levees twenty feet in height. The traveller from the deck of the steamer, as from some floating castle top, overlooks the whole country for miles and miles around. Tom, therefore, had spread out full before him, in plantation after plantation, a map of the life to which he was approaching.

He saw the distant slaves at their toil; he saw afar their villages of huts gleaming out in long rows on many a plantation, distant from the stately mansions and pleasure-grounds of the master;—and as the moving picture passed on, his poor, foolish heart would be turning backward to the Kentucky farm, with its old shadowy beeches,—to the

3 The memory, like the Shelby home itself, is bankrupt.

4 This passing reference to Chloe refers only to her passion for cooking.

5 Marcus Tullius Cicero (106–43 B.C.), Roman politician, renowned orator, and writer. Cicero predated Christ and thus the Christian promise of an afterlife with God in heaven.

master's house, with its wide, cool halls, and, near by, the little cabin, overgrown with the multiflora and bignonia.[3] There he seemed to see familiar faces of comrades, who had grown up with him from infancy; he saw his busy wife, bustling in her preparations for his evening meals;[4] he heard the merry laugh of his boys at their play, and the chirrup of the baby at his knee; and then, with a start, all faded, and he saw again the cane-brakes and cypresses and gliding plantations, and heard again the creaking and groaning of the machinery, all telling him too plainly that all that phase of life had gone by forever.

In such a case, you write to your wife, and send messages to your children; but Tom could not write,—the mail for him had no existence, and the gulf of separation was unbridged by even a friendly word or signal.

Is it strange, then, that some tears fall on the pages of his Bible, as he lays it on the cotton-bale, and, with patient finger, threading his slow way from word to word, traces out its promises? Having learned late in life, Tom was but a slow reader, and passed on laboriously from verse to verse. Fortunate for him was it that the book he was intent on was one which slow reading cannot injure,—nay, one whose words, like ingots of gold, seem often to need to be weighed separately, that the mind may take in their priceless value. Let us follow him a moment, as, pointing to each word, and pronouncing each half aloud, he reads,

"Let—not—your—heart—be—troubled. In—my Father's —house—are—many—mansions. I—go—to—prepare— a—place—for—you."

Cicero,[5] when he buried his darling and only daughter, had a heart as full of honest grief as poor Tom's,—perhaps no fuller, for both were only men;—but Cicero could pause over no such sublime words of hope, and look to no such future reunion; and if he *had* seen them, ten to one he would not have believed,—he must fill his head first with a thousand questions of authenticity of manuscript, and correctness of translation. But, to poor Tom, there it lay, just what he needed, so evidently true and divine that the possibility of a question never entered his simple head. It must be true; for, if not true, how could he live?

As for Tom's Bible, though it had no annotations and helps in margin from learned commentators, still it had been embellished with certain way-marks and guide-boards of Tom's own invention, and which helped him more than the most learned expositions could have done. It had been his custom to get the Bible read to him by his master's children, in particular by young Master George; and, as they read, he would designate, by bold, strong marks and dashes, with pen and ink, the passages which more particularly gratified his ear or affected his heart. His Bible was thus marked through, from one end to the other, with a variety of styles and designations; so he could in a moment seize upon his favorite passages, without the labor of spelling out what lay between them;—and while it lay there before him, every passage breathing of some old home scene, and recalling some past enjoyment, his Bible seemed to him all of this life that remained, as well as the promise of a future one.

Among the passengers on the boat was a young gentleman of fortune and family, resident in New Orleans, who bore the name of St. Clare. He had with him a daughter between five and six years of age, together with a lady who seemed to claim relationship to both, and to have the little one especially under her charge.

Tom had often caught glimpses of this little girl,—for she was one of those busy, tripping creatures, that can be no more contained in one place than a sunbeam or a summer breeze,—nor was she one that, once seen, could be easily forgotten.

Her form was the perfection of childish beauty, without its usual chubbiness and squareness of outline. There was about it an undulating and aerial grace, such as one might dream of for some mythic and allegorical being. Her face was remarkable less for its perfect beauty of feature than for a singular and dreamy earnestness of expression, which made the ideal start when they looked at her, and by which the dullest and most literal were impressed, without exactly knowing why. The shape of her head and the turn of her neck and bust was peculiarly noble, and the long golden-brown hair that floated like a cloud around it, the deep spiritual gravity of her violet blue eyes, shaded by heavy fringes of golden brown,—all marked her out from other children, and made every one turn and look after her, as she glided hither and thither on the boat. Nevertheless, the little one was not what you would have called either a grave child or a sad one. On the contrary, an airy and innocent playfulness seemed to flicker like the shadow of summer leaves over her childish face, and around her buoyant figure. She was always in motion, always with a half smile on her rosy mouth, flying hither and thither, with an undulating and cloud-like tread, singing to herself as she moved as in a happy dream. Her father and female guardian were incessantly

"First Meeting of Uncle Tom and Eva." Lithograph by Thomas W. Strong. With his flowing garb and pedagogical demeanor, Tom seems more like a Greek philosopher than a slave being taught to read. We almost don't notice his chains and bare feet. Note the three Stoics in the background. Eva is described as having "long golden-brown hair" and "violet blue eyes." This noble combination of purple and gold will recur in the sky at the climax of Tom's life.

busy in pursuit of her,—but, when caught, she melted from them again like a summer cloud; and as no word of chiding or reproof ever fell on her ear for whatever she chose to do, she pursued her own way all over the boat. Always dressed in white, she seemed to move like a shadow through all sorts of places, without contracting spot or stain; and there was not a corner or nook, above or below, where those fairy footsteps had not glided, and that visionary golden head, with its deep blue eyes, fleeted along.

The fireman, as he looked up from his sweaty toil, sometimes found those eyes looking wonderingly into the raging depths of the furnace, and fearfully and pityingly at him, as if she thought him in some dreadful danger. Anon the steersman at the wheel paused and smiled, as the picture-like head gleamed through the window of the round house, and in a moment was gone again. A thousand times a day rough voices blessed her, and smiles of unwonted softness stole over hard faces, as she passed; and when she tripped fearlessly over dangerous places, rough, sooty hands were stretched involuntarily out to save her, and smooth her path.

Tom, who had the soft, impressible nature of his kindly race, ever yearning toward the simple and childlike, watched the little creature with daily increasing interest. To him she seemed something almost divine; and whenever her golden head and deep blue eyes peered out upon him from behind some dusky cotton-bale, or looked down upon him over some ridge of packages, he half believed that he saw one of the angels stepped out of his New Testament.

Often and often she walked mournfully round the place where Haley's gang of men and women sat in their chains. She would glide in among them, and look at them with an air of perplexed and sorrowful earnestness; and sometimes she would lift their chains with her slender hands, and then sigh woefully, as she glided away. Several times she appeared suddenly among them, with her hands full of candy, nuts, and oranges, which she would distribute joyfully to them, and then be gone again.

Tom watched the little lady a great deal, before he ventured on any overtures towards acquaintanceship. He knew an abundance of simple acts to propitiate and invite the approaches of the little people, and he resolved to play his part right skillfully. He could cut cunning little baskets out of cherry-stones, could make grotesque faces on hickory-nuts, or odd-jumping figures out of elder-pith, and he was a very Pan in the manufacture of whistles of all sizes and sorts. His pockets were full of miscellaneous articles of attraction, which he had hoarded in days of old for his master's children, and which he now produced, with commendable prudence and economy, one by one, as overtures for acquaintance and friendship.

The little one was shy, for all her busy interest in everything going on, and it was not easy to tame her. For a while, she would perch like a canary-bird on some box or package near Tom, while busy in the little arts aforenamed, and take from him, with a kind of grave bashfulness, the little articles he offered. But at last they got on quite confidential terms.

"What's little missy's name?" said Tom, at last, when he thought matters were ripe to push such an inquiry.

"Evangeline St. Clare," said the little one, "though papa and everybody else call me Eva. Now, what's your name?"

"My name's Tom; the little chil'en used to call me Uncle Tom, way back thar in Kentuck."

"Then I mean to call you Uncle Tom, because, you see, I like you," said Eva. "So, Uncle Tom, where are you going?"

"I don't know, Miss Eva."

"Don't know?" said Eva.

"No. I am going to be sold to somebody. I don't know who."

"My papa can buy you," said Eva, quickly; "and if he buys you, you will have good times. I mean to ask him to, this very day."

"Thank you, my little lady," said Tom.

The boat here stopped at a small landing to take in wood, and Eva, hearing her father's voice, bounded nimbly away. Tom rose up, and went forward to offer his service in wooding, and soon was busy among the hands.

Eva and her father were standing together by the railings to see the boat start from the landing-place, the wheel had made two or three revolutions in the water, when, by some sudden movement, the little one suddenly lost her balance, and fell sheer over the side of the boat into the water. Her father, scarce knowing what he did, was plunging in after her, but was held back by some behind him, who saw that more efficient aid had followed his child.

Tom was standing just under her on the lower deck, as she fell. He saw her strike the water, and sink, and was after her in a moment. A broad-chested, strong-armed fellow, it was nothing for him to keep afloat in the water,[6] till, in a moment or two, the child rose to the surface, and

6 No sign of rheumatism in this scene. Stowe is particularly shrewd in this episode—we don't get to see whether St. Clare would have bought Tom before the dramatic rescue of Little Eva. He gets little credit for buying him afterward; some gesture was required of a gentleman.

"Uncle Tom Saving Eva from a Watery Grave." Engraving by T. Williams, "after George Cruikshank." Eva is utterly limp. Tom appears particularly competent compared to the puffy, clownish bystanders peering over the railing. From *Uncle Tom's Cabin*, John Cassell, London, 1852

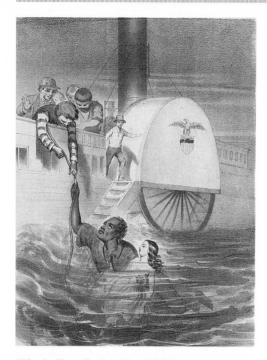

"Uncle Tom Saving Eva." Lithograph by Thomas W. Strong. The scene is strikingly mythological. Tom's strength and competence dominate the image. Eva, doll-like and unruffled, appears to be merely asleep. Circa 1853.

he caught her in his arms, and, swimming with her to the boat-side, handed her up, all dripping, to the grasp of hundreds of hands, which, as if they had all belonged to one man, were stretched eagerly out to receive her. A few moments more, and her father bore her, dripping and senseless, to the ladies' cabin, where, as is usual in cases of the kind, there ensued a very well-meaning and kind-hearted strife among the female occupants generally, as to who should do the most things to make a disturbance, and to hinder her recovery in every way possible.

It was a sultry, close day, the next day, as the steamer drew near to New Orleans. A general bustle of expectation and preparation was spread through the boat; in the cabin, one and another were gathering their things together, and arranging them, preparatory to going ashore. The steward and chambermaid, and all, were busily engaged in cleaning, furbishing, and arranging the splendid boat, preparatory to a grand entree.

On the lower deck sat our friend Tom, with his arms folded, and anxiously, from time to time, turning his eyes towards a group on the other side of the boat.

There stood the fair Evangeline, a little paler than the day before, but otherwise exhibiting no traces of the accident which had befallen her. A graceful, elegantly-formed young man stood by her, carelessly leaning one elbow on a bale of cotton, while a large pocket-book lay open before him. It was quite evident, at a glance, that the gentleman was Eva's father. There was the same noble cast of head, the same large blue eyes, the same golden-brown hair; yet the expression was wholly different. In the large, clear blue eyes, though in form and color exactly similar, there was wanting that misty, dreamy depth of expression; all was clear, bold, and bright, but with a light wholly of this world: the beautifully cut mouth had a proud and somewhat sarcastic expression, while an air of free-and-easy superiority sat not ungracefully in every turn and movement of his fine form. He was listening, with a good-humored, negligent air, half comic, half contemptuous, to Haley, who was very volubly expatiating on the quality of the article for which they were bargaining.

"All the moral and Christian virtues bound in black morocco, complete!" he said, when Haley had finished. "Well, now, my good fellow, what's the damage, as they say in Kentucky; in short, what's to be paid out for this business? How much are you going to cheat me, now? Out with it!"

"Wal," said Haley, "if I should say thirteen hundred dollars for that ar fellow, I shouldn't but just save myself; I shouldn't, now, re'ly."

"Poor fellow!" said the young man, fixing his keen, mocking blue eye on him; "but I suppose you'd let me have him for that, out of a particular regard for me."

"Well, the young lady here seems to be sot on him, and nat'lly enough."

"O! certainly, there's a call on your benevolence, my friend. Now, as a matter of Christian charity, how cheap could you afford to let him go, to oblige a young lady that's particular sot on him?"

"Wal, now, just think on 't," said the trader; "just look at them limbs,—broad-chested, strong as a horse. Look at his head; them high forrads allays shows calculatin niggers, that'll do any kind o' thing. I've marked that ar. Now, a nigger of that ar heft and build is worth considerable, just, as you may say, for his body, supposin he's stupid; but come to put in his calculatin faculties, and them which I can show he has oncommon, why, of course, it makes him come higher. Why, that ar fellow managed his master's whole farm. He has a strornary talent for business."

"Bad, bad, very bad; knows altogether too much!" said the young man, with the same mocking smile playing about his mouth. "Never will do, in the world. Your smart fellows are always running off, stealing horses, and raising the devil generally. I think you'll have to take off a couple of hundred for his smartness."

"Wal, there might be something in that ar, if it warnt for his character; but I can show recommends from his master and others, to prove he is one of your real pious,—the most humble, prayin, pious crittur ye ever did see. Why, he's been called a preacher in them parts he came from."

"And I might use him for a family chaplain, possibly," added the young man, dryly. "That's quite an idea. Religion is a remarkably scarce article at our house."

"You're joking, now."

"How do you know I am? Didn't you just warrant him for a preacher? Has he been examined by any synod or council? Come, hand over your papers."

If the trader had not been sure, by a certain good-humored twinkle in the large blue eye, that all this banter was sure, in the long run, to turn out a cash concern, he might have been somewhat out of patience; as it was, he laid down a greasy pocket-book on the cotton-bales, and began anxiously studying over certain papers in it, the young man standing by, the while, looking down on him with an air of careless, easy drollery.

"Papa, do buy him! it's no matter what you pay," whispered Eva, softly, getting up on a package, and putting her arm around her father's neck. "You have money enough, I know. I want him."

"What for, pussy? Are you going to use him for a rattle-box, or a rocking-horse, or what?"

"I want to make him happy."[7]

"An original reason, certainly."

Here the trader handed up a certificate, signed by Mr. Shelby, which the young man took with the tips of his long fingers, and glanced over carelessly.

"A gentlemanly hand," he said, "and well spelt, too. Well, now, but I'm not sure, after all, about this religion," said he, the old wicked expression returning to his eye; "the country is almost ruined with pious white people: such pious politicians as we have just before elections,— such pious goings on in all departments of church and state, that a fellow does not know who'll cheat him next. I don't know, either, about religion's being up in the market, just now. I have not looked in the papers lately, to see how it sells. How many hundred dollars, now, do you put on for this religion?"

"You like to be a jokin, now," said the trader; "but, then, there's *sense* under all that ar. I know there's differences in religion. Some kinds is mis'rable: there's your meetin pious; there's your singin, roarin pious; them ar an't no account, in black or white;—but these rayly is; and I've seen it in niggers as often as any, your rail softly, quiet, stiddy, honest, pious, that the hull world couldn't tempt 'em to do nothing that they thinks is wrong; and ye see in this letter what Tom's old master says about him."

"Now," said the young man, stooping gravely over his book of bills, "if you can assure me that I really can buy *this* kind of pious, and that it will be set down to my account in the book up above, as something belonging to me, I wouldn't care if I did go a little extra for it. How d' ye say?"

"Wal, raily, I can't do that," said the trader. "I'm a thinkin that every man'll have to hang on his own hook, in them ar quarters."

"Rather hard on a fellow that pays extra on religion, and can't trade with it in the state where he wants it most, an't it, now?" said the young man, who had been making out a roll of bills while he was speaking. "There, count your money, old boy!" he added, as he handed the roll to the trader.

"All right," said Haley, his face beaming with delight; and pulling out an old inkhorn, he proceeded to fill out a bill of sale, which, in a few moments, he handed to the young man.

"I wonder, now, if I was divided up and inventoried," said the latter, as he ran over the paper, "how much I might bring. Say so much for the shape of my head, so much for a high forehead, so much for arms, and hands, and legs, and then so much for education, learning, talent, honesty, religion! Bless me! there would be small charge on that last, I'm thinking. But come, Eva," he said; and taking the hand of his daughter, he stepped across the boat, and carelessly putting the tip of his finger under Tom's chin, said good-humoredly, "Look up, Tom, and see how you like your new master."

Tom looked up. It was not in nature to look into that gay, young, handsome face, without a feeling of pleasure; and Tom felt the tears start in his eyes as he said, heartily, "God bless you, Mas'r!"

"Well, I hope he will. What's your name? Tom? Quite as likely to do it for your asking as mine, from all accounts. Can you drive horses, Tom?"

"I've been allays used to horses," said Tom. "Mas'r Shelby raised heaps on 'em."

"Well, I think I shall put you in coachy, on condition that you won't be drunk more than once a week, unless in cases of emergency, Tom."[8]

Tom looked surprised, and rather hurt, and said, "I never drink, Mas'r."

"I've heard that story before, Tom; but then we'll see. It will be a special accommodation to all concerned, if you don't. Never mind, my boy," he added, good-humoredly, seeing Tom still looked grave; "I don't doubt you mean to do well."

"I sartin do, Mas'r," said Tom.

"And you shall have good times," said Eva. "Papa is very good to everybody, only he always will laugh at them."

"Papa is much obliged to you for his recommendation," said St. Clare, laughing, as he turned on his heel and walked away.

8 St. Clare's humor takes Tom by surprise but signals to Stowe's readers the laxity of the St. Clare household, which is used to employing drunken drivers.

# CHAPTER 15

## Of Tom's New Master, and Various Other Matters[1]

**S**ince the thread of our humble hero's life has now become inter-woven with that of higher ones, it is necessary to give some brief introduction to them.

Augustine St. Clare was the son of a wealthy planter of Louisiana. The family had its origin in Canada. Of two brothers, very similar in temperament and character, one had settled on a flourishing farm in Vermont, and the other became an opulent planter in Louisiana. The mother of Augustine was a Huguenot French lady,[2] whose family had emigrated to Louisiana during the days of its early settlement. Augustine and another brother were the only children of their parents. Having inherited from his mother an exceeding delicacy of constitution, he was, at the instance of physicians, during many years of his boyhood, sent to the care of his uncle in Vermont, in order that his constitution might be strengthened by the cold of a more bracing climate.

In childhood, he was remarkable for an extreme and marked sensitiveness of character, more akin to the softness of woman than the ordinary hardness of his own sex. Time, however, overgrew this softness with the rough bark of manhood, and but few knew how living and fresh it still lay at the core. His talents were of the very first order, although his mind showed a preference always for the ideal and the aesthetic, and there was about him that repugnance to the actual business of life which is the common result of this balance of the faculties. Soon after

1 The "various other matters" include the backgrounds of both St. Clare's wife, Marie, and his cousin Ophelia, as well as an overview of St. Clare's "Southern residence."

2 Stowe's novel is populated with a range of Christian religions, and the Huguenots are yet another. The Huguenots were French Protestants who fled religious persecution, especially after King Louis XIV's 1685 Edict. They assimilated easily into what would become the United States. Louisiana became a territory of the United States in 1803, purchased from France. Note that Stowe calls Augustine's mother a "lady," an important signal to her readers of the woman's aristocratic status. Stowe will employ popular American antipathy toward aristocrats in her descriptions of Augustine St. Clare.

the completion of his college course, his whole nature was kindled into one intense and passionate effervescence of romantic passion. His hour came,—the hour that comes only once; his star rose in the horizon,—that star that rises so often in vain, to be remembered only as a thing of dreams; and it rose for him in vain. To drop the figure,— he saw and won the love of a high-minded and beautiful woman, in one of the northern states, and they were affianced. He returned south to make arrangements for their marriage, when, most unexpectedly, his letters were returned to him by mail, with a short note from her guardian, stating to him that ere this reached him the lady would be the wife of another. Stung to madness, he vainly hoped, as many another has done, to fling the whole thing from his heart by one desperate effort. Too proud to supplicate or seek explanation, he threw himself at once into a whirl of fashionable society, and in a fortnight from the time of the fatal letter was the accepted lover of the reigning belle of the season; and as soon as arrangements could be made, he became the husband of a fine figure, a pair of bright dark eyes, and a hundred thousand dollars; and, of course, everybody thought him a happy fellow.

The married couple were enjoying their honeymoon, and entertaining a brilliant circle of friends in their splendid villa, near Lake Pontchartrain, when, one day, a letter was brought to him in *that* well-remembered writing. It was handed to him while he was in full tide of gay and successful conversation, in a whole room-full of company. He turned deadly pale when he saw the writing, but still preserved his composure, and finished the playful warfare of badinage which he was at the moment carrying on with a lady opposite; and, a short time after, was missed from the circle. In his room, alone, he opened and read the letter, now worse than idle and useless to be read. It was from her, giving a long account of a persecution to which she had been exposed by her guardian's family, to lead her to unite herself with their son: and she related how, for a long time, his letters had ceased to arrive; how she had written time and again, till she became weary and doubtful; how her health had failed under her anxieties, and how, at last, she had discovered the whole fraud which had been practised on them both. The letter ended with expressions of hope and thankfulness, and professions of undying affection, which were more bitter than death to the unhappy young man.[3] He wrote to her immediately:

"I have received yours,—but too late. I believed all I

3 It's an old story, but it retains its power even here. James Baldwin, himself a novelist of thwarted love from time to time (see *Another Country*), is silent on St. Clare's romantic history.

heard. I was desperate. *I am married*, and all is over. Only forget,—it is all that remains for either of us."

And thus ended the whole romance and ideal of life for Augustine St. Clare. But the *real* remained,—the *real*, like the flat, bare, oozy tide-mud, when the blue sparkling wave, with all its company of gliding boats and white-winged ships, its music of oars and chiming waters, has gone down, and there it lies, flat, slimy, bare,—exceedingly real.

Of course, in a novel, people's hearts break, and they die, and that is the end of it; and in a story this is very convenient. But in real life we do not die when all that makes life bright dies to us. There is a most busy and important round of eating, drinking, dressing, walking, visiting, buying, selling, talking, reading, and all that makes up what is commonly called *living,* yet to be gone through; and this yet remained to Augustine. Had his wife been a whole woman, she might yet have done something—as woman can—to mend the broken threads of life, and weave again into a tissue of brightness. But Marie St. Clare could not even see that they had been broken. As before stated, she consisted of a fine figure, a pair of splendid eyes, and a hundred thousand dollars; and none of these items were precisely the ones to minister to a mind diseased.

When Augustine, pale as death, was found lying on the sofa, and pleaded sudden sick-headache as the cause of his distress, she recommended to him to smell of hartshorn; and when the paleness and headache came on week after week, she only said that she never thought Mr. St. Clare was sickly; but it seems he was very liable to sick-headaches, and that it was a very unfortunate thing for her, because he didn't enjoy going into company with her, and it seemed odd to go so much alone, when they were just married. Augustine was glad in his heart that he had married so undiscerning a woman; but as the glosses and civilities of the honeymoon wore away, he discovered that a beautiful young woman, who has lived all her life to be caressed and waited on, might prove quite a hard mistress in domestic life. Marie never had possessed much capability of affection, or much sensibility, and the little that she had, had been merged into a most intense and unconscious selfishness; a selfishness the more hopeless, from its quiet obtuseness, its utter ignorance of any claims but her own. From her infancy, she had been surrounded with servants, who lived only to study her caprices; the idea that they had either feelings or rights had never dawned upon her, even in distant perspective. Her father, whose only child she had been, had never denied her anything that lay within the compass of human possibility; and when she entered life, beautiful, accomplished, and an heiress, she had, of course, all the eligibles and non-eligibles of the other sex sighing at her feet, and she had no doubt that Augustine was a most fortunate man in having obtained her. It is a great mistake to suppose that a woman with no heart will be an easy creditor in the exchange of affection. There is not on earth a more merciless exactor of love from others than a thoroughly selfish woman; and the more unlovely she grows, the more jealously and scrupulously she exacts love, to the uttermost farthing. When, therefore, St. Clare began to drop off those gallantries and small attentions which flowed at first through the habitude of courtship, he found his sultana no way ready to resign her slave; there were abundance of tears, poutings, and small tempests, there were discontents, pinings, upbraidings. St. Clare was good-natured and self-indulgent, and sought to buy off with presents and flatteries; and when Marie became mother to a beautiful daughter, he really felt awakened, for a time, to something like tenderness.

St. Clare's mother had been a woman of uncommon elevation and purity of character, and he gave to this child his mother's name, fondly fancying that she would prove a reproduction of her image. The thing had been remarked with petulant jealousy by his wife, and she regarded her husband's absorbing devotion to the child with suspicion and dislike; all that was given to her seemed so much taken from herself. From the time of the birth of this child, her health gradually sunk. A life of constant inaction, bodily and mental,—the friction of ceaseless ennui and discontent, united to the ordinary weakness which attended the period of maternity,—in course of a few years changed the blooming young belle into a yellow, faded, sickly woman, whose time was divided among a variety of fanciful diseases, and who considered herself, in every sense, the most ill-used and suffering person in existence.

There was no end of her various complaints; but her principal forte appeared to lie in sick-headache, which sometimes would confine her to her room three days out of six. As, of course, all family arrangements fell into the hands of servants, St. Clare found his menage anything but comfortable. His only daughter was exceedingly delicate, and he feared that, with no one to look after her and attend to her, her health and life might yet fall a sacrifice

Illustrators have paid very little attention to Marie St. Clare. This comic-book scene emphasizes the weakness and selfishness that characterize the St. Clare household. From Classics Illustrated Classic Comic Book no. 15, *Uncle Tom's Cabin*, 1943

**4** Stowe is referring to *The Ancient History* ten volumes (1730–1738) by Charles Rollin (1661–1741) and to *Scott's Family Bible* (1788–1792), edited with notes by Thomas Scott (1747–1821).

**5** The contrast between Ophelia's former home in Vermont and her new residence in the Deep South of New Orleans is at once a comparison of North and South and of American labor and European aristocracy. The labor is particularly feminine—housekeeping—and as such aimed to appeal to every woman, wife, and mother. Although we can draw connections to domestic slave labor, Stowe frames this description as female labor.

to her mother's inefficiency. He had taken her with him on a tour to Vermont, and had persuaded his cousin, Miss Ophelia St. Clare, to return with him to his southern residence; and they are now returning on this boat, where we have introduced them to our readers.

And now, while the distant domes and spires of New Orleans rise to our view, there is yet time for an introduction to Miss Ophelia.

Whoever has travelled in the New England States will remember, in some cool village, the large farm-house, with its clean-swept grassy yard, shaded by the dense and massive foliage of the sugar maple; and remember the air of order and stillness, of perpetuity and unchanging repose, that seemed to breathe over the whole place. Nothing lost, or out of order; not a picket loose in the fence, not a particle of litter in the turfy yard, with its clumps of lilac-bushes growing up under the windows. Within, he will remember wide, clean rooms, where nothing ever seems to be doing or going to be done, where everything is once and forever rigidly in place, and where all household arrangements move with the punctual exactness of the old clock in the corner. In the family "keeping-room," as it is termed, he will remember the staid respectable old bookcase, with its glass doors, where Rollin's History, Milton's Paradise Lost, Bunyan's Pilgrim's Progress, and Scott's Family Bible,**4** stand side by side in decorous order, with multitudes of other books, equally solemn and respectable. There are no servants in the house, but the lady in the snowy cap, with the spectacles, who sits sewing every afternoon among her daughters, as if nothing ever had been done, or were to be done,—she and her girls, in some long-forgotten fore part of the day, "*did up the work*," and for the rest of the time, probably, at all hours when you would see them, it is "*done up*." The old kitchen floor never seems stained or spotted; the tables, the chairs, and the various cooking utensils, never seem deranged or disordered; though three and sometimes four meals a day are got there, though the family washing and ironing is there performed, and though pounds of butter and cheese are in some silent and mysterious manner there brought into existence.**5**

On such a farm, in such a house and family, Miss Ophelia had spent a quiet existence of some forty-five years, when her cousin invited her to visit his southern mansion. The eldest of a large family, she was still considered by her father and mother as one of "the children," and the proposal that she should go to *Orleans* was a most momentous one to the family circle. The old gray-headed father took down Morse's Atlas out of the book-case, and looked out the exact latitude and longitude; and read Flint's Travels in the South and West,[6] to make up his own mind as to the nature of the country.

The good mother inquired, anxiously, "if Orleans wasn't an awful wicked place," saying, "that it seemed to her most equal to going to the Sandwich Islands, or anywhere among the heathen."

It was known at the minister's, and at the doctor's, and at Miss Peabody's milliner shop, that Ophelia St. Clare was "talking about" going away down to Orleans with her cousin; and of course the whole village could do no less than help this very important process of *talking about* the matter. The minister, who inclined strongly to abolitionist views, was quite doubtful whether such a step might not tend somewhat to encourage the southerners in holding on to their slaves; while the doctor, who was a staunch colonizationist, inclined to the opinion that Miss Ophelia ought to go, to show the Orleans people that we don't think hardly of them, after all. He was of opinion, in fact, that southern people needed encouraging. When, however, the fact that she had resolved to go was fully before the public mind, she was solemnly invited out to tea by all her friends and neighbors for the space of a fortnight, and her prospects and plans duly canvassed and inquired into. Miss Moseley, who came into the house to help to do the dress-making, acquired daily accessions of importance from the developments with regard to Miss Ophelia's wardrobe which she had been enabled to make. It was credibly ascertained that Squire Sinclare, as his name was commonly contracted in the neighborhood, had counted out fifty dollars, and given them to Miss Ophelia, and told her to buy any clothes she thought best; and that two new silk dresses, and a bonnet, had been sent for from Boston. As to the propriety of this extraordinary outlay, the public mind was divided,—some affirming that it was well enough, all things considered, for once in one's life, and others stoutly affirming that the money had better have been sent to the missionaries; but all parties agreed that there had been no such parasol seen in those parts as had been sent on from New York, and that she had one silk dress that might fairly be trusted to stand alone, whatever might be said of its mistress. There were credible rumors, also, of a hemstitched pocket-handkerchief; and report

6 Stowe is referring to *The Cerographic Atlas of the United States* (1842–1845) by Samuel Breese and Sidney Edwards Morse (1794–1871), brother of the painter-inventor Samuel F. B. Morse; and to *Recollections of the Last Ten Years* (1826) by Timothy Flint (1780–1840). Stowe does not mention Flint's *The Shoshonee Valley* (1830), which featured several examples of interracial love and marriage.

7 Stowe clearly enjoys satirizing the commentary by this Greek chorus of parsimonious Yankee females on extravagant preparations and purchases for Ophelia's traveling to New Orleans. The spinster woman enjoys all the grandeur of a bride's trousseau, even though her silks seem to outshine their owner.

8 Ophelia is the stereotypical New England spinster: tall and thin, with high moral standards and education to match, and most of all a sense of duty. Behind this stereotype lay a reality: that unmarried women could not inherit property and were often seen as a burden to their families. The sense of duty was aimed at giving their lives value in a culture where to be a woman was to be a wife and mother. I have always read Stowe's move to the present tense ("as you now behold her") as emphasizing that the reader should see Ophelia, not see events through her eyes. We are not, that is, to assume that Ophelia stands in for Harriet Beecher Stowe.

even went so far as to state that Miss Ophelia had one pocket-handkerchief with lace all around it,—it was even added that it was worked in the corners; but this latter point was never satisfactorily ascertained, and remains, in fact, unsettled to this day.[7]

Miss Ophelia, as you now behold her, stands before you, in a very shining brown linen travelling-dress, tall, square-formed, and angular. Her face was thin, and rather sharp in its outlines; the lips compressed, like those of a person who is in the habit of making up her mind definitely on all subjects; while the keen, dark eyes had a peculiarly searching, advised movement, and travelled over everything, as if they were looking for something to take care of.[8]

All her movements were sharp, decided, and energetic; and, though she was never much of a talker, her words were remarkably direct, and to the purpose, when she did speak.

In her habits, she was a living impersonation of order, method, and exactness. In punctuality, she was as inevitable as a clock, and as inexorable as a railroad engine; and she held in most decided contempt and abomination anything of a contrary character.

The great sin of sins, in her eyes,—the sum of all evils,—was expressed by one very common and important word in her vocabulary—"shiftlessness." Her finale and ultimatum of contempt consisted in a very emphatic pronunciation of the word "shiftless;" and by this she characterized all modes of procedure which had not a direct and inevitable relation to accomplishment of some purpose then definitely had in mind. People who did nothing, or who did not know exactly what they were going to do, or who did not take the most direct way to accomplish what they set their hands to, were objects of her entire contempt,—a contempt shown less frequently by anything she said, than by a kind of stony grimness, as if she scorned to say anything about the matter.

As to mental cultivation,—she had a clear, strong, active mind, was well and thoroughly read in history and the older English classics, and thought with great strength within certain narrow limits. Her theological tenets were all made up, labelled in most positive and distinct forms, and put by, like the bundles in her patch trunk; there were just so many of them, and there were never to be any more. So, also, were her ideas with regard to most matters of practical life,—such as housekeeping in all its branches, and the various political relations of her native village. And, underlaying all, deeper than anything else, higher and broader, lay the strongest principle of her being—conscientiousness. Nowhere is conscience so dominant and all-absorbing as with New England women. It is the granite formation, which lies deepest, and rises out, even to the tops of the highest mountains.

Miss Ophelia was the absolute bond-slave of the "*ought*." Once make her certain that the "path of duty," as she commonly phrased it, lay in any given direction, and fire and water could not keep her from it. She would walk straight down into a well, or up to a loaded cannon's mouth, if she were only quite sure that there the path lay. Her standard of right was so high, so all-embracing, so minute, and making so few concessions to human frailty, that, though she strove with heroic ardor to reach it, she never actually did so, and of course was burdened with a constant and often harassing sense of deficiency;—this gave a severe and somewhat gloomy cast to her religious character.

But, how in the world can Miss Ophelia get along with Augustine St. Clare,—gay, easy, unpunctual, unpractical, sceptical,—in short, walking with impudent and nonchalant freedom over every one of her most cherished habits and opinions?[9]

To tell the truth, then, Miss Ophelia loved him. When a boy, it had been hers to teach him his catechism, mend his clothes, comb his hair, and bring him up generally in the way he should go; and her heart having a warm side to it, Augustine had, as he usually did with most people, monopolized a large share of it for himself, and therefore it was that he succeeded very easily in persuading her that the "path of duty" lay in the direction of New Orleans, and that she must go with him to take care of Eva, and keep everything from going to wreck and ruin during the frequent illnesses of his wife. The idea of a house without anybody to take care of it went to her heart; then she loved the lovely little girl, as few could help doing; and though she regarded Augustine as very much of a heathen, yet she loved him, laughed at his jokes, and forbore with his failings, to an extent which those who knew him thought perfectly incredible. But what more or other is to be known of Miss Ophelia our reader must discover by a personal acquaintance.

There she is, sitting now in her state-room, surrounded by a mixed multitude of little and big carpet-bags, boxes,

9 As a direct contrast to the hardworking New England Ophelia, Augustine is shiftless, easygoing, and free to the point of carelessness. Readers know that he was a bit slow to rescue his drowning daughter and will hear shortly that he has left Eva in a carriage driven by a drunken fellow.

baskets, each containing some separate responsibility which she is tying, binding up, packing, or fastening, with a face of great earnestness.

"Now, Eva, have you kept count of your things? Of course you haven't,—children never do: there's the spotted carpet-bag and the little blue band-box with your best bonnet,—that's two; then the India rubber satchel is three; and my tape and needle box is four; and my band-box, five; and my collar-box, six; and that little hair trunk, seven. What have you done with your sunshade? Give it to me, and let me put a paper round it, and tie it to my umbrella with my shade;—there, now."

"Why, aunty, we are only going up home;—what is the use?"

"To keep it nice, child; people must take care of their things, if they ever mean to have anything; and now, Eva, is your thimble put up?"

"Really, aunty, I don't know."

"Well, never mind; I'll look your box over,—thimble, wax, two spools, scissors, knife, tape-needle; all right,—put it in here. What did you ever do, child, when you were coming on with only your papa. I should have thought you'd a lost everything you had."

"Well, aunty, I did lose a great many; and then, when we stopped anywhere, papa would buy some more of whatever it was."

"Mercy on us, child,—what a way!"

"It was a very easy way, aunty," said Eva.

"It's a dreadful shiftless one," said aunty.

"Why, aunty, what'll you do now?" said Eva; "that trunk is too full to be shut down."

"It *must* shut down," said aunty, with the air of a general, as she squeezed the things in, and sprung upon the lid;—still a little gap remained about the mouth of the trunk.

"Get up here, Eva!" said Miss Ophelia, courageously; "what has been done can be done again. This trunk has *got to be* shut and locked—there are no two ways about it."

And the trunk, intimidated, doubtless, by this resolute statement, gave in. The hasp snapped sharply in its hole, and Miss Ophelia turned the key, and pocketed it in triumph.

"Now we're ready. Where's your papa? I think it time this baggage was set out. Do look out, Eva, and see if you see your papa."

"O, yes, he's down the other end of the gentlemen's cabin, eating an orange."

"He can't know how near we are coming," said aunty; "hadn't you better run and speak to him?"

"Papa never is in a hurry about anything," said Eva, "and we haven't come to the landing. Do step on the guards, aunty. Look! there's our house, up that street!"

The boat now began, with heavy groans, like some vast, tired monster, to prepare to push up among the multiplied steamers at the levee. Eva joyously pointed out the various spires, domes, and way-marks, by which she recognized her native city.

"Yes, yes, dear; very fine," said Miss Ophelia. "But mercy on us! the boat has stopped! where is your father?"

And now ensued the usual turmoil of landing—waiters running twenty ways at once—men tugging trunks, carpet-bags, boxes—women anxiously calling to their children, and everybody crowding in a dense mass to the plank towards the landing.

Miss Ophelia seated herself resolutely on the lately vanquished trunk, and marshalling all her goods and chattels in fine military order, seemed resolved to defend them to the last.

"Shall I take your trunk, ma'am?" "Shall I take your baggage?" "Let me 'tend to your baggage, Missis?" "Shan't I carry out these yer, Missis?" rained down upon her unheeded. She sat with grim determination, upright as a darning-needle stuck in a board, holding on her bundle of umbrella and parasols, and replying with a determination that was enough to strike dismay even into a hackman, wondering to Eva, in each interval, "what upon earth her papa could be thinking of; he couldn't have fallen over, now,—but something must have happened;"—and just as she had begun to work herself into a real distress, he came up, with his usually careless motion, and giving Eva a quarter of the orange he was eating, said,

"Well, Cousin Vermont, I suppose you are all ready."

"I've been ready, waiting, nearly an hour," said Miss Ophelia; "I began to be really concerned about you."

"That's a clever fellow, now," said he. "Well, the carriage is waiting, and the crowd are now off, so that one can walk out in a decent and Christian manner, and not be pushed and shoved. Here," he added to a driver who stood behind him, "take these things."

"I'll go and see to his putting them in," said Miss Ophelia.

"O, pshaw, cousin, what's the use?" said St. Clare.

"Well, at any rate, I'll carry this, and this, and this," said Miss Ophelia, singling out three boxes and a small carpet-bag.

"My dear Miss Vermont, positively, you mustn't come the Green Mountains over us that way. You must adopt at least a piece of a southern principle, and not walk out under all that load. They'll take you for a waiting-maid; give them to this fellow; he'll put them down as if they were eggs, now."

Miss Ophelia looked despairingly, as her cousin took all her treasures from her, and rejoiced to find herself once more in the carriage with them, in a state of preservation.

"Where's Tom?" said Eva.

"O, he's on the outside, Pussy. I'm going to take Tom up to mother for a peace-offering, to make up for that drunken fellow that upset the carriage."

"O, Tom will make a splendid driver, I know," said Eva; "he'll never get drunk."

The carriage stopped in front of an ancient mansion, built in that odd mixture of Spanish and French style, of which there are specimens in some parts of New Orleans. It was built in the Moorish fashion,—a square building enclosing a court-yard, into which the carriage drove through an arched gateway. The court, in the inside, had evidently been arranged to gratify a picturesque and voluptuous ideality. Wide galleries ran all around the four sides, whose Moorish arches, slender pillars, and arabesque ornaments, carried the mind back, as in a dream, to the reign of oriental romance in Spain. In the middle of the court, a fountain threw high its silvery water, falling in a never-ceasing spray into a marble basin, fringed with a deep border of fragrant violets. The water in the fountain, pellucid as crystal, was alive with myriads of gold and silver fishes, twinkling and darting through it like so many living jewels. Around the fountain ran a walk, paved with a mosaic of pebbles, laid in various fanciful patterns; and this, again, was surrounded by turf, smooth as green velvet, while a carriage-drive enclosed the whole. Two large orange-trees, now fragrant with blossoms, threw a delicious shade; and, ranged in a circle round upon the turf, were marble vases of arabesque sculpture, containing the choicest flowering plants of the tropics. Huge pomegranate trees, with their glossy leaves and flame-colored flowers, dark-leaved Arabian jessamines, with their silvery stars, geraniums, luxuriant roses bending beneath their heavy abundance of flowers, golden jessamines, lemon-scented verbenum, all united their bloom and fragrance, while here and there a mystic old aloe, with its strange, massive leaves, sat looking like some hoary old enchanter, sitting in weird grandeur among the more perishable bloom and fragrance around it.

The galleries that surrounded the court were festooned with a curtain of some kind of Moorish stuff, and could be drawn down at pleasure, to exclude the beams of the sun. On the whole, the appearance of the place was luxurious and romantic.[10]

As the carriage drove in, Eva seemed like a bird ready to burst from a cage, with the wild eagerness of her delight.

"O, isn't it beautiful, lovely! my own dear, darling home!" she said to Miss Ophelia. "Isn't it beautiful?"

" 'Tis a pretty place," said Miss Ophelia, as she alighted; "though it looks rather old and heathenish to me."

Tom got down from the carriage, and looked about with an air of calm, still enjoyment. The negro, it must be remembered, is an exotic of the most gorgeous and superb countries of the world, and he has, deep in his heart, a passion for all that is splendid, rich, and fanciful; a passion which, rudely indulged by an untrained taste, draws on them the ridicule of the colder and more correct white race.[11]

St. Clare, who was in his heart a poetical voluptuary,[12] smiled as Miss Ophelia made her remark on his premises, and, turning to Tom, who was standing looking round, his beaming black face perfectly radiant with admiration, he said,

"Tom, my boy, this seems to suit you."

"Yes, Mas'r, it looks about the right thing," said Tom.

All this passed in a moment, while trunks were being hustled off, hackman paid, and while a crowd, of all ages and sizes,—men, women, and children,—came running through the galleries, both above and below, to see Mas'r come in. Foremost among them was a highly-dressed young mulatto man, evidently a very *distingue* personage, attired in the ultra extreme of the mode, and gracefully waving a scented cambric handkerchief in his hand.[13]

This personage had been exerting himself, with great alacrity, in driving all the flock of domestics to the other end of the verandah.

"Back! all of you. I am ashamed of you," he said, in a tone of authority. "Would you intrude on Master's domestic relations, in the first hour of his return?"

All looked abashed at this elegant speech, delivered with quite an air, and stood huddled together at a respectful distance, except two stout porters, who came up and began conveying away the baggage.

10 The opulent decor of the St. Clare residence marks it as an exotic, otherworldly place and hints at the decadence readers will find within. It is certainly a far cry from Vermont!

11 The description of the St. Clare residence also allows Stowe to comment on both Ophelia's inability to derive aesthetic pleasure and, in another racist generalization, on "the negro's" natural appreciation of and "untrained taste" for visual splendor.

12 St. Clare is being skewered here.

13 To the modern reader, Adolph is unmistakably "metrosexual"—a well-groomed dandy—if not actually gay. Yes, he is ridiculous, but is he any more ridiculous than Ophelia or St. Clare? Stowe introduces him as a dramatic type just after the long description of the luxurious house. Unfortunately, there are few images of Adolph; he has not had a successful life in the public imagination.

**14** Even this unhappy couple is overtly labeled as husband and wife. Only Tom and Chloe are not.

Owing to Mr. Adolph's systematic arrangements, when St. Clare turned round from paying the hackman, there was nobody in view but Mr. Adolph himself, conspicuous in satin vest, gold guard-chain, and white pants, and bowing with inexpressible grace and suavity.

"Ah, Adolph, is it you?" said his master, offering his hand to him; "how are you, boy?" while Adolph poured forth, with great fluency, an extemporary speech, which he had been preparing, with great care, for a fortnight before.

"Well, well," said St. Clare, passing on, with his usual air of negligent drollery, "that's very well got up, Adolph. See that the baggage is well bestowed. I'll come to the people in a minute;" and, so saying, he led Miss Ophelia to a large parlor that opened on to the verandah.

While this had been passing, Eva had flown like a bird, through the porch and parlor, to a little boudoir opening likewise on the verandah.

A tall, dark-eyed, sallow woman, half rose from a couch on which she was reclining.

"Mamma!" said Eva, in a sort of a rapture, throwing herself on her neck, and embracing her over and over again.

"That'll do,—take care, child,—don't, you make my head ache," said the mother, after she had languidly kissed her.

St. Clare came in, embraced his wife in true, orthodox, husbandly fashion,**14** and then presented to her his cousin. Marie lifted her large eyes on her cousin with an air of some curiosity, and received her with languid politeness. A crowd of servants now pressed to the entry door, and among them a middle-aged mulatto woman, of very respectable appearance, stood foremost, in a tremor of expectation and joy, at the door.

"O, there's Mammy!" said Eva, as she flew across the room; and, throwing herself into her arms, she kissed her repeatedly.

This woman did not tell her that she made her head ache, but, on the contrary, she hugged her, and laughed, and cried, till her sanity was a thing to be doubted of; and when released from her, Eva flew from one to another, shaking hands and kissing, in a way that Miss Ophelia afterwards declared fairly turned her stomach.

"Well!" said Miss Ophelia, "you southern children can do something that *I* couldn't."

"What, now, pray?" said St. Clare.

"Well, I want to be kind to everybody, and I wouldn't have anything hurt; but as to kissing—"

"Niggers," said St. Clare, "that you're not up to,—hey?"

"Yes, that's it. How can she?"

St. Clare laughed, as he went into the passage. "Halloa, here, what's to pay out here? Here, you all—Mammy, Jimmy, Polly, Sukey—glad to see Mas'r?" he said, as he went shaking hands from one to another. "Look out for the babies!" he added, as he stumbled over a sooty little urchin, who was crawling upon all fours. "If I step upon anybody, let 'em mention it."

There was an abundance of laughing and blessing Mas'r, as St. Clare distributed small pieces of change among them.

"Come, now, take yourselves off, like good boys and girls," he said; and the whole assemblage, dark and light, disappeared through a door into a large verandah, followed by Eva, who carried a large satchel, which she had been filling with apples, nuts, candy, ribbons, laces, and toys of every description, during her whole homeward journey.

As St. Clare turned to go back, his eye fell upon Tom, who was standing uneasily, shifting from one foot to the other, while Adolph stood negligently leaning against the banisters, examining Tom through an opera-glass, with an air that would have done credit to any dandy living.

"Puh! you puppy," said his master, striking down the opera glass; "is that the way you treat your company? Seems to me, Dolph," he added, laying his finger on the elegant figured satin vest that Adolph was sporting, "seems to me that's *my* vest."

"O! Master, this vest all stained with wine; of course, a gentleman in Master's standing never wears a vest like this. I understood I was to take it. It does for a poor nigger-fellow, like me."

And Adolph tossed his head, and passed his fingers through his scented hair, with a grace.

"So, that's it, is it?" said St. Clare, carelessly. "Well, here, I'm going to show this Tom to his mistress, and then you take him to the kitchen; and mind you don't put on any of your airs to him. He's worth two such puppies as you."

"Master always will have his joke," said Adolph, laughing. "I'm delighted to see Master in such spirits."

"Here, Tom," said St. Clare, beckoning.

Tom entered the room. He looked wistfully[15] on the velvet carpets, and the before unimagined splendors of mirrors, pictures, statues, and curtains, and, like the Queen of Sheba before Solomon, there was no more spirit in him. He looked afraid even to set his feet down.

15 I.e., amazed and looking intently. In Stowe's time, "wistful" meant "attentive" rather than "mournful." The biblical reference is to the visit of the Queen of Sheba (Saba) to Solomon "to try him with hard questions" (1 Kings 10:4–5): "And when the queen of Saba saw all the wisdom of Solomon, and the house which he had built, and the meat of his table, and the apartments of his servants, and the order of his ministers, and their apparel, and the cupbearers, and the holocausts [burnt offerings], which he offered in the house of the Lord: she had no longer any spirit in her." Stowe's irony in this reference highlights the lack of wisdom and order in the opulent St. Clare house.

16 Named for the inventor of the process, Louis-Jacques-Mandé Daguerre (1789–1851), the daguerrotype was an early type of photograph, often in sepia tones (*Shorter Oxford*).

Anonymous lithograph of a spoiled, luxuriating Marie, reclining on her bed.

"See here, Marie," said St. Clare to his wife, "I've bought you a coachman, at last, to order. I tell you, he's a regular hearse for blackness and sobriety, and will drive you like a funeral, if you want. Open your eyes, now, and look at him. Now, don't say I never think about you when I'm gone."

Marie opened her eyes, and fixed them on Tom, without rising.

"I know he'll get drunk," she said.

"No, he's warranted a pious and sober article."

"Well, I hope he may turn out well," said the lady; "it's more than I expect, though."

"Dolph," said St. Clare, "show Tom down stairs; and, mind yourself," he added; "remember what I told you."

Adolph tripped gracefully forward, and Tom, with lumbering tread, went after.

"He's a perfect behemoth!" said Marie.

"Come, now, Marie," said St. Clare, seating himself on a stool beside her sofa, "be gracious, and say something pretty to a fellow."

"You've been gone a fortnight beyond the time," said the lady, pouting.

"Well, you know I wrote you the reason."

"Such a short, cold letter!" said the lady.

"Dear Me! the mail was just going, and it had to be that or nothing."

"That's just the way, always," said the lady; "always something to make your journeys long, and letters short."

"See here, now," he added, drawing an elegant velvet case out of his pocket, and opening it, "here's a present I got for you in New York."

It was a daguerreotype,**16** clear and soft as an engraving, representing Eva and her father sitting hand in hand.

Marie looked at it with a dissatisfied air.

"What made you sit in such an awkward position?" she said.

"Well, the position may be a matter of opinion; but what do you think of the likeness?"

"If you don't think anything of my opinion in one case, I suppose you wouldn't in another," said the lady, shutting the daguerreotype.

"Hang the woman!" said St. Clare, mentally; but aloud he added, "Come, now, Marie, what do you think of the likeness? Don't be nonsensical, now."

"It's very inconsiderate of you, St. Clare," said the lady, "to insist on my talking and looking at things. You know I've been lying all day with the sick-headache; and there's been such a tumult made ever since you came, I'm half dead."

"You're subject to the sick-headache, ma'am?" said Miss Ophelia, suddenly rising from the depths of the large armchair, where she had sat quietly, taking an inventory of the furniture, and calculating its expense.

"Yes, I'm a perfect martyr to it," said the lady.

"Juniper-berry tea is good for sick-headache," said Miss Ophelia; "at least, Auguste, Deacon Abraham Perry's wife, used to say so; and she was a great nurse."

"I'll have the first juniper-berries that get ripe in our garden by the lake brought in for that especial purpose," said St. Clare, gravely pulling the bell as he did so; "meanwhile, cousin, you must be wanting to retire to your apartment, and refresh yourself a little, after your journey. Dolph," he added, "tell Mammy to come here." The decent mulatto woman whom Eva had caressed so rapturously soon entered; she was dressed neatly, with a high red and yellow turban on her head, the recent gift of Eva, and which the child had been arranging on her head. "Mammy," said St. Clare, "I put this lady under your care; she is tired, and wants rest; take her to her chamber, and be sure she is made comfortable;" and Miss Ophelia disappeared in the rear of Mammy.

# CHAPTER 16

## *Tom's Mistress and Her Opinions*[1]

1 As the wife of Tom's legal master, Marie St. Clare functions as Tom's mistress. The hard-hearted Southern mistress is a convention in abolitionist literature, her cruelty made worse by her lack of "natural" womanly feelings. Stowe's depiction of Marie's selfishness begins over the top and remains there. We learned in the last chapter that Augustine had been in love with a Northern woman, that he had married Marie on the rebound, as it were, and that she was pouty, undiscerning, and utterly self-centered. Now we see the material effects of these traits on her slaves and feel how her presence bodes evil for Tom.

2 As part of their rule of the domestic sphere, nineteenth-century ladies held the keys to all the locks of the household stores; occasionally, as here with Ophelia, the keys were delivered over to a trusted housekeeper. Stowe also alludes to Matt. 16:18–19: "Thou art Peter, and upon this rock I will build my church; and the gates of hell shall not prevail against it. And I will give unto thee the keys of the kingdom of heaven."

"And now, Marie," said St. Clare, "your golden days are dawning. Here is our practical, business-like New England cousin, who will take the whole budget of cares off your shoulders, and give you time to refresh yourself, and grow young and handsome. The ceremony of delivering the keys had better come off forthwith."[2]

This remark was made at the breakfast-table, a few mornings after Miss Ophelia had arrived.

"I'm sure she's welcome," said Marie, leaning her head languidly on her hand. "I think she'll find one thing, if she does, and that is, that it's we mistresses that are the slaves, down here."

"O, certainly, she will discover that, and a world of wholesome truths besides, no doubt," said St. Clare.

"Talk about our keeping slaves, as if we did it for our *convenience*," said Marie. "I'm sure, if we consulted *that,* we might let them all go at once."

Evangeline fixed her large, serious eyes on her mother's face, with an earnest and perplexed expression, and said, simply, "What do you keep them for, mamma?"

"I don't know, I'm sure, except for a plague; they are the plague of my life. I believe that more of my ill health is caused by them than by any one thing; and ours, I know, are the very worst that ever anybody was plagued with."

"O, come, Marie, you've got the blues, this morning," said St. Clare. "You know't isn't so. There's Mammy, the best creature living,—what could you do without her?"

"Mammy is the best I ever knew," said Marie; "and yet Mammy, now, is selfish—dreadfully selfish; it's the fault of the whole race."**3**

"Selfishness *is* a dreadful fault," said St. Clare, gravely.

"Well, now, there's Mammy," said Marie, "I think it's selfish of her to sleep so sound nights; she knows I need little attentions almost every hour, when my worst turns are on, and yet she's so hard to wake. I absolutely am worse, this very morning, for the efforts I had to make to wake her last night."

"Hasn't she sat up with you a good many nights, lately, mamma?" said Eva.

"How should you know that?" said Marie, sharply; "she's been complaining, I suppose."

"She didn't complain; she only told me what bad nights you'd had,—so many in succession."

"Why don't you let Jane or Rosa take her place, a night or two," said St. Clare, "and let her rest?"

"How can you propose it?" said Marie. "St. Clare, you really are inconsiderate. So nervous as I am, the least breath disturbs me; and a strange hand about me would drive me absolutely frantic. If Mammy felt the interest in me she ought to, she'd wake easier,—of course, she would. I've heard of people who had such devoted servants, but it never was *my* luck;" and Marie sighed.

Miss Ophelia had listened to this conversation with an air of shrewd, observant gravity; and she still kept her lips tightly compressed, as if determined fully to ascertain her longitude and position,**4** before she committed herself.

"Now Mammy has a *sort* of goodness," said Marie; "she's smooth and respectful, but she's selfish at heart. Now, she never will be done fidgeting and worrying about that husband of hers. You see, when I was married and came to live here, of course, I had to bring her with me, and her husband my father couldn't spare.**5** He was a blacksmith, and, of course, very necessary; and I thought and said, at the time, that Mammy and he had better give each other up, as it wasn't likely to be convenient for them ever to live together again. I wish, now, I'd insisted on it, and married Mammy to somebody else; but I was foolish and indulgent, and didn't want to insist. I told Mammy, at the time, that she mustn't ever expect to see him more than once or twice in her life again, for the air of father's place doesn't agree with my health, and I can't go there; and I advised her to take up with somebody else; but no— she wouldn't. Mammy has a kind of obstinacy about her, in spots, that everybody don't see as I do."

3 Throughout this chapter, Marie St. Clare voices racist stereotypes, many of which reflect most often her own character flaws. Marie thinks, strangely enough, that her slaves sleep too much. Stowe's most self-centered character focuses not only on Mammy's perceived flaws but also on the perceived selfishness of African Americans as a race. We cannot help but see the irony.

4 Stowe brings the New England seagoing heritage into her description of Ophelia's assessment of her place in the St. Clare household: "her longitude and position."

5 In keeping with the pattern, Stowe gives Mammy a husband too. He is a blacksmith, and they have two children. Throughout *Uncle Tom's Cabin*, Stowe shows a wide range of horrors created by the ownership of human beings granted by slavery. Here the reader sees not only the use of slaves as transferable and inheritable property but, more significantly, one of the ways in which the core of domestic life—marriage and children—is destroyed at the whim of a selfish mistress. Stowe emphasizes to her reader that every character, no matter how minor, is part of a web of relationships that do not center on the master and his needs. Every slave, she insists, would rather be doing something else.

6 In these early passages, Ophelia says little. She observes the St. Clares, and we observe her. Stowe is careful to ensure that we do not mistake Ophelia for the author; she accomplishes this by her repeated depiction of how Ophelia reacts to Marie and others.

7 St. Clare's sarcastic asides are crucial to his development as a character. Stowe must show him to be an acute critic of slavery with firsthand knowledge and a passive, morally weak individual. However, he must remain likeable. Stowe knows that we cannot help but smile at St. Clare's dry wit; we indulge his weakness for the next twelve chapters.

8 Slaveowners who did not brutalize their slaves often took comfort in the boast that their slaves were not abused. Stowe means us to see through Marie's treatment of Mammy. Marie's comment about Mammy's use of "white sugar," one of the staples of the slave trade, highlights the inescapable complicity in slavery. Spoiled children are anathema to Stowe's readers. Marie's racist remark again reflects on her own failings.

9 Stowe consistently reminds her readers of Eva's uncannily sensitive reactions to suffering, a nineteenth-century Romantic convention that would signal that Eva is not long for this world.

"Has she children?" said Miss Ophelia.

"Yes; she has two."

"I suppose she feels the separation from them?"

"Well, of course, I couldn't bring them. They were little dirty things—I couldn't have them about; and, besides, they took up too much of her time; but I believe that Mammy has always kept up a sort of sulkiness about this. She won't marry anybody else; and I do believe, now, though she knows how necessary she is to me, and how feeble my health is, she would go back to her husband to-morrow, if she only could. I *do*, indeed," said Marie; "they are just so selfish, now, the best of them."[6]

"It's distressing to reflect upon," said St. Clare, dryly.[7]

Miss Ophelia looked keenly at him, and saw the flush of mortification and repressed vexation, and the sarcastic curl of the lip, as he spoke.

"Now, Mammy has always been a pet with me," said Marie. "I wish some of your northern servants could look at her closets of dresses,—silks and muslins, and one real linen cambric, she has hanging there. I've worked sometimes whole afternoons, trimming her caps, and getting her ready to go to a party. As to abuse, she don't know what it is. She never was whipped more than once or twice in her whole life. She has her strong coffee or her tea every day, with white sugar in it. It's abominable, to be sure; but St. Clare will have high life below-stairs, and they every one of them live just as they please. The fact is, our servants are over-indulged. I suppose it is partly our fault that they are selfish, and act like spoiled children; but I've talked to St. Clare till I am tired."[8]

"And I, too," said St. Clare, taking up the morning paper.

Eva, the beautiful Eva, had stood listening to her mother, with that expression of deep and mystic earnestness which was peculiar to her.[9] She walked softly round to her mother's chair, and put her arms round her neck.

"Well, Eva, what now?" said Marie.

"Mamma, couldn't I take care of you one night—just one? I know I shouldn't make you nervous, and I shouldn't sleep. I often lie awake nights, thinking—"

"O, nonsense, child—nonsense!" said Marie; "you are such a strange child!"

"But may I, mamma? I think," she said, timidly, "that Mammy isn't well. She told me her head ached all the time, lately."

"O, that's just one of Mammy's fidgets! Mammy is just like all the rest of them—makes such a fuss about every little head-ache or finger-ache; it'll never do to encourage it—never! I'm principled about this matter," said she, turning to Miss Ophelia; "you'll find the necessity of it. If you encourage servants in giving way to every little disagreeable feeling, and complaining of every little ailment, you'll have your hands full. I never complain myself—nobody knows what I endure. I feel it a duty to bear it quietly, and I do."

Miss Ophelia's round eyes expressed an undisguised amazement at this peroration, which struck St. Clare as so supremely ludicrous, that he burst into a loud laugh.

"St. Clare always laughs when I make the least allusion to my ill health," said Marie, with the voice of a suffering martyr. "I only hope the day won't come when he'll remember it!" and Marie put her handkerchief to her eyes.

Of course, there was rather a foolish silence.[10] Finally, St. Clare got up, looked at his watch, and said he had an engagement down street. Eva tripped away after him, and Miss Ophelia and Marie remained at the table alone.

"Now, that's just like St. Clare!" said the latter, withdrawing her handkerchief with somewhat of a spirited flourish when the criminal to be affected by it was no longer in sight. "He never realizes, never can, never will, what I suffer, and have, for years. If I was one of the complaining sort, or ever made any fuss about my ailments, there would be some reason for it. Men do get tired, naturally, of a complaining wife. But I've kept things to myself, and borne, and borne, till St. Clare has got in the way of thinking I can bear anything."

Miss Ophelia did not exactly know what she was expected to answer to this.

While she was thinking what to say, Marie gradually wiped away her tears, and smoothed her plumage in a general sort of way, as a dove might be supposed to make toilet after a shower, and began a house-wifely chat with Miss Ophelia, concerning cupboards, closets, linen-presses, store-rooms, and other matters, of which the latter was, by common understanding, to assume the direction,—giving her so many cautious directions and charges, that a head less systematic and business-like than Miss Ophelia's would have been utterly dizzied and confounded.

"And now," said Marie, "I believe I've told you everything; so that, when my next sick turn comes on, you'll be able to go forward entirely, without consulting me;—only about Eva,—she requires watching."

"She seems to be a good child, very," said Miss Ophelia; "I never saw a better child."

10 "Of course" there is a foolish silence. Stowe's portrait of St. Clare is admirably consistent: He is a man who will not speak the awful truth to those who most need it. He is the sort of gentleman to avoid conflict at all costs.

11 An evergreen climbing jasmine whose white flowers were used to flavor tea.

"Eva's peculiar," said her mother, "very. There are things about her so singular; she isn't like me, now, a particle;" and Marie sighed, as if this was a truly melancholy consideration.

Miss Ophelia in her own heart said, "I hope she isn't," but had prudence enough to keep it down.

"Eva always was disposed to be with servants; and I think that well enough with some children. Now, I always played with father's little negroes—it never did me any harm. But Eva somehow always seems to put herself on an equality with every creature that comes near her. It's a strange thing about the child. I never have been able to break her of it. St. Clare, I believe, encourages her in it. The fact is, St. Clare indulges every creature under this roof but his own wife."

Again Miss Ophelia sat in blank silence.

"Now, there's no way with servants," said Marie, "but to *put them down*, and keep them down. It was always natural to me, from a child. Eva is enough to spoil a whole house-full. What she will do when she comes to keep house herself, I'm sure I don't know. I hold to being *kind* to servants—I always am; but you must make 'em *know their place.* Eva never does; there's no getting into the child's head the first beginning of an idea what a servant's place is! You heard her offering to take care of me nights, to let Mammy sleep! That's just a specimen of the way the child would be doing all the time, if she was left to herself."

"Why," said Miss Ophelia, bluntly, "I suppose you think your servants are human creatures, and ought to have some rest when they are tired."

"Certainly, of course. I'm very particular in letting them have everything that comes convenient,—anything that doesn't put one at all out of the way, you know. Mammy can make up her sleep, some time or other; there's no difficulty about that. She's the sleepiest concern that ever I saw; sewing, standing, or sitting, that creature will go to sleep, and sleep anywhere and everywhere. No danger but Mammy gets sleep enough. But this treating servants as if they were exotic flowers, or china vases, is really ridiculous," said Marie, as she plunged languidly into the depths of a voluminous and pillowy lounge, and drew towards her an elegant cut-glass vinaigrette.

"You see," she continued, in a faint and lady-like voice, like the last dying breath of an Arabian jessamine,[11] or something equally ethereal, "you see, Cousin Ophelia, I don't often speak of myself. It isn't my *habit*; 'tisn't agreeable to me. In fact, I haven't strength to do it. But there are

points where St. Clare and I differ. St. Clare never understood me, never appreciated me. I think it lies at the root
of all my ill health. St. Clare means well, I am bound to
believe; but men are constitutionally selfish and inconsiderate to woman. That, at least, is my impression."

Miss Ophelia, who had not a small share of the genuine
New England caution, and a very particular horror of
being drawn into family difficulties, now began to foresee
something of this kind impending; so, composing her face
into a grim neutrality,[12] and drawing out of her pocket
about a yard and a quarter of stocking, which she kept as
a specific against what Dr. Watts asserts to be a personal
habit of Satan when people have idle hands,[13] she proceeded to knit most energetically, shutting her lips
together in a way that said, as plain as words could, "You
needn't try to make me speak. I don't want anything to do
with your affairs,"—in fact, she looked about as sympathizing as a stone lion. But Marie didn't care for that. She
had got somebody to talk to, and she felt it her duty to
talk, and that was enough; and reinforcing herself by
smelling again at her vinaigrette, she went on.

"You see, I brought my own property and servants into
the connection,[14] when I married St. Clare, and I am
legally entitled to manage them my own way. St. Clare had
his fortune and his servants, and I'm well enough content
he should manage them his way; but St. Clare will be
interfering. He has wild, extravagant notions about
things, particularly about the treatment of servants. He
really does act as if he set his servants before me, and
before himself, too; for he lets them make him all sorts of
trouble, and never lifts a finger. Now, about some things,
St. Clare is really frightful—he frightens me—good-
natured as he looks, in general. Now, he has set down his
foot that, come what will, there shall not be a blow struck
in this house, except what he or I strike; and he does it in
a way that I really dare not cross him. Well, you may see
what that leads to; for St. Clare wouldn't raise his hand,
if every one of them walked over him, and I—you see how
cruel it would be to require me to make the exertion.
Now, you know these servants are nothing but grown-up
children."[15]

"I don't know anything about it, and I thank the Lord
that I don't!" said Miss Ophelia, shortly.

"Well, but you will have to know something, and know
it to your cost, if you stay here. You don't know what a
provoking, stupid, careless, unreasonable childish,
ungrateful set of wretches they are."

12 Stowe will skewer the limits on Ophelia's
"mind one's own business" policy. That is,
Stowe will suggest that it is not only misguided but also immoral for good people to do
nothing.

13 An allusion to Isaac Watts's 1715 *Divine
Songs* 20: "For Satan finds some mischief still
for idle hands to do."

14 Here Stowe elaborates on the division of
property. Note that in discussing the dowry
she brought into her marriage, Marie distinguishes property from servants (slaves). We
are forewarned that Marie understands well
what is legally hers.

15 Marie articulates the racist stereotype
that slaves, coddled or not, are at best children, and at worst ungrateful wretches.
James Baldwin writes in his essay "In Search
of a Majority" that this stereotype persisted
into the twentieth century because it
remained convenient for whites: "In a way,
the Negro tells us where the bottom is:
because he is there, and where he is, beneath
us, we know where the limits are and how far
we must not fall. We must not fall beneath
him. We must never allow ourselves to fall
that low" (*James Baldwin: Collected Essays*).

16 St. Clare, then, shares the philosophy of sympathy that fuels Stowe's sentimental strategy: that readers not only can but should reason from their own situation to those in slavery. The conversation between Marie and Ophelia gives Stowe's readers a point-by-point outline of the arguments in support of slavery as well as a plethora of racist stereotypes. Crucially, the voice of the slaveowner is that of a white female.

17 An ironic passage, given that Stowe once wrote that it was her experience as a grieving mother at the loss of one of her children in the Cincinnati plague that first led her to realize the pain the slave mother must feel at the loss of hers in slavery (see "Harriet Beecher Stowe and 'The Man That Was a Thing,' " p. xxxv).

18 There is as much satirical playfulness in this exchange between Ophelia and Marie as there was between Sam and Andy in earlier chapters. While twentieth-century readers find Sam and Andy to be stereotyped, bigoted caricatures, nineteenth-century readers said the same about Ophelia and Marie.

19 The division of social life in the nineteenth century into separate spheres of male and female domain led to comparison between mistresses/mothers and their slaves/children. Terms such as "rule" and "government" were common in descriptions of the domestic sphere.

Marie seemed wonderfully supported, always, when she got upon this topic; and she now opened her eyes, and seemed quite to forget her languor.

"You don't know, and you can't, the daily, hourly trials that beset a housekeeper from them, everywhere and every way. But it's no use to complain to St. Clare. He talks the strangest stuff. He says we have made them what they are, and ought to bear with them. He says their faults are all owing to us, and that it would be cruel to make the fault and punish it too. He says we shouldn't do any better, in their place; just as if one could reason from them to us, you know."[16]

"Don't you believe that the Lord made them of one blood with us?" said Miss Ophelia, shortly.

"No, indeed, not I! A pretty story, truly! They are a degraded race."

"Don't you think they've got immortal souls?" said Miss Ophelia, with increasing indignation.

"O, well," said Marie, yawning, "that, of course—nobody doubts that. But as to putting them on any sort of equality with us, you know, as if we could be compared, why, it's impossible! Now, St. Clare really has talked to me as if keeping Mammy from her husband was like keeping me from mine. There's no comparing in this way. Mammy couldn't have the feelings that I should. It's a different thing altogether,—of course, it is,—and yet St. Clare pretends not to see it. And just as if Mammy could love her little dirty babies as I love Eva![17] Yet St. Clare once really and soberly tried to persuade me that it was my duty, with my weak health, and all I suffer, to let Mammy go back, and take somebody else in her place. That was a little too much even for *me* to bear. I don't often show my feelings. I make it a principle to endure everything in silence; it's a wife's hard lot, and I bear it. But I did break out, that time; so that he has never alluded to the subject since. But I know by his looks, and little things that he says, that he thinks so as much as ever; and it's so trying, so provoking!"

Miss Ophelia looked very much as if she was afraid she should say something; but she rattled away with her needles in a way that had volumes of meaning in it, if Marie could only have understood it.[18]

"So, you just see," she continued, "what you've got to manage. A household without any rule; where servants have it all their own way, do what they please, and have what they please, except so far as I, with my feeble health, have kept up government.[19] I keep my cowhide about, and sometimes I do lay it on; but the exertion is always too much for me. If St. Clare would only have this thing done as others do—"

"And how's that?"

"Why, send them to the calaboose,[20] or some of the other places to be flogged. That's the only way. If I wasn't such a poor, feeble piece, I believe I should manage with twice the energy that St. Clare does."

"And how does St. Clare contrive to manage?" said Miss Ophelia. "You say he never strikes a blow."

"Well, men have a more commanding way, you know; it is easier for them; besides, if you ever looked full in his eye, it's peculiar,—that eye,—and if he speaks decidedly, there's a kind of flash. I'm afraid of it, myself; and the servants know they must mind. I couldn't do as much by a regular storm and scolding as St. Clare can by one turn of his eye, if once he is in earnest. O, there's no trouble about St. Clare; that's the reason he's no more feeling for me. But you'll find, when you come to manage, that there's no getting along without severity,—they are so bad, so deceitful, so lazy."

"The old tune," said St. Clare, sauntering in. "What an awful account these wicked creatures will have to settle, at last, especially for being lazy! You see, cousin," said he, as he stretched himself at full length on a lounge opposite to Marie, "it's wholly inexcusable in them, in the light of the example that Marie and I set them,—this laziness."

"Come, now, St. Clare, you are too bad!" said Marie.

"Am I, now? Why, I thought I was talking good, quite remarkably for me. I try to enforce your remarks, Marie, always."

"You know you meant no such thing, St. Clare," said Marie.

"O, I must have been mistaken, then. Thank you, my dear, for setting me right."

"You do really try to be provoking," said Marie.

"O, come, Marie, the day is growing warm, and I have just had a long quarrel with Dolph, which has fatigued me excessively; so, pray be agreeable, now, and let a fellow repose in the light of your smile."

"What's the matter about Dolph?" said Marie. "That fellow's impudence has been growing to a point that is perfectly intolerable to me. I only wish I had the undisputed management of him a while. I'd bring him down!"

"What you say, my dear, is marked with your usual acuteness and good sense," said St. Clare. "As to Dolph, the case is this: that he has so long been engaged in imi-

20 Literally, a dungeon (Spanish). It was the term used for the local lockup in the South that employed men for whipping slaves sent in by their owners. Marie is not unlike her husband in wanting to outsource as much of the dirty work of keeping slaves as possible. Gentle people cannot be expected to do their own flogging.

**21** The character of Adolph would be perfectly at home in any twenty-first-century television sitcom. The cambric of St. Clare's handkerchiefs is fine white linen. Dolph's dandified affecting of his master's habits was a familiar comic bit in minstrel shows. James Baldwin seems to have taken no notice of him at all.

**22** Stowe has accomplished a moment of accord between Ophelia and Marie: They both disapprove of St. Clare giving fine things to Adolph, but for completely different reasons. Marie disapproves of luxurious things for servants, and Ophelia disapproves of luxurious things.

**23** This does not refer to a particular person but speaks to St. Clare's continued interest in things Northern.

**24** The piano was an important part of the Victorian home, used to play both classical and religious music. Stowe adds these familiar details in order to drive home the point of St. Clare's moral failures.

tating my graces and perfections, that he has, at last, really mistaken himself for his master; and I have been obliged to give him a little insight into his mistake."

"How?" said Marie.

"Why, I was obliged to let him understand explicitly that I preferred to keep *some* of my clothes for my own personal wearing; also, I put his magnificence upon an allowance of cologne-water, and actually was so cruel as to restrict him to one dozen of my cambric handkerchiefs. Dolph was particularly huffy about it, and I had to talk to him like a father, to bring him round."[21]

"O! St. Clare, when will you learn how to treat your servants? It's abominable, the way you indulge them!" said Marie.

"Why, after all, what's the harm of the poor dog's wanting to be like his master; and if I haven't brought him up any better than to find his chief good in cologne and cambric handkerchiefs, why shouldn't I give them to him?"

"And why haven't you brought him up better?" said Miss Ophelia, with blunt determination.[22]

"Too much trouble,—laziness, cousin, laziness,—which ruins more souls than you can shake a stick at. If it weren't for laziness, I should have been a perfect angel, myself. I'm inclined to think that laziness is what your old Dr. Botherem, up in Vermont,[23] used to call the 'essence of moral evil.' It's an awful consideration, certainly."

"I think you slaveholders have an awful responsibility upon you," said Miss Ophelia. "I wouldn't have it, for a thousand worlds. You ought to educate your slaves, and treat them like reasonable creatures,—like immortal creatures, that you've got to stand before the bar of God with. That's my mind," said the good lady, breaking suddenly out with a tide of zeal that had been gaining strength in her mind all the morning.

"O! come, come," said St. Clare, getting up quickly; "what do you know about us?" And he sat down to the piano,[24] and rattled a lively piece of music. St. Clare had a decided genius for music. His touch was brilliant and firm, and his fingers flew over the keys with a rapid and bird-like motion, airy, and yet decided. He played piece after piece, like a man who is trying to play himself into a good humor. After pushing the music aside, he rose up, and said, gayly, "Well, now, cousin, you've given us a good talk, and done your duty; on the whole, I think the better of you for it. I make no manner of doubt that you threw a very diamond of truth at me, though you see it hit me so directly in the face that it wasn't exactly appreciated, at first."

"For my part, I don't see any use in such sort of talk," said Marie. "I'm sure, if anybody does more for servants than we do, I'd like to know who; and it don't do em a bit good,—not a particle,—they get worse and worse. As to talking to them, or anything like that, I'm sure I have talked till I was tired and hoarse, telling them their duty, and all that; and I'm sure they can go to church when they like, though they don't understand a word of the sermon, more than so many pigs,**25**—so it isn't of any great use for them to go, as I see; but they do go, and so they have every chance; but, as I said before, they are a degraded race, and always will be, and there isn't any help for them; you can't make anything of them, if you try. You see, Cousin Ophelia, I've tried, and you haven't; I was born and bred among them, and I know."

Miss Ophelia thought she had said enough, and therefore sat silent. St. Clare whistled a tune.

"St. Clare, I wish you wouldn't whistle," said Marie; "it makes my head worse."

"I won't," said St. Clare. "Is there anything else you wouldn't wish me to do?"

"I wish you *would* have some kind of sympathy for my trials; you never have any feeling for me."

"My dear accusing angel!" said St. Clare.

"It's provoking to be talked to in that way."

"Then, how will you be talked to? I'll talk to order,—any way you'll mention,—only to give satisfaction."

A gay laugh from the court rang through the silken curtains of the verandah. St. Clare stepped out, and lifting up the curtain, laughed too.

"What is it?" said Miss Ophelia, coming to the railing.

There sat Tom, on a little mossy seat in the court, every one of his button-holes stuck full of cape jessamines, and Eva, gayly laughing, was hanging a wreath of roses round his neck; and then she sat down on his knee, like a chip-sparrow, still laughing.

"O, Tom, you look so funny!"

Tom had a sober, benevolent smile, and seemed, in his quiet way, to be enjoying the fun quite as much as his little mistress. He lifted his eyes, when he saw his master, with a half-deprecating, apologetic air.

"How can you let her?" said Miss Ophelia.

"Why not?" said St. Clare.

"Why, I don't know, it seems so dreadful!"**26**

"You would think no harm in a child's caressing a large dog, even if he was black; but a creature that can think, and reason, and feel, and is immortal, you shudder at; con-

25 Another in a host of racist stereotypes that compared African Americans to animals. Marie will end with the trump card for any Southerner in an argument with a Northerner about slavery: "I was born and bred among them, and I know."

26 With this scene, Stowe contrasts the "natural" decorative instinct of Eva with both the artificial indulgence of Marie (and Adolph) and the self-denial of Ophelia. Thesis, antithesis, synthesis.

"Eva Dressing Uncle Tom." Wood engraving by T. Williams, "after George Cruikshank." "There sat Tom, on a little mossy seat in the court, every one of his button-holes stuck full of cape jessamines, and Eva, gaily laughing, was hanging a wreath of roses round his neck; and then she sat down on his knee, like a chip-sparrow, still laughing." From *Uncle Tom's Cabin*, John Cassell, London, 1852

27 St. Clare teases Ophelia about her "Northern" sense of decorum, using the argument that there is no personal prejudice in Southerners' actions, just habit. His convoluted logic suggests that Southerners consider slaves to be as natural a part of their families as a pet dog. With this passage, Stowe calls her Northern readers to task about their own prejudices in supporting blacks only in the abstract or at a distance.

28 One of the many legacies of Jean Jacques Rousseau's writings (particularly *Emile*, published in 1762) was a new and widespread belief that children were naturally innocent and that parents and teachers should work to make childhood a pure and natural time. This philosophy sat uneasily with those who embraced the notion that children were little heathens, and that to spare the rod was to spoil the child. Many teachers and religious thinkers in the nineteenth century, the scholar Karen Sanchez-Eppler writes, "held an unstable double vision of children's relation to religion, at once seeing the child as naturally depraved and as naturally angelic" ("Raising Empires Like Children: Race, Nation, and Religious Education"). In *Uncle Tom's Cabin*, Stowe brings to life this double vision with the characters of Eva and, in chapter 20, Topsy.

29 St. Clare may be extolling the virtues of childhood, but Tom functions simply as a new and exotic entertainment for his little daughter.

30 Showing her (and St. Clare's) love of Shakespeare, Stowe refers here to *The Merchant of Venice* (1.2.17–18). Shakespeare's most famous heroine, Portia, speaks to Nerissa in this scene; the speech begins "If to do were as easy as to know what were good to do, chapels had been churches and poor men's cottages princes' palaces."

31 James Baldwin also admired Shakespeare's efforts "to defeat all labels and complicate all battles," as he writes in "This Nettle, Danger." "Shakespeare knew, and all artists know, that evil comes into the world by means of some vast, inexplicable and probably ineradicable human fault. That is to say: the evil is, in some sense, ours, and we help to feed it by failing so often in our private lives to deal with our private truth—our

fess it, cousin. I know the feeling among some of you northerners well enough.[27] Not that there is a particle of virtue in our not having it; but custom with us does what Christianity ought to do,—obliterates the feeling of personal prejudice. I have often noticed, in my travels north, how much stronger this was with you than with us. You loathe them as you would a snake or a toad, yet you are indignant at their wrongs. You would not have them abused; but you don't want to have anything to do with them yourselves. You would send them to Africa, out of your sight and smell, and then send a missionary or two to do up all the self-denial of elevating them compendiously. Isn't that it?"

"Well, cousin," said Miss Ophelia, thoughtfully, "there may be some truth in this."

"What would the poor and lowly do, without children?" said St. Clare, leaning on the railing, and watching Eva, as she tripped off, leading Tom with her. "Your little child is your only true democrat.[28] Tom, now, is a hero to Eva; his stories are wonders in her eyes, his songs and Methodist hymns are better than an opera, and the traps and little bits of trash in his pocket a mine of jewels, and he the most wonderful Tom that ever wore a black skin.[29] This is one of the roses of Eden that the Lord has dropped down expressly for the poor and lowly, who get few enough of any other kind."

"It's strange, cousin," said Miss Ophelia; "one might almost think you were a *professor*, to hear you talk."

"A professor?" said St. Clare.

"Yes; a professor of religion."

"Not at all; not a professor, as your town-folks have it; and, what is worse, I'm afraid, not a *practiser*, either."

"What makes you talk so, then?"

"Nothing is easier than talking," said St. Clare. "I believe Shakespeare makes somebody say, 'I could sooner show twenty what were good to be done, than be one of the twenty to follow my own showing.'[30] Nothing like division of labor. My forte lies in talking, and yours, cousin, lies in doing."[31]

In Tom's external situation, at this time, there was, as the world says, nothing to complain of. Little Eva's fancy for him—the instinctive gratitude and loveliness of a noble nature—had led her to petition her father that he might be her especial attendant, whenever she needed the escort of a servant, in her walks or rides; and Tom had general orders to let everything else go, and attend to

Miss Eva whenever she wanted him,—orders which our readers may fancy were far from disagreeable to him. He was kept well dressed, for St. Clare was fastidiously particular on this point. His stable services were merely a sinecure, and consisted simply in a daily care and inspection, and directing an under-servant in his duties; for Marie St. Clare declared that she could not have any smell of the horses about him when he came near her, and that he must positively not be put to any service that would make him unpleasant to her, as her nervous system was entirely inadequate to any trial of that nature; one snuff of anything disagreeable being, according to her account, quite sufficient to close the scene, and put an end to all her earthly trials at once. Tom, therefore, in his well-brushed broadcloth suit, smooth beaver, glossy boots, faultless wristbands and collar, with his grave, good-natured black face, looked respectable enough to be a Bishop of Carthage,[32] as men of his color were, in other ages.

Then, too, he was in a beautiful place, a consideration to which his sensitive race are never indifferent; and he did enjoy with a quiet joy the birds, the flowers, the fountains, the perfume, and light and beauty of the court, the silken hangings, and pictures, and lustres, and statuettes, and gilding, that made the parlors within a kind of Aladdin's palace[33] to him.

If ever Africa shall show an elevated and cultivated race,—and come it must, some time, her turn to figure in the great drama of human improvement,—life will awake there with a gorgeousness and splendor of which our cold western tribes faintly have conceived.[34] In that far-off mystic land of gold, and gems, and spices, and waving palms, and wondrous flowers, and miraculous fertility, will awake new forms of art, new styles of splendor; and the negro race, no longer despised and trodden down, will, perhaps, show forth some of the latest and most magnificent revelations of human life. Certainly they will, in their gentleness, their lowly docility of heart, their aptitude to repose on a superior mind and rest on a higher power, their childlike simplicity of affection, and facility of forgiveness. In all these they will exhibit the highest form of the peculiarly *Christian life*, and, perhaps, as God chasteneth whom he loveth,[35] he hath chosen poor Africa in the furnace of affliction, to make her the highest and noblest in that kingdom which he will set up, when every other kingdom has been tried, and failed; for the first shall be last, and the last first.[36]

own experience" (*James Baldwin: Collected Essays*).

32 Stowe probably has in mind Thascius Caecilius Cyprianus (200–258). Cyprianus was leader of the Christian church in Africa, made bishop of Carthage in 248. Tom's outfit consists of a suit of finely twilled wool, a hat made of wool resembling beaver fur, well-shined boots, and cuffs and neckband (commonly worn by men at the time instead of a shirt).

33 Reference to the cave of riches found by Aladdin, a character in *Arabian Nights*. (The stories had become popular in England and America after the publication of Sir Richard Burton's famous 1850 translation.) In this repetition of the scene in which Tom first entered the opulent St. Clare household, Stowe voices the racist belief that slaves, like children, were naturally attracted to beautiful things.

34 Stowe reflects the nineteenth-century racialist belief that civilizations, like people, had inherent qualities that were necessary to the continued progress of the world. The cold Anglo-Saxon had little capacity for pleasure and beauty. The idea that others—"simpler folk"—had unique contributions for the world that Western civilization had built would have significant force, especially after World War I. The question of what was to be done with emancipated slaves formed a great debate of the nineteenth century. Here Stowe focuses on such "inherent" qualities as gentle simplicity and a forgiving nature to assuage whites' fears of retribution in a post-slavery country.

35 Prov. 13:24: "He that spareth his rod hateth his son; but he that loveth him chasteneth him betimes." Here, and in the next scriptural reference, Stowe seems to be suggesting that Africa will be rewarded for its suffering.

36 Jesus' words in Matt. 19:30: "Many that are first shall be last; and the last shall be first."

**37** One of many hints to Stowe's readers that Eva is not long for this world.

**38** In the nineteenth century, because women were prone to swooning (as a result of shock or, more often, tight corsets), they carried with them their vinaigrette, a bottle containing a sponge soaked with smelling salts. Stowe contrasts Marie's nervous condition with Ophelia's obscene good health.

Was this what Marie St. Clare was thinking of, as she stood, gorgeously dressed, on the verandah, on Sunday morning, clasping a diamond bracelet on her slender wrist? Most likely it was. Or, if it wasn't that, it was something else; for Marie patronized good things, and she was going now, in full force,—diamonds, silk, and lace, and jewels, and all,—to a fashionable church, to be very religious. Marie always made a point to be very pious on Sundays. There she stood, so slender, so elegant, so airy and undulating in all her motions, her lace scarf enveloping her like a mist. She looked a graceful creature, and she felt very good and very elegant indeed. Miss Ophelia stood at her side, a perfect contrast. It was not that she had not as handsome a silk dress and shawl, and as fine a pocket-handkerchief; but stiffness and squareness, and bolt-uprightness, enveloped her with as indefinite yet appreciable a presence as did grace her elegant neighbor; not the grace of God, however,—that is quite another thing!

"Where's Eva?" said Marie.

"The child stopped on the stairs, to say something to Mammy."

And what was Eva saying to Mammy on the stairs? Listen, reader, and you will hear, though Marie does not.**37**

"Dear Mammy, I know your head is aching dreadfully."

"Lord bless you, Miss Eva! my head allers aches lately. You don't need to worry."

"Well, I'm glad you're going out; and here,"—and the little girl threw her arms around her,—"Mammy, you shall take my vinaigrette."**38**

"What! your beautiful gold thing, thar, with them diamonds! Lor, Miss, 't wouldn't be proper, no ways."

"Why not? You need it, and I don't. Mamma always uses it for headache, and it'll make you feel better. No, you shall take it, to please me, now."

"Do hear the darlin talk!" said Mammy, as Eva thrust it into her bosom, and, kissing her, ran down stairs to her mother.

"What were you stopping for?"

"I was just stopping to give Mammy my vinaigrette, to take to church with her."

"Eva!" said Marie, stamping impatiently,—"your gold vinaigrette to *Mammy*! When will you learn what's *proper*? Go right and take it back, this moment!"

Eva looked downcast and aggrieved, and turned slowly.

"I say, Marie, let the child alone; she shall do as she pleases," said St. Clare.

"St. Clare, how will she ever get along in the world?" said Marie.

"The Lord knows," said St. Clare; "but she'll get along in heaven better than you or I."

"O, papa, don't," said Eva, softly touching his elbow; "it troubles mother."

"Well, cousin, are you ready to go to meeting?" said Miss Ophelia, turning square about on St. Clare.

"I'm not going, thank you."

"I do wish St. Clare ever would go to church," said Marie; "but he hasn't a particle of religion about him. It really isn't respectable."

"I know it," said St. Clare. "You ladies go to church to learn how to get along in the world, I suppose, and your piety sheds respectability on us. If I did go at all, I would go where Mammy goes; there's something to keep a fellow awake there, at least."[39]

"What! those shouting Methodists? Horrible!" said Marie.

"Anything but the dead sea of your respectable churches, Marie. Positively, it's too much to ask of a man. Eva, do you like to go? Come, stay at home and play with me."

"Thank you, papa; but I'd rather go to church."

"Isn't it dreadful tiresome?" said St. Clare.

"I think it is tiresome, some," said Eva; "and I am sleepy, too, but I try to keep awake."

"What do you go for, then?"

"Why, you know, papa," she said, in a whisper, "cousin told me that God wants to have us; and he gives us everything, you know; and it isn't much to do it, if he wants us to. It isn't so very tiresome, after all."

"You sweet, little obliging soul!" said St. Clare, kissing her; "go along, that's a good girl, and pray for me."

"Certainly, I always do," said the child, as she sprang after her mother into the carriage.

St. Clare stood on the steps and kissed his hand to her, as the carriage drove away; large tears were in his eyes.

"O, Evangeline! rightly named," he said; "hath not God made thee an evangel to me?"[40]

So he felt a moment; and then he smoked a cigar, and read the Picayune,[41] and forgot his little gospel. Was he much unlike other folks?

"You see, Evangeline," said her mother, "it's always right and proper to be kind to servants, but it isn't proper to treat them *just* as we would our relations, or people in our own class of life. Now, if Mammy was sick, you wouldn't want to put her in your own bed."

39 St. Clare voices the attraction many whites felt for the more exuberant religious meetings held by the slaves. Recall George Shelby's interest in Tom's prayer meeting in chapter 4. Note that while St. Clare is not a strong believer in things religious, he thinks the services are beneficial as entertainment.

40 Again, recall that the name Evangeline comes from "evangel," meaning the bringer of good news (the gospel).

41 The Picayune is the local paper. The word "picayune" refers both to a coin and to a person of small value.

42 The following episode—particularly the dialogue—is one of the weakest in the novel. Stowe is seeking to skewer the Southern minister's weekly endeavor to justify slavery by reference to the Bible, a widespread practice in the antebellum South. But the episode is plodding. I confess that my eyes glaze over.

43 Most likely, Dr. G——'s text is from Eccles. 3:1: "To every thing there is a season, and a time to every purpose under heaven." The text allows an interpretation that what men do is natural and actually a part of God's unseen plan.

"I should feel just like it, mamma," said Eva, "because then it would be handier to take care of her, and because, you know, my bed is better than hers."

Marie was in utter despair at the entire want of moral perception evinced in this reply.

"What can I do to make this child understand me?" she said.

"Nothing," said Miss Ophelia, significantly.

Eva looked sorry and disconcerted for a moment; but children, luckily, do not keep to one impression long, and in a few moments she was merrily laughing at various things which she saw from the coach-windows, as it rattled along.

"Well, ladies," said St. Clare, as they were comfortably seated at the dinner-table, "and what was the bill of fare at church to-day?"[42]

"O, Dr. G— preached a splendid sermon,"[43] said Marie. "It was just such a sermon as you ought to hear; it expressed all my views exactly."

"It must have been very improving," said St. Clare. "The subject must have been an extensive one."

"Well, I mean all my views about society, and such things," said Marie. "The text was, 'He hath made everything beautiful in its season;' and he showed how all the orders and distinctions in society came from God; and that it was so appropriate, you know, and beautiful, that some should be high and some low, and that some were born to rule and some to serve, and all that, you know; and he applied it so well to all this ridiculous fuss that is made about slavery, and he proved distinctly that the Bible was on our side, and supported all our institutions so convincingly. I only wish you'd heard him."

"O, I didn't need it," said St. Clare. "I can learn what does me as much good as that from the Picayune, any time, and smoke a cigar besides; which I can't do, you know, in a church."

"Why," said Miss Ophelia, "don't you believe in these views?"

"Who,—I? You know I'm such a graceless dog that these religious aspects of such subjects don't edify me much. If I was to say anything on this slavery matter, I would say out, fair and square, 'We're in for it; we've got 'em, and mean to keep 'em,—it's for our convenience and our interest;' for that's the long and short of it,—that's just the whole of what all this sanctified stuff amounts to, after all; and I think that will be intelligible to everybody, everywhere."

"I do think, Augustine, you are so irreverent!" said Marie. "I think it's shocking to hear you talk."

"Shocking! it's the truth. This religious talk on such matters,—why don't they carry it a little further, and show the beauty, in its season, of a fellow's taking a glass too much, and sitting a little too late over his cards, and various providential arrangements of that sort, which are pretty frequent among us young men;-we'd like to hear that those are right and godly, too."

"Well," said Miss Ophelia, "do you think slavery right or wrong?"

"I'm not going to have any of your horrid New England directness, cousin," said St. Clare, gayly. "If I answer that question, I know you'll be at me with half a dozen others, each one harder than the last; and I'm not a going to define my position. I am one of the sort that lives by throwing stones at other people's glass houses, but I never mean to put up one for them to stone."[44]

"That's just the way he's always talking," said Marie; "you can't get any satisfaction out of him. I believe it's just because he don't like religion, that he's always running out in this way he's been doing."

"Religion!" said St. Clare, in a tone that made both ladies look at him. "Religion! Is what you hear at church religion? Is that which can bend and turn, and descend and ascend, to fit every crooked phase of selfish, worldly society, religion? Is that religion which is less scrupulous, less generous, less just, less considerate for man, than even my own ungodly, worldly, blinded nature? No! When I look for a religion, I must look for something above me, and not something beneath."

"Then you don't believe that the Bible justifies slavery," said Miss Ophelia.

"The Bible was my *mother's* book," said St. Clare. "By it she lived and died, and I would be very sorry to think it did. I'd as soon desire to have it proved that my mother could drink brandy, chew tobacco, and swear, by way of satisfying me that I did right in doing the same. It wouldn't make me at all more satisfied with these things in myself, and it would take from me the comfort of respecting her; and it really is a comfort, in this world, to have anything one can respect. In short, you see," said he, suddenly resuming his gay tone, "all I want is that different things be kept in different boxes. The whole frame-

44  In his *Jacula Prudentum* 196, George Herbert (1593–1633) rephrases a proverb, "Whose house is of glass, must not throw stones at another."

**45** St. Clare's rejection of Christianity is based on the self-interested interpretations of the Bible by pro-slavery ministers.

work of society, both in Europe and America, is made up of various things which will not stand the scrutiny of any very ideal standard of morality. It's pretty generally understood that men don't aspire after the absolute right, but only to do about as well as the rest of the world. Now, when any one speaks up, like a man, and says slavery is necessary to us, we can't get along without it, we should be beggared if we give it up, and, of course, we mean to hold on to it,—this is strong, clear, well-defined language; it has the respectability of truth to it; and if we may judge by their practice, the majority of the world will bear us out in it. But when he begins to put on a long face, and snuffle, and quote Scripture, I incline to think he isn't much better than he should be. "

"You are very uncharitable," said Marie.

"Well," said St. Clare, "suppose that something should bring down the price of cotton once and forever, and make the whole slave property a drug in the market, don't you think we should soon have another version of the Scripture doctrine? What a flood of light would pour into the church, all at once, and how immediately it would be discovered that everything in the Bible and reason went the other way!"**45**

"Well, at any rate," said Marie, as she reclined herself on a lounge, "I'm thankful I'm born where slavery exists; and I believe it's right,—indeed, I feel it must be; and, at any rate, I'm sure I couldn't get along without it."

"I say, what do you think, Pussy?" said her father to Eva, who came in at this moment, with a flower in her hand.

"What about, papa?"

"Why, which do you like the best,—to live as they do at your uncle's, up in Vermont, or to have a house-full of servants, as we do?"

"O, of course, our way is the pleasantest," said Eva.

"Why so?" said St. Clare, stroking her head.

"Why, it makes so many more round you to love, you know," said Eva, looking up earnestly.

"Now, that's just like Eva," said Marie; "just one of her odd speeches."

"Is it an odd speech, papa?" said Eva, whisperingly, as she got upon his knee.

"Rather, as this world goes, Pussy," said St. Clare. "But where has my little Eva been, all dinner-time?"

"O, I've been up in Tom's room, hearing him sing, and Aunt Dinah gave me my dinner."

"Hearing Tom sing, hey?"

"O, yes! he sings such beautiful things about the New Jerusalem, and bright angels, and the land of Canaan."[46]

"I dare say; it's better than the opera, isn't it?"

"Yes, and he's going to teach them to me."

"Singing lessons, hey?—you *are* coming on."

"Yes, he sings for me, and I read to him in my Bible; and he explains what it means, you know."

"On my word," said Marie, laughing, "that is the latest joke of the season."

"Tom isn't a bad hand, now, at explaining Scripture, I'll dare swear," said St. Clare. "Tom has a natural genius for religion. I wanted the horses out early, this morning, and I stole up to Tom's cubiculum[47] there, over the stables, and there I heard him holding a meeting by himself; and, in fact, I haven't heard anything quite so savory as Tom's prayer, this some time. He put in for me, with a zeal that was quite apostolic."

"Perhaps he guessed you were listening. I've heard of that trick before."

"If he did, he wasn't very politic; for he gave the Lord his opinion of me, pretty freely. Tom seemed to think there was decidedly room for improvement in me, and seemed very earnest that I should be converted."

"I hope you'll lay it to heart," said Miss Ophelia.

"I suppose you are much of the same opinion," said St. Clare. "Well, we shall see,—shan't we, Eva?"

46 Little Eva does not know the code that Uncle Tom is singing is about the North and freedom. Whether Tom knows the code is a different question.

47 Sleeping quarter; small room partitioned off from the main building. Root word of today's office "cubicle."

# CHAPTER 17

———

## *The Freeman's Defence*[1]

1 The title of this chapter refers to the necessity of free Northerners to defend themselves against harboring slaves under the Fugitive Slave Act of 1850. Section 6 of the act, the first of two critical parts, reads:

> And be it further enacted, That when a person held to service or labor in any State or Territory of the United States, has heretofore or shall hereafter escape into another State or Territory of the United States, the person or persons to whom such service or labor may be due, or his, her, or their agent or attorney, duly authorized, by power of attorney, in writing, acknowledged and certified under the seal of some legal officer or court of the State or Territory in which the same may be executed, may pursue and reclaim such fugitive person, either by procuring a warrant from some one of the courts, judges, or commissioners aforesaid, of the proper circuit, district, or county, for the apprehension of such fugitive from service or labor, or by seizing and arresting such fugitive, where the same can be done without process, and by taking, or causing such person to be taken, forthwith before such court, judge, or commissioner, whose duty it shall be to hear and determine the case of such claimant in a summary manner. . . .

There was a gentle bustle at the Quaker house, as the afternoon drew to a close. Rachel Halliday moved quietly to and fro, collecting from her household stores such needments[2] as could be arranged in the smallest compass, for the wanderers who were to go forth that night. The afternoon shadows stretched eastward, and the round red sun stood thoughtfully on the horizon, and his beams shone yellow and calm into the little bed-room where George and his wife were sitting. He was sitting with his child on his knee, and his wife's hand in his. Both looked thoughtful and serious, and traces of tears were on their cheeks.

"Yes, Eliza," said George, "I know all you say is true. You are a good child,—a great deal better than I am; and I will try to do as you say. I'll try to act worthy of a free man. I'll try to feel like a Christian. God Almighty knows that I've meant to do well,—tried hard to do well,—when everything has been against me; and now I'll forget all the past, and put away every hard and bitter feeling, and read my Bible, and learn to be a good man."

"And when we get to Canada," said Eliza, "I can help you. I can do dress-making very well; and I understand fine washing and ironing; and between us we can find something to live on."

"Yes, Eliza, so long as we have each other and our boy. O! Eliza, if these people only knew what a blessing it is for a man to feel that his wife and child belong to *him*! I've often wondered to see men that could call their wives and children *their own* fretting and worrying about anything else.[3] Why, I feel rich and strong, though we have nothing but our bare hands. I feel as if I could scarcely ask God for any more. Yes, though I've worked hard every day, till I am twenty-five years old, and have not a cent of money, nor a roof to cover me, nor a spot of land to call my own, yet, if they will only let me alone now, I will be satisfied—thankful; I will work, and send back the money for you and my boy. As to my old master, he has been paid five times over for all he ever spent for me. I don't owe him anything."

"But yet we are not quite out of danger," said Eliza; "we are not yet in Canada."

"True," said George, "but it seems as if I smelt the free air, and it makes me strong."

At this moment, voices were heard in the outer apartment, in earnest conversation, and very soon a rap was heard on the door. Eliza started and opened it.

Simeon Halliday was there, and with him a Quaker brother,[4] whom he introduced as Phineas Fletcher. Phineas was tall and lathy,[5] red-haired, with an expression of great acuteness and shrewdness in his face. He had not the placid, quiet, unworldly air of Simeon Halliday; on the contrary, a particularly wide-awake and *au fait*[6] appearance, like a man who rather prides himself on knowing what he is about, and keeping a bright look-out ahead; peculiarities which sorted rather oddly with his broad brim and formal phraseology.

"Our friend Phineas hath discovered something of importance to the interests of thee and thy party, George," said Simeon; "it were well for thee to hear it."

"That I have," said Phineas, "and it shows the use of a man's always sleeping with one ear open, in certain places, as I've always said. Last night I stopped at a little lone tavern, back on the road. Thee remembers the place, Simeon, where we sold some apples, last year, to that fat woman, with the great ear-rings. Well, I was tired with hard driving; and, after my supper, I stretched myself down on a pile of bags in the corner, and pulled a buffalo[7] over me, to wait till my bed was ready; and what does I do, but get fast asleep."

"With one ear open, Phineas?" said Simeon, quietly.

"No; I slept, ears and all, for an hour or two, for I was pretty well tired; but when I came to myself a little, I found that there were some men in the room, sitting round a table, drinking and talking; and I thought, before I made much muster,[8] I'd just see what they were up to, especially

Section 7, perhaps more worrisome to Northerners, stated:

And be it further enacted, That any person who shall knowingly and willingly obstruct, hinder, or prevent such claimant, his agent or attorney, or any person or persons lawfully assisting him, her, or them, from arresting such a fugitive from service or labor, either with or without process as aforesaid, or shall rescue, or attempt to rescue, such fugitive from service or labor, from the custody of such claimant, his or her agent or attorney, or other person or persons lawfully assisting as aforesaid, when so arrested, pursuant to the authority herein given and declared; or shall aid, abet, or assist such person so owing service or labor as aforesaid, directly or indirectly, to escape from such claimant, his agent or attorney, or other person or persons legally authorized as aforesaid; or shall harbor or conceal such fugitive, so as to prevent the discovery and arrest of such person, after notice or knowledge of the fact that such person was a fugitive from service or labor as aforesaid, shall, for either of said offences, be subject to a fine not exceeding one thousand dollars, and imprisonment not exceeding six months. . . .

Many Northerners and states-rights advocates were outraged by the long arm of the new law. In 1851 Boston, a vigilante group of free blacks stormed a courtroom and spirited away Shadrach Minkins, a fugitive slave, from his federal pursuers. Minkins managed to reach Canada, where he married and raised a family.

2 Stowe adopts an archaic language here that highlights the speech of the Quakers. Thus, "needments" for "necessities."

3 Modern readers may wince at the idea that George Harris in his freedom enjoys his *ownership* of his wife and child.

4 Here "brother" is Quaker terminology for a member of the congregation.

5 I.e., lanky.

6 French for "skillful."

7 The skin of a buffalo, used as a blanket for warmth.

8 Ironically, a military term for "show one-self."

9 Stowe makes use of the dramatic scene to create a tableau—almost a stage—for her readers to view.

as I heard them say something about the Quakers. 'So,' says one, 'they are up in the Quaker settlement, no doubt,' says he. Then I listened with both ears, and I found that they were talking about this very party. So I lay and heard them lay off all their plans. This young man, they said, was to be sent back to Kentucky, to his master, who was going to make an example of him, to keep all niggers from running away; and his wife two of them were going to run down to New Orleans to sell, on their own account, and they calculated to get sixteen or eighteen hundred dollars for her; and the child, they said, was going to a trader, who had bought him; and then there was the boy, Jim, and his mother, they were to go back to their masters in Kentucky. They said that there were two constables, in a town a little piece ahead, who would go in with 'em to get 'em taken up, and the young woman was to be taken before a judge; and one of the fellows, who is small and smooth-spoken, was to swear to her for his property, and get her delivered over to him to take south. They've got a right notion of the track we are going tonight; and they'll be down after us, six or eight strong. So, now, what's to be done?"

The group that stood in various attitudes,[9] after this communication, were worthy of a painter. Rachel Halliday, who had taken her hands out of a batch of biscuit, to hear the news, stood with them upraised and floury, and with a face of the deepest concern. Simeon looked profoundly thoughtful; Eliza had thrown her arms around her husband, and was looking up to him. George stood with clenched hands and glowing eyes, and looking as any other man might look, whose wife was to be sold at auction, and son sent to a trader, all under the shelter of a Christian nation's laws.

"What *shall* we do, George?" said Eliza, faintly.

"I know what *I* shall do," said George, as he stepped into the little room, and began examining his pistols.

"Ay, ay," said Phineas, nodding his head to Simeon; "thou seest, Simeon, how it will work."

"I see," said Simeon, sighing; "I pray it come not to that."

"I don't want to involve any one with or for me," said George. "If you will lend me your vehicle and direct me, I will drive alone to the next stand. Jim is a giant in strength, and brave as death and despair, and so am I."

"Ah, well, friend," said Phineas, "but thee'll need a driver, for all that. Thee's quite welcome to do all the fighting, thee knows; but I know a thing or two about the road, that thee doesn't."

"But I don't want to involve you," said George.

"Involve," said Phineas, with a curious and keen expression of face. "When thee does involve me, please to let me know."

"Phineas is a wise and skilful man," said Simeon. "Thee does well, George, to abide by his judgment; and," he added, laying his hand kindly on George's shoulder, and pointing to the pistols, "be not over hasty with these,—young blood is hot."

"I will attack no man," said George. "All I ask of this country is to be let alone, and I will go out peaceably; but,"—he paused, and his brow darkened and his face worked,—"I've had a sister sold in that New Orleans market. I know what they are sold for; and am I going to stand by and see them take my wife and sell her, when God has given me a pair of strong arms to defend her? No; God help me! I'll fight to the last breath, before they shall take my wife and son. Can you blame me?"[10]

"Mortal man cannot blame thee, George. Flesh and blood could not do otherwise," said Simeon. "Woe unto the world because of offences, but woe unto them through whom the offence cometh."

"Would not even you, sir, do the same, in my place?"

"I pray that I be not tried," said Simeon; "the flesh is weak."

"I think my flesh would be pretty tolerable strong, in such a case," said Phineas, stretching out a pair of arms like the sails of a windmill. "I an't sure, friend George, that I shouldn't hold a fellow for thee, if thee had any accounts to settle with him."

"If man should *ever* resist evil," said Simeon, "then George should feel free to do it now: but the leaders of our people taught a more excellent way; for the wrath of man worketh not the righteousness of God;[11] but it goes sorely against the corrupt will of man, and none can receive it save they to whom it is given. Let us pray the Lord that we be not tempted."

"And so *I* do," said Phineas; "but if we are tempted too much—why, let them look out, that's all."

"It's quite plain thee wasn't born a Friend,"[12] said Simeon, smiling. "The old nature hath its way in thee pretty strong as yet."

To tell the truth, Phineas had been a hearty, two-fisted backwoodsman, a vigorous hunter, and a dead shot at a buck; but, having wooed a pretty Quakeress, had been moved by the power of her charms to join the society in his neighborhood; and though he was an honest, sober,

10 George Harris embodies the manhood that many abolitionists hoped slaves would display in fighting for their cause. Henry Highland Garnet, in his 1843 address, exhorts slaves: "In the name of God, we ask, are you men? Where is the blood of your fathers? Has it all run out of your veins? Awake, awake, millions of voices are calling you!" George Harris repeats that he does not want to force the pacifist Quakers to be involved in fighting on his behalf.

11 James 1:19–20: "Be swift to hear, slow to speak, slow to wrath: For the wrath of man worketh not the righteousness of God."

12 I.e., a Quaker, member of the Society of Friends.

13 Rachel's cooking recollects Aunt Chloe's.

and efficient member, and nothing particular could be alleged against him, yet the more spiritual among them could not but discern an exceeding lack of savor in his developments.

"Friend Phineas will ever have ways of his own," said Rachel Halliday, smiling; "but we all think that his heart is in the right place, after all."

"Well," said George, "isn't it best that we hasten our flight?"

"I got up at four o'clock, and came on with all speed, full two or three hours ahead of them, if they start at the time they planned. It isn't safe to start till dark, at any rate; for there are some evil persons in the villages ahead, that might be disposed to meddle with us, if they saw our wagon, and that would delay us more than the waiting; but in two hours I think we may venture. I will go over to Michael Cross, and engage him to come behind on his swift nag, and keep a bright look-out on the road, and warn us if any company of men come on. Michael keeps a horse that can soon get ahead of most other horses; and he could shoot ahead and let us know, if there were any danger. I am going out now to warn Jim and the old woman to be in readiness, and to see about the horse. We have a pretty fair start, and stand a good chance to get to the stand before they can come up with us. So, have good courage, friend George; this isn't the first ugly scrape that I've been in with thy people," said Phineas, as he closed the door.

"Phineas is pretty shrewd," said Simeon. "He will do the best that can be done for thee, George."

"All I am sorry for," said George, "is the risk to you."

"Thee'll much oblige us, friend George, to say no more about that. What we do we are conscience bound to do; we can do no other way. And now, mother," said he, turning to Rachel, "hurry thy preparations for these friends, for we must not send them away fasting."

And while Rachel and her children were busy making corncake, and cooking ham and chicken, and hurrying on the *et ceteras* of the evening meal,[13] George and his wife sat in their little room, with their arms folded about each other, in such talk as husband and wife have when they know that a few hours may part them forever.

"Eliza," said George, "people that have friends, and houses, and lands, and money, and all those things, *can't* love as we do, who have nothing but each other. Till I knew you, Eliza, no creature ever had loved me, but my poor, heartbroken mother and sister. I saw poor Emily that morning the trader carried her off. She came to the corner where I was lying asleep, and said, 'Poor George, your last friend is going. What will become of you, poor boy?' And I got up and threw my arms round her, and cried and sobbed, and she cried too; and those were the last kind words I got for ten long years; and my heart all withered up, and felt as dry as ashes, till I met you. And your loving me,—why, it was almost like raising one from the dead! I've been a new man ever since! And now, Eliza, I'll give my last drop of blood, but they *shall not* take you from me. Whoever gets you must walk over my dead body."

"O Lord, have mercy!" said Eliza, sobbing. "If he will only let us get out of this country together, that is all we ask."

"Is God on their side?" said George, speaking less to his wife than pouring out his own bitter thoughts. "Does he see all they do? Why does he let such things happen? And they tell us that the Bible is on their side; certainly all the power is. They are rich, and healthy, and happy; they are members of churches, expecting to go to heaven; and they get along so easy in the world, and have it all their own way; and poor, honest, faithful Christians,—Christians as good or better than they,—are lying in the very dust under their feet. They buy 'em and sell 'em, and make trade of their heart's blood, and groans and tears,—and God *lets* them."

"Friend George," said Simeon, from the kitchen, "listen to this Psalm; it may do thee good."[14]

George drew his seat near the door, and Eliza, wiping her tears, came forward also to listen, while Simeon read as follows:

"But as for me, my feet were almost gone; my steps had well-nigh slipped. For I was envious of the foolish, when I saw the prosperity of the wicked. They are not in trouble like other men, neither are they plagued like other men. Therefore, pride compasseth them as a chain; violence covereth them as a garment. Their eyes stand out with fatness; they have more than heart could wish. They are corrupt, and speak wickedly concerning oppression; they speak loftily. Therefore his people return, and the waters of a full cup are wrung out to them, and they say, How doth God know? and is there knowledge in the Most High?"

"Is not that the way thee feels, George?"

"It is so, indeed," said George,—"as well as I could have written it myself."

"Then, hear," said Simeon: "When I thought to know

14 Psalm 73, "The End of the Wicked Contrasted with That of the Righteous."

201

**15** Stowe's description of the calm, pious Quaker family is designed to contrast with the luxurious excesses of the St. Clare household. How much happier Tom would be among Rachel, Ruth, Simeon, and Phineas! Sadly, Tom never encounters any of these or similar Friends.

**16** Seed-cake is a cake flavored with seeds, caraway or sesame.

this, it was too painful for me until I went unto the sanctuary of God. Then understood I their end. Surely thou didst set them in slippery places, thou castedst them down to destruction. As a dream when one awaketh, so, oh Lord, when thou awakest, thou shalt despise their image. Nevertheless, I am continually with thee; thou hast holden me by my right hand. Thou shalt guide me by thy counsel, and afterwards receive me to glory. It is good for me to draw near unto God. I have put my trust in the Lord God."

The words of holy trust, breathed by the friendly old man, stole like sacred music over the harassed and chafed spirit of George; and after he ceased, he sat with a gentle and subdued expression on his fine features.**15**

"If this world were all, George," said Simeon, "thee might, indeed, ask, where is the Lord? But it is often those who have least of all in this life whom he chooseth for the kingdom. Put thy trust in him, and, no matter what befalls thee here, he will make all right hereafter."

If these words had been spoken by some easy, self-indulgent exhorter, from whose mouth they might have come merely as pious and rhetorical flourish, proper to be used to people in distress, perhaps they might not have had much effect; but coming from one who daily and calmly risked fine and imprisonment for the cause of God and man, they had a weight that could not but be felt, and both the poor, desolate fugitives found calmness and strength breathing into them from it.

And now Rachel took Eliza's hand kindly, and led the way to the supper-table. As they were sitting down, a light tap sounded at the door, and Ruth entered.

"I just ran in," she said, "with these little stockings for the boy,—three pair, nice, warm woollen ones. It will be so cold, thee knows, in Canada. Does thee keep up good courage, Eliza?" she added, tripping round to Eliza's side of the table, and shaking her warmly by the hand, and slipping a seed-cake**16** into Harry's hand. "I brought a little parcel of these for him," she said, tugging at her pocket to get out the package. "Children, thee knows, will always be eating."

"O, thank you; you are too kind," said Eliza.

"Come, Ruth, sit down to supper," said Rachel.

"I couldn't, any way. I left John with the baby, and some biscuits in the oven; and I can't stay a moment, else John will burn up all the biscuits, and give the baby all the sugar in the bowl. That's the way he does," said the little Quakeress, laughing. "So, good-by, Eliza; good-by, George; the Lord grant thee a safe journey;" and, with a few tripping steps, Ruth was out of the apartment.

A little while after supper, a large covered-wagon drew up before the door; the night was clear starlight; and Phineas jumped briskly down from his seat to arrange his passengers. George walked out of the door, with his child on one arm and his wife on the other. His step was firm, his face settled and resolute. Rachel and Simeon came out after them.

"You get out, a moment," said Phineas to those inside, "and let me fix the back of the wagon, there, for the womenfolks and the boy."

"Here are the two buffaloes," said Rachel. "Make the seats as comfortable as may be; it's hard riding all night."

Jim came out first, and carefully assisted out his old mother, who clung to his arm, and looked anxiously about, as if she expected the pursuer every moment.

"Jim, are your pistols all in order?" said George, in a low, firm voice.

"Yes, indeed," said Jim.

"And you've no doubt what you shall do, if they come?"

"I rather think I haven't," said Jim, throwing open his broad chest, and taking a deep breath. "Do you think I'll let them get mother again?"

During this brief colloquy, Eliza had been taking her leave of her kind friend, Rachel, and was handed into the carriage by Simeon, and, creeping into the back part with her boy, sat down among the buffalo skins. The old woman was next handed in and seated, and George and Jim placed on a rough board seat front of them, and Phineas mounted in front.

"Farewell, my friends," said Simeon, from without.

"God bless you!" answered all from within.

And the wagon drove off, rattling and jolting over the frozen road.

There was no opportunity for conversation, on account of the roughness of the way and the noise of the wheels. The vehicle, therefore, rumbled on, through long, dark stretches of woodland,—over wide, dreary plains,—up hills, and down valleys,—and on, on, on they jogged, hour after hour. The child soon fell asleep, and lay heavily in his mother's lap. The poor, frightened old woman at last forgot her fears; and, even Eliza, as the night waned, found all her anxieties insufficient to keep her eyes from closing. Phineas seemed, on the whole, the briskest of the company, and beguiled his long drive with whistling certain very unquaker-like songs, as he went on.

But about three o'clock George's ear caught the hasty and decided click of a horse's hoof coming behind them at

17 The pursuing horsemen seen on the horizon is a familiar scene that never loses its dramatic strength. The chase scene became a staple of early-nineteenth-century popular fiction, particularly in works by Emerson Bennett, Robert Montgomery Bird, James Fenimore Cooper, Timothy Flint, James Hall, Charles Fenno Hoffman, Henry William Herbert, J. H. Ingraham, Washington Irving, John Pendleton Kennedy, George Lippard, William Gilmore Simms, James Kirk Paulding, and Walter Scott.

some distance, and jogged Phineas by the elbow. Phineas pulled up his horses, and listened.

"That must be Michael," he said; "I think I know the sound of his gallop;" and he rose up and stretched his head anxiously back over the road.

A man riding in hot haste was now dimly descried at the top of a distant hill.

"There he is, I do believe!" said Phineas. George and Jim both sprang out of the wagon, before they knew what they were doing. All stood intensely silent, with their faces turned towards the expected messenger. On he came. Now he went down into a valley, where they could not see him; but they heard the sharp, hasty tramp, rising nearer and nearer; at last they saw him emerge on the top of an eminence, within hail.

"Yes, that's Michael!" said Phineas; and, raising his voice, "Halloa, there, Michael!"

"Phineas! is that thee?"

"Yes; what news—they coming?"

"Right on behind, eight or ten of them, hot with brandy, swearing and foaming like so many wolves."

And, just as he spoke, a breeze brought the faint sound of galloping horsemen towards them.

"In with you,—quick, boys, *in*!" said Phineas. "If you must fight, wait till I get you a piece ahead." And, with the word, both jumped in, and Phineas lashed the horses to a run, the horseman keeping close beside them. The wagon rattled, jumped, almost flew, over the frozen ground; but plainer, and still plainer, came the noise of pursuing horsemen behind. The women heard it, and, looking anxiously out, saw, far in the rear, on the brow of a distant hill, a party of men looming up against the red-streaked sky of early dawn.[17] Another hill, and their pursuers had evidently caught sight of their wagon, whose white cloth-covered top made it conspicuous at some distance, and a loud yell of brutal triumph came forward on the wind. Eliza sickened, and strained her child closer to her bosom; the old woman prayed and groaned, and George and Jim clenched their pistols with the grasp of despair. The pursuers gained on them fast; the carriage made a sudden turn, and brought them near a ledge of a steep overhanging rock, that rose in an isolated ridge or clump in a large lot, which was, all around it, quite clear and smooth. This isolated pile, or range of rocks, rose up black and heavy against the brightening sky, and seemed to promise shelter and concealment. It was a place well known to Phineas, who had been familiar with the spot in his hunting days; and it was to gain this point he had been racing his horses.[18]

"Now for it!" said he, suddenly checking his horses, and springing from his seat to the ground. "Out with you, in a twinkling, every one, and up into these rocks with me. Michael, thee tie thy horse to the wagon, and drive ahead to Amariah's, and get him and his boys to come back and talk to these fellows."

In a twinkling they were all out of the carriage.

"There," said Phineas, catching up Harry, "you, each of you, see to the women; and run, *now*, if you ever *did* run!"

There needed no exhortation. Quicker than we can say it, the whole party were over the fence, making with all speed for the rocks, while Michael, throwing himself from his horse, and fastening the bridle to the wagon, began driving it rapidly away.

"Come ahead," said Phineas, as they reached the rocks, and saw, in the mingled starlight and dawn, the traces of a rude but plainly marked foot-path leading up among them; "this is one of our old hunting-dens. Come up!"

Phineas went before, springing up the rocks like a goat, with the boy in his arms. Jim came second, bearing his trembling old mother over his shoulder, and George and Eliza brought up the rear. The party of horsemen came up to the fence, and, with mingled shouts and oaths, were dismounting, to prepare to follow them. A few moments' scrambling brought them to the top of the ledge; the path then passed between a narrow defile, where only one could walk at a time, till suddenly they came to a rift or chasm more than a yard in breadth, and beyond which lay a pile of rocks, separate from the rest of the ledge, standing full thirty feet high, with its sides steep and perpendicular as those of a castle. Phineas easily leaped the chasm, and sat down the boy on a smooth, flat platform of crisp white moss, that covered the top of the rock.

"Over with you!" he called; "spring, now, once, for your lives!" said he, as one after another sprang across. Several fragments of loose stone formed a kind of breastwork, which sheltered their position from the observation of those below.

"Well, here we all are," said Phineas, peeping over the stone breastwork to watch the assailants, who were coming tumultuously up under the rocks. "Let 'em get us, if they can. Whoever comes here has to walk single file between those two rocks, in fair range of your pistols, boys, d'ye see?"

18 One forgets, during scenes such as this, that Stowe is a middle-aged mother. Her action scenes are as well described and plotted as Cooper's. However, there was some criticism at the time (perhaps tongue-in-cheek) that Stowe could have used some technical advice on firearm use here. An anonymous writer to *Frederick Douglass' Paper* wrote the following on July 29, 1852:

[E]very one who has ever seen the use of pistols with which weapons the authoress of *Uncle Tom's Cabin* arms George, knows that they are not reliable, unless very large for any considerable distance, say ten steps;—small ones are so notoriously inaccurate that no resolute man regards them, and at hand to hand they are less efficient than the bowie knife or any other kind of broad heavy dagger: the pistol, if so it be named, ought to be *very large* or in other words, it should be a *short gun*, as long as could be consistent with convenience and concealment and carrying an ounce ball; such a weapon for distance and such a companion for it as the heavy bowie knife for a *close fight*, [should have been put] in the hands of each determined man.

"I do see," said George; "and now, as this matter is ours, let us take all the risk, and do all the fighting."

"Thee's quite welcome to do the fighting, George," said Phineas, chewing some checkerberry-leaves as he spoke;

"The Freeman's Defence." George Harris and the Quaker men protecting Eliza and the other runaway slaves from Loker, Marks, and their gang. Although George passes as white in the novel, he appears quite dark in this engraving, as does Eliza.    From *Uncle Tom's Cabin,* John P. Jewett & Co., 1852

"but I may have the fun of looking on, I suppose. But see, these fellows are kinder debating down there, and looking up, like hens when they are going to fly up on to the roost. Hadn't thee better give 'em a word of advice, before they come up, just to tell 'em handsomely they'll be shot if they do?"

The party beneath, now more apparent in the light of the dawn, consisted of our old acquaintances, Tom Loker and Marks, with two constables, and a posse consisting of such rowdies at the last tavern as could be engaged by a little brandy to go and help the fun of trapping a set of niggers.

"Well, Tom, yer coons are farly treed," said one.

"Yes, I see 'em go up right here," said Tom; "and here's a path. I'm for going right up. They can't jump down in a hurry, and it won't take long to ferret 'em out."

"But, Tom, they might fire at us from behind the rocks," said Marks. "That would be ugly, you know."

"Ugh!" said Tom, with a sneer. "Always for saving your skin, Marks! No danger! niggers are too plaguy scared!"

"I don't know why I *shouldn't* save my skin," said Marks. "It's the best I've got; and niggers *do* fight like the devil, sometimes."

At this moment, George appeared on the top of a rock above them, and, speaking in a calm, clear voice, said,

"Gentlemen, who are you, down there, and what do you want?"

"We want a party of runaway niggers," said Tom Loker. "One George Harris, and Eliza Harris, and their son, and Jim Selden, and an old woman. We've got the officers, here, and a warrant to take 'em; and we're going to have 'em, too. D'ye hear? An't you George Harris, that belongs to Mr. Harris, of Shelby county, Kentucky?"

"I am George Harris. A Mr. Harris, of Kentucky, did call me his property. But now I'm a free man, standing on God's free soil; and my wife and my child I claim as mine. Jim and his mother are here. We have arms to defend ourselves, and we mean to do it. You can come up, if you like; but the first one of you that comes within the range of our bullets is a dead man, and the next, and the next; and so on till the last."

"O, come! come!" said a short, puffy man, stepping forward, and blowing his nose as he did so. "Young man, this an't no kind of talk at all for you. You see, we're officers of justice. We've got the law on our side, and the power, and so forth; so you'd better give up peaceably, you see; for you'll certainly have to give up, at last."

"I know very well that you've got the law on your side, and the power,"[19] said George, bitterly. "You mean to take my wife to sell in New Orleans, and put my boy like a calf in a trader's pen, and send Jim's old mother to the brute that whipped and abused her before, because he couldn't abuse her son. You want to send Jim and me back to be whipped and tortured, and ground down under the heels of them that you call masters; and your laws *will* bear you out in it,—more shame for you and them! But you haven't got us. We don't own your laws; we don't own your country; we stand here as free, under God's sky, as you are; and, by the great God that made us, we'll fight for our liberty till we die."[20]

George stood out in fair sight, on the top of the rock, as he made his declaration of independence; the glow of dawn gave a flush to his swarthy cheek, and bitter indignation and despair gave fire to his dark eye; and, as if appealing from man to the justice of God, he raised his hand to heaven as he spoke.

If it had been only a Hungarian youth, now bravely defending in some mountain fastness the retreat of fugitives escaping from Austria into America,[21] this would have been sublime heroism; but as it was a youth of African descent, defending the retreat of fugitives through America into Canada, of course we are too well instructed and patriotic to see any heroism in it; and if any of our readers do, they must do it on their own private responsibility. When despairing Hungarian fugitives make their way, against all the search-warrants and authorities of their lawful government, to America, press and political cabinet ring with applause and welcome. When despairing African fugitives do the same thing,—it is—what *is* it?

Be it as it may, it is certain that the attitude, eye, voice, manner, of the speaker, for a moment struck the party below to silence. There is something in boldness and determination that for a time hushes even the rudest

19 George is a bit too talky in this scene.

20 See Patrick Henry's *Speech in Virginia Convention*, given in Richmond on March 23, 1775: "Is life so dear or peace so sweet as to be purchased at the price of chains and slavery? Forbid it, Almighty God. I know not what course others may take, but as for me, give me liberty or give me death!" (W. W. Henry, *Patrick Henry; Life, Correspondence and Speeches*). As one might imagine, many abolitionists seized upon these words for the anti-slavery cause.

21 Stowe sets George Harris's quest for independence against that of the Hungarians exiled in the United States. Throughout *Uncle Tom's Cabin*, as a worldly parallel to the apocalyptic warning to Christians, Stowe exploits the volatility of international politics of recent years (especially since 1847) to remind her readers of the likelihood of upheavals in the United States as well. The year 1847, for example, saw Liberia proclaimed as an independent republic, the capture of Mexico City by U.S. forces, and a war in Switzerland. The year 1848 saw the rise and suppression of revolts in Paris and Rome, multiple revolutions in Vienna, Berlin, Milan, Parma, and Prague, the second Sikh War, and the abolition of serfdom in Austria. Also in 1848, with the Treaty of Guadalupe Hidalgo, the United States acquired Texas, New Mexico, California, Utah, Nevada, Arizona, and parts of Colorado and Wyoming from Mexico. The year 1849 saw Hungary proclaim independence from Austria with Lajos Kossuth as governor-president and by year's end capitulate to Austria, sending well over a thousand Hungarians fleeing—some, as Stowe describes here, to the United States. Revolts and rebellions continued on the world stage in the years preceding *Uncle Tom's Cabin*.

nature. Marks was the only one who remained wholly untouched. He was deliberately cocking his pistol, and, in the momentary silence that followed George's speech, he fired at him.

"Ye see ye get jist as much for him dead as alive in Kentucky," he said, coolly, as he wiped his pistol on his coat-sleeve.

George sprang backward,—Eliza uttered a shriek,—the ball had passed close to his hair, had nearly grazed the cheek of his wife, and struck in the tree above.

"It's nothing, Eliza," said George, quickly.

"Thee'd better keep out of sight, with thy speechifying," said Phineas; "they're mean scamps."

"Now, Jim," said George, "look that your pistols are all right, and watch that pass with me. The first man that shows himself I fire at; you take the second, and so on. It won't do, you know, to waste two shots on one."

"But what if you don't hit?"

"I *shall* hit," said George, coolly.

"Good! now, there's stuff in that fellow," muttered Phineas, between his teeth.

The party below, after Marks had fired, stood, for a moment, rather undecided.

"I think you must have hit some on 'em," said one of the men. "I heard a squeal!"

"I'm going right up for one," said Tom. "I never was afraid of niggers, and I an't going to be now. Who goes after?" he said, springing up the rocks.

George heard the words distinctly. He drew up his pistol, examined it, pointed it towards that point in the defile where the first man would appear.

One of the most courageous of the party followed Tom, and, the way being thus made, the whole party began pushing up the rock,—the hindermost pushing the front ones faster than they would have gone of themselves. On they came, and in a moment the burly form of Tom appeared in sight, almost at the verge of the chasm.

George fired,—the shot entered his side,—but, though wounded, he would not retreat, but, with a yell like that of a mad bull, he was leaping right across the chasm into the party.

"Friend," said Phineas, suddenly stepping to the front, and meeting him with a push from his long arms, "thee isn't wanted here."

Down he fell into the chasm, crackling down among trees, bushes, logs, loose stones, till he lay, bruised and groaning, thirty feet below. The fall might have killed him, had it not been broken and moderated by his clothes catching in the branches of a large tree; but he came down with some force, however,—more than was at all agreeable or convenient.

"Lord help us, they are perfect devils!" said Marks, heading the retreat down the rocks with much more of a will than he had joined the ascent, while all the party came tumbling precipitately after him,—the fat constable, in particular, blowing and puffing in a very energetic manner.

"I say, fellers," said Marks, "you jist go round and pick up Tom, there, while I run and get on to my horse, to go back for help,—that's you;" and, without minding the hootings and jeers of his company, Marks was as good as his word, and was soon seen galloping away.

"Was ever such a sneaking varmint?" said one of the men; "to come on his business, and he clear out and leave us this yer way!"

"Well, we must pick up that feller," said another. "Cuss me if I much care whether he is dead or alive."

This image features a very dark George Harris being held back by one of the Quaker men as a startlingly simian Tom Loker falls from the precipice.

The men, led by the groans of Tom, scrambled and crackled through stumps, logs and bushes, to where that hero lay groaning and swearing, with alternate vehemence.

"Ye keep it agoing pretty loud, Tom," said one. "Ye much hurt?"

"Don't know. Get me up, can't ye? Blast that infernal Quaker! If it hadn't been for him, I'd a pitched some on 'em down here, to see how they liked it."

With much labor and groaning, the fallen hero was assisted to rise; and, with one holding him up under each shoulder, they got him as far as the horses.

"If you could only get me a mile back to that ar tavern. Give me a handkerchief or something, to stuff into this place, and stop this infernal bleeding."

George looked over the rocks, and saw them trying to lift the burly form of Tom into the saddle. After two or three ineffectual attempts, he reeled, and fell heavily to the ground.

"O, I hope he isn't killed!" said Eliza, who, with all the party, stood watching the proceeding.

**22** Leaving a wounded man is the lowest of the low acts.

**23** Stowe rarely misses the chance to give a male character a loving mother (or wife) as evidence of possible redemption.

"Why not?" said Phineas; "serves him right."

"Because, after death comes the judgment," said Eliza.

"Yes," said the old woman, who had been groaning and praying, in her Methodist fashion, during all the encounter, "it's an awful case for the poor crittur's soul."

"On my word, they're leaving him, I do believe," said Phineas.**22**

It was true; for after some appearance of irresolution and consultation, the whole party got on their horses and rode away. When they were quite out of sight, Phineas began to bestir himself.

"Well, we must go down and walk a piece," he said. "I told Michael to go forward and bring help, and be along back here with the wagon; but we shall have to walk a piece along the road, I reckon, to meet them. The Lord grant he be along soon! It's early in the day; there won't be much travel afoot yet a while; we an't much more than two miles from our stopping-place. If the road hadn't been so rough last night, we could have outrun 'em entirely."

As the party neared the fence, they discovered in the distance, along the road, their own wagon coming back, accompanied by some men on horseback.

"Well, now, there's Michael, and Stephen, and Amariah," exclaimed Phineas, joyfully. "Now we *are* made,—as safe as if we'd got there."

"Well, do stop, then," said Eliza, "and do something for that poor man; he's groaning dreadfully."

"It would be no more than Christian," said George; "let's take him up and carry him on."

"And doctor him up among the Quakers!" said Phineas; "pretty well, that! Well, I don't care if we do. Here, let's have a look at him;" and Phineas, who, in the course of his hunting and backwoods life, had acquired some rude experience of surgery, kneeled down by the wounded man, and began a careful examination of his condition.

"Marks," said Tom, feebly, "is that you, Marks?"

"No; I reckon 'tan't, friend," said Phineas. "Much Marks cares for thee, if his own skin's safe. He's off, long ago."

"I believe I'm done for," said Tom. "The cussed sneaking dog, to leave me to die alone! My poor old mother always told me 'twould be so."**23**

"La sakes! jist hear the poor crittur. He's got a mammy, now," said the old negress. "I can't help kinder pityin' on him."

"Softly, softly; don't thee snap and snarl, friend," said Phineas, as Tom winced and pushed his hand away. "Thee

210

has no chance, unless I stop the bleeding." And Phineas busied himself with making some off-hand surgical arrangements with his own pocket-handkerchief, and such as could be mustered in the company.

"You pushed me down there," said Tom, faintly.

"Well, if I hadn't, thee would have pushed us down, thee sees," said Phineas, as he stooped to apply his bandage. "There, there,—let me fix this bandage. We mean well to thee; we bear no malice. Thee shall be taken to a house where they'll nurse thee first rate,—as well as thy own mother could."

Tom groaned, and shut his eyes. In men of his class, vigor and resolution are entirely a physical matter, and ooze out with the flowing of the blood; and the gigantic fellow really looked piteous in his helplessness.

The other party now came up. The seats were taken out of the wagon. The buffalo-skins, doubled in fours, were spread all along one side, and four men, with great difficulty, lifted the heavy form of Tom into it. Before he was gotten in, he fainted entirely. The old negress, in the abundance of her compassion, sat down on the bottom, and took his head in her lap. Eliza, George and Jim, bestowed themselves, as well as they could, in the remaining space, and the whole party set forward.

"What do you think of him?" said George, who sat by Phineas in front.

"Well, it's only a pretty deep flesh-wound; but, then, tumbling and scratching down that place didn't help him much. It has bled pretty freely,—pretty much dreaned him out, courage and all,—but he'll get over it, and may be learn a thing or two by it."

"I'm glad to hear you say so," said George. "It would always be a heavy thought to me, if I'd caused his death, even in a just cause."[24]

"Yes," said Phineas, "killing is an ugly operation, any way they'll fix it,—man or beast. I've been a great hunter, in my day, and I tell thee I've seen a buck that was shot down, and a dying, look that way on a feller with his eye, that it reely most made a feller feel wicked for killing on him; and human creatures is a more serious consideration yet, bein', as thy wife says, that the judgment comes to 'em after death. So I don't know as our people's notions on these matters is too strict; and, considerin' how I was raised, I fell in with them pretty considerably."

"What shall you do with this poor fellow?" said George.

"O, carry him along to Amariah's. There's old Grandmam Stephens there,—Dorcas, they call her,—she's most

24 Quaker nonviolence refuses the concept of "just cause."

25 Since we've already heard of one convert to the Quaker teachings—Phineas—we should be prepared for a second conversion to the Friends.

an amazin' nurse. She takes to nursing real natural, and an't never better suited than when she gets a sick body to tend. We may reckon on turning him over to her for a fortnight or so."

A ride of about an hour more brought the party to a neat farm-house, where the weary travellers were received to an abundant breakfast. Tom Loker was soon carefully deposited in a much cleaner and softer bed than he had ever been in the habit of occupying.[25] His wound was carefully dressed and bandaged, and he lay languidly opening and shutting his eyes on the white window-curtains and gently-gliding figures of his sick room, like a weary child. And here, for the present, we shall take our leave of one party.

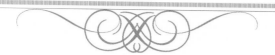

# CHAPTER 18

## Miss Ophelia's Experiences and Opinions[1]

Our friend Tom,[2] in his own simple musings, often compared his more fortunate lot, in the bondage into which he was cast, with that of Joseph in Egypt;[3] and, in fact, as time went on, and he developed more and more under the eye of his master, the strength of the parallel increased.

St. Clare was indolent and careless of money. Hitherto the providing and marketing had been principally done by Adolph, who was, to the full, as careless and extravagant as his master; and, between them both, they had carried on the dispersing process with great alacrity. Accustomed, for many years, to regard his master's property as his own care, Tom saw, with an uneasiness he could scarcely repress, the wasteful expenditure of the establishment; and, in the quiet, indirect way which his class often acquire, would sometimes make his own suggestions.

St. Clare at first employed him occasionally; but, struck with his soundness of mind and good business capacity, he confided in him more and more, till gradually all the marketing and providing for the family were intrusted to him.

"No, no, Adolph," he said, one day, as Adolph was deprecating the passing of power out of his hands; "let Tom alone. You only understand what you want; Tom understands cost and come to; and there may be some end to money, bye and bye if we don't let somebody do that."

Trusted to an unlimited extent by a careless master, who handed him a bill without looking at it, and pocketed

1 In this chapter title, Stowe signals that we will see events primarily through the eyes of a Northerner.

2 How quickly we go from Tom among Friends to "our friend Tom." It is curious that in this early part of the chapter, Stowe dispenses with the term "Uncle." I recall Baldwin's observation in "In Search of a Majority": "Uncle Tom is, for example, if he is called uncle, a kind of saint. He is there, he endures, he will forgive us, and this is a key to that image. . . . When he is Uncle Tom he has no sex—when he is Tom, he does" (*James Baldwin: Collected Essays*).

3 Gen. 37–50. Joseph, son of Jacob, sold by his brothers into Egypt, was appointed by Pharoah to be in charge of Egypt. "Tell my father of my splendor in Egypt, and of all that you have seen" (45:13). Stowe is alluding to Joseph's managerial skills, which brought him some success in Potiphar's household, although unlike Joseph, Tom is not likely to get into any difficulty with his boss's wife (see Gen. 39:8–9).

4 Latin, the distinction between me and you. Scholar Michael Borgstrom has written that the character of Adolph "stands in the continuum of caricatures offered as comic relief in a novel inundated with tears" ("Passing Over: Setting the Record Straight in *Uncle Tom's Cabin*").

5 I.e., St. Clare is drunk. Some film versions of the novel, particularly Geza Radvanyi's 1969 version (with Eartha Kitt as Cassy!), make much of St. Clare's nighttime activities. In this film, poor Eva consoles herself with Uncle Tom largely because her father is rarely home in the evening. Stowe herself suggests that St. Clare has some sort of regular nocturnal activities.

the change without counting it, Tom had every facility and temptation to dishonesty; and nothing but an impregnable simplicity of nature, strengthened by Christian faith, could have kept him from it. But, to that nature, the very unbounded trust reposed in him was bond and seal for the most scrupulous accuracy.

With Adolph the case had been different. Thoughtless and self-indulgent, and unrestrained by a master who found it easier to indulge than to regulate, he had fallen into an absolute confusion as to *meum tuum*[4] with regard to himself and his master, which sometimes troubled even St. Clare. His own good sense taught him that such a training of his servants was unjust and dangerous. A sort of chronic remorse went with him everywhere, although not strong enough to make any decided change in his course; and this very remorse reacted again into indulgence. He passed lightly over the most serious faults, because he told himself that, if he had done his part, his dependents had not fallen into them.

Tom regarded his gay, airy, handsome young master with an odd mixture of fealty, reverence, and fatherly solicitude. That he never read the Bible; never went to church; that he jested and made free with any and every thing that came in the way of his wit; that he spent his Sunday evenings at the opera or theatre; that he went to wine parties, and clubs, and suppers, oftener than was at all expedient,—were all things that Tom could see as plainly as anybody, and on which he based a conviction that "Mas'r wasn't a Christian;"—a conviction, however, which he would have been very slow to express to any one else, but on which he founded many prayers, in his own simple fashion, when he was by himself in his little dormitory. Not that Tom had not his own way of speaking his mind occasionally, with something of the tact often observable in his class; as, for example, the very day after the Sabbath we have described, St. Clare was invited out to a convivial party of choice spirits, and was helped home, between one and two o'clock at night, in a condition when the physical had decidedly attained the upper hand of the intellectual.[5] Tom and Adolph assisted to get him composed for the night, the latter in high spirits, evidently regarding the matter as a good joke, and laughing heartily at the rusticity of Tom's horror, who really was simple enough to lie awake most of the rest of the night, praying for his young master.

"Well, Tom, what are you waiting for?" said St. Clare, the next day, as he sat in his library, in dressing-gown and slippers. St. Clare had just been intrusting Tom with some money, and various commissions. "Isn't all right there, Tom?" he added, as Tom still stood waiting.

"I'm 'fraid not, Mas'r," said Tom, with a grave face.

St. Clare laid down his paper, and set down his coffee-cup, and looked at Tom.

"Why, Tom, what's the case? You look as solemn as a coffin."

"I feel very bad, Mas'r. I allays have thought that Mas'r would be good to everybody."

"Well, Tom, haven't I been? Come, now, what do you want? There's something you haven't got, I suppose, and this is the preface."

"Mas'r allays been good to me. I haven't nothing to complain of, on that head. But there is one that Mas'r isn't good to."

"Why, Tom, what's got into you? Speak out; what do you mean?"

"Last night, between one and two, I thought so. I studied upon the matter then. Mas'r isn't good to *himself*."

Tom said this with his back to his master, and his hand on the door-knob. St. Clare felt his face flush crimson, but he laughed.

"O, that's all, is it?" he said, gayly.

"All!" said Tom, turning suddenly round and falling on his knees. "O, my dear young Mas'r! I'm 'fraid it will be *loss of all—all*—body and soul. The good Book says, 'it biteth like a serpent and stingeth like an adder!' my dear Mas'r!"**6**

Tom's voice choked, and the tears ran down his cheeks.

"You poor, silly fool!" said St. Clare, with tears in his own eyes. "Get up, Tom. I'm not worth crying over."

But Tom wouldn't rise, and looked imploring.

"Well, I won't go to any more of their cursed nonsense, Tom," said St. Clare; "on my honor, I won't. I don't know why I haven't stopped long ago. I've always despised *it,* and myself for it,—so now, Tom, wipe up your eyes, and go about your errands. Come, come," he added, "no blessings. I'm not so wonderfully good, now," he said, as he gently pushed Tom to the door. "There, I'll pledge my honor to you, Tom, you don't see me so again," he said; and Tom went off, wiping his eyes, with great satisfaction.

"I'll keep my faith with him, too," said St. Clare, as he closed the door.

And St. Clare did so,—for gross sensualism, in any form, was not the peculiar temptation of his nature.

But, all this time, who shall detail the tribulations man-

6 Prov. 23:31–32: "Look thou not upon the wine when it is red, when it giveth his color in the cup, when it moveth itself aright. At the last it biteth like a serpent, and stingeth like an adder."

**7** Stowe extols the housekeeper as commander of the domestic sphere.

**8** Stowe praises Mrs. Shelby as a good housekeeper, though we remember that she was tragically ignorant of the state of her household's finances.

**9** I.e., a frame or receptacle for pressing or holding linens such as bedsheets, shirts, undergarments (*Shorter Oxford*).

**10** A rather playful way for Stowe to let her readers know the thoroughness of Ophelia's housecleaning. Consider the voice of Ophelia emerging here, evoking the Christian traditions of good and evil as darkness and light and of the celestial hierarchy. The kitchen and upstairs servants are of sixth and seventh rank in the ninefold hierarchy of seraphim, cherubim, thrones, dominations, virtues, principalities, powers, archangels, and angels. See Rom. 8:38–39: "Neither death, nor life, nor angels, nor principalities, nor powers, nor things present, nor things to come, Nor height, nor depth, nor any other creature, shall be able to separate us from the love of God, which is in Christ Jesus our Lord." Then Stowe moves easily from heaven to earth as the household slaves now become presidential cabinet members. In a few sentences, Stowe has ranged from heaven to earth and, in this reference to the English charter obtained in 1215 from King John establishing personal and political liberty, back in time.

ifold of our friend Miss Ophelia, who had begun the labors of a Southern housekeeper?

There is all the difference in the world in the servants of Southern establishments, according to the character and capacity of the mistresses who have brought them up.

South as well as north, there are women who have an extraordinary talent for command,**7** and tact in educating. Such are enabled, with apparent ease, and without severity, to subject to their will, and bring into harmonious and systematic order, the various members of their small estate,—to regulate their peculiarities, and so balance and compensate the deficiencies of one by the excess of another, as to produce a harmonious and orderly system.

Such a housekeeper was Mrs. Shelby,**8** whom we have already described; and such our readers may remember to have met with. If they are not common at the South, it is because they are not common in the world. They are to be found there as often as anywhere; and, when existing, find in that peculiar state of society a brilliant opportunity to exhibit their domestic talent.

Such a housekeeper Marie St. Clare was not, nor her mother before her. Indolent and childish, unsystematic and improvident, it was not to be expected that servants trained under her care should not be so likewise; and she had very justly described to Miss Ophelia the state of confusion she would find in the family, though she had not ascribed it to the proper cause.

The first morning of her regency, Miss Ophelia was up at four o'clock; and having attended to all the adjustments of her own chamber, as she had done ever since she came there, to the great amazement of the chamber-maid, she prepared for a vigorous onslaught on the cupboards and closets of the establishment of which she had the keys.

The store-room, the linen-presses,**9** the china-closet, the kitchen and cellar, that day, all went under an awful review. Hidden things of darkness were brought to light to an extent that alarmed all the principalities and powers of kitchen and chamber, and caused many wonderings and murmurings about "dese yer northern ladies" from the domestic cabinet.**10**

Old Dinah, the head cook, and principal of all rule and authority in the kitchen department, was filled with wrath at what she considered an invasion of privilege. No feudal baron in *Magna Charta* times could have more thoroughly resented some incursion of the crown.

Dinah was a character in her own way, and it would be injustice to her memory not to give the reader a little idea of her. She was a native and essential cook, as much as Aunt Chloe,—cooking being an indigenous talent of the African race;[11] but Chloe was a trained and methodical one, who moved in an orderly domestic harness, while Dinah was a self-taught genius, and, like geniuses in general, was positive, opinionated and erratic, to the last degree.

Like a certain class of modern philosophers, Dinah perfectly scorned logic and reason in every shape, and always took refuge in intuitive certainty; and here she was perfectly impregnable. No possible amount of talent, or authority, or explanation, could ever make her believe that any other way was better than her own, or that the course she had pursued in the smallest matter could be in the least modified. This had been a conceded point with her old mistress, Marie's mother; and "Miss Marie," as Dinah always called her young mistress, even after her marriage, found it easier to submit than contend; and so Dinah had ruled supreme. This was the easier, in that she was perfect mistress of that diplomatic art which unites the utmost subservience of manner with the utmost inflexibility as to measure.

Dinah was mistress of the whole art and mystery of excuse-making, in all its branches. Indeed, it was an axiom with her that the cook can do no wrong; and a cook in a Southern kitchen finds abundance of heads and shoulders on which to lay off every sin and frailty, so as to maintain her own immaculateness entire. If any part of the dinner was a failure, there were fifty indisputably good reasons for it; and it was the fault undeniably of fifty other people, whom Dinah berated with unsparing zeal.

But it was very seldom that there was any failure in Dinah's last results. Though her mode of doing everything was peculiarly meandering and circuitous, and without any sort of calculation as to time and place,—though her kitchen generally looked as if it had been arranged by a hurricane blowing through it, and she had about as many places for each cooking utensil as there were days in the year,—yet, if one would have patience to wait her own good time, up would come her dinner in perfect order, and in a style of preparation with which an epicure could find no fault.

It was now the season of incipient preparation for dinner. Dinah, who required large intervals of reflection and repose, and was studious of ease in all her arrangements, was seated on the kitchen floor, smoking a short, stumpy pipe, to which she was much addicted, and which she

11 Another racist observation about "native talent," this time cooking. Thus, Dinah will not be compared to a white cook but to a fellow member of her race. Dinah has been with Marie's family since before the marriage, with absolute rule over her kitchen.

217

**12** Dinah's languid invoking of the "domestic Muses" is contrasted with Ophelia's Protestant work ethic.

**13** Ophelia, as a typical New England spinster, enjoys reforms of all kinds. The nineteenth century saw a blossoming of reforming zeal. Organizations and movements to improve and change society formed for purposes as diverse as expanding women's voting rights, promoting free love and temperance, and founding religious missions in Africa. Famous female reformers included women's rights advocates Elizabeth Cady Stanton (1815–1902) and Susan B. Anthony (1820–1906), educator and intellectual Margaret Fuller (1810–1850), Quaker abolitionist sisters Angelina Grimké Weld (1805–1879) and Sarah Moore Grimké (1792–1873), and abolitionist and women's rights advocate Lucretia Mott (1793–1880).

**14** Stowe's allusion to Edward Bouverie Pusey (1800–1882), a strict Anglican champion of orthodoxy, demonstrates her knowledge of various religious movements and trends in Britain as well as America. William Wells Brown made it a point to visit Dr. Pusey in Oxford in 1851 and said that he was pleased to find "a colored man" among the students there (*The American Fugitive in Europe. Sketches of Places and People Abroad*).

**15** Variant of *virtu*, French for objects of art.

**16** The trope of ridiculing another woman's housekeeping style is very old. Stowe's readers would react with equal parts laughter and sympathy for poor Dinah.

always kindled up, as a sort of censer, whenever she felt the need of an inspiration in her arrangements. It was Dinah's mode of invoking the domestic Muses.[12]

Seated around her were various members of that rising race with which a Southern household abounds, engaged in shelling peas, peeling potatoes, picking pin-feathers out of fowls, and other preparatory arrangements,—Dinah every once in a while interrupting her meditations to give a poke, or a rap on the head, to some of the young operators, with the pudding-stick that lay by her side. In fact, Dinah ruled over the woolly heads of the younger members with a rod of iron, and seemed to consider them born for no earthly purpose but to "save her steps," as she phrased it. It was the spirit of the system under which she had grown up, and she carried it out to its full extent.

Miss Ophelia, after passing on her reformatory tour[13] through all the other parts of the establishment, now entered the kitchen. Dinah had heard, from various sources, what was going on, and resolved to stand on defensive and conservative ground,—mentally determined to oppose and ignore every new measure, without any actual and observable contest.

The kitchen was a large brick-floored apartment, with a great old-fashioned fireplace stretching along one side of it,—an arrangement which St. Clare had vainly tried to persuade Dinah to exchange for the convenience of a modern cook-stove. Not she. No Puseyite,[14] or conservative of any school, was ever more inflexibly attached to time-honored inconveniencies than Dinah.

When St. Clare had first returned from the north, impressed with the system and order of his uncle's kitchen arrangements, he had largely provided his own with an array of cupboards, drawers, and various apparatus, to induce systematic regulation, under the sanguine illusion that it would be of any possible assistance to Dinah in her arrangements. He might as well have provided them for a squirrel or a magpie. The more drawers and closets there were, the more hiding-holes could Dinah make for the accommodation of old rags, hair-combs, old shoes, ribbons, cast-off artificial flowers, and other articles of *vertu*,[15] wherein her soul delighted.

When Miss Ophelia entered the kitchen, Dinah did not rise, but smoked on in sublime tranquillity, regarding her movements obliquely out of the corner of her eye, but apparently intent only on the operations around her.[16]

Miss Ophelia commenced opening a set of drawers.

"What is this drawer for, Dinah?" she said.

"It's handy for most anything, Missis," said Dinah. So it appeared to be. From the variety it contained, Miss Ophelia pulled out first a fine damask table-cloth stained with blood, having evidently been used to envelop some raw meat.

"What's this, Dinah? You don't wrap up meat in your mistress' best table-cloths?"

"O Lor, Missis, no; the towels was all a missin',—so I jest did it. I laid out to wash that ar,—that's why I put it thar."

"Shif'less!" said Miss Ophelia to herself, proceeding to tumble over[17] the drawer, where she found a nutmeg-grater and two or three nutmegs, a Methodist hymn-book, a couple of soiled Madras handkerchiefs, some yarn and knitting-work, a paper of tobacco and a pipe, a few crackers, one or two gilded china-saucers with some pomade in them, one or two thin old shoes, a piece of flannel carefully pinned up enclosing some small white onions, several damask table-napkins, some coarse crash towels, some twine and darning-needles, and several broken papers, from which sundry sweet herbs were sifting into the drawer.

"Where do you keep your nutmegs, Dinah?" said Miss Ophelia, with the air of one who prayed for patience.

"Most anywhar, Missis; there's some in that cracked teacup, up there, and there's some over in that ar cupboard."

"Here are some in the grater," said Miss Ophelia, holding them up.

"Laws, yes, I put 'em there this morning,—I likes to keep my things handy," said Dinah. "You, Jake! what are you stopping for! You'll cotch it! Be still, thar!" she added, with a dive of her stick at the criminal.

"What's this?" said Miss Ophelia, holding up the saucer of pomade.

"Laws, it's my har *grease*;—I put it thar to have it handy."

"Do you use your mistress' best saucers for that?"

"Law! it was cause I was driv, and in sich a hurry;—I was gwine to change it this very day."

"Here are two damask table-napkins."

"Them table-napkins I put thar, to get 'em washed out, some day."

"Don't you have some place here on purpose for things to be washed?"

"Well, Mas'r St. Clare got dat ar chest, he said, for dat; but I likes to mix up biscuit and hev my things on it some days, and then it an't handy a liftin' up the lid."

17 I.e., violently attack the cleaning and rearranging of things in the kitchen.

"Why don't you mix your biscuits on the pastry-table, there?"

"Law, Missis, it gets sot so full of dishes, and one thing and another, der ant no room, noways—"

"But you should *wash* your dishes, and clear them away."

"Wash my dishes!" said Dinah, in a high key, as her wrath began to rise over her habitual respect of manner; "what does ladies know 'bout work, I want to know? When'd Mas'r ever get his dinner, if I was to spend all my time a washin' and a puttin' up dishes? Miss Marie never told me so, nohow."

"Well, here are these onions."

"Laws, yes!" said Dinah; "thar *is* whar I put 'em, now. I couldn't 'member. Them's particular onions I was a savin' for dis yer very stew. I'd forgot they was in dat ar old flannel."

Miss Ophelia lifted out the sifting papers of sweet herbs.

"I wish Missis wouldn't touch dem ar. I likes to keep my things where I knows whar to go to 'em," said Dinah, rather decidedly.

"But you don't want these holes in the papers."

"Them's handy for siftin' on 't out," said Dinah.

"But you see it spills all over the drawer."

"Laws, yes! if Missis will go a tumblin' things all up so, it will. Missis has spilt lots dat ar way," said Dinah, coming uneasily to the drawers. "If Missis only will go up stars till my clarin' up time comes, I'll have everything right; but I can't do nothin' when ladies is round, a henderin'. You, Sam, don't you gib the baby dat ar sugar-bowl! I'll crack ye over, if ye don't mind!"

"I'm going through the kitchen, and going to put everything in order, *once*, Dinah; and then I'll expect you to *keep* it so."

"Lor, now! Miss Phelia; dat ar an't no way for ladies to do. I never did see ladies doin' no sich; my old Missis nor Miss Marie never did, and I don't see no kinder need on 't;" and Dinah stalked indignantly about, while Miss Ophelia piled and sorted dishes, emptied dozens of scattering bowls of sugar into one receptacle, sorted napkins, table-cloths, and towels, for washing; washing, wiping, and arranging with her own hands, and with a speed and alacrity which perfectly amazed Dinah.

"Lor, now! if dat ar de way dem northern ladies do, dey an't ladies, nohow," she said to some of her satellites, when at a safe hearing distance. "I has things as straight as anybody, when my clarin' up time comes; but I don't want ladies round, a henderin', and getting my things all where I can't find 'em."

To do Dinah justice, she had, at irregular periods, paroxysms of reformation and arrangement, which she called "clarin' up times," when she would begin with great zeal, and turn every drawer and closet wrong side outward, on to the floor or tables, and make the ordinary confusion seven-fold more confounded. Then she would light her pipe, and leisurely go over her arrangements, looking things over, and discoursing upon them; making all the young fry scour most vigorously on the tin things, and keeping up for several hours a most energetic state of confusion, which she would explain to the satisfaction of all inquirers, by the remark that she was a "clarin' up." "She couldn't hev things a gwine on so as they had been, and she was gwine to make these yer young ones keep better order;" for Dinah herself, somehow, indulged the illusion that she, herself, was the soul of order, and it was only the *young uns*, and the everybody else in the house, that were the cause of anything that fell short of perfection in this respect. When all the tins were scoured, and the tables scrubbed snowy white, and everything that could offend tucked out of sight in holes and corners, Dinah would dress herself up in a smart dress, clean apron, and high, brilliant Madras turban, and tell all marauding "young uns" to keep out of the kitchen, for she was gwine to have things kept nice. Indeed, these periodic seasons were often an inconvenience to the whole household; for Dinah would contract such an immoderate attachment to her scoured tin, as to insist upon it that it shouldn't be used again for any possible purpose,—at least, till the ardor of the "clarin' up" period abated.

Miss Ophelia, in a few days, thoroughly reformed every department of the house to a systematic pattern; but her labors in all departments that depended on the cooperation of servants were like those of Sisyphus or the Danaides.[18] In despair, she one day appealed to St. Clare.

"There is no such thing as getting anything like system in this family!"

"To be sure, there isn't," said St. Clare.

"Such shiftless management, such waste, such confusion, I never saw!"

"I dare say you didn't."

"You would not take it so coolly, if you were housekeeper."

"My dear cousin, you may as well understand, once for

18 I.e., an impossible task. From Greek mythology, figures condemned to endless toil in Hades. Corinthian King Sisyphus was condemned perpetually to roll a large stone up a steep cliff; the Danaides had to fill up a constantly emptying barrel.

19 Curiously, St. Clare can see no other "discipline" but the extreme of violent whippings. Stowe begins to show her readers more cracks in St. Clare's ethical makeup.

20 Stowe stakes out the argument between St. Clare and Ophelia as a sectional one between South and North.

21 Given that St. Clare has just called his slaves "poor devils," his choice of allusion is significant. See Milton's *Paradise Lost,* Book I, where Satan gathers his fellow fallen angels to find their new world in Chaos and build his palace, called Pandemonium. "Sonorous metal blowing martial sounds: / At which the universal host up sent / A shout that tore hell's concave, and beyond / Frighted the reign of Chaos and Old Night."

all, that we masters are divided into two classes, oppressors and oppressed. We who are good-natured and hate severity make up our minds to a good deal of inconvenience. If we *will keep* a shambling, loose, untaught set in the community, for our convenience, why, we must take the consequence. Some rare cases I have seen, of persons, who, by a peculiar tact, can produce order and system without severity; but I'm not one of them,—and so I made up my mind, long ago, to let things go just as they do. I will not have the poor devils thrashed and cut to pieces, and they know it,—and, of course, they know the staff is in their own hands."[19]

"But to have no time, no place, no order,—all going on in this shiftless way!"

"My dear Vermont, you natives up by the North Pole set an extravagant value on time![20] What on earth is the use of time to a fellow who has twice as much of it as he knows what to do with? As to order and system, where there is nothing to be done but to lounge on the sofa and read, an hour sooner or later in breakfast or dinner isn't of much account. Now, there's Dinah gets you a capital dinner,—soup, ragout, roast fowl, dessert, ice-creams and all,—and she creates it all out of chaos and old night[21] down there, in that kitchen. I think it really sublime, the way she manages. But, Heaven bless us! if we are to go down there, and view all the smoking and squatting about, and hurryscurryation of the preparatory process, we should never eat more! My good cousin, absolve yourself from that! It's more than a Catholic penance, and does no more good. You'll only lose your own temper, and utterly confound Dinah. Let her go her own way."

"But, Augustine, you don't know how I found things."

"Don't I? Don't I know that the rolling-pin is under her bed, and the nutmeg-grater in her pocket with her tobacco,—that there are sixty-five different sugar-bowls, one in every hole in the house,—that she washes dishes with a dinner-napkin one day, and with a fragment of an old petticoat the next? But the upshot is, she gets up glorious dinners, makes superb coffee; and you must judge her as warriors and statesmen are judged, by *her success.*"

"But the waste,—the expense!"

"O, well! Lock everything you can, and keep the key. Give out by driblets, and never inquire for odds and ends,—it isn't best."

"That troubles me, Augustine. I can't help feeling as if these servants were not *strictly honest*. Are you sure they can be relied on?"

Augustine laughed immoderately at the grave and anxious face with which Miss Ophelia propounded the question.

"O, cousin, that's too good,—*honest!*—as if that's a thing to be expected! Honest!—why, of course, they arn't. Why should they be? What upon earth is to make them so?"

"Why don't you instruct?"

"Instruct! O, fiddlestick! What instructing do you think I should do? I look like it! As to Marie, she has spirit enough, to be sure, to kill off a whole plantation, if I'd let her manage; but she wouldn't get the cheatery out of them."

"Are there no honest ones?"

"Well, now and then one, whom Nature makes so impracticably simple, truthful and faithful, that the worst possible influence can't destroy it in. But, you see, from the mother's breast the colored child feels and sees that there are none but underhand ways open to it. It can get along no other way with its parents, its mistress, its young master and missie play-fellows. Cunning and deception become necessary, inevitable habits. It isn't fair to expect anything else of him. He ought not to be punished for it. As to honesty, the slave is kept in that dependent, semi-childish state, that there is no making him realize the rights of property, or feel that his master's goods are not his own, if he can get them. For my part, I don't see how they *can* be honest. Such a fellow as Tom, here, is—is a moral miracle!"[22]

"And what becomes of their souls?" said Miss Ophelia.

"That isn't my affair as I know of," said St. Clare; "I am only dealing in facts of the present life. The fact is, that the whole race are pretty generally understood to be turned over to the devil, for our benefit, in this world, however it may turn out in another!"

"This is perfectly horrible!" said Miss Ophelia; "you ought to be ashamed of yourselves!"

"I don't know as I am. We are in pretty good company, for all that," said St. Clare, "as people in the broad road generally are. Look at the high and the low, all the world over, and it's the same story,—the lower class used up, body, soul and spirit, for the good of the upper.[23] It is so in England; it is so everywhere; and yet all Christendom stands aghast, with virtuous indignation, because we do the thing in a little different shape from what they do it."

"It isn't so in Vermont."

"Ah, well, in New England, and in the free States, you

22 St. Clare's speech demonstrates Stowe's ability to get inside another's head and speak in ways that are simultaneously believable and horrible. St. Clare voices two nineteenth-century beliefs promoted by the female abolitionists (and difficult to contradict): that the mother is the moral influence on her child and that slavery destroys morality.

23 Again, more evidence that St. Clare has at least some familiarity with class rhetoric, as has Stowe.

**24** Once again, St. Clare portrays the differences between himself and Ophelia as natural, growing out of their respective environments (sections) of South and North.

**25** Prue carries her wares, as do African women today, in a basket on her head. A rusk was a twice-baked bread, often used for teething children—an apt item for the grieving Prue. Notice a few lines down that Prue also squats like an African woman.

have the better of us, I grant. But there's the bell; so, Cousin, let us for a while lay aside our sectional prejudices, and come out to dinner."**24**

As Miss Ophelia was in the kitchen in the latter part of the afternoon, some of the sable children called out, "La, sakes! thar's Prue a coming, grunting along like she allers does."

A tall, bony colored woman now entered the kitchen, bearing on her head a basket of rusks and hot rolls.**25**

"Ho, Prue! you've come," said Dinah.

Prue had a peculiar scowling expression of countenance, and a sullen, grumbling voice. She set down her basket, squatted herself down, and resting her elbows on her knees said,

"O Lord! I wish't I's dead!"

"Why do you wish you were dead?" said Miss Ophelia.

"I'd be out o' my misery," said the woman, gruffly, without taking her eyes from the floor.

"What need you getting drunk, then, and cutting up, Prue?" said a spruce quadroon chambermaid, dangling, as she spoke, a pair of coral ear-drops.

The woman looked at her with a sour, surly glance.

"Maybe you'll come to it, one of these yer days. I'd be glad to see you, I would; then you'll be glad of a drop, like me, to forget your misery."

"Come, Prue," said Dinah, "let's look at your rusks. Here's Missis will pay for them."

Miss Ophelia took out a couple of dozen.

"Thar's some tickets in that ar old cracked jug on the top shelf," said Dinah. "You, Jake, climb up and get it down."

"Tickets,—what are they for?" said Miss Ophelia.

"We buys tickets of her Mas'r, and she gives us bread for 'em."

"And they counts my money and tickets, when I gets home, to see if I's got the change; and if I han't, they half kills me."

"And serves you right," said Jane, the pert chambermaid, "if you will take their money to get drunk on. That's what she does, Missis."

"And that's what I *will* do,—I can't live no other ways,—drink and forget my misery."

"You are very wicked and very foolish," said Miss Ophelia, "to steal your master's money to make yourself a brute with."

"It's mighty likely, Missis; but I will do it,—yes, I will. O Lord! I wish I's dead, I do,—I wish I's dead, and out of my misery!" and slowly and stiffly the old creature rose, and got her basket on her head again; but before she went out, she looked at the quadroon girl, who still stood playing with her ear-drops.

"Ye think ye're mighty fine with them ar, a frolickin' and a tossin' your head, and a lookin' down on everybody. Well, never mind,—you may live to be a poor, old, cut-up crittur, like me. Hope to the Lord ye will, I do; then see if ye won't drink,—drink,—drink,—yerself into torment; and sarve ye right, too—ugh!" and, with a malignant howl, the woman left the room.

"Disgusting old beast!" said Adolph, who was getting his master's shaving-water. "If I was her master, I'd cut her up worse than she is."

"Ye couldn't do that ar, no ways," said Dinah. "Her back's a far sight now,—she can't never get a dress together over it."

"I think such low creatures ought not to be allowed to go round to genteel families," said Miss Jane. "What do you think, Mr. St. Clare?" she said, coquettishly tossing her head at Adolph.[26]

It must be observed that, among other appropriations from his master's stock, Adolph was in the habit of adopting his name and address; and that the style under which he moved, among the colored circles of New Orleans, was that of *Mr. St. Clare.*

"I'm certainly of your opinion, Miss Benoir," said Adolph.

Benoir was the name of Marie St. Clare's family, and Jane was one of her servants.[27]

"Pray, Miss Benoir, may I be allowed to ask if those drops are for the ball, to-morrow night? They are certainly bewitching!"

"I wonder, now, Mr. St. Clare, what the impudence of you men will come to!" said Jane, tossing her pretty head till the ear-drops twinkled again. "I shan't dance with you for a whole evening, if you go to asking me any more questions."

"O, you couldn't be so cruel, now! I was just dying to know whether you would appear in your pink tarletane,[28]" said Adolph.

"What is it?" said Rosa, a bright, piquant[29] little quadroon, who came skipping down stairs at this moment.

"Why, Mr. St. Clare's so impudent!"

"On my honor," said Adolph, "I'll leave it to Miss Rosa, now."

"I know he's always a saucy creature," said Rosa, pois-

26 Stowe demonstrates differences between slaves, giving us this brief portrait of an upstairs servant, fourth generation of white-and-black marriages, of neat appearance. She is a female Adolph. Stowe introduces her for the purpose of criticizing Prue and allowing both Ophelia and Dinah to share the sympathetic role.

27 Marie Benoir St. Clare's slaves are distinguished from St. Clare's, though both Jane and Adolph are snobs. Personal house servants were usually light skinned and often mimicked their white masters. The "light-colored balls" Stowe refers to below and societies were an insidious legacy of racism that prized whiteness above all; they would continue into the twentieth century. An excellent tale on colorism is the short story "The Wife of His Youth" by Charles W. Chesnutt (1858–1932). In a compelling essay entitled "This Promiscuous Housekeeping: Death, Transgression, and Homoeroticism in *Uncle Tom's Cabin*," scholar P. Gabrielle Foreman takes particular note of the sexuality swirling around Tom, Eva, Marie, Augustine, and Ophelia.

28 A stiff, open-weave fabric used for ball-dresses (*Shorter Oxford*).

29 "Bright" was often used to denote the lightness of the skin of a female slave. "Piquant" means "charming." Rosa is presented as Jane's rival. Both Jane and Rosa show the sexuality associated with light-skinned female slaves. Several late film versions of *Uncle Tom's Cabin* create subplots involving St. Clare and these attractive slaves. Is Stowe to think that St. Clare has no interest in these women, or that they are not interested in him?

30 Again, Stowe's women characters play out yet another aspect of whiter-is-better: Bad hair is kinky "wool"; good hair is straight and silky.

31 The naïveté of the statement is startling after Prue's litany of woes. In the next paragraph, the word "ugly" can mean physical or moral repulsiveness. Given the preceding conversation of Dinah, Jane, and Rosa, readers are apt to focus more on the physical. But Tom's caution to Prue about "body and soul" brings both meanings into play.

ing herself on one of her little feet, and looking maliciously at Adolph. "He's always getting me so angry with him."

"O! ladies, ladies, you will certainly break my heart, between you," said Adolph. "I shall be found dead in my bed, some morning, and you'll have it to answer for."

"Do hear the horrid creature talk!" said both ladies, laughing immoderately.

"Come,—clar out, you! I can't have you cluttering up the kitchen," said Dinah; "in my way, foolin' round here."

"Aunt Dinah's glum, because she can't go to the ball," said Rosa.

"Don't want none o' your light-colored balls," said Dinah; "cuttin' round, makin' b'lieve you's white folks. Arter all, you's niggers, much as I am."

"Aunt Dinah greases her wool stiff, every day, to make it lie straight," said Jane.

"And it will be wool, after all," said Rosa, maliciously shaking down her long, silky curls.**30**

"Well, in the Lord's sight, an't wool as good as har, any time?" said Dinah. "I'd like to have Missis say which is worth the most,—a couple such as you, or one like me. Get out wid ye, ye trumpery,—I won't have ye round!"

Here the conversation was interrupted in a two-fold manner. St. Clare's voice was heard at the head of the stairs, asking Adolph if he meant to stay all night with his shaving-water; and Miss Ophelia, coming out of the dining-room, said,

"Jane and Rosa, what are you wasting your time for, here? Go in and attend to your muslins."

Our friend Tom, who had been in the kitchen during the conversation with the old rusk-woman, had followed her out into the street. He saw her go on, giving every once in a while a suppressed groan. At last she set her basket down on a door-step, and began arranging the old, faded shawl which covered her shoulders.

"I'll carry your basket a piece," said Tom, compassionately.

"Why should ye?" said the woman. "I don't want no help."

"You seem to be sick, or in trouble, or somethin'," said Tom.

"I an't sick," said the woman, shortly.

"I wish," said Tom, looking at her earnestly,—"I wish I could persuade you to leave off drinking. Don't you know it will be the ruin of ye, body and soul?"**31**

"I knows I'm gwine to torment," said the woman, sullenly. "Ye don't need to tell me that ar. I's ugly,—I's wicked,—I's gwine straight to torment. O, Lord! I wish I's thar!"

Tom shuddered at these frightful words, spoken with a sullen, impassioned earnestness.

"O, Lord have mercy on ye! poor crittur. Han't ye never heard of Jesus Christ?"

"Jesus Christ,—who's he?"

"Why, he's *the Lord*," said Tom.

"I think I've hearn tell o' the Lord, and the judgment and torment. I've heard o' that."

"But didn't anybody ever tell you of the Lord Jesus, that loved us poor sinners, and died for us?"

"Don't know nothin' 'bout that," said the woman; "nobody han't never loved me, since my old man died."

"Where was you raised?" said Tom.

"Up in Kentuck.[32] A man kept me to breed chil'en for market, and sold 'em as fast as they got big enough; last of all, he sold me to a speculator, and my Mas'r got me o' him."

"What set you into this bad way of drinkin'?"

"To get shet o' my misery. I had one child after I come here; and I thought then I'd have one to raise, cause Mas'r wasn't a speculator.[33] It was de peartest little thing! and Missis she seemed to think a heap on 't, at first; it never cried,—it was likely and fat. But Missis tuck sick, and I tended her; and I tuck the fever, and my milk all left me, and the child it pined to skin and bone, and Missis wouldn't buy milk for it. She wouldn't hear to me, when I told her I hadn't milk. She said she knowed I could feed it on what other folks eat; and the child kinder pined, and cried, and cried, and cried, day and night, and got all gone to skin and bones, and Missis got sot agin it, and she said 'twan't nothin' but crossness. She wished it was dead, she said; and she wouldn't let me have it o' nights, cause, she said, it kept me awake, and made me good for nothing. She made me sleep in her room; and I had to put it away off in a little kind o' garret, and thar it cried itself to death, one night. It did; and I tuck to drinkin', to keep its crying out of my ears! I did,—and I will drink! I will, if I do go to torment for it! Mas'r says I shall go to torment, and I tell him I've got thar now!"

"O, ye poor crittur!" said Tom, "han't nobody never told ye how the Lord Jesus loved ye, and died for ye? Han't they told ye that he'll help ye, and ye can go to heaven, and have rest, at last?"

"I looks like gwine to heaven," said the woman; "an't

**32** The slave mother kept as a breeder, whose children were sold away, is an abolitionist mainstay, but notice that Prue's master was one of those fine, kind Kentucky men.

**33** Stowe rises to the challenge of presenting what to at least some of her readers is a well-known fact of the slave mother's life: that her mistress often asks her to neglect her own child to serve the whites. Stowe moves from the selling of slave children to a larger, more personal story meant to raise sympathy in white mothers. Not only would white mothers know the anxiety of "losing one's milk" (i.e., the incapacity to continue to breastfeed one's infant), but many of them had most likely lost a child to illness, listening to its dying cries.

34 The reluctance of the would-be-Christian slave upon hearing that master and mistress might also be in heaven is a bit of comic relief. In Harriet Wilson's 1859 novel *Our Nig*, the young heroine, Frado, voices similar disgust at the idea of a heaven with all the white folks.

35 A plant with a tuberous root, cultivated for its waxy white, funnel-shaped, fragrant flowers (*Shorter Oxford*).

36 Stowe reminds her readers once again that Eva is marked for early death.

thar where white folks is gwine? S'pose they'd have me thar? I'd rather go to torment, and get away from Mas'r and Missis.[34] I had *so*," she said, as, with her usual groan, she got her basket on her head, and walked sullenly away.

Tom turned, and walked sorrowfully back to the house. In the court he met little Eva,—a crown of tuberoses[35] on her head, and her eyes radiant with delight.

"O, Tom! here you are. I'm glad I've found you. Papa says you may get out the ponies, and take me in my little new carriage," she said, catching his hand. "But what's the matter, Tom?—you look sober."

"I feel bad, Miss Eva," said Tom, sorrowfully. "But I'll get the horses for you."

"But do tell me, Tom, what is the matter. I saw you talking to cross old Prue."

Tom, in simple, earnest phrase, told Eva the woman's history. She did not exclaim, or wonder, or weep, as other children do.[36] Her cheeks grew pale, and a deep, earnest shadow passed over her eyes. She laid both hands on her bosom, and sighed heavily.

## VOLUME II

### CHAPTER 19

## Miss Ophelia's Experiences and Opinions, Continued[1]

"Tom, you needn't get me the horses. I don't want to go," she said.

"Why not, Miss Eva?"

"These things sink into my heart, Tom,"[2] said Eva,— "they sink into my heart," she repeated, earnestly. "I don't want to go;" and she turned from Tom, and went into the house.

A few days after, another woman came, in old Prue's place, to bring the rusks; Miss Ophelia was in the kitchen.

"Lor!" said Dinah, "what's got Prue?"

"Prue isn't coming any more," said the woman, mysteriously.

"Why not?" said Dinah. "She an't dead, is she?"

"We doesn't exactly know. She's down cellar," said the woman, glancing at Miss Ophelia.

After Miss Ophelia had taken the rusks, Dinah followed the woman to the door.

"What *has* got Prue, any how?" she said.

The woman seemed desirous, yet reluctant, to speak, and answered, in a low, mysterious tone.

"Well, you mustn't tell nobody. Prue, she got drunk agin,—and they had her down cellar,—and thar they left her all day,—and I hearn 'em saying that the *flies had got to her,—and she's dead!*"[3]

Dinah held up her hands, and, turning, saw close by her side the spirit-like form of Evangeline, her large, mystic

1 This scene is broken into two chapters, for no apparent reason.

2 We get yet another hint of Eva's early demise. It seems odd that we are given so many reminders of Eva's mortality unless we remember that there can be no drama surrounding this tragedy. The central story is Tom's life and death.

3 Stowe's purpose in telling the story of poor Prue is twofold: to give her readers yet another story of slavery's horrors and to show the influence of these scenes on Eva and Ophelia. Eva's response is mystic and melancholy; Ophelia becomes angry. Prue was left in the cellar to die, much like her baby was left in the garret.

**4** The horrors of slavery are literally killing Eva.

**5** This passage is the low point in Stowe's portrayal of St. Clare. Perhaps not surprisingly, we have never seen an illustration of these conversational scenes in any of the various editions of the novel we've examined. How does one draw a philosophical discussion?

**6** St. Clare is presented as a fatalist, the opposite of Ophelia, who actively searches for some solution to any problem. Is this fatalism another response to his early romantic disappointment?

eyes dilated with horror, and every drop of blood driven from her lips and cheeks.**4**

"Lor bless us! Miss Eva's gwine to faint away! What got us all, to let her har such talk? Her pa'll be rail mad."

"I shan't faint, Dinah," said the child, firmly; "and why shouldn't I hear it? It an't so much for me to hear it, as for poor Prue to suffer it."

"*Lor sakes!* it isn't for sweet, delicate young ladies, like you,—these yer stories isn't; it's enough to kill 'em!"

Eva sighed again, and walked up stairs with a slow and melancholy step.

Miss Ophelia anxiously inquired the woman's story. Dinah gave a very garrulous version of it, to which Tom added the particulars which he had drawn from her that morning.

"An abominable business,—perfectly horrible!" she exclaimed, as she entered the room where St. Clare lay reading his paper.

"Pray, what iniquity has turned up now?" said he.

"What now? why, those folks have whipped Prue to death!" said Miss Ophelia, going on, with great strength of detail, into the story, and enlarging on its most shocking particulars.

"I thought it would come to that, some time," said St. Clare, going on with his paper.**5**

"Thought so!—an't you going to *do* anything about it?" said Miss Ophelia. "Haven't you got any *selectmen*, or anybody, to interfere and look after such matters?"

"It's commonly supposed that the *property* interest is a sufficient guard in these cases. If people choose to ruin their own possessions, I don't know what's to be done. It seems the poor creature was a thief and a drunkard; and so there won't be much hope to get up sympathy for her."

"It is perfectly outrageous,—it is horrid, Augustine! It will certainly bring down vengeance upon you."

"My dear cousin, I didn't do it, and I can't help it; I would, if I could. If low-minded, brutal people will act like themselves, what am I to do? They have absolute control; they are irresponsible despots. There would be no use in interfering; there is no law that amounts to anything practically, for such a case. The best we can do is to shut our eyes and ears, and let it alone. It's the only resource left us."

"How can you shut your eyes and ears? How can you let such things alone?"**6**

"My dear child, what do you expect? Here is a whole class,—debased, uneducated, indolent, provoking,—put, without any sort of terms or conditions, entirely into the hands of such people as the majority in our world are; people who have neither consideration nor self-control, who haven't even an enlightened regard to their own interest,—for that's the case with the largest half of mankind. Of course, in a community so organized, what can a man of honorable and humane feelings do, but shut his eyes all he can, and harden his heart? I can't buy every poor wretch I see. I can't turn knight-errant,[7] and undertake to redress every individual case of wrong in such a city as this. The most I can do is to try and keep out of the way of it."

St. Clare's fine countenance was for a moment overcast; he looked annoyed, but suddenly calling up a gay smile, he said,

"Come, cousin, don't stand there looking like one of the Fates;[8] you've only seen a peep through the curtain,—a specimen of what is going on, the world over, in some shape or other. If we are to be prying and spying into all the dismals of life, we should have no heart to anything. 'Tis like looking too close into the details of Dinah's kitchen;" and St. Clare lay back on the sofa, and busied himself with his paper.

Miss Ophelia sat down, and pulled out her knitting-work, and sat there grim with indignation. She knit and knit, but while she mused the fire burned; at last she broke out—

"I tell you, Augustine, I can't get over things so, if you can. It's a perfect abomination for you to defend such a system,—that's *my* mind!"

"What now?" said St. Clare, looking up. "At it again, hey?"

"I say it's perfectly abominable for you to defend such a system!" said Miss Ophelia, with increasing warmth.

"*I* defend it, my dear lady? Who ever said I did defend it?" said St, Clare.

"Of course, you defend it,—you all do,—all you Southerners. What do you have slaves for, if you don't?"

"Are you such a sweet innocent as to suppose nobody in this world ever does what they don't think is right?[9] Don't you, or didn't you ever, do anything that you did not think quite right?"

"If I do, I repent of it, I hope," said Miss Ophelia, rattling her needles with energy.

"So do I," said St. Clare, peeling his orange; "I'm repenting of it all the time."

"What do you keep on doing it for?"

7 In medieval times, the knight-errant wandered in search of chivalrous adventures. The novels of Sir Walter Scott—particularly *Ivanhoe*—were popular in the South, which liked to think of itself as a culture that had much in common with knights and ladies of yore. Northern abolitionists often chuckled at the notion of Southern chivalry.

8 Goddesses of destiny in Greek and Roman mythology, Clotho, Lachesis, and Atropos.

9 Like other women, Ophelia lives in the domestic sphere. Here, St. Clare hints at the public sphere. It's a jungle out there!

10 A pang for those readers who had disapproved of Ophelia's meddling.

11 I.e., to provoke or tease you. Stowe suggests that St. Clare is bored. Compare his "good-for-nothing" demeanor with Ophelia's constant industry, or, later in the chapter, with Tom and Eva's earnest studying.

12 We see that Augustine, like Mr. Shelby, appreciates food while discoursing on slavery.

13 Here St. Clare parodies the opening lines of the Declaration of Independence.

"Didn't you ever keep on doing wrong, after you'd repented, my good cousin?"

"Well, only when I've been very much tempted," said Miss Ophelia.

"Well, I'm very much tempted," said St. Clare; "that's just my difficulty."

"But I always resolve I won't, and I try to break off."

"Well, I have been resolving I won't, off and on, these ten years," said St. Clare; "but I haven't, some how, got clear. Have you got clear of all your sins, cousin?"

"Cousin Augustine," said Miss Ophelia, seriously, and laying down her knitting-work, "I suppose I deserve that you should reprove my short-comings. I know all you say is true enough; nobody else feels them more than I do; but it does seem to me, after all, there is some difference between me and you. It seems to me I would cut off my right hand sooner than keep on, from day to day, doing what I thought was wrong. But, then, my conduct is so inconsistent with my profession, I don't wonder you reprove me."[10]

"O, now, cousin," said Augustine, sitting down on the floor, and laying his head back in her lap, "don't take on so awfully serious! You know what a good-for-nothing, saucy boy I always was. I love to poke you up,[11]—that's all,—just to see you get earnest. I do think you are desperately, distressingly good; it tires me to death to think of it."

"But this is a serious subject, my boy, Auguste," said Miss Ophelia, laying her hand on his forehead.

"Dismally so," said he; "and I—well, I never want to talk seriously in hot weather. What with mosquitos and all, a fellow can't get himself up to any very sublime moral flights; and I believe," said St. Clare, suddenly rousing himself up, "there's a theory, now! I understand now why northern nations are always more virtuous than southern ones,—I see into that whole subject."

"O, Auguste, you are a sad rattle-brain!"

"Am I? Well, so I am, I suppose; but for once I will be serious, now; but you must hand me that basket of oranges;—you see, you'll have to 'stay me with flagons and comfort me with apples,[12]' if I'm going to make this effort. Now," said Augustine, drawing the basket up, "I'll begin: When, in the course of human events, it becomes necessary for a fellow to hold two or three dozen of his fellow-worms in captivity, a decent regard to the opinions of society requires—"[13]

"I don't see that you are growing more serious," said Miss Ophelia.

"Wait,—I'm coming on,—you'll hear. The short of the matter is, cousin," said he, his handsome face suddenly settling into an earnest and serious expression, "on this abstract question of slavery there can, as I think, be but one opinion. Planters, who have money to make by it,—clergymen, who have planters to please,—politicians, who want to rule by it,—may warp and bend language and ethics to a degree that shall astonish the world at their ingenuity; they can press nature and the Bible, and nobody knows what else, into the service; but, after all, neither they nor the world believe in it one particle the more. It comes from the devil, that's the short of it;—and, to my mind, it's a pretty respectable specimen of what he can do in his own line."

Miss Ophelia stopped her knitting, and looked surprised; and St. Clare, apparently enjoying her astonishment, went on.

"You seem to wonder; but if you will get me fairly at it, I'll make a clean breast of it.[14] This cursed business, accursed of God and man, what is it? Strip it of all its ornament, run it down to the root and nucleus of the whole, and what is it? Why, because my brother Quashy is ignorant and weak, and I am intelligent and strong,—because I know how, and *can* do it,—therefore, I may steal all he has, keep it, and give him only such and so much as suits my fancy. Whatever is too hard, too dirty, too disagreeable, for me, I may set Quashy to doing. Because I don't like work, Quashy shall work. Because the sun burns me, Quashy shall stay in the sun. Quashy shall earn the money, and I will spend it. Quashy shall lie down in every puddle, that I may walk over dry-shod. Quashy shall do my will, and not his, all the days of his mortal life, and have such chance of getting to heaven, at last, as I find convenient. This I take to be about what slavery *is*. I defy anybody on earth to read our slave-code, as it stands in our law-books, and make anything else of it. Talk of the *abuses* of slavery! Humbug! The *thing itself* is the essence of all abuse! And the only reason why the land don't sink under it, like Sodom and Gomorrah, is because it is *used* in a way infinitely better than it is. For pity's sake, for shame's sake, because we are men born of women, and not savage beasts, many of us do not, and dare not,—we would *scorn* to use the full power which our savage laws put into our hands. And he who goes the furthest, and does the worst, only uses within limits the power that the law gives him."

St. Clare had started up, and, as his manner was when excited, was walking, with hurried steps, up and down the

14 St. Clare's speech is sharply brilliant, of course, but it is also hypocritical coming from the mouth of a slaveowner.

**15** By comparing St. Clare's looks to a Greek statue, Stowe is partly critiquing the Classical standard of beauty and worth; she would prefer a value system based on Christianity, not on Greek ideals. But Stowe would also like us to visualize a really good looking man in this scene: How else could she get her overworked nineteenth-century housewife-readers to sit through the whole of St. Clare's overwrought lament?

**16** St. Clare's apathy, he claims, is born of despair.

**17** This is an interesting comment, inasmuch as the Greek statue displayed the ideal man whereas the Roman figure represented the unique individual, often warts and all.

**18** The representation of maternal love is crucial to Stowe's appeal to her audience of white Christian Northern women. The housewife-readers who might have wearied of St. Clare's fervor would be won back by his passionate remembrance of his mother. "*She* was *divine*! . . . O, mother! mother!" he cries. Luckily Marie seems to be out of earshot.

floor. His fine face, classic as that of a Greek statue,**15** seemed actually to burn with the fervor of his feelings. His large blue eyes flashed, and he gestured with an unconscious eagerness. Miss Ophelia had never seen him in this mood before, and she sat perfectly silent.

"I declare to you," said he, suddenly stopping before his cousin "(it's no sort of use to talk or to feel on this subject), but I declare to you, there have been times when I have thought, if the whole country would sink, and hide all this injustice and misery from the light, I would willingly sink with it. When I have been travelling up and down on our boats, or about on my collecting tours, and reflected that every brutal, disgusting, mean, low-lived fellow I met, was allowed by our laws to become absolute despot of as many men, women and children, as he could cheat, steal, or gamble money enough to buy,—when I have seen such men in actual ownership of helpless children, of young girls and women,—I have been ready to curse my country, to curse the human race!"**16**

"Augustine! Augustine!" said Miss Ophelia, "I'm sure you've said enough. I never, in my life, heard anything like this, even at the North."

"At the North!" said St. Clare, with a sudden change of expression, and resuming something of his habitual careless tone. "Pooh! your northern folks are cold-blooded; you are cool in everything! You can't begin to curse up hill and down as we can, when we get fairly at it."

"Well, but the question is," said Miss Ophelia.

"O, yes, to be sure, the *question is*,—and a deuce of a question it is! How came *you* in this state of sin and misery? Well, I shall answer in the good old words you used to teach me, Sundays. I came so by ordinary generation. My servants were my father's, and, what is more, my mother's; and now they are mine, they and their increase, which bids fair to be a pretty considerable item. My father, you know, came first from New England; and he was just such another man as your father,—a regular old Roman,**17**—upright, energetic, noble-minded, with an iron will. Your father settled down in New England, to rule over rocks and stones, and to force an existence out of Nature; and mine settled in Louisiana, to rule over men and women, and force existence out of them. My mother,"**18** said St. Clare, getting up and walking to a picture at the end of the room, and gazing upward with a face fervent with veneration, "*she* was *divine*! Don't look at me so!—you know what I mean! She probably was of mortal birth; but, as far as ever I could observe, there was no trace of any human weakness or error about her; and everybody that lives to remember her, whether bond or free, servant, acquaintance, relation, all say the same. Why, cousin, that mother has been all that has stood between me and utter unbelief for years. She was a direct embodiment and personification of the New Testament,—a living fact, to be accounted for, and to be accounted for in no other way than by its truth. O, mother! mother!" said St. Clare, clasping his hands, in a sort of transport; and then suddenly checking himself, he came back, and seating himself on an ottoman, he went on:

"My brother and I were twins;[19] and they say, you know, that twins ought to resemble each other; but we were in all points a contrast. He had black, fiery eyes, coal-black hair, a strong, fine Roman profile, and a rich brown complexion. I had blue eyes, golden hair, a Greek outline, and fair complexion. He was active and observing, I dreamy and inactive. He was generous to his friends and equals, but proud, dominant, overbearing, to inferiors, and utterly unmerciful to whatever set itself up against him. Truthful we both were; he from pride and courage, I from a sort of abstract ideality. We loved each other about as boys generally do,—off and on, and in general;—he was my father's pet, and I my mother's.

"There was a morbid sensitiveness and acuteness of feeling in me on all possible subjects, of which he and my father had no kind of understanding, and with which they could have no possible sympathy. But mother did; and so, when I had quarrelled with Alfred, and father looked sternly on me, I used to go off to mother's room, and sit by her. I remember just how she used to look, with her pale cheeks, her deep, soft, serious eyes, her white dress,—she always wore white; and I used to think of her whenever I read in Revelations about the saints that were arrayed in fine linen, clean and white. She had a great deal of genius[20] of one sort and another, particularly in music; and she used to sit at her organ, playing fine old majestic music of the Catholic church, and singing with a voice more like an angel than a mortal woman; and I would lay my head down on her lap, and cry, and dream, and feel,—oh, immeasurably!—things that I had no language to say!

"In those days, this matter of slavery had never been canvassed[21] as it has now; nobody dreamed of any harm in it.

"My father was a born aristocrat. I think, in some pre-existent state, he must have been in the higher circles of spirits, and brought all his old court pride along with him;

19 Again, our eyes tend to glaze over during this long, long monologue. What do we really gain from learning even more about St. Clare's personal history? What is Tom doing all this time? What about Eva? What's Dinah cooking in the kitchen?

20 I.e., talent. St. Clare enthusiastically itemizes her abilities.

21 I.e., had the pros and cons weighed.

**22** St. Clare is careful to insist that he is an aristocrat, not a democrat, by birth; his prejudices spring from both class and race.

**23** St. Clare suggests that part of the problem was automation; that is, the assembly-line aspects of running a plantation.

**24** I.e., senseless.

**25** I.e., evade work—anathema to the Northern work ethic! With the wonderful excess of these paragraphs—the thesauruslike abundance of synonyms such as "inflexible, driving, punctilious," "lazy, twaddling, shiftless" —Stowe now provides a semantic incentive to keep us plodding through this chapter.

**26** The description of the "slab-sided, two-fisted renegade" overseer prefigures Simon Legree. Stowe's use of the term "apprenticeship" is an interesting irony—as though brutality and hardness were a skilled profession for which one must train.

**27** I.e., domination.

**28** Much of this entire speech could be deleted; this paragraph would be the first to go. Without good looks or interesting verbiage to keep us interested, I am close to turning the page. Perhaps Stowe has learned too well from Jane Austen, whose long monologues of Miss Bates (in *Emma*) bore us silly. We are beginning to feel jealous of Ophelia: At least she has her knitting to keep her busy.

for it was ingrain, bred in the bone, though he was originally of poor and not in any way of noble family. My brother was begotten in his image.

"Now, an aristocrat, you know, the world over, has no human sympathies, beyond a certain line in society.**22** In England the line is in one place, in Burmah in another, and in America in another; but the aristocrat of all these countries never goes over it. What would be hardship and distress and injustice in his own class, is a cool matter of course in another one. My father's dividing line was that of color. *Among his equals*, never was a man more just and generous; but he considered the negro, through all possible gradations of color, as an intermediate link between man and animals, and graded all his ideas of justice or generosity on this hypothesis. I suppose, to be sure, if anybody had asked him, plump and fair, whether they had human immortal souls, he might have hemmed and hawed, and said yes. But my father was not a man much troubled with spiritualism; religious sentiment he had none, beyond a veneration for God, as decidedly the head of the upper classes.

"Well, my father worked some five hundred negroes; he was an inflexible, driving, punctilious business man; everything was to move by system,—to be sustained with unfailing accuracy and precision.**23** Now, if you take into account that all this was to be worked out by a set of lazy, twaddling,**24** shiftless laborers, who had grown up, all their lives, in the absence of every possible motive to learn how to do anything but 'shirk,'**25** as you Vermonters say, and you'll see that there might naturally be, on his plantation, a great many things that looked horrible and distressing to a sensitive child, like me.

"Besides all, he had an overseer,—a great, tall, slab-sided, two-fisted renegade son of Vermont—(begging your pardon),—who had gone through a regular apprenticeship in hardness and brutality, and taken his degree to be admitted to practice.**26** My mother never could endure him, nor I; but he obtained an entire ascendency**27** over my father; and this man was the absolute despot of the estate.

"I was a little fellow then, but I had the same love that I have now for all kinds of human things,—a kind of passion for the study of humanity, come in what shape it would.**28** I was found in the cabins and among the field-hands a great deal, and, of course, was a great favorite; and all sorts of complaints and grievances were breathed in my ear; and I told them to mother, and we, between us, formed a sort of committee for a redress of grievances. We hindered and repressed a great deal of cruelty, and congratulated ourselves on doing a vast deal of good, till, as often happens, my zeal overacted. Stubbs complained to my father that he couldn't manage the hands, and must resign his position. Father was a fond, indulgent husband, but a man that never flinched from anything that he thought necessary; and so he put down his foot, like a rock, between us and the field-hands. He told my mother, in language perfectly respectful and deferential, but quite explicit, that over the house-servants she should be entire mistress, but that with the field-hands he could allow no interference. He revered and respected her above all living beings; but he would have said it all the same to the virgin Mary herself, if she had come in the way of his system.

"I used sometimes to hear my mother reasoning cases with him,—endeavoring to excite his sympathies. He would listen to the most pathetic appeals with the most discouraging politeness and equanimity. 'It all resolves itself into this,' he would say; 'must I part with Stubbs, or keep him? Stubbs is the soul of punctuality, honesty, and efficiency,—a thorough business hand, and as humane as the general run. We can't have perfection; and if I keep him, I must sustain his administration as a *whole*, even if there are, now and then, things that are exceptionable. All government includes some necessary hardness. General rules will bear hard on particular cases.' This last maxim my father seemed to consider a settler in most alleged cases of cruelty. After he had said *that*, he commonly drew up his feet on the sofa, like a man that has disposed of a business, and betook himself to a nap, or the newspaper, as the case might be.

"The fact is, my father showed the exact sort of talent for a statesman. He could have divided Poland as easily as an orange, or trod on Ireland as quietly and systematically as any man living. At last my mother gave up, in despair. It never will be known, till the last account, what noble and sensitive natures like hers have felt, cast, utterly helpless, into what seems to them an abyss of injustice and cruelty, and which seems so to nobody about them. It has been an age of long sorrow of such natures, in such a hell-begotten sort of world as ours. What remained for her, but to train her children in her own views and sentiments?[29] Well, after all you say about training, children will grow up substantially what they *are* by nature, and only that. From the cradle, Alfred was an aristocrat; and as he grew up, instinctively, all his sympathies and all his reasonings were in that line, and all mother's exhortations went to

29 St. Clare weighs in on the nature/nurture debate. Mark Twain picks up the theme again, in relation to slavery, in his 1894 novel *Pudd'nhead Wilson*, perhaps best known as a story about fingerprints.

**30** St. Clare thinks much better of himself than the reader does at this point. This speech has much in common with many of Robert Browning's long dramatic monologues ("My Last Duchess," for example) and would be of more literary merit taken out of the novel and put into such a form. As it is, it drags.

**31** And yet, St. Clare has just said it is nature, not nurture, that matters.

**32** I.e., to raise an objection.

the winds. As to me, they sunk deep into me. She never contradicted, in form, anything that my father said, or seemed directly to differ from him; but she impressed, burnt into my very soul, with all the force of her deep, earnest nature, an idea of the dignity and worth of the meanest human soul. I have looked in her face with solemn awe, when she would point up to the stars in the evening, and say to me, 'See there, Auguste! the poorest, meanest soul on our place will be living, when all these stars are gone forever,—will live as long as God lives!'**30**

"She had some fine old paintings; one, in particular, of Jesus healing a blind man. They were very fine, and used to impress me strongly. 'See there, Auguste,' she would say; 'the blind man was a beggar, poor and loathsome; therefore, he would not heal him *afar off*! He called him to him, and put *his hands on him*! Remember this, my boy.' If I had lived to grow up under her care, she might have stimulated me to I know not what of enthusiasm. I might have been a saint, reformer, martyr,—but, alas! alas! I went from her when I was only thirteen, and I never saw her again!"**31**

St. Clare rested his head on his hands, and did not speak for some minutes. After a while, he looked up, and went on:

"What poor, mean trash this whole business of human virtue is! A mere matter, for the most part, of latitude and longitude, and geographical position, acting with natural temperament. The greater part is nothing but an accident! Your father, for example, settles in Vermont, in a town where all are, in fact, free and equal; becomes a regular church member and deacon, and in due time joins an Abolition society, and thinks us all little better than heathens. Yet he is, for all the world, in constitution and habit, a duplicate of my father. I can see it leaking out in fifty different ways,—just that same strong, overbearing, dominant spirit. You know very well how impossible it is to persuade some of the folks in your village that Squire Sinclair does not feel above them. The fact is, though he has fallen on democratic times, and embraced a democratic theory, he is to the heart an aristocrat, as much as my father, who ruled over five or six hundred slaves."

Miss Ophelia felt rather disposed to cavil**32** at this picture, and was laying down her knitting to begin, but St. Clare stopped her.

"Now, I know every word you are going to say. I do not say they *were* alike, in fact. One fell into a condition where everything acted against the natural tendency, and the other where everything acted for it; and so one turned out a pretty wilful, stout, overbearing old democrat, and the other a wilful, stout old despot. If both had owned plantations in Louisiana, they would have been as like as two old bullets cast in the same mould."

"What an undutiful boy you are!" said Miss Ophelia.

"I don't mean them any disrespect," said St. Clare. "You know reverence is not my forte. But, to go back to my history:

"When father died, he left the whole property to us twin boys, to be divided as we should agree. There does not breathe on God's earth a nobler-souled, more generous fellow, than Alfred, in all that concerns his equals; and we got on admirably with this property question, without a single unbrotherly word or feeling. We undertook to work the plantation together; and Alfred, whose outward life and capabilities had double the strength of mine, became an enthusiastic planter, and a wonderfully successful one.

"But two years' trial satisfied me that I could not be a partner in that matter. To have a great gang of seven hundred, whom I could not know personally, or feel any individual interest in, bought and driven, housed, fed, worked like so many horned cattle, strained up to military precision,—the question of how little of life's commonest enjoyments would keep them in working order being a constantly recurring problem,—the *necessity* of drivers and overseers,—the ever-necessary whip, first, last, and only argument,—the whole thing was insufferably disgusting and loathsome to me; and when I thought of my mother's estimate of one poor human soul, it became even frightful!

"It's all nonsense to talk to me about slaves *enjoying* all this! To this day, I have no patience with the unutterable trash that some of your patronizing Northerners have made up, as in their zeal to apologize for our sins. We all know better. Tell me that any man living wants to work all his days, from day-dawn till dark, under the constant eye of a master, without the power of putting forth one irresponsible volition,[33] on the same dreary, monotonous, unchanging toil, and all for two pairs of pantaloons and a pair of shoes a year, with enough food and shelter to keep him in working order! Any man who thinks that human beings can, as a general thing, be made about as comfortable that way as any other, I wish he might try it. I'd buy the dog, and work him, with a clear conscience!"

33 I.e., frivolous wish.

239

34 The relationship between slave and master, between laborer and capitalist, between nonwhite and white will continue to be seen as a natural division well into the twentieth century.

35 Once again, Stowe shows her readers that both she and St. Clare have steeped themselves in the contemporary political discourse of workers, the masses, capitalism, exploitation, and labor.

"I always have supposed," said Miss Ophelia, "that you, all of you, approved of these things, and thought them *right*,—according to Scripture."

"Humbug! We are not quite reduced to that yet. Alfred, who is as determined a despot as ever walked, does not pretend to this kind of defence;—no, he stands, high and haughty, on that good old respectable ground, *the right of the strongest*; and he says, and I think quite sensibly, that the American planter is 'only doing, in another form, what the English aristocracy and capitalists are doing by the lower classes;' that is, I take it, *appropriating* them, body and bone, soul and spirit, to their use and convenience.**34** He defends both,—and I think, at least, *consistently*. He says that there can be no high civilization without enslavement of the masses, either nominal or real. There must, he says, be a lower class, given up to physical toil and confined to an animal nature; and a higher one thereby acquires leisure and wealth for a more expanded intelligence and improvement, and becomes the directing soul of the lower. So he reasons, because, as I said, he is born an aristocrat;—so I don't believe, because I was born a democrat."

"How in the world can the two things be compared?" said Miss Ophelia. "The English laborer is not sold, traded, parted from his family, whipped."

"He is as much at the will of his employer as if he were sold to him. The slave-owner can whip his refractory slave to death,—the capitalist can starve him to death. As to family security, it is hard to say which is the worst,—to have one's children sold, or see them starve to death at home."**35**

"But it's no kind of apology for slavery, to prove that it isn't worse than some other bad thing."

"I didn't give it for one,—nay, I'll say, besides, that ours is the more bold and palpable infringement of human rights; actually buying a man up, like a horse,—looking at his teeth, cracking his joints, and trying his paces, and then paying down for him,—having speculators, breeders, traders, and brokers in human bodies and souls,—sets the thing before the eyes of the civilized world in a more tangible form, though the thing done be, after all, in its nature, the same; that is, appropriating one set of human beings to the use and improvement of another, without any regard to their own."

"I never thought of the matter in this light," said Miss Ophelia.

"Well, I've travelled in England some, and I've looked

over a good many documents as to the state of their lower classes; and I really think there is no denying Alfred, when he says that his slaves are better off than a large class of the population of England. You see, you must not infer, from what I have told you, that Alfred is what is called a hard master; for he isn't. He is despotic, and unmerciful to insubordination; he would shoot a fellow down with as little remorse as he would shoot a buck, if he opposed him. But, in general, he takes a sort of pride in having his slaves comfortably fed and accommodated.

"When I was with him, I insisted that he should do something for their instruction; and, to please me, he did get a chaplain, and used to have them catechized[36] Sunday, though, I believe, in his heart, that he thought it would do about as much good to set a chaplain over his dogs and horses. And the fact is, that a mind stupefied and animalized by every bad influence from the hour of birth, spending the whole of every week-day in unreflecting toil, cannot be done much with by a few hours on Sunday.[37] The teachers of Sunday-schools among the manufacturing population of England, and among plantation-hands in our country, could perhaps testify to the same result, *there and here*. Yet some striking exceptions there are among us, from the fact that the negro is naturally more impressible to religious sentiment than the white."

"Well," said Miss Ophelia, "how came you to give up your plantation life?"

"Well, we jogged on[38] together some time, till Alfred saw plainly that I was no planter. He thought it absurd, after he had reformed, and altered, and improved everywhere, to suit my notions, that I still remained unsatisfied. The fact was, it was, after all, the THING that I hated,—the using these men and women, the perpetuation of all this ignorance, brutality and vice,—just to make money for me!

"Besides, I was always interfering in the details. Being myself one of the laziest of mortals, I had altogether too much fellow-feeling for the lazy; and when poor, shiftless dogs put stones at the bottom of their cotton-baskets to make them weigh heavier, or filled their sacks with dirt, with cotton at the top, it seemed so exactly like what I should do if I were they, I couldn't and wouldn't have them flogged[39] for it. Well, of course, there was an end of plantation discipline; and Alf and I came to about the same point that I and my respected father did, years before. So he told me that I was a womanish sentimentalist,[40] and would never do for business life; and advised me to take the bank-stock and the New Orleans family mansion, and

36 I.e., taught the fundamentals of religion and the Bible.

37 St. Clare voices the racist belief in the childlike impressionability of the slaves even as he admits to the brutalizing effects of their uninterrupted toil.

38 I.e., trudged along.

39 I.e., whipped. Whose side are we really to be on here, however?

40 I.e., too soft.

**41** Here is a second low point in our assessment of St. Clare.

**42** St. Clare dismisses his youthful idealism as a passing emotional reaction to a fever.

**43** Ophelia's harsh criticism of her cousin is evident in the complete verse from Luke 9:62: "No man, having put his hand to the plow, and looking back, is fit for the kingdom of heaven."

**44** Stowe is brilliant here. Having become sick and tired of St. Clare's justifications, we almost nod when he says "bad as it is for the slave, it is worse, if anything, for the master." Well that depends on what is "bad" and what is "worse." Physical abuse, sexual abuse, and the wrenching apart of families are bad; is being a perpetrator of these horrors even worse? This is indeed Stowe's question.

**45** Smallpox was a serious, often fatal, disease in the nineteenth century.

go to writing poetry, and let him manage the plantation. So we parted, and I came here."

"But why didn't you free your slaves?"

"Well, I wasn't up to that.**41** To hold them as tools for money-making, I could not;—have them to help spend money, you know, didn't look quite so ugly to me. Some of them were old house-servants, to whom I was much attached; and the younger ones were children to the old. All were well satisfied to be as they were." He paused, and walked reflectively up and down the room.

"There was," said St. Clare, "a time in my life when I had plans and hopes of doing something in this world, more than to float and drift. I had vague, indistinct yearnings to be a sort of emancipator,—to free my native land from this spot and stain. All young men have had such fever-fits,**42** I suppose, some time,—but then—"

"Why didn't you?" said Miss Ophelia;—"you ought not to put your hand to the plough, and look back."**43**

"O, well, things didn't go with me as I expected, and I got the despair of living that Solomon did. I suppose it was a necessary incident to wisdom in us both; but, some how or other, instead of being actor and regenerator in society, I became a piece of drift-wood, and have been floating and eddying about, ever since. Alfred scolds me, every time we meet; and he has the better of me, I grant,— for he really does something; his life is a logical result of his opinions, and mine is a contemptible *non sequitur*."

"My dear cousin, can you be satisfied with such a way of spending your probation?"

"Satisfied! Was I not just telling you I despised it? But, then, to come back to this point,—we were on this liberation business. I don't think my feelings about slavery are peculiar. I find many men who, in their hearts, think of it just as I do. The land groans under it; and, bad as it is for the slave, it is worse, if anything, for the master.**44** It takes no spectacles to see that a great class of vicious, improvident, degraded people, among us, are an evil to us, as well as to themselves. The capitalist and aristocrat of England cannot feel that as we do, because they do not mingle with the class they degrade as we do. They are in our houses; they are the associates of our children, and they form their minds faster than we can; for they are a race that children always will cling to and assimilate with. If Eva, now, was not more angel than ordinary, she would be ruined. We might as well allow the small-pox**45** to run among them, and think our children would not take it, as to let them be uninstructed and vicious, and think our children will not be affected by that. Yet our laws positively and utterly forbid any efficient general educational system, and they do it wisely, too; for, just begin and thoroughly educate one generation, and the whole thing would be blown sky high. If we did not give them liberty, they would take it."[46]

"And what do you think will be the end of this?" said Miss Ophelia.

"I don't know. One thing is certain,—that there is a mustering among the masses, the world over; and there is a *dies iræ*[47] coming on, sooner or later. The same thing is working in Europe, in England, and in this country. My mother used to tell me of a millennium that was coming, when Christ should reign, and all men should be free and happy. And she taught me, when I was a boy, to pray, 'Thy kingdom come.' Sometimes I think all this sighing, and groaning, and stirring among the dry bones foretells what she used to tell me was coming. But who may abide the day of His appearing?"[48]

"Augustine, sometimes I think you are not far from the kingdom," said Miss Ophelia, laying down her knitting, and looking anxiously at her cousin.

"Thank you for your good opinion; but it's up and down with me,—up to heaven's gate in theory, down in earth's dust in practice. But there's the tea-bell,[49]—do let's go,— and don't say, now, I haven't had one down-right serious talk, for once in my life."

At table, Marie alluded to the incident of Prue. "I suppose you'll think, cousin," she said, "that we are all barbarians."

"I think that's a barbarous thing," said Miss Ophelia, "but I don't think you are all barbarians."

"Well, now," said Marie, "I know it's impossible to get along with some of these creatures. They are so bad they ought not to live. I don't feel a particle of sympathy for such cases. If they'd only behave themselves, it would not happen."

"But, mamma," said Eva, "the poor creature was unhappy; that's what made her drink."

"O fiddlestick! as if that were any excuse! I'm unhappy, very often. I presume," she said, pensively, "that I've had greater trials than ever she had. It's just because they are so bad. There's some of them that you cannot break in by any kind of severity. I remember father had a man that was so lazy he would run away just to get rid of work, and lie round in the swamps, stealing and doing all sorts of horrid things. That man was caught and whipped, time and again, and it never did him any good; and the last time

46 James Baldwin may have also sensed Stowe's embrace of radical rhetoric. In *The Devil Finds Work*, Baldwin writes that "[I] read *Uncle Tom's Cabin* compulsively. . . . I was trying to find out something, sensing something in the book of some immense import for me: which, however I knew I did not really understand." Baldwin hints at what it might have been in the next paragraph, without returning to Stowe: "Revolution was the only hope of the American working class—the *proletariat*; and worldwide revolution was the only hope of the world" (*James Baldwin: Collected Essays*).

47 Day of judgment. Literally, "day of wrath," Latin. Baldwin continues, in *The Devil Finds Work*: "Because Uncle Tom would not take vengeance into his own hands, he was not a hero for me."

48 St. Clare voices an anxiety general among Christians in Stowe's time: that the end of the world was near.

49 Again, like Mr. Shelby, St. Clare regularly consoles himself with food.

**50** The term, from taming wild horses, referred to the breaking of the will of slaves.

**51** Finally, Stowe gives us a scene in this chapter worthy of illustration! The name "Scipio" comes from Scipio Africanus the Elder (234–183 B.C.E.), considered the greatest Roman general before Julius Caesar. His name was widely used for slaves of "pure African blood" who often were portrayed as "noble savages."

**52** The hunt metaphor—dogs chasing their prey, whether stag or slave—is common in Southern literature well into the twentieth century. The story of this chase serves also to remind us that George and Eliza are still in danger.

"Scipio hunted 'as men hunt a deer!'" Wood engraving by M. Jackson, "after George Cruikshank." Note the dead dogs. The white man gesturing to the other not to shoot appears to be Augustine St. Clare. The caricatured representation of a trapped Scipio is at odds with St. Clare's description of the native-born African's "rude instinct of freedom."

he crawled off, though he couldn't but just go, and died in the swamp. There was no sort of reason for it, for father's hands were always treated kindly."

"I broke a fellow in,**50** once," said St. Clare, "that all the overseers and masters had tried their hands on in vain."

"You!" said Marie; "well, I'd be glad to know when *you* ever did anything of the sort."

"Well, he was a powerful, gigantic fellow,—a native-born African; and he appeared to have the rude instinct of freedom in him to an uncommon degree. He was a regular African lion. They called him Scipio.**51** Nobody could do anything with him; and he was sold round from overseer to overseer, till at last Alfred bought him, because he thought he could manage him. Well, one day he knocked down the overseer, and was fairly off into the swamps. I was on a visit to Alf's plantation, for it was after we had dissolved partnership. Alfred was greatly exasperated; but I told him that it was his own fault, and laid him any wager that I could break the man; and finally it was agreed that, if I caught him, I should have him to experiment on. So they mustered out a party of some six or seven, with guns and dogs, for the hunt.**52** People, you know, can get up just as much enthusiasm in hunting a man as a deer, if it is only customary; in fact, I got a little excited myself, though I had only put in as a sort of mediator, in case he was caught.

"Well, the dogs bayed and howled, and we rode and scampered, and finally we started him. He ran and bounded like a buck, and kept us well in the rear for some time; but at last he got caught in an impenetrable thicket of cane; then he turned to bay, and I tell you he fought the dogs right gallantly. He dashed them to right and left, and actually killed three of them with only his naked fists, when a shot from a gun brought him down, and he fell, wounded and bleeding, almost at my feet. The poor fellow looked up at me with manhood and despair both in his eye. I kept back the dogs and the party, as they came pressing up, and claimed him as my prisoner. It was all I could do to keep them from shooting him, in the flush of success;

but I persisted in my bargain, and Alfred sold him to me. Well, I took him in hand, and in one fortnight I had him tamed down as submissive and tractable as heart could desire."

"What in the world did you do to him?" said Marie.

"Well, it was quite a simple process. I took him to my own room, had a good bed made for him, dressed his wounds, and tended him myself, until he got fairly on his feet again. And, in process of time, I had free papers made out for him, and told him he might go where he liked."

"And did he go?" said Miss Ophelia.

"No. The foolish fellow tore the paper in two, and absolutely refused to leave me.[53] I never had a braver, better fellow,—trusty and true as steel. He embraced Christianity afterwards, and became as gentle as a child. He used to oversee my place on the lake, and did it capitally, too. I lost him the first cholera season. In fact, he laid down his life for me. For I was sick, almost to death; and when, through the panic, everybody else fled, Scipio worked for me like a giant, and actually brought me back into life again. But, poor fellow! he was taken, right after, and there was no saving him. I never felt anybody's loss more."

Eva had come gradually nearer and nearer to her father, as he told the story,—her small lips apart, her eyes wide and earnest with absorbing interest.

As he finished, she suddenly threw her arms around his neck, burst into tears, and sobbed convulsively.

"Eva, dear child! what is the matter?" said St. Clare, as the child's small frame trembled and shook with the violence of her feelings. "This child," he added, "ought not to hear any of this kind of thing,—she's nervous."

"No, papa, I'm not nervous," said Eva, controlling herself, suddenly, with a strength of resolution singular in such a child. "I'm not nervous, but these things *sink into my heart*."[54]

"What do you mean, Eva?"

"I can't tell you, papa. I think a great many thoughts. Perhaps some day I shall tell you."

"Well, think away, dear,—only don't cry and worry your papa," said St. Clare. "Look here,—see what a beautiful peach I have got for you!"[55]

Eva took it, and smiled, though there was still a nervous twitching about the corners of her mouth.

"Come, look at the gold-fish," said St. Clare, taking her hand and stepping on to the verandah. A few

[53] Stowe gives us a Romantic story typical of Lord Byron.

[54] With the signature phrase—"these things *sink into my heart*"—readers are reminded of Eva's mysterious seriousness and her impending death.

[55] Again with the food!

**56** I.e., the courtyard. Stowe brings us back to Tom by means of a house tour. We step onto the verandah and away from the silken curtains, and only then can we be reminded of the humble Tom, who we learn lives in a "little loft over the stable." Like the abodes of all good characters in Stowe's novel, Tom's room is simple and decent, with Bible and hymnbook open and at hand. A perfect Victorian bachelor pad.

**57** This is a bit out of the blue, but Stowe shows not only that Tom's literacy is not as strong as a child's but that, unlike many slaves, Tom has a willing tutor. Neither seems to realize that Eva's assistance is illegal.

**58** The cost of paper and ink made the use of a small chalkboard ("slate") common in schoolhouses and homes.

moments, and merry laughs were heard through the silken curtains, as Eva and St. Clare were pelting each other with roses, and chasing each other among the alleys of the court.**56**

There is danger that our humble friend Tom be neglected amid the adventures of the higher born; but, if our readers will accompany us up to a little loft over the stable, they may, perhaps, learn a little of his affairs. It was a decent room, containing a bed, a chair, and a small, rough stand, where lay Tom's Bible and hymn-book; and where he sits, at present, with his slate before him, intent on something that seems to cost him a great deal of anxious thought.

The fact was, that Tom's home-yearnings had become so strong, that he had begged a sheet of writing-paper of Eva, and, mustering up all his small stock of literary attainment acquired by Mas'r George's instructions, he conceived the bold idea of writing a letter;**57** and he was busy now, on his slate,**58** getting out his first draft. Tom was in a good deal of trouble, for the forms of some of the letters he had forgotten entirely; and of what he did remember, he did not know exactly which to use. And while he was working, and breathing very hard, in his earnestness, Eva alighted, like a bird, on the round of his chair behind him, and peeped over his shoulder.

"O, Uncle Tom! what funny things you *are* making, there!"

"I'm trying to write to my poor old woman, Miss Eva, and my little chil'en," said Tom, drawing the back of his hand over his eyes; "but, some how, I'm feard I shan't make it out."

"I wish I could help you, Tom! I've learnt to write some. Last year I could make all the letters, but I'm afraid I've forgotten."

So Eva put her little golden head close to his, and the two commenced a grave and anxious discussion, each one equally earnest, and about equally ignorant; and, with a deal of consulting and advising over every word, the composition began, as they both felt very sanguine, to look quite like writing.

"Yes, Uncle Tom, it really begins to look beautiful," said Eva, gazing delightedly on it. "How pleased your wife'll be, and the poor little children! O, it's a shame you ever had to go away from them! I mean to ask papa to let you go back, some time."

"Missis said that she would send down money for me, as soon as they could get it together," said Tom. "I'm 'spectin' she will. Young Mas'r George, he said he'd come for me; and he gave me this yer dollar as a sign;" and Tom drew from under his clothes the precious dollar.

"O, he'll certainly come, then!" said Eva. "I'm so glad!"

"And I wanted to send a letter, you know, to let 'em know whar I was, and tell poor Chloe that I was well off,—cause she felt so drefful, poor soul!"

"I say, Tom!" said St. Clare's voice, coming in the door at this moment.

Tom and Eva both started.

"What's here?" said St. Clare, coming up and looking at the slate.

"O, it's Tom's letter. I'm helping him to write it," said Eva; "isn't it nice?"

"I wouldn't discourage either of you," said St. Clare, "but I rather think, Tom, you'd better get me to write your letter for you. I'll do it, when I come home from my ride."

"It's very important he should write," said Eva, "because his mistress is going to send down money to redeem him, you know, papa; he told me they told him so."

St. Clare thought, in his heart, that this was probably only one of those things which good-natured owners say to their servants, to alleviate their horror of being sold, without any intention of fulfilling the expectation thus excited. But he did not make any audible comment upon it,—only ordered Tom to get the horses out for a ride.

Tom's letter was written in due form for him that evening, and safely lodged in the post-office.

Miss Ophelia still persevered in her labors in the house-keeping line. It was universally agreed, among all the household, from Dinah down to the youngest urchin, that Miss Ophelia was decidedly "curis,"**59**—a term by which a southern servant implies that his or her betters don't exactly suit them.

The higher circle in the family—to wit, Adolph, Jane and Rosa—agreed that she was no lady; ladies never kept working about as she did;—that she had no *air* at all; and they were surprised that she should be any relation of the St. Clares. Even Marie declared that it was absolutely fatiguing to see Cousin Ophelia always so busy. And, in fact, Miss Ophelia's industry**60** was so incessant as to lay some foundation for the complaint. She sewed and stitched away, from daylight till dark, with the energy of

59 I.e., strange.

60 I.e., hard work.

one who is pressed on by some immediate urgency; and then, when the light faded, and the work was folded away, with one turnout came the ever-ready knitting-work, and there she was again, going on as briskly as ever. It really was a labor to see her.

# CHAPTER 20

## Topsy[1]

One morning, while Miss Ophelia was busy in some of her domestic cares, St. Clare's voice was heard, calling her at the foot of the stairs.

"Come down here, Cousin; I've something to show you."

"What is it?" said Miss Ophelia, coming down, with her sewing in her hand.

"I've made a purchase for your department,—see here," said St. Clare; and, with the word, he pulled along a little negro girl, about eight or nine years of age.

She was one of the blackest of her race; and her round, shining eyes, glittering as glass beads, moved with quick and restless glances over everything in the room. Her mouth, half open with astonishment at the wonders of the new Mas'r's parlor, displayed a white and brilliant set of teeth. Her woolly hair was braided in sundry little tails, which stuck out in every direction. The expression of her face was an odd mixture of shrewdness and cunning, over which was oddly drawn, like a kind of veil, an expression of the most doleful gravity and solemnity. She was dressed in a single filthy, ragged garment, made of bagging; and stood with her hands demurely folded before her. Altogether, there was something odd and goblin-like about her appearance,[2]—something, as Miss Ophelia afterwards said, "so heathenish," as to inspire that good lady with utter dismay; and, turning to St. Clare, she said,

"Augustine, what in the world have you brought that thing here for?"

St. Claire introducing Topsy to Miss Ophelia. Notice that Ophelia has what appears to be knitting in her never-idle hands. Drawing by A. Bonamore, circa 1900. Source unknown

1 Topsy, the cartoon little slave girl, has taken on iconic status. George Sand, in her famous "Review of *Uncle Tom's Cabin*," remarks on Stowe's extraordinary success in creating child characters: "Children are the true heroes of Mrs. Stowe. Her soul, the most maternal that ever was, has conceived all the little beings in the very light of Heaven, (rayon de la grace,) George Shelby, little Harry, the cousin of Eva, the baby of the little wife of the Senator, and Topsey [*sic*], the poor, devilish, and excellent Topsey, those that are seen, and those that are not seen in this romance, but of which only three words are spoken by their desolate mothers—are a world of little white and black angels, in which every woman recognises the object of her love, the source of her joys and her tears. In taking form in the mind of Mrs. Stowe, these children, without ceasing to be children, take also ideal proportions, and come to interest us more than all the personages in love romances."

2 In this dehumanizing description of Topsy, Stowe lets her readers see the expected racist attribute of keen manipulation beneath the "veil" before she pulls it closed, undercutting from the outset Topsy's grave appearance.

3 In presenting the "Jim Crow" antics of Topsy, St. Clare echoes Mr. Shelby's behavior in calling on little Harry to perform for Haley. Topsy became famous immediately, and songs such as this one, writen by Eliza Cook and published in *Frederick Douglass' Paper* on August 12, 1852, appeared in America and Britain.

Little Topsy's Song

Topsy was neber born,
Neber had a moder.
Spects I growed a nigger brat,
Jist like any oder.

Whip me till the blood pours down
Ole missus used to do it.
She said she'd cut my heart right out,
But neber could get to do it.

Got no heart, I don't beheb
Niggers do widout 'em.
Neber heard of God or love,
So can't tell much about 'em.

[Chorus]

"For you to educate, to be sure, and train in the way she should go. I thought she was rather a funny specimen in the Jim Crow line. Here, Topsy," he added, giving a whistle, as a man would to call the attention of a dog, "give us a song, now, and show us some of your dancing."[3]

The black, glassy eyes glittered with a kind of wicked drollery, and the thing struck up, in a clear shrill voice, an odd negro melody, to which she kept time with her hands and feet, spinning round, clapping her hands, knocking her knees together, in a wild, fantastic sort of time, and producing in her throat all those odd guttural sounds which distinguish the native music of her race; and finally, turning a summerset or two, and giving a prolonged closing note, as odd and unearthly as that of a steam-whistle, she came suddenly down on the carpet, and stood with her hands folded, and a most sanctimonious expression of meekness and solemnity over her face, only broken by the cunning glances which she shot askance from the corners of her eyes.

Miss Ophelia stood silent, perfectly paralyzed with amazement.[4]

St. Clare, like a mischievous fellow as he was, appeared to enjoy her astonishment; and, addressing the child again, said,

"Topsy, this is your new mistress. I'm going to give you up to her; see now that you behave yourself."[5]

"Yes, Mas'r," said Topsy, with sanctimonious gravity, her wicked eyes twinkling as she spoke.

"You're going to be good, Topsy, you understand," said St. Clare.

"O yes, Mas'r," said Topsy, with another twinkle, her hands still devoutly folded.

"Now, Augustine, what upon earth is this for?" said Miss Ophelia. "Your house is so full of these little plagues, now, that a body can't set down their foot without treading on 'em. I get up in the morning, and find one asleep behind the door, and see one black head poking out from under the table, one lying on the door-mat,—and they are mopping and mowing and grinning between all the railings, and tumbling over the kitchen floor! What on earth did you want to bring this one for?"

"For you to educate—didn't I tell you? You're always preaching about educating. I thought I would make you a present of a fresh-caught specimen, and let you try your hand on her, and bring her up in the way she should go."

"*I* don't want her, I am sure;—I have more to do with 'em now than I want to."

"That's you Christians, all over!—you'll get up a society, and get some poor missionary to spend all his days among just such heathen. But let me see one of you that would take one into your house with you, and take the labor of their conversion on yourselves! No; when it comes to that, they are dirty and disagreeable, and it's too much care, and so on."

"Augustine, you know I didn't think of it in that light," said Miss Ophelia, evidently softening. "Well, it might be a real missionary work," said she, looking rather more favorably on the child.[6]

St. Clare had touched the right string. Miss Ophelia's conscientiousness was ever on the alert. "But," she added, "I really didn't see the need of buying this one;—there are enough now, in your house, to take all my time and skill."

"Well, then, Cousin," said St. Clare, drawing her aside; "I ought to beg your pardon for my good-for-nothing speeches. You are so good, after all, that there's no sense in them. Why, the fact is, this concern belonged to a couple of drunken creatures that keep a low restaurant that I have to pass by every day, and I was tired of hearing her screaming, and them beating and swearing at her. She looked bright and funny, too, as if something might be made of her;—so I bought her, and I'll give her to you. Try, now, and give her a good orthodox New England bringing up, and see what it'll make of her. You know I haven't any gift that way; but I'd like you to try."

"Well, I'll do what I can," said Miss Ophelia; and she approached her new subject very much as a person might be supposed to approach a black spider, supposing them to have benevolent designs toward it.[7]

"She's dreadfully dirty, and half naked," she said.

"Well, take her down stairs, and make some of them clean and clothe her up."

Miss Ophelia carried her to the kitchen regions.

"Don't see what Mas'r St. Clare wants of 'nother nigger!" said Dinah, surveying the new arrival with no friendly air. "Won't have her round under *my* feet, *I* know!"

"Pah!" said Rosa and Jane, with supreme disgust; "let her keep out of our way! What in the world Mas'r wanted another of these low niggers for, I can't see!"[8]

"You go long! No more nigger dan you be, Miss Rosa," said Dinah, who felt this last remark a reflection on herself. "You seem to tink yourself white folks. You an't nerry one, black *nor* white. I'd like to be one or turrer."

Miss Ophelia saw that there was nobody in the camp that would undertake to oversee the cleansing and dress-

Miguel Covarrubias offers an angry, sullen Topsy and a pinched-faced, wholly unfriendly Ophelia.   From *Uncle Tom's Cabin: or, Life Among the Lowly*, Heritage Press edition, 1938

This is Topsy's savage song,
Topsy's cute and clever.
Hurrah, then, for the white man's right
Slavery forever!

I 'spects I'se very wicked,
That's just what I am.
Ony you jist give me a chance,
Won't I rouse Ole Sam?

'T ain't no use in being good,
Cos I'se black you see.
I neber cared for nothin yet,
And nothin cares for me.

Ha! Ha! Ha! Miss Feely's hand
Dun know how to grip me.
Neber likes to do no work,
And won't widout they whip me.

This is Topsy's savage song,
Topsy's cute and clever.
Hurrah, then, for the white man's right
Slavery forever!

Don't you die, Miss Evy,
Else I go dead too.
I knows I'se wicked but I'll try
And be all good to you.

You hab taught me better things,
Though I'se nigger skin.
You hab found poor Topsy's heart,
Spite of all its sin.

Don't you die Miss Evy dear,
Else I go dead too.
Though I'se black, I'se sure that God
Will let me go wid you.

This is Topsy's human song,
Under Love's endeavor.
Hurrah, then, for the white child's work
Humanity forever!

4 We haven't seen Ophelia express much but exasperation and pity for the St. Clare slaves, but Stowe means to open up a touchy subject—the aversion Northern whites feel about associating with African Americans. Suddenly, Ophelia refers to Topsy and the other slave children as "thing" and "plagues."

5 St. Clare's flippant language appears to be an attempt at humor. Stowe still needs to work to make St. Clare likable, but he is generally too abstract for real humor.

6 Thus, Ophelia can relate to Topsy only as missionary work.

7 An anonymous *Times* (London) review in 1852 argued that America's whites were not ready for freeing the slaves because the vast majority had a "horror of black blood." Topsy, no matter what Ophelia's missionary zeal, still seems to her "a black spider." But readers everywhere loved her strangeness. The archbishop of Dublin, Lord Denman, formerly chief justice, published a pamphlet in 1853 praising Mrs. Stowe and singling out Topsy as the novel's most original character (*Uncle Tom's Cabin, Bleak House, Slavery and Slave Trade*). Likewise Lord Morpeth, in the preface to an 1852 British edition of the novel, wrote: "In Aunt Chloe, and much of the interior economy of the Shelby household, and especially in the bright, blue-eyed Eva, have we not repeated glimpses of Mr. Charles Dickens? In the tea-table dialogue of the Ohio Senator and his wife, and in the self-portraying complaints of Mrs. St. Clare, are we not vividly reminded of our admirable Miss Austen? I think Topsy may challenge the honors of entire originality."

8 Dinah, Rosa, and Jane's disgust at Topsy—and their refusal to help bathe her—serve a number of narrative purposes. First, we gain more evidence of the slackness of the St. Clare household; second, we understand why Tom has made no friends in his new home; and third, Ophelia is left to do the work of washing.

ing of the new arrival; and so she was forced to do it herself, with some very ungracious and reluctant assistance from Jane.

It is not for ears polite to hear the particulars of the first toilet of a neglected, abused child. In fact, in this world, multitudes must live and die in a state that it would be too great a shock to the nerves of their fellow-mortals even to hear described. Miss Ophelia had a good, strong, practical deal of resolution; and she went through all the disgusting details with heroic thoroughness, though, it must be confessed, with no very gracious air,—for endurance was the utmost to which her principles could bring her. When she saw, on the back and shoulders of the child, great welts and calloused spots, ineffaceable marks of the system under which she had grown up thus far, her heart became pitiful within her.[9]

"See there!" said Jane, pointing to the marks, "don't that show she's a limb?[10] We'll have fine works with her, I reckon. I hate these nigger young uns! so disgusting! I wonder that Mas'r would buy her!"

The "young un" alluded to heard all these comments with the subdued and doleful air which seemed habitual to her, only scanning, with a keen and furtive glance of her flickering eyes, the ornaments which Jane wore in her ears. When arrayed at last in a suit of decent and whole clothing, her hair cropped short to her head,[11] Miss Ophelia, with some satisfaction, said she looked more Christian-like than she did, and in her own mind began to mature some plans for her instruction.

Sitting down before her, she began to question her.

"How old are you, Topsy?"

"Dun no, Missis," said the image, with a grin that showed all her teeth.

"Don't know how old you are? Didn't anybody ever tell you? Who was your mother?"

"Never had none!" said the child, with another grin.

"Never had any mother? What do you mean? Where were you born?"[12]

"Never was born!" persisted Topsy, with another grin, that looked so goblin-like, that, if Miss Ophelia had been at all nervous, she might have fancied that she had got hold of some sooty gnome from the land of Diablerie;[13] but Miss Ophelia was not nervous, but plain and business-like, and she said, with some sternness,

"You mustn't answer me in that way, child; I'm not playing with you. Tell me where you were born, and who your father and mother were."

9 Stowe gives her readers not a description of the first bath Topsy has had in a while, if ever, but rather of Ophelia's heroic efforts to rise above her revulsion. Such intimacy, however, brings its reward in her softening feelings after seeing Topsy's scars.

10 A mischievous child, "the devil's limb." Characterizing Topsy as a devilish heathen will make her conversion seem even more profound.

11 Topsy is stripped of a mark of her heritage—the woolly braids and tails. Thus shorn, she is ready for Ophelia's Christianizing. James Baldwin writes in "Everybody's Protest Novel": "This tableau . . . is the heritage of the Negro in America: *Wash me*, cried the slave to his Maker, *and I shall be whiter, whiter than snow*! For black is the color of evil; only the robes of the saved are white" (*James Baldwin: Collected Essays*).

12 Lack of knowledge as to their origins was common among slaves, as Frederick Douglass's and many other slave narratives attest. Here, the horror at such ignorance is somewhat displaced onto the reaction of our New England spinster and softened by the comical delivery by Topsy.

13 I.e., the land of sorcery (dealings with the devil).

**14** Through Topsy, Stowe gives us the child's perspective on slavery, recounted as the facts of her life. A common practice in slavery was to put the children in the care of an old woman no longer able to do fieldwork, in order to free up their mothers for labor.

**15** Topsy's disconcerting answer to Ophelia's catechism question—"I spect I grow'd"—has become a classic, largely because of the quick change of subject to sewing. Stowe is a confident writer and knows when to leave a phrase ringing in the readers' ears.

**16** St. Clare's version of tabula rasa, the blank slate.

"Never was born," reiterated the creature, more emphatically; "never had no father nor mother, nor nothin'. I was raised by a speculator, with lots of others. Old Aunt Sue used to take car on us."**14**

The child was evidently sincere; and Jane, breaking into a short laugh, said,

"Laws, Missis, there's heaps of 'em. Speculators buys 'em up cheap, when they's little, and gets 'em raised for market."

"How long have you lived with your master and mistress?"

"Dun no, Missis."

"Is it a year, or more, or less?"

"Dun no, Missis."

"Laws, Missis, those low negroes,—they can't tell; they don't know anything about time," said Jane; "they don't know what a year is; they don't know their own ages."

"Have you ever heard anything about God, Topsy?"

The child looked bewildered, but grinned as usual.

"Do you know who made you?"

"Nobody, as I knows on," said the child, with a short laugh.

The idea appeared to amuse her considerably; for her eyes twinkled, and she added,

"I spect I grow'd. Don't think nobody never made me."**15**

"Do you know how to sew?" said Miss Ophelia, who thought she would turn her inquiries to something more tangible.

"No, Missis."

"What can you do?—what did you do for your master and mistress?"

"Fetch water, and wash dishes, and rub knives, and wait on folks."

"Were they good to you?"

"Spect they was," said the child, scanning Miss Ophelia cunningly.

Miss Ophelia rose from this encouraging colloquy; St. Clare was leaning over the back of her chair.

"You find virgin soil there, Cousin; put in your own ideas,—you won't find many to pull up."**16**

Miss Ophelia's ideas of education, like all her other ideas, were very set and definite; and of the kind that prevailed in New England a century ago, and which are still preserved in some very retired and unsophisticated parts, where there are no railroads. As nearly as could be expressed, they could be comprised in very few words: to teach them to mind when they were spoken to; to teach them the catechism, sewing, and reading; and to whip them if they told lies. And though, of course, in the flood of light that is now poured on education, these are left far away in the rear, yet it is an undisputed fact that our grandmothers raised some tolerably fair men and women under this régime, as many of us can remember and testify.[17] At all events, Miss Ophelia knew of nothing else to do; and, therefore, applied her mind to her heathen with the best diligence she could command.

The child was announced and considered in the family as Miss Ophelia's girl; and, as she was looked upon with no gracious eye in the kitchen, Miss Ophelia resolved to confine her sphere of operation and instruction chiefly to her own chamber. With a self-sacrifice which some of our readers will appreciate, she resolved, instead of comfortably making her own bed, sweeping and dusting her own chamber,—which she had hitherto done, in utter scorn of all offers of help from the chambermaid of the establishment,—to condemn herself to the martyrdom of instructing Topsy to perform these operations,—ah, woe the day! Did any of our readers ever do the same, they will appreciate the amount of her self-sacrifice.

Miss Ophelia began with Topsy by taking her into her chamber, the first morning, and solemnly commencing a course of instruction in the art and mystery of bed-making.

Behold, then, Topsy, washed and shorn of all the little braided tails wherein her heart had delighted, arrayed in a clean gown, with well-starched apron, standing reverently before Miss Ophelia, with an expression of solemnity well befitting a funeral.

"Now, Topsy, I'm going to show you just how my bed is to be made. I am very particular about my bed. You must learn exactly how to do it."

"Yes, ma'am," says Topsy, with a deep sigh, and a face of woful earnestness.

"Now, Topsy, look here;—this is the hem of the sheet,—this is the right side of the sheet, and this is the wrong;—will you remember?"

"Yes, ma'am," says Topsy, with another sigh.

"Well, now, the under sheet you must bring over the bolster,—so,—and tuck it clear down under the mattress nice and smooth,—so,—do you see?"

"Yes, ma'am," said Topsy, with profound attention.

"But the upper sheet," said Miss Ophelia, "must be brought down in this way, and tucked under firm and smooth at the foot,—so,—the narrow hem at the foot."

17 Yet another appeal to Stowe's female readers.

This chubby Topsy (at least she looks a little more well fed in her demure smock) is still impish and strangely inhuman. Note how Ophelia's corkscrew hairstyle is not entirely unlike Topsy's.

**18** I.e., the bedclothes.

**19** We are to laugh a bit at Ophelia's utter seriousness in this exercise.

**20** The moniker "Miss Feely" is wonderfully ironic. Are we to even consider that the scene we are witnessing is almost flirtatious? We have seen a bath followed by bed-making followed by a coy lifting of ribbons and feigned innocence. Are we to consider and then soundly reject any hint of what this scene truly is—the beginning of a romance between these two characters?

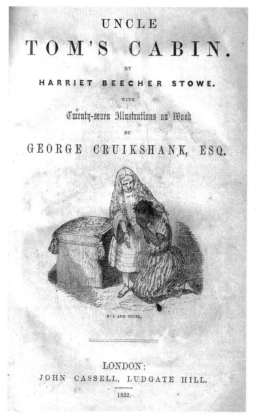

George Cruikshank's cover image from the first British edition of *Uncle Tom's Cabin*, featuring Eva and Topsy. By contrast, the American edition featured Uncle Tom's cabin. The sentimental image of these two girls beckons the sympathy of the reader. Eva looks like Alice (in Wonderland). From *Uncle Tom's Cabin*, John Cassell, London, 1852

"Yes, ma'am," said Topsy, as before;—but we will add, what Miss Ophelia did not see, that, during the time when the good lady's back was turned, in the zeal of her manipulations, the young disciple had contrived to snatch a pair of gloves and a ribbon, which she had adroitly slipped into her sleeves, and stood with her hands dutifully folded, as before.

"Now, Topsy, let's see *you* do this," said Miss Ophelia, pulling off the clothes,[18] and seating herself.

Topsy, with great gravity and adroitness, went through the exercise completely to Miss Ophelia's satisfaction; smoothing the sheets, patting out every wrinkle, and exhibiting, through the whole process, a gravity and seriousness with which her instructress was greatly edified.[19] By an unlucky slip, however, a fluttering fragment of the ribbon hung out of one of her sleeves, just as she was finishing, and caught Miss Ophelia's attention. Instantly she pounced upon it. "What's this? You naughty, wicked child,—you've been stealing this!"

The ribbon was pulled out of Topsy's own sleeve, yet was she not in the least disconcerted; she only looked at it with an air of the most surprised and unconscious innocence.

"Laws! why, that ar's Miss Feely's[20] ribbon, an't it? How could it a got caught in my sleeve?"

"Topsy, you naughty girl, don't you tell me a lie,—you stole that ribbon!"

"Missis, I declar for 't, I didn't;—never seed it till dis yer blessed minnit."

"Topsy," said Miss Ophelia, "don't you know it's wicked to tell lies?"

"I never tells no lies, Miss Feely," said Topsy, with virtuous gravity; "it's jist the truth I've been a tellin now, and an't nothin else."

"Topsy, I shall have to whip you, if you tell lies so."

"Laws, Missis, if you's to whip all day, couldn't say no other way," said Topsy, beginning to blubber. "I never seed dat ar,—it must a got caught in my sleeve. Miss Feely must have left it on the bed, and it got caught in the clothes, and so got in my sleeve."

Miss Ophelia was so indignant at the barefaced lie, that she caught the child and shook her.

"Don't you tell me that again!"

The shake brought the gloves on to the floor, from the other sleeve.

"There, you!" said Miss Ophelia, "will you tell me now, you didn't steal the ribbon?"

Topsy now confessed to the gloves, but still persisted in denying the ribbon.

"Now, Topsy," said Miss Ophelia, "if you'll confess all about it, I won't whip you this time." Thus adjured, Topsy confessed to the ribbon and gloves, with woful protestations of penitence.

"Well, now, tell me. I know you must have taken other things since you have been in the house, for I let you run about all day yesterday. Now, tell me if you took anything, and I shan't whip you."

"Laws, Missis! I took Miss Eva's red thing she wars on her neck."

"You did, you naughty child!—Well, what else?"

"I took Rosa's yer-rings,—them red ones."

"Go bring them to me this minute, both of 'em."

"Laws, Missis! I can't,—they's burnt up!"

"Burnt up!—what a story! Go get 'em, or I'll whip you."

Topsy, with loud protestations, and tears, and groans, declared that she *could* not. "They's burnt up,—they was."

"What did you burn 'em up for?" said Miss Ophelia.

"Cause I's wicked,—I is. I's mighty wicked, any how. I can't help it."

Just at this moment, Eva came innocently into the room, with the identical coral necklace on her neck.

"Why, Eva, where did you get your necklace?" said Miss Ophelia.

"Get it? Why, I've had it on all day," said Eva.

"Did you have it on yesterday?"

"Yes; and what is funny, Aunty, I had it on all night. I forgot to take it off when I went to bed."

Miss Ophelia looked perfectly bewildered; the more so, as Rosa, at that instant, came into the room, with a basket of newly-ironed linen poised on her head, and the coral ear-drops shaking in her ears!

"I'm sure I can't tell anything what to do with such a child!" she said, in despair. "What in the world did you tell me you took those things for, Topsy?"

"Why, Missis said I must 'fess; and I couldn't think of nothin' else to 'fess," said Topsy, rubbing her eyes.

"Eva and Topsy." This color lithograph by Louisa Corbaux is one of the many popular responses capitalizing on Stowe's story. This is one of the few images in which Topsy is represented in a fairly realistic manner, rather than as a conventional stereotype.    Published in London by C. Jefferys, 1852

21 I.e., humbled. Stowe plants the seeds of Eva's power over Topsy from their early meeting.

22 Stowe pauses to drive home the emblematic nature of these two children as symbols of their races. The effusive description of the Saxon child contrasts with a short, negative one of the Afric. In her sweep of centuries of history, Stowe gives a common racist reading of the natural positions of the races, banishing the common American heritage of both girls.

23 Spoke at length.

"Eva Stood Looking at Topsy." Topsy appears to be returning Eva's gaze as an equal, suggesting the doubled or mirrored nature of black-white relations under slavery. Artist unknown.   From *Uncle Tom's Cabin, or, Life Among the Lowly*, Grosset and Dunlap, n.d.

"But, of course, I didn't want you to confess things you didn't do," said Miss Ophelia; "that's telling a lie, just as much as the other."

"Laws, now, is it?" said Topsy, with an air of innocent wonder.

"La, there an't any such thing as truth in that limb," said Rosa, looking indignantly at Topsy. "If I was Mas'r St. Clare, I'd whip her till the blood run. I would,—I'd let her catch it!"

"No, no, Rosa," said Eva, with an air of command, which the child could assume at times; "you mustn't talk so, Rosa. I can't bear to hear it."

"La sakes! Miss Eva, you's so good, you don't know nothing how to get along with niggers. There's no way but to cut 'em well up, I tell ye."

"Rosa!" said Eva, "hush! Don't you say another word of that sort!" and the eye of the child flashed, and her cheek deepened its color.

Rosa was cowed[21] in a moment.

"Miss Eva has got the St. Clare blood in her, that's plain. She can speak, for all the world, just like her papa," she said, as she passed out of the room.

Eva stood looking at Topsy.

There stood the two children, representatives of the two extremes of society.[22] The fair, high-bred child, with her golden head, her deep eyes, her spiritual, noble brow, and prince-like movements; and her black, keen, subtle, cringing, yet acute neighbor. They stood the representatives of their races. The Saxon, born of ages of cultivation, command, education, physical and moral eminence; the Afric, born of ages of oppression, submission, ignorance, toil, and vice!

Something, perhaps, of such thoughts struggled through Eva's mind. But a child's thoughts are rather dim, undefined instincts; and in Eva's noble nature many such were yearning and working, for which she had no power of utterance. When Miss Ophelia expatiated[23] on Topsy's naughty, wicked conduct, the child looked perplexed and sorrowful, but said, sweetly,

"Poor Topsy, why need you steal? You're going to be taken good care of, now. I'm sure I'd rather give you anything of mine, than have you steal it."

It was the first word of kindness the child had ever heard in her life; and the sweet tone and manner struck strangely on the wild, rude heart, and a sparkle of something like a tear shone in the keen, round, glittering eye;

but it was followed by the short laugh and habitual grin. No! the ear that has never heard anything but abuse is strangely incredulous of anything so heavenly as kindness; and Topsy only thought Eva's speech something funny and inexplicable,—she did not believe it.

But what was to be done with Topsy? Miss Ophelia found the case a puzzler; her rules for bringing up didn't seem to apply. She thought she would take time to think of it; and, by the way of gaining time, and in hopes of some indefinite moral virtues supposed to be inherent in dark closets,[24] Miss Ophelia shut Topsy up in one till she had arranged her ideas further on the subject.

"I don't see," said Miss Ophelia to St. Clare, "how I'm going to manage that child, without whipping her."

"Well, whip her, then, to your heart's content; I'll give you full power to do what you like."

"Children always have to be whipped," said Miss Ophelia; "I never heard of bringing them up without."

"O, well, certainly," said St. Clare: "do as you think best. Only I'll make one suggestion: I've seen this child whipped with a poker, knocked down with the shovel or tongs, whichever came handiest, & c.; and, seeing that she is used to that style of operation, I think your whippings will have to be pretty energetic, to make much impression."

"What is to be done with her, then?" said Miss Ophelia.

"You have started a serious question," said St. Clare; "I wish you'd answer it. What is to be done with a human being that can be governed only by the lash,—*that* fails,—it's a very common state of things down here!"

"I'm sure I don't know; I never saw such a child as this."

"Such children are very common among us, and such men and women, too. How are they to be governed?" said St. Clare.

"I'm sure it's more than I can say," said Miss Ophelia.

"Or I either," said St. Clare. "The horrid cruelties and outrages that once and a while find their way into the papers,—such cases as Prue's, for example,—what do they come from? In many cases, it is a gradual hardening process on both sides,—the owner growing more and more cruel, as the servant more and more callous. Whipping and abuse are like laudanum[25] you have to double the dose as the sensibilities decline. I saw this very early when I became an owner; and I resolved never to begin, because I did not know when I should stop,—and I resolved, at least, to protect my own moral nature. The consequence is, that

24 A contemporary punishment for unruly children was to lock them in a dark small room. See, for example, Charlotte Brontë's *Jane Eyre* (1847).

25 Laudanum was an opium-based painkiller introduced by Swiss alchemist and surgeon Paracelsus in the sixeenth century. It was widely prescribed in the nineteenth century for a variety of ailments.

This is one of the most curious cover images of Topsy and Eva: This depiction of an odd sisterhood is remarkably modern.   From *Altemus's Young People's Library: Uncle Tom's Cabin; or, Life Among the Lowly*, 1900

**26** In spite of continuing analogies to animals (cats, monkeys, and serpent), the reader might notice that Topsy shows great aptitude for attaining skills important to her own growth—reading and writing—but ineptitude when faced with a skill, such as sewing, that would make her a good servant.

**27** Roots doctor or, more likely here, a magician. Stowe continues to emphasize Topsy's heathenish nature.

**28** I.e., joking.

**29** An echo of the earlier comparison of Eva and Topsy as Saxon and Afric.

**30** I.e., enjoy her company.

Miguel Covarrubias depicts Topsy encountering her mirror image. The quest for self-identity is a leitmotif of Stowe's novel.   From *Uncle Tom's Cabin: or, Life Among the Lowly*, Heritage Press edition, 1938

my servants act like spoiled children; but I think that better than for us both to be brutalized together. You have talked a great deal about our responsibilities in educating, Cousin. I really wanted you to *try* with one child, who is a specimen of thousands among us."

"It is your system makes such children," said Miss Ophelia.

"I know it; but they are *made,*—they exist,—and what *is* to be done with them?"

"Well, I can't say I thank you for the experiment. But, then, as it appears to be a duty, I shall persevere and try, and do the best I can," said Miss Ophelia; and Miss Ophelia, after this, did labor, with a commendable degree of zeal and energy, on her new subject. She instituted regular hours and employments for her, and undertook to teach her to read and to sew.

In the former art, the child was quick enough. She learned her letters as if by magic, and was very soon able to read plain reading; but the sewing was a more difficult matter. The creature was as lithe as a cat, and as active as a monkey,**26** and the confinement of sewing was her abomination; so she broke her needles, threw them slyly out of windows, or down in chinks of the walls; she tangled, broke, and dirtied her thread, or, with a sly movement, would throw a spool away altogether. Her motions were almost as quick as those of a practised conjurer,**27** and her command of her face quite as great; and though Miss Ophelia could not help feeling that so many accidents could not possibly happen in succession, yet she could not, without a watchfulness which would leave her no time for anything else, detect her.

Topsy was soon a noted character in the establishment. Her talent for every species of drollery,**28** grimace, and mimicry,—for dancing, tumbling, climbing, singing, whistling, imitating every sound that hit her fancy,—seemed inexhaustible. In her play-hours, she invariably had every child in the establishment at her heels, open-mouthed with admiration and wonder,—not excepting Miss Eva, who appeared to be fascinated by her wild diablerie, as a dove is sometimes charmed by a glittering serpent.**29** Miss Ophelia was uneasy that Eva should fancy Topsy's society**30** so much, and implored St. Clare to forbid it.

"Poh! let the child alone," said St. Clare. "Topsy will do her good."

"But so depraved a child,—are you not afraid she will teach her some mischief?"

"She can't teach her mischief; she might teach it to

some children, but evil rolls off Eva's mind like dew off a cabbage-leaf,—not a drop sinks in."

"Don't be too sure," said Miss Ophelia. "I know I'd never let a child of mine play with Topsy."

"Well, your children needn't," said St. Clare, "but mine may; if Eva could have been spoiled, it would have been done years ago."

Topsy was at first despised and contemned[31] by the upper servants. They soon found reason to alter their opinion. It was very soon discovered that whoever cast an indignity on Topsy was sure to meet with some inconvenient accident shortly after;—either a pair of ear-rings or some cherished trinket would be missing, or an article of dress would be suddenly found utterly ruined, or the person would stumble accidentally into a pail of hot water, or a libation of dirty slop would unaccountably deluge them from above when in full gala dress;—and on all these occasions, when investigation was made, there was nobody found to stand sponsor for the indignity.[32] Topsy was cited, and had up before all the domestic judicatories, time and again; but always sustained her examinations with most edifying innocence and gravity of appearance. Nobody in the world ever doubted who did the things; but not a scrap of any direct evidence could be found to establish the suppositions, and Miss Ophelia was too just to feel at liberty to proceed to any lengths without it.[33]

The mischiefs done were always so nicely timed, also, as further to shelter the aggressor. Thus, the times for revenge on Rosa and Jane, the two chamber-maids, were always chosen in those seasons when (as not unfrequently happened) they were in disgrace with their mistress, when any complaint from them would of course meet with no sympathy. In short, Topsy soon made the household understand the propriety of letting her alone; and she was let alone accordingly.

Topsy was smart and energetic in all manual operations, learning everything that was taught her with surprising quickness. With a few lessons, she had learned to do the proprieties of Miss Ophelia's chamber[34] in a way with which even that particular lady could find no fault. Mortal hands could not lay spread smoother, adjust pillows more accurately, sweep and dust and arrange more perfectly, than Topsy, when she chose,—but she didn't very often choose. If Miss Ophelia, after three or four days of careful and patient supervision, was so sanguine as to suppose that Topsy had at last fallen into her way, could

31 i.e., condemned.

32 I.e., to claim responsibility for the practical joke.

33 Note Stowe's comic use of mock-legalese. Like Charles Dickens, Stowe uses inappropriately formal language—"domestic judicatories," "establish the suppositions"—to describe a unique scene as a general occurrence.

34 I.e., bedroom.

"Topsy at Her Tricks" ("I'm nothing but a Nigger nohow"). Color lithograph by Louisa Corbaux, 1852. This Topsy is sweetly demure, prefiguring Shirley Temple's later depictions of Eva.

**35** Notice the irony here: Ophelia's beatings pale in comparison to those of Topsy's former master; Miss Feely's wouldn't kill a mosquito!

"On one occasion, Miss Ophelia found Topsy with her very best scarlet India Canton crape shawl wound round her head for a turban." Wood engraving by T. Williams, "after George Cruikshank." This Topsy is wild and primitive.   From *Uncle Tom's Cabin*, John Cassell, London, 1852

do without overlooking, and so go off and busy herself about something else, Topsy would hold a perfect carnival of confusion, for some one or two hours. Instead of making the bed, she would amuse herself with pulling off the pillow-cases, butting her woolly head among the pillows, till it would sometimes be grotesquely ornamented with feathers sticking out in various directions; she would climb the posts, and hang head downward from the tops; flourish the sheets and spreads all over the apartment; dress the bolster up in Miss Ophelia's night-clothes, and enact various scenic performances with that,—singing and whistling, and making grimaces at herself in the looking-glass; in short, as Miss Ophelia phrased it, "raising Cain" generally.

On one occasion, Miss Ophelia found Topsy with her very best scarlet India Canton crape shawl wound round her head for a turban, going on with her rehearsals before the glass in great style,—Miss Ophelia having, with carelessness most unheard-of in her, left the key for once in her drawer.

"Topsy!" she would say, when at the end of all patience, "what does make you act so?"

"Dunno, Missis,—I spects cause I's so wicked!"

"I don't know anything what I shall do with you, Topsy."

"Law, Missis, you must whip me; my old Missis allers whipped me. I an't used to workin' unless I gets whipped."

"Why, Topsy, I don't want to whip you. You can do well, if you've a mind to; what is the reason you won't?"

"Laws, Missis, I's used to whippin'; I spects it's good for me."

Miss Ophelia tried the recipe, and Topsy invariably made a terrible commotion, screaming, groaning and imploring, though half an hour afterwards, when roosted on some projection of the balcony, and surrounded by a flock of admiring "young uns," she would express the utmost contempt of the whole affair.

"Law, Miss Feely whip!—wouldn't kill a skeeter, her whippins. Oughter see how old Mas'r made the flesh fly; old Mas'r know'd how!"**35**

Topsy always made great capital of her own sins and enormities, evidently considering them as something peculiarly distinguishing.

"Law, you niggers," she would say to some of her auditors, "does you know you's all sinners? Well, you is—everybody is. White folks is sinners too,—Miss Feely says so; but I spects niggers is the biggest ones; but lor! ye an't any on ye up to me. I's so awful wicked there can't nobody do nothin' with me. I used to keep old Missis a swarin' at me half de time. I spects I's the wickedest critter in the world;" and Topsy would cut a summerset, and come up brisk and shining on to a higher perch, and evidently plume herself on the distinction.

Miss Ophelia busied herself very earnestly on Sundays, teaching Topsy the catechism. Topsy had an uncommon verbal memory, and committed with a fluency that greatly encouraged her instructress.

"What good do you expect it is going to do her?" said St. Clare.

"Why, it always has done children good. It's what children always have to learn, you know," said Miss Ophelia.

"Understand it or not," said St. Clare.

"O, children never understand it at the time; but, after they are grown up, it'll come to them."

"Mine hasn't come to me yet," said St. Clare, "though I'll bear testimony that you put it into me pretty thoroughly when I was a boy."

"Ah, you were always good at learning, Augustine. I used to have great hopes of you," said Miss Ophelia.

"Well, haven't you now?" said St. Clare.

"I wish you were as good as you were when you were a boy, Augustine."

"So do I, that's a fact, Cousin," said St. Clare. "Well, go ahead and catechize Topsy; may be you'll make out something yet."

Topsy, who had stood like a black statue during this discussion, with hands decently folded, now, at a signal from Miss Ophelia, went on:

"Our first parents, being left to the freedom of their own will, fell from the state wherein they were created."

Topsy's eyes twinkled, and she looked inquiringly.

"What is it, Topsy?" said Miss Ophelia.

"Please, Missis, was dat ar state Kintuck?"

"What state, Topsy?"

"Dat state dey fell out of. I used to hear Mas'r tell how we came down from Kintuck."[36]

St. Clare laughed.

"You'll have to give her a meaning, or she'll make one," said he. "There seems to be a theory of emigration suggested there."

"O! Augustine, be still," said Miss Ophelia; "how can I do anything, if you will be laughing?"

"Well, I won't disturb the exercises again, on my honor;" and St. Clare took his paper into the parlor, and sat down, till Topsy had finished her recitations. They were all very

**36** This is one of the funniest comic exchanges between Ophelia and Topsy. Note that Topsy's twinkling eyes and teasing function as a kind of flirtation.

This print by Vic Arnold is romantic and inviting, defying contemporary caricatures. Published in 1886 by A. S. Seer's Union Square Print, NY

37 The comic antics of Topsy are darkened for the modern reader by Ophelia and St. Clare's racist comparisons—to a plague, a parrot, a dog. Such dehumanizing was reflected in public policy for the next hundred years. "Today, to be sure, we know that the Negro is not biological or mentally inferior," Baldwin writes in "Many Thousands Gone." "Yet, in our most recent war [World War II], his blood was segregated as was, for the most part, his person" (*James Baldwin: Collected Essays*).

38 Company of supporting dancers in a ballet. Stowe makes another uneasy exit from one scene to the next.

Woodcut by William Luson Thomas. This formidable and sober Topsy is older and less frivolous than her typical depictions. Courtesy of British Museum

well, only that now and then she would oddly transpose some important words, and persist in the mistake, in spite of every effort to the contrary; and St. Clare, after all his promises of goodness, took a wicked pleasure in these mistakes, calling Topsy to him whenever he had a mind to amuse himself, and getting her to repeat the offending passages, in spite of Miss Ophelia's remonstrances.

"How do you think I can do anything with the child, if you will go on so, Augustine?" she would say.

"Well, it is too bad,—I won't again; but I do like to hear the droll little image stumble over those big words!"

"But you confirm her in the wrong way."

"What's the odds? One word is as good as another to her."

"You wanted me to bring her up right; and you ought to remember she is a reasonable creature, and be careful of your influence over her."

"O, dismal! so I ought; but, as Topsy herself says, 'I's so wicked!'"

In very much this way Topsy's training proceeded, for a year or two,—Miss Ophelia worrying herself, from day to day, with her, as a kind of chronic plague, to whose inflictions she became, in time, as accustomed, as persons sometimes do to the neuralgia or sick head-ache.

St. Clare took the same kind of amusement in the child that a man might in the tricks of a parrot or a pointer.[37] Topsy, whenever her sins brought her into disgrace in other quarters, always took refuge behind his chair; and St. Clare, in one way or other, would make peace for her. From him she got many a stray picayune, which she laid out in nuts and candies, and distributed, with careless generosity, to all the children in the family; for Topsy, to do her justice, was good-natured and liberal, and only spiteful in self-defence. She is fairly introduced into our *corps de ballet*,[38] and will figure, from time to time, in her turn, with other performers.

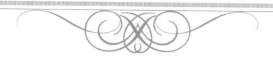

# CHAPTER 21

## *Kentuck*[1]

Our readers may not be unwilling to glance back, for a brief interval, at Uncle Tom's Cabin, on the Kentucky farm, and see what has been transpiring among those whom he had left behind.

It was late in the summer afternoon, and the doors and windows of the large parlor all stood open, to invite any stray breeze, that might feel in a good humor, to enter. Mr. Shelby sat in a large hall opening into the room, and running through the whole length of the house, to a balcony on either end. Leisurely tipped back in one chair, with his heels in another, he was enjoying his after-dinner cigar.[2] Mrs. Shelby sat in the door, busy about some fine sewing; she seemed like one who had something on her mind, which she was seeking an opportunity to introduce.

"Do you know," she said, "that Chloe has had a letter from Tom?"

"Ah! has she? Tom's got some friend there, it seems. How is the old boy?"

"He has been bought by a very fine family, I should think," said Mrs. Shelby,—"is kindly treated, and has not much to do."

"Ah! well, I'm glad of it,—very glad," said Mr. Shelby, heartily. "Tom, I suppose, will get reconciled to a Southern residence;—hardly want to come up here again."

"On the contrary, he inquires very anxiously," said Mrs. Shelby, "when the money for his redemption is to be raised."

1 In Topsy's formulation, "Kentuck" is either Eden or metaphorically the state of grace. We feel a bit disoriented in this sudden lurching back to Chloe and Uncle Tom's cabin. Have we forgotten his old home? Should we be nostalgic about the place from which he was sold? The scene opens in the Big House, not in the cabin, where Mr. Shelby sits at leisure; we recall that it was the sale of Tom that has allowed him to be more at ease, or at least on somewhat less precarious financial footing. We find that our nostalgia has suddenly vanished.

2 Once again, Mr. Shelby is putting something in his mouth.

3 I.e., disorderly haste. Mr. Shelby would like the leisure to smoke his cigar and not be bothered by his outstanding debts. Apparently the sale of Tom has not helped as much as Tom would have liked: The cash raised by selling Tom to Haley was supposed to have put Mr. Shelby on better financial footing.

4 Mr. Shelby is quick to dismiss the idea that a household economy might be a model for business economy, even though he does not seem to have a keen grasp of his own affairs.

5 Mrs. Shelby, for all her good intentions, has been creating an illusion for herself and the Shelby slaves that denies the realities of slavery. Even so, she is presented much more sympathetically here than Mr. Shelby. A few lines later, we are asked to imagine Tom taking another wife! Especially when we readers know he is quite happy with his Little Eva.

"I'm sure *I* don't know," said Mr. Shelby. "Once get business running wrong, there does seem to be no end to it. It's like jumping from one bog to another, all through a swamp; borrow of one to pay another, and then borrow of another to pay one,—and these confounded notes falling due before a man has time to smoke a cigar and turn round,—dunning letters and dunning messages,—all scamper and hurry-scurry."**3**

"It does seem to me, my dear, that something might be done to straighten matters. Suppose we sell off all the horses, and sell one of your farms, and pay up square?"

"O, ridiculous, Emily! You are the finest woman in Kentucky; but still you haven't sense to know that you don't understand business;—women never do, and never can."

"But, at least," said Mrs. Shelby, "could not you give me some little insight into yours; a list of all your debts, at least, and of all that is owed to you, and let me try and see if I can't help you to economize."

"O, bother! don't plague me, Emily!—I can't tell exactly. I know somewhere about what things are likely to be; but there's no trimming and squaring my affairs, as Chloe trims crust off her pies. You don't know anything about business, I tell you."**4**

And Mr. Shelby, not knowing any other way of enforcing his ideas, raised his voice,—a mode of arguing very convenient and convincing, when a gentleman is discussing matters of business with his wife.

Mrs. Shelby ceased talking, with something of a sigh. The fact was, that though her husband had stated she was a woman, she had a clear, energetic, practical mind, and a force of character every way superior to that of her husband; so that it would not have been so very absurd a supposition, to have allowed her capable of managing, as Mr. Shelby supposed. Her heart was set on performing her promise to Tom and Aunt Chloe, and she sighed as discouragements thickened around her.**5**

"Don't you think we might in some way contrive to raise that money? Poor Aunt Chloe! her heart is so set on it!"

"I'm sorry, if it is. I think I was premature in promising. I'm not sure, now, but it's the best way to tell Chloe, and let her make up her mind to it. Tom'll have another wife, in a year or two; and she had better take up with somebody else."

"Mr. Shelby, I have taught my people that their marriages are as sacred as ours. I never could think of giving Chloe such advice."

"It's a pity, wife, that you have burdened them with a

morality above their condition and prospects. I always thought so."

"It's only the morality of the Bible, Mr. Shelby."

"Well, well, Emily, I don't pretend to interfere with your religious notions; only they seem extremely unfitted for people in that condition."

"They are, indeed," said Mrs. Shelby, "and that is why, from my soul, I hate the whole thing. I tell you, my dear, *I* cannot absolve myself from the promises I make to these helpless creatures. If I can get the money no other way, I will take music-scholars;—I could get enough, I know, and earn the money myself."

"You wouldn't degrade yourself that way, Emily? I never could consent to it."

"Degrade! would it degrade me as much as to break my faith with the helpless? No, indeed!"

"Well, you are always heroic and transcendental," said Mr. Shelby, "but I think you had better think before you undertake such a piece of Quixotism."**6**

Here the conversation was interrupted by the appearance of Aunt Chloe, at the end of the verandah.

"If you please, Missis," said she.

"Well, Chloe, what is it?" said her mistress, rising, and going to the end of the balcony.

"If Missis would come and look at dis yer lot o' poetry."

Chloe had a particular fancy for calling poultry poetry,**7**—an application of language in which she always persisted, notwithstanding frequent corrections and advisings from the young members of the family.

"La sakes!" she would say, "I can't see; one jis good as turry,**8**—poetry suthin good, any how;" and so poetry Chloe continued to call it.

Mrs. Shelby smiled as she saw a prostrate lot of chickens and ducks, over which Chloe stood, with a very grave face of consideration.

"I'm a thinkin whether Missis would be a havin a chicken pie o' dese yer."

"Really, Aunt Chloe, I don't much care;—serve them any way you like."

Chloe stood handling them over abstractedly; it was quite evident that the chickens were not what she was thinking of. At last, with the short laugh with which her tribe**9** often introduce a doubtful proposal, she said,

"Laws me, Missis! what should Mas'r and Missis be a troublin theirselves 'bout de money, and not a usin what's right in der hands?" and Chloe laughed again.

"I don't understand you, Chloe," said Mrs. Shelby, noth-

6 I.e., naïve idealism. From the eponymous would-be knight in *Don Quixote* (1605, 1615) by Miguel Cervantes. Mr. Shelby's dismissal of Quixotism recollects St. Clare's suggestion that one can't be a knight-errant. That is, chivalry is admirable in fiction but not in real life—not, at least, until the Civil War.

7 An interesting episode of personalized language, especially following so closely on the reference to *Don Quixote*. One of the guiding principles of writing for Cervantes was to re-create various languages and dialects, which in his estimation were formative of world views. Stowe possesses similar gifts.

8 I.e., the other.

9 Which tribe? Black cooks, slaves? "Tribe" is used figuratively here.

**10** Malapropism for confectioners (bakers). I've always wondered why Stowe chooses to poke fun at Chloe at this moment, when Chloe's scheme of working for four to five years, earning two hundred dollars per year, is already heartbreakingly ridiculous.

ing doubting, from her knowledge of Chloe's manner, that she had heard every word of the conversation that had passed between her and her husband.

"Why, laws me, Missis!" said Chloe, laughing again, "other folks hires out der niggers and makes money on 'em! Don't keep sich a tribe eatin 'em out of house and home."

"Well, Chloe, who do you propose that we should hire out?"

"Laws! I an't a proposin nothin; only Sam he said der was one of dese yer *perfectioners*,**10** dey calls 'em, in Louisville, said he wanted a good hand at cake and pastry; and said he'd give four dollars a week to one, he did."

"Well, Chloe."

"Well, laws, I's a thinkin, Missis, it's time Sally was put along to be doin' something. Sally's been under my care, now, dis some time, and she does most as well as me, considerin; and if Missis would only let me go, I would help fetch up de money. I an't afraid to put my cake, nor pies nother, 'long side no *perfectioner's*."

"Confectioner's, Chloe."

"Law sakes, Missis! 'tan't no odds;—words is so curis, can't never get 'em right!"

"But, Chloe, do you want to leave your children?"

"Laws, Missis! de boys is big enough to do day's works; dey does well enough; and Sally, she'll take de baby,—she's such a peart young un, she won't take no lookin arter."

"Louisville is a good way off."

"Law sakes! who's afeard?—it's down river, somer near my old man, perhaps?" said Chloe, speaking the last in the tone of a question, and looking at Mrs. Shelby.

"No, Chloe; it's many a hundred miles off," said Mrs. Shelby.

Chloe's countenance fell.

"Never mind; your going there shall bring you nearer, Chloe. Yes, you may go; and your wages shall every cent of them be laid aside for your husband's redemption."

As when a bright sunbeam turns a dark cloud to silver, so Chloe's dark face brightened immediately,—it really shone.

"Laws! if Missis isn't too good! I was thinking of dat ar very thing; cause I shouldn't need no clothes, nor shoes, nor nothin,—I could save every cent. How many weeks is der in a year, Missis?"

"Fifty-two," said Mrs. Shelby.

"Laws! now, dere is? and four dollars for each on 'em. Why, how much'd dat ar be?"

"Two hundred and eight dollars," said Mrs. Shelby.

"Why-e!" said Chloe, with an accent of surprise and delight; "and how long would it take me to work it out, Missis?"

"Some four or five years, Chloe; but, then, you needn't do it all,—I shall add something to it."

"I wouldn't hear to Missis' givin lessons nor nothin. Mas'r's quite right in dat ar;—'t wouldn't do, no ways. I hope none our family ever be brought to dat ar, while I's got hands."

"Don't fear, Chloe; I'll take care of the honor of the family," said Mrs. Shelby, smiling. "But when do you expect to go?"

"Well, I want spectin nothin; only Sam, he's a gwine to de river with some colts, and he said I could go long with him; so I jes put my things together. If Missis was willin, I'd go with Sam to-morrow morning, if Missis would write my pass, and write me a commendation."[11]

"Well, Chloe, I'll attend to it, if Mr. Shelby has no objections. I must speak to him."

Mrs. Shelby went up stairs, and Aunt Chloe, delighted, went out to her cabin, to make her preparation.

"Law sakes, Mas'r George! ye didn't know I's a gwine to Louisville tomorrow!" she said to George, as, entering her cabin, he found her busy in sorting over her baby's clothes. "I thought I'd jis look over sis's things, and get 'em straightened up. But I'm gwine, Mas'r George,—gwine to have four dollars a week; and Missis is gwine to lay it all up, to buy back my old man agin!"

"Whew!" said George, "here's a stroke of business, to be sure! How are you going?"

"To-morrow, wid Sam. And now, Mas'r George, I knows you'll jis sit down and write to my old man, and tell him all about it,—won't ye?"

"To be sure," said George; "Uncle Tom'll be right glad to hear from us. I'll go right in the house, for paper and ink; and then, you know, Aunt Chloe, I can tell about the new colts and all."

"Sartin, sartin,[12] Mas'r George; you go 'long, and I'll get ye up a bit o'chicken, or some sich; ye won't have many more suppers wid yer poor old aunty."

11 I.e., a signed permission to travel from her owner's house and a letter of reference. Any individual of African descent, free or slave, traveling without legal papers, particularly after the Fugitive Slave Act of 1850, was liable to be stopped and imprisoned.

12 I.e., certainly, certainly. Poor Chloe's last labor is making chicken for Mas'r George.

# CHAPTER 22

## *"The Grass Withereth—*
## *the Flower Fadeth"*[1]

1 "The grass withereth, the flower fadeth; but the word of our God shall stand for ever" (Isa. 40:8). In a paragraph of purple prose we learn that two years have passed, and "though parted from all his soul held dear," Tom was not "positively and consciously miserable." I have never quite understood whether to take Stowe at her word here. "Sartin" some of the many illustrations of Tom with Eva show a man who is not entirely content, but many others show a jolly Tom, a dapper Tom, at worst a pensive Tom. Perhaps it is just too difficult to portray a man as depressed when there is a lovely blonde perched on his knee.

2 The line is either from "Juno and the Peacock," in *Aesop's Fables* ("Be content with your lot; one cannot be first in everything") or from Phil. 4:11 ("for I have learned, in whatsoever state I am, therewith to be content"). Neither passage promotes revolutionary action.

Life passes, with us all, a day at a time; so it passed with our friend Tom, till two years were gone. Though parted from all his soul held dear, and though often yearning for what lay beyond, still was he never positively and consciously miserable; for, so well is the harp of human feeling strung, that nothing but a crash that breaks every string can wholly mar its harmony; and, on looking back to seasons which in review appear to us as those of deprivation and trial, we can remember that each hour, as it glided, brought its diversions and alleviations, so that, though not happy wholly, we were not, either, wholly miserable.

Tom read, in his only literary cabinet, of one who had "learned in whatsoever state he was, therewith to be content."[2] It seemed to him good and reasonable doctrine, and accorded well with the settled and thoughtful habit which he had acquired from the reading of that same book.

His letter homeward, as we related in the last chapter, was in due time answered by Master George, in a good, round, school-boy hand, that Tom said might be read "most acrost the room." It contained various refreshing items of home intelligence, with which our reader is fully acquainted: stated how Aunt Chloe had been hired out to a confectioner in Louisville, where her skill in the pastry line was gaining wonderful sums of money, all of which, Tom was informed, was to be laid up to go to make up the sum of his redemption money; Mose and Pete were thriv-

270

ing, and the baby was trotting all about the house, under the care of Sally and the family generally.

Tom's cabin was shut up for the present; but George expatiated brilliantly on ornaments and additions to be made to it when Tom came back.[3]

The rest of this letter gave a list of George's school studies, each one headed by a flourishing capital; and also told the names of four new colts that appeared on the premises since Tom left; and stated, in the same connection, that father and mother were well. The style of the letter was decidedly concise and terse; but Tom thought it the most wonderful specimen of composition that had appeared in modern times. He was never tired of looking at it, and even held a council with Eva on the expediency of getting it framed, to hang up in his room. Nothing but the difficulty of arranging it so that both sides of the page would show at once stood in the way of this undertaking.

The friendship between Tom and Eva had grown with the child's growth. It would be hard to say what place she held in the soft, impressible[4] heart of her faithful attendant. He loved her as something frail and earthly, yet almost worshipped her as something heavenly and divine. He gazed on her as the Italian sailor gazes on his image of the child Jesus,—with a mixture of reverence and tenderness; and to humor her graceful fancies, and meet those thousand simple wants which invest childhood like a many-colored rainbow, was Tom's chief delight. In the market, at morning, his eyes were always on the flower-stalls for rare bouquets for her, and the choicest peach or orange was slipped into his pocket to give to her when he came back; and the sight that pleased him most was her sunny head looking out the gate for his distant approach, and her childish question,—"Well, Uncle Tom, what have you got for me to-day?"

Nor was Eva less zealous in kind offices, in return. Though a child, she was a beautiful reader;—a fine musical ear, a quick poetic fancy, and an instinctive sympathy with what is grand and noble, made her such a reader of the Bible as Tom had never before heard. At first, she read to please her humble friend; but soon her own earnest

3 Where are Chloe's children being housed while the cabin is shut up? Where will the money for renovations come from?

4 I.e., impressionable. Stowe uses nineteenth-century formulation that imagines ideas and habits as stamped onto nerves and organs.

Hammatt Billings's version of Little Eva and Uncle Tom holding hands in the arbor. Tom is dressed as a Southern gentleman and appears almost like a father figure, leaning toward Eva. Again, Eva looks uncannily like later images of Alice (in Wonderland). From *Uncle Tom's Cabin,* John P. Jewett & Co., 1852

Another version of Tom and Eva in the arbor. Wood engraving by W. Measom, "after George Cruikshank." Tom is dressed and well shod, but in this image there is a greater physical distance between Tom and Eva than on the previous page. From *Uncle Tom's Cabin*, John Cassell, London, 1852

5 Lake Pontchartrain is a large lake north of New Orleans, then and now used as a summer resort for the wealthy seeking escape from the urban heat. The St. Clare "villa," Stowe tells us, is an East Indian cottage, as exotic and luxurious as the house in New Orleans. This is a far cry from Tom's cabin in Kentucky and from the Quaker settlement in Ohio.

nature threw out its tendrils, and wound itself around the majestic book; and Eva loved it, because it woke in her strange yearnings, and strong, dim emotions, such as impassioned, imaginative children love to feel.

The parts that pleased her most were the Revelations and the Prophecies,—parts whose dim and wondrous imagery, and fervent language, impressed her the more, that she questioned vainly of their meaning;—and she and her simple friend, the old child and the young one, felt just alike about it. All that they knew was, that they spoke of a glory to be revealed,—a wondrous something yet to come, wherein their soul rejoiced, yet knew not why; and though it be not so in the physical, yet in moral science that which cannot be understood is not always profitless. For the soul awakes, a trembling stranger, between two dim eternities,—the eternal past, the eternal future. The light shines only on a small space around her; therefore, she needs must yearn towards the unknown; and the voices and shadowy movings which come to her from out the cloudy pillar of inspiration have each one echoes and answers in her own expecting nature. Its mystic imagery are so many talismans and gems inscribed with unknown hieroglyphics; she folds them in her bosom, and expects to read them when she passes beyond the veil.

At this time in our story, the whole St. Clare establishment is, for the time being, removed to their villa on Lake Pontchartrain.[5] The heats of summer had driven all who were able to leave the sultry and unhealthy city, to seek the shores of the lake, and its cool sea-breezes.

St. Clare's villa was an East

This advertisement for the Boston Theatre Company's rendition of *Uncle Tom's Cabin* uses Hammatt Billings's version of Little Eva and Uncle Tom holding hands in the arbor. Notice the main attraction of this extended run is Lotta's performance of Topsey [*sic*]. Such posters today are extremely rare and fetch extremely high prices from collectors.

Indian cottage, surrounded by light verandahs of bamboo-work, and opening on all sides into gardens and pleasure-grounds. The common sitting-room opened on to a large garden, fragrant with every picturesque plant and flower of the tropics, where winding paths ran down to the very shores of the lake, whose silvery sheet of water lay there, rising and falling in the sunbeams,—a picture never for an hour the same, yet every hour more beautiful.

It is now one of those intensely golden sunsets which kindles the whole horizon into one blaze of glory, and makes the water another sky. The lake lay in rosy or golden streaks, save where white-winged vessels glided hither and thither,[6] like so many spirits, and little golden stars twinkled through the glow, and looked down at themselves as they trembled in the water.

Tom and Eva were seated on a little mossy seat, in an arbor, at the foot of the garden. It was Sunday evening, and Eva's Bible lay open on her knee. She read,—"And I saw a sea of glass, mingled with fire."

"Tom," said Eva, suddenly stopping, and pointing to the lake, "there 'tis."

"What, Miss Eva?"

"Don't you see,—there?" said the child, pointing to the glassy water, which, as it rose and fell, reflected the golden glow of the sky. "There's a 'sea of glass, mingled with fire.' "[7]

"True enough, Miss Eva," said Tom; and Tom sang—

> *"O, had I the wings of the morning,*
> *I'd fly away to Canaan's shore;*
> *Bright angels should convey me home,*
> *To the new Jerusalem."*

"Where do you suppose new Jerusalem is, Uncle Tom?" said Eva.

"O, up in the clouds, Miss Eva."

"Then I think I see it," said Eva. "Look in those clouds!—they look like great gates of pearl; and you can see beyond them—far, far off—it's all gold. Tom, sing about 'spirits bright.' "

UNCLE TOM AND LITTLE EVA.

"Uncle Tom and Little Eva." Lithograph by E. C. Kellog & Co. Unlike the W. Measom image on page 272, in this romantic image, Tom is dressed in the garb of a field hand rather than a house servant. From *Uncle Tom's Cabin*, Horace Thayer & Co., 1852–56

6 I.e., here and there.

7 Tom and Eva share verses and hymns based on Revelation.

Tom sung the words of a well-known Methodist hymn,

> *"I see a band of spirits bright,*
> *That taste the glories there;*
> *They all are robed in spotless white,*
> *And conquering palms they bear."*

"Uncle Tom, I've seen *them*," said Eva.

Tom had no doubt of it at all; it did not surprise him in the least. If Eva had told him she had been to heaven, he would have thought it entirely probable.

"They come to me sometimes in my sleep, those spirits;" and Eva's eyes grew dreamy, and she hummed, in a low voice,

> *They all are robed in spotless white,*
> *And conquering palms they bear."*

"Uncle Tom," said Eva, "I'm going there."

"Where, Miss Eva?"

The child rose, and pointed her little hand to the sky; the glow of evening lit her golden hair and flushed cheek with a kind of unearthly radiance, and her eyes were bent earnestly on the skies.

"I'm going *there*," she said, "to the spirits bright, Tom; *I'm going, before long.*"

The faithful old heart felt a sudden thrust; and Tom thought how often he had noticed, within six months, that Eva's little hands had grown thinner, and her skin more transparent, and her breath shorter; and how, when she ran or played in the garden, as she once could for hours, she became soon so tired and languid. He had heard Miss Ophelia speak often of a cough, that all her medicaments could not cure; and even now that fervent cheek and little hand were burning with hectic fever; and yet the thought that Eva's

Miguel Covarrubias imagines a stoic, strong, and silent Tom both protecting and listening to Eva. Tom's nobility loses nothing from being read to by the narrow-waisted Eva.
From *Uncle Tom's Cabin: or, Life Among the Lowly,* Heritage Press edition, 1938

By 1943, Tom's inherent nobility is manifested in his outward bearing, grace, and charm—a function of the nascent Civil Rights movement.   From Classics Illustrated Classic Comic Book no. 15, *Uncle Tom's Cabin,* 1943

This cover image of Eva and Tom has the pair sitting on what appears to be the front stoop of a cabin. Eva is dressed like a little girl in postwar England; Tom—strong, handsome, and masculine—is colorfully yet tastefully dressed. From *Uncle Tom's Cabin*, Ward, Lock & Co., n.d.

words suggested had never come to him till now.

Has there ever been a child like Eva?[8] Yes, there have been; but their names are always on grave-stones, and their sweet smiles, their heavenly eyes, their singular words and ways, are among the buried treasures of yearning hearts.[9] In how many families do you hear the legend that all the goodness and graces of the living are nothing to the peculiar charms of one who *is not*. It is as if heaven had an especial band of angels, whose office it was to sojourn for a season here, and endear to them the wayward human heart, that they might bear it upward with them in their homeward flight. When you see that deep, spiritual light in the eye,—when the little soul reveals itself in words sweeter and wiser than the ordinary words of children,—hope not to retain that child; for the seal of heaven is on it, and the light of immortality looks out from its eyes.

Even so, beloved Eva! fair star of thy dwelling! Thou art passing away; but they that love thee dearest know it not.

The colloquy between Tom and Eva was interrupted by a hasty call from Miss Ophelia.

"Eva—Eva!—why, child, the dew is falling; you mustn't be out there!"

Eva and Tom hastened in.

Miss Ophelia was old, and skilled in the tactics of nursing. She was from New England, and knew well the first guileful footsteps of that soft, insidious disease, which sweeps away so many of the fairest and loveliest, and

[8] Yes, there have been children like Eva: Charles Dickens's Little Nell, from his 1841 novel *The Old Curiosity Shop*, for example. Everybody who had read Dickens's novel saw the resemblance, including Dickens himself, who wrote to a friend that although he liked *Uncle Tom's Cabin*, he thought Stowe was "a leetle unscrupulous in the appropriatin' way" (Harry Stone, "Charles Dickens and Harriet Beecher Stowe").

[9] Given the high infant and child mortality rates, this passage would have touched the heart of every mother in Stowe's audience.

The cover image of this edition shows Tom as an old man, white-haired and stooped, though with an interesting gleam in his eye. Could this man have rescued Eva from "her watery grave" several chapters earlier? Eva is striking a coy pose, and her legs are wrapped around one of Tom's. This is in stark contrast to Topsy's bowlegged prancing. From *Uncle Tom's Cabin, or, Life Among the Lowly*, Grosset and Dunlap, n.d.

The cover image of this *Young Folks Edition* features a solid, well-dressed, bespectacled Tom with Eva perched on his knee. Eva's outfit is oddly suggestive of the Moulin Rouge.
From *Uncle Tom's Cabin, Young Folks Edition*, M. A. Donohue & Co., circa 1900

10 These symptoms suggest that Eva most likely has tuberculosis. Ophelia's skills at nursing stand in contrast to Marie's uselessness in all things domestic.

11 I.e., be speaking dismally.

12 A drug made according to a recipe.

before one fibre of life seems broken, seals them irrevocably for death.

She had noted the slight, dry cough, the daily brightening cheek; nor could the lustre of the eye, and the airy buoyancy born of fever, deceive her.[10]

She tried to communicate her fears to St. Clare; but he threw back her suggestions with a restless petulance, unlike his usual careless good humor.

"Don't be croaking,[11] Cousin,—I hate it!" he would say; "don't you see that the child is only growing. Children always lose strength when they grow fast."

"But she has that cough!"

"O! nonsense of that cough!—it is not anything. She has taken a little cold, perhaps."

"Well, that was just the way Eliza Jane was taken, and Ellen and Maria Sanders."

"O! stop these hobgoblin' nurse legends. You old hands got so wise, that a child cannot cough, or sneeze, but you see desperation and ruin at hand. Only take care of the child, keep her from the night air, and don't let her play too hard, and she'll do well enough."

So St. Clare said; but he grew nervous and restless. He watched Eva feverishly day by day, as might be told by the frequency with which he repeated over that "the child was quite well"—that there wasn't anything in that cough, —it was only some little stomach affection, such as children often had. But he kept by her more than before, took her oftener to ride with him, brought home every few days some receipt[12] or strengthening mixture, —"not," he said, "that the child *needed* it, but then it would not do her any harm."

If it must be told, the thing that struck a deeper pang to his heart than anything else was the daily

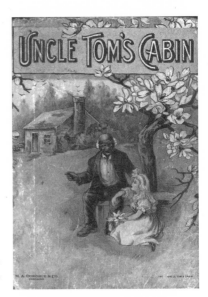

In this cover, also by M. A. Donohue & Co., Tom is depicted as a black Benjamin Franklin. Eva is kneeling at Tom's knee, holding a magnolia blossom.
From *Uncle Tom's Cabin*, M. A. Donohue & Co., circa 1900

increasing maturity of the child's mind and feelings. While still retaining all a child's fanciful graces, yet she often dropped, unconsciously, words of such a reach of thought, and strange unworldly wisdom, that they seemed to be an inspiration. At such times, St. Clare would feel a sudden thrill, and clasp her in his arms, as if that fond clasp could save her; and his heart rose up with wild determination to keep her, never to let her go.

The child's whole heart and soul seemed absorbed in works of love and kindness. Impulsively generous she had always been; but there was a touching and womanly thoughtfulness about her now, that every one noticed. She still loved to play with Topsy, and the various colored children; but she now seemed rather a spectator than an actor of their plays, and she would sit for half an hour at a time, laughing at the odd tricks of Topsy,—and then a shadow would seem to pass across her face, her eyes grew misty, and her thoughts were afar.

"Mamma," she said, suddenly, to her mother, one day, "why don't we teach our servants to read?"

"What a question, child! People never do."

"Why don't they?" said Eva.

"Because it is no use for them to read. It don't help them to work any better, and they are not made for anything else."

"But they ought to read the Bible, mamma, to learn God's will."

"O! they can get that read to them all *they* need."

"It seems to me, mamma, the Bible is for every one to read themselves. They need it a great many times when there is nobody to read it."

"Eva, you are an odd child," said her mother.

"Miss Ophelia has taught Topsy to read," continued Eva.

"Yes, and you see how much good it does. Topsy is the worst creature I ever saw!"

"Here's poor Mammy!" said Eva. "She does love the Bible so much, and wishes so she could read! And what will she do when I can't read to her?"[13]

Marie was busy, turning over the contents of a drawer, as she answered,

"Well, of course, by and by, Eva, you will have other things to think of, besides reading the Bible round to servants. Not but that is very proper; I've done it myself, when I had health. But when you come to be dressing and going into company, you won't have time. See here!" she added, "these jewels I'm going to give you when you come out. I wore them to my first ball. I can tell you, Eva, I made a sensation."

13 Eva voices the most effective argument made for slave literacy: that slaveowners not be held accountable (by God) for the loss of their slaves' souls.

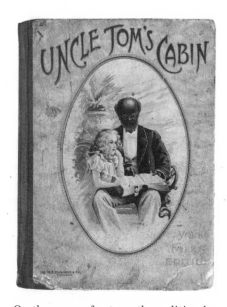

On the cover of yet another edition by M. A. Donohue & Co., Tom is a grandfatherly tutor. From *Uncle Tom's Cabin, Young Folks Edition*, M. A. Donohue & Co., circa 1900

14 Again, Eva's lessons to Tom and Mammy could potentially land her in jail; Louisiana's laws prohibiting teaching slaves to read were among the strictest in the nation (see chapter 3, note 4).

In this edition, a dandified Tom wears lederhosen and is bedecked by a lei of flowers. From *Onkel Toms Hütte, oder Negerleben in den Sklavenstaaten von Nordamerika*, Konstanz Christlicher Buch- und Kunstverlag, Carl Hirsch A.G., circa 1924

Eva took the jewel-case, and lifted from it a diamond necklace. Her large, thoughtful eyes rested on them, but it was plain her thoughts were elsewhere.

"How sober you look, child!" said Marie.

"Are these worth a great deal of money, mamma?"

"To be sure, they are. Father sent to France for them. They are worth a small fortune."

"I wish I had them," said Eva, "to do what I pleased with!"

"What would you do with them?"

"I'd sell them, and buy a place in the free states, and take all our people there, and hire teachers, to teach them to read and write."14

Eva was cut short by her mother's laughing.

"Set up a boarding-school! Wouldn't you teach them to play on the piano, and paint on velvet?"

"I'd teach them to read their own Bible, and write their own letters, and read letters that are written to them," said Eva, steadily. "I know, mamma, it does come very hard on them, that they can't do these things. Tom feels it,—Mammy does,—a great many of them do. I think it's wrong."

"Come, come, Eva; you are only a child! You don't know anything about these things," said Marie; "besides, your talking makes my head ache."

Marie always had a head-ache on hand for any conversation that did not exactly suit her.

Eva stole away; but after that, she assiduously gave Mammy reading lessons.

This Uncle Tom looks like a merchant or European banker going over books with his sweet daughter. From *Uncle Tom's Cabin*, James Nisbet & Co., Ltd., London

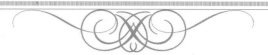

# CHAPTER 23

## *Henrique*[1]

About this time, St. Clare's brother Alfred, with his eldest son, a boy of twelve, spent a day or two with the family at the lake.

No sight could be more singular and beautiful than that of these twin brothers. Nature, instead of instituting resemblances between them, had made them opposites on every point; yet a mysterious tie seemed to unite them in a closer friendship than ordinary.

They used to saunter, arm in arm, up and down the alleys and walks of the garden. Augustine, with his blue eyes and golden hair, his ethereally flexible form and vivacious features; and Alfred, dark-eyed, with haughty Roman profile, firmly-knit limbs, and decided bearing. They were always abusing each other's opinions and practices,[2] and yet never a whit the less absorbed in each other's society; in fact, the very contrariety seemed to unite them, like the attraction between opposite poles of the magnet.

Henrique, the eldest son of Alfred, was a noble, dark-eyed, princely boy, full of vivacity and spirit; and, from the first moment of introduction, seemed to be perfectly fascinated by the spirituelle[3] graces of his cousin Evangeline.

Eva had a little pet pony, of a snowy whiteness. It was easy as a cradle, and as gentle as its little mistress; and this pony was now brought up to the back verandah by Tom, while a little mulatto boy of about thirteen led along

1 The French name signals Stowe's use of French terms throughout this chapter on the visit of Eva's aristocratic uncle and cousin. Is Stowe being ironic or serious when she writes "No sight could be more singular and beautiful than that of these twin brothers"? None of the novel's many illustrators agree: They have found the pairing of Tom and Eva or Topsy and Eva to be far more singular.

2 I.e., disagreeing with.

3 Not spiritual but refined and lively.

4 The interest in foreheads and brows (or more pseudo-accurately, the "science" of phrenology) throughout *Uncle Tom's Cabin* reflects the nineteenth-century belief that the size of the cranium denotes the size of the brain. Not surprisingly, Dodo has not only "a high, bold forehead" but also white blood.

a small black Arabian, which had just been imported, at a great expense, for Henrique.

Henrique had a boy's pride in his new possession; and, as he advanced and took the reins out of the hands of his little groom, he looked carefully over him, and his brow darkened.

"What's this, Dodo, you little lazy dog! you haven't rubbed my horse down, this morning."

"Yes, Mas'r," said Dodo, submissively; "he got that dust on his own self."

"You rascal, shut your mouth!" said Henrique, violently raising his riding-whip. "How dare you speak?"

The boy was a handsome, bright-eyed mulatto, of just Henrique's size, and his curling hair hung round a high, bold forehead.4 He had white blood in his veins, as could be seen by the quick flush in his cheek, and the sparkle of his eye, as he eagerly tried to speak.

"Mas'r Henrique!—" he began.

Henrique struck him across the face with his riding-whip, and, seizing one of his arms, forced him on to his knees, and beat him till he was out of breath.

"There, you impudent dog! Now will you learn not to answer back when I speak to you? Take the horse back, and clean him properly. I'll teach you your place!"

"Young Mas'r," said Tom, "I specs what he was gwine to say was, that the horse would roll when he was bringing him up from the stable; he's so full of spirits,—that's the way he got that dirt on him; I looked to his cleaning."

"You hold your tongue till you're asked to speak!" said Henrique, turning on his heel, and walking up the steps to speak to Eva, who stood in her riding-dress.

"Dear Cousin, I'm sorry this stupid fellow has kept you waiting," he said. "Let's sit down here, on this seat, till they come. What's the matter, Cousin?—you look sober."

"How could you be so cruel and wicked to poor Dodo?" said Eva.

"Cruel,—wicked!" said the boy, with unaffected surprise. "What do you mean, dear Eva?"

"I don't want you to call me dear Eva, when you do so," said Eva.

"Dear Cousin, you don't know Dodo; it's the only way to manage him, he's so full of lies and excuses. The only way is to put him down at once,—not let him open his mouth; that's the way papa manages."

"But Uncle Tom said it was an accident, and he never tells what isn't true."

"He's an uncommon old nigger, then!" said Henrique. "Dodo will lie as fast as he can speak."

"You frighten him into deceiving, if you treat him so."

"Why, Eva, you've really taken such a fancy to Dodo, that I shall be jealous."[5]

"But you beat him,—and he didn't deserve it."

"O, well, it may go for some time when he does, and don't get it. A few cuts never come amiss with Dodo,—he's a regular spirit, I can tell you; but I won't beat him again before you, if it troubles you."

Eva was not satisfied, but found it in vain to try to make her handsome cousin understand her feelings.

Dodo soon appeared, with the horses.

"Well, Dodo, you've done pretty well, this time," said his young master, with a more gracious air. "Come, now, and hold Miss Eva's horse, while I put her on to the saddle."

Dodo came and stood by Eva's pony. His face was troubled; his eyes looked as if he had been crying.

Henrique, who valued himself on his gentlemanly adroitness in all matters of gallantry, soon had his fair cousin in the saddle, and, gathering the reins, placed them in her hands.

But Eva bent to the other side of the horse, where Dodo was standing, and said, as he relinquished the reins,—"That's a good boy, Dodo;—thank you!"

Dodo looked up in amazement into the sweet young face; the blood rushed to his cheeks, and the tears to his eyes.

"Here, Dodo," said his master, imperiously.

Dodo sprang and held the horse, while his master mounted.

"There's a picayune[6] for you to buy candy with, Dodo," said Henrique; "go get some."

And Henrique cantered down the walk after Eva. Dodo stood looking after the two children. One had given him money; and one had given him what he wanted far more,—a kind word, kindly spoken. Dodo had been only a few months away from his mother. His master had bought him at a slave warehouse, for his handsome face, to be a match to the handsome pony; and he was now getting his breaking-in, at the hands of his young master.

The scene of the beating had been witnessed by the two brothers St. Clare, from another part of the garden.

Augustine's cheek flushed; but he only observed, with his usual sarcastic carelessness,

"I suppose that's what we may call republican education, Alfred?"

5 Eva and Henrique are acting out a game much more dangerous in adults: white jealousy over supposed black sexuality. Henrique slaps Dodo because he can. Henrique vows that he won't slap him again because he can—only free individuals can make vows. Henrique tosses Dodo a coin because he can.

6 The parting insult is that Dodo would rather buy candy than anything else.

7 I.e., the rabble (French, from the Italian *canaglia*, literally "pack of dogs").

8 Marked by its history of colonization by Spain and France, Santo Domingo exterminated its native Indian population, imported black slaves for its burgeoning plantation economy, and suffered uprisings and rebellions, as did neighboring Haiti. Santo Domingo declared its independence and became the Dominican Republic in 1844. The unrest would continue throughout the nineteenth century.

"Henrique is a devil of a fellow, when his blood's up," said Alfred, carelessly.

"I suppose you consider this an instructive practice for him," said Augustine, drily.

"I couldn't help it, if I didn't. Henrique is a regular little tempest;—his mother and I have given him up, long ago. But, then, that Dodo is a perfect sprite,—no amount of whipping can hurt him."

"And this by way of teaching Henrique the first verse of a republican's catechism, 'All men are born free and equal!' "

"Poh!" said Alfred; "one of Tom Jefferson's pieces of French sentiment and humbug. It's perfectly ridiculous to have that going the rounds among us, to this day."

"I think it is," said St. Clare, significantly.

"Because," said Alfred, "we can see plainly enough that all men are *not* born free, nor born equal; they are born anything else. For my part, I think half this republican talk sheer humbug. It is the educated, the intelligent, the wealthy, the refined, who ought to have equal rights, and not the canaille."[7]

"'If you can keep the canaille of that opinion," said Augustine. "They took *their* turn once, in France."

"Of course, they must be *kept* down, consistently, steadily, as I *should*," said Alfred, setting his foot hard down, as if he were standing on somebody.

"It makes a terrible slip when they get up," said Augustine,—"in St. Domingo,[8] for instance."

"Poh!" said Alfred, "we'll take care of that, in this country. We must set our face against all this educating, elevating talk, that is getting about now; the lower class must not be educated."

"That is past praying for," said Augustine; "educated they will be, and we have only to say how. Our system is educating them in barbarism and brutality. We are breaking all humanizing ties, and making them brute beasts; and, if they get the upper hand, such we shall find them."

"They never shall get the upper hand!" said Alfred.

"That's right," said St. Clare; "put on the steam, fasten down the escape-valve, and sit on it, and see where you'll land."

"Well," said Alfred, "we *will* see. I'm not afraid to sit on the escape-valve, as long as the boilers are strong, and the machinery works well."

"The nobles in Louis XVI.'s time thought just so; and Austria and Pius IX. think so now; and, some pleasant morning, you may all be caught up to meet each other in the air, *when the boilers burst.*"[9]

"*Dies declarabit,*"[10] said Alfred, laughing.

"I tell you," said Augustine, "if there is anything that is revealed with the strength of a divine law in our times, it is that the masses are to rise, and the under class become the upper one."[11]

"That's one of your red republican humbugs, Augustine! Why didn't you ever take to the stump;—you'd make a famous stump orator![12] Well, I hope I shall be dead before this millennium of your greasy masses comes on."

"Greasy or not greasy, they will govern *you*, when their time comes," said Augustine; "and they will be just such rulers as you make them. The French noblesse chose to have the people '*sans culottes*,' and they had '*sans culotte*' governors to their hearts' content. The people of Hayti—"

"O, come, Augustine! as if we hadn't had enough of that abominable, contemptible Hayti![13] The Haytiens were not Anglo Saxons; if they had been, there would have been another story. The Anglo Saxon is the dominant race of the world, and *is to be so.*"

"Well, there is a pretty fair infusion of Anglo Saxon blood among our slaves, now," said Augustine. "There are plenty among them who have only enough of the African to give a sort of tropical warmth and fervor to our calculating firmness and foresight. If ever the San Domingo hour comes, Anglo Saxon blood will lead on the day. Sons of white fathers, with all our haughty feelings burning in their veins, will not always be bought and sold and traded. They will rise, and raise with them their mother's race."[14]

"Stuff!—nonsense!"

"Well," said Augustine, "there goes an old saying to this effect 'As it was in the days of Noah, so shall it be;—they ate, they drank, they planted, they builded, and knew not till the flood came and took them.' "

"On the whole, Augustine, I think your talents might do for a circuit rider,"[15] said Alfred, laughing. "Never you fear for us; possession is our nine points. We've got the power. This subject race," said he, stamping firmly, "is down, and shall *stay* down! We have energy enough to manage our own powder."

"Sons trained like your Henrique will be grand guardians of your powder-magazines," said Augustine,— "so cool and self-possessed! The proverb says, 'They that cannot govern themselves cannot govern others.' "

"There is a trouble there," said Alfred, thoughtfully;

9 Augustine St. Clare cites revolutionary events, reminding Stowe's readers of world-wide volatile political conditions. The French Revolution resulted in Louis XVI and his wife, Marie Antoinette, being guillotined in 1793. In 1849 Austria had defeated Hungary's bid for independence, and the French had restored Pius IX in Rome after defeating the republic declared after the 1848 revolt. Prince Louis Napoleon Bonaparte was elected president of the French Republic in December 1848 by universal suffrage.

10 Latin, "Time will tell."

11 Apparently, political writings about the conditions of the working classes are more important to St. Clare than the Bible.

12 In suggesting that his brother could be a political speechmaker, Alfred reveals that he listens to the form and dismisses the content of Augustine's arguments. The *Manifesto of the Communist Party*, by Karl Marx and Friedrich Engels, was first published in English in 1850 in the journal *Red Republican*, translated by Helen Macfarlane. Alfred's use of the epithet "red republican" most likely refers to the red caps worn by republican radicals in France, however, not to the English Chartist publication.

13 In August 1791, spurred by the French Revolution, Haitian slaves rebelled violently against their masters. The "Emperor" Dessalines, who came to power in 1804, killed many of the white residents of the island.

14 A common racist belief: that white blood contains the impetus to freedom. In speaking of "their mother's race," Augustine evokes the law developed to solve the problem created by "the mixing of the races" in a country where inheritance came through the father. With so many slaves with white fathers, it was decided that "the condition of the child follows the condition of the mother."

15 A circuit rider was an itinerant entertainer who traveled "circuit" finding work. Augustine remembers his Bible when he's with his brother. Perhaps it's the memory of their mother; but he sounds like Ophelia. The apocalyptic reference to unpreparedness for the "flood" certainly echoes these admonitions.

16 Augustine's lament that "one man can do nothing, against the whole action of a community" is a third low point in Stowe's portrayal of Eva's father. Nevertheless, St. Clare's statement shows the importance of community and the rationale for Stowe's strategy in *Uncle Tom's Cabin* to create a community that embraces former slaves, to wit: Liberia.

"there's no doubt that our system is a difficult one to train children under. It gives too free scope to the passions, altogether, which, in our climate, are hot enough. I find trouble with Henrique. The boy is generous and warm-hearted, but a perfect fire-cracker when excited. I believe I shall send him North for his education, where obedience is more fashionable, and where he will associate more with equals, and less with dependants."

"Since training children is the staple work of the human race," said Augustine, "I should think it something of a consideration that our system does not work well there."

"It does not for some things," said Alfred; "for others, again, it does. It makes boys manly and courageous; and the very vices of an abject race tend to strengthen in them the opposite virtues. I think Henrique, now, has a keener sense of the beauty of truth, from seeing lying and deception the universal badge of slavery."

"A Christian-like view of the subject, certainly!" said Augustine.

"It's true, Christian-like or not; and is about as Christian-like as most other things in the world," said Alfred.

"That may be," said St. Clare.

"Well, there's no use in talking, Augustine. I believe we've been round and round this old track five hundred times, more or less. What do you say to a game of backgammon?"

The two brothers ran up the verandah steps, and were soon seated at a light bamboo stand, with the backgammon-board between them. As they were setting their men, Alfred said,

"I tell you, Augustine, if I thought as you do, I should do something."

"I dare say you would,—you are one of the doing sort,—but what?"

"Why, elevate your own servants, for a specimen," said Alfred, with a half-scornful smile.

"You might as well set Mount Ætna on them flat, and tell them to stand up under it, as tell me to elevate my servants under all the super-incumbent mass of society upon them. One man can do nothing, against the whole action of a community.[16] Education, to do anything, must be a state education; or there must be enough agreed in it to make a current. "

"You take the first throw," said Alfred; and the brothers were soon lost in the game, and heard no more till the scraping of horses' feet was heard under the verandah.

"There come the children," said Augustine, rising. "Look here, Alf! Did you ever see anything so beautiful?" And, in truth, it *was* a beautiful sight. Henrique, with his bold brow, and dark, glossy curls, and glowing cheek, was laughing gayly, as he bent towards his fair cousin, as they came on. She was dressed in a blue riding-dress, with a cap of the same color. Exercise had given a brilliant hue to her cheeks, and heightened the effect of her singularly transparent skin, and golden hair.

"Good heavens! what perfectly dazzling beauty!" said Alfred. "I tell you, Auguste, won't she make some hearts ache, one of these days?"

"She will, too truly,—God knows I'm afraid so!" said St. Clare, in a tone of sudden bitterness, as he hurried down to take her off her horse.

"Eva, darling! you're not much tired?" he said, as he clasped her in his arms.

"No, papa," said the child; but her short, hard breathing alarmed her father.

"How could you ride so fast, dear?—you know it's bad for you."

"I felt so well, papa, and liked it so much, I forgot."

St. Clare carried her in his arms into the parlor, and laid her on the sofa.

"Henrique, you must be careful of Eva," said he; "you mustn't ride fast with her."

"I'll take her under my care," said Henrique, seating himself by the sofa, and taking Eva's hand.

Eva soon found herself much better. Her father and uncle resumed their game, and the children were left together.

"Do you know, Eva, I'm so sorry papa is only going to stay two days here, and then I shan't see you again for ever so long! If I stay with you, I'd try to be good, and not be cross to Dodo, and so on. I don't mean to treat Dodo ill; but, you know, I've got such a quick temper. I'm not really bad to him, though. I give him a picayune, now and then; and you see he dresses well. I think, on the whole, Dodo's pretty well off."

"Would you think you were well off, if there were not one creature in the world near you to love you?"

"I?—Well, of course not."

"And you have taken Dodo away from all the friends he ever had, and now he has not a creature to love him;—nobody can be good that way."

"Well, I can't help it, as I know of. I can't get his mother, and I can't love him myself, nor anybody else, as I know of."

"Why can't you?" said Eva.

"*Love* Dodo! Why, Eva, you wouldn't have me! I may *like* him well enough; but you don't *love* your servants."

"I do, indeed."

"How odd!"

"Don't the Bible say we must love everybody?"

"O, the Bible! To be sure, it says a great many such things; but, then, nobody ever thinks of doing them,—you know, Eva, nobody does."

Eva did not speak; her eyes were fixed and thoughtful, for a few moments.

"At any rate," she said, "dear Cousin, do love poor Dodo, and be kind to him, for my sake!"

"I could love anything, for your sake, dear Cousin; for I really think you are the loveliest creature that I ever saw!" And Henrique spoke with an earnestness that flushed his handsome face. Eva received it with perfect simplicity, without even a change of feature; merely saying, "I'm glad you feel so, dear Henrique! I hope you will remember."

The dinner-bell put an end to the interview.

# CHAPTER 24

## *Foreshadowings*

Two days after this, Alfred St. Clare and Augustine parted; and Eva, who had been stimulated, by the society of her young cousin, to exertions beyond her strength, began to fail rapidly. St. Clare was at last willing to call in medical advice,—a thing from which he had always shrunk, because it was the admission of an unwelcome truth.

But, for a day or two, Eva was so unwell as to be confined to the house; and the doctor was called.

Marie St. Clare had taken no notice of the child's gradually decaying health and strength, because she was completely absorbed in studying out two or three new forms of disease to which she believed she herself was a victim.[1] It was the first principle of Marie's belief that nobody ever was or could be so great a sufferer as *herself*; and, therefore, she always repelled quite indignantly any suggestion that any one around her could be sick. She was always sure, in such a case, that it was nothing but laziness, or want of energy; and that, if they had had the suffering *she* had, they would soon know the difference.

Miss Ophelia had several times tried to awaken her maternal fears about Eva; but to no avail.

"I don't see as anything ails the child," she would say; "she runs about, and plays."

"But she has a cough."

"Cough! you don't need to tell *me* about a cough. I've always been subject to a cough, all my days. When I was of

1 Marie has unwittingly diagnosed Eva as consumptive—which was probably true—but in her utter self-centeredness, Marie ignores her own insight. The very bad mother!

Eva's age, they thought I was in a consumption. Night after night, Mammy used to sit up with me. O! Eva's cough is not anything."

"But she gets weak, and is short-breathed."

"Law! I've had that, years and years; it's only a nervous affection."

"But she sweats so, nights!"

"Well, I have, these ten years. Very often, night after night, my clothes will be wringing wet. There won't be a dry thread in my night-clothes, and the sheets will be so that Mammy has to hang them up to dry! Eva doesn't sweat anything like that!"

Miss Ophelia shut her mouth for a season. But, now that Eva was fairly and visibly prostrated, and a doctor called, Marie, all on a sudden, took a new turn.

"She knew it," she said; "she always felt it, that she was destined to be the most miserable of mothers. Here she was, with her wretched health, and her only darling child going down to the grave before her eyes;"—and Marie routed up Mammy nights, and rumpussed and scolded, with more energy than ever, all day, on the strength of this new misery.

"My dear Marie, don't talk so!" said St. Clare. "You ought not to give up the case so, at once."

"You have not a mother's feelings, St. Clare! You never could understand me!—you don't now."

"But don't talk so, as if it were a gone case!"

"I can't take it as indifferently as you can, St. Clare. If *you* don't feel when your only child is in this alarming state, *I* do. It's a blow too much for me, with all I was bearing before."

"It's true," said St. Clare, "that Eva is very delicate, *that* I always knew; and that she has grown so rapidly as to exhaust her strength; and that her situation is critical. But just now she is only prostrated by the heat of the weather, and by the excitement of her cousin's visit, and the exertions she made. The physician says there is room for hope."

"Well, of course, if you can look on the bright side, pray do; it's a mercy if people haven't sensitive feelings, in this world. I am sure I wish I didn't feel as I do; it only makes me completely wretched! I wish I *could* be as easy as the rest of you!"

And the "rest of them" had good reason to breathe the same prayer, for Marie paraded her new misery as the reason and apology for all sorts of inflictions on every one about her. Every word that was spoken by anybody, everything that was done or was not done everywhere, was only a new proof that she was surrounded by hard-hearted, insensible beings, who were unmindful of her peculiar sorrows. Poor Eva heard some of these speeches; and nearly cried her little eyes out, in pity for her mamma, and in sorrow that she should make her so much distress.

In a week or two, there was a great improvement of symptoms,—one of those deceitful lulls, by which her inexorable disease so often beguiles the anxious heart, even on the verge of the grave. Eva's step was again in the garden,—in the balconies; she played and laughed again,—and her father, in a transport, declared that they should soon have her as hearty as anybody. Miss Ophelia and the physician alone felt no encouragement from this illusive truce. There was one other heart, too, that felt the same certainty, and that was the little heart of Eva. What is it that sometimes speaks in the soul so calmly, so clearly, that its earthly time is short? Is it the secret instinct of decaying nature, or the soul's impulsive throb, as immortality draws on? Be it what it may, it rested in the heart of Eva, a calm, sweet, prophetic certainty that Heaven was near; calm as the light of sunset, sweet as the bright stillness of autumn, there her little heart reposed, only troubled by sorrow for those who loved her so dearly.

For the child, though nursed so tenderly, and though life was unfolding before her with every brightness that love and wealth could give, had no regret for herself in dying.

In that book which she and her simple old friend had read so much together, she had seen and taken to her young heart the image of one who loved the little child; and, as she gazed and mused, He had ceased to be an image and a picture of the distant past, and come to be a living, all-surrounding reality. His love enfolded her child-ish heart with more than mortal tenderness; and it was to Him, she said, she was going, and to his home.

But her heart yearned with sad tenderness for all that she was to leave behind. Her father most,—for Eva, though she never distinctly thought so, had an instinctive perception that she was more in his heart than any other. She loved her mother because she was so loving a crea-ture, and all the selfishness that she had seen in her only saddened and perplexed her; for she had a child's implicit trust that her mother could not do wrong. There was something about her that Eva never could make out; and she always smoothed it over with thinking that, after all, it was mamma, and she loved her very dearly indeed.

She felt, too, for those fond, faithful servants, to whom she was as daylight and sunshine. Children do not usually generalize; but Eva was an uncommonly mature child, and the things that she had witnessed of the evils of the system under which they were living had fallen, one by one, into the depths of her thoughtful, pondering heart. She had vague longings to do something for them,—to bless and save not only them, but all in their condition,—longings that contrasted sadly with the feebleness of her little frame.

"Uncle Tom," she said, one day, when she was reading to her friend, "I can understand why Jesus *wanted* to die for us."

"Why, Miss Eva?"

"Because I've felt so, too."

"What is it, Miss Eva?—I don't understand."

"I can't tell you; but, when I saw those poor creatures on the boat, you know, when you came up and I,—some had lost their mothers, and some their husbands, and some mothers cried for their little children,—and when I heard about poor Prue,—oh, wasn't that dreadful!—and a great many other times, I've felt that I would be glad to die, if my dying could stop all this misery. I *would die* for them, Tom, if I could," said the child, earnestly, laying her little thin hand on his.

Tom looked at the child with awe; and when she, hearing her father's voice, glided away, he wiped his eyes many times, as he looked after her.

"It's jest no use tryin' to keep Miss Eva here," he said to Mammy, whom he met a moment after. "She's got the Lord's mark in her forehead."

"Ah, yes, yes," said Mammy, raising her hands; "I've allers said so. She wasn't never like a child that's to live—there was allers something deep in her eyes. I've told Missis so, many the time; it's a comin' true,—we all sees it,—dear, little, blessed lamb!"

Eva came tripping up the verandah steps to her father. It was late in the afternoon, and the rays of the sun formed a kind of glory behind her, as she came forward in her white dress, with her golden hair and glowing cheeks, her eyes unnaturally bright with the slow fever that burned in her veins.

St. Clare had called her to show a statuette that he had been buying for her; but her appearance, as she came on, impressed him suddenly and painfully. There is a kind of beauty so intense, yet so fragile, that we cannot bear to look at it. Her father folded her suddenly in his arms, and almost forgot what he was going to tell her.[2]

"Eva, dear, you are better now-a-days,—are you not?"

"Papa," said Eva, with sudden firmness, "I've had things I wanted to say to you, a great while. I want to say them now, before I get weaker."

St. Clare trembled as Eva seated herself in his lap. She laid her head on his bosom, and said,

"It's all no use, papa, to keep it to myself any longer. The time is coming that I am going to leave you. I am going, and never to come back!" and Eva sobbed.

"O, now, my dear little Eva!" said St. Clare, trembling as he spoke, but speaking cheerfully, "you've got nervous and low-spirited; you mustn't indulge such gloomy thoughts. See here, I've bought a statuette for you!"

"No, papa," said Eva, putting it gently away, "don't deceive yourself!—I am *not* any better, I know it perfectly well,—and I am going, before long. I am not nervous,—I am not low-spirited. If it were not for you, papa, and my friends, I should be perfectly happy. I want to go,—I long to go!"

"Why, dear child, what has made your poor little heart so sad? You have had everything, to make you happy, that could be given you."

"I had rather be in heaven; though, only for my friends' sake, I would be willing to live. There are a great many things here that make me sad, that seem dreadful to me; I had rather be there; but I don't want to leave you,—it almost breaks my heart!"

"What makes you sad, and seems dreadful, Eva?"

"O, things that are done, and done all the time. I feel sad for our poor people; they love me dearly, and they are all good and kind to me. I wish, papa, they were all *free*."

"Why, Eva, child, don't you think they are well enough off now?"

"O, but, papa, if anything should happen to you, what would become of them? There are very few men like you, papa. Uncle Alfred isn't like you, and mamma isn't; and then, think of poor old Prue's owners! What horrid things people do, and can do!" and Eva shuddered.

"My dear child, you are too sensitive. I'm sorry I ever let you hear such stories."

"O, that's what troubles me, papa. You want me to live so happy, and never to have any pain,—never suffer anything,—not even hear a sad story, when other poor creatures have nothing but pain and sorrow, all their lives;—it

2 If Marie is blinded to Eva's rapidly deteriorating condition by her selfishness, her husband simply ignores truths. His elation, as with most of his moods, is fleeting.

seems selfish. I ought to know such things, I ought to feel about them! Such things always sunk into my heart; they went down deep; I've thought and thought about them. Papa, isn't there any way to have all slaves made free?"

"That's a difficult question, dearest. There's no doubt that this way is a very bad one; a great many people think so; I do myself. I heartily wish that there were not a slave in the land; but, then, I don't know what is to be done about it!"

"Papa, you are such a good man, and so noble, and kind, and you always have a way of saying things that is so pleasant, couldn't you go all round and try to persuade people to do right about this? When I am dead, papa, then you will think of me, and do it for my sake. I would do it, if I could."

"When you are dead, Eva," said St. Clare, passionately. "O, child, don't talk to me so! You are all I have on earth."

"Poor old Prue's child was all that she had,—and yet she had to hear it crying, and she couldn't help it! Papa, these poor creatures love their children as much as you do me. O! do something for them! There's poor Mammy loves her children; I've seen her cry when she talked about them. And Tom loves his children; and it's dreadful, papa, that such things are happening, all the time!"

"There, there, darling," said St. Clare, soothingly; "only don't distresss yourself, and don't talk of dying, and I will do anything you wish."

"And promise me, dear father, that Tom shall have his freedom as soon as"—she stopped, and said, in a hesitating tone—"I am gone!"

"Yes, dear, I will do anything in the world,—anything you could ask me to."

"Dear papa," said the child, laying her burning cheek against his, "how I wish we could go together!"

"Where, dearest?" said St. Clare.

"To our Saviour's home; it's so sweet and peaceful there—it is all so loving there!" The child spoke unconsciously, as of a place where she had often been. "Don't you want to go, papa?" she said.

St. Clare drew her closer to him, but was silent.

"You will come to me," said the child, speaking in a voice of calm certainty which she often used unconsciously.

"I shall come after you. I shall not forget you."

The shadows of the solemn evening closed round them deeper and deeper, as St. Clare sat silently holding the little frail form to his bosom. He saw no more the deep eyes, but the voice came over him as a spirit voice, and, as in a sort of judgment vision, his whole past life rose in a moment before his eyes: his mother's prayers and hymns; his own early yearnings and aspirings for good; and, between them and this hour, years of worldliness and scepticism, and what man calls respectable living. We can think *much*, very much, in a moment. St. Clare saw and felt many things, but spoke nothing; and, as it grew darker, he took his child to her bedroom; and, when she was prepared for rest, he sent away the attendants, and rocked her in his arms, and sung to her till she was asleep.[3]

3 Stowe gives St. Clare a second chance at redemption with his deathbed promise to his little angel. This chapter and the next one, also dealing with Little Eva's illness, do not feature the usual abundance of biblical quotations found in most other chapters of the novel.

## CHAPTER 25

### *The Little Evangelist*

It was Sunday afternoon. St. Clare was stretched on a bamboo lounge in the verandah, solacing himself with a cigar. Marie lay reclined on a sofa, opposite the window opening on the verandah, closely secluded, under an awning of transparent gauze, from the outrages of the mosquitos, and languidly holding in her hand an elegantly bound prayer-book. She was holding it because it was Sunday, and she imagined she had been reading it,—though, in fact, she had been only taking a succession of short naps, with it open in her hand.

Miss Ophelia, who, after some rummaging, had hunted up a small Methodist meeting within riding distance, had gone out, with Tom as driver, to attend it; and Eva had accompanied them.

"I say, Augustine," said Marie after dozing a while, "I must send to the city after my old Doctor Posey; I'm sure I've got the complaint of the heart."

"Well; why need you send for him? This doctor that attends Eva seems skilful."

"I would not trust him in a critical case," said Marie; "and I think I may say mine is becoming so! I've been thinking of it, these two or three nights past; I have such distressing pains, and such strange feelings."

"O, Marie, you are blue; I don't believe it's heart complaint."

"I dare say *you* don't," said Marie; "I was prepared to expect *that*. You can be alarmed enough, if Eva coughs, or has the least thing the matter with her; but you never think of me."

"If it's particularly agreeable to you to have heart disease, why, I'll try and maintain you have it," said St. Clare; "I didn't know it was."

"Well, I only hope you won't be sorry for this, when it's too late!" said Marie; "but, believe it or not, my distress about Eva, and the exertions I have made with that dear child, have developed what I have long suspected."

What the *exertions* were which Marie referred to, it would have been difficult to state. St. Clare quietly made this commentary to himself, and went on smoking, like a hard-hearted wretch of a man as he was, till a carriage drove up before the verandah, and Eva and Miss Ophelia alighted.

Miss Ophelia marched straight to her own chamber, to put away her bonnet and shawl, as was always her manner, before she spoke a word on any subject; while Eva came, at St. Clare's call, and was sitting on his knee, giving him an account of the services they had heard.

They soon heard loud exclamations from Miss Ophelia's room, which, like the one in which they were sitting, opened on to the verandah, and violent reproof addressed to somebody.

"What new witchcraft has Tops been brewing?" asked St. Clare. "That commotion is of her raising, I'll be bound!"

And, in a moment after, Miss Ophelia, in high indignation, came dragging the culprit along.

"Come out here, now!" she said. "I *will* tell your master!"[1]

"What's the case now?" asked Augustine.

"The case is, that I cannot be plagued with this child, any longer! It's past all bearing; flesh and blood cannot endure it! Here, I locked her up, and gave her a hymn to study; and what does she do, but spy out where I put my key, and has gone to my bureau, and got a bonnet-trimming, and cut it all to pieces, to make dolls' jackets! I never saw anything like it, in my life!"

"I told you, Cousin," said Marie, "that you'd find out that these creatures can't be brought up, without severity. If I had *my* way, now," she said, looking reproachfully at St. Clare, "I'd send that child out, and have her thoroughly whipped; I'd have her whipped till she couldn't stand!"

"I don't doubt it," said St. Clare. "Tell me of the lovely rule of woman! I never saw above a dozen women that wouldn't half kill a horse, or a servant, either, if they had their own way with them!—let alone a man."

"There is no use in this shilly-shally[2] way of yours, St.

1 Although Topsy was given to Ophelia as a present, Ophelia apparently was not given any papers for her. St. Clare remains Topsy's master for the moment.

2 I.e., indecisive.

Clare!" said Marie. "Cousin is a woman of sense, and she sees it now, as plain as I do."

Miss Ophelia had just the capability of indignation that belongs to the thorough-paced housekeeper, and this had been pretty actively roused by the artifice and wastefulness of the child; in fact, many of my lady readers must own that they should have felt just so in her circumstances; but Marie's words went beyond her, and she felt less heat.

"I wouldn't have the child treated so, for the world," she said; "but, I am sure, Augustine, I don't know what to do. I've taught and taught; I've talked till I'm tired; I've whipped her; I've punished her in every way I can think of, and still she's just what she was at first."

"Come here, Tops, you monkey!" said St. Clare, calling the child up to him.

Topsy came up; her round, hard eyes glittering and blinking with a mixture of apprehensiveness and their usual odd drollery.

"What makes you behave so?" said St. Clare, who could not help being amused with the child's expression.

"Spects it's my wicked heart," said Topsy, demurely; "Miss Feely says so."

"Don't you see how much Miss Ophelia has done for you? She says she has done everything she can think of."

"Lor, yes, Mas'r! old Missis used to say so, too. She whipped me a heap harder, and used to pull my har, and knock my head agin the door; but it didn't do me no good! I spects, if they's to pull every spear o' har out of my head, it wouldn't do no good, neither,—I's so wicked! Laws! I's nothin but a nigger, no ways!"

"Well, I shall have to give her up," said Miss Ophelia; "I can't have that trouble any longer."

"Well, I'd just like to ask one question," said St. Clare.

"What is it?"

"Why, if your Gospel is not strong enough to save one heathen child, that you can have at home here, all to yourself, what's the use of sending one or two poor missionaries off with it among thousands of just such? I suppose this child is about a fair sample of what thousands of your heathen are."

Miss Ophelia did not make an immediate answer; and Eva, who had stood a silent spectator of the scene thus far, made a silent sign to Topsy to follow her. There was a little glass-room at the corner of the verandah, which St. Clare used as a sort of reading-room; and Eva and Topsy disappeared into this place.

"What's Eva going about, now?" said St. Clare; "I mean to see."

And, advancing on tiptoe, he lifted up a curtain that covered the glass door, and looked in. In a moment, laying his finger on his lips, he made a silent gesture to Miss Ophelia to come and look. There sat the two children on the floor, with their side faces towards them. Topsy, with her usual air of careless drollery and unconcern; but, opposite to her, Eva, her whole face fervent with feeling, and tears in her large eyes.

"What does make you so bad, Topsy? Why won't you try and be good? Don't you love *anybody*, Topsy?"

"Donno nothing 'bout love; I loves candy and sich, that's all," said Topsy.

"But you love your father and mother?"

"Never had none, ye know. I telled ye that, Miss Eva."

"O, I know," said Eva, sadly; "but hadn't you any brother, or sister, or aunt, or—"

"No, none on 'em,—never had nothing nor nobody."

"But, Topsy, if you'd only try to be good, you might—"

"Couldn't never be nothin' but a nigger, if I was ever so good," said Topsy. "If I could be skinned, and come white, I'd try then."

"But people can love you, if you are black, Topsy. Miss Ophelia would love you, if you were good."

Topsy gave the short, blunt laugh that was her common mode of expressing incredulity.

"Don't you think so?" said Eva.

"No; she can't bar me, 'cause I'm a nigger!—she'd 's soon have a toad touch her! There can't nobody love niggers, and niggers can't do nothin'! *I* don't care," said Topsy, beginning to whistle.

"O, Topsy, poor child, *I* love you!" said Eva, with a sudden burst of feeling, and laying her little thin, white hand on Topsy's shoulder; "I love you, because you haven't had any father, or mother, or friends;—because you've been a poor, abused child! I love you, and I want you to be good. I am very unwell, Topsy, and I think I shan't live a great while; and it really grieves me, to have you be so naughty. I wish you would try to be good, for my sake;—it's only a little while I shall be with you."

The round, keen eyes of the black child were overcast with tears;—large, bright drops rolled heavily down, one by one, and fell on the little white hand. Yes, in that moment, a ray of real belief, a ray of heavenly love, had penetrated the darkness of her heathen soul! She laid her head down between her knees, and wept and sobbed,—

"Eva and Topsy." "O Topsy, poor child, *I* love you!" says an angelic Eva. Wood engraving by T. Williams, "after George Cruikshank." From *Uncle Tom's Cabin*, John Cassell, London, 1852

3 The love of Jesus is the great equalizer, yet in Eva's formulation it seems that Topsy too can be white. The Rev. John Angell James of Birmingham wrote a letter to Stowe in 1853, republished in *Frederick Douglass' Paper* (April 1, 1853) praising Topsy:

> Another character which has pleased me above most, is that little imp of wickedness and mischief, from which slavery had almost crushed out the remains of humanity. O my dear Madam, I rose in a kind of rapture from the wondrous and felicitous skill of the mind and pen which could make even poor Topsy start up at the touch of the magic wand of love, a new creature in Christ Jesus. What an illustration, thought I, is here, of a passage of Scripture which contain the true philosophy both of humanity and the Gospel—"I drew them with cords of a man, with bands of love." Never was the motive power of man's nature more beautifully illustrated. You have taught the world a new lesson, how man is to be reformed and governed, even when sunk by oppression and by crime into this lowest depth of degradation, by the omnipotence of God.

4 It is important to note, historian Ann Douglas writes, "that Little Eva doesn't actually convert anyone. Her sainthood is there to precipitate our nostalgia and our narcissism." Moreover, Douglas continues, "if 'camp' is art that is too excessive to be taken seriously . . . then Little Eva suggests Christianity beginning to function as camp" (*The Feminization of American Culture*).

while the beautiful child, bending over her, looked like the picture of some bright angel stooping to reclaim a sinner.

"Poor Topsy!" said Eva, "don't you know that Jesus loves all alike?[3] He is just as willing to love you, as me. He loves you just as I do,—only more, because he is better. He will help you to be good; and you can go to Heaven at last, and be an angel forever, just as much as if you were white. Only think of it, Topsy!—*you* can be one of those spirits bright, Uncle Tom sings about."

"O, dear Miss Eva, dear Miss Eva!" said the child; "I will try, I will try; I never did care nothin' about it before."

St. Clare, at this instant, dropped the curtain. "It puts me in mind of mother," he said to Miss Ophelia. "It is true what she told me; if we want to give sight to the blind, we must be willing to do as Christ did,—call them to us, and *put our hands on them.*"

"I've always had a prejudice against negroes," said Miss Ophelia, "and it's a fact, I never could bear to have that child touch me; but, I didn't think she knew it."

"Trust any child to find that out," said St. Clare; "there's no keeping it from them. But I believe that all the trying in the world to benefit a child, and all the substantial favors you can do them, will never excite one emotion of gratitude, while that feeling of repugnance remains in the heart;—it's a queer kind of a fact,—but so it is."

"I don't know how I can help it," said Miss Ophelia; "they *are* disagreeable to me,—this child in particular,—how can I help feeling so?"

"Eva does, it seems."

"Well, she's so loving! After all, though, she's no more than Christ-like," said Miss Ophelia; "I wish I were like her. She might teach me a lesson."[4]

"It wouldn't be the first time a little child had been used to instruct an old disciple, if it *were* so," said St. Clare.

# CHAPTER 26

## Death

*"Weep not for those whom the veil of the tomb,*
*In life's early morning, hath hid from our eyes."*[1]

Eva's bed-room was a spacious apartment, which,
like all the other rooms in the house, opened on to the
broad verandah. The room communicated, on one side,
with her father and mother's apartment; on the other,
with that appropriated to Miss Ophelia. St. Clare had
gratified his own eye and taste, in furnishing this room in
a style that had a peculiar keeping with the character of
her for whom it was intended. The windows were hung
with curtains of rose-colored and white muslin, the floor
was spread with a matting which had been ordered in
Paris, to a pattern of his own device, having round it a
border of rose-buds and leaves, and a centre-piece with
full-blown[2] roses. The bedstead, chairs, and lounges, were
of bamboo, wrought in peculiarly graceful and fanciful
patterns. Over the head of the bed was an alabaster
bracket, on which a beautiful sculptured angel stood, with
drooping wings, holding out a crown of myrtle-leaves.[3]
From this depended, over the bed, light curtains of rose-
colored gauze, striped with silver, supplying that protection from mosquitos which is an indispensable addition to
all sleeping accommodation in that climate. The graceful
bamboo lounges were amply supplied with cushions of
rose-colored damask, while over them, depending from the

1  "Weep Not for Those," a poem by the Irish
Romantic poet Thomas Moore (1779–1852).
The whole of the poem is as follows.

Weep not for those whom the veil of the
  tomb,
In life's happy morning, hath hid from
  our eyes,
Ere sin threw a blight o'er the spirit's
  young bloom,
Or earth had profaned what was born for
  the skies.
Death chilled the fair fountain, ere sor-
  row had stained it;
'Twas frozen in all the pure light of its
  course,
And but sleeps till the sunshine of
  Heaven has unchained it,
To water that Eden where first was its
  source.
Weep not for those whom the veil of the
  tomb,
In life's happy morning, hath hid from
  our eyes,
Ere sin threw a blight o'er the spirit's
  young bloom,
Or earth had profaned what was born for
  the skies.

Mourn not for her, the young Bride of
  the Vale,
Our gayest and loveliest, lost to us now,

Ere life's early lustre had time to grow
pale,
And the garland of Love was yet fresh on
her brow.
Oh, then was her moment, dear spirit, for
flying
From this gloomy world, while its gloom
was unknown—
And the wild hymns she warbled so
sweetly, in dying,
Were echoed in Heaven by lips like her
own.
Weep not for her—in her springtime she
flew
To that land where the wings of the soul
are unfurled;
And now, like a star beyond evening's
cold dew,
Looks radiantly down on the tears of
this world.

Most collections of Moore's poems include a note by Moore that the second verse "alludes to the fate of a very lovely and amiable girl, the daughter of the late Colonel Bainbrigge, who was married in Ashbourne church, October 18, 1815, and died of a fever in a few weeks after. The sound of her marriage-bells seemed scarcely out of our ears when we heard of her death. During her last delirium she sung several hymns, in a voice even clearer and sweeter than usual, and among them were some from the present collection, (particularly, 'There's nothing bright but Heaven,') which this very interesting girl had often heard me sing during the summer."

2 I.e., in full bloom.

3 Myrtle leaves were deep green. Although a standard decorative element, the crown also alludes to Revelation, as in 2:10: "Do not fear what you are about to suffer. Behold, the devil is about to throw some of you into prison, that you may be tested, and for ten days you will have tribulation. Be faithful unto death, and I will give you the crown of life."

4 A vase common in the nineteenth century, made of unglazed white porcelain made to resemble marble from the Aegean island of Paros.

5 The word "baggage" can mean "rubbish" but also "whore." Marie's choice of insult for

hands of sculptured figures, were gauze curtains similar to those of the bed. A light, fanciful bamboo table stood in the middle of the room, where a Parian vase,[4] wrought in the shape of a white lily, with its buds, stood, ever filled with flowers. On this table lay Eva's books and little trinkets, with an elegantly wrought alabaster writing-stand, which her father had supplied to her when he saw her trying to improve herself in writing. There was a fireplace in the room, and on the marble mantle above stood a beautifully wrought statuette of Jesus receiving little children, and on either side marble vases, for which it was Tom's pride and delight to offer bouquets every morning. Two or three exquisite paintings of children, in various attitudes, embellished the wall. In short, the eye could turn nowhere without meeting images of childhood, of beauty, and of peace. Those little eyes never opened, in the morning light, without falling on something which suggested to the heart soothing and beautiful thoughts.

The deceitful strength which had buoyed Eva up for a little while was fast passing away; seldom and more seldom her light footstep was heard in the verandah, and oftener and oftener she was found reclined on a little lounge by the open window, her large, deep eyes fixed on the rising and falling waters of the lake.

It was towards the middle of the afternoon, as she was so reclining,—her Bible half open, her little transparent fingers lying listlessly between the leaves,—suddenly she heard her mother's voice, in sharp tones, in the verandah.

"What now, you baggage![5]—what new piece of mischief! You've been picking the flowers, hey?" and Eva heard the sound of a smart slap.

"Law, Missis!—they's for Miss Eva," she heard a voice say, which she knew belonged to Topsy.

"Miss Eva! A pretty excuse!—you suppose she wants *your* flowers, you good-for-nothing nigger! Get along off with you!"

In a moment, Eva was off from her lounge, and in the verandah.

"O, don't, mother! I should like the flowers; do give them to me; I want them!"

"Why, Eva, your room is full now. "

"I can't have too many," said Eva. "Topsy, do bring them here."

Topsy, who had stood sullenly, holding down her head, now came up and offered her flowers. She did it with a look of hesitation and bashfulness, quite unlike the eldrich[6] boldness and brightness which was usual with her.

"It's a beautiful bouquet!" said Eva, looking at it.

It was rather a singular one,—a brilliant scarlet geranium, and one single white japonica, with its glossy leaves. It was tied up with an evident eye to the contrast of color, and the arrangement of every leaf had carefully been studied.

Topsy looked pleased, as Eva said,—"Topsy, you arrange flowers very prettily. Here," she said, "is this vase I haven't any flowers for. I wish you'd arrange something every day for it."

"Well, that's odd!" said Marie. "What in the world do you want that for?"

"Never mind, mamma; you'd as lief as not[7] Topsy should do it,—had you not?"

"Of course, anything you please, dear! Topsy, you hear your young mistress;—see that you mind."

Topsy made a short courtesy, and looked down; and, as she turned away, Eva saw a tear roll down her dark cheek.

"You see, mamma, I knew poor Topsy wanted to do something for me," said Eva to her mother.

"O, nonsense! it's only because she likes to do mischief. She knows she mustn't pick flowers,—so she does it; that's all there is to it. But, if you fancy to have her pluck them, so be it."

"Mamma, I think Topsy is different from what she used to be; she's trying to be a good girl."

"She'll have to try a good while before *she* gets to be good," said Marie, with a careless laugh.

"Well, you know, mamma, poor Topsy! everything has always been against her."

"Not since she's been here, I'm sure. If she hasn't been talked to, and preached to, and every earthly thing done that anybody could do;—and she's just so ugly,[8] and always will be; you can't make anything of the creature!"

"But, mamma, it's so different to be brought up as I've been, with so many friends, so many things to make me good and happy; and to be brought up as she's been, all the time, till she came here!"

"Most likely," said Marie, yawning,—"dear me, how hot it is!"

"Mamma, you believe, don't you, that Topsy could become an angel, as well as any of us, if she were a Christian?"

"Topsy! what a ridiculous idea! Nobody but you would ever think of it. I suppose she could, though."

"But, mamma, isn't God her father, as much as ours? Isn't Jesus her Saviour?"

Topsy reflects her mistress's own lack of refinement.

6 I.e., weird or unnatural. Topsy's strange and mystical facility with flowers and arranging is a kind of material version of Eva's unworldliness.

7 I.e., be happier if.

8 I.e., offensive—to the eye, to the sense of morality or of refinement.

**9** In the nineteenth century, mourners were often given a lock of the deceased's hair as a memento. Eva wants to decide who gets her hair. (As Ann Douglas has wryly observed, however, "Little Eva manages to give away on her deathbed innumerable locks of her hair to her family, friends, and slaves, and still go apparently unshorn to the grave" [*The Feminization of American Culture*].)

"Well, that may be. I suppose God made everybody," said Marie. "Where is my smelling-bottle?"

"It's such a pity,—oh! *such* a pity!" said Eva, looking out on the distant lake, and speaking half to herself.

"What's a pity?" said Marie.

"Why, that any one, who could be a bright angel, and live with angels, should go all down, down, down, and nobody help them!—oh, dear!"

"Well, we can't help it; it's no use worrying, Eva! I don't know what's to be done; we ought to be thankful for our own advantages."

"I hardly can be," said Eva, "I'm so sorry to think of poor folks that haven't any."

"That's odd enough," said Marie;—"I'm sure my religion makes me thankful for my advantages."

"Mamma," said Eva, "I want to have some of my hair cut off,—a good deal of it."

"What for?" said Marie.

"Mamma, I want to give some away to my friends, while I am able to give it to them myself.**9** Won't you ask aunty to come and cut it for me?"

Marie raised her voice, and called Miss Ophelia, from the other room.

The child half rose from her pillow as she came in, and, shaking down her long golden-brown curls, said, rather playfully, "Come, aunty, shear the sheep!"

"What's that?" said St. Clare, who just then entered with some fruit he had been out to get for her.

"Papa, I just want aunty to cut off some of my hair;—there's too much of it, and it makes my head hot. Besides, I want to give some of it away."

Miss Ophelia came, with her scissors.

"Take care,—don't spoil the looks of it!" said her father; "cut underneath, where it won't show. Eva's curls are my pride."

"O, papa!" said Eva, sadly.

"Yes, and I want them kept handsome against the time I take you up to your uncle's plantation, to see Cousin Henrique," said St. Clare, in a gay tone.

"I shall never go there, papa;—I am going to a better country. O, do believe me! Don't you see, papa, that I get weaker, every day?"

"Why do you insist that I shall believe such a cruel thing, Eva?" said her father.

"Only because it is *true*, papa: and, if you will believe it now, perhaps you will get to feel about it as I do."

St. Clare closed his lips, and stood gloomily eying the

long, beautiful curls, which, as they were separated from the child's head, were laid, one by one, in her lap. She raised them up, looked earnestly at them, twined them around her thin fingers, and looked, from time to time, anxiously at her father.

"It's just what I've been foreboding!" said Marie; "it's just what has been preying on my health, from day to day, bringing me downward to the grave, though nobody regards it. I have seen this, long. St. Clare, you will see, after a while, that I was right."[10]

"Which will afford you great consolation, no doubt!" said St. Clare, in a dry, bitter tone.

Marie lay back on a lounge, and covered her face with her cambric handkerchief.

Eva's clear blue eye looked earnestly from one to the other. It was the calm, comprehending gaze of a soul half loosed from its earthly bonds; it was evident she saw, felt, and appreciated, the difference between the two.

She beckoned with her hand to her father. He came, and sat down by her.

"Papa, my strength fades away every day, and I know I must go. There are some things I want to say and do,—that I ought to do; and you are so unwilling to have me speak a word on this subject. But it must come; there's no putting it off. Do be willing I should speak now!"

"My child, I *am* willing!" said St. Clare, covering his eyes with one hand, and holding up Eva's hand with the other.

"Then, I want to see all our people together. I have some things I *must* say to them," said Eva.

"*Well*," said St. Clare, in a tone of dry endurance.

Miss Ophelia despatched a messenger, and soon the whole of the servants were convened in the room.

Eva lay back on her pillows; her hair hanging loosely about her face, her crimson cheeks contrasting painfully with the intense whiteness of her complexion and the thin contour of her limbs and features, and her large, soul-like eyes fixed earnestly on every one.

The servants were struck with a sudden emotion. The spiritual face, the long locks of hair cut off and lying by her, her father's averted face, and Marie's sobs, struck at once upon the feelings of a sensitive and impressible race;[11] and, as they came in, they looked one on another, sighed, and shook their heads. There was a deep silence, like that of a funeral.

Eva raised herself, and looked long and earnestly round at every one. All looked sad and apprehensive. Many of the women hid their faces in their aprons.

10 Marie shows no maternal concern at her daughter's deathbed, insisting only that she was "right" and that the grief she feels will kill her. Can one imagine a more unfeeling mother?

11 Readers might more readily imagine that Marie's real sobs, rather than touching the feelings of the "over-sensitive" slaves, would put them into shock.

**12** Eva's deathbed words to those gathered echo Christ's words to his apostles at the Last Supper: "Little children, yet a little while I am with you" (John 13:33).

**13** Those slaves trained in religion know the proper response is "Amen," not sobs.

"Eva's last gifts." Eva gives locks of her hair to all of the St. Clare household. Wood engraving, 1852, by M. Jackson, "after George Cruikshank." This image recollects the earlier image in chapter 4 of the prayer meeting in Uncle Tom's cabin. Eva is remarkably, transcendently composed, compared to everyone else in the room. From *Uncle Tom's Cabin*, John Cassell, London, 1852

"I sent for you all, my dear friends," said Eva, "because I love you. I love you all; and I have something to say to you, which I want you always to remember. . . . . . . I am going to leave you. In a few more weeks, you will see me no more—"**12**

Here the child was interrupted by bursts of groans, sobs, and lamentations, which broke from all present, and in which her slender voice was lost entirely. She waited a moment, and then, speaking in a tone that checked the sobs of all, she said,

"If you love me, you must not interrupt me so. Listen to what I say.

I want to speak to you about your souls. . . . . . . Many of you, I am afraid, are very careless. You are thinking only about this world. I want you to remember that there is a beautiful world, where Jesus is. I am going there, and you can go there. It is for you, as much as me. But, if you want to go there, you must not live idle, careless, thoughtless lives. You must be Christians. You must remember that each one of you can become angels, and be angels forever. . . . . . . If you want to be Christians, Jesus will help you. You must pray to him; you must read—"

The child checked herself, looked piteously at them, and said, sorrowfully,

"O, dear! you *can't* read,—poor souls!" and she hid her face in the pillow and sobbed, while many a smothered sob from those she was addressing, who were kneeling on the floor, aroused her.

"Never mind," she said, raising her face and smiling brightly through her tears, "I have prayed for you; and I know Jesus will help you, even if you can't read. Try all to do the best you can; pray every day; ask Him to help you, and get the Bible read to you whenever you can; and I think I shall see you all in heaven."

"Amen," was the murmured response from the lips of Tom and Mammy, and some of the elder ones, who belonged to the Methodist church.**13** The younger and more thoughtless ones, for the time completely overcome, were sobbing, with their heads bowed upon their knees.

"I know," said Eva, "you all love me."

Sheet music from the 1923 Duncan Sisters' musical *Topsy and Eva*.
© Irving Berlin, Inc. Music Publishers

Uncle Tom Bourbon Whiskey.
Courtesy of Larry Vincent Buster Collection, New Rochelle, NY

Postcard titled " 'Uncle Tom.' An Old-Fashioned Southern Negro."
Originally printed by the Asheville Post Card Co., Asheville, NC

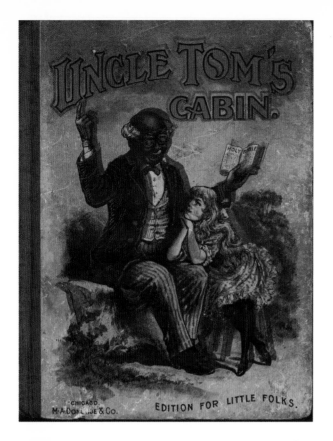

Here are three separate covers of the *Young Folks Edition* from M. A. Donohue. Each features a well-dressed Tom, as anesthetized and grandfatherly as he's ever been. *Uncle Tom's Cabin* (Chicago: M. A. Donohue, circa 1900).

The cover image of this edition shows Tom as an old man, white-haired and stooped,
though with an interesting gleam in his eye. From *Uncle Tom's Cabin, or,
Life Among the Lowly* (New York: Grosset and Dunlap, n.d.).

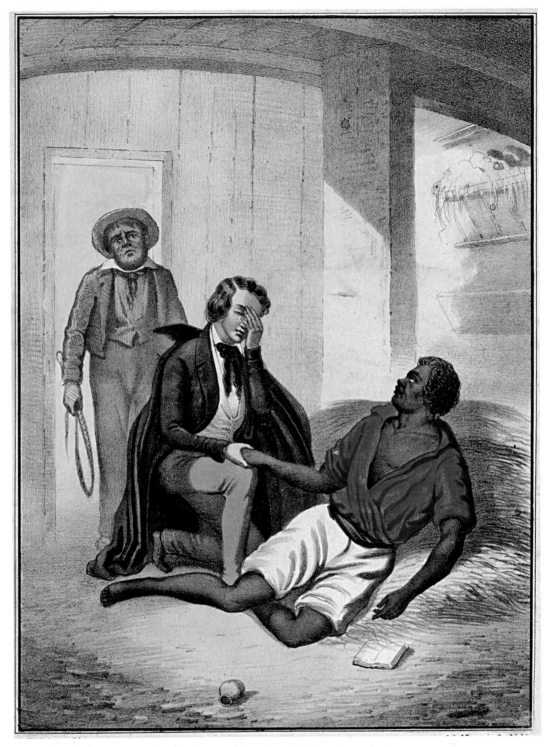

"Death of Uncle Tom." Lithograph by Thomas W. Strong.
National Museum of American History. Smithsonian Institution. Behring Center

"First Meeting of Uncle Tom and Eva." Lithograph by Thomas W. Strong.
National Museum of American History. Smithsonian Institution. Behring Center

"Uncle Tom Saving Eva." Lithograph by Thomas W. Strong.
National Museum of American History. Smithsonian Institution. Behring Center

"Uncle Tom and Little Eva."
Lithograph by E. C. Kellog & Co. From *Uncle Tom's Cabin*
(Horace Thayer & Co., 1852–56).
National Museum of American History. Smithsonian Institution. Behring Center

"Yes; oh, yes! indeed we do! Lord bless her!" was the involuntary answer of all.

"Yes, I know you do! There isn't one of you that hasn't always been very kind to me; and I want to give you something that, when you look at, you shall always remember me. I'm going to give all of you a curl of my hair; and, when you look at it, think that I loved you and am gone to heaven, and that I want to see you all there."

It is impossible to describe the scene, as, with tears and sobs, they gathered round the little creature, and took from her hands what seemed to them a last mark of her love. They fell on their knees; they sobbed, and prayed, and kissed the hem of her garment;[14] and the elder ones poured forth words of endearment, mingled in prayers and blessings, after the manner of their susceptible race.[15]

As each one took their gift, Miss Ophelia, who was apprehensive for the effect of all this excitement on her little patient, signed[16] to each one to pass out of the apartment.

At last, all were gone but Tom and Mammy.

"Here, Uncle Tom," said Eva, "is a beautiful one for you. O, I am so happy, Uncle Tom, to think I shall see you in heaven,—for I'm sure I shall; and Mammy,—dear, good, kind Mammy!" she said, fondly throwing her arms round her old nurse,—"I know you'll be there, too."

"O, Miss Eva, don't see how I can live without ye, no how!" said the faithful creature. " 'Pears like it's just taking everything off the place to oncet!"[17] and Mammy gave way to a passion of grief.

Miss Ophelia pushed her and Tom gently from the apartment, and thought they were all gone; but, as she turned, Topsy was standing there.

"Where did you start up from?" she said, suddenly.

"I was here," said Topsy, wiping the tears from her eyes. "O, Miss Eva, I've been a bad girl; but won't you give *me* one, too?"

"Yes, poor Topsy! to be sure, I will. There—every time you look at that, think that I love you, and wanted you to be a good girl!"

"O, Miss Eva, I *is* tryin!" said Topsy, earnestly; "but, Lor, it's so hard to be good! 'Pears like I an't used to it, no ways!"

"Jesus knows it, Topsy; he is sorry for you; he will help you."

Topsy, with her eyes hid in her apron, was silently passed from the apartment by Miss Ophelia; but, as she went, she hid the precious curl in her bosom.

14 Stowe's word choices ("kissed the hem of her garment") emphasize the Christ-like character of Eva.

15 Although trained in the proper religious behavior at deathbeds—"prayers and blessings"—Mammy, Tom, and the other elders also tell Eva their feelings, a decidedly un-Saxon trait!

16 I.e., signaled or motioned.

17 I.e., all at once.

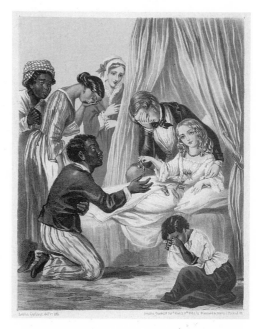

"Eva's Farewell." Color lithograph by Louisa Corbaux, 1852. In this intimate depiction, a young Tom kneels devoutly; Eva appears to be beatified.

All being gone, Miss Ophelia shut the door. That worthy lady had wiped away many tears of her own, during the scene; but concern for the consequence of such an excitement to her young charge was uppermost in her mind.

St. Clare had been sitting, during the whole time, with his hand shading his eyes, in the same attitude. When they were all gone, he sat so still.

"Papa!" said Eva, gently, laying her hand on his.

He gave a sudden start and shiver; but made no answer.

"Dear papa!" said Eva.

"I *cannot*," said St. Clare, rising, "I *cannot* have it so! The Almighty hath dealt *very bitterly* with me!" and St. Clare pronounced these words with a bitter emphasis, indeed.

"Augustine! has not God a right to do what he will with his own?" said Miss Ophelia.

"Perhaps so; but that doesn't make it any easier to bear," said he, with a dry, hard, tearless manner, as he turned away.

"Papa, you break my heart!" said Eva, rising and throwing herself into his arms; "you must not feel so!" and the child sobbed and wept with a violence which alarmed them all, and turned her father's thoughts at once to another channel.

"There, Eva,—there, dearest! Hush! hush! I was wrong; I was wicked. I will feel any way, do any way,—only don't distress yourself; don't sob so. I will be resigned; I was wicked to speak as I did."

Eva soon lay like a wearied dove[18] in her father's arms; and he, bending over her, soothed her by every tender word he could think of.

Marie rose and threw herself out[19] of the apartment into her own, when she fell into violent hysterics.

"You didn't give me a curl, Eva," said her father, smiling sadly.

"They are all yours, papa," said she, smiling,—"yours and mamma's; and you must give dear aunty as many as she wants. I only gave them to our poor people myself, because you know, papa, they might be forgotten when I am gone, and because I hoped it might help them remember. . . . . . You are a Christian, are you not, papa?" said Eva, doubtfully.

"Why do you ask me?"

"I don't know. You are so good, I don't see how you can help it."

"What is being a Christian, Eva?"

"Loving Christ most of all," said Eva.

"Do you, Eva?"

"Certainly I do."

"You never saw him," said St. Clare.

"That makes no difference," said Eva. "I believe him, and in a few days I shall *see* him;" and the young face grew fervent, radiant with joy.

St. Clare said no more. It was a feeling which he had seen before in his mother; but no chord within vibrated to it.

Eva, after this, declined rapidly; there was no more any doubt of the event; the fondest hope could not be blinded.[20] Her beautiful room was avowedly a sick room; and Miss Ophelia day and night performed the duties of a nurse,—and never did her friends appreciate her value more than in that capacity. With so well-trained a hand and eye, such perfect adroitness and practice in every art which could promote neatness and comfort, and keep out of sight every disagreeable incident of sickness,[21]—with such a perfect sense of time, such a clear, untroubled head, such exact accuracy in remembering every prescription and direction of the doctors,—she was everything to him. They who had shrugged their shoulders at her little peculiarities and setnesses,[22] so unlike the careless freedom of southern manners, acknowledged that now she was the exact person that was wanted.

Uncle Tom was much in Eva's room. The child suffered much from nervous restlessness, and it was a relief to her to be carried; and it was Tom's greatest delight to carry her little frail form in his arms, resting on a pillow, now up and down her room, now out into the verandah; and when the fresh sea-breezes blew from the lake,—and the child felt freshest in the morning,—he would sometimes walk with her under the orange-trees in the garden, or, sitting down in some of their old seats, sing to her their favorite old hymns.

Her father often did the same thing; but his frame was slighter, and when he was weary, Eva would say to him,

"O, papa, let Tom take me. Poor fellow! it pleases him; and you know it's all he can do now, and he wants to do something!"

"So do I, Eva!" said her father.

"Well, papa, you can do everything, and are everything to me. You read to me,—you sit up nights,—and Tom has only this one thing, and his singing; and I know, too, he does it easier than you can. He carries me so strong!"

The desire to do something was not confined to Tom. Every servant in the establishment showed the same feeling, and in their way did what they could.

20  Even St. Clare cannot deny the truth that Eva is dying.

21  A sign of discretion on both Ophelia and Stowe's parts: to spare, respectively, the household and the readers the graphic details of a child's dying days. Those mothers who have lost a child will already know.

22  I.e., strange and inflexible ideas.

**23** Here the slave mother is kept away even from her "adopted" child.

**24** I.e., small boat.

**25** Stowe injects a *Walden*-like appreciation of nature here.

Poor Mammy's heart yearned towards her darling; but she found no opportunity, night or day, as Marie declared that the state of her mind was such, it was impossible for her to rest; and, of course, it was against her principles to let any one else rest.**23** Twenty times in a night, Mammy would be roused to rub her feet, to bathe her head, to find her pocket-handkerchief, to see what the noise was in Eva's room, to let down a curtain because it was too light, or to put it up because it was too dark; and, in the day-time, when she longed to have some share in the nursing of her pet, Marie seemed unusually ingenious in keeping her busy anywhere and everywhere all over the house, or about her own person; so that stolen interviews and momentary glimpses were all she could obtain. "I feel it my duty to be particularly careful of myself, now," she would say, "feeble as I am, and with the whole care and nursing of that dear child upon me."

"Indeed, my dear," said St. Clare, "I thought our cousin relieved you of that."

"You talk like a man, St. Clare,—just as if a mother *could* be relieved of the care of a child in that state; but, then, it's all alike,—no one ever knows what I feel! I can't throw things off, as you do."

St. Clare smiled. You must excuse him, he couldn't help it,—for St. Clare could smile yet. For so bright and placid was the farewell voyage of the little spirit,—by such sweet and fragrant breezes was the small bark**24** borne towards the heavenly shores,—that it was impossible to realize that it was death that was approaching. The child felt no pain,—only a tranquil, soft weakness, daily and almost insensibly increasing; and she was so beautiful, so loving, so trustful, so happy, that one could not resist the sooth-ing influence of that air of innocence and peace which seemed to breathe around her. St. Clare found a strange calm coming over him. It was not hope,—that was impos-sible; it was not resignation; it was only a calm resting in the present, which seemed so beautiful that he wished to think of no future. It was like that hush of spirit which we feel amid the bright, mild woods of autumn, when the bright hectic flush is on the trees, and the last lingering flowers by the brook; and we joy in it all the more, because we know that soon it will all pass away.**25**

The friend who knew most of Eva's own imaginings and foreshadowings was her faithful bearer, Tom. To him she said what she would not disturb her father by saying. To him she imparted those mysterious intimations which the soul feels, as the cords begin to unbind, ere it leaves its clay[26] forever.

Tom, at last, would not sleep in his room, but lay all night in the outer verandah, ready to rouse at every call.

"Uncle Tom, what alive[27] have you taken to sleeping anywhere and everywhere, like a dog, for?" said Miss Ophelia. "I thought you was one of the orderly sort, that liked to lie in bed in a Christian way."

"I do, Miss Feely," said Tom, mysteriously. "I do, but now—"

"Well, what now?"

"We mustn't speak loud; Mas'r St. Clare won't hear on't; but Miss Feely, you know there must be somebody watchin' for the bridegroom."

"What do you mean, Tom?"

"You know it says in Scripture, 'At midnight there was a great cry made. Behold, the bridegroom cometh.'[28] That's what I'm spectin now, every night, Miss Feely,—and I couldn't sleep out o' hearin, no ways."

"Why, Uncle Tom, what makes you think so?"

"Miss Eva, she talks to me. The Lord, he sends his messenger in the soul. I must be thar, Miss Feely; for when that ar blessed child goes into the kingdom, they'll open the door so wide, we'll all get a look in at the glory, Miss Feely."

"Uncle Tom, did Miss Eva say she felt more unwell than usual tonight?"

"No; but she told me, this morning, she was coming nearer,—thar's them that tells it to the child, Miss Feely. It's the angels,—'it's the trumpet sound afore the break o' day,' " said Tom, quoting from a favorite hymn.[29]

This dialogue passed between Miss Ophelia and Tom, between ten and eleven, one evening, after her arrangements had all been made for the night, when, on going to bolt her outer door, she found Tom stretched along by it, in the outer verandah.

She was not nervous or impressible; but the solemn, heartfelt manner struck her. Eva had been unusually bright and cheerful, that afternoon, and had sat raised in her bed, and looked over all her little trinkets and precious things, and designated the friends to whom she would have them given; and her manner was more animated, and her voice more natural, than they had known it for weeks. Her father had been in, in the evening, and had said that Eva appeared more like her former self than ever she had done since her sickness; and when he kissed

26 I.e., the body, the soul's earthly vessel.

27 "Alive" is an expression of surprise.

28 "Then shall the kingdom of heaven be likened unto ten virgins, which took their lamps, and went forth to meet the bridegroom" (Matt. 25:1).

29 Perhaps "Steal Away to Jesus": "My Lord, He calls me, / He calls me by the thunder, / The trumpet sounds within-a my soul, I ain't got long to stay here."

**30** St. Claire sees the look of death upon Eva's face, a look apparently quite familiar to him. Oscar Wilde famously remarked that "one must have a heart of stone to read the death of Little Nell [from Charles Dickens's *The Old Curiosity Shop* (1841)] without laughing" (Hesketh Pearson, *Oscar Wilde: His Life and Wit*). Many readers have had a similar response to this scene.

her for the night, he said to Miss Ophelia,—"Cousin, we may keep her with us, after all; she is certainly better;" and he had retired with a lighter heart in his bosom than he had had there for weeks.

But at midnight,—strange, mystic hour!—when the veil between the frail present and the eternal future grows thin,—then came the messenger!

There was a sound in that chamber, first of one who stepped quickly. It was Miss Ophelia, who had resolved to sit up all night with her little charge, and who, at the turn of the night, had discerned what experienced nurses significantly call "a change." The outer door was quickly opened, and Tom, who was watching outside, was on the alert, in a moment.

"Go for the doctor, Tom! lose not a moment," said Miss Ophelia, and, stepping across the room, she rapped at St. Clare's door.

"Cousin," she said, "I wish you would come."

Those words fell on his heart like clods upon a coffin. Why did they? He was up and in the room in an instant, and bending over Eva, who still slept.

What was it he saw that made his heart stand still? Why was no word spoken between the two? Thou canst say, who hast seen that same expression on the face dearest to thee;—that look indescribable, hopeless, unmistakable, that says to thee that thy beloved is no longer thine.[30]

On the face of the child, however, there was no ghastly imprint,—only a high and almost sublime expression,—the overshadowing presence of spiritual natures, the dawning of immortal life in that childish soul.

They stood there so still, gazing upon her, that even the ticking of the watch seemed too loud. In a few moments, Tom returned, with the doctor. He entered, gave one look, and stood silent as the rest.

"When did this change take place?" said he, in a low whisper, to Miss Ophelia.

"About the turn of the night," was the reply.

Marie, roused by the entrance of the doctor, appeared, hurriedly, from the next room.

"Augustine! Cousin!—O!—what!" she hurriedly began.

"Hush!" said St. Clare, hoarsely; "*she is dying!*"

Mammy heard the words, and flew to awaken the servants. The house was soon roused,—lights were seen, footsteps heard, anxious faces thronged the verandah, and looked tearfully through the glass doors; but St. Clare heard and said nothing,—he saw only *that look* on the face of the little sleeper.

"O, if she would only wake, and speak once more!" he said; and, stooping over her, he spoke in her ear,—"Eva, darling!"

The large blue eyes unclosed,—a smile passed over her face;—she tried to raise her head, and to speak.

"Do you know me, Eva?"

"Dear papa," said the child, with a last effort, throwing her arms about his neck. In a moment they dropped again; and, as St. Clare raised his head, he saw a spasm of mortal agony pass over the face,—she struggled for breath, and threw up her little hands.

"O, God, this is dreadful!" he said, turning away in agony, and wringing Tom's hand, scarce conscious what he was doing. "O, Tom, my boy, it is killing me!"

Tom had his master's hands between his own; and, with tears streaming down his dark cheeks, looked up for help where he had always been used to look.

"Pray that this may be cut short!" said St. Clare,—"this wrings my heart."

"O, bless the Lord! it's over,—it's over, dear Master!" said Tom; "look at her."

A blackface Topsy and graying Tom bend over a Gibson Girl Eva in this Duncan Sisters production.

While Stowe did not describe angels, many of her readers would have imagined them throughout her text.

In this Miguel Covarrubias illustration, Tom prays as Eva's spirit ascends to heaven. St. Clare sobs.
From *Uncle Tom's Cabin: or, Life Among the Lowly*, Heritage Press edition, 1938

The child lay panting on her pillows, as one exhausted,—the large clear eyes rolled up and fixed. Ah, what said those eyes, that spoke so much of heaven? Earth was past, and earthly pain; but so solemn, so mysterious, was the triumphant brightness of that face, that it checked even the sobs of sorrow. They pressed around her, in breathless stillness.

"Eva," said St. Clare, gently.

She did not hear.

"O, Eva, tell us what you see! What is it?" said her father.

A bright, a glorious smile passed over her face, and she said, brokenly,—"O! love,—joy,—peace!" gave one sigh, and passed from death unto life!

"Farewell, beloved child! the bright, eternal doors have closed after thee; we shall see thy sweet face no more. O, woe for them who watched thy entrance into heaven, when they shall wake and find only the cold gray sky of daily life, and thou gone forever!"

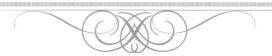

## CHAPTER 27

*"This Is the Last of Earth."*

*—John Q. Adams*[1]

The statuettes and pictures in Eva's room were shrouded in white napkins, and only hushed breathings and muffled foot-falls were heard there, and the light stole in solemnly through windows partially darkened by closed blinds.[2]

The bed was draped in white; and there, beneath the drooping angel-figure, lay a little sleeping form,—sleeping never to waken!

There she lay, robed in one of the simple white dresses she had been wont to wear when living; the rose-colored light through the curtains cast over the icy coldness of death a warm glow. The heavy eyelashes drooped softly on the pure cheek; the head was turned a little to one side, as if in natural sleep, but there was diffused over every lineament of the face that high celestial expression, that mingling of rapture and repose, which showed it was no earthly or temporary sleep, but the long, sacred rest which "He giveth to his beloved."

There is no death to such as thou, dear Eva! neither darkness nor shadow of death; only such a bright fading as when the morning star fades in the golden dawn. Thine is the victory without the battle,—the crown without the conflict.

So did St. Clare think, as, with folded arms, he stood there gazing. Ah! who shall say what he did think? for, from the hour that voices had said, in the dying chamber, "she is gone," it had been all a dreary mist, a heavy "dim-

John Quincy Adams, sixth U.S. president (1825–29) and member of Congress (1803–8 and 1831–48). Adams was from Massachusetts, which, like Ohio, was a vanguard state in the battle against slavery. Few American presidents have ever had as remarkable a post–White House career as Adams.

1 "This is the last of Earth! I am content," were the final words of John Quincy Adams, uttered on February 21, 1848. The sixth president of the United States (1825–1829) after serving in the Senate and as secretary of state to President James Monroe, Adams returned to Congress in 1831, serving until his death in 1848. Although he had not been especially energetic opposing slavery as president, Adams earned the nickname "Old Man Eloquent" during his congressional career for his passionate antislavery speeches. He became especially beloved by antislavery advocates when he argued before the United States Supreme Court in 1841 in support of a group of Africans captured aboard the schooner *Amistad* and imprisoned in New London, Connecticut. (Steven Spielberg's powerful 1997 film *Amistad* features Anthony Hopkins as Adams.) Frederick Douglass's warm tribute to John Quincy Adams in the *North Star* on March 10, 1848, offers evidence of the former president's stature:

> The recent decease of this venerable statesman, scholar and patriot, has called forth one general voice of mourning throughout our widely-extended country. The press teems with brilliant eulogies of his character, and legislative halls reverberate with eloquent expressions of honor for his memory. Each incident of his long and eventful life, is seized upon with avidity, and every effort is made to magnify and extend his fame. This feeling of respect and veneration, is not felt entirely by white persons, but is shared, to a considerable degree, by the oppressed and despised colored people. They remember, with characteristic gratitude, the heroic conduct of the deceased, in defending the sacred right of petition; his mighty exposures of the slave power, and its aggressions on the rights of the North; the glorious victory achieved over the slave oligarchy in Congress, with the infamous mobocrat, Thomas Marshall [representative from Kentucky] at its head; his unwearied exertions against the annexation of Texas; and they can never forget his grand effort in behalf of the *Amistad* captives. These facts in the history of this great man, made him loved and venerated by the oppressed while living, and

ness of anguish." He had heard voices around him; he had had questions asked, and answered them; they had asked him when he would have the funeral, and where they should lay her; and he had answered, impatiently, that he cared not.

Adolph and Rosa had arranged the chamber; volatile, fickle and childish, as they generally were, they were softhearted and full of feeling; and, while Miss Ophelia presided over the general details of order and neatness, it was their hands that added those soft, poetic touches to the arrangements, that took from the death-room the grim and ghastly air which too often marks a New England funeral.

There were still flowers on the shelves,—all white, delicate and fragrant, with graceful, drooping leaves. Eva's little table, covered with white, bore on it her favorite vase, with a single white moss rose-bud in it. The folds of the drapery, the fall of the curtains, had been arranged and rearranged, by Adolph and Rosa, with that nicety of eye which characterizes their race. Even now, while St. Clare stood there thinking, little Rosa tripped softly into the chamber with a basket of white flowers. She stepped back when she saw St. Clare, and stopped respectfully; but, seeing that he did not observe her, she came forward to place them around the dead. St. Clare saw her as in a dream, while she placed in the small hands a fair cape jessamine, and, with admirable taste, disposed other flowers around the couch.

The door opened again, and Topsy, her eyes swelled with crying, appeared, holding something under her apron. Rosa made a quick, forbidding gesture; but she took a step into the room.

"You must go out," said Rosa, in a sharp, positive whisper; "*you* haven't any business here!"

"O, do let me! I brought a flower,—such a pretty one!" said Topsy, holding up a half-blown tea rose-bud. "Do let me put just one there."

"Get along!" said Rosa, more decidedly.

"Let her stay!" said St. Clare, suddenly stamping his foot. "She shall come."

Rosa suddenly retreated, and Topsy came forward and laid her offering at the feet of the corpse; then suddenly, with a wild and bitter cry, she threw herself on the floor alongside the bed, and wept, and moaned aloud.

Miss Ophelia hastened into the room, and tried to raise and silence her; but in vain.

"O, Miss Eva! oh, Miss Eva! I wish I's dead, too,—I do!"

There was a piercing wildness in the cry; the blood flushed into St. Clare's white, marble-like face, and the first tears he had shed since Eva died stood in his eyes.[3]

"Get up, child," said Miss Ophelia, in a softened voice; "don't cry so. Miss Eva is gone to heaven; she is an angel."

"But I can't see her!" said Topsy. "I never shall see her!" and she sobbed again.

They all stood a moment in silence.

"*She* said she *loved* me," said Topsy,—"she did! O, dear! oh, dear! there an't *nobody* left now,—there an't!"

"That's true enough," said St. Clare; "but do," he said to Miss Ophelia, "see if you can't comfort the poor creature."

"I jist wish I hadn't never been born," said Topsy. "I didn't want to be born, no ways; and I don't see no use on't."

Miss Ophelia raised her gently, but firmly, and took her from the room; but, as she did so, some tears fell from her eyes.

"Topsy, you poor child," she said, as she led her into her room, "don't give up! *I* can love you, though I am not like that dear little child. I hope I've learnt something of the love of Christ from her. I can love you; I do, and I'll try to help you to grow up a good Christian girl."

Miss Ophelia's voice was more than her words, and more than that were the honest tears that fell down her face. From that hour, she acquired an influence over the mind of the destitute child that she never lost.

"O, my Eva, whose little hour on earth did so much of good," thought St. Clare, "what account have I to give for my long years?"

There were, for a while, soft whisperings and foot-falls in the chamber, as one after another stole in, to look at the dead; and then came the little coffin; and then there was a funeral, and carriages drove to the door, and strangers came and were seated; and there were white scarfs and ribbons, and crape bands, and mourners dressed in black crape; and there were words read from the Bible, and prayers offered; and St. Clare lived, and walked, and moved, as one who has shed every tear;—to the last he saw only one thing, that golden head in the coffin; but then he saw the cloth spread over it, the lid of the coffin closed; and he walked, when he was put beside the others, down to a little place at the bottom of the garden, and there, by the mossy seat where she and Tom had talked, and sung, and read so often, was the little grave. St. Clare stood beside it,—looked vacantly down; he saw them lower the little coffin; he heard, dimly, the solemn words, "I am the resurrection and the Life; he that believeth in me, though

lead them to cherish and honor his memory, now that he is dead.

We give in another column of this week's paper, the proceedings of a meeting of our colored friends and fellow-citizens, at Buffalo, in honor of the illustrious departed, as evincing the feelings of the oppressed in this country with respect to his worth. ("John Quincy Adams")

Despite Adams's beloved status among abolitionists, we must note that this is a curious chapter title/epigraph. Stowe seems to be indicating, somewhat sadly, the distance between what one has accomplished and what needs yet to be accomplished. Even after a lifetime of service to the United States of America, could Adams really be "content" with the state of slavery, even upon his deathbed? In fact, historian Paul Nagel states that some of those gathered by Adams's side at his death report that he said "composed," not "content." As Nagel writes, "Both dying assertions were widely repeated, although the second seems more likely correct. In all his life, Adams was never content" (*John Quincy Adams: A Public Life, A Private Life*).

2 Throughout this chapter, Stowe describes common nineteenth-century white Christian funeral practices, some of which survive into our own time in changed form. All decorations and mirrors were removed or covered in the deathbed room. The dead body was dressed, laid out in her bed now decorated as a funeral bed. Heavy-scented flowers were placed around the room and over the body, and were constantly refreshed (to hide the smell of decay in the unembalmed body). The wake and funeral took place in this room; the body was moved for the funeral to a coffin still in the room. Religious services took place at graveside, and mourners stayed to watch the grave filled in. African-American funeral practices were markedly different, influenced by Christian practices, African customs, and the exigencies of slavery. Often slaves were buried with the last item they used before they died, or with speaking tubes and mirrors to communicate between the world of the dead and the living.

3 Stowe's novel does not attend to differences between slave and white funeral prac-

tices. However, Stowe suggests there may be some differences, such as when she shows Topsy breaking the strict and formal mourning ritual with her wild laments. Topsy's outburst breaks the wall of silence and allows St. Clare to mourn outwardly.

4 Stowe deftly finds a way to thwart any sympathizing for Marie, who, though selfish, is a mother who has just lost a child. By jumping quickly away from Marie's sobs to the ironic assertion that her servants "really thought that Missis was the principal sufferer in the case," Stowe gently suggests that for once we should ignore the mother's pain.

5 I.e., rubbing or massaging to help blood circulation. Stowe continues her effort to keep our focus off the mother by offering another Dickensian moment of universalizing humor, with the flood of participles ("running," "scampering," "chafing," "fussing") suggesting that everywhere there are people as selfish as Marie, and everywhere their servants will suffer.

6 "Weed" is the term for the black cloth (usually crepe) band worn on a hat or arm to signify that one is in mourning. "Widow's weeds" refers to the black clothing worn by a woman whose husband has died. The weed signals to the larger community that one has experienced a death in the family.

7 I.e., odd or unusual. Marie means this critically, but Marie's criticisms of her husband are typically cloaked in ambiguity. This wifely reticence in part reflects Stowe's complex understanding of communication between husband and wife, but it also reveals Stowe's skill in investing small interactions with larger meaning.

he were dead, yet shall he live;" and, as the earth was cast in and filled up the little grave, he could not realize that it was his Eva that they were hiding from his sight.

Nor was it!—not Eva, but only the frail seed of that bright, immortal form with which she shall yet come forth, in the day of the Lord Jesus!

And then all were gone, and the mourners went back to the place which should know her no more; and Marie's room was darkened, and she lay on the bed, sobbing and moaning in uncontrollable grief, and calling every moment for the attentions of all her servants. Of course, they had no time to cry,—why should they? the grief was *her* grief, and she was fully convinced that nobody on earth did, could, or would feel it as she did.

"St. Clare did not shed a tear," she said; "he didn't sympathize with her; it was perfectly wonderful to think how hard-hearted and unfeeling he was, when he must know how she suffered."

So much are people the slave of their eye and ear, that many of the servants really thought that Missis was the principal sufferer in the case,[4] especially as Marie began to have hysterical spasms, and sent for the doctor, and at last declared herself dying; and, in the running and scampering, and bringing up hot bottles, and heating of flannels, and chafing,[5] and fussing, that ensued, there was quite a diversion.

Tom, however, had a feeling at his own heart, that drew him to his master. He followed him wherever he walked, wistfully and sadly; and when he saw him sitting, so pale and quiet, in Eva's room, holding before his eyes her little open Bible, though seeing no letter or word of what was in it, there was more sorrow to Tom in that still, fixed, tearless eye, than in all Marie's moans and lamentations.

In a few days the St. Clare family were back again in the city; Augustine, with the restlessness of grief, longing for another scene, to change the current of his thoughts. So they left the house and garden, with its little grave, and came back to New Orleans; and St. Clare walked the streets busily, and strove to fill up the chasm in his heart with hurry and bustle, and change of place; and people who saw him in the street, or met him at the café, knew of his loss only by the weed[6] on his hat; for there he was, smiling and talking, and reading the newspaper, and speculating on politics, and attending to business matters; and who could see that all this smiling outside was but a hollow shell over a heart that was a dark and silent sepulchre?

"Mr. St. Clare is a singular[7] man," said Marie to Miss

Ophelia, in a complaining tone. "I used to think, if there was anything in the world he did love, it was our dear little Eva; but he seems to be forgetting her very easily. I cannot ever get him to talk about her. I really did think he would show more feeling!"

"Still waters run deepest, they used to tell me," said Miss Ophelia, oracularly.

"O, I don't believe in such things; it's all talk. If people have feeling, they will show it,—they can't help it; but, then, it's a great misfortune to have feeling. I'd rather have been made like St. Clare. My feelings prey upon me so!"

"Sure, Missis, Mas'r St. Clare is gettin' thin as a shader. They say, he don't never eat nothin'," said Mammy. "I know he don't forget Miss Eva; I know there couldn't nobody,—dear, little, blessed cretur!" she added, wiping her eyes.

"Well, at all events, he has no consideration for me," said Marie; "he hasn't spoken one word of sympathy, and he must know how much more a mother feels than any man can."

"The heart knoweth its own bitterness," said Miss Ophelia, gravely.[8]

"That's just what I think. I know just what I feel,—nobody else seems to. Eva used to, but she is gone!" and Marie lay back on her lounge, and began to sob disconsolately.

Marie was one of those unfortunately constituted mortals, in whose eyes whatever is lost and gone assumes a value which it never had in possession. Whatever she had, she seemed to survey only to pick flaws in it; but, once fairly away, there was no end to her valuation of it.

While this conversation was taking place in the parlor, another was going on in St. Clare's library.

Tom, who was always uneasily following his master about, had seen him go to his library, some hours before; and, after vainly waiting for him to come out, determined, at last, to make an errand in. He entered softly. St. Clare lay on his lounge, at the further end of the room. He was lying on his face, with Eva's Bible open before him, at a little distance. Tom walked up, and stood by the sofa. He hesitated; and, while he was hesitating, St. Clare suddenly raised himself up. The honest face, so full of grief, and with such an imploring expression of affection and sympathy, struck his master. He laid his hand on Tom's, and bowed down his forehead on it.

"O, Tom, my boy, the whole world is as empty as an eggshell."

8 Prov. 14:10: "The heart knows its own bitterness, and no stranger shares its joy. The house of the wicked will be destroyed, but the tent of the upright will flourish." With this subtle allusion to the destruction of the Big House and the flourishing of more modest dwellings, Stowe, through Ophelia, reminds us that the central character in this story is Tom. The quote also contains the hint of St. Clare's passing.

9 Tom is in a strange position vis-à-vis his master: Tom is comforter, teacher, and guide. In quick succession he quotes Matt. 11:25, Mark 9:23–24, and Eph. 3:19. Tom's lament about being sold away from his old woman and children is the only thing that prevents later readers from recalling Huckleberry Finn's synopsis of John Bunyan's *The Pilgrim's Progress*: "about a man that left his family, it didn't say why" (chapter 17; Mark Twain's *Huckleberry Finn* was published in 1884).

"I know it, Mas'r,—I know it," said Tom; "but, oh, if Mas'r could only look up,—up where our dear Miss Eva is,—up to the dear Lord Jesus!"

"Ah, Tom! I do look up; but the trouble is, I don't see anything, when I do. I wish I could."

Tom sighed heavily.

"It seems to be given to children, and poor, honest fellows, like you, to see what we can't," said St. Clare. "How comes it?"

"Thou hast 'hid from the wise and prudent, and revealed unto babes,' " murmured Tom; " 'even so, Father, for so it seemed good in thy sight.' "9

"Tom, I don't believe,—I can't believe,—I've got the habit of doubting," said St. Clare. "I want to believe this Bible,—and I can't."

"Dear Mas'r, pray to the good Lord,—'Lord, I believe; help thou my unbelief.' "

"Who knows anything about anything?" said St. Clare, his eyes wandering dreamily, and speaking to himself. "Was all that beautiful love and faith only one of the ever-shifting phases of human feeling, having nothing real to rest on, passing away with the little breath? And is there no more Eva,—no heaven,—no Christ,—nothing?"

"O, dear Mas'r, there is! I know it; I'm sure of it," said Tom, falling on his knees. "Do, do, dear Mas'r, believe it!"

"How do you know there's any Christ, Tom? You never saw the Lord."

"Felt Him in my soul, Mas'r,—feel Him now! O, Mas'r, when I was sold away from my old woman and the children, I was jest a most broke up. I felt as if there warn't nothin' left; and then the good Lord, he stood by me, and he says, 'Fear not, Tom;' and he brings light and joy into a poor feller's soul,—makes all peace; and I's so happy, and loves everybody, and feels willin' jest to be the Lord's, and have the Lord's will done, and be put jest where the Lord wants to put me. I know it couldn't come from me, cause I's a poor, complainin' cretur; it comes from the Lord; and I know He's willin' to do for Mas'r."

Tom spoke with fast-running tears and choking voice. St. Clare leaned his head on his shoulder, and wrung the hard, faithful, black hand.

"Tom, you love me," he said.

"I's willin' to lay down my life, this blessed day, to see Mas'r a Christian."

"Poor, foolish boy!" said St. Clare, half-raising himself. "I'm not worth the love of one good, honest heart, like yours."

"O, Mas'r, dere's more than me loves you,—the blessed Lord Jesus loves you."

"How do you know that, Tom?" said St. Clare.

"Feels it in my soul. O, Mas'r! 'the love of Christ, that passeth knowledge.' "[10]

"Singular!" said St. Clare, turning away, "that the story of a man that lived and died eighteen hundred years ago can affect people so yet. But he was no man," he added, suddenly. "No man ever had such long and living power! O, that I could believe what my mother taught me, and pray as I did when I was a boy!"

"If Mas'r pleases," said Tom, "Miss Eva used to read this so beautifully. I wish Mas'r'd be so good as read it. Don't get no readin', hardly, now Miss Eva's gone."

The chapter was the eleventh of John,—the touching account of the raising of Lazarus. St. Clare read it aloud, often pausing to wrestle down feelings which were roused by the pathos of the story. Tom knelt before him, with clasped hands, and with an absorbed expression of love, trust, adoration, on his quiet face.

"Tom," said his Master, "this is all *real* to you!"

"I can jest fairly *see* it, Mas'r," said Tom.

"I wish I had your eyes, Tom."

"I wish, to the dear Lord, Mas'r had!"

"But, Tom, you know that I have a great deal more knowledge than you; what if I should tell you that I don't believe this Bible?"

"O, Mas'r!" said Tom, holding up his hands, with a deprecating gesture.

"Wouldn't it shake your faith some, Tom?"

"Not a grain," said Tom.

"Why, Tom, you must know I know the most."

"O, Mas'r, haven't you jest read how he hides from the wise and prudent, and reveals unto babes? But Mas'r wasn't in earnest, for sartin, now?" said Tom, anxiously.

"No, Tom, I was not. I don't disbelieve, and I think there is reason to believe; and still I don't. It's a troublesome bad habit I've got, Tom."

"If Mas'r would only pray!"

"How do you know I don't, Tom?"

"Does Mas'r?"

"I would, Tom, if there was anybody there when I pray; but it's all speaking unto nothing, when I do. But come, Tom, you pray, now, and show me how."

Tom's heart was full; he poured it out in prayer, like waters that have been long suppressed. One thing was plain enough; Tom thought there was somebody to hear,

10 See Phil. 4:7: "The peace of God, which passeth all understanding, shall keep your hearts and minds through Jesus Christ."

whether there were or not. In fact, St. Clare felt himself borne, on the tide of his faith and feeling, almost to the gates of that heaven he seemed so vividly to conceive. It seemed to bring him nearer to Eva.

"Thank you, my boy," said St. Clare, when Tom rose. "I like to hear you, Tom; but go, now, and leave me alone; some other time, I'll talk more."

Tom silently left the room.

# CHAPTER 28

## *Reunion*

Week after week glided away in the St. Clare mansion, and the waves of life settled back to their usual flow, where that little bark had gone down. For how imperiously, how coolly, in disregard of all one's feeling, does the hard, cold, uninteresting course of daily realities move on! Still must we eat, and drink, and sleep, and wake again,—still bargain, buy, sell, ask and answer questions,—pursue, in short, a thousand shadows, though all interest in them be over; the cold mechanical habit of living remaining, after all vital interest in it has fled.

All the interests and hopes of St. Clare's life had unconsciously wound themselves around this child. It was for Eva that he had managed his property; it was for Eva that he had planned the disposal of his time; and, to do this and that for Eva,—to buy, improve, alter, and arrange, or dispose something[1] for her,—had been so long his habit, that now she was gone, there seemed nothing to be thought of, and nothing to be done.

True, there was another life,—a life which, once believed in, stands as a solemn, significant figure before the otherwise unmeaning ciphers of time, changing them to orders of mysterious, untold value. St. Clare knew this well; and often, in many a weary hour, he heard that slender, childish voice calling him to the skies, and saw that little hand pointing to him the way of life; but a heavy lethargy of sorrow lay on him,—he could not arise. He had one of those natures which could better and more

1 I.e., prepare something. Poor St. Clare has sunk into a selfish torpor that is oddly worse than that of his wife, Marie. Stowe's blithe inclusion of the loaded term "property" serves as a subtle reminder that St. Clare has not done a very admirable job "managing his property" according to Eva's wishes. The reader knows that St. Clare's most important piece of property, Tom, for too long (fourteen chapters!) the understudy savior, will now do his best to help St. Clare.

2 The poets Thomas Moore (1779–1852) and Lord Byron (1788–1824), and the German Romantic Johann Wolfgang von Goethe (1749–1832), all celebrated human individualism and higher spiritual understanding. In 1833 Moore published a satirical poem, "Epistle of Condolence from a Slave-Lord to a Cotton-Lord," comparing factories employing children to Southern plantations, in the face of British outrage against both forms of exploitation:

> Alas! my dear friend, what a state of
>   affairs!
> How unjustly we both are despoil'd of
>   our rights!
> Not a pound of black flesh shall I leave
>   to my heirs,
> Nor must you any more work to death lit-
>   tle whites.
>
> Both forced to submit to that general
>   controller
> Of King, Lords, and cotton-mills—
>   Public Opinion;
> No more shall you beat with a big billy-
>   roller,
> Nor I with the cart-whip assert my
>   dominion.
>
> Whereas, were we suffered to do as we
>   please
> With our Blacks and our Whites, as of
>   yore we were let,
> We might range them alternate, like
>   harpsichord keys,
> And between us thump out a good
>   piebald duet.
>
> But this fun is all over;—farewell to the
>   zest
> Which Slavery now lends to each cup we
>   sip;
> Which makes still the cruellest coffee
>   the best,
> And that sugar the sweetest which
>   smacks of the whip.
>
> Farewell, too, the Factory's white pick-
>   aninnies,
> Small, living machines, which, if flogg'd
>   to their tasks,
> Mix so well with their namesakes, the
>   billies and jennies,
> That which have got souls in 'em nobody
>   asks;

clearly conceive of religious things from its own perceptions and instincts, than many a matter-of-fact and practical Christian. The gift to appreciate and the sense to feel the finer shades and relations of moral things, often seems an attribute of those whose whole life shows a careless disregard of them. Hence Moore, Byron, Goethe,2 often speak words more wisely descriptive of the true religious sentiment, than another man, whose whole life is governed by it. In such minds, disregard of religion is a more fearful treason,—a more deadly sin.

St. Clare had never pretended to govern himself by any religious obligation; and a certain fineness of nature gave him such an instinctive view of the extent of the requirements of Christianity, that he shrank, by anticipation, from what he felt would be the exactions of his own conscience, if he once did resolve to assume them. For, so inconsistent is human nature, especially in the ideal, that not to undertake a thing at all seems better than to undertake and come short.

Still St. Clare was, in many respects, another man. He read his little Eva's Bible seriously and honestly; he thought more soberly and practically of his relations to his servants,—enough to make him extremely dissatisfied with both his past and present course; and one thing he did, soon after his return to New Orleans, and that was to commence the legal steps necessary to Tom's emancipation, which was to be perfected as soon as he could get through the necessary formalities.3 Meantime, he attached himself to Tom more and more, every day. In all the wide world, there was nothing that seemed to remind him so much of Eva; and he would insist on keeping him constantly about him, and, fastidious and unapproachable as he was with regard to his deeper feelings, he almost thought aloud to Tom. Nor would any one have wondered at it, who had seen the expression of affection and devotion with which Tom continually followed his young master.

"Well, Tom," said St. Clare, the day after he had commenced the legal formalities for his enfranchisement, "I'm going to make a free man of you;—so, have your trunk packed, and get ready to set out for Kentuck. "

The sudden light of joy that shone in Tom's face as he raised his hands to heaven, his emphatic "Bless the Lord!" rather discomposed St. Clare; he did not like it that Tom should be so ready to leave him.

"You haven't had such very bad times here, that you need be in such a rapture, Tom," he said, drily.4

"No, no, Mas'r! 'tan't that,—it's bein' a *free man*! That's what I'm joyin' for."

"Why, Tom, don't you think, for your own part, you've been better off than to be free?"

"*No, indeed,* Mas'r St. Clare," said Tom, with a flash of energy. "No, indeed!"

"Why, Tom, you couldn't possibly have earned, by your work, such clothes and such living as I have given you."

"Knows all that, Mas'r St. Clare; Mas'r's been too good; but, Mas'r, I'd rather have poor clothes, poor house, poor everything, and have 'em *mine,* than have the best, and have 'em any man's else,—I had *so,* Mas'r; I think it's natur Mas'r."

"I suppose so, Tom, and you'll be going off and leaving me, in a month or so," he added, rather discontentedly. "Though why you shouldn't, no mortal knows," he said, in a gayer tone; and, getting up, he began to walk the floor.

"Not while Mas'r is in trouble," said Tom. "I'll stay with Mas'r as long as he wants me,—so as I can be any use."

"Not while I'm in trouble, Tom?" said St. Clare, looking sadly out of the window. . . . . . ."And when will *my* trouble be over?"

"When Mas'r St. Clare's a Christian," said Tom.

"And you really mean to stay by till that day comes?" said St. Clare, half smiling, as he turned from the window, and laid his hand on Tom's shoulder. "Ah, Tom, you soft, silly boy! I won't keep you till that day. Go home to your wife and children, and give my love to all."

"I's faith to believe that day will come," said Tom, earnestly, and with tears in his eyes; "the Lord has a work for Mas'r."

"A work, hey?" said St. Clare; "well, now, Tom, give me your views on what sort of a work it is;—let's hear."

"Why, even a poor fellow like me has a work from the Lord; and Mas'r St. Clare, that has larnin,[5] and riches, and friends,—how much he might do for the Lord!"

"Tom, you seem to think the Lord needs a great deal done for him," said St. Clare, smiling.

"We does for the Lord when we does for his critturs," said Tom.

"Good theology, Tom; better than Dr. B. preaches, I dare swear," said St. Clare.

The conversation was here interrupted by the announcement of some visitors.

Marie St. Clare felt the loss of Eva as deeply as she could feel anything; and, as she was a woman that had a

Little Maids of the Mill, who, themselves but ill fed,
Are oblig'd, 'mong their other benevo-
      lent cares,
To keep "feeding the scribblers,"*—and
      better, 'tis said,
Than old Blackwood or Fraser have ever
      fed theirs.

All this is now o'er, and so dismal *my* loss
      is,
So hard 'tis to part from the smack of the
      thong,
That I mean (from pure love for the old
      whipping process)
To take to whipt syllabub all my life long.

* Child workers

3 With this diction of bureaucratic delay, Stowe reminds her readers that freeing slaves is not a simple and easy task in the contemporary legal environment.

4 St. Clare's pain at Tom's readiness to leave him (to return to his wife and children) recalls Circe's anger at Odysseus's desire to return to Penelope. St. Clare's discomfort and priggish diction ("such very bad times") provide evidence that he too suffers under the system of slavery. We may understand the emotions underneath St. Clare's sarcasm, but Stowe challenges us to reject any sympathy.

5 I.e., education ("learning"). Stowe is very careful in her depiction of Tom to limit his dropped consonants and poor grammar to moments when he is not quoting scripture. When he does quote biblical passages, he quotes them almost verbatim. Stowe does not explain this discrepancy.

**6** The reader feels the unfairness of Marie's treatment of Mammy, all the more painful in the context of being reminded of Mammy's own children, from whom she is separated.

**7** I.e., impudence ("sauce"). In the many scenes between Topsy and the other servants, Stowe distinguishes between perceived malevolence (Topsy's mischievousness) and real malevolence (Rosa's lack of fellow-feeling for Topsy). The shock elicited by the sudden appearance of Eva's curl foreshadows Legree's startled reaction in chapter 35.

great faculty of making everybody unhappy when she was, her immediate attendants had still stronger reason to regret the loss of their young mistress, whose winning ways and gentle intercessions had so often been a shield to them from the tyrannical and selfish exactions of her mother. Poor old Mammy, in particular, whose heart, severed from all natural domestic ties, had consoled itself with this one beautiful being, was almost heart-broken. She cried day and night, and was, from excess of sorrow, less skilful and alert in her ministrations on her mistress than usual, which drew down a constant storm of invectives on her defenceless head.**6**

Miss Ophelia felt the loss; but, in her good and honest heart, it bore fruit unto everlasting life. She was more softened, more gentle; and, though equally assiduous in every duty, it was with a chastened and quiet air, as one who communed with her own heart not in vain. She was more diligent in teaching Topsy,—taught her mainly from the Bible,—did not any longer shrink from her touch, or manifest an ill-repressed disgust, because she felt none. She viewed her now through the softened medium that Eva's hand had first held before her eyes, and saw in her only an immortal creature, whom God had sent to be led by her to glory and virtue. Topsy did not become at once a saint; but the life and death of Eva did work a marked change in her. The callous indifference was gone; there was now sensibility, hope, desire, and the striving for good,—a strife irregular, interrupted, suspended oft, but yet renewed again.

One day, when Topsy had been sent for by Miss Ophelia, she came, hastily thrusting something into her bosom.

"What are you doing there, you limb? You've been stealing something, I'll be bound," said the imperious little Rosa, who had been sent to call her, seizing her, at the same time, roughly by the arm.

"You go 'long, Miss Rosa!" said Topsy, pulling from her; " 'tan't none o' your business!"

"None o' your sa'ce!"**7** said Rosa. "I saw you hiding something,—I know yer tricks," and Rosa seized her arm, and tried to force her hand into her bosom, while Topsy, enraged, kicked and fought valiantly for what she considered her rights. The clamor and confusion of the battle drew Miss Ophelia and St. Clare both to the spot.

"She's been stealing!" said Rosa.

"I han't, neither!" vociferated Topsy, sobbing with passion.

"Give me that, whatever it is!" said Miss Ophelia, firmly.

Topsy hesitated; but, on a second order, pulled out of her bosom a little parcel done up in the foot of one of her own old stockings.

Miss Ophelia turned it out. There was a small book, which had been given to Topsy by Eva, containing a single verse of Scripture, arranged for every day in the year, and in a paper the curl of hair that she had given her on that memorable day when she had taken her last farewell.

St. Clare was a good deal affected at the sight of it; the little book had been rolled in a long strip of black crape, torn from the funeral weeds.

"What did you wrap *this* round the book for?" said St. Clare, holding up the crape.

"Cause,—cause,—cause 'twas Miss Eva. O, don't take 'em away, please!" she said; and, sitting flat down on the floor, and putting her apron over her head, she began to sob vehemently.

It was a curious mixture of the pathetic and the ludicrous,—the little old stocking,—black crape,—text-book,—fair soft curl,—and Topsy's utter distress.

St. Clare smiled; but there were tears in his eyes, as he said,

"Come, come,—don't cry; you shall have them!" and, putting them together, he threw them into her lap, and drew Miss Ophelia with him into the parlor.

"I really think you can make something of that concern," he said, pointing with his thumb backward over his shoulder. "Any mind that is capable of a *real sorrow* is capable of good. You must try and do something with her."

"The child has improved greatly," said Miss Ophelia. "I have great hopes of her; but, Augustine," she said, laying her hand on his arm, "one thing I want to ask; whose is this child to be?—yours or mine?"

"Why, I gave her to *you*," said Augustine.

"But not legally;—I want her to be mine legally," said Miss Ophelia.

"Whew! cousin," said Augustine. "What will the Abolition Society think? They'll have a day of fasting appointed for this backsliding, if you become a slave-holder!"

"O, nonsense! I want her mine, that I may have a right to take her to the free States, and give her her liberty, that all I am trying to do be not undone."

"O, cousin, what an awful 'doing evil that good may come'![8] I can't encourage it."

"I don't want you to joke, but to reason," said Miss Ophelia. "There is no use in my trying to make this child a Christian child, unless I save her from all the chances

8 See Shakespeare's *The Life of Henry the Fifth*, 4.1.4: "There is some soul of goodness in things evil, / Would men observingly distill it out."

9 With this reference to St. Clare's "class of mind," Stowe again contrasts Southern diffidence to Northern action, embodied by Ophelia. Action, obviously, is preferable, as events will show.

10 We can perhaps consider this to be another illusion to Shakespeare's *The Merchant of Venice*, in which Shylock demands a pound of flesh as the default interest on a loan. If so, the allusion is rather ironic in that Ophelia here wishes to "buy" several pounds of flesh in the person of Topsy.

11 St. Clare concedes Ophelia's point that the possession of life is only God's, but he reminds her that, even though they may dismiss it as fiction, the law is a reality that cannot be ignored. How are we to read the fact that poor Ophelia has broken her own moral code in order to protect the unprotected? How are we to read the fact that her request, however unseemly, *worked*? St. Clare dashes off a "deed of gift" that saves Topsy from the auction block. How are we to read his next comment: "There, isn't that black and white, now, Miss Vermont?" Or, the line a few moments later: "she's yours by a fiction of law, then"? All of the philosophical discussions between St. Clare and Ophelia in this middle part of the novel have been leading up to this exchange—by which is meant both the present debate and the "gifting" of Topsy. However, although this episode is crucial, illustrators have taken little notice.

and reverses of slavery; and, if you really are willing I should have her, I want you to give me a deed of gift, or some legal paper."

"Well, well," said St. Clare, "I will;" and he sat down, and unfolded a newspaper to read.

"But I want it done now," said Miss Ophelia.

"What's your hurry?"

"Because now is the only time there ever is to do a thing in," said Miss Ophelia. "Come, now, here's paper, pen, and ink; just write a paper."

St. Clare, like most men of his class of mind, cordially hated the present tense of action, generally; and, therefore, he was considerably annoyed by Miss Ophelia's downrightness.[9]

"Why, what's the matter?" said he. "Can't you take my word? One would think you had taken lessons of the Jews,[10] coming at a fellow so!"

"I want to make sure of it," said Miss Ophelia. "You may die, or fail, and then Topsy be hustled off to auction, spite of all I can do."

"Really, you are quite provident. Well, seeing I'm in the hands of a Yankee, there is nothing for it but to concede;" and St. Clare rapidly wrote off a deed of gift, which, as he was well versed in the forms of law, he could easily do, and signed his name to it in sprawling capitals, concluding by a tremendous flourish.

"There, isn't that black and white, now, Miss Vermont?" he said, as he handed it to her.

"Good boy," said Miss Ophelia, smiling. "But must it not be witnessed?"

"O, bother!—yes. Here," he said, opening the door into Marie's apartment, "Marie, Cousin wants your autograph; just put your name down here."

"What's this?" said Marie, as she ran over the paper. "Ridiculous! I thought Cousin was too pious for such horrid things," she added, as she carelessly wrote her name, "but, if she has a fancy for that article, I am sure she's welcome."

"There, now, she's yours, body and soul," said St. Clare, handing the paper.

"No more mine now than she was before," said Miss Ophelia. "Nobody but God has a right to give her to me; but I can protect her now."

"Well, she's yours by a fiction of law, then," said St. Clare, as he turned back into the parlor, and sat down to his paper.[11]

Miss Ophelia, who seldom sat much in Marie's company, followed him into the parlor, having first carefully laid away the paper.

"Augustine," she said, suddenly, as she sat knitting, "have you ever made any provision for your servants, in case of your death?"

"No," said St. Clare, as he read on.

"Then all your indulgence to them may prove a great cruelty, by and by."

St. Clare had often thought the same thing himself; but he answered, negligently,

"Well, I mean to make a provision, by and by."

"When?" said Miss Ophelia.

"O, one of these days."

"What if you should die first?"

"Cousin, what's the matter?" said St. Clare, laying down his paper and looking at her. "Do you think I show symptoms of yellow fever or cholera, that you are making post mortem arrangements with such zeal?"

" 'In the midst of life we are in death,' "[12] said Miss Ophelia.

St. Clare rose up, and laying the paper down, carelessly, walked to the door that stood open on the verandah, to put an end to a conversation that was not agreeable to him. Mechanically, he repeated the last word again,— "*Death*!"—and, as he leaned against the railings, and watched the sparkling water as it rose and fell in the fountain; and, as in a dim and dizzy haze, saw flowers and trees and vases of the courts, he repeated again the mystic word so common in every mouth, yet of such fearful power,— "DEATH!" "Strange that there should be such a word," he said, "and such a thing, and we ever forget it; that one should be living, warm and beautiful, full of hopes, desires and wants, one day, and the next be gone, utterly gone, and forever!"

It was a warm, golden evening; and, as he walked to the other end of the verandah, he saw Tom busily intent on his Bible, pointing, as he did so, with his finger to each successive word, and whispering them to himself with an earnest air.

"Want me to read to you, Tom?" said St. Clare, seating himself carelessly by him.

"If Mas'r pleases," said Tom, gratefully, "Mas'r makes it so much plainer."

St. Clare took the book and glanced at the place, and began reading one of the passages which Tom had designated by the heavy marks around it. It ran as follows:[13]

"When the Son of man shall come in his glory, and all

12 *The Book of Common Prayer*, a line from the prayers used for the burial of the dead. Thus, Ophelia reminds St. Clare (and most of her readers) of Eva's death.

13 St. Clare reads from Matt. 25:31–41, passages that deal with the Last Judgment. Stowe underscores the extent to which these verses have affected St. Clare by telling us that he did not hear the tea-bell.

14 The Aeolian harp was a popular instrument in the nineteenth century; usually constructed out of a small box and strings, the harp would be placed in a windowsill where it would play music when exposed to the wind. (Aeolius was god of the winds.) We will see this instrument in another form in chapter 39.

15 Stowe's use of Mozart's *Requiem* opens up a brilliant cluster of images. The musical genius died young, in the midst of his last work (unfinished), a funeral mass. The pieces chosen from the *Requiem* would have been well known to Stowe's readers and would evoke the fear and sympathy she needs. And, as the translation below makes clear, not only is it Jesus whose mercy the petitioner asks; to be remembered is also part of the plea. In a nineteenth-century culture that saves the locks of dead children, to be remembered would strike at the heart. The *National Era* of May 27, 1847, carried a story of the dying Mozart and his young daughter that curiously prefigures the relationship between St. Clare and Eva:

History informs us that Wolfgang Mozart, the great German composer, died at Vienna in 1791. There is something strikingly beautiful and touching in the circumstances of his death. His sweetest song was the last he sung, the "Requiem." He had been employed on this exquisite piece for several weeks, his soul filled with inspiration of richest melody, and already claiming kindred with immortality. After giving it its last touch, and breathing into it that undying spirit of song which was to consecrate it through all time as his eyenean strain, he fell into a gentle and quiet slumber. At length the light footsteps of his daughter Emilie awoke him. "Come hither, Emilie," said he, "my task is done; the Requiem—my Requiem—is finished."

"Say not so, dear father," said the gentle girl, interrupting him, as tears stood in her eyes. "You must be better—you look better, for even now your cheek has a glow upon it. I am sure we will nurse you well again. Let me bring you something refreshing."

"Do not deceive yourself, my love," said the dying father; "this wasted form can never be restored by human aid. From

his holy angels with him, then shall he sit upon the throne of his glory: and before him shall be gathered all nations; and he shall separate them one from another, as a shepherd divideth his sheep from the goats." St. Clare read on in an animated voice, till he came to the last of the verses.

"Then shall the king say unto them on his left hand, Depart from me, ye cursed, into everlasting fire: for I was an hungered, and ye gave me no meat: I was thirsty, and ye gave me no drink: I was a stranger, and ye took me not in: naked, and ye clothed me not: I was sick, and in prison, and ye visited me not. Then shall they answer unto Him, Lord when saw we thee an hungered, or athirst, or a stranger, or naked, or sick, or in prison, and did not minister unto thee? Then shall he say unto them, Inasmuch as ye did it not to one of the least of these my brethren, ye did it not to me."

St. Clare seemed struck with this last passage, for he read it twice,—the second time slowly, and as if he were revolving the words in his mind.

"Tom," he said, "these folks that get such hard measure seem to have been doing just what I have,—living good, easy, respectable lives; and not troubling themselves to inquire how many of their brethren were hungry or athirst, or sick, or in prison."

Tom did not answer.

St. Clare rose up and walked thoughtfully up and down the verandah, seeming to forget everything in his own thoughts; so absorbed was he, that Tom had to remind him twice that the tea-bell had rung, before he could get his attention.

St. Clare was absent and thoughtful, all tea-time. After tea, he and Marie and Miss Ophelia took possession of the parlor, almost in silence.

Marie disposed herself on a lounge, under a silken mosquito curtain, and was soon sound asleep. Miss Ophelia silently busied herself with her knitting. St. Clare sat down to the piano, and began playing a soft and melancholy movement with the Æolian[14] accompaniment. He seemed in a deep reverie, and to be soliloquizing to himself by music. After a little, he opened one of the drawers, took out an old music-book whose leaves were yellow with age, and began turning it over.

"There," he said to Miss Ophelia, "this was one of my mother's books,—and here is her handwriting,—come and look at it. She copied and arranged this from Mozart's Requiem."[15] Miss Ophelia came accordingly.

"It was something she used to sing often," said St. Clare. "I think I can hear her now."

He struck a few majestic chords, and began singing that grand old Latin piece, the "Dies Iræ."[16]

Tom, who was listening in the outer verandah, was drawn by the sound to the very door, where he stood earnestly. He did not understand the words, of course; but the music and manner of singing appeared to affect him strongly, especially when St. Clare sang the more pathetic parts. Tom would have sympathized more heartily, if he had known the meaning of the beautiful words:

> *Recordare Jesu pie*
> *Quod sum causa tuæ viæ*
> *Ne me perdas, illa die*
> *Quærens me sedisti lassus*
> *Redemisti crucem passus*
> *Tantus labor non sit cassus.*[17]

St. Clare threw a deep and pathetic expression into the words; for the shadowy veil of years seemed drawn away, and he seemed to hear his mother's voice leading his. Voice and instrument seemed both living, and threw out with vivid sympathy those strains which the ethereal Mozart first conceived as his own dying requiem.

When St. Clare had done singing, he sat leaning his head upon his hand a few moments, and then began walking up and down the floor.

"What a sublime conception is that of a last judgment!" said he,—"a righting of all the wrongs of ages!—a solving of all moral problems, by an unanswerable wisdom! It is, indeed, a wonderful image."

"It is a fearful one to us," said Miss Ophelia.

"It ought to be to me, I suppose," said St Clare, stopping, thoughtfully. "I was reading to Tom, this afternoon, that chapter in Matthew that gives an account of it, and I have been quite struck with it. One should have expected some terrible enormities charged to those who are excluded from Heaven, as the reason; but no,—they are condemned for *not* doing positive good, as if that included every possible harm."

"Perhaps," said Miss Ophelia, "it is impossible for a person who does no good not to do harm."

"And what," said St. Clare, speaking abstractedly, but with deep feeling, "what shall be said of one whose own heart, whose education, and the wants of society, have

heaven's mercy alone do I look for aid in this my dying hour. You spoke of refreshment, my Emilie; take these my last notes, sit down to my piano here—sing with them the hymn of your sainted mother; let me once more hear those tones which have been my solace and delight."

Emilie obeyed, and with tenderest emotion sang the following stanzas.

> Spirit! thy labor is o'er,
> Thy term of probation is run,
> Thy steps are now bound for the untrodden shore,
> And the race of immortals begun.
>
> Spirit! look not on the strife
> Or the pleasures of earth with regret;
> Pause not on the threshold of limitless life,
> To mourn for the day that is set.
>
> Spirit! no fetters can bind,
> No wicked have power to molest;
> There the weary like thee, the wretched, shall find
> A heaven, a mansion of rest.
>
> Spirit! how bright is the road
> For which thou art now on the wing!
> Thy home it will be with thy Saviour and God,
> Their loud hallelujah to sing.

As she concluded, says an account before us, she dwelt for a moment upon the low, melancholy notes of the piece, and then, turning from the instrument, looked in silence for the approving smile of her father. It was the still, passionless smile which the rapt and joyful spirit had left, with the seal of death upon those features. ("The Dying Mozart")

16 "Day of Wrath." Stowe's novel could not be any more clear as to what St. Clare's fate will be.

17 Stowe added a note to her text that these lines "have been thus rather inadequately translated" (by which I presume the translation is Stowe's own):

> Think, O Jesus, for what reason
> Thou endured'st earth's spite and treason,
> Nor me lose, in that dread season;
> Seeking me, thy worn feet hasted,

On the cross thy soul death tasted,
Let not all these toils be wasted.

Regardless of the translation, those familiar with Mozart's *Requiem* would recognize the pathos of "Dies Irae" in this context.

18 St. Clare's statement confirms a belief common among pious Christians: that the hypocrisy of their fellow Christians is responsible for turning would-be believers away from redemption. St. Clare's (intentionally funny?) comment a few paragraphs below about the futility of training Rosa, Jane, or Adolph for any productive work raises some interesting questions that Stowe does not get around to answering. What will happen to these three? Are they less deserving of our sympathy than the other slave characters in the novel?

called in vain to some noble purpose; who has floated on, a dreamy, neutral spectator of the struggles, agonies, and wrongs of man, when he should have been a worker?"

"I should say," said Miss Ophelia, "that he ought to repent, and begin now."

"Always practical and to the point!" said St. Clare, his face breaking out into a smile. "You never leave me any time for general reflections, Cousin; you always bring me short up against the actual present; you have a kind of eternal *now,* always in your mind."

"*Now* is all the time I have anything to do with," said Miss Ophelia.

"Dear little Eva,—poor child!" said St. Clare, "she had set her little simple soul on a good work for me."

It was the first time since Eva's death that he had ever said as many words as these of her, and he spoke now evidently repressing very strong feeling.

"My view of Christianity is such," he added, "that I think no man can consistently profess it without throwing the whole weight of his being against this monstrous system of injustice that lies at the foundation of all our society; and, if need be, sacrificing himself in the battle. That is, I mean that *I* could not be a Christian otherwise, though I have certainly had intercourse with a great many enlightened and Christian people who did no such thing; and I confess that the apathy of religious people on this subject, their want of perception of wrongs that filled me with horror, have engendered in me more scepticism than any other thing."[18]

"If you knew all this," said Miss Ophelia, "why didn't you do it?"

"O, because I have had only that kind of benevolence which consists in lying on a sofa, and cursing the church and clergy for not being martyrs and confessors. One can see, you know, very easily, how others ought to be martyrs."

"Well, are you going to do differently now?" said Miss Ophelia.

"God only knows the future," said St. Clare. "I am braver than I was, because I have lost all; and he who has nothing to lose can afford all risks."

"And what are you going to do?"

"My duty, I hope, to the poor and lowly, as fast as I find it out," said St. Clare, "beginning with my own servants, for whom I have yet done nothing; and, perhaps, at some future day, it may appear that I can do something for a whole class; something to save my country from the disgrace of that false position in which she now stands before all civilized nations."

"Do you suppose it possible that a nation ever will voluntarily emancipate?" said Miss Ophelia.

"I don't know," said St. Clare. "This is a day of great deeds. Heroism and disinterestedness are rising up, here and there, in the earth. The Hungarian nobles set free millions of serfs, at an immense pecuniary loss; and, perhaps, among us may be found generous spirits, who do not estimate honor and justice by dollars and cents."

"I hardly think so," said Miss Ophelia.

"But, suppose we should rise up to-morrow and emancipate, who would educate these millions, and teach them how to use their freedom? They never would rise to do much among us. The fact is, we are too lazy and unpractical, ourselves, ever to give them much of an idea of that industry and energy which is necessary to form them into men. They will have to go north, where labor is the fashion,—the universal custom; and tell me, now, is there enough Christian philanthropy, among your northern states, to bear with the process of their education and elevation? You send thousands of dollars to foreign missions; but could you endure to have the heathen sent into your towns and villages, and give your time, and thoughts, and money, to raise them to the Christian standard? That's what I want to know. If we emancipate, are you willing to educate? How many families, in your town, would take in a negro man and woman, teach them, bear with them, and seek to make them Christians?[19] How many merchants would take Adolph, if I wanted to make him a clerk; or mechanics, if I wanted him taught a trade? If I wanted to put Jane and Rosa to a school, how many schools are there in the northern states that would take them in? how many families that would board them? and yet they are as white as many a woman, north or south. You see, Cousin, I want justice done us. We are in a bad position. We are the more *obvious* oppressors of the negro; but the unchristian prejudice of the north is an oppressor almost equally severe."

"Well, Cousin, I know it is so," said Miss Ophelia,—"I know it was so with me, till I saw that it was my duty to overcome it; but, I trust I have overcome it; and I know there are many good people at the north, who in this matter need only to be *taught* what their duty is, to do it. It would certainly be a greater self-denial to receive heathen among us, than to send missionaries to them; but I think we would do it."

19 Once again, St. Clare calls the North to task for its own complicity in racism. Note that he cannot let go of his paternalism: He must call Tom "boy," and even in his imagination, he must retain the power of deciding if and how his slaves will be educated.

**20** Stowe often halts the action of her novel to give her readers a description of something or other or to philosophize, but here, almost out of the blue, she offers some hint of what is inside Tom's head. Tom's reverie is so sentimental that one prefers to skip over it quickly, but it deserves some scrutiny. He begins by thinking of home, his family, his ability to work, and then feels his own muscular body. From there he thinks of young George Shelby and then Little Eva. Poor Chloe, unnamed, has receded again into the background! Now dreaming, Tom envisions Eva's golden beauty running toward him . . . and, sadly, wakes to disaster.

"*You* would, I know," said St. Clare. "I'd like to see anything you wouldn't do, if you thought it your duty!"

"Well, I'm not uncommonly good," said Miss Ophelia. "Others would, if they saw things as I do. I intend to take Topsy home, when I go. I suppose our folks will wonder, at first; but I think they will be brought to see as I do. Besides, I know there are many people at the north who do exactly what you said."

"Yes, but they are a minority; and, if we should begin to emancipate to any extent, we should soon hear from you."

Miss Ophelia did not reply. There was a pause of some moments; and St. Clare's countenance was overcast by a sad, dreamy expression.

"I don't know what makes me think of my mother so much, to-night," he said. "I have a strange kind of feeling, as if she were near me. I keep thinking of things she used to say. Strange, what brings these past things so vividly back to us, sometimes!"

St. Clare walked up and down the room for some minutes more, and then said,

"I believe I'll go down street, a few moments, and hear the news, to-night."

He took his hat, and passed out.

Tom followed him to the passage, out of the court, and asked if he should attend him.

"No, my boy," said St. Clare. "I shall be back in an hour."

Tom sat down in the verandah.**20** It was a beautiful moonlight evening, and he sat watching the rising and falling spray of the fountain, and listening to its murmur. Tom thought of his home, and that he should soon be a free man, and able to return to it at will. He thought how he should work to buy his wife and boys. He felt the muscles of his brawny arms with a sort of joy, as he thought they would soon belong to himself, and how much they could do to work out the freedom of his family. Then he thought of his noble young master, and, ever second to that, came the habitual prayer that he had always offered for him; and then his thoughts passed on to the beautiful Eva, whom he now thought of among the angels; and he thought till he almost fancied that that bright face and golden hair were looking upon him, out of the spray of the fountain. And, so musing, he fell asleep, and dreamed he saw her coming bounding towards him, just as she used to come, with a wreath of jessamine in her hair, her cheeks bright, and her eyes radiant with delight; but, as he looked, she seemed to rise from the ground; her cheeks wore a paler hue,—her eyes had a deep, divine radiance, a golden halo seemed around her head,—and she vanished from his sight; and Tom was awakened by a loud knocking, and a sound of many voices at the gate.

He hastened to undo it; and, with smothered voices and heavy tread, came several men, bringing a body, wrapped in a cloak, and lying on a shutter. The light of the lamp fell full on the face; and Tom gave a wild cry of amazement and despair, that rung through all the galleries, as the men advanced, with their burden, to the open parlor door, where Miss Ophelia still sat knitting.

St. Clare had turned into a café, to look over an evening paper. As he was reading, an affray arose between two gentlemen in the room, who were both partially intoxicated. St. Clare and one or two others made an effort to separate them, and St. Clare received a fatal stab in the side with a bowie-knife, which he was attempting to wrest from one of them.

The house was full of cries and lamentations, shrieks and screams; servants frantically tearing their hair, throwing themselves on the ground, or running distractedly about, lamenting. Tom and Miss Ophelia alone seemed to have any presence of mind; for Marie was in strong hysteric convulsions. At Miss Ophelia's direction, one of the lounges in the parlor was hastily prepared, and the bleeding form laid upon it. St. Clare had fainted, through pain and loss of blood; but, as Miss Ophelia applied restoratives, he revived, opened his eyes, looked fixedly on them, looked earnestly around the room, his eyes travelling wistfully over every object, and finally they rested on his mother's picture.

The physician now arrived, and made his examination. It was evident, from the expression of his face, that there was no hope; but he applied himself to dressing the wound, and he and Miss Ophelia and Tom proceeded composedly with this work, amid the lamentations and sobs and cries of the affrighted servants, who had clustered about the doors and windows of the verandah.

"Now," said the physician, "we must turn all these creatures out; all depends on his being kept quiet."

St. Clare opened his eyes, and looked fixedly on the distressed beings, whom Miss Ophelia and the doctor were trying to urge from the apartment. "Poor creatures!" he said, and an expression of bitter self-reproach passed over his face. Adolph absolutely refused to go. Terror had deprived him of all presence of mind; he threw himself along on the floor, and nothing could persuade him to rise. The rest yielded to Miss Ophelia's urgent representa-

"The Death of Augustine St. Clare." Wood engraving, 1852, by T. Williams, "after George Cruikshank." Tom is again on his knees. From *Uncle Tom's Cabin*, John Cassell, London, 1852

**21** Stowe's dramatic sense is equaled perhaps only by Charles Dickens, who also serialized his novels. Even today's readers can easily imagine the strains of "Dies Irae" playing in the background in this scene.

**22** With St. Clare's last word—"*Mother!*"—we understand that the meaning of the chapter title, "Reunion," refers to St. Clare's various reunions in heaven. Stowe's optimistic readers were, perhaps, hoping for a reunion of Tom and Chloe, but alas.

In this depiction of Tom's master's death, St. Clare is dressed as a Dickensian gentleman. A coldhearted Marie stares into a mirror as she says that blacks were not meant to be free.   From Classics Illustrated Classic Comic Book no. 15, *Uncle Tom's Cabin*, 1943

tions, that their master's safety depended on their stillness and obedience.

St. Clare could say but little; he lay with his eyes shut, but it was evident that he wrestled with bitter thoughts. After a while, he laid his hand on Tom's, who was kneeling beside him, and said, "Tom! poor fellow!"

"What, Mas'r?" said Tom, earnestly.

"I am dying!" said St. Clare, pressing his hand; "pray!"

"If you would like a clergyman—" said the physician.

St. Clare hastily shook his head, and said again to Tom, more earnestly, "Pray!"

And Tom did pray, with all his mind and strength, for the soul that was passing,—the soul that seemed looking so steadily and mournfully from those large, melancholy blue eyes. It was literally prayer offered with strong crying and tears.

When Tom ceased to speak, St. Clare reached out and took his hand, looking earnestly at him, but saying nothing.**21** He closed his eyes, but still retained his hold; for, in the gates of eternity, the black hand and the white hold each other with an equal clasp. He murmured softly to himself, at broken intervals,

*"Recordare Jesu pie—*

• • • •

*Ne me perdas—ille die*
*Quærens me—sedisti lassus."*

It was evident that the words he had been singing that evening were passing through his mind,—words of entreaty addressed to Infinite Pity. His lips moved at intervals, as parts of the hymn fell brokenly from them.

"His mind is wandering," said the doctor.

"No! it is coming HOME, at last!" said St. Clare, energetically; "at last! at last!"

The effort of speaking exhausted him. The sinking paleness of death fell on him; but with it there fell, as if shed from the wings of some pitying spirit, a beautiful expression of peace, like that of a wearied child who sleeps.

So he lay for a few moments. They saw that the mighty hand was on him. Just before the spirit parted, he opened his eyes, with a sudden light, as of joy and recognition, and said "*Mother!*"**22** and then he was gone!

# CHAPTER 29

## *The Unprotected*[1]

We hear often of the distress of the negro servants, on the loss of a kind master; and with good reason, for no creature on God's earth is left more utterly unprotected and desolate than the slave in these circumstances.

The child who has lost a father has still the protection of friends, and of the law; he is something, and can do something,—has acknowledged rights and position; the slave has none. The law regards him, in every respect, as devoid of rights as a bale of merchandise. The only possible acknowledgment of any of the longings and wants of a human and immortal creature, which are given to him, comes to him through the sovereign and irresponsible will of his master; and when that master is stricken down, nothing remains.

The number of those men who know how to use wholly irresponsible power humanely and generously is small. Everybody knows this, and the slave knows it best of all; so that he feels that there are ten chances of his finding an abusive and tyrannical master, to one of his finding a considerate and kind one. Therefore is it that the wail over a kind master is loud and long, as well it may be.

When St. Clare breathed his last, terror and consternation took hold of all his household. He had been stricken down so in a moment, in the flower and strength of his youth! Every room and gallery of the house resounded with sobs and shrieks of despair.

Marie, whose nervous system had been enervated by a

1 Stowe begins the chapter by contrasting the lack of legal protection for slaves with the network of laws and relationships protecting children, but her purpose here is primarily to pause after the death of St. Clare and give her readers time to let the import of his death sink in. The readers know full well that Uncle Tom is unprotected and that things look bad for him.

2 Marie is choosing her "widow's weeds," mourning clothes traditionally made from these two fabrics. We recall that Mrs. Bird gave Eliza her bombazine cloak and note the difference between Marie and the noble-minded senator's wife.

constant course of self-indulgence, had nothing to support the terror of the shock, and, at the time her husband breathed his last, was passing from one fainting fit to another; and he to whom she had been joined in the mysterious tie of marriage passed from her forever, without the possibility of even a parting word.

Miss Ophelia, with characteristic strength and self-control, had remained with her kinsman to the last,—all eye, all ear, all attention; doing everything of the little that could be done, and joining with her whole soul in the tender and impassioned prayers which the poor slave had poured forth for the soul of his dying master.

When they were arranging him for his last rest, they found upon his bosom a small, plain miniature case, opening with a spring. It was the miniature of a noble and beautiful female face; and on the reverse, under a crystal, a lock of dark hair. They laid them back on the lifeless breast,—dust to dust,—poor mournful relics of early dreams, which once made that cold heart beat so warmly!

Tom's whole soul was filled with thoughts of eternity; and while he ministered around the lifeless clay, he did not once think that the sudden stroke had left him in hopeless slavery. He felt at peace about his master; for in that hour, when he had poured forth his prayer into the bosom of his Father, he had found an answer of quietness and assurance springing up within himself. In the depths of his own affectionate nature, he felt able to perceive something of the fulness of Divine love; for an old oracle hath thus written,—"He that dwelleth in love dwelleth in God, and God in him." Tom hoped and trusted, and was at peace.

But the funeral passed, with all its pageant of black crape, and prayers, and solemn faces; and back rolled the cool, muddy waves of every-day life; and up came the everlasting hard inquiry of "What is to be done next?"

It rose to the mind of Marie, as, dressed in loose morning-robes, and surrounded by anxious servants, she sat up in a great easy-chair, and inspected samples of crape and bombazine.[2] It rose to Miss Ophelia, who began to turn her thoughts towards her northern home. It rose, in silent terrors, to the minds of the servants, who well knew the unfeeling, tyrannical character of the mistress in whose hands they were left. All knew, very well, that the indulgences which had been accorded to them were not from their mistress, but from their master; and that, now he was gone, there would be no screen between them and every tyrannous infliction which a temper soured by affliction might devise.

It was about a fortnight after the funeral, that Miss Ophelia, busied one day in her apartment, heard a gentle tap at the door. She opened it, and there stood Rosa, the pretty young quadroon, whom we have before often noticed, her hair in disorder, and her eyes swelled with crying.

"O, Miss Feely," she said, falling on her knees, and catching the skirt of her dress, "*do, do go* to Miss Marie for me! do plead for me! She's goin' to send me out to be whipped,—look there!" And she handed to Miss Ophelia a paper.

It was an order, written in Marie's delicate Italian hand, to the master of a whipping-establishment, to give the bearer fifteen lashes.

"What have you been doing?" said Miss Ophelia.

"You know, Miss Feely, I've got such a bad temper; it's very bad of me. I was trying on Miss Marie's dress, and she slapped my face; and I spoke out before I thought, and was saucy; and she said that she'd bring me down, and have me know, once for all, that I wasn't going to be so topping as I had been; and she wrote this, and says I shall carry it. I'd rather she'd kill me, right out."

Miss Ophelia stood considering, with the paper in her hand.

"You see, Miss Feely," said Rosa, "I don't mind the whipping so much, if Miss Marie or you was to do it; but, to be sent to a *man*! and such a horrid man,—the shame of it, Miss Feely!"[3]

Miss Ophelia well knew that it was the universal custom to send women and young girls to whipping-houses, to the hands of the lowest of men,—men vile enough to make this their profession,—there to be subjected to brutal exposure and shameful correction. She had *known* it before; but hitherto she had never realized it, till she saw the slender form of Rosa almost convulsed with distress. All the honest blood of womanhood, the strong New England blood of liberty, flushed to her cheeks, and throbbed bitterly in her indignant heart; but, with habitual prudence and self-control, she mastered herself, and, crushing the paper firmly in her hand, she merely said to Rosa,

"Sit down, child, while I go to your mistress."

"Shameful! monstrous! outrageous!" she said to herself, as she was crossing the parlor.

She found Marie sitting up in her easy-chair, with

3 The slave must have a bare back for whipping, so the public whipping of a female slave was a peep show as well. Ophelia will argue this point to Marie later in this chapter.

4 Stowe contrasts one scene of brazenly familiar touching—two female slaves ministering to Marie's hair and feet—to the image of a half-naked Rosa being whipped by a vulgar man. How quickly things change after Eva and St. Clare's deaths! Marie's desire to shame her slave probably has something to do with Rosa's youth and beauty.

5 I.e., corrupt her moral character.

6 Another instance of a racist stereotype; but by this point in the story, readers might not consider Marie a reliable observer, given that she missed the symptoms of her own child.

Mammy standing by her, combing her hair; Jane sat on the ground before her, busy in chafing her feet.4

"How do you find yourself, to-day?" said Miss Ophelia.

A deep sigh, and a closing of the eyes, was the only reply, for a moment; and then Marie answered, "O, I don't know, Cousin; I suppose I'm as well as I ever shall be!" and Marie wiped her eyes with a cambric handkerchief, bordered with an inch deep of black.

"I came," said Miss Ophelia, with a short, dry cough, such as commonly introduces a difficult subject,—"I came to speak with you about poor Rosa."

Marie's eyes were open wide enough now, and a flush rose to her sallow cheeks, as she answered, sharply,

"Well, what about her?"

"She is very sorry for her fault."

"She is, is she? She'll be sorrier, before I've done with her! I've endured that child's impudence long enough; and now I'll bring her down,—I'll make her lie in the dust!"

"But could not you punish her some other way,—some way that would be less shameful?"

"I mean to shame her; that's just what I want. She has all her life presumed on her delicacy, and her good looks, and her lady-like airs, till she forgets who she is;—and I'll give her one lesson that will bring her down, I fancy!"

"But, Cousin, consider that, if you destroy delicacy and a sense of shame in a young girl, you deprave her very fast."5

"Delicacy!" said Marie, with a scornful laugh,—"a fine word for such as she! I'll teach her, with all her airs, that she's no better than the raggedest black wench that walks the streets! She'll take no more airs with me!"

"You will answer to God for such cruelty!" said Miss Ophelia, with energy.

"Cruelty,—I'd like to know what the cruelty is! I wrote orders for only fifteen lashes, and told him to put them on lightly. I'm sure there's no cruelty there!"

"No cruelty!" said Miss Ophelia. "I'm sure any girl might rather be killed outright!"

"It might seem so to anybody with your feeling; but all these creatures get used to it; it's the only way they can be kept in order.6 Once let them feel that they are to take any airs about delicacy, and all that, and they'll run all over you, just as my servants always have. I've begun now to bring them under; and I'll have them all to know that I'll send one out to be whipped, as soon as another, if they don't mind themselves!" said Marie, looking around her decidedly.

Jane hung her head and cowered at this, for she felt as if

it was particularly directed to her. Miss Ophelia sat for a moment, as if she had swallowed some explosive mixture, and were ready to burst. Then, recollecting the utter uselessness of contention with such a nature, she shut her lips resolutely, gathered herself up, and walked out of the room.

It was hard to go back and tell Rosa that she could do nothing for her; and, shortly after, one of the man-servants came to say that her mistress had ordered him to take Rosa with him to the whipping-house, whither she was hurried, in spite of her tears and entreaties.

A few days after, Tom was standing musing by the balconies, when he was joined by Adolph, who, since the death of his master, had been entirely crest-fallen and disconsolate. Adolph knew that he had always been an object of dislike to Marie; but while his master lived he had paid but little attention to it. Now that he was gone, he had moved about in daily dread and trembling, not knowing what might befall him next. Marie had held several consultations with her lawyer; after communicating with St. Clare's brother, it was determined to sell the place, and all the servants, except her own personal property,[7] and these she intended to take with her, and go back to her father's plantation.

"Do ye know, Tom, that we've all got to be sold?" said Adolph.

"How did you hear that?" said Tom.

"I hid myself behind the curtains when Missis was talking with the lawyer. In a few days we shall all be sent off to auction, Tom."

"The Lord's will be done!" said Tom, folding his arms and sighing heavily.

"We'll never get another such a master," said Adolph, apprehensively; "but I'd rather be sold than take my chance under Missis."

Tom turned away; his heart was full. The hope of liberty, the thought of distant wife and children, rose up before his patient soul, as to the mariner shipwrecked almost in port rises the vision of the church-spire and loving roofs of his native village, seen over the top of some black wave only for one last farewell.[8] He drew his arms tightly over his bosom, and choked back the bitter tears, and tried to pray. The poor old soul had such a singular, unaccountable prejudice in favor of liberty, that it was a hard wrench for him; and the more he said, "Thy will be done," the worse he felt.

He sought Miss Ophelia, who, ever since Eva's death, had treated him with marked and respectful kindness.

7 That "personal property" consists primarily of the slaves Marie brought into her marriage to St. Clare. Although under English common law a married woman's rights were traditionally subordinated to her husband, in 1839 Mississippi, with the passage of the Married Woman's Property Act, American women slowly began to enjoy the rights to control real and personal property after their marriage, to enjoy the profits of their labor, to be parties to law suits and contracts, and to execute their own wills. (The rationale behind the Mississippi law was to prevent property—particularly slaves—from being seized to pay for debts incurred by husbands.) Tom's initial response to the news of his sale—"The Lord's will be done!"—is quickly overtaken by sorrow and tears. This is perhaps the first evidence that Tom is actually *human*, that he does not always have the strength to be so *good*, that he harbors strong inner feelings.

8 A New England metaphor. Ophelia will try to compensate for the lack of written documentation to give Tom his freedom by sitting down promptly and writing to the Shelbys. As this comes at the end of an emotion-filled chapter, we almost forget about it until George arrives many chapters later.

9 Perhaps we do not need so many scenes of Marie choosing mourning clothes, but if Stowe did not emphasize Marie's childishness, the reader might blame Tom's misfortune on the impotent Ophelia or, worse, on Tom's own passivity.

"Miss Feely," he said, "Mas'r St. Clare promised me my freedom. He told me that he had begun to take it out for me; and now, perhaps, if Miss Feely would be good enough to speak about it to Missis, she would feel like goin' on with it, as it was Mas'r St. Clare's wish."

"I'll speak for you, Tom, and do my best," said Miss Ophelia; "but, if it depends on Mrs. St. Clare, I can't hope much for you;—nevertheless, I will try."

This incident occurred a few days after that of Rosa, while Miss Ophelia was busied in preparations to return north.

Seriously reflecting within herself, she considered that perhaps she had shown too hasty a warmth of language in her former interview with Marie; and she resolved that she would now endeavor to moderate her zeal, and to be as conciliatory as possible. So the good soul gathered herself up, and, taking her knitting, resolved to go into Marie's room, be as agreeable as possible, and negotiate Tom's case with all the diplomatic skill of which she was mistress.

She found Marie reclining at length upon a lounge, supporting herself on one elbow by pillows, while Jane, who had been out shopping, was displaying before her certain samples of thin black stuffs.[9]

"That will do," said Marie, selecting one; "only I'm not sure about its being properly mourning."

"Laws, Missis," said Jane, volubly, "Mrs. General Derbennon wore just this very thing, after the General died, last summer; it makes up lovely!"

"What do you think?" said Marie to Miss Ophelia.

"It's a matter of custom, I suppose," said Miss Ophelia. "You can judge about it better than I."

"The fact is," said Marie, "that I haven't a dress in the world that I can wear; and, as I am going to break up the establishment, and go off, next week, I must decide upon something."

"Are you going so soon?"

"Yes. St. Clare's brother has written, and he and the lawyer think that the servants and furniture had better be put up at auction, and the place left with our lawyer."

"There's one thing I wanted to speak with you about," said Miss Ophelia. "Augustine promised Tom his liberty, and began the legal forms necessary to it. I hope you will use your influence to have it perfected."

"Indeed, I shall do no such thing!" said Marie, sharply. "Tom is one of the most valuable servants on the place,— it couldn't be afforded, any way. Besides, what does he want of liberty? He's a great deal better off as he is."

"But he does desire it, very earnestly, and his master promised it," said Miss Ophelia.

"I dare say he does want it," said Marie; "they all want it, just because they are a discontented set,—always wanting what they haven't got. Now, I'm principled against emancipating, in any case. Keep a negro under the care of a master, and he does well enough, and is respectable; but set them free, and they get lazy, and won't work, and take to drinking, and go all down to be mean, worthless fellows. I've seen it tried, hundreds of times. It's no favor to set them free."

"But Tom is so steady, industrious, and pious."

"O, you needn't tell me! I've seen a hundred like him. He'll do very well, as long as he's taken care of,—that's all."

"But, then, consider," said Miss Ophelia, "when you set him up for sale, the chances of his getting a bad master."

"O, that's all humbug!" said Marie; "it isn't one time in a hundred that a good fellow gets a bad master; most masters are good, for all the talk that is made. I've lived and grown up here, in the South, and I never yet was acquainted with a master that didn't treat his servants well,—quite as well as is worth while. I don't feel any fears on that head."

"Well," said Miss Ophelia, energetically, "I know it was one of the last wishes of your husband that Tom should have his liberty; it was one of the promises that he made to dear little Eva on her death-bed, and I should not think you would feel at liberty to disregard it."

Marie had her face covered with her handkerchief at this appeal, and began sobbing and using her smelling-bottle, with great vehemence.

"Everybody goes against me!" she said. "Everybody is so inconsiderate! I shouldn't have expected that *you* would bring up all these remembrances of my troubles to me,—it's so inconsiderate! But nobody ever does consider,—my trials are so peculiar! It's so hard, that when I had only one daughter, she should have been taken!—and when I had a husband that just exactly suited me,—and I'm so hard to be suited!—he should be taken! And you seem to have so little feeling for me, and keep bringing it up to me so carelessly,—when you know how it overcomes me! I suppose you mean well; but it is very inconsiderate,—very!" And Marie sobbed, and gasped for breath, and called Mammy to open the window, and to bring her the camphor-bottle, and to bathe her head, and unhook her dress. And, in the general confusion that ensued, Miss Ophelia made her escape to her apartment.

She saw, at once, that it would do no good to say anything more; for Marie had an indefinite capacity for hysteric fits; and, after this, whenever her husband's or Eva's wishes with regard to the servants were alluded to, she always found it convenient to set one in operation. Miss Ophelia, therefore, did the next best thing she could for Tom,—she wrote a letter to Mrs. Shelby for him, stating his troubles, and urging them to send to his relief.

The next day, Tom and Adolph, and some half a dozen other servants, were marched down to a slave-warehouse, to await the convenience of the trader, who was going to make up a lot for auction.

## CHAPTER 30

### *The Slave Warehouse*

A slave warehouse! Perhaps some of my readers conjure up horrible visions of such a place. They fancy some foul, obscure den, some horrible *Tartarus "informis, ingens, cui lumen ademptum."*[1] But no, innocent friend; in these days men have learned the art of sinning expertly and genteelly, so as not to shock the eyes and senses of respectable society. Human property is high in the market; and is, therefore, well fed, well cleaned, tended, and looked after, that it may come to sale sleek, and strong, and shining. A slave-warehouse in New Orleans is a house externally not much unlike many others, kept with neatness; and where every day you may see arranged, under a sort of shed along the outside, rows of men and women, who stand there as a sign of the property sold within.

Then you shall be courteously entreated to call and examine, and shall find an abundance of husbands, wives, brothers, sisters, fathers, mothers, and young children,[2] to be "sold separately, or in lots to suit the convenience of the purchaser;" and that soul immortal, once bought with blood and anguish by the Son of God, when the earth shook, and the rocks rent, and the graves were opened, can be sold, leased, mortgaged, exchanged for groceries or dry goods, to suit the phases of trade, or the fancy of the purchaser.

It was a day or two after the conversation between Marie and Miss Ophelia, that Tom, Adolph, and about half a dozen others of the St. Clare estate, were turned

1 Zeus imprisoned the Titans in Tartarus, a dark abyss "misshapen, monstrous, devoid of light" (Virgil, *The Aeneid*, book 3, line 658). Stowe understands the profound power of the slave warehouse image, as do so many illustrators. A slave warehouse features human relationships in every form: horizontal relations of kinship, marriage, and friendship between and among slaves; vertical relations between parents and children, the old and the young, the sellers, traders, dealers, and the property; contractual relations between buyers and sellers. Among the slaves, there will be heartbreaking emotions—tears, desperation, frustration, anger, fear, defiance, panic—and incongruous behaviors: bickering, tale-telling, confessions of love. Some people will cluster together; others will sit apart. Some will clutch, and others will push away. There will be foul acts and heroic; malice and kindness; brutality and benevolence. Everyone, however, will play the role he is supposed to: This is the real horror of the scene.

2 Stowe deliberately uses relational terms rather than simply "men, women, and children." All of these individuals, she insists, have lives and histories. They are not simply slaves.

3 In the nineteenth century, "Sambo" was a derogatory nickname for an extremely subservient slave.

4 I.e., silliness. Tom's seriousness is contrasted with the low antics of the other slaves.

5 Most slave narratives describe such scenes. As a Northern, white woman, Stowe knows that there is much at stake in portraying the chaos and horror of the auction house realistically while retaining her focus on individual suffering, and she takes pains to intermix sentiment with detailed depiction.

"The Slave Warehouse." Wood engraving, 1852, by T. Williams, "after George Cruikshank." The scene is more evocative of a dockyard in England than of a slave warehouse.   From *Uncle Tom's Cabin*, John Cassell, London, 1852

over to the loving kindness of Mr. Skeggs, the keeper of a depot on————street, to await the auction, next day.

Tom had with him quite a sizable trunk full of clothing, as had most others of them. They were ushered, for the night, into a long room, where many other men, of all ages, sizes and shades of complexion, were assembled, and from which roars of laughter and unthinking merriment were proceeding.

"Ah, ha! that's right. Go it, boys,—go it!" said Mr. Skeggs, the keeper. "My people are always so merry! Sambo,[3] I see!" he said, speaking approvingly to a burly negro who was performing tricks of low buffoonery,[4] which occasioned the shouts which Tom had heard.

As might be imagined, Tom was in no humor to join these proceedings; and, therefore, setting his trunk as far as possible from the noisy group, he sat down on it, and leaned his face against the wall.

The dealers in the human article make scrupulous and systematic efforts to promote noisy mirth among them, as a means of drowning reflection, and rendering them insensible to their condition.[5] The whole object of the training to which the negro is put, from the time he is sold in the northern market till he arrives south, is systematically directed towards making him callous, unthinking, and brutal. The slave-dealer collects his gang in Virginia or Kentucky, and drives them to some convenient, healthy place,— often a watering place,—to be fattened. Here they are fed full daily; and, because some incline to pine, a fiddle is kept commonly going among them, and they are made to dance daily; and he who refuses to be merry—in whose soul thoughts of wife, or child, or home, are too strong for him to be gay—is marked as sullen and dangerous, and subjected to all the evils which the ill will of an utterly irresponsible and hardened man can inflict upon him. Briskness, alertness, and cheerfulness of appearance, especially before observers, are constantly enforced upon them, both by the hope of thereby getting a good master, and the fear of all that the driver may bring upon them, if they prove unsalable.

"What dat ar nigger doin here?" said Sambo, coming up

to Tom, after Mr. Skeggs had left the room. Sambo was a full black, of great size, very lively, voluble, and full of trick and grimace.

"What you doin here?" said Sambo, coming up to Tom, and poking him facetiously in the side. "Meditatin', eh?"

"I am to be sold at the auction, to-morrow!" said Tom, quietly.

"Sold at auction,—haw! haw! boys, an't this yer fun? I wish't I was gwine that ar way!—tell ye, wouldn't I make em laugh? But how is it,—dis yer whole lot gwine to-morrow?" said Sambo, laying his hand freely on Adolph's shoulder.[6]

"Please to let me alone!" said Adolph, fiercely, straightening himself up, with extreme disgust.

"Law, now, boys! dis yer's one o' yer white niggers,[7]— kind o' cream color, ye know, scented!" said he, coming up to Adolph and snuffing. "O, Lor! he'd do for a tobaccershop; they could keep him to scent snuff! Lor, he'd keep a whole shope agwine,—he would!"

"I say, keep off, can't you?" said Adolph, enraged.

"Lor, now, how touchy we is,—we white niggers! Look at us, now!" and Sambo gave a ludicrous imitation of Adolph's manner; "here's de airs and graces. We's been in a good family, I specs."

"Yes," said Adolph; "I had a master that could have bought you all for old truck!"[8]

"Laws, now, only think," said Sambo, "the gentlemens that we is!"

"I belonged to the St. Clare family," said Adolph, proudly.

"Lor, you did! Be hanged if they ar'n't lucky to get shet of ye. Spects they's gwine to trade ye off with a lot o' cracked tea-pots and sich like!" said Sambo, with a provoking grin.

Adolph, enraged at this taunt, flew furiously at his adversary, swearing and striking on every side of him. The rest laughed and shouted, and the uproar brought the keeper to the door.

"What now, boys? Order,—order!" he said, coming in and flourishing a large whip.

All fled in different directions, except Sambo, who, presuming on the favor which the keeper had to him as a licensed wag, stood his ground, ducking his head with a facetious grin, whenever the master made a dive at him.

"Lor, Mas'r, 'tan't us,—we's reglar stiddy,—it's these yer new hands; they's real aggravating—kinder pickin' at us, all time!"

The keeper, at this, turned upon Tom and Adolph, and

6 In this scene between Adolph and Sambo, Stowe responds to the pro-slavery argument that most slaveholders are as kind and indulgent as St. Clare, and that most slaves are as comfortable as Adolph and live better than they would as Northern domestics or wage laborers. What side do the slavery proponents take in this scene? They could point to Sambo and argue that certainly this character is not a poster child for abolition (to put it bluntly), but they cannot say that Adolph is better off now, as a result of the coddling and finery. There is nothing benevolent and paternalistic about a slave auction. But is Stowe asking us to conclude that Adolph should have spent less time in front of a mirror and more time reading the Bible (or otherwise planning for his future)?

7 The term "white niggers" was not a very widely used term in the mid-nineteenth century; when it was used, it referred to lightskinned slaves. One of its earliest uses in the antislavery press occurred in this item from Frederick Douglass's the *North Star* from a New Hampshire correspondent, in a November 24, 1848, piece entitled "The South As It Is":

I have been made astonished since I have been in Appalachicola to see so many "white niggers" and mulattoes—"creoles," they call them. The farther south you come the more white slaves you will find. It would be a low estimate to say that three-fourths of the slaves in the Southern States have white blood. Many attempt to justify slavery on the ground that the "niggers" are another and inferior race. If none were slaves but full blooded Africans there would at least, be three-fourths less than there now are. This excuse, however, is one peculiar to the North. I never hear it given here. Men do not attempt to justify it on the ground of "race" or "color." This would not do here; for if the slaveholders denied their slaves as belonging to the human family, of course, they must deny that their children do also. I do not make this insinuation without some knowledge of the matter. I know—and it is publicly known, that masters do cohabit with their slaves—raise children by their slaves and sell their own flesh and blood as slaves. In towns of two or three thou-

345

sand inhabitants (by towns I mean what would be called in New England, villages), almost every single man, and many married ones, keep a black or mulatto woman, as a mistress—do it openly and unblushingly, too. The offspring become slaves to the owner of the mother. Such things are common and well known, and the reputation of such men, rarely, if ever, suffers from such an imputation.

8  I.e., junk. Stowe depicts the bankruptcy of Adolph's pegging his worth to the position of his former master.

9  Stowe reminds her readers that even Christian church-going Northerners are implicated in a financial network that allows the buying and selling of human beings.

distributing a few kicks and cuffs without much inquiry, and leaving general orders for all to be good boys and go to sleep, left the apartment.

While this scene was going on in the men's sleeping-room, the reader may be curious to take a peep at the corresponding apartment allotted to the women. Stretched out in various attitudes over the floor, he may see numberless sleeping forms of every shade of complexion, from the purest ebony to white, and of all years, from childhood to old age, lying now asleep. Here is a fine bright girl, of ten years, whose mother was sold out yesterday, and who tonight cried herself to sleep when nobody was looking at her. Here, a worn old negress, whose thin arms and callous fingers tell of hard toil, waiting to be sold to-morrow, as a castoff article, for what can be got for her; and some forty or fifty others, with heads variously enveloped in blankets or articles of clothing, lie stretched around them. But, in a corner, sitting apart from the rest, are two females of a more interesting appearance than common. One of these is a respectably-dressed mulatto woman between forty and fifty, with soft eyes and a gentle and pleasing physiognomy. She has on her head a high-raised turban, made of a gay red Madras handkerchief, of the first quality, and her dress is neatly fitted, and of good material, showing that she has been provided for with a careful hand. By her side, and nestling closely to her, is a young girl of fifteen,—her daughter. She is a quadroon, as may be seen from her fairer complexion, though her likeness to her mother is quite discernible. She has the same soft, dark eye, with longer lashes, and her curling hair is of a luxuriant brown. She also is dressed with great neatness, and her white, delicate hands betray very little acquaintance with servile toil. These two are to be sold to-morrow, in the same lot with the St. Clare servants; and the gentleman to whom they belong, and to whom the money for their sale is to be transmitted, is a member of a Christian church in New York, who will receive the money, and go thereafter to the sacrament of his Lord and theirs, and think no more of it.[9]

These two, whom we shall call Susan and Emmeline, had been the personal attendants of an amiable and pious lady of New Orleans, by whom they had been carefully and piously instructed and trained. They had been taught to read and write, diligently instructed in the truths of religion, and their lot had been as happy an one as in their condition it was possible to be. But the only son of their protectress had the management of her property; and, by carelessness and extravagance involved it to a large amount, and at last failed.[10] One of the largest creditors was the respectable firm of B. & Co., in New York. B. & Co. wrote to their lawyer in New Orleans, who attached the real estate (these two articles and a lot of plantation hands formed the most valuable part of it), and wrote word to that effect to New York. Brother B., being, as we have said, a Christian man, and a resident in a free State, felt some uneasiness on the subject. He didn't like trading in slaves and souls of men,—of course, he didn't; but, then, there were thirty thousand dollars in the case, and that was rather too much money to be lost for a principle; and so, after much considering, and asking advice from those that he knew would advise to suit him, Brother B. wrote to his lawyer to dispose of the business in the way that seemed to him the most suitable, and remit the proceeds.

The day after the letter arrived in New Orleans, Susan and Emmeline were attached, and sent to the depot to await a general auction on the following morning; and as they glimmer faintly upon us in the moonlight which steals through the grated window, we may listen to their conversation. Both are weeping, but each quietly, that the other may not hear.

"Mother, just lay your head on my lap, and see if you can't sleep a little," says the girl, trying to appear calm.

"I haven't any heart to sleep, Em; I can't; it's the last night we may be together!"

"O, mother, don't say so! perhaps we shall get sold together,—who knows?"

"If't was anybody's else case, I should say so, too, Em," said the woman; "but I'm so feard of losin' you that I don't see anything but the danger."

"Why, mother, the man said we were both likely, and would sell well."

Susan remembered the man's looks and words. With a deadly sickness at her heart, she remembered how he had looked at Emmeline's hands, and lifted up her curly hair, and pronounced her a first-rate article. Susan had been trained as a Christian, brought up in the daily reading of the Bible, and had the same horror of her child's being sold to a life of shame that any other Christian mother might have; but she had no hope,—no protection.[11]

"Mother, I think we might do first rate, if you could get a place as cook, and I as chamber-maid or seamstress, in some family. I dare say we shall. Let's both look as bright and lively as we can, and tell all we can do, and perhaps we shall," said Emmeline.

10 In other words, the pious lady's son mortgaged all of their property in order to finance his high living and managed to go bankrupt, necessitating the sale of these two "items." Stowe shows how "respectable firms" such as ones any Northerner would do business with can profit from slavery. The contemporary argument to keep their finances separate from the slave economy has recently been revived in calls to boycott consumer products made by sweatshop labor.

11 In 1861, Harriet Jacobs would make the lack of protection of women from sexual assault under slavery a central part of her slave narrative, *Incidents in the Life of a Slave Girl*.

**12** Susan attempts to hide her daughter's hair because it is a selling point for buyers who seek sexual slaves. Stowe shows her readers the downside of having such beautiful hair as Rosa and Jane were so proud to sport.

**13** From Matt. 18:6 (and also Luke 17:2). Susan does not pray for help; rather, she pointedly lays all of the blame for Emmeline's potential "sin" (being used sexually by a new master) on herself. Susan laments that she will cause her daughter to sin, and she feels it would be better to be dead. Stowe is baiting her female readers to argue against the mother's culpability.

"I want you to brush your hair all back straight, to-morrow," said Susan.**12**

"What for, mother? I don't look near so well, that way."

"Yes, but you'll sell better so."

"I don't see why!" said the child.

"Respectable families would be more apt to buy you, if they saw you looked plain and decent, as if you wasn't trying to look handsome. I know their ways better 'n you do," said Susan.

"Well, mother, then I will."

"And, Emmeline, if we shouldn't ever see each other again, after to-morrow,—if I'm sold way up on a plantation somewhere, and you somewhere else,—always remember how you've been brought up, and all Missis has told you; take your Bible with you, and your hymn-book; and if you're faithful to the Lord, he'll be faithful to you."

So speaks the poor soul, in sore discouragement; for she knows that to-morrow any man, however vile and brutal, however godless and merciless, if he only has money to pay for her, may become owner of her daughter, body and soul; and then, how is the child to be faithful? She thinks of all this, as she holds her daughter in her arms, and wishes that she were not handsome and attractive. It seems almost an aggravation to her to remember how purely and piously, how much above the ordinary lot, she has been brought up. But she has no resort but to *pray*; and many such prayers to God have gone up from those same trim, neatly-arranged, respectable slave-prisons,—prayers which God has not forgotten, as a coming day shall show; for it is written, "Whoso causeth one of these little ones to offend, it were better for him that a millstone were hanged about his neck, and that he were drowned in the depths of the sea."**13**

The soft, earnest, quiet moonbeam looks in fixedly marking the bars of the grated windows on the prostrate, sleeping forms. The mother and daughter are singing together a wild and melancholy dirge, common as a funeral hymn among the slaves:

*"O, where is weeping Mary?*
*O, where is weeping Mary?*
*'Rived in the goodly land.*
*She is dead and gone to Heaven;*
*She is dead and gone to Heaven;*
*'Rived in the goodly land."*

These words, sung by voices of a peculiar and melancholy sweetness, in an air which seemed like the sighing of earthly despair after heavenly hope, floated through the dark prison rooms with a pathetic cadence, as verse after verse was breathed out:

> *"O, where are Paul and Silas?*
> *O, where are Paul and Silas?*
> *Gone to the goodly land.*
> *They are dead and gone to Heaven;*
> *They are dead and gone to Heaven;*
> *'Rived in the goodly land."*

Sing on, poor souls! The night is short, and the morning will part you forever!

But now it is morning, and everybody is astir; and the worthy Mr. Skeggs is busy and bright, for a lot of goods is to be fitted out for auction.

There is a brisk look-out on the toilet; injunctions passed around to every one to put on their best face and be spry; and now all are arranged in a circle for a last review, before they are marched up to the Bourse.[14]

Mr. Skeggs, with his palmetto[15] on and his cigar in his mouth, walks around to put farewell touches on his wares.

"How's this?" he said, stepping in front of Susan and Emmeline. "Where's your curls, gal?"

The girl looked timidly at her mother, who, with the smooth adroitness common among her class, answers,

"I was telling her, last night, to put up her hair smooth and neat, and not havin' it flying about in curls; looks more respectable so."

"Bother!" said the man, peremptorily, turning to the girl; "you go right along, and curl yourself real smart!" He added, giving a crack to a rattan[16] he held in his hand, "And be back in quick time, too!"

"You go and help her," he added, to the mother. "Them curls may make a hundred dollars difference in the sale of her."

Beneath a splendid dome were men of all nations, moving to and fro, over the marble pave.[17] On every side of the circular area were little tribunes, or stations, for the use of speakers and auctioneers. Two of these, on opposite sides of the area, were now occupied by brilliant and talented gentlemen, enthusiastically forcing up, in English and French commingled, the bids of connoisseurs in their various wares. A third one, on the other side, still unoccupied, was surrounded by a group, waiting the moment of sale to begin. And here we may recognize the St. Clare ser-

14 The Bourse is the money market; here, place for auction.

15 I.e., hat made out of palm leaves. We recall Sam's hat from those days gone by on the Shelby plantation.

16 A rattan is a stem from a climbing palm, used as a walking stick or for punishment. Skeggs kindly puts a price on Emmeline's sexual appeal. Mary Boykin Chesnut, a slavery-hating wife of a South Carolina senator, plantation owner, and Confederate general, writes passionately of sexual abuse of slave women in her diary (*A Diary from Dixie*, 1905):

> You say there are no more fallen women on a plantation than in London in proportion to numbers. But what do you say to this—to a magnate who runs a hideous black harem, with its consequences, under the same roof with his lovely white wife and his beautiful and accomplished daughters? He holds his head high and poses as the model of all human virtues to these poor women whom God and the laws have given him. From the height of his awful majesty he scolds and thunders at them as if he never did wrong in his life. Fancy such a man finding his daughter reading Don Juan. "You with that immoral book!" he would say, and then he would order her out of his sight.

17 I.e., flooring.

349

**18** I.e., a dandy (one dressed fancily). Adolph himself could be considered a "dandy." There is a sadistic undercurrent in this scene; the "exquisite's" primary purpose in buying Adolph seems to be to break him.

**19** A calaboose is place for public whipping of slaves. The origins of the term are from the Spanish *calabozo*, "dungeon."

**20** Tom's examination of the faces of his potential buyers is unsettling and strangely sexual. The depiction of faces and looks forewarns us that Tom's fate will be bound up in his next owner's character.

Simon Legree. Note how simian and ugly he looks. Tom is wearing a nice jacket, compared with the other slaves' naked chests and Legree's work shirt. Legree is portrayed as a mean farmhand, not as a plantation owner. The other purchasers are in finery. From Classics Illustrated Classic Comic Book no. 15, *Uncle Tom's Cabin*, 1943

vants,—Tom, Adolph, and others; and there, too, Susan and Emmeline, awaiting their turn with anxious and dejected faces. Various spectators, intending to purchase, or not intending, as the case might be, gathered around the group, handling, examining, and commenting on their various points and faces with the same freedom that a set of jockeys discuss the merits of a horse.

"Hulloa, Alf! what brings you here?" said a young exquisite,[18] slapping the shoulder of a sprucely-dressed young man, who was examining Adolph through an eye-glass.

"Well, I was wanting a valet, and I heard that St. Clare's lot was going. I thought I'd just look at his—"

"Catch me ever buying any of St. Clare's people! Spoilt niggers, every one. Impudent as the devil!" said the other.

"Never fear that!" said the first. "If I get 'em, I'll soon have their airs out of them; they'll soon find that they've another kind of master to deal with than Monsieur St. Clare. 'Pon my word, I'll buy that fellow. I like the shape of him."

"You'll find it'll take all you've got to keep him. He's deucedly extravagant!"

"Yes, but my lord will find that he *can't* be extravagant with *me*. Just let him be sent to the calaboose[19] a few times, and thoroughly dressed down! I'll tell you if it don't bring him to a sense of his ways! O, I'll reform him, up hill and down,—you'll see. I buy him, that's flat!"

Tom had been standing wistfully examining the multitude of faces thronging around him, for one whom he would wish to call master. And if you should ever be under the necessity, sir, of selecting, out of two hundred men, one who was to become your absolute owner and disposer, you would, perhaps, realize, just as Tom did, how few there were that you would feel at all comfortable in being made over to. Tom saw abundance of men,—great, burly, gruff men; little, chirping, dried men; long-favored, lank, hard men; and every variety of stubbed-looking, commonplace men, who pick up their fellow-men as one picks up chips, putting them into the fire or a basket with equal unconcern, according to their convenience; but he saw no St. Clare.[20]

A little before the sale commenced, a short, broad, muscular man, in a checked shirt considerably open at the bosom, and pantaloons much the worse for dirt and wear, elbowed his way through the crowd, like one who is going actively into a business; and, coming up to the group, began to examine them systematically. From the moment that Tom saw him approaching, he felt an immediate and revolting horror at him, that increased as he came near. He was evidently, though short, of gigantic strength. His round, bullet head, large, light-gray eyes, with their shaggy, sandy eye-brows, and stiff, wiry, sun-burned hair, were rather unprepossessing items, it is to be confessed; his large, coarse mouth was distended with tobacco, the juice of which, from time to time, he ejected from him with great decision and explosive force; his hands were immensely large, hairy, sunburned, freckled, and very dirty, and garnished with long nails, in a very foul condition. This man proceeded to a very free personal examination of the lot. He seized Tom by the jaw, and pulled open his mouth to inspect his teeth; made him strip up his sleeve, to show his muscle; turned him round, made him jump and spring, to show his paces.[21]

"Where was you raised?" he added, briefly, to these investigations.

"In Kintuck, Mas'r," said Tom, looking about, as if for deliverance.

"What have you done?"

"Had care of Mas'r's farm," said Tom.

"Likely story!" said the other, shortly, as he passed on. He paused a moment before Dolph; then spitting a discharge of tobacco-juice on his well-blacked boots, and giving a contemptuous umph, he walked on. Again he stopped before Susan and Emmeline. He put out his heavy, dirty hand, and drew the girl towards him; passed it over her neck and bust, felt her arms, looked at her teeth, and then pushed her back against her mother, whose patient face showed the suffering she had been going through at every motion of the hideous stranger.[22]

The girl was frightened, and began to cry.

"Stop that, you minx!"[23] said the salesman; "no whimpering here,—the sale is going to begin." And accordingly the sale begun.

Adolph was knocked off, at a good sum, to the young gentleman who had previously stated his intention of buying him; and the other servants of the St. Clare lot went to various bidders.

"Now, up with you, boy! d'ye hear?" said the auctioneer to Tom.

Tom stepped upon the block, gave a few anxious looks round; all seemed mingled in a common, indistinct noise,—the clatter of the salesman crying off his qualifi-

**21** Thus, quite late in the novel, we are introduced to the infamous Simon Legree. For readers who have come to *Uncle Tom's Cabin* after learning of it through popular culture, the lateness of Legree's appearance seems surprising. Legree is perhaps the most well known character, after Uncle Tom and Little Eva (and perhaps Topsy). His was the part that most actors yearned to play in the Tom shows. Stowe's first adjectives to describe him are "short, broad, muscular." She repeats "short" later in the paragraph. Compare Stowe's first description of Tom: "large, broad-chested, powerfully-made."

**22** Stowe's straightforward description serves to underscore Legree's brutal indifference to Emmeline's humanity.

**23** I.e., hussy or prostitute. The term is ironic: Legree has handled her mercilessly with his dirty hands; Emmeline's whimpering is a natural response. Stowe's depiction of

In this Miguel Covarrubias depiction, a strong, barebacked Tom is sold and we can see why he might fetch a very high price: His back is muscular and unmarked; his head is bowed respectfully. This image evokes that of folk character and hero John Henry. From *Uncle Tom's Cabin: or, Life Among the Lowly*, Heritage Press edition, 1938

Legree's hardness is designed to leave her readers flushed with worry. Will mother and daughter be wrenched apart? Who, then, will protect the daughter? Will Legree manhandle her again? Perhaps the bitterest (and most well known) assessment of Legree was offered by Mary Boykin Chesnut (*Diary*): "You see, Mrs. Stowe did not hit the sorest spot. She made Legree a bachelor." Chesnut writes that she knew "a Legree": "He was high and mighty, but the kindest creature to his slaves. And the unfortunate results of his bad ways were not sold, had not to jump over ice-blocks. They were kept in full view, and provided for handsomely in his will."

**24** The "bullet-head" is stubborn and has much more money to spend than he lets on. Legree's stinginess serves to mitigate our worry about Emmeline's bodily safety, however. That is, while Stowe warns her readers of the probability that Emmeline will be raped ("he has got the girl, body and soul"), she also suggests that Legree's passions flow in another direction: money and alcohol.

"Emeline [*sic*] Sold." Color lithograph by Louisa Corbaux, 1852. Emmeline looks white and very young; once again, she could be mistaken for any Victorian heroine.

cations in French and English, the quick fire of French and English bids; and almost in a moment came the final thump of the hammer, and the clear ring on the last syllable of the word "*dollars*," as the auctioneer announced his price, and Tom was made over.—He had a master!

He was pushed from the block;—the short, bullet-headed man seizing him roughly by the shoulder, pushed him to one side, saying, in a harsh voice, "Stand there, *you*!"

Tom hardly realized anything; but still the bidding went on,—rattling, clattering, now French, now English. Down goes the hammer again,—Susan is sold! She goes down from the block, stops, looks wistfully back,—her daughter stretches her hands towards her. She looks with agony in the face of the man who has bought her,—a respectable middle-aged man, of benevolent countenance.

"O, Mas'r, please do buy my daughter!"

"I'd like to, but I'm afraid I can't afford it!" said the gentleman, looking, with painful interest, as the young girl mounted the block, and looked around her with a frightened and timid glance.

The blood flushes painfully in her otherwise colorless cheek, her eye has a feverish fire, and her mother groans to see that she looks more beautiful than she ever saw her before. The auctioneer sees his advantage, and expatiates volubly in mingled French and English, and bids rise in rapid succession.

"I'll do anything in reason," said the benevolent-looking gentleman, pressing in and joining with the bids. In a few moments they have run beyond his purse. He is silent; the auctioneer grows warmer; but bids gradually drop off. It lies now between an aristocratic old citizen and our bullet-headed acquaintance. The citizen bids for a few turns, contemptuously measuring his opponent; but the bullet-head has the advantage over him, both in obstinacy and concealed length of purse,**24** and the controversy lasts but a moment; the hammer falls,—he has got the girl, body and soul, unless God help her!

Her master is Mr. Legree, who owns a cotton plantation on the Red river. She is pushed along into the same lot with Tom and two other men, and goes off, weeping as she goes.

The benevolent gentleman is sorry; but, then, the thing happens every day! One sees girls and mothers crying, at these sales, *always*! it can't be helped, &c; and he walks off, with his acquisition, in another direction.

Two days after, the lawyer of the Christian firm of B. &

Co., New York, sent on their money to them. On the reverse of that draft, so obtained, let them write these words of the great Paymaster, to whom they shall make up their account in a future day: "*When he maketh inquisition for blood, he forgetteth not the cry of the humble!*"[25]

25 "When he maketh inquisition for blood . . ." comes from Psalm 9:12. The thrust of this psalm is that God keeps accounts and will judge eventually. Stowe's use of the term "Paymaster" to refer to God provides a brilliant ending to a chapter devoted to the buying and selling of human beings.

# CHAPTER 31

## *The Middle Passage*[1]

[1] The *OED* credits Thomas Clarkson with first using the term "middle passage" in 1788 in *An Essay on the Impolicy of the African Slave Trade*: "The captain of a ship, then on the middle passage, had lost a considerable number of his slaves by death." The term appeared frequently in the American press in the early nineteenth century. In this piece from the *New York Evangelist*, reprinted in the *Colored American* (April 15, 1837), the term is already marked with quotes as a euphemism:

> It would seem by a statement in a late Natchez *Courier*, that now, since the African slave trade is declared to be piracy, the American slave trade has assumed a vigor and magnitude that far outstrips the palmiest days of the trade across the "Middle Passage." The statement referred to is, that there have been transported from the older slave states to Alabama, Mississippi, Louisiana, and Arkansas, during the year 1836, the enormous number of two hundred and fifty thousand slaves! Remember, Congress has direct power over all the "commerce between the several states." Mark that! ("The American Slave Trade")

The epigraph, a verse from one of the more obscure texts of the Hebrew bible, the book of Habakkuk, seems an odd choice. But the

"Thou art of purer eyes than to behold evil, and canst not look upon iniquity: wherefore lookest thou upon them that deal treacherously, and holdest thy tongue when the wicked devoureth the man that is more righteous than he?"—HAB. 1:13.

On the lower part of a small, mean boat, on the Red river, Tom sat,—chains on his wrists, chains on his feet, and a weight heavier than chains lay on his heart. All had faded from his sky,—moon and star; all had passed by him, as the trees and banks were now passing, to return no more. Kentucky home, with wife and children, and indulgent owners; St. Clare home, with all its refinements and splendors; the golden head of Eva, with its saint-like eyes; the proud, gay, handsome, seemingly careless, yet ever-kind St. Clare; hours of ease and indulgent leisure,—all gone! and in place thereof, *what* remains?

It is one of the bitterest apportionments of a lot of slavery, that the negro, sympathetic and assimilative, after acquiring, in a refined family, the tastes and feelings which form the atmosphere of such a place, is not the less liable to become the bond-slave of the coarsest and most brutal,—just as a chair or table, which once decorated the superb saloon, comes, at last, battered and defaced, to the bar-room of some filthy tavern, or some low haunt of vulgar debauchery. The great difference is, that the table and chair cannot feel, and the *man* can; for even a legal enactment that he shall be "taken, reputed, adjudged in law, to be a chattel personal,"[2] cannot blot out his soul, with its own private little world of memories, hopes, loves, fears, and desires.

Mr. Simon Legree, Tom's master, had purchased slaves at one place and another, in New Orleans, to the number of eight, and driven them, handcuffed, in couples of two and two, down to the good steamer Pirate, which lay at the levee, ready for a trip up the Red river.

Having got them fairly on board, and the boat being off, he came round, with that air of efficiency which ever characterized him, to take a review of them. Stopping opposite to Tom, who had been attired for sale in his best broadcloth suit, with well-starched linen and shining boots, he briefly expressed himself as follows:

"Stand up."

Tom stood up.

"Take off that stock!"[3] and, as Tom, encumbered by his fetters, proceeded to do it, he assisted him, by pulling it, with no gentle hand, from his neck, and putting it in his pocket.

Legree now turned to Tom's trunk, which, previous to this, he had been ransacking, and, taking from it a pair of old pantaloons and a dilapidated coat, which Tom had been wont to put on about his stable-work, he said, liberating Tom's hands from the handcuffs, and pointing to a recess in among the boxes,

"You go there, and put these on."

Tom obeyed, and in a few moments returned.

"Take off your boots," said Mr. Legree.

Tom did so.

"There," said the former, throwing him a pair of coarse, stout shoes, such as were common among the slaves, "put these on."

In Tom's hurried exchange, he had not forgotten to transfer his cherished Bible to his pocket. It was well he did so; for Mr. Legree, having refitted Tom's handcuffs, proceeded deliberately to investigate the contents of his pockets. He drew out a silk handkerchief, and put it into his own pocket. Several little trifles, which Tom had treasured, chiefly because they had amused Eva, he looked upon with a contemptuous grunt, and tossed them over his shoulder into the river.

Tom's Methodist hymn-book, which, in his hurry, he had forgotten, he now held up and turned over.

"Humph! pious, to be sure. So, what's yer name,—you belong to the church, eh?"

lines that follow return to the image of painful and wasteful loss at sea and offer some consolation: "He brings all of them up with a hook, he drags them out with his net, he gathers them in his seine; so he rejoices and exults" (Hab. 1:15).

2 This quote refers to state slave codes defining slave chattel. Tom's desires, it would seem, still involve the "golden head of Eva." What would James Baldwin say?

3 I.e., those clothes. Tom's pockets are full not only with his Bible but also with "trifles" that have meaning because they belonged to Eva. Where, one asks again, are the things that remind him of Chloe?

4 With this quote from Isa. 43:1, Tom comforts himself that his soul is God's. Legree's hatred of religion is cleverly designed to raise the hackles of Stowe's Northern Christian female readers (though one expects that their hackles were quite elevated already). Moreover, the assertion "you've got to be as *I* say" sounds chillingly like the demand of an oppressive husband or father.

5 Historian John Ashworth writes that "abolitionists never doubted that men's consciences were on their side. . . . Harriet Beecher Stowe, author of *Uncle Tom's Cabin*, reflects this view in the novel. when she makes it clear that all slaveholders are afflicted by attacks of conscience, to escape from which they resort to drink or other diversions. The thoroughly evil slaveholder like Simon Legree rejects his conscience outright, precisely as he rejects antislavery" (*Slavery, Capitalism, and Politics in the Antebellum Republic*).

6 I.e., the forward part of the ship, below deck, where the sailors live. Baldwin might argue that Tom is wholly passive here, mouthing biblical phrases rather than relying on his own voice and his own physical strength to protect himself from Legree. However, Stowe would like us to see Tom's forbearance as an expression of his own force of will.

7 I.e., cheerful.

"Yes, Mas'r," said Tom, firmly.

"Well, I'll soon have *that* out of you. I have none o' yer bawling, praying, singing niggers on my place; so remember. Now, mind yourself," he said, with a stamp and a fierce glance of his gray eye, directed at Tom, "*I'm* your church now! You understand,—you've got to be as *I* say."

Something within the silent black man answered *No!* and, as if repeated by an invisible voice, came the words of an old prophetic scroll, as Eva had often read them to him,—"Fear not! for I have redeemed thee. I have called thee by my name. Thou art MINE!"[4]

But Simon Legree heard no voice. That voice is one he never shall hear.[5] He only glared for a moment on the downcast face of Tom, and walked off. He took Tom's trunk, which contained a very neat and abundant wardrobe, to the forecastle,[6] where it was soon surrounded by various hands of the boat. With much laughing, at the expense of niggers who tried to be gentlemen, the articles very readily were sold to one and another, and the empty trunk finally put up at auction. It was a good joke, they all thought, especially to see how Tom looked after his things, as they were going this way and that; and then the auction of the trunk, that was funnier than all, and occasioned abundant witticisms.

This little affair being over, Simon sauntered up again to his property.

"Now, Tom, I've relieved you of any extra baggage, you see. Take mighty good care of them clothes. It'll be long enough 'fore you get more. I go in for making niggers careful; one suit has to do for one year, on my place."

Simon next walked up to the place where Emmeline was sitting, chained to another woman.

"Well, my dear," he said, chucking her under the chin, "keep up your spirits."

The involuntary look of horror, fright and aversion, with which the girl regarded him, did not escape his eye. He frowned fiercely.

"None o' your shines, gal! you's got to keep a pleasant face, when I speak to ye,—d'ye hear? And you, you old yellow poco moonshine!" he said, giving a shove to the mulatto woman to whom Emmeline was chained, "don't you carry that sort of face! You's got to look chipper,[7] I tell ye!"

"I say, all on ye," he said retreating a pace or two back, "look at me,—look at me,—look me right in the eye,—*straight*, now!" said he, stamping his foot at every pause.

As by a fascination, every eye was now directed to the glaring greenish-gray eye of Simon.

"Now," said he, doubling his great, heavy fist into something resembling a blacksmith's hammer, "d'ye see this fist? Heft it!"[8] he said, bringing it down on Tom's hand. "Look at these yer bones! Well, I tell ye this yer fist has got as hard as iron *knocking down niggers.* I never see the nigger, yet, I couldn't bring down with one crack," said he, bringing his fist down so near to the face of Tom that he winked[9] and drew back. "I don't keep none o' yer cussed overseers; I does my own overseeing; and I tell you things *is* seen to. You's every one on ye got to toe the mark, I tell ye; quick,—straight,—the moment I speak. That's the way to keep in with me. Ye won't find no soft spot in me, nowhere. So, now, mind yerselves; for I don't show no mercy!"

The women involuntarily drew in their breath, and the whole gang sat with downcast, dejected faces. Meanwhile, Simon turned on his heel, and marched up to the bar of the boat for a dram.[10]

"That's the way I begin with my niggers," he said, to a gentlemanly man, who had stood by him during his speech. "It's my system to begin strong,—just let 'em know what to expect."

"Indeed!" said the stranger, looking upon him with the curiosity of a naturalist studying some out-of-the-way specimen.

"Yes, indeed. I'm none o' yer gentlemen planters, with lily fingers, to slop round and be cheated by some old cuss of an overseer! Just feel of my knuckles, now; look at my fist. Tell ye, sir, the flesh on 't has come jest like a stone,[11] practising on niggers,—feel on it."

The stranger applied his fingers to the implement in question, and simply said,

" 'T is hard enough; and, I suppose," he added, "practice has made your heart just like it."

"Why, yes, I may say so," said Simon, with a hearty laugh. "I reckon there's as little soft in me as in any one going. Tell you, nobody comes it over me![12] Niggers never gets round me, neither with squalling nor soft soap,— that's a fact."

"You have a fine lot there."

"Real," said Simon. "There's that Tom, they told me he was suthin' uncommon. I paid a little high for him, tendin' him for a driver and a managing chap; only get the notions out that he's larnt by bein' treated as niggers never ought to be, he'll do prime! The yellow woman I got took in in. I rayther think she's sickly, but I shall put her through for what she's worth; she may last a year or two. I don't go for

8 I.e., feel the weight of it. Legree's maniacal outburst and obscene display of strength serve not only to scare the slaves in his entourage but also to contrast him with St. Clare. "I'm none o' yer gentlemen planters, with lily fingers," he says a few paragraphs later. Which sort of owner would be worse, the reader is provoked to wonder? And in fact readers did wonder. For instance, the *National Era* published the following letter on February 24, 1853:

> In reading that admirable production, *Uncle Tom's Cabin*, I was struck with the utter contempt in which the slave-trader is held by the respectable slaveholder, and it awakened reflections in this wise: If it was not for such characters as Shelby and St. Clair, and respectable slaveholders generally, such characters as Haley, and others of his class, together with the overseers, (Sambo and Quimbo, for instance,) could not exist. They are part and portion of the system; it cannot exist without them. So also, we hate slavery and condemn slaveholders as being in the wrong; yet if it was not for us, they could not maintain the sys-

Here Tom almost looks, appropriately enough, like the modern marketing images of Founding Father—and slaveholder—Samuel Adams. By the turn of the twentieth century, Uncle Tom had become such an icon that he even appeared on whiskey bottles, like this one from the United Distilling Company of Cincinnati.

tem which degrades man to a level with the brute, makes him a subject of property, with the separation of families, and all the other evils which are part and parcel of the system. I say, that if we did not patronize them, by buying their products of unrequited toil, (I mean the people of the free States,) they could not maintain the system; so that we bear the same relation to the slaveholder that he does to the trader in the bodies of his fellow-men.

9 I.e., blinked.

10 I.e., a small drink of whiskey. Stowe consistently drops hints that Legree's primary vice is drink, not sex.

11 I.e., become as hard as a stone. Surely, Baldwin's complaint that in Stowe's novel "black equates with evil and white with grace" does not hold true ("Everybody's Protest Novel," in *James Baldwin: Collected Essays*).

12 I.e., nobody fools me! With these moments of exuberant self-expression, Simon Legree wills himself into literary existence, thrusting himself into the consciousness of those around him. Legree is a powerful fictional character primarily because of how he articulates himself. His passion to speak, to pronounce his creed, to show off his power, to describe his own nature, is compelling.

13 Legree's verbal outbursts also afford the opportunity to show him being overheard by others on the boat. And once again, in the paragraphs that follow, Stowe shows that slavery creates discord among Southern whites. The young man's allusion to millstones recollects Susan's lament that it would be better to drown with a millstone around her neck than allow a child to sin. But these Southern "gentlemen" aren't incited to act; rather, they "color"—that is, blush—and turn to board games.

savin' niggers. Use up, and buy more, 's my way;—makes you less trouble, and I'm quite sure it comes cheaper in the end;" and Simon sipped his glass.

"And how long do they generally last?" said the stranger.

"Well, donno; 'cordin' as their constitution is. Stout fellers last six or seven years; trashy ones gets worked up in two or three. I used to, when I fust begun, have considerable trouble fussin' with 'em and trying to make 'em hold out,—doctorin' on 'em up when they's sick, and givin' on 'em clothes and blankets, and what not, tryin' to keep 'em all sort o' decent and comfortable. Law, 't wasn't no sort o' use; I lost money on 'em, and 't was heaps o' trouble. Now, you see, I just put 'em straight through, sick or well. When one nigger's dead, I buy another; and I find it comes cheaper and easier, every way."13

The stranger turned away, and seated himself beside a gentleman, who had been listening to the conversation with repressed uneasiness.

"You must not take that fellow to be any specimen of Southern planters," said he.

"I should hope not," said the young gentleman, with emphasis.

"He is a mean, low, brutal fellow!" said the other.

"And yet your laws allow him to hold any number of human beings subject to his absolute will, without even a shadow of protection; and, low as he is, you cannot say that there are not many such."

"Well," said the other, "there are also many considerate and humane men among planters."

"Granted," said the young man; "but, in my opinion, it is you considerate, humane men, that are responsible for all the brutality and outrage wrought by these wretches; because, if it were not for your sanction and influence, the whole system could not keep foot-hold for an hour. If there were no planters except such as that one," said he, pointing with his finger to Legree, who stood with his back to them, "the whole thing would go down like a millstone. It is your respectability and humanity that licenses and protects his brutality."

"You certainly have a high opinion of my good nature," said the planter, smiling; "but I advise you not to talk quite so loud, as there are people on board the boat who might not be quite so tolerant to opinion as I am. You had better wait till I get up to my plantation, and there you may abuse us all, quite at your leisure."

The young gentleman colored and smiled, and the two were soon busy in a game of backgammon. Meanwhile, another conversation was going on in the lower part of the boat, between Emmeline and the mulatto woman with whom she was confined. As was natural, they were exchanging with each other some particulars of their history.

"Who did you belong to?" said Emmeline.

"Well, my Mas'r was Mr. Ellis,—lived on Levee-street. P'raps you've seen the house."

"Was he good to you?" said Emmeline.

"Mostly, till he tuk sick. He's lain sick, off and on, more than six months, and been orful[14] oneasy. 'Pears like he warnt willin' to have nobody rest, day nor night; and got so curous,[15] there couldn't nobody suit him. 'Pears like he just grew crosser, every day; kep me up nights till I got farly beat out, and couldn't keep awake no longer; and cause I got to sleep, one night, Lors, he talk so orful to me, and he tell me he'd sell me to just the hardest master he could find; and he'd promised me my freedom, too, when he died."

"Had you any friends?" said Emmeline.

"Yes, my husband,—he's a blacksmith.[16] Mas'r gen'ly hired him out. They took me off so quick, I didn't even have time to see him; and I's got four children. O, dear me!" said the woman, covering her face with her hands.

It is a natural impulse, in every one, when they hear a tale of distress, to think of something to say by way of consolation. Emmeline wanted to say something, but she could not think of anything to say. What was there to be said? As by a common consent, they both avoided, with fear and dread, all mention of the horrible man who was now their master.

True, there is religious trust for even the darkest hour. The mulatto woman was a member of the Methodist church, and had an unenlightened but very sincere spirit of piety. Emmeline had been educated much more intelligently,—taught to read and write, and diligently instructed in the Bible, by the care of a faithful and pious mistress; yet, would it not try the faith of the firmest Christian, to find themselves abandoned, apparently, of God, in the grasp of ruthless violence? How much more must it shake the faith of Christ's poor little ones, weak in knowledge and tender in years!

The boat moved on,—freighted with its weight of sorrow—up the red, muddy, turbid current, through the abrupt, tortuous windings of the Red river; and sad eyes gazed wearily on the steep red-clay banks, as they glided by in dreary sameness. At last the boat stopped at a small town, and Legree, with his party, disembarked.

14 I.e., terribly ("awful"). Note the ease with which Stowe's pen turns from Legree's dialect to the words of a more educated Southerner to her own narrative voice and then to the colloquial idiom of one suffering slave woman to another.

15 I.e., strange.

16 Again, Stowe insists that there are no minor characters whose stories are irrelevant to the larger picture: She provides the mulatto woman with a husband (a blacksmith) and four children.

# CHAPTER 32

## *Dark Places*

1 The chapter title is given biblical meaning with this epigraph, from Psalm 74:20. James Baldwin objected deeply to the heavenly binary in which dark is bad and light is good (see chapter 31, note 11).

2 I.e., roughly made. But we feel the presence of the secondary meaning: offensive. The two women, seated with the baggage, are further dehumanized.

3 Stowe uses small details such as these to evoke the dismal and poisonous atmosphere of Legree's plantation.

"The dark places of the earth are full of the habitations of cruelty."[1]

Trailing wearily behind a rude[2] wagon, and over a ruder road, Tom and his associates faced onward.

In the wagon was seated Simon Legree; and the two women, still fettered together, were stowed away with some baggage in the back part of it, and the whole company were seeking Legree's plantation, which lay a good distance off.

It was a wild, forsaken road, now winding through dreary pine barrens, where the wind whispered mournfully, and now over log causeways, through long cypress swamps, the doleful trees rising out of the slimy, spongy ground, hung with long wreaths of funereal black moss, while ever and anon the loathsome form of the moccasin snake[3] might be seen sliding among broken stumps and shattered branches that lay here and there, rotting in the water.

It is disconsolate enough, this riding, to the stranger, who, with well-filled pocket and well-appointed horse, threads the lonely way on some errand of business; but wilder, drearier, to the man enthralled, whom every weary step bears further from all that man loves and prays for.

So one should have thought, that witnessed the sunken and dejected expression on those dark faces; the wistful, patient weariness with which those sad eyes rested on object after object that passed them in their sad journey.

Simon rode on, however, apparently well pleased, occasionally pulling away at a flask of spirit, which he kept in his pocket.

"I say, *you*!" he said, as he turned back and caught a glance at the dispirited faces behind him! "Strike up a song, boys,—come!"

The men looked at each other, and the "*come*" was repeated, with a smart crack of the whip which the driver carried in his hands. Tom began a Methodist hymn,[4]

> *"Jerusalem, my happy home,*
> *Name ever dear to me!*
> *When shall my sorrows have an end,*
> *Thy joys when shall—"*

"Shut up, you black cuss!" roared Legree; "did ye think I wanted any o' yer infernal old Methodism? I say, tune up, now, something real rowdy,—quick!"

One of the other men struck up one of those unmeaning songs, common among the slaves.[5]

> *"Mas'r see'd me cotch a coon,*
> *High boys, high!*
> *He laughed to split,—d'ye see the moon,*
> *Ho! ho! ho! boys, ho!*
> *Ho! yo! hi—e! oh!"*

The singer appeared to make up the song to his own pleasure, generally hitting on rhyme, without much attempt at reason; and all the party took up the chorus, at intervals,

> *"Ho! ho! ho! boys, ho!*
> *High—e—oh! high—e—oh!"*

It was sung very boisterously, and with a forced attempt at merriment; but no wail of despair, no words of impassioned prayer, could have had such a depth of woe in them as the wild notes of the chorus. As if the poor, dumb heart, threatened,—prisoned,—took refuge in that inarticulate sanctuary of music, and found there a language in which to breathe its prayer to God! There was a prayer in it, which Simon could not hear. He only heard the boys singing noisily, and was well pleased; he was making them "keep up their spirits."

4 "Jerusalem, my happy home" was a sixteenth-century hymn sung to the tune of "St. Stephen."

5 Frederick Douglass wrote of these songs in his 1845 *Narrative*: "I did not, when a slave, understand the deep meaning of those rude and apparently incoherent songs. . . . Those songs still follow me, to deepen my hatred of slavery, and quicken my sympathy for my brethren in bonds."

6 I.e., a room for growing plants, attached to a house. Stowe's quick movement from Emmeline's revulsion at Legree's drunken touch to the description of a ruined garden prevents us once again from focusing too much on potential rape. Stowe needs to keep the focus on Legree's general cruelty, not merely his potential sexual cruelty.

"Well, my little dear," said he, turning to Emmeline, and laying his hand on her shoulder, "we're almost home!"

When Legree scolded and stormed, Emmeline was terrified; but when he laid his hand on her, and spoke as he now did, she felt as if she had rather he would strike her. The expression of his eyes made her soul sick, and her flesh creep. Involuntarily she clung closer to the mulatto woman by her side, as if she were her mother.

"You didn't ever wear ear-rings," he said, taking hold of her small ear with his coarse fingers.

"No, Mas'r!" said Emmeline, trembling and looking down.

"Well, I'll give you a pair, when we get home, if you're a good girl. You needn't be so frightened; I don't mean to make you work very hard. You'll have fine times with me, and live like a lady,—only be a good girl."

Legree had been drinking to that degree that he was inclining to be very gracious; and it was about this time that the enclosures of the plantation rose to view. The estate had formerly belonged to a gentleman of opulence and taste, who had bestowed some considerable attention to the adornment of his grounds. Having died insolvent, it had been purchased, at a bargain, by Legree, who used it, as he did everything else, merely as an implement for money-making. The place had that ragged, forlorn appearance, which is always produced by the evidence that the care of the former owner has been left to go to utter decay.

What was once a smooth-shaven lawn before the house, dotted here and there with ornamental shrubs, was now covered with frowsy tangled grass, with horse-posts set up, here and there, in it, where the turf was stamped away, and the ground littered with broken pails, cobs of corn, and other slovenly remains. Here and there, a mildewed jessamine or honeysuckle hung raggedly from some ornamental support, which had been pushed to one side by being used as a horse-post. What once was a large garden was now all grown over with weeds, through which, here and there, some solitary exotic reared its forsaken head. What had been a conservatory[6] had now no window-sashes, and on the mouldering shelves stood some dry, forsaken flower-pots, with sticks in them, whose dried leaves showed they had once been plants.

The wagon rolled up a weedy gravel walk, under a noble avenue of China trees, whose graceful forms and ever-springing foliage seemed to be the only things there that neglect could not daunt or alter,—like noble spirits, so deeply rooted in goodness, as to flourish and grow stronger amid discouragement and decay.

The house had been large and handsome. It was built in a manner common at the South; a wide verandah of two stories running round every part of the house, into which every outer door opened, the lower tier being supported by brick pillars.

But the place looked desolate and uncomfortable; some windows stopped up with boards, some with shattered panes, and shutters hanging by a single hinge,—all telling of coarse neglect and discomfort.

Bits of board, straw, old decayed barrels and boxes, garnished the ground in all directions; and three or four ferocious-looking dogs, roused by the sound of the wagon-wheels, came tearing out, and were with difficulty restrained from laying hold of Tom and his companions, by the effort of the ragged servants who came after them.

"Ye see what ye'd get!" said Legree, caressing the dogs with grim satisfaction, and turning to Tom and his companions. "Ye see what ye'd get, if ye try to run off. These yer dogs has been raised to track niggers; and they'd jest as soon chaw one on ye up as eat their supper. So, mind yerself! How now, Sambo!"[7] he said, to a ragged fellow, without any brim to his hat, who was officious in his attentions. "How have things been going?"

"Fust rate, Mas'r."

"Quimbo," said Legree to another, who was making zealous demonstrations to attract his attention, "ye minded what I telled ye?"

"Guess I did, didn't I?"

These two colored men were the two principal hands on the plantation.[8] Legree had trained them in savageness and brutality as systematically as he had his bull-dogs; and, by long practice in hardness and cruelty, brought their whole nature to about the same range of capacities. It is a common remark, and one that is thought to militate strongly against the character of the race, that the negro overseer is always more tyrannical and cruel than the white one. This is simply saying that the negro mind has been more crushed and debased than the white. It is no more true of this race than of every oppressed race, the world over. The slave is always a tyrant, if he can get a chance to be one.

Legree, like some potentates we read of in history, governed his plantation by a sort of resolution of forces. Sambo and Quimbo cordially hated each other; the plantation hands, one and all, cordially hated them; and, by

7 This derogatory nickname was used in chapter 30 for the "buffoon" who watched over the slaves; here, it may or may not be this man's name.

8 Sambo and Quimbo serve as bookends to Sam and Andy. They remind us of the pair on Shelby's plantation, but the rivalry between them, Stowe suggests, is not playful. The two are compared to bulldogs; not surprisingly, we will see them used to track fugitives.

**9** With this scene, Stowe again depicts the blithe sexual abuse of slave women, in this case by a fellow slave. Legree's emphasis on the word "*you*" makes it clear that he has purchased Emmeline for a similar purpose.

playing off one against another, he was pretty sure, through one or the other of the three parties, to get informed of whatever was on foot in the place.

Nobody can live entirely without social intercourse; and Legree encouraged his two black satellites to a kind of coarse familiarity with him,—a familiarity, however, at any moment liable to get one or the other of them into trouble; for, on the slightest provocation, one of them always stood ready, at a nod, to be a minister of his vengeance on the other.

As they stood there now by Legree, they seemed an apt illustration of the fact that brutal men are lower even than animals. Their coarse, dark, heavy features; their great eyes, rolling enviously on each other; their barbarous, guttural, half-brute intonation; their dilapidated garments fluttering in the wind,—were all in admirable keeping with the vile and unwholesome character of everything about the place.

"Here, you Sambo," said Legree, "take these yer boys down to the quarters; and here's a gal I've got for *you*,"**9** said he, as he separated the mulatto woman from Emmeline, and pushed her towards him;—"I promised to bring you one, you know."

The woman gave a sudden start, and, drawing back, said, suddenly,

"O, Mas'r! I left my old man in New Orleans."

"What of that, you———; won't you want one here? None o' your words,—go long!" said Legree, raising his whip.

"Come, mistress," he said to Emmeline, "you go in here with me."

A dark, wild face was seen, for a moment, to glance at the window of the house; and, as Legree opened the door, a female voice said something, in a quick, imperative tone. Tom, who was looking, with anxious interest, after Emmeline, as she went in, noticed this, and heard Legree answer, angrily, "You may hold your tongue! I'll do as I please, for all you!"

Tom heard no more; for he was soon following Sambo to the quarters. The quarters was a little sort of street of rude shanties, in a row, in a part of the plantation, far off from the house. They had a forlorn, brutal, forsaken air. Tom's heart sunk when he saw them. He had been comforting himself with the thought of a cottage, rude, indeed, but one which he might make neat and quiet, and where he might have a shelf for his Bible, and a place to be alone out of his laboring hours. He looked into several; they were mere rude shells, destitute of any species of furniture, except a heap of straw, foul with dirt, spread confusedly over the floor, which was merely the bare ground, trodden hard by the tramping of innumerable feet.

"Which of these will be mine?" said he, to Sambo, submissively.

"Dunno; ken turn in here, I spose," said Sambo; "spects thar's room for another thar; thar's a pretty smart heap o' niggers to each on 'em, now; sure, I dunno what I's to do with more."

It was late in the evening when the weary occupants of the shanties came flocking home,—men and women, in soiled and tattered garments, surly and uncomfortable, and in no mood to look pleasantly on new-comers. The small village was alive with no inviting sounds; hoarse, guttural voices contending at the hand-mills[10] where their morsel of hard corn was yet to be ground into meal, to fit it for the cake that was to constitute their only supper. From the earliest dawn of the day, they had been in the fields, pressed to work under the driving lash of the overseers; for it was now in the very heat and hurry of the season, and no means was left untried to press every one up to the top of their capabilities. "True," says the negligent lounger; "picking cotton isn't hard work." Isn't it? And it isn't much inconvenience, either, to have one drop of water fall on your head; yet the worst torture of the inquisition is produced by drop after drop, drop after drop, falling moment after moment, with monotonous succession, on the same spot; and work, in itself not hard, becomes so, by being pressed, hour after hour, with unvarying, unrelenting sameness, with not even the consciousness of free-will to take from its tediousness. Tom looked in vain among the gang, as they poured along, for companionable faces. He saw only sullen, scowling, imbruted men, and feeble, discouraged women, or women that were not women,—the strong pushing away the weak,—the gross, unrestricted animal selfishness of human beings, of whom nothing good was expected and desired; and who, treated in every way like brutes, had sunk as nearly to their level as it was possible for human beings to do. To a late hour in the night the sound of the grinding was protracted; for the mills were few in number compared with the grinders, and the weary and feeble ones were driven back by the strong, and came on last in their turn.

"Ho yo!" said Sambo, coming to the mulatto woman, and

10 I.e., two small millstones used one against the other to grind grain by hand. Stowe's female readers will understand the extent of work that these slaves will have to do in order to eat, even at the end of a long day in the cotton fields.

11 About eight quarts.

12 I.e., dying embers. This is a particularly Romantic image. Tom's kindness to Lucy is paternal; he no longer seems like the childish servant that he did in Little Eva's presence.

"Tom Reading His Bible." Wood engraving by W. Measom, "after George Cruikshank." The cabin here is odd, with its fireplace and open door. Tom's demeanor is brooding rather than praying.

throwing down a bag of corn before her; "what a cuss yo name?"

"Lucy," said the woman.

"Wal, Lucy, yo my woman now. Yo grind dis yer corn, and get *my* supper baked, ye har?"

"I an't your woman, and I won't be!" said the woman, with the sharp, sudden courage of despair; "you go long!"

"I'll kick yo, then!" said Sambo, raising his foot threateningly.

"Ye may kill me, if ye choose,—the sooner the better! Wish't I was dead!" said she.

"I say, Sambo, you go to spilin' the hands, I'll tell Mas'r o' you," said Quimbo, who was busy at the mill, from which he had viciously driven two or three tired women, who were waiting to grind their corn.

"And I'll tell him ye won't let the women come to the mills, yo old nigger!" said Sambo. "Yo jes keep to yo own row."

Tom was hungry with his day's journey, and almost faint for want of food.

"Thar, yo!" said Quimbo, throwing down a coarse bag, which contained a peck[11] of corn; "thar, nigger, grab, take car on 't,—yo won't get no more, *dis* yer week."

Tom waited till a late hour, to get a place at the mills; and then, moved by the utter weariness of two women, whom he saw trying to grind their corn there, he ground for them, put together the decaying brands[12] of the fire, where many had baked cakes before them, and then went about getting his own supper. It was a new kind of work there,—a deed of charity, small as it was; but it woke an answering touch in their hearts,—an expression of womanly kindness came over their hard faces; they mixed his cake for him, and tended its baking; and Tom sat down by the light of the fire, and drew out his Bible,—for he had need of comfort.

"What's that?" said one of the women.

"A Bible," said Tom.

"Good Lord! han't seen un since I was in Kentuck."

"Was you raised in Kentuck?" said Tom, with interest.

"Yes, and well raised, too; never 'spected to come to dis yer!" said the woman, sighing.

"What's dat ar book, any way?" said the other woman.

"Why, the Bible."

"Laws a me! what's dat?" said the woman.

"Do tell! you never hearn on 't?" said the other woman. "I used to har Missis a readin' on 't, sometimes, in Kentuck; but, laws o' me! we don't har nothin' here but crackin' and swarin'."

"Read a piece, anyways!" said the first woman, curiously, seeing Tom attentively poring over it.

Tom read,—"Come unto ME, all ye that labor and are heavy laden, and I will give you rest."**13**

"Them's good words, enough," said the woman; "who says 'em?"

"The Lord," said Tom.

"I jest wish I know'd whar to find Him," said the woman. "I would go; 'pears like I never should get rested agin. My flesh is fairly sore, and I tremble all over, every day, and Sambo's allers a jawin'**14** at me, 'cause I doesn't pick faster; and nights it's most midnight 'fore I can get my supper; and den 'pears like I don't turn over and shut my eyes, 'fore I hear de horn blow to get up, and at it agin in de mornin'. If I knew whar de Lor was, I'd tell him."

"He's here, he's everywhere," said Tom.

"Lor, you an't gwine to make me believe dat ar! I know de Lord an't here," said the woman; "'t an't no use talking, though. I's jest gwine to camp down, and sleep while I ken."

The women went off to their cabins, and Tom sat alone, by the smouldering fire, that flickered up redly in his face.

The silver, fair-browed moon rose in the purple sky, and looked down, calm and silent, as God looks on the scene of misery and oppression,—looked calmly on the lone black man, as he sat, with his arms folded, and his Bible on his knee.

"Is God HERE?" Ah, how is it possible for the untaught heart to keep its faith, unswerving, in the face of dire misrule, and palpable, unrebuked injustice? In that simple heart waged a fierce conflict: the crushing sense of wrong, the foreshadowing of a whole life of future misery, the wreck of all past hopes, mournfully tossing in the soul's sight, like dead corpses of wife, and child, and friend, rising from the dark wave, and surging in the face of the half-drowned mariner! Ah, was it easy *here* to believe and hold fast the great password of Christian faith, that "God IS, and is the REWARDER of them that diligently seek Him"?

Tom rose, disconsolate, and stumbled into the cabin that had been allotted to him. The floor was already strewn with weary sleepers, and the foul air of the place almost repelled him; but the heavy night-dews were chill, and his limbs weary, and, wrapping about him a tattered blanket, which formed his only bed-clothing, he stretched himself in the straw and fell asleep.

In dreams, a gentle voice came over his ear; he was sitting on the mossy seat in the garden by Lake Pontchar-

13 This verse is from Matt. 11:28–30, a typically consoling choice for Tom to reflect upon.

14 I.e., always yelling.

**15** Stowe shows Tom turning to Isa. 43 (verses 2–3) not only for comfort but also in direct answer to the narrator's question: "Is God HERE?" Once again, we see Tom dreaming of his golden Eva; what about poor Chloe?

**16** Harriet Beecher Stowe herself wrote these lines, which suggest that it is only natural that one should dream about the dead rather than the living.

A dead slave lies bound in front of a plantation, suggestive of the White House as well, in this striking lithograph by Miguel Covarrubias. This image evokes the horrors of the Middle Passage.   From *Uncle Tom's Cabin: or, Life Among the Lowly*, Heritage Press edition, 1938

train, and Eva, with her serious eyes bent downward, was reading to him from the Bible; and he heard her read,

"When thou passest through the waters, I will be with thee, and the rivers they shall not overflow thee; when thou walkest through the fire, thou shalt not be burned, neither shall the flame kindle upon thee; for I am the Lord thy God, the Holy One of Israel, thy Saviour."[15]

Gradually the words seemed to melt and fade, as in a divine music; the child raised her deep eyes, and fixed them lovingly on him, and rays of warmth and comfort seemed to go from them to his heart; and, as if wafted on the music, she seemed to rise on shining wings, from which flakes and spangles of gold fell off like stars, and she was gone.

Tom woke. Was it a dream? Let it pass for one. But who shall say that that sweet young spirit, which in life so yearned to comfort and console the distressed, was forbidden of God to assume this ministry after death?

*It is a beautiful belief,*
*That ever round our head*
*Are hovering, on angel wings,*
*The spirits of the dead.*[16]

# CHAPTER 33

## *Cassy*[1]

"And behold, the tears of such as were oppressed, and they had no comforter; and on the side of their oppressors there was *power,* but they had no comforter."—ECCL. 4:1.

It took but a short time to familiarize Tom with all that was to be hoped or feared in his new way of life. He was an expert and efficient workman in whatever he undertook; and was, both from habit and principle, prompt and faithful. Quiet and peaceable in his disposition, he hoped, by unremitting diligence, to avert from himself at least a portion of the evils of his condition. He saw enough of abuse and misery to make him sick and weary; but he determined to toil on, with religious patience, committing himself to Him that judgeth righteously, not without hope that some way of escape might yet be opened to him.

Legree took silent note of Tom's availability. He rated him as a first-class hand; and yet he felt a secret dislike to him,—the native antipathy of bad to good. He saw, plainly, that when, as was often the case, his violence and brutality fell on the helpless, Tom took notice of it; for, so subtle is the atmosphere of opinion, that it will make itself felt, without words; and the opinion even of a slave may annoy a master. Tom in various ways manifested a tenderness of feeling, a commiseration for his fellow-sufferers, strange

1 Before we learn about the Cassy of the chapter title, we learn that Legree has a rather good sense of what makes a "first-class hand." Legree is not a bad manager of people, though his philosophy of enlightened self-interest runs into trouble with both Tom and Cassy. Like Tom, Cassy is first described physically; only later does Stowe reveal Cassy's interior complexities.

The epigraph, from Ecclesiastes, is not one that Tom would quote; it is perhaps too accusatory. It is important to note that whereas both Stowe and Tom draw on the Bible, they do it in different ways for different purposes. In general, Stowe uses the Bible to teach, Tom to comfort himself and others.

and new to them, which was watched with a jealous eye by Legree. He had purchased Tom with a view of eventually making him a sort of overseer, with whom he might, at times, intrust his affairs, in short absences; and, in his view, the first, second, and third requisite for that place, was *hardness*. Legree made up his mind, that, as Tom was not hard to his hand, he would harden him forthwith; and some few weeks after Tom had been on the place, he determined to commence the process.

One morning, when the hands were mustered for the field, Tom noticed, with surprise, a new comer among them, whose appearance excited his attention. It was a woman, tall and slenderly formed, with remarkably delicate hands and feet, and dressed in neat and respectable garments. By the appearance of her face, she might have been between thirty-five and forty; and it was a face that, once seen, could never be forgotten,—one of those that, at a glance, seem to convey to us an idea of a wild, painful, and romantic history. Her forehead was high, and her eyebrows marked with beautiful clearness. Her straight, well-formed nose, her finely-cut mouth, and the graceful contour of her head and neck, showed that she must once have been beautiful; but her face was deeply wrinkled with lines of pain, and of proud and bitter endurance. Her complexion was sallow and unhealthy, her cheeks thin, her features sharp, and her whole form emaciated. But her eye was the most remarkable feature,—so large, so heavily black, overshadowed by long lashes of equal darkness, and so wildly, mournfully despairing. There was a fierce pride and defiance in every line of her face, in every curve of the flexible lip, in every motion of her body; but in her eye was a deep, settled night of anguish,—an expression so hopeless and unchanging as to contrast fearfully with the scorn and pride expressed by her whole demeanor.

Where she came from, or who she was, Tom did not know. The first he did know, she was walking by his side, erect and proud, in the dim gray of the dawn. To the gang, however, she was known; for there was much looking and turning of heads, and a smothered yet apparent exultation among the miserable, ragged, half-starved creatures by whom she was surrounded.

"Got to come to it, at last,—glad of it!" said one.

"He! he! he!" said another; "you'll know how good it is, Misse!"

"We'll see her work!"

"Wonder if she'll get a cutting up, at night, like the rest of us!"

"I'd be glad to see her down for a flogging, I'll bound!" said another.

The woman took no notice of these taunts, but walked on, with the same expression of angry scorn, as if she heard nothing. Tom had always lived among refined and cultivated people, and he felt intuitively, from her air and bearing, that she belonged to that class; but how or why she could be fallen to those degrading circumstances, he could not tell. The woman neither looked at him nor spoke to him, though, all the way to the field, she kept close at his side.

Tom was soon busy at his work; but, as the woman was at no great distance from him, he often glanced an eye to her, at her work. He saw, at a glance, that a native adroitness and handiness made the task to her an easier one than it proved to many. She picked very fast and very clean, and with an air of scorn, as if she despised both the work and the disgrace and humiliation of the circumstances in which she was placed.

In the course of the day, Tom was working near the mulatto woman who had been bought in the same lot with himself. She was evidently in a condition of great suffering, and Tom often heard her praying, as she wavered and trembled, and seemed about to fall down. Tom silently, as he came near to her, transferred several handfuls of cotton from his own sack to hers.

"O, don't, don't!" said the woman, looking surprised; "it'll get you into trouble."

Just then Sambo came up. He seemed to have a special spite against this woman; and, flourishing his whip, said, in brutal, guttural tones, "What dis yer, Luce,—foolin' a'?" and, with the word, kicking the woman with his heavy cowhide shoe, he struck Tom across the face with his whip.

Tom silently resumed his task; but the woman, before at the last point of exhaustion, fainted.

"I'll bring her to!" said the driver, with a brutal grin. "I'll give her something better than camphire!"[2] and, taking a pin from his coat-sleeve, he buried it to the head in her flesh. The woman groaned, and half rose. "Get up, you beast, and work, will yer; or I'll show yer a trick more!"

The woman seemed stimulated, for a few moments, to an unnatural strength, and worked with desperate eagerness.

"See that you keep to dat ar," said the man, "or yer'll wish yer's dead to-night, I reckin!"

"That I do now!" Tom heard her say; and again he heard her say, "O, Lord, how long! O, Lord, why don't you help us?"

2 Camphor was commonly used as a smelling salt to revive a person who had fainted. Such a ladylike substance will not be wasted on Lucy.

3 Stowe thus depicts Uncle Tom's first overtly disobedient act. We might note, *pace* Baldwin, that it is a positive act, not a passive one.

At the risk of all that he might suffer, Tom came forward again, and put all the cotton in his sack into the woman's.[3]

"O, you mustn't! you donno what they'll do to ye!" said the woman.

"I can bar it!" said Tom, "better'n you;" and he was at his place again. It passed in a moment.

Suddenly, the stranger woman whom we have described, and who had, in the course of her work, come near enough to hear Tom's last words, raised her heavy black eyes, and fixed them, for a second, on him; then, taking a quantity of cotton from her basket, she placed it in his.

"You know nothing about this place," she said, "or you wouldn't have done that. When you've been here a month, you'll be done helping anybody; you'll find it hard enough to take care of your own skin!"

"The Lord forbid, Missis!" said Tom, using instinctively to his field companion the respectful form proper to the high bred with whom he had lived.

"The Lord never visits these parts," said the woman, bitterly, as she went nimbly forward with her work; and again the scornful smile curled her lips.

But the action of the woman had been seen by the driver, across the field; and flourishing his whip, he came up to her.

"What! what!" he said to the woman, with an air of triumph, "YOU a foolin'? Go along! yer under me now,—mind yourself, or yer'll cotch it!"

A glance like sheet-lightning suddenly flashed from those black eyes; and, facing about, with quivering lip and dilated nostrils, she drew herself up, and fixed a glance, blazing with rage and scorn, on the driver.

"Dog!" she said, "touch *me,* if you dare! I've power enough, yet, to have you torn by the dogs, burnt alive, cut to inches! I've only to say the word!"

"What de devil you here for, den?" said the man, evidently cowed, and sullenly retreating a step or two. "Didn't mean no harm, Misse Cassy!"

"Keep your distance, then!" said the woman. And, in truth, the man seemed greatly inclined to attend to something at the other end of the field, and started off in quick time.

The woman suddenly turned to her work, and labored with a despatch that was perfectly astonishing to Tom. She seemed to work by magic. Before the day was through, her basket was filled, crowded down, and piled, and she had several times put largely into Tom's. Long after dusk, the whole weary train, with their baskets on their heads, defiled[4] up to the building appropriated to the storing and weighing the cotton. Legree was there, busily conversing with the two drivers.

"Dat ar Tom's gwine to make a powerful deal o' trouble; kept a puttin' into Lucy's basket.—One o' these yer dat will get all der niggers to feelin' 'bused, if Mas'r don't watch him!" said Sambo.

"Hey-dey! The black cuss!" said Legree. "He'll have to get a breakin' in, won't he, boys?"

Both negroes grinned a horrid grin, at this intimation.

"Ay, ay! let Mas'r Legree alone, for breakin' in! De debil heself couldn't beat Mas'r at dat!" said Quimbo.

"Wal, boys, the best way is to give him the flogging to do, till he gets over his notions. Break him in!"

"Lord, Mas'r 'll have hard work to get dat out o' him!"

"It'll have to come out of him, though!" said Legree, as he rolled his tobacco in his mouth.

"Now, dar's Lucy,—de aggravatinest, ugliest wench on de place!" pursued Sambo.

"Take care, Sam; I shall begin to think what's the reason for your spite agin Lucy."

"Well, Mas'r knows she sot herself up agin Mas'r, and wouldn't have me, when he told her to."

"I'd a flogged her into 't," said Legree, spitting, "only there's such a press o' work, it don't seem wuth a while to upset her jist now. She's slender; but these yer slender gals will bear half killin' to get their own way!"

"Wal, Lucy was real aggravatin' and lazy, sulkin' round; wouldn't do nothin',—and Tom he tuck up for her."

"He did, eh! Wal, then, Tom shall have the pleasure of flogging her. It'll be a good practice for him, and he won't put it on to the gal like you devils, neither."

"Ho, ho! haw! haw! haw!" laughed both the sooty wretches; and the diabolical sounds seemed, in truth, a not unapt expression of the fiendish character which Legree gave them.

"Wal, but, Mas'r, Tom and Misse Cassy, and dey among 'em, filled Lucy's basket. I ruther guess der weight's in it, Mas'r!"

"*I do the weighing*!" said Legree, emphatically.

Both the drivers again laughed their diabolical laugh.

"So!" he added, "Misse Cassy did her day's work."

"She picks like de debil and all his angels!"

"She's got 'em all in her, I believe!" said Legree; and,

4 I.e., filed one by one. Stowe uses small details such as this to paint a realistic picture of life in the fields.

Cassy leading the others in carrying her cotton to be weighed. The curling whip in the background adds an extra sting to the image.   From *Uncle Tom's Cabin: or, Life Among the Lowly*, Heritage Press edition, 1938

This undated photograph shows the gritty realities of picking cotton; note the young age of the children in the field.

growling a brutal oath, he proceeded to the weighing-room.

Slowly the weary, dispirited creatures, wound their way into the room, and, with crouching reluctance, presented their baskets to be weighed.

Legree noted on a slate, on the side of which was pasted a list of names, the amount.

Tom's basket was weighed and approved; and he looked, with an anxious glance, for the success of the woman he had befriended.

Tottering with weakness, she came forward, and delivered her basket. It was of full weight, as Legree well perceived; but, affecting anger, he said,

"What, you lazy beast! short again! stand aside, you'll catch it, pretty soon!"

The woman gave a groan of utter despair, and sat down on a board.

The person who had been called Misse Cassy now came forward, and, with a haughty, negligent air, delivered her basket. As she delivered it, Legree looked in her eyes with a sneering yet inquiring glance.

She fixed her black eyes steadily on him, her lips moved slightly, and she said something in French. What it was, no one knew; but Legree's face became perfectly demoniacal in its expression, as she spoke; he half raised his hand, as if to strike,—a gesture which she regarded with fierce disdain, as she turned and walked away.

"And now," said Legree, "come here, you Tom. You see, I told ye I didn't buy ye jest for the common work; I mean to promote ye, and make a driver of ye; and to-night ye may jest as well begin to get yer hand in. Now, ye jest take this yer gal and flog her; ye've seen enough on 't to know how."

"I beg Mas'r's pardon," said Tom; "hopes Mas'r won't set me at that. It's what I an't used to,—never did,—and can't do, no way possible."

"Ye'll larn a pretty smart chance of things ye never did know, before I've done with ye!" said Legree, taking up a cow-hide, and striking Tom a heavy blow across the cheek, and following up the infliction by a shower of blows.

"There!" he said, as he stopped to rest; "now, will ye tell me ye can't do it?"

"Yes, Mas'r," said Tom, putting up his hand, to wipe the blood, that trickled down his face. "I'm willin' to work, night and day, and work while there's life and breath in me; but this yer thing I can't feel it right to do;—and, Mas'r, I *never* shall do it,—*never!*"[5]

Tom had a remarkably smooth, soft voice, and a habitually respectful manner, that had given Legree an idea that he would be cowardly, and easily subdued. When he spoke these last words, a thrill of amazement went through every one; the poor woman clasped her hands, and said, "O Lord!" and every one involuntarily looked at each other and drew in their breath, as if to prepare for the storm that was about to burst.

Legree looked stupefied and confounded; but at last burst forth,—

"What! ye blasted black beast! tell *me* ye don't think it *right* to do what I tell ye! What have any of you cussed cattle to do with thinking what's right? I'll put a stop to it! Why, what do ye think ye are? May be ye think ye'r a gentleman, master Tom, to be a telling your master what's right, and what an't! So you pretend it's wrong to flog the gal!"

"I think so, Mas'r," said Tom; "the poor crittur's sick and feeble; 't would be downright cruel, and it's what I never will do, nor begin to. Mas'r, if you mean to kill me, kill me; but, as to my raising my hand agin any one here, I never shall,—I'll die first!"

Tom spoke in a mild voice, but with a decision that could not be mistaken. Legree shook with anger; his greenish eyes glared fiercely, and his very whiskers seemed to curl with passion; but, like some ferocious beast, that plays with its victim before he devours it, he kept back his strong impulse to proceed to immediate violence, and broke out into bitter raillery.

"Well, here's a pious dog, at last, let down among us sinners!—a saint, a gentleman, and no less, to talk to us sinners about our sins! Powerful holy critter, he must be! Here, you rascal, you make believe to be so pious,—didn't you never hear, out of yer Bible, 'Servants, obey yer masters'?[6] An't I yer master? Didn't I pay down twelve hundred dollars, cash, for all there is inside yer old cussed black shell? An't yer mine, now, body and soul?" he said, giving Tom a violent kick with his heavy boot; "tell me!"

In the very depth of physical suffering, bowed by brutal oppression, this question shot a gleam of joy and triumph through Tom's soul. He suddenly stretched himself up, and, looking earnestly to heaven, while the tears and blood that flowed down his face mingled, he exclaimed,

"No! no! no! my soul an't yours, Mas'r! You haven't

**5** This is the second time that Tom is overtly disobedient—this time, however, he is defiantly refusing to act. Tom's halting diction reinforces his utter shock at being asked to participate in something that he considers morally reprehensible, but his smooth, soft, mild manner inflames Legree's rage.

**6** Legree shows that he, too, can quote the Bible. His verse is from Eph. 6:5 or Col. 3:22. But Legree's knowledge is limited. The verse he quotes is followed by the decree that masters should also be kind, since they too have a Master. Col. 4:1 reads, "Masters, treat your slaves justly and fairly, knowing that you also have a Master in heaven."

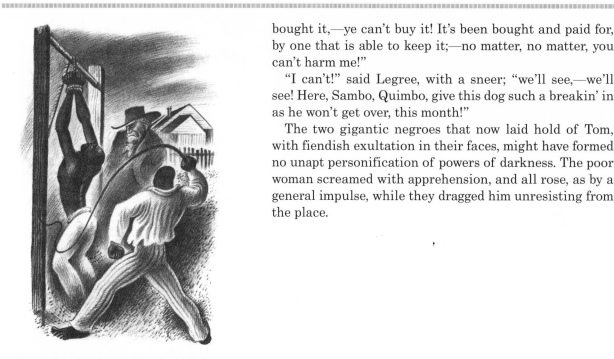

Tom's bare back now sports painful stripes. We can feel Tom strain at his bonds as Sambo whips him and Legree looks on.

bought it,—ye can't buy it! It's been bought and paid for, by one that is able to keep it;—no matter, no matter, you can't harm me!"

"I can't!" said Legree, with a sneer; "we'll see,—we'll see! Here, Sambo, Quimbo, give this dog such a breakin' in as he won't get over, this month!"

The two gigantic negroes that now laid hold of Tom, with fiendish exultation in their faces, might have formed no unapt personification of powers of darkness. The poor woman screamed with apprehension, and all rose, as by a general impulse, while they dragged him unresisting from the place.

# CHAPTER 34

## *The Quadroon's Story*[1]

"And behold the tears of such as are oppressed; and on the side of their oppressors there was power. Wherefore I praised the dead that are already dead more than the living that are yet alive."—Eccl. 4:1.

It was late at night, and Tom lay groaning and bleeding alone, in an old forsaken room of the gin-house, among pieces of broken machinery, piles of damaged cotton, and other rubbish which had there accumulated.

The night was damp and close, and the thick air swarmed with myriads of mosquitos, which increased the restless torture of his wounds; whilst a burning thirst—a torture beyond all others—filled up the utter most measure of physical anguish.

"O, good Lord! *Do* look down,—give me the victory!—give me the victory over all!" prayed poor Tom, in his anguish.

A footstep entered the room, behind him, and the light of a lantern flashed on his eyes.

"Who's there? O, for the Lord's massy, please give me some water!"

1 This chapter title signals that we will finally hear about the mysterious Cassy's past. The epigraph is the same verse from Ecclesiastes that Stowe used for the last chapter. Stowe's setting of these final scenes in the gin house is not accidental: In the mid-nineteenth century, it was becoming a commonplace among abolitionists that the growth of the cotton industry (made prof-

Illustration by Hammatt Billings of Cassy bringing a drink to Uncle Tom. Stowe writes that Cassy pours water for Uncle Tom from a bottle, but here it looks like she is bringing Tom brandy. Cassy's features are pointy and white.   From *Uncle Tom's Cabin,* John P. Jewett & Co., 1852

itable by Eli Whitney's invention of the cotton gin in 1794) was largely responsible for the increase of slavery. The following excerpt is from an article entitled "Revolution of the Spindles, for the Overthrow of American Slavery" which appeared in Frederick Douglass's the *North Star* on June 23, 1848:

Little dreamed the ingenious Eli Whitney, when riveting the teeth on his admirable invention, the cotton-gin, that he was at the same time riveting the fetters on the slave, and the foulest of institutions on the framework of American society. On this subject, we quote an article in The Friend, No. 64, being an abridgement from the twenty-first volume of "Silliman's Journal:"

"Negro slavery existed in the United States long before the cotton-gin was brought into use, yet at the time of its invention, the market was glutted with all those articles which were suited to the soil and climate of Georgia, and it was difficult to find profitable employment for the slaves. Under these circumstances, slavery must have languished,

George Cruikshank's image of Cassy tending Tom also features a bottle: This one looks like an Italian wine bottle. Although Cruikshank's Cassy is not as haggard as Billings's, she is equally unattractive.   From *Uncle Tom's Cabin,* John Cassell, London, 1852

The woman Cassy—for it was she—set down her lantern, and, pouring water from a bottle, raised his head, and gave him drink. Another and another cup were drained, with feverish eagerness.

"Drink all ye want," she said; "I knew how it would be. It isn't the first time I've been out in the night, carrying water to such as you."

"Thank you, Missis," said Tom, when he had done drinking.

"Don't call me Missis! I'm a miserable slave, like yourself,—a lower one than you can ever be!" said she, bitterly; "but now," said she, going to the door, and dragging in a small pallaise, over which she had spread linen cloths wet with cold water, "try, my poor fellow, to roll yourself on to this."

Stiff with wounds and bruises, Tom was a long time in accomplishing this movement; but, when done, he felt a sensible relief from the cooling application to his wounds.

The woman, whom long practice with the victims of brutality had made familiar with many healing arts, went on to make many applications to Tom's wounds, by means of which he was soon somewhat relieved.

"Now," said the woman, when she had raised his head on a roll of damaged cotton, which served for a pillow, "there's the best I can do for you."

Tom thanked her; and the woman, sitting down on the floor, drew up her knees, and embracing them with her arms, looked fixedly before her, with a bitter and painful expression of countenance. Her bonnet fell back, and long wavy streams of black hair fell around her singular and melancholy face.

"It's no use, my poor fellow!" she broke out, at last, "it's of no use, this you've been trying to do. You were a brave fellow,—you had the right on your side; but it's all in vain, and out of the question, for you to struggle. You are in the devil's hands;—he is the strongest, and you must give up!"

Give up! and, had not human weakness and physical agony whispered that, before? Tom started; for the bitter woman, with her wild eyes and melancholy voice, seemed to him an embodiment of the temptation with which he had been wrestling.

"O Lord! O Lord!" he groaned, "how can I give up?"

"There's no use calling on the Lord,—he never hears," said the woman, steadily; "there isn't any God, I believe; or, if there is, he's taken sides against us. All goes against us, heaven and earth. Everything is pushing us into hell. Why shouldn't we go?"

Tom closed his eyes, and shuddered at the dark, atheistic words.

"You see," said the woman, "*you* don't know anything about it;—I do. I've been on this place five years, body and soul, under this man's foot; and I hate him as I do the devil! Here you are, on a lone plantation, ten miles from any other, in the swamps; not a white person here, who could testify, if you were burned alive,—if you were scalded, cut into inch-pieces, set up for the dogs to tear, or hung up and whipped to death. There's no law here, of God or man, that can do you, or any one of us, the least good; and, this man! there's no earthly thing that he's too good to do.[2] I could make any one's hair rise, and their teeth chatter, if I should only tell what I've seen and been knowing to, here,—and it's no use resisting! Did I *want* to live with him? Wasn't I a woman delicately bred; and he— God in heaven! what was he, and is he? And yet, I've lived with him, these five years, and cursed every moment of my life,—night and day! And now, he's got a new one,—a young thing, only fifteen, and she brought up, she says, piously. Her good mistress taught her to read the Bible; and she's brought her Bible here—to hell with her!"—and the woman laughed a wild and doleful laugh, that rung, with a strange, supernatural sound, through the old ruined shed.

Tom folded his hands; all was darkness and horror.

"O Jesus! Lord Jesus! have you quite forgot us poor critturs?" burst forth, at last;—"help, Lord, I perish!"

The woman sternly continued:

"And what are these miserable low dogs you work with, that you should suffer on their account? Every one of them would turn against you, the first time they got a chance. They are all of 'em as low and cruel to each other as they can be; there's no use in your suffering to keep from hurting them."

"Poor critturs!" said Tom,—"what made 'em cruel?— and, if I give out, I shall get used to't, and grow, little by little, just like 'em! No, no, Missis! I've lost everything,— wife, and children, and home, and a kind Mas'r,—and he would have set me free, if he'd only lived a week longer; I've lost everything in *this* world, and it's clean gone, for-ever,—and now I *can't* lose Heaven, too; no, I can't get to be wicked, besides all!"

"But it can't be that the Lord will lay sin to our account," said the woman; "he won't charge it to us, when we're forced to it; he'll charge it to them that drove us to it."

"Yes," said Tom; "but that won't keep us from growing

and the pecuniary value of slaves have suffered a great decline; and experience sufficiently proves that when the price of slaves is low, emancipations become frequent. But the invention of the cotton-gin, by opening a new source of profit from the labor of slaves, enhanced their value, and gave an impulse to the traffic in their persons from the exhausted slave States of the north to those further south and west, impulse which continues to the present day."

We learn from the same source, that the invention of the cotton-gin (which is the machine used in separating the seed from the fibre,) took place about the year 1793. The marvellous impetus given to the cotton trade by this invention, may be judged of from the fact, that while in the year immediately preceding, that is, in 1792, the total weight of cotton raised in the United States, was estimated at three millions of pounds; in 1800, it was reported at thirty-five millions; in 1810, at eighty-five millions; in 1820, at one hundred and sixty millions; in 1830, at three hundred and fifty millions; in 1840, at seven hundred and ninety millions; and in 1847, (as per report of the Patent-office, quoted in the Standard,) at one thousand and forty-one millions.

Still more clearly to elucidate the cotemporaneous [*sic*] growth of slavery and the cotton-trade, we give two tables, compiled by the intelligent editor of the North of Scotland Gazette, and published in that paper of November 30th, 1847:

Exports of Cotton from the U. States.

| Year. | Lbs. |
|---|---|
| 1790, | 189,316 |
| 1800, | 20,911,201 |
| 1810, | 62,911,201 |
| 1820, | 124,893,405 |
| 1830, | 270,979,784 |
| 1840, | 540,957,568 |
| 1843, | 1,081,919,136 |
| 1846, | 1,250,500,000 |

Slave Population in the United States.

| Year. | Population |
|---|---|
| 1790, | - - - 657,437 |
| 1800, | - - - 866,582 |
| 1810, | - - - 1,299,872 |
| 1820, | - - - 1,733,162 |
| 1830, | - - - 2,310,882 |
| 1840, | - - - 2,485,685 |
| 1843, | - - - 2,847,810 |
| 1846 | - - - 3,000,000 |

After considering these statements, who is there that can resist the conclusion that American slavery derives its vitality from the cotton trade?

The comic-book version of Cassy tending Tom features a more innocent-looking pitcher.   From Classics Illustrated Classic Comic Book no. 15, *Uncle Tom's Cabin*, 1943

2 As many scholars have noted, the horrifying description of Cassy's life with Legree prefigures the isolated domain of Mr. Kurtz in Joseph Conrad's *Heart of Darkness* (1902).

3 Luke 23:34. Not surprisingly, the verse makes Cassy cry. Stowe portrays her as hardened but not evil. Cassy's tragic life, Stowe suggests, is partly a function of her privileged upbringing as the child of a wealthy slaveholder and a slave. Untrained for anything else but enjoying luxury, what can she do but become the lover of her next master?

wicked. If I get to be as hard-hearted as that ar' Sambo, and as wicked, it won't make much odds to me how I come so; it's the *bein' so,*—that ar's what I'm a dreadin'."

The woman fixed a wild and startled look on Tom, as if a new thought had struck her; and then, heavily groaning, said,

"O God a' mercy! you speak the truth! O—O—O!"—and, with groans, she fell on the floor, like one crushed and writhing under the extremity of mental anguish.

There was a silence, a while, in which the breathing of both parties could be heard, when Tom faintly said, "O, please, Missis!"

The woman suddenly rose up, with her face composed to its usual stern, melancholy expression.

"Please, Missis, I saw 'em throw my coat in that ar' corner, and in my coat-pocket is my Bible;—if Missis would please get it for me."

Cassy went and got it. Tom opened, at once, to a heavily marked passage, much worn, of the last scenes in the life of Him by whose stripes we are healed.

"If Missis would only be so good as read that ar',—it's better than water."

Cassy took the book, with a dry, proud air, and looked over the passage. She then read aloud, in a soft voice, and with a beauty of intonation that was peculiar, that touching account of anguish and of glory. Often, as she read, her voice faltered, and sometimes failed her altogether, when she would stop, with an air of frigid composure, till she had mastered herself. When she came to the touching words, "Father forgive them, for they know not what they do,"[3] she threw down the book, and, burying her face in the heavy masses of her hair, she sobbed aloud, with a convulsive violence.

Tom was weeping, also, and occasionally uttering a smothered ejaculation.

"If we only could keep up to that ar'!" said Tom;—"it seemed to come so natural to him, and we have to fight so hard for 't! O Lord, help us! O blessed Lord Jesus, do help us!"

"Missis," said Tom, after a while, "I can see that, some how, you're quite 'bove me in everything; but there's one thing Missis might learn even from poor Tom. Ye said the Lord took sides against us, because he lets us be 'bused and knocked round; but ye see what come on his own Son,—the blessed Lord of Glory,—wan't he allays poor? and have we, any on us, yet come so low as he come? The Lord han't forgot us,—I'm sartin' o' that ar'. If we suffer with him, we shall also reign, Scripture says; but, if we deny Him, he also will deny us. Didn't they all suffer?— the Lord and all his? It tells how they was stoned and sawn asunder, and wandered about in sheep-skins and goat-skins, and was destitute, afflicted, tormented. Sufferin' an't no reason to make us think the Lord's turned agin us; but jest the contrary, if only we hold on to him, and doesn't give up to sin."

"But why does he put us where we can't help but sin?" said the woman.

"I think we *can* help it," said Tom.

"You'll see," said Cassy; "what'll you do? To-morrow they'll be at you again. I know 'em; I've seen all their doings; I can't bear to think of all they'll bring you to;— and they'll make you give out, at last!"

"Lord Jesus!" said Tom, "you *will* take care of my soul? O Lord, do!—don't let me give out!"

"O dear!" said Cassy; "I've heard all this crying and praying before; and yet, they've been broken down, and brought under. There's Emmeline, she's trying to hold on, and you're trying,—but what use? You must give up, or be killed by inches."

"Well, then, I *will* die!" said Tom. "Spin it out as long as they can, they can't help my dying, some time!—and, after that, they can't do no more. I'm clar, I'm set! I *know* the Lord'll help me, and bring me through."

The woman did not answer; she sat with her black eyes intently fixed on the floor.

"May be it's the way," she murmured to herself; "but those that *have* given up, there's no hope for them!—none! We live in filth, and grow loathsome, till we loathe ourselves! And we long to die, and we don't dare to kill ourselves!—No hope! no hope! no hope!—this girl now,—just as old as I was!

"You see me now," she said, speaking to Tom very rapidly; "see what I am! Well, I was brought up in luxury; the first I remember is, playing about, when I was a child, in splendid parlors;—when I was kept dressed up like a doll, and company and visiters used to praise me. There was a garden opening from the saloon windows; and there I used to play hide-and-go-seek, under the orange-trees, with my brothers and sisters. I went to a convent, and there I learned music, French and embroidery, and what not; and when I was fourteen, I came out to my father's funeral. He died very suddenly, and when the property came to be settled, they found that there was scarcely enough to cover the debts; and when the creditors took an inventory of the

**4** A tropical disease transmitted by mosquitoes and causing liver and kidney degeneration, yellow fever is characterized by the yellow skin of jaundice. Neither the cause nor the cure was known in Stowe's time. Cassy's status as a *mother* adds to her story's pathos.

property, I was set down in it. My mother was a slave woman, and my father had always meant to set me free; but he had not done it, and so I was set down in the list. I'd always known who I was, but never thought much about it. Nobody ever expects that a strong, healthy man is a going to die. My father was a well man only four hours before he died;—it was one of the first cholera cases in New Orleans. The day after the funeral, my father's wife took her children, and went up to her father's plantation. I thought they treated me strangely, but didn't know. There was a young lawyer who they left to settle the business; and he came every day, and was about the house, and spoke very politely to me. He brought with him, one day, a young man, whom I thought the handsomest I had ever seen. I shall never forget that evening. I walked with him in the garden. I was lonesome and full of sorrow, and he was so kind and gentle to me; and he told me that he had seen me before I went to the convent, and that he had loved me a great while, and that he would be my friend and protector;—in short, though he didn't tell me, he had paid two thousand dollars for me, and I was his property,—I became his willingly, for I loved him. Loved!" said the woman, stopping. "O, how I *did* love that man! How I love him now,—and always shall, while I breathe! He was so beautiful, so high, so noble! He put me into a beautiful house, with servants, horses, and carriages, and furniture, and dresses. Everything that money could buy, he gave me; but I didn't set any value on all that,—I only cared for him. I loved him better than my God and my own soul; and, if I tried, I couldn't do any other way from what he wanted me to.

"I wanted only one thing—I did want him to *marry* me. I thought, if he loved me as he said he did, and if I was what he seemed to think I was, he would be willing to marry me and set me free. But he convinced me that it would be impossible; and he told me that, if we were only faithful to each other, it was marriage before God. If that is true, wasn't I that man's wife? Wasn't I faithful? For seven years, didn't I study every look and motion, and only live and breathe to please him? He had the yellow fever,[4] and for twenty days and nights I watched with him. I alone,—and gave him all his medicine, and did everything for him; and then he called me his good angel, and said I'd saved his life. We had two beautiful children. The first was a boy, and we called him Henry. He was the image of his father,—he had such beautiful eyes, such a forehead, and his hair hung all in curls around it; and he had all his father's spirit, and his talent, too. Little Elise, he said, looked like me. He used to tell me that I was the most beautiful woman in Louisiana, he was so proud of me and the children. He used to love to have me dress them up, and take them and me about in an open carriage, and hear the remarks that people would make on us; and he used to fill my ears constantly with the fine things that were said in praise of me and the children. O, those were happy days! I thought I was as happy as any one could be; but then there came evil times. He had a cousin come to New Orleans, who was his particular friend,—he thought all the world of him;—but, from the first time I saw him, I couldn't tell why, I dreaded him; for I felt sure he was going to bring misery on us. He got Henry to going out with him, and often he would not come home nights till two or three o'clock. I did not dare say a word; for Henry was so high-spirited, I was afraid to. He got him to the gaming-houses;[5] and he was one of the sort that, when he once got a going there, there was no holding back. And then he introduced him to another lady, and I saw soon that his heart was gone from me. He never told me, but I saw it,—I knew it, day after day,—I felt my heart breaking, but I could not say a word! At this, the wretch offered to buy me and the children of Henry, to clear off his gambling debts, which stood in the way of his marrying as he wished;—and *he sold us*. He told me, one day, that he had business in the country, and should be gone two or three weeks. He spoke kinder than usual, and said he should come back; but it didn't deceive me. I knew that the time had come; I was just like one turned into stone; I couldn't speak, nor shed a tear. He kissed me and kissed the children, a good many times, and went out. I saw him get on his horse, and I watched him till he was quite out of sight; and then I fell down, and fainted.

"Then *he* came, the cursed wretch! he came to take possession.[6] He told me that he had bought me and my children; and showed me the papers. I cursed him before God, and told him I'd die sooner than live with him.

" 'Just as you please,' said he; 'but, if you don't behave reasonably, I'll sell both the children, where you shall never see them again.' He told me that he always had meant to have me, from the first time he saw me; and that he had drawn Henry on, and got him in debt, on purpose to make him willing to sell me. That he got him in love with another woman; and that I might know, after all that, that he should not give up for a few airs and tears, and things of that sort.

5 I.e., gambling. As with Mr. Shelby, financial irresponsibility leads to tragedy for "property."

6 Literally, to take ownership; however, in this case "possession" means both demonic possession as well as sexual intercourse. Stowe is as frank as she can be about what Cassy means by "submissive." More than likely, nineteenth-century women readers who had no choice but to submit to husbands not of their choosing or for whom there was no love or respect recognized Cassy's chilling plight.

7 Ie., suffer physically. Stowe is careful not to allow Cassy's painful story to numb the reader: The moments of horror are leavened with moments of hope; the reader hangs on every word.

"I gave up, for my hands were tied. He had my children;—whenever I resisted his will anywhere, he would talk about selling them, and he made me as submissive as he desired. O, what a life it was! to live with my heart breaking, every day,—to keep on, on, on, loving, when it was only misery; and to be bound, body and soul, to one I hated. I used to love to read to Henry, to play to him, to waltz with him, and sing to him; but everything I did for this one was a perfect drag,—yet I was afraid to refuse anything. He was very imperious, and harsh to the children. Elise was a timid little thing; but Henry was bold and high-spirited, like his father, and he had never been brought under, in the least, by any one. He was always finding fault, and quarrelling with him; and I used to live in daily fear and dread. I tried to make the child respectful;—I tried to keep them apart, for I held on to those children like death; but it did no good. *He sold both those children.* He took me to ride, one day, and when I came home, they were nowhere to be found! He told me he had sold them; he showed me the money, the price of their blood. Then it seemed as if all good forsook me. I raved and cursed,—cursed God and man; and, for a while, I believe, he really was afraid of me. But he didn't give up so. He told me that my children were sold, but whether I ever saw their faces again, depended on him; and that, if I wasn't quiet, they should smart[7] for it. Well, you can do anything with a woman, when you've got her children. He made me submit; he made me be peaceable; he flattered me with hopes that, perhaps, he would buy them back; and so things went on, a week or two. One day, I was out walking, and passed by the calaboose; I saw a crowd about the gate, and heard a child's voice,—and suddenly my Henry broke away from two or three men who were holding him, and ran, screaming, and caught my dress. They came up to him, swearing dreadfully; and one man, whose face I shall never forget, told him that he wouldn't get away so; that he was going with him into the calaboose, and he'd get a lesson there he'd never forget. I tried to beg and plead,—they only laughed; the poor boy screamed and looked into my face, and held on to me, until, in tearing him off, they tore the skirt of my dress half away; and they carried him in, screaming 'Mother! mother! mother!' There was one man stood there seemed to pity me. I offered him all the money I had, if he'd only interfere. He shook his head, and said that the man said the boy had been impudent and disobedient, ever since he bought him; that he was going to break him in, once for all. I turned and ran; and every step of the way, I thought that I heard him scream. I got into the house; ran, all out of breath, to the parlor, where I found Butler. I told him, and begged him to go and interfere. He only laughed, and told me the boy had got his deserts. He'd got to be broken in,—the sooner the better; 'what did I expect?' he asked.

"It seemed to me something in my head snapped, at that moment. I felt dizzy and furious. I remember seeing a great sharp bowie-knife on the table; I remember something about catching it, and flying upon him; and then all grew dark, and I didn't know any more—not for days and days.

When I came to myself, I was in a nice room,—but not mine. An old black woman tended me; and a doctor came to see me, and there was a great deal of care taken of me. After a while, I found that he had gone away, and left me at this house to be sold; and that's why they took such pains with me.

"I didn't mean to get well, and hoped I shouldn't; but, in spite of me, the fever went off, and I grew healthy, and finally got up. Then, they made me dress up, every day; and gentlemen used to come in and stand and smoke their cigars, and look at me, and ask questions, and debate my price. I was so gloomy and silent, that none of them wanted me. They threatened to whip me, if I wasn't gayer, and didn't take some pains to make myself agreeable. At length, one day, came a gentleman named Stuart. He seemed to have some feeling for me; he saw that something dreadful was on my heart, and he came to see me alone, a great many times, and finally persuaded me to tell him. He bought me, at last, and promised to do all he could to find and buy back my children. He went to the hotel where my Henry was; they told him he had been sold to a planter up on Pearl river; that was the last that I ever heard. Then he found where my daughter was; an old woman was keeping her. He offered an immense sum for her, but they would not sell her. Butler found out that it was for me he wanted her; and he sent me word that I should never have her. Captain Stuart was very kind to me; he had a splendid plantation, and took me to it. In the course of a year, I had a son born. O, that child!—how I loved it! How just like my poor Henry the little thing looked! But I had made up my mind,—yes, I had. I would never again let a child live to grow up! I took the little fellow in my arms, when he was two weeks old, and kissed him, and cried over him; and then I gave him laudanum,[8] and held him close to my bosom, while he slept to death. How I mourned and cried

8 Cassy's decision to use laudanum to kill her child by her next master rather than let him grow up in slavery was a common thought of slave mothers, many of whom followed with action.

9 Tom was distracted from his pain for a long while.

10 I.e., to hell.

over it! and who ever dreamed that it was anything but a mistake, that had made me give it the laudanum? but it's one of the few things that I'm glad of, now. I am not sorry, to this day; he, at least, is out of pain. What better than death could I give him, poor child! After a while, the cholera came, and Captain Stuart died; everybody died that wanted to live,—and I,—I, though I went down to death's door,—*I lived*! Then I was sold, and passed from hand to hand, till I grew faded and wrinkled, and I had a fever; and then this wretch bought me, and brought me here,—and here I am!"

The woman stopped. She had hurried on through her story, with a wild, passionate utterance; sometimes seeming to address it to Tom, and sometimes speaking as in a soliloquy. So vehement and overpowering was the force with which she spoke, that, for a season, Tom was beguiled even from the pain of his wounds,[9] and, raising himself on one elbow, watched her as she paced restlessly up and down, her long black hair swaying heavily about her, as she moved.

"You tell me," she said, after a pause, "that there is a God,—a God that looks down and sees all these things. May be it's so. The sisters in the convent used to tell me of a day of judgment, when everything is coming to light;— won't there be vengeance, then!

"They think it's nothing, what we suffer,—nothing, what our children suffer! It's all a small matter; yet I've walked the streets when it seemed as if I had misery enough in my one heart to sink the city. I've wished the houses would fall on me, or the stones sink under me. Yes! and, in the judgment day, I will stand up before God, a witness against those that have ruined me and my children, body and soul!

"When I was a girl, I thought I was religious; I used to love God and prayer. Now, I'm a lost soul, pursued by devils that torment me day and night; they keep pushing me on and on—and I'll do it, too, some of these days!" she said, clenching her hand, while an insane light glanced in her heavy black eyes. "I'll send him where he belongs,[10]— a short way, too—one of these nights, if they burn me alive for it!" A wild, long laugh, rang through the deserted room, and ended in a hysteric sob; she threw herself on the floor, in convulsive sobbings and struggles.

In a few moments the frenzy fit seemed to pass off; she rose slowly, and seemed to collect herself.

"Can I do anything more for you, my poor fellow?" she

said, approaching where Tom lay; "shall I give you some more water?"

There was a graceful and compassionate sweetness in her voice and manner, as she said this, that formed a strange contrast with the former wildness.

Tom drank the water, and looked earnestly and pitifully into her face.

"O, Missis, I wish you'd go to him[11] that can give you living waters!"

"Go to him! Where is he? Who is he?" said Cassy.

"Him that you read of to me,—the Lord."

"I used to see the picture of him, over the altar, when I was a girl," said Cassy, her dark eyes fixing themselves in an expression of mournful reverie; "but, *he isn't here*! there's nothing here, but sin and long, long, long despair! O!" She laid her hand on her breast and drew in her breath, as if to lift a heavy weight.

Tom looked as if he would speak again; but she cut him short, with a decided gesture.

"Don't talk, my poor fellow. Try to sleep, if you can." And, placing water in his reach, and making whatever little arrangements for his comfort she could, Cassy left the shed.

11  I.e., Jesus.

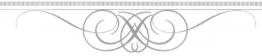

## CHAPTER 35

### *The Tokens*

1 *Childe Harold's Pilgrimage* by Lord Byron, begun in 1809 and finished in 1818, was a poem of four cantos following the wanderings of a disillusioned young man. The poem made Byron famous and his melancholy hero a Romantic figure. Stowe was fascinated with Lord Byron and his poetry, and also with his long-suffering wife. Stowe would go on to write "The True Story of Lady Byron's Life" and *Lady Byron Vindicated*.

*"And slight, withal, may be the things that bring*
*Back on the heart the weight which it would fling*
*Aside forever; it may be a sound,*
*A flower, the wind, the ocean, which shall wound,—*
*Striking the electric chain wherewith we're darkly*
 *bound."*
—*Childe Harold's Pilgrimage*, Can. 4.[1]

The sitting-room of Legree's establishment was a large, long room, with a wide, ample fireplace. It had once been hung with a showy and expensive paper, which now hung mouldering, torn and discolored, from the damp walls. The place had that peculiar sickening, unwholesome smell, compounded of mingled damp, dirt and decay, which one often notices in close old houses. The wall-paper was defaced, in spots, by slops of beer and wine; or garnished with chalk memorandums, and long sums footed up, as if somebody had been practising arithmetic there. In the fireplace stood a brazier full of burning charcoal; for, though the weather was not cold, the evenings always seemed damp and chilly in that great room; and Legree, moreover, wanted a place to light his cigars, and heat his water for punch. The ruddy glare of the charcoal displayed the confused and unpromising aspect of the room,—saddles, bridles, several sorts of harness, riding-whips, overcoats, and various articles of clothing, scattered up and down the room in confused variety; and the dogs, of whom we have before spoken, had encamped themselves among them, to suit their own taste and convenience.

Legree was just mixing himself a tumbler of punch,[2] pouring his hot water from a cracked and broken-nosed pitcher, grumbling, as he did so,

"Plague on that Sambo, to kick up this yer row between me and the new hands! The fellow won't be fit to work for a week, now,—right in the press of the season!"

"Yes, just like you," said a voice, behind his chair. It was the woman Cassy, who had stolen upon his soliloquy.

"Hah! you she-devil! you've come back, have you?"

"Yes, I have," she said, coolly; "come to have my own way, too!"

"You lie, you jade![3] I'll be up to my word. Either behave yourself, or stay down to the quarters, and fare and work with the rest."

"I'd rather, ten thousand times," said the woman, "live in the dirtiest hole at the quarters, than be under your hoof!"

"But you *are* under my hoof, for all that," said he, turning upon her, with a savage grin; "that's one comfort. So, sit down here on my knee, my dear, and hear to reason," said he, laying hold on her wrist.

"Simon Legree, take care!" said the woman, with a sharp flash of her eye, a glance so wild and insane in its light as to be almost appalling. "You're afraid of me, Simon," she said, deliberately; "and you've reason to be! But be careful, for I've got the devil in me!"

The last words she whispered in a hissing tone, close to his ear.

"Get out! I believe, to my soul, you have!" said Legree, pushing her from him, and looking uncomfortably at her. "After all, Cassy," he said, "why can't you be friends with me, as you used to?"[4]

"Used to!" said she, bitterly. She stopped short,—a world of choking feelings, rising in her heart, kept her silent.

Cassy had always kept over Legree the kind of influence that a strong, impassioned woman can ever keep over the most brutal man; but, of late, she had grown more and more irritable and restless, under the hideous yoke of her servitude, and her irritability, at times, broke out into raving insanity; and this liability made her a sort of object of dread to Legree, who had that superstitious horror of insane persons which is common to coarse and uninstructed minds. When Legree brought Emmeline to the

2 I.e., a mixed drink (likely with rum or whiskey). Clearly, Legree's home is a step down from St. Clare's plantation. Better a humble but neat abode than a filthy, seedy, decrepit mansion.

3 I.e., you hussy. Cassy is a complicated character who is crucial to many plotlines. Here, she plays a crucial role in depicting the limits of Legree's power.

4 Legree's sense that there should be no antagonism between master and slave, that they should be "friends," is clearly laughable.

**5** I.e., squabble.

**6** Stowe's description of Eva's hair "like a living thing" recalls the scene at the end of the last chapter where Tom asks Cassy to go to him who gives "living waters." We are to see Eva's hair as having a supernatural, Christ-like energy that burns Legree. The action prefigures similar scenes of vampires cringing and jumping back at the sight of a crucifix.

house, all the smouldering embers of womanly feeling flashed up in the worn heart of Cassy, and she took part with the girl; and a fierce quarrel ensued between her and Legree. Legree, in a fury, swore she should be put to field service, if she would not be peaceable. Cassy, with proud scorn, declared she *would* go to the field. And she worked there one day, as we have described, to show how perfectly she scorned the threat.

Legree was secretly uneasy, all day; for Cassy had an influence over him from which he could not free himself. When she presented her basket at the scales, he had hoped for some concession, and addressed her in a sort of half conciliatory, half scornful tone; and she had answered with the bitterest contempt.

The outrageous treatment of poor Tom had roused her still more; and she had followed Legree to the house, with no particular intention, but to upbraid him for his brutality.

"I wish, Cassy," said Legree, "you'd behave yourself decently."

"*You* talk about behaving decently! And what have you been doing?—you, who haven't even sense enough to keep from spoiling one of your best hands, right in the most pressing season, just for your devilish temper!"

"I was a fool, it's a fact, to let any such brangle[5] come up," said Legree; "but, when the boy set up his will, he had to be broke in."

"I reckon you won't break *him* in!"

"Won't I?" said Legree, rising, passionately. "I'd like to know if I won't? He'll be the first nigger that ever came it round me! I'll break every bone in his body, but he *shall* give up!"

Just then the door opened, and Sambo entered. He came forward, bowing, and holding out something in a paper.

"What's that, you dog?" said Legree.

"It's a witch thing, Mas'r!"

"A what?"

"Something that niggers gets from witches. Keeps 'em from feelin' when they's flogged. He had it tied round his neck, with a black string."

Legree, like most godless and cruel men, was superstitious. He took the paper, and opened it uneasily.

There dropped out of it a silver dollar, and a long, shining curl of fair hair,—hair which, like a living thing, twined itself round Legree's fingers.[6]

"Damnation!" he screamed, in sudden passion, stamping on the floor, and pulling furiously at the hair, as if it burned him. "Where did this come from? Take it off!—burn it up!—burn it up!" he screamed, tearing it off, and throwing it into the charcoal. "What did you bring it to me for?"

Sambo stood, with his heavy mouth wide open, and aghast with wonder; and Cassy, who was preparing to leave the apartment, stopped, and looked at him in perfect amazement.

"Don't you bring me any more of your devilish things!" said he, shaking his fist at Sambo, who retreated hastily towards the door; and, picking up the silver dollar, he sent it smashing through the window-pane, out into the darkness.

Sambo was glad to make his escape. When he was gone, Legree seemed a little ashamed of his fit of alarm. He sat doggedly down in his chair, and began sullenly sipping his tumbler of punch.

Cassy prepared herself for going out, unobserved by him; and slipped away to minister to poor Tom, as we have already related.

And what was the matter with Legree? and what was there in a simple curl of fair hair to appall that brutal man, familiar with every form of cruelty? To answer this, we must carry the reader backward in his history. Hard and reprobate as the godless man seemed now, there had been a time when he had been rocked on the bosom of a mother,—cradled with prayers and pious hymns,[7]—his now seared brow bedewed with the waters of holy baptism. In early childhood, a fair-haired woman had led him, at the sound of Sabbath bell, to worship and to pray. Far in New England that mother had trained her only son, with long, unwearied love, and patient prayers.[8] Born of a hard-tempered sire, on whom that gentle woman had wasted a world of unvalued love, Legree had followed in the steps of his father. Boisterous, unruly, and tyrannical, he despised all her counsel, and would none of her reproof; and, at an early age, broke from her, to seek his fortunes at sea. He never came home but once, after; and then, his mother, with the yearning of a heart that must love something, and has nothing else to love, clung to him, and sought, with passionate prayers and entreaties, to win him from a life of sin, to his soul's eternal good.

That was Legree's day of grace; then good angels called him; then he was almost persuaded, and mercy held him by the hand. His heart inly relented,—there was a conflict,—but sin got the victory, and he set all the force of his rough nature against the conviction of his conscience.

7 Like St. Clare, Legree had a pious mother. Stowe's inclusion of this fact seems odd here: Unlike St. Clare's mother, who evidently died too early to do her son lasting good, Legree's mother wasted her love on a hard-tempered man.

8 As historian Emory Thomas remarks, "The 'moonlight and magnolia' romantic image of Southern life not only prescribed a large portion of the Southerner's concept of himself, it affected Northerners as well. Perhaps no one paid higher tribute to Southern Romanticism than Harriet Beecher Stowe when she made Simon Legree, the irredeemable villain of *Uncle Tom's Cabin*, a Yankee" (*The Confederacy As a Revolutionary Experience*). As expected, Southern readers leapt on the fact that the novel's villain hailed from New England.

9 I.e., magic, especially communication with the dead.

10 Stowe makes her reader shudder for Emmeline with this threat.

11 I.e., a burial chamber, wholly or partially underground.

He drank and swore,—was wilder and more brutal than ever. And, one night, when his mother, in the last agony of her despair, knelt at his feet he spurned her from him,—threw her senseless on the floor, and, with brutal curses, fled to his ship. The next Legree heard of his mother was, when, one night, as he was carousing among drunken companions, a letter was put into his hand. He opened it, and a lock of long, curling hair fell from it, and twined about his fingers. The letter told him his mother was dead, and that, dying, she blest and forgave him.

There is a dread, unhallowed necromancy of evil,[9] that turns things sweetest and holiest to phantoms of horror and affright. That pale, loving mother,—her dying prayers, her forgiving love,—wrought in that demoniac heart of sin only as a damning sentence, bringing with it a fearful looking for of judgment and fiery indignation. Legree burned the hair, and burned the letter; and when he saw them hissing and crackling in the flame, inly shuddered as he thought of everlasting fires. He tried to drink, and revel, and swear away the memory; but often, in the deep night, whose solemn stillness arraigns the bad soul in forced communion with herself, he had seen that pale mother rising by his bedside, and felt the soft twining of that hair around his fingers, till the cold sweat would roll down his face, and he would spring from his bed in horror. Ye who have wondered to hear, in the same evangel, that God is love, and that God is a consuming fire, see ye not how, to the soul resolved in evil, perfect love is the most fearful torture, the seal and sentence of the direst despair?

"Blast it!" said Legree to himself, as he sipped his liquor; "where did he get that? If it didn't look just like—whoo! I thought I'd forgot that. Curse me, if I think there's any such thing as forgetting anything, any how,—hang it! I'm lonesome! I mean to call Em. She hates me—the monkey! I don't care,—I'll *make* her come!"[10]

Legree stepped out into a large entry, which went up stairs, by what had formerly been a superb winding staircase; but the passage-way was dirty and dreary, encumbered with boxes and unsightly litter. The stairs, uncarpeted, seemed winding up, in the gloom, to nobody knew where! The pale moonlight streamed through a shattered fanlight over the door; the air was unwholesome and chilly, like that of a vault.[11]

Legree stopped at the foot of the stairs, and heard a voice singing. It seemed strange and ghostlike in that dreary old house, perhaps because of the already tremulous state of his nerves. Hark! what is it?[12]

A wild, pathetic voice, chants a hymn common among the slaves:

*"O there'll be mourning, mourning, mourning,*
*O there'll be mourning, at the judgment-seat of Christ!"*

"Blast the girl!" said Legree. "I'll choke her.—Em! Em!" he called, harshly; but only a mocking echo from the walls answered him. The sweet voice still sung on:

> *"Parents and children there shall part!*
> *Parents and children there shall part!*
> *Shall part to meet no more!"*

And clear and loud swelled through the empty halls the refrain,

*"O there'll be mourning, mourning, mourning,*
*O there'll be mourning, at the judgment-seat of Christ!"*

Legree stopped. He would have been ashamed to tell of it, but large drops of sweat stood on his forehead, his heart beat heavy and thick with fear; he even thought he saw something white rising and glimmering in the gloom before him, and shuddered to think what if the form of his dead mother should suddenly appear to him.

"I know one thing," he said to himself, as he stumbled back in the sitting-room, and sat down; "I'll let that fellow alone, after this! What did I want of his cussed paper? I b'lieve I am bewitched, sure enough! I've been shivering and sweating, ever since! Where did he get that hair? It couldn't have been *that*! I burnt *that* up, I know I did! It would be a joke, if hair could rise from the dead!"

Ah, Legree! that golden tress *was* charmed; each hair had in it a spell of terror and remorse for thee, and was used by a mightier power to bind thy cruel hands from inflicting uttermost evil on the helpless!

"I say," said Legree, stamping and whistling to the dogs, "wake up, some of you, and keep me company!" but the dogs only opened one eye at him, sleepily, and closed it again.

"I'll have Sambo and Quimbo up here, to sing and dance one of their hell dances, and keep off these horrid notions," said Legree; and, putting on his hat, he went on

12 Stowe leaves Legree's vision ambiguous. Does he see something? Is it his conscience?

**13** I.e., accustomed. Again, Legree's sense that there should be no discord on the plantation is ironic.

**14** A "worthy" is a distinguished person; Stowe is playful here.

**15** Cassy's question is important: Her rejection of the idea of killing Legree demonstrates her goodness and allows Stowe to more easily facilitate her reintroduction to the moral family circle at the end of the novel.

to the verandah, and blew a horn, with which he commonly summoned his two sable drivers.

Legree was often wont,[13] when in a gracious humor, to get these two worthies[14] into his sitting-room, and, after warming them up with whiskey, amuse himself by setting them to singing, dancing or fighting, as the humor took him.

It was between one and two o'clock at night, as Cassy was returning from her ministrations to poor Tom, that she heard the sound of wild shrieking, whooping, halloing, and singing, from the sitting-room, mingled with the barking of dogs, and other symptoms of general uproar.

She came up on the verandah steps, and looked in. Legree and both the drivers, in a state of furious intoxication, were singing, whooping, upsetting chairs, and making all manner of ludicrous and horrid grimaces at each other.

She rested her small, slender hand on the window-blind, and looked fixedly at them;—there was a world of anguish, scorn, and fierce bitterness, in her black eyes, as she did so. "Would it be a sin to rid the world of such a wretch?" she said to herself.[15]

She turned hurriedly away, and, passing round to a back door, glided up stairs, and tapped at Emmeline's door.

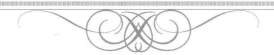

# CHAPTER 36

## *Emmeline and Cassy*[1]

Cassy entered the room, and found Emmeline sitting, pale with fear, in the furthest corner of it. As she came in, the girl started up nervously; but, on seeing who it was, rushed forward, and catching her arm, said, "O, Cassy, is it you? I'm so glad you've come! I was afraid it was—. O, you don't know what a horrid noise there has been, down stairs, all this evening!"

"I ought to know," said Cassy, dryly. "I've heard it often enough."

"O Cassy! do tell me,—couldn't we get away from this place? I don't care where,—into the swamp among the snakes,—anywhere! *Couldn't* we get *somewhere* away from here?"

"Nowhere, but into our graves," said Cassy.

"Did you ever try?"

"I've seen enough of trying, and what comes of it," said Cassy.

"I'd be willing to live in the swamps, and gnaw the bark from trees. I an't afraid of snakes! I'd rather have one near me than him," said Emmeline, eagerly.

"There have been a good many here of your opinion," said Cassy; "but you couldn't stay in the swamps,—you'd be tracked by the dogs, and brought back, and then—then—"

"What would he do?" said the girl, looking, with breathless interest, into her face.

"What *wouldn't* he do, you'd better ask," said Cassy.

1 As the chapter titled indicates, Stowe will be focusing on friendship. Although Cassy is not yet wholly open to any intimacy, these will be the first warm scenes between women since Eliza and Ruth were together in the Quaker settlement.

**2** The description of swamps, snakes, and scenes of horror adds to the overall tone of despair. Despite Legree's spoken desire for amity on his plantation, he has clearly presided over horrendous abuse.

"He's learned his trade well, among the pirates in the West Indies. You wouldn't sleep much, if I should tell you things I've seen,—things that he tells of, sometimes, for good jokes. I've heard screams here that I haven't been able to get out of my head for weeks and weeks. There's a place way out down by the quarters, where you can see a black, blasted tree, and the ground all covered with black ashes. Ask any one what was done there, and see if they will dare to tell you."**2**

"O! what do you mean?"

"I won't tell you. I hate to think of it. And I tell you, the Lord only knows what we may see to-morrow, if that poor fellow holds out as he's begun."

"Horrid!" said Emmeline, every drop of blood receding from her cheeks. "O, Cassy, do tell me what I shall do!"

"What I've done. Do the best you can,—do what you must,—and make it up in hating and cursing."

"He wanted to make me drink some of his hateful brandy," said Emmeline; "and I hate it so—"

"You'd better drink," said Cassy. "I hated it, too; and now I can't live without it. One must have something;—things don't look so dreadful, when you take that."

"Mother used to tell me never to touch any such thing," said Emmeline.

"*Mother* told you!" said Cassy, with a thrilling and bitter emphasis on the word mother. "What use is it for mothers to say anything? You are all to be bought and paid for, and your souls belong to whoever gets you. That's the way it goes. I say, *drink* brandy; drink all you can, and it'll make things come easier."

"O, Cassy! do pity me!"

"Pity you!—don't I? Haven't I a daughter,—Lord knows where she is, and whose she is, now,—going the way her mother went, before her, I suppose, and that her children must go, after her! There's no end to the curse—forever!"

"I wish I'd never been born!" said Emmeline, wringing her hands.

"That's an old wish with me," said Cassy. "I've got used to wishing that. I'd die, if I dared to," she said, looking out into the darkness, with that still, fixed despair which was the habitual expression of her face when at rest.

"It would be wicked to kill one's self," said Emmeline.

"I don't know why,—no wickeder than things we live and do, day after day. But the sisters told me things, when I was in the convent, that make me afraid to die. If it would only be the end of us, why, then—"

Emmeline turned away, and hid her face in her hands.

While this conversation was passing in the chamber, Legree, overcome with his carouse, had sank to sleep in the room below. Legree was not an habitual drunkard. His coarse, strong nature craved, and could endure, a continual stimulation, that would have utterly wrecked and crazed a finer one. But a deep, underlying spirit of cautiousness prevented his often yielding to appetite in such measure as to lose control of himself.

This night, however, in his feverish efforts to banish from his mind those fearful elements of woe and remorse which woke within him, he had indulged more than common; so that, when he had discharged his sable attendants, he fell heavily on a settle in the room, and was sound asleep.

O! how dares the bad soul to enter the shadowy world of sleep?—that land whose dim outlines lie so fearfully near to the mystic scene of retribution! Legree dreamed. In his heavy and feverish sleep, a veiled form stood beside him, and laid a cold, soft hand upon him. He thought he knew who it was; and shuddered, with creeping horror, though the face was veiled. Then he thought he felt *that hair* twining round his fingers; and then, that it slid smoothly round his neck, and tightened and tightened, and he could not draw his breath; and then he thought voices *whispered* to him,—whispers that chilled him with horror. Then it seemed to him he was on the edge of a frightful abyss, holding on and struggling in mortal fear, while dark hands stretched up, and were pulling him over; and Cassy came behind him laughing, and pushed him. And then rose up that solemn veiled figure, and drew aside the veil. It was his mother; and she turned away from him, and he fell down, down, down, amid a confused noise of shrieks, and groans, and shouts of demon laughter,—and Legree awoke.

Calmly the rosy hue of dawn was stealing into the room. The morning star stood, with its solemn, holy eye of light, looking down on the man of sin, from out the brightening sky. O, with what freshness, what solemnity and beauty, is each new day born; as if to say to insensate man, "Behold! thou hast one more chance! *Strive* for immortal glory!" There is no speech nor language where this voice is not heard; but the bold, bad man heard it not. He woke with an oath and a curse. What to him was the gold and purple, the daily miracle of morning! What to him the sanctity of that star which the Son of God has hallowed as his own emblem?[3] Brute-like, he saw without perceiving; and, stumbling forward, poured out a tumbler of brandy, and drank half of it.

3 Stowe's prose becomes as purple as the "gold and purple" miracle of morning when she describes the transition between sleep and waking for Legree.

4 I.e., urgent situation. Legree needs to get his cotton to market.

"I've had a h—l of a night!" he said to Cassy, who just then entered from an opposite door.

"You'll get plenty of the same sort, by and by," said she, dryly.

"What do you mean, you minx?"

"You'll find out, one of these days," returned Cassy, in the same tone. "Now, Simon, I've one piece of advice to give you."

"The devil, you have!"

"My advice is," said Cassy, steadily, as she began adjusting some things about the room, "that you let Tom alone."

"What business is't of yours?"

"What? To be sure, I don't know what it should be. If you want to pay twelve hundred for a fellow, and use him right up in the press of the season, just to serve your own spite, it's no business of mine. I've done what I could for him."

"You have? What business have you meddling in my matters?"

"None, to be sure. I've saved you some thousands of dollars, at different times, by taking care of your hands,—that's all the thanks I get. If your crop comes shorter into market than any of theirs, you won't lose your bet, I suppose? Tompkins won't lord it over you, I suppose,—and you'll pay down your money like a lady, won't you? I think I see you doing it!"

Legree, like many other planters, had but one form of ambition,—to have in the heaviest crop of the season,—and he had several bets on this very present season pending in the next town. Cassy, therefore, with woman's tact, touched the only string that could be made to vibrate.

"Well, I'll let him off at what he's got," said Legree; "but he shall beg my pardon, and promise better fashions."

"That he won't do," said Cassy.

"Won't,—eh?"

"No, he won't," said Cassy.

"I'd like to know *why,* Mistress," said Legree, in the extreme of scorn.

"Because he's done right, and he knows it, and won't say he's done wrong."

"Who a cuss cares what he knows? The nigger shall say what I please, or—"

"Or, you'll lose your bet on the cotton crop, by keeping him out of the field, just at this very press.4"

"But he *will* give up,—course, he will; don't I know what niggers is? He'll beg like a dog, this morning."

"He won't, Simon; you don't know this kind. You may

kill him by inches,—you won't get the first word of confession out of him."

"We'll see;—where is he?" said Legree, going out.

"In the waste-room of the gin-house," said Cassy.

Legree, though he talked so stoutly to Cassy, still sallied forth from the house with a degree of misgiving which was not common with him. His dreams of the past night, mingled with Cassy's prudential suggestions, considerably affected his mind. He resolved that nobody should be witness of his encounter with Tom; and determined, if he could not subdue him by bullying, to defer his vengeance, to be wreaked in a more convenient season.

The solemn light of dawn—the angelic glory of the morning-star—had looked in through the rude window of the shed where Tom was lying; and, as if descending on that star-beam, came the solemn words, "I am the root and offspring of David, and the bright and morning star."[5] The mysterious warnings and intimations of Cassy, so far from discouraging his soul, in the end had roused it as with a heavenly call. He did not know but that the day of his death was dawning in the sky; and his heart throbbed with solemn throes of joy and desire, as he thought that the wondrous *all*, of which he had often pondered,—the great white throne, with its ever radiant rainbow; the white-robed multitude, with voices as many waters; the crowns, the palms, the harps,—might all break upon his vision before that sun should set again. And, therefore, without shuddering or trembling, he heard the voice of his persecutor, as he drew near.

"Well, my boy," said Legree, with a contemptuous kick, "how do you find yourself? Didn't I tell yer I could larn yer a thing or two? How do yer like it,—eh? How did yer whaling agree with yer, Tom? An't quite so crank as ye was last night. Ye couldn't treat a poor sinner, now, to a bit of a sermon, could ye,—eh?"

Tom answered nothing.

"Get up, you beast!" said Legree, kicking him again.

This was a difficult matter for one so bruised and faint; and, as Tom made efforts to do so, Legree laughed brutally.

"What makes ye so spry,[6] this morning, Tom? Cotched cold, may be, last night."

Tom by this time had gained his feet, and was confronting his master with a steady, unmoved front.

"The devil, you can!" said Legree, looking him over. "I believe you haven't got enough yet. Now, Tom, get right down on yer knees and beg my pardon, for yer shines last night."

5 The same dawn as woke Legree, but now described as "the angelic glory of the morning-star," shines on Tom as Legree kicks him awake.

6 I.e., impudently high-spirited. Legree immediately enters into a religious discourse with Tom; Stowe begins setting up the final showdown of good and evil.

Tom did not move.

"Down, you dog!" said Legree, striking him with his riding-whip.

"Mas'r Legree," said Tom, "I can't do it. I did only what I thought was right. I shall do just so again, if ever the time comes. I never will do a cruel thing, come what may."

"Yes, but ye don't know what may come, Master Tom. Ye think what you've got is something. I tell you 't an't anything,—nothing 't all. How would ye like to be tied to a tree, and have a slow fire lit up around ye;—wouldn't that be pleasant,—eh, Tom?"

"Mas'r," said Tom, "I know ye can do dreadful things, but,"—he stretched himself upward and clasped his hands,—"but, after ye've killed the body, there an't no more ye can do. And O, there's all ETERNITY to come, after that!"

ETERNITY,—the word thrilled through the black man's soul with light and power, as he spoke; it thrilled through the sinner's soul, too, like the bite of a scorpion. Legree gnashed on him with his teeth, but rage kept him silent; and Tom, like a man disenthralled, spoke, in a clear and cheerful voice,

"Mas'r Legree, as ye bought me, I'll be a true and faithful servant to ye. I'll give ye all the work of my hands, all my time, all my strength; but my soul I won't give up to mortal man. I will hold on to the Lord, and put his commands before all,—die or live; you may be sure on 't. Mas'r Legree, I an't a grain afeard to die. I'd as soon die as not. Ye may whip me, starve me, burn me,—it'll only send me sooner where I want to go."

"I'll make ye give out, though, 'fore I've done!" said Legree, in a rage.

"I shall have *help*," said Tom; "you'll never do it."

"Who the devil's going to help you?" said Legree, scornfully.

"The Lord Almighty," said Tom.

"D—n you!" said Legree, as with one blow of his fist he felled Tom to the earth.

A cold soft hand fell on Legree's, at this moment. He turned,—it was Cassy's; but the cold soft touch recalled his dream of the night before, and, flashing through the chambers of his brain, came all the fearful images of the night-watches, with a portion of the horror that accompanied them.

"Will you be a fool?" said Cassy, in French. "Let him go! Let me alone to get him fit to be in the field again. Isn't it just as I told you?"

They say the alligator, the rhinoceros, though enclosed in bullet-proof mail, have each a spot where they are vulnerable; and fierce, reckless, unbelieving reprobates, have commonly this point in superstitious dread.

Legree turned away, determined to let the point go for the time.

"Well, have it your own way," he said, doggedly, to Cassy.

"Hark, ye!" he said to Tom; "I won't deal with ye now, because the business is pressing, and I want all my hands; but I *never* forget. I'll score it against ye, and sometime I'll have my pay out o' yer old black hide,—mind ye!"

Legree turned, and went out.

"There you go," said Cassy, looking darkly after him; "your reckoning's to come, yet!—My poor fellow, how are you?"

"The Lord God hath sent his angel, and shut the lion's mouth, for this time," said Tom.[7]

"For this time, to be sure," said Cassy; "but now you've got his ill will upon you, to follow you day in, day out, hanging like a dog on your throat,—sucking your blood, bleeding away your life, drop by drop. I know the man."

7 Dan. 6:23. Continuing the theme of gold and purple, Tom quotes from the book of Daniel, who before being thrown in with the lions had been clothed in gold and purple. Note once again that in quoting this verse there are no markers of Tom's dialect.

# CHAPTER 37

## Liberty

1 John Philpot Curran (1750–1817), Irish orator and judge who worked for Catholic emancipation. He was beloved in antislavery circles for his role in the James Somerset case (1772), in which a Jamaican slave, brought to England by his master, declared himself free.

2 Stowe simply pulls the curtain closed on Tom and Cassy to wrench our attention back to George and Eliza. Meanwhile, back at the farmhouse, there is another Tom groaning, but this time it is Tom Loker in a clean Quaker bed. The fall of one Tom and the rise of another is evidence of Stowe's concern with narrative structure. Stowe also contrasts the squalor of Legree's plantation with the snowy cleanliness of the Quaker cottage.

"No matter with what solemnities he may have been devoted upon the altar of slavery, the moment he touches the sacred soil of Britain, the altar and the God sink together in the dust, and he stands redeemed, regenerated, and disenthralled, by the irresistible genius of universal emancipation."
—CURRAN.[1]

A while we must leave Tom in the hands of his persecutors, while we turn to pursue the fortunes of George and his wife, whom we left in friendly hands, in a farmhouse on the road-side.[2]

Tom Loker we left groaning and touzling in a most immaculately clean Quaker bed, under the motherly supervision of Aunt Dorcas, who found him to the full as tractable a patient as a sick bison.

Imagine a tall, dignified, spiritual woman, whose clear muslin cap shades waves of silvery hair, parted on a broad, clear forehead, which overarches thoughtful gray eyes. A snowy handkerchief of lisse crape is folded neatly across her bosom; her glossy brown silk dress rustles peacefully, as she glides up and down the chamber.

"The devil!" says Tom Loker, giving a great throw to the bed-clothes.

"I must request thee, Thomas, not to use such language," says Aunt Dorcas, as she quietly rearranged the bed.

"Well, I won't, granny, if I can help it," says Tom; "but it is enough to make a fellow swear,—so cursedly hot!"

Dorcas removed a comforter from the bed, straightened the clothes again, and tucked them in till Tom looked something like a chrysalis; remarking, as she did so,

"I wish, friend, thee would leave off cursing and swearing, and think upon thy ways."

"What the devil," said Tom, "should I think of *them* for? Last thing ever *I* want to think of—hang it all!" And Tom flounced over, untucking and disarranging everything, in a manner frightful to behold.

"That fellow and gal are here, I 'spose," said he, sullenly, after a pause.

"They are so," said Dorcas.

"They'd better be off up to the lake," said Tom; "the quicker the better."

"Probably they will do so," said Aunt Dorcas, knitting peacefully.

"And hark ye," said Tom; "we've got correspondents in Sandusky, that watch the boats for us. I don't care if I tell, now. I hope they *will* get away, just to spite Marks,—the cursed puppy!—d—n him!"

"Thomas!" said Dorcas.

"I tell you, granny, if you bottle a fellow up too tight, I shall split," said Tom. "But about the gal,—tell 'em to dress her up some way, so's to alter her. Her description's out in Sandusky."

"We will attend to that matter," said Dorcas, with characteristic composure.

As we at this place take leave of Tom Loker, we may as well say, that, having lain three weeks at the Quaker dwelling, sick with a rheumatic fever, which set in, in company with his other afflictions, Tom arose from his bed a somewhat sadder and wiser man; and, in place of slave-catching, betook himself to life in one of the new settlements, where his talents developed themselves more happily in trapping bears, wolves, and other inhabitants of the forest, in which he made himself quite a name in the land. Tom always spoke reverently of the Quakers. "Nice people," he would say; "wanted to convert me, but couldn't come it, exactly. But, tell ye what, stranger, they do fix up a sick fellow first rate,—no mistake. Make jist the tallest kind o' broth and knicknacks."

As Tom had informed them that their party would be looked for in Sandusky, it was thought prudent to divide them. Jim, with his old mother, was forwarded separately; and a night or two after, George and Eliza, with their

3 Here Stowe seems to be channeling Sir Walter Scott reading any one of many verse romances. Stowe's poetic and patriotic waxings allow us to catch our breath after the drama of the last chapter.

4 Eliza's disguise evokes the famous escape of Ellen Craft and her husband William in 1848. Ellen cut off her hair, changed her gait, and bandaged her face to hide her smooth chin. She played the part of a white slaveholder; William was her slave. The pair traveled undetected from Georgia to Philadelphia, where they told their story. The Crafts fled America for England after the passage of the Fugitive Slave Law in 1850.

child, were driven privately into Sandusky, and lodged beneath a hospitable roof, preparatory to taking their last passage on the lake.

Their night was now far spent, and the morning star of liberty rose fair before them. Liberty!—electric word! What is it? Is there anything more in it than a name—a rhetorical flourish? Why, men and women of America, does your heart's blood thrill at that word, for which your fathers bled, and your braver mothers were willing that their noblest and best should die?

Is there anything in it glorious and dear for a nation, that is not also glorious and dear for a man? What is freedom to a nation, but freedom to the individuals in it? What is freedom to that young man, who sits there, with his arms folded over his broad chest, the tint of African blood in his cheek, its dark fires in his eye,—what is freedom to George Harris? To your fathers, freedom was the right of a nation to be a nation.[3] To him, it is the right of a man to be a man, and not a brute; the right to call the wife of his bosom his wife, and to protect her from lawless violence; the right to protect and educate his child; the right to have a home of his own, a religion of his own, a character of his own, unsubject to the will of another. All these thoughts were rolling and seething in George's breast, as he was pensively leaning his head on his hand, watching his wife, as she was adapting to her slender and pretty form the articles of man's attire, in which it was deemed safest she should make her escape.

"Now for it," said she, as she stood before the glass, and shook down her silky abundance of black curly hair. "I say, George, it's almost a pity, isn't it," she said, as she held up some of it, playfully,—"pity it's all got to come off?"

George smiled sadly, and made no answer.

Eliza turned to the glass, and the scissors glittered as one long lock after another was detached from her head.[4]

"There, now, that'll do," she said, taking up a hairbrush; "now for a few fancy touches."

"There, an't I a pretty young fellow?" she said, turning around to her husband, laughing and blushing at the same time.

"You always will be pretty, do what you will," said George.

"What does make you so sober?" said Eliza, kneeling on one knee, and laying her hand on his. "We are only within twenty-four hours of Canada, they say. Only a day and a night on the lake, and then—oh, then!—"

"O, Eliza!" said George, drawing her towards him; "that is it! Now my fate is all narrowing down to a point. To come so near, to be almost in sight, and then lose all. I should never live under it, Eliza."

"Don't fear," said his wife, hopefully. "The good Lord would not have brought us so far, if he didn't mean to carry us through. I seem to feel him with us, George."

"You are a blessed woman, Eliza!" said George, clasping her with a convulsive grasp. "But,—oh, tell me! can this great mercy be for us? Will these years and years of misery come to an end?—shall we be free?"

"I am sure of it, George," said Eliza, looking upward, while tears of hope and enthusiasm shone on her long, dark lashes. "I feel it in me, that God is going to bring us out of bondage, this very day."

"I will believe you, Eliza," said George, rising suddenly up. "I will believe,—come, let's be off. Well, indeed," said he, holding her off at arm's length, and looking admiringly at her, "you *are* a pretty little fellow. That crop of little, short curls, is quite becoming. Put on your cap. So—a little to one side. I never saw you look quite so pretty. But, it's almost time for the carriage;—I wonder if Mrs. Smyth has got Harry rigged?"

The door opened, and a respectable, middle-aged woman entered, leading little Harry, dressed in girl's clothes.[5]

"What a pretty girl he makes," said Eliza, turning him round. "We call him Harriet, you see;—don't the name come nicely?"

The child stood gravely regarding his mother in her new and strange attire, observing a profound silence, and occasionally drawing deep sighs, and peeping at her from under his dark curls.

"Does Harry know mamma?" said Eliza, stretching her hands toward him.

The child clung shyly to the woman.

"Come, Eliza, why do you try to coax him, when you know that he has got to be kept away from you?"

"I know it's foolish," said Eliza; "yet, I can't bear to have him turn away from me. But come,—where's my cloak? Here,—how is it men put on cloaks, George?"

"You must wear it so," said her husband, throwing it over his shoulders.

"So, then," said Eliza, imitating the motion,—"and I must stamp, and take long steps, and try to look saucy."

"Don't exert yourself," said George. "There is, now and then, a modest young man; and I think it would be easier for you to act that character."

"And these gloves! mercy upon us!" said Eliza; "why, my hands are lost in them."

5 Stowe adds a Mrs. Smyth to this cross-dressing party. She remains mysterious, even in the illustrations.

"I advise you to keep them on pretty strictly," said George. "Your little slender paw might bring us all out. Now, Mrs. Smyth, you are to go under our charge, and be our aunty,—you mind."

"I've heard," said Mrs. Smyth, "that there have been men down, warning all the packet captains against a man and woman, with a little boy."

"They have!" said George. "Well, if we see any such people, we can tell them."

A hack now drove to the door, and the friendly family who had received the fugitives crowded around them with farewell greetings.

The disguises the party had assumed were in accordance with the hints of Tom Loker. Mrs. Smyth, a respectable woman from the settlement in Canada, whither they were fleeing, being fortunately about crossing the lake to return thither, had consented to appear as the aunt of little Harry; and, in order to attach him to her, he had been allowed to remain, the two last days, under her sole charge; and an extra amount of petting, joined to an indefinite amount of seedcake and candy, had cemented a very close attachment on the part of the young gentleman.

The hack drove to the wharf. The two young men, as they appeared, walked up the plank into the boat, Eliza gallantly giving her arm to Mrs. Smyth, and George attending to their baggage.

George was standing at the captain's office, settling for his party, when he overheard two men talking by his side.

"I've watched every one that came on board," said one, "and I know they're not on this boat."

The voice was that of the clerk of the boat. The speaker whom he addressed was our sometimes friend Marks, who, with that valuable perseverance which characterized him, had come on to Sandusky, seeking whom he might devour.

"You would scarcely know the woman from a white one," said Marks. "The man is a very light mulatto; he has a brand in one of his hands."

The hand with which George was taking the tickets and change trembled a little; but he turned coolly around, fixed an unconcerned glance on the face of the speaker,

In this Hammatt Billings illustration, George, Eliza, and little Harry are safe. The Harris family is decidedly middle class. They have "passed" successfully.   From *Uncle Tom's Cabin,* John P. Jewett & Co., 1852

and walked leisurely toward another part of the boat, where Eliza stood waiting for him.

Mrs. Smyth, with little Harry, sought the seclusion of the ladies' cabin, where the dark beauty of the supposed little girl drew many flattering comments from the passengers.

George had the satisfaction, as the bell rang out its farewell peal, to see Marks walk down the plank to the shore, and drew a long sigh of relief, when the boat had put a returnless distance between them.

It was a superb day. The blue waves of Lake Erie danced, rippling and sparkling, in the sun-light. A fresh breeze blew from the shore, and the lordly boat ploughed her way right gallantly onward.

O, what an untold world there is in one human heart! Who thought, as George walked calmly up and down the deck of the steamer, with his shy companion at his side, of all that was burning in his bosom? The mighty good that seemed approaching seemed too good, too fair, even to be a reality; and he felt a jealous dread, every moment of the day, that something would rise to snatch it from him.

But the boat swept on. Hours fleeted, and, at last, clear and full rose the blessed English shores; shores charmed by a mighty spell,—with one touch to dissolve every incantation of slavery, no matter in what language pronounced, or by what national power confirmed.

George and his wife stood arm in arm, as the boat neared the small town of Amherstberg, in Canada. His breath grew thick and short; a mist gathered before his eyes; he silently pressed the little hand that lay trembling on his arm. The bell rang; the boat stopped. Scarcely seeing what he did, he looked out his baggage, and gathered his little party. The little company were landed on the shore. They stood still till the boat had cleared; and then, with tears and embracings, the husband and wife, with their wondering child in their arms, knelt down and lifted up their hearts to God!

> " 'Twas something like the burst from death to life
>     From the grave's cerements to the robes of heaven;
> From sin's dominion, and from passion's strife,
>     To the pure freedom of a soul forgiven;
>     Where all the bonds of death and hell are riven,
>     And mortal puts on immortality,
>     When Mercy's hand hath turned the golden key,
>     And Mercy's voice hath said, Rejoice, thy soul is
>       free."

"Flight of Fugitives to Canada, Guided by the North Star." Wood engraving by George Cruikshank. These people look more like Chaucer's pilgrims than fugitive slaves. From *The Uncle Tom's Cabin Almanack, or, Abolitionist Memento*, 1853

**6** With her repetition of the word "little," Stowe seems to suggest that we temper our happiness at George and Eliza's successful escape. We know we will still be back with Tom, Cassy, and the other slaves under Legree's hard fist.

**7** This verse and the ones above appear to have been written by Stowe herself.

The little party[6] were soon guided, by Mrs. Smyth, to the hospitable abode of a good missionary, whom Christian charity has placed here as a shepherd to the out-cast and wandering, who are constantly finding an asylum on this shore.

Who can speak the blessedness of that first day of freedom? Is not the *sense* of liberty a higher and a finer one than any of the five? To move, speak and breathe,—go out and come in unwatched, and free from danger! Who can speak the blessings of that rest which comes down on the free man's pillow, under laws which insure to him the rights that God has given to man? How fair and precious to that mother was that sleeping child's face, endeared by the memory of a thousand dangers! How impossible was it to sleep, in the exuberant possession of such blessedness! And yet, these two had not one acre of ground,—not a roof that they could call their own,—they had spent their all, to the last dollar. They had nothing more than the birds of the air, or the flowers of the field,—yet they could not sleep for joy. "O, ye who take freedom from man, with what words shall ye answer it to God?"[7]

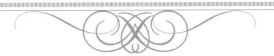

# CHAPTER 38

## *The Victory*[1]

"Thanks be unto God, who giveth us the victory."[2]

Have not many of us, in the weary way of life, felt, in some hours, how far easier it were to die than to live?

The martyr, when faced even by a death of bodily anguish and horror, finds in the very terror of his doom a strong stimulant and tonic. There is a vivid excitement, a thrill and fervor, which may carry through any crisis of suffering that is the birth-hour of eternal glory and rest.

But to live,—to wear on, day after day, of mean, bitter, low, harassing servitude, every nerve dampened and depressed, every power of feeling gradually smothered,— this long and wasting heart-martyrdom, this slow, daily bleeding away of the inward life, drop by drop, hour after hour,—this is the true searching test of what there may be in man or woman.

When Tom stood face to face with his persecutor, and heard his threats, and thought in his very soul that his hour was come, his heart swelled bravely in him, and he thought he could bear torture and fire, bear anything, with the vision of Jesus and heaven but just a step beyond; but, when he was gone, and the present excitement passed off, came back the pain of his bruised and weary limbs,—came back the sense of his utterly degraded, hopeless, forlorn estate; and the day passed wearily enough.

1 The victory is the believer's triumph over death. There has been little opportunity for any sort of temporal victory in the novel; there is no contest on earth, Stowe insists, as important as the contest of truth over corruption, of belief over cynicism.

2 The verse is from 1 Cor. 15:57. An earlier part of the passage may be more familiar: "O death, where is thy victory? O death, where is thy sting?"

3 This literal dying away of the warmth underscores Tom's awful recognition that there will be no return to his life on the Shelby plantation. But, we see, he still has his Bible.

Long before his wounds were healed, Legree insisted that he should be put to the regular field-work; and then came day after day of pain and weariness, aggravated by every kind of injustice and indignity that the ill-will of a mean and malicious mind could devise. Whoever, in *our* circumstances, has made trial of pain, even with all the alleviations which, for us, usually attend it, must know the irritation that comes with it. Tom no longer wondered at the habitual surliness of his associates; nay, he found the placid, sunny temper, which had been the habitude of his life, broken in on, and sorely strained, by the inroads of the same thing. He had flattered himself on leisure to read his Bible; but there was no such thing as leisure there. In the height of the season, Legree did not hesitate to press all his hands through, Sundays and week-days alike. Why shouldn't he?—he made more cotton by it, and gained his wager; and if it wore out a few more hands, he could buy better ones. At first, Tom used to read a verse or two of his Bible, by the flicker of the fire, after he had returned from his daily toil; but, after the cruel treatment he received, he used to come home so exhausted, that his head swam and his eyes failed when he tried to read; and he was fain to stretch himself down, with the others, in utter exhaustion.

Is it strange that the religious peace and trust, which had upborne him hitherto, should give way to tossings of soul and despondent darkness? The gloomiest problem of this mysterious life was constantly before his eyes,—souls crushed and ruined, evil triumphant, and God silent. It was weeks and months that Tom wrestled, in his own soul, in darkness and sorrow. He thought of Miss Ophelia's letter to his Kentucky friends, and would pray earnestly that God would send him deliverance. And then he would watch, day after day, in the vague hope of seeing somebody sent to redeem him; and, when nobody came, he would crush back to his soul bitter thoughts,—that it was vain to serve God, that God had forgotten him. He sometimes saw Cassy; and sometimes, when summoned to the house, caught a glimpse of the dejected form of Emmeline, but held very little communion with either; in fact, there was no time for him to commune with anybody.

One evening, he was sitting, in utter dejection and prostration, by a few decaying brands,[3] where his coarse supper was baking. He put a few bits of brushwood on the fire, and strove to raise the light, and then drew his worn Bible from his pocket. There were all the marked passages, which had thrilled his soul so often,—words of patriarchs

and seers, poets and sages, who from early time had spoken courage to man,—voices from the great cloud of witnesses who ever surround us in the race of life. Had the
word lost its power, or could the failing eye and weary
sense no longer answer to the touch of that mighty inspiration? Heavily sighing, he put it in his pocket. A coarse
laugh roused him; he looked up,—Legree was standing
opposite to him.

"Well, old boy," he said, "you find your religion don't
work, it seems! I thought I should get that through your
wool, at last!"[4]

The cruel taunt was more than hunger and cold and
nakedness. Tom was silent.

"You were a fool," said Legree; "for I meant to do well by
you, when I bought you. You might have been better off
than Sambo, or Quimbo either, and had easy times; and,
instead of getting cut up and thrashed, every day or two,
ye might have had liberty to lord it round, and cut up the
other niggers; and ye might have had, now and then, a
good warming of whiskey punch. Come, Tom, don't you
think you'd better be reasonable?—heave that ar old pack
of trash in the fire,[5] and join my church!"

"The Lord forbid!" said Tom, fervently.

"You see the Lord an't going to help you; if he had been,
he wouldn't have let *me* get you! This yer religion is all a
mess of lying trumpery,[6] Tom. I know all about it. Ye'd better hold to me; I'm somebody, and can do something!"

"No, Mas'r," said Tom; "I'll hold on. The Lord may help
me, or not help; but I'll hold to him, and believe him to the
last!"

"The more fool you!" said Legree, spitting scornfully at
him, and spurning him with his foot. "Never mind; I'll
chase you down, yet, and bring you under,—you'll see!"
and Legree turned away.

When a heavy weight presses the soul to the lowest level
at which endurance is possible, there is an instant and
desperate effort of every physical and moral nerve to
throw off the weight; and hence the heaviest anguish
often precedes a return tide of joy and courage. So was it
now with Tom. The atheistic taunts of his cruel master
sunk his before dejected soul to the lowest ebb; and,
though the hand of faith still held to the eternal rock, it
was with a numb, despairing grasp. Tom sat, like one
stunned, at the fire. Suddenly everything around him
seemed to fade, and a vision rose before him of one
crowned with thorns, buffeted and bleeding. Tom gazed, in
awe and wonder, at the majestic patience of the face; the

4 Once again, Legree immediately launches
into the subject of religion when he speaks to
Tom.

5 Legree's suggestion that Tom throw his
Bible—"that ar old pack of trash"—in the
fire backfires spectacularly. Tom triumphs
over the despair of having been abandoned by
the Shelbys.

6 I.e., superstitious nonsense.

**7** This passage is from Rev. 3:21.

**8** These verses are from John Newton's famous hymn "Amazing Grace" (1722), originally entitled "Faith's Review and Expectation." These three stanzas, written by Newton, are not typically included in most versions of the hymn.

**9** "Psychologist" was a relatively new term in the nineteenth century; the poet Robert Southey used it in 1836, for example, as a synonym for "metaphysician." Psychology was considered a science in much the same way that phrenology (the now-debunked theory of mental faculties) was. In 1851, the *National Era* ran ads for the *Phrenological Journal*, "devoted to the Moral and Intellectual development of Man. Psychology, Magnetism, Physiognomy, and all that relates to MIND."

deep, pathetic eyes thrilled him to his inmost heart; his soul woke, as, with floods of emotion, he stretched out his hands and fell upon his knees,—when, gradually, the vision changed: the sharp thorns became rays of glory; and, in splendor inconceivable, he saw that same face bending compassionately towards him, and a voice said, "He that overcometh shall sit down with me on my throne, even as I also overcame, and am set down with my Father on his throne."[7]

How long Tom lay there, he knew not. When he came to himself, the fire was gone out, his clothes were wet with the chill and drenching dews; but the dread soul-crisis was past, and, in the joy that filled him, he no longer felt hunger, cold, degradation, disappointment, wretchedness. From his deepest soul, he that hour loosed and parted from every hope in the life that now is, and offered his own will an unquestioning sacrifice to the Infinite. Tom looked up to the silent, everliving stars,—types of the angelic hosts who ever look down on man; and the solitude of the night rung with the triumphant words of a hymn, which he had sung often in happier days, but never with such feeling as now:

> "*The earth shall be dissolved like snow,*
> *The sun shall cease to shine;*
> *But God, who called me here below,*
> *Shall be forever mine.*
>
> "*And when this mortal life shall fail,*
> *And flesh and sense shall cease,*
> *I shall possess within the veil*
> *A life of joy and peace.*
>
> "*When we've been there ten thousand years,*
> *Bright shining like the sun,*
> *We've no less days to sing God's praise*
> *Than when we first begun.*"[8]

Those who have been familiar with the religious histories of the slave population know that relations like what we have narrated are very common among them. We have heard some from their own lips, of a very touching and affecting character. The psychologist[9] tells us of a state, in which the affections and images of the mind become so dominant and overpowering, that they press into their service the outward senses, and make them give tangible shape to the inward imagining. Who shall measure what an all-pervading Spirit may do with these capabilities of our mortality, or the ways in which He may encourage the desponding souls of the desolate? If the poor forgotten slave believes that Jesus hath appeared and spoken to him, who shall contradict him? Did He not say that his mission, in all ages, was to bind up the broken-hearted, and set at liberty them that are bruised?

When the dim gray of dawn woke the slumberers to go forth to the field, there was among those tattered and shivering wretches one who walked with an exultant tread; for firmer than the ground he trod on was his strong faith in Almighty, eternal love. Ah, Legree, try all your forces now! Utmost agony, woe, degradation, want, and loss of all things, shall only hasten on the process by which he shall be made a king and a priest unto God!

From this time, an inviolable sphere of peace encompassed the lowly heart of the oppressed one,—an ever-present Saviour hallowed it as a temple. Past now the bleeding of earthly regrets; past its fluctuations of hope, and fear, and desire; the human will, bent, and bleeding, and struggling long, was now entirely merged in the Divine. So short now seemed the remaining voyage of life,—so near, so vivid, seemed eternal blessedness,—that life's uttermost woes fell from him unharming.

All noticed the change in his appearance. Cheerfulness and alertness seemed to return to him, and a quietness which no insult or injury could ruffle seemed to possess him.

"What the devil's got into Tom?" Legree said to Sambo. "A while ago he was all down in the mouth, and now he's peart as a cricket."

"Dunno, Mas'r; gwine to run off, mebbe."

"Like to see him try that," said Legree, with a savage grin, "wouldn't we, Sambo?"

"Guess we would! Haw! haw! ho!" said the sooty gnome, laughing obsequiously. "Lord, de fun! To see him stickin' in de mud,—chasin' and tarin' through de bushes, dogs a holdin' on to him! Lord, I laughed fit to split, dat ar time we cotched Molly. I thought they'd a had her all stripped up afore I could get 'em off. She car's de marks o' dat ar spree yet."

"I reckon she will, to her grave," said Legree. "But now, Sambo, you look sharp. If the nigger's got anything of this sort going, trip him up."

"Mas'r, let me lone for dat," said Sambo. "I'll tree de coon. Ho, ho, ho!"

This was spoken as Legree was getting on to his horse,

**10** This hymn by Isaac Watts was found in many of the southern country songbooks of the antebellum period and was particularly popular among slaves and abolitionists, perhaps because of the metaphor of "title."

**11** I.e., shut your old trap (mouth). Even James Baldwin must have recognized that Tom's "cheerful" response cannot be considered wholly passive. Tom actively distances himself from Legree with his mood, which provokes yet more violence. Tom is clearly the most powerful character in this scene.

to go to the neighboring town. That night, as he was returning, he thought he would turn his horse and ride round the quarters, and see if all was safe.

It was a superb moonlight night, and the shadows of the graceful China trees lay minutely pencilled on the turf below, and there was that transparent stillness in the air which it seems almost unholy to disturb. Legree was at a little distance from the quarters, when he heard the voice of some one singing. It was not a usual sound there, and he paused to listen. A musical tenor voice sang,

> *"When I can read my title clear*
> *To mansions in the skies,*
> *I'll bid farewell to every fear,*
> *And wipe my weeping eyes.*
>
> *"Should earth against my soul engage,*
> *And hellish darts be hurled,*
> *Then I can smile at Satan's rage,*
> *And face a frowning world.*
>
> *"Let cares like a wild deluge come,*
> *And storms of sorrow fall,*
> *May I but safely reach my home,*
> *My God, my Heaven, my All."***10**

"So ho!" said Legree to himself, "he thinks so, does he? How I hate these cursed, Methodist hymns! Here, you nigger," said he, coming suddenly out upon Tom, and raising his riding-whip, "how dare you be gettin' up this yer row, when you ought to be in bed? Shut yer old black gash,**11** and get along in with you!"

"Yes, Mas'r," said Tom, with ready cheerfulness, as he rose to go in.

Legree was provoked beyond measure by Tom's evident happiness; and, riding up to him, belabored him over his head and shoulders.

"There, you dog," he said, "see if you'll feel so comfortable, after that!"

But the blows fell now only on the outer man, and not, as before, on the heart. Tom stood perfectly submissive; and yet Legree could not hide from himself that his power over his bond thrall was somehow gone. And, as Tom disappeared in his cabin, and he wheeled his horse suddenly round, there passed through his mind one of those vivid flashes that often send the lightning of conscience across the dark and wicked soul. He understood full well that it was GOD who was standing between him and his victim, and he blasphemed him. That submissive and silent man, whom taunts, nor threats, nor stripes, nor cruelties, could disturb, roused a voice within him, such as of old his Master roused in the demoniac soul, saying, "What have we to do with thee, thou Jesus of Nazareth?—art thou come to torment us before the time?"

Tom's whole soul overflowed with compassion and sympathy for the poor wretches by whom he was surrounded. To him it seemed as if his life-sorrows were now over, and as if, out of that strange treasury of peace and joy, with which he had been endowed from above, he longed to pour out something for the relief of their woes. It is true, opportunities were scanty; but, on the way to the fields, and back again, and during the hours of labor, chances fell in his way of extending a helping-hand to the weary, the disheartened and discouraged. The poor, worn-down, brutalized creatures, at first, could scarce comprehend this; but, when it was continued week after week, and month after month, it began to awaken long-silent chords in their benumbed hearts. Gradually and imperceptibly the strange, silent, patient man, who was ready to bear every one's burden, and sought help from none,—who stood aside for all, and came last, and took least, yet was foremost to share his little all with any who needed,—the man who, in cold nights, would give up his tattered blanket to add to the comfort of some woman who shivered with sickness, and who filled the baskets of the weaker ones in the field, at the terrible risk of coming short in his own measure,—and who, though pursued with unrelenting cruelty by their common tyrant, never joined in uttering a word of reviling or cursing,—this man, at last, began to have a strange power over them; and, when the more pressing season was past, and they were allowed again their Sundays for their own use, many would gather together to hear from him of Jesus. They would gladly have met to hear, and pray, and sing, in some place, together; but Legree would not permit it, and more than once broke up such attempts, with oaths and brutal execrations,—so that the blessed news had to circulate from individual to individual. Yet who can speak the simple joy with which some of those poor outcasts, to whom life was a joyless journey to a dark unknown, heard of a compassionate Redeemer and a heavenly home? It is the statement of missionaries, that, of all races of the earth, none have received the Gospel with such eager docility as the African. The principle of reliance and unquestioning

**12** Tom is no longer the "Uncle" of the Shelby and St. Clare plantations. Now Cassy gives him the respectful title "Father."

**13** Atypically, Tom uses his physical strength here to keep Cassy from committing what he considers an immoral act.

faith, which is its foundation, is more a native element in this race than any other; and it has often been found among them, that a stray seed of truth, borne on some breeze of accident into hearts the most ignorant, has sprung up into fruit, whose abundance has shamed that of higher and more skilful culture.

The poor mulatto woman, whose simple faith had been well-nigh crushed and overwhelmed, by the avalanche of cruelty and wrong which had fallen upon her, felt her soul raised up by the hymns and passages of Holy Writ, which this lowly missionary breathed into her ear in intervals, as they were going to and returning from work; and even the halfcrazed and wandering mind of Cassy was soothed and calmed by his simple and unobtrusive influences.

Stung to madness and despair by the crushing agonies of a life, Cassy had often resolved in her soul an hour of retribution, when her hand should avenge on her oppressor all the injustice and cruelty to which she had been witness, or which *she* had in her own person suffered.

One night, after all in Tom's cabin were sunk in sleep, he was suddenly aroused by seeing her face at the hole between the logs, that served for a window. She made a silent gesture for him to come out.

Tom came out the door. It was between one and two o'clock at night,—broad, calm, still moonlight. Tom remarked, as the light of the moon fell upon Cassy's large, black eyes, that there was a wild and peculiar glare in them, unlike their wonted fixed despair.

"Come here, Father Tom,"**12** she said, laying her small hand on his wrist, and drawing him forward with a force as if the hand were of steel; "come here,—I've news for you."

"What, Misse Cassy?" said Tom, anxiously.

"Tom, wouldn't you like your liberty?"

"I shall have it, Misse, in God's time," said Tom.

"Ay, but you may have it to-night," said Cassy, with a flash of sudden energy. "Come on."

Tom hesitated.

"Come!" said she, in a whisper, fixing her black eyes on him. "Come along! He's asleep—sound. I put enough into his brandy to keep him so. I wish I'd had more,—I shouldn't have wanted you. But come, the back door is unlocked; there's an axe there, I put it there,—his room door is open; I'll show you the way. I'd a done it myself, only my arms are so weak. Come along!"

"Not for ten thousand worlds, Misse!" said Tom, firmly, stopping and holding her back, as she was pressing forward.**13**

"But think of all these poor creatures," said Cassy. "We might set them all free, and go somewhere in the swamps, and find an island, and live by ourselves; I've heard of its being done. Any life is better than this."

"No!" said Tom, firmly. "No! good never comes of wickedness. I'd sooner chop my right hand off!"

"Then *I* shall do it," said Cassy, turning.

"O, Misse Cassy!" said Tom, throwing himself before her, "for the dear Lord's sake that died for ye, don't sell your precious soul to the devil, that way! Nothing but evil will come of it. The Lord hasn't called us to wrath. We must suffer, and wait his time."

"Wait!" said Cassy. "Haven't I waited?—waited till my head is dizzy and my heart sick? What has he made me suffer? What has he made hundreds of poor creatures suffer? Isn't he wringing the life-blood out of you? I'm called on; they call me! His time's come, and I'll have his heart's blood!"

"No, no, no!" said Tom, holding her small hands, which were clenched with spasmodic violence. "No, ye poor, lost soul, that ye mustn't do. The dear, blessed Lord never shed no blood but his own, and that he poured out for us when we was enemies. Lord, help us to follow his steps, and love our enemies."

"Love!" said Cassy, with a fierce glare; "love *such* enemies! It isn't in flesh and blood."

"No, Misse, it isn't," said Tom, looking up; "but *He* gives it to us, and that's the *victory*. When we can love and pray over all and through all, the battle's past, and the victory's come,—glory be to God!" And, with streaming eyes and choking voice, the black man looked up to heaven.

And this, oh Africa! latest called of nations,—called to the crown of thorns, the scourge, the bloody sweat, the cross of agony,—this is to be *thy* victory; by this shalt thou reign with Christ when his kingdom shall come on earth.

The deep fervor of Tom's feelings, the softness of his voice, his tears, fell like dew on the wild, unsettled spirit of the poor woman. A softness gathered over the lurid fires of her eye; she looked down, and Tom could feel the relaxing muscles of her hands, as she said,

"Didn't I tell you that evil spirits followed me? O! Father Tom, I can't pray,—I wish I could. I never have prayed since my children were sold! What you say must be right, I know it must; but when I try to pray, I can only hate and curse. I can't pray!"

"Poor soul!" said Tom, compassionately. "Satan desires to have ye, and sift ye as wheat. I pray the Lord for ye. O!

Misse Cassy, turn to the dear Lord Jesus. He came to bind up the broken-hearted, and comfort all that mourn."

Cassy stood silent, while large, heavy tears dropped from her downcast eyes.

"Misse Cassy," said Tom, in a hesitating tone, after surveying her a moment in silence, "if ye only could get away from here,—if the thing was possible,—I'd 'vise ye and Emmeline to do it; that is, if ye could go without blood-guiltiness,—not otherwise."

"Would you try it with us, Father Tom?"

"No," said Tom; "time was when I would; but the Lord's given me a work among these yer poor souls, and I'll stay with 'em and bear my cross with 'em till the end. It's different with you; it's a snare to you,—it's more 'n you can stand,—and you'd better go, if you can."

"I know no way but through the grave," said Cassy. "There's no beast or bird but can find a home somewhere; even the snakes and the alligators have their places to lie down and be quiet; but there's no place for us. Down in the darkest swamps, their dogs will hunt us out, and find us. Everybody and everything is against us; even the very beasts side against us,—and where shall we go?"

Tom stood silent; at length he said,

"Him that saved Daniel in the den of lions,—that saved the children in the fiery furnace,—Him that walked on the sea, and bade the winds be still,—He's alive yet; and I've faith to believe he can deliver you. Try it, and I'll pray, with all my might, for you."

By what strange law of mind is it that an idea long overlooked, and trodden under foot as a useless stone, suddenly sparkles out in new light, as a discovered diamond?

Cassy had often revolved, for hours, all possible or probable schemes of escape, and dismissed them all, as hopeless and impracticable; but at this moment there flashed through her mind a plan, so simple and feasible in all its details, as to awaken an instant hope.

"Father Tom, I'll try it!" she said, suddenly.

"Amen!" said Tom; "the Lord help ye!"

# CHAPTER 39

## *The Stratagem*

"The way of the wicked is as darkness; he knoweth not at what he stumbleth."[1]

The garret[2] of the house that Legree occupied, like most other garrets, was a great, desolate space, dusty, hung with cobwebs, and littered with cast-off lumber. The opulent family that had inhabited the house in the days of its splendor had imported a great deal of splendid furniture, some of which they had taken away with them, while some remained standing desolate in mouldering, unoccupied rooms, or stored away in this place. One or two immense packing-boxes, in which this furniture was brought, stood against the sides of the garret. There was a small window there, which let in, through its dingy, dusty panes, a scanty, uncertain light on the tall, high-backed chairs and dusty tables, that had once seen better days. Altogether, it was a weird and ghostly place; but, ghostly as it was, it wanted not in legends among the superstitious negroes, to increase its terrors. Some few years before, a negro woman, who had incurred Legree's displeasure, was confined there for several weeks. What passed there, we do not say; the negroes used to whisper darkly to each other; but it was known that the body of the unfortunate creature was one day taken down from there, and buried; and, after that, it was said that oaths and cursings and the sound of violent blows, used to ring

1 The epigraph, which once again uses the metaphor of darkness to represent wickedness, is from Prov. 4:19. Stowe's chapter title refers to Cassy's plan to trick Legree.

2 I.e., the attic. Stowe is tantalizingly vague about what, exactly, occurred with the woman who "incurred Legree's displeasure." The story may be more than a little melodramatic here, but given Legree's recent brutality toward Tom, we still feel the icy thrill Stowe wants us to feel at the mention of buried bodies and groans of despair.

3 I.e., disuse.

4 The story of the murdered woman in the attic also allows Stowe to jump from Tom's sermon in the last chapter back to Cassy's life with Legree. Stowe uses the term "suddenly" to suggest that we are not to see Cassy's plotting as incited by Tom's words.

through that old garret, and mingled with wailings and groans of despair. Once, when Legree chanced to overhear something of this kind, he flew into a violent passion, and swore that the next one that told stories about that garret should have an opportunity of knowing what was there, for he would chain them up there for a week. This hint was enough to repress talking, though, of course, it did not disturb the credit of the story in the least.

Gradually, the staircase that led to the garret, and even the passageway to the staircase, were avoided by every one in the house, from every one fearing to speak of it, and the legend was gradually falling into desuetude.[3] It had suddenly occurred to Cassy to make use of the superstitious excitability, which was so great in Legree, for the purpose of her liberation, and that of her fellow-sufferer.

The sleeping-room of Cassy was directly under the garret. One day, without consulting Legree, she suddenly[4] took it upon her, with some considerable ostentation, to change all the furniture and appurtenances of the room to one at some considerable distance. The under-servants, who were called on to effect this movement, were running and bustling about with great zeal and confusion, when Legree returned from a ride.

"Hallo! you Cass!" said Legree, "what's in the wind now?"

"Nothing; only I choose to have another room," said Cassy, doggedly.

"And what for, pray?" said Legree.

"I choose to," said Cassy.

"The devil you do! and what for?"

"I'd like to get some sleep, now and then."

"Sleep! well, what hinders your sleeping?"

"I could tell, I suppose, if you want to hear," said Cassy, dryly.

"Speak out, you minx!" said Legree.

"O! nothing. I suppose it wouldn't disturb *you!* Only groans, and people scuffling, and rolling round on the garret floor, half the night, from twelve to morning!"

"People up garret!" said Legree, uneasily, but forcing a laugh; "who are they, Cassy?"

Cassy raised her sharp, black eyes, and looked in the face of Legree, with an expression that went through his bones, as she said, "To be sure, Simon, who are they? I'd like to have *you* tell me. You don't know, I suppose!"

With an oath, Legree struck at her with his riding-whip; but she glided to one side, and passed through the door, and looking back, said, "If you'll sleep in that room, you'll know all about it. Perhaps you'd better try it!" and then immediately she shut and locked the door.

Legree blustered and swore, and threatened to break down the door; but apparently thought better of it, and walked uneasily into the sitting-room. Cassy perceived that her shaft had struck home; and, from that hour, with the most exquisite address, she never ceased to continue the train of influences she had begun.[5]

In a knot-hole in the garret she had inserted the neck of an old bottle, in such a manner that when there was the least wind, most doleful and lugubrious wailing sounds proceeded from it, which, in a high wind, increased to a perfect shriek, such as to credulous and superstitious ears might easily seem to be that of horror and despair.[6]

These sounds were, from time to time, heard by the servants, and revived in full force the memory of the old ghost legend. A superstitious creeping horror seemed to fill the house; and though no one dared to breathe it to Legree, he found himself encompassed by it, as by an atmosphere.

No one is so thoroughly superstitious as the godless man. The Christian is composed by the belief of a wise, all-ruling Father, whose presence fills the void unknown with light and order; but to the man who has dethroned God, the spirit-land is, indeed, in the words of the Hebrew poet, "a land of darkness and the shadow of death," without any order, where the light is as darkness.[7] Life and death to him are haunted grounds, filled with goblin forms of vague and shadowy dread.

Legree had had the slumbering moral element in him roused by his encounters with Tom,—roused, only to be resisted by the determinate force of evil; but still there was a thrill and commotion of the dark, inner world, produced by every word, or prayer, or hymn, that reacted in superstitious dread.

The influence of Cassy over him was of a strange and singular kind. He was her owner, her tyrant and tormentor. She was, as he knew, wholly, and without any possibility of help or redress, in his hands; and yet so it is, that the most brutal man cannot live in constant association with a strong female influence, and not be greatly controlled by it.[8] When he first bought her, she was, as she had said, a woman delicately bred; and then he crushed her, without scruple, beneath the foot of his brutality. But, as time, and debasing influences, and despair, hardened womanhood

5 Cassy's role as trickster recollects the antics of Sam and Andy in chapter 6.

6 Nineteenth-century readers would be familiar with the image of the Aeolean harp (see chapter 28, note 14). Cassy's trick with the bottle demonstrates her understanding of the concept.

7 Stowe's verse here is from the book of Job, the end of chapter 10, when Job is remonstrating with God. "Why didst thou bring me forth from the womb? . . . Let me alone, that I may find a little comfort before I go whence I shall not return, to the land of gloom and deep darkness, the land of gloom and chaos, where light is as darkness."

8 Stowe knows that the description of Cassy's life of torment and degradation will resonate with female readers. Like a nineteenth-century Oprah, Stowe appeals to her readership by offering stories that are simultaneously awful and familiar. Cassy's experience in being a "delicately bred" woman bought by Legree and physically humiliated year after year may have sparked more than an impersonal outrage in Stowe's thousands of readers. I wonder whether these readers found themselves murmuring the 1850's equivalent of "You go, sister!" under their breath.

9 I.e., expressed contempt and sneered.

within her, and waked the fires of fiercer passions, she had become in a measure his mistress, and he alternately tyrannized over and dreaded her.

This influence had become more harassing and decided, since partial insanity had given a strange, weird, unsettled cast to all her words and language.

A night or two after this, Legree was sitting in the old sitting-room, by the side of a flickering wood fire, that threw uncertain glances round the room. It was a stormy, windy night, such as raises whole squadrons of nondescript noises in rickety old houses. Windows were rattling, shutters flapping, the wind carousing, rumbling, and tumbling down the chimney, and, every once in a while, puffing out smoke and ashes, as if a legion of spirits were coming after them. Legree had been casting up accounts and reading newspapers for some hours, while Cassy sat in the corner, sullenly looking into the fire. Legree laid down his paper, and seeing an old book lying on the table, which he had noticed Cassy reading, the first part of the evening, took it up, and began to turn it over. It was one of those collections of stories of bloody murders, ghostly legends, and supernatural visitations, which, coarsely got up and illustrated, have a strange fascination for one who once begins to read them.

Legree poohed and pished,[9] but read, turning page after page, till, finally, after reading some way, he threw down the book, with an oath.

"You don't believe in ghosts, do you, Cass?" said he, taking the tongs and settling the fire. "I thought you'd more sense than to let noises scare *you*."

"No matter what I believe," said Cassy, sullenly.

"Fellows used to try to frighten me with their yarns at sea," said Legree. "Never come it round me that way. I'm too tough for any such trash, tell ye."

Cassy sat looking intensely at him in the shadow of the corner. There was that strange light in her eyes that always impressed Legree with uneasiness.

"Them noises was nothing but rats and the wind," said Legree. "Rats will make a devil of a noise. I used to hear 'em sometimes down in the hold of the ship; and wind,— Lord's sake! ye can make anything out o' wind."

Cassy knew Legree was uneasy under her eyes, and, therefore, she made no answer, but sat fixing them on him, with that strange, unearthly expression, as before.

"Come, speak out, woman,—don't you think so?" said Legree.

"Can rats walk down stairs, and come walking through

the entry, and open a door when you've locked it and set a chair against it?" said Cassy; "and come walk, walk, walking right up to your bed, and put out their hand, so?"

Cassy kept her glittering eyes fixed on Legree, as she spoke, and he stared at her like a man in the nightmare, till, when she finished by laying her hand, icy cold, on his, he sprung back, with an oath.

"Woman! what do you mean? Nobody did?"—

"O, no,—of course not,—did I say they did?" said Cassy, with a smile of chilling derision.

"But—did—have you really seen?—Come, Cass, what is it, now,—speak out!"

"You may sleep there, yourself," said Cassy, "if you want to know."

"Did it come from the garret, Cassy?"

"*It,*—what?" said Cassy.

"Why, what you told of—"

"I didn't tell you anything," said Cassy, with dogged sullenness.

Legree walked up and down the room, uneasily.

"I'll have this yer thing examined. I'll look into it, this very night. I'll take my pistols—"

"Do," said Cassy; "sleep in that room. I'd like to see you doing it. Fire your pistols,—do!"

Legree stamped his foot, and swore violently.

"Don't swear," said Cassy; "nobody knows who may be hearing you. Hark! What was that?"

"What?" said Legree, starting.

A heavy old Dutch clock, that stood in the corner of the room, began, and slowly struck twelve.

For some reason or other, Legree neither spoke nor moved; a vague horror fell on him; while Cassy, with a keen, sneering glitter in her eyes, stood looking at him, counting the strokes.

"Twelve o'clock; well, *now* we'll see," said she, turning, and opening the door into the passage-way, and standing as if listening.

"Hark! What's that?" said she, raising her finger.

"It's only the wind," said Legree. "Don't you hear how cursedly it blows?"

"Simon, come here," said Cassy, in a whisper, laying her hand on his, and leading him to the foot of the stairs: "do you know what *that* is? Hark!"

A wild shriek came pealing down the stairway. It came from the garret. Legree's knees knocked together; his face grew white with fear.

"Hadn't you better get your pistols?" said Cassy, with a

sneer that froze Legree's blood. "It's time this thing was looked into, you know. I'd like to have you go up now; *they're at it.*"

"I won't go!" said Legree, with an oath.

"Why not? There an't any such thing as ghosts, you know! Come!" and Cassy flitted up the winding stairway, laughing, and looking back after him. "Come on."

"I believe you *are* the devil!" said Legree. "Come back, you hag,—come back, Cass! You shan't go!"

But Cassy laughed wildly, and fled on. He heard her open the entry doors that led to the garret. A wild gust of wind swept down, extinguishing the candle he held in his hand, and with it the fearful, unearthly screams; they seemed to be shrieked in his very ear.

Legree fled frantically into the parlor, whither, in a few moments, he was followed by Cassy, pale, calm, cold as an avenging spirit, and with that same fearful light in her eye.

"I hope you are satisfied," said she.

"Blast you, Cass!" said Legree.

"What for?" said Cassy. "I only went up and shut the doors. *What's the matter with that garret,* Simon, do you suppose?" said she.

"None of your business!" said Legree.

"O, it an't? Well," said Cassy, "at any rate, I'm glad *I* don't sleep under it."

Anticipating the rising of the wind, that very evening, Cassy had been up and opened the garret window. Of course, the moment the doors were opened, the wind had drafted down, and extinguished the light.

This may serve as a specimen of the game that Cassy played with Legree, until he would sooner have put his head into a lion's mouth than to have explored that garret. Meanwhile, in the night, when everybody else was asleep, Cassy slowly and carefully accumulated there a stock of provisions sufficient to afford subsistence for some time; she transferred, article by article, a greater part of her own and Emmeline's wardrobe. All things being arranged, they only waited a fitting opportunity to put their plan in execution.

By cajoling Legree, and taking advantage of a good-natured interval, Cassy had got him to take her with him to the neighboring town, which was situated directly on the Red river. With a memory sharpened to almost preter-natural clearness, she remarked[10] every turn in the road, and formed a mental estimate of the time to be occupied in traversing it.

At the time when all was matured for action, our readers may, perhaps, like to look behind the scenes, and see the final *coup d'état.*

It was now near evening. Legree had been absent, on a ride to a neighboring farm. For many days Cassy had been unusually gracious and accommodating in her humors; and Legree and she had been, apparently, on the best of terms. At present, we may behold her and Emmeline in the room of the latter, busy in sorting and arranging two small bundles.

"There, these will be large enough," said Cassy. "Now put on your bonnet, and let's start: it's just about the right time."

"Why, they can see us yet," said Emmeline.

"I mean they shall," said Cassy, coolly. "Don't you know that they must have their chase after us, at any rate? The way of the thing is to be just this:—We will steal out of the back door, and run down by the quarters. Sambo or Quimbo will be sure to see us. They will give chase, and we will get into the swamp; then, they can't follow us any further till they go up and give the alarm, and turn out the dogs, and so on; and, while they are blundering round, and tumbling over each other, as they always do,[11] you and I will just slip along to the creek, that runs back of the house, and wade along in it, till we get opposite the back door. That will put the dogs all at fault; for scent won't lie in the water. Every one will run out of the house to look after us, and then we'll whip in at the back door, and up into the garret, where I've got a nice bed made up in one of the great boxes. We must stay in that garret a good while; for, I tell you, he will raise heaven and earth after us. He'll muster some of those old overseers on the other plantations, and have a great hunt; and they'll go over every inch of ground in that swamp. He makes it his boast that nobody ever got away from him. So let him hunt at his leisure."

"Cassy, how well you have planned it!" said Emmeline. "Who ever would have thought of it, but you?"

There was neither pleasure nor exultation in Cassy's eyes,—only a despairing firmness.

"Come," she said, reaching her hand to Emmeline.

The two fugitives glided noiselessly from the house, and flitted, through the gathering shadows of evening, along by the quarters. The crescent moon, set like a silver signet in the western sky, delayed a little the approach of night. As Cassy expected, when quite near the verge of the swamps that encircled the plantation, they heard a voice

11 Stowe paints this scene as a malevolent version of Sam and Andy's high jinks in chasing Eliza on her flight from the Shelby plantation.

Legree with his dogs pursuing Cassy and Emmeline in this Miguel Covarrubias lithograph.   From *Uncle Tom's Cabin: or, Life Among the Lowly,* Heritage Press edition, 1938

**12** I.e., torches.

calling to them to stop. It was not Sambo, however, but Legree, who was pursuing them with violent execrations. At the sound, the feebler spirit of Emmeline gave way; and, laying hold of Cassy's arm, she said, "O, Cassy, I'm going to faint!"

"If you do, I'll kill you!" said Cassy, drawing a small, glittering stiletto, and flashing it before the eyes of the girl.

The diversion accomplished the purpose. Emmeline did not faint, and succeeded in plunging, with Cassy, into a part of the labyrinth of swamp, so deep and dark that it was perfectly hopeless for Legree to think of following them, without assistance.

"Well," said he, chuckling brutally; "at any rate, they've got themselves into a trap now—the baggages! They're safe enough. They shall sweat for it!"

"Hulloa, there! Sambo! Quimbo! All hands!" called Legree, coming to the quarters, when the men and women were just returning from work. "There's two runaways in the swamps. I'll give five dollars to any nigger as catches 'em. Turn out the dogs! Turn out Tiger, and Fury, and the rest!"

The sensation produced by this news was immediate. Many of the men sprang forward, officiously, to offer their services, either from the hope of the reward, or from that cringing subserviency which is one of the most baleful effects of slavery. Some ran one way, and some another. Some were for getting flambeaux of pine-knots.[12] Some were uncoupling the dogs, whose hoarse, savage bay added not a little to the animation of the scene.

"Mas'r, shall we shoot 'em, if we can't cotch 'em?" said Sambo, to whom his master brought out a rifle.

"You may fire on Cass, if you like; it's time she was gone to the devil, where she belongs; but the gal, not," said Legree. "And now, boys, be spry and smart. Five dollars for him that gets 'em; and a glass of spirits to every one of you, anyhow."

The whole band, with the glare of blazing torches, and whoop, and shout, and savage yell, of man and beast, proceeded down to the swamp, followed, at some distance, by every servant in the house. The establishment was, of a consequence, wholly deserted, when Cassy and Emmeline glided into it the back way. The whooping and shouts of their pursuers were still filling the air; and, looking from the sitting-room windows, Cassy and Emmeline could see the troop, with their flambeaux, just dispersing themselves along the edge of the swamp.

"See there!" said Emmeline, pointing to Cassy; "the

hunt is begun! Look how those lights dance about! Hark! the dogs! Don't you hear? If we were only *there,* our chance wouldn't be worth a picayune. O, for pity's sake, do let's hide ourselves. Quick!"

"There's no occasion for hurry," said Cassy, coolly; "they are all out after the hunt,—that's the amusement of the evening! We'll go up stairs, by and by. Meanwhile," said she, deliberately taking a key from the pocket of a coat that Legree had thrown down in his hurry, "meanwhile I shall take something to pay our passage."

She unlocked the desk, took from it a roll of bills, which she counted over rapidly.

"O, don't let's do that!" said Emmeline.

"Don't!" said Cassy; "why not? Would you have us starve in the swamps, or have that that will pay our way to the free states? Money will do anything, girl." And, as she spoke, she put the money in her bosom.

"It would be stealing," said Emmeline, in a distressed whisper.

"Stealing!" said Cassy, with a scornful laugh. "They who steal body and soul needn't talk to us. Every one of these bills is stolen,—stolen from poor, starving, sweating creatures, who must go to the devil at last, for his profit.[13] Let *him* talk about stealing! But come, we may as well go up garret; I've got a stock of candles there, and some books to pass away the time. You may be pretty sure they won't come *there* to inquire after us. If they do, I'll play ghost for them."

When Emmeline reached the garret, she found an immense box, in which some heavy pieces of furniture had once been brought, turned on its side, so that the opening faced the wall, or rather the eaves. Cassy lit a small lamp, and, creeping round under the eaves, they established themselves in it. It was spread with a couple of small mattresses and some pillows; a box near by was plentifully stored with candles, provisions, and all the clothing necessary to their journey, which Cassy had arranged into bundles of an astonishingly small compass.

"There," said Cassy, as she fixed the lamp into a small hook, which she had driven into the side of the box for that purpose; "this is to be our home for the present. How do you like it?"

"Are you sure they won't come and search the garret?"

"I'd like to see Simon Legree doing that," said Cassy. "No, indeed; he will be too glad to keep away. As to the servants, they would any of them stand and be shot, sooner than show their faces here."

13 Cassy is apparently well read in the contemporary discourse of labor and exploitation. Moments later, she settles down and reads a French book, demonstrating her education and perhaps her familiarity with French labor politics.

Somewhat reassured, Emmeline settled herself back on her pillow.

"What did you mean, Cassy, by saying you would kill me?" she said, simply.

"I meant to stop your fainting," said Cassy, "and I did do it. And now I tell you, Emmeline, you must make up your mind *not* to faint, let what will come; there's no sort of need of it. If I had not stopped you, that wretch might have had his hands on you now."

Emmeline shuddered.

The two remained some time in silence. Cassy busied herself with a French book; Emmeline, overcome with the exhaustion, fell into a doze, and slept some time. She was awakened by loud shouts and outcries, the tramp of horses' feet, and the baying of dogs. She started up, with a faint shriek.

"Only the hunt coming back," said Cassy, coolly; "never fear. Look out of this knot-hole. Don't you see 'em all down there? Simon has to give it up, for this night. Look, how muddy his horse is, flouncing about in the swamp; the dogs, too, look rather crest-fallen. Ah, my good sir, you'll have to try the race again and again,—the game isn't there."

"O, don't speak a word!" said Emmeline; "what if they should hear you?"

"If they do hear anything, it will make them very particular to keep away," said Cassy. "No danger; we may make any noise we please, and it will only add to the effect."

At length the stillness of midnight settled down over the house. Legree, cursing his ill luck, and vowing dire vengeance on the morrow, went to bed.

# CHAPTER 40

## The Martyr

*"Deem not the just by Heaven forgot!*
  *Though life its common gifts deny,—*
*Though, with a crushed and bleeding heart,*
  *And spurned of man, he goes to die!*
*For God hath marked each sorrowing day,*
  *And numbered every bitter tear;*
*And heaven's long years of bliss shall pay*
  *For all his children suffer here."*
—BRYANT.[1]

The longest way must have its close,—the gloomiest night will wear on to a morning. An eternal, inexorable lapse of moments is ever hurrying the day of the evil to an eternal night, and the night of the just to an eternal day. We have walked with our humble friend thus far in the valley of slavery; first through flowery fields of ease and indulgence, then through heart-breaking separations from all that man holds dear.[2] Again, we have waited with him in a sunny island, where generous hands concealed his chains with flowers;[3] and, lastly, we have followed him when the last ray of earthly hope went out in night, and seen how, in the blackness of earthly darkness,[4] the firmament of the unseen has blazed with stars of new and significant lustre.

The morning-star now stands over the tops of the moun-

1 This poem by William Cullen Bryant, American poet, critic, newspaper editor, and Free Soil antislavery advocate, appears to be an early version of "Blessed Are They That Mourn," which may have appeared in a newspaper or magazine.

2 Stowe offers a brief history of Tom's experiences thus far. The "flowery fields" from which he was separated refer, of course, to the Shelby plantation. It is unclear whether we are to read the description "ease and indulgence" as ironic. Certainly this description fits the Shelbys' life in the Big House.

3 This line refers to Tom's life on the St. Clare plantation with his beloved Eva. Note the wonderful description of chains concealed with flowers.

4 Now that he is under Legree's thumb, the bleakness of Tom's earthly existence puts in stark relief the loveliness of the heavenly home awaiting him. Legree, we see in the description of his nocturnal teeth-gnashing just following, is outraged by Tom's allegiance to a greater Master.

tains, and gales and breezes, not of earth, show that the gates of day are unclosing.

The escape of Cassy and Emmeline irritated the before surly temper of Legree to the last degree; and his fury, as was to be expected, fell upon the defenceless head of Tom. When he hurriedly announced the tidings among his hands, there was a sudden light in Tom's eye, a sudden upraising of his hands, that did not escape him. He saw that he did not join the muster of the pursuers. He thought of forcing him to do it; but, having had, of old, experience of his inflexibility when commanded to take part in any deed of inhumanity, he would not, in his hurry, stop to enter into any conflict with him.

Tom, therefore, remained behind, with a few who had learned of him to pray, and offered up prayers for the escape of the fugitives.

When Legree returned, baffled and disappointed, all the long-working hatred of his soul towards his slave began to gather in a deadly and desperate form. Had not this man braved him,—steadily, powerfully, resistlessly,—ever since he bought him? Was there not a spirit in him which, silent as it was, burned on him like the fires of perdition?

"I *hate* him!" said Legree, that night, as he sat up in his bed; "I *hate* him! And isn't he MINE? Can't I do what I like with him? Who's to hinder, I wonder?" And Legree clenched his fist, and shook it, as if he had something in his hands that he could rend in pieces.

But, then, Tom was a faithful, valuable servant; and, although Legree hated him the more for that, yet the consideration was still somewhat of a restraint to him.

The next morning, he determined to say nothing, as yet; to assemble a party, from some neighboring plantations, with dogs and guns; to surround the swamp, and go about the hunt systematically. If it succeeded, well and good; if not, he would summon Tom before him, and—his teeth clenched and his blood boiled—*then* he would break that fellow down, or—there was a dire inward whisper, to which his soul assented.

Ye say that the *interest* of the master is a sufficient safeguard for the slave. In the fury of man's mad will, he will wittingly, and with open eye, sell his own soul to the devil to gain his ends; and will he be more careful of his neighbor's body?

"Well," said Cassy, the next day, from the garret, as she reconnoitred through the knot-hole, "the hunt's going to begin again, to-day!"

Three or four mounted horsemen were curvetting[5] about, on the space front of the house; and one or two leashes of strange dogs were struggling with the negroes who held them, baying and barking at each other.

The men are, two of them, overseers of plantations in the vicinity; and others were some of Legree's associates at the tavern-bar of a neighboring city, who had come for the interest of the sport. A more hard-favored set, perhaps, could not be imagined. Legree was serving brandy, profusely, round among them, as also among the negroes, who had been detailed from the various plantations for this service; for it was an object to make every service of this kind, among the negroes, as much of a holiday as possible.

Cassy placed her ear at the knot-hole; and, as the morning air blew directly towards the house, she could overhear a good deal of the conversation. A grave sneer overcast the dark, severe gravity of her face, as she listened, and heard them divide out the ground, discuss the rival merits of the dogs, give orders about firing, and the treatment of each, in case of capture.

Cassy drew back; and, clasping her hands, looked upward, and said, "O, great Almighty God! we are *all* sinners; but what have *we* done, more than all the rest of the world, that we should be treated so?"

There was a terrible earnestness in her face and voice, as she spoke.

"If it wasn't for *you*, child," she said, looking at Emmeline, "I'd *go* out to them; and I'd thank any one of them that *would* shoot me down; for what use will freedom be to me? Can it give me back my children, or make me what I used to be?"

Emmeline, in her child-like simplicity, was half afraid of the dark moods of Cassy. She looked perplexed, but made no answer. She only took her hand, with a gentle, caressing movement.

"Don't!" said Cassy, trying to draw it away; "you'll get me to loving you; and I never mean to love anything, again!"

"Poor Cassy!" said Emmeline, "don't feel so! If the Lord gives us liberty, perhaps he'll give you back your daughter; at any rate, I'll be like a daughter to you. I know I'll never see my poor old mother again! I shall love you, Cassy, whether you love me or not!"

The gentle, child-like spirit conquered. Cassy sat down by her, put her arm round her neck, stroked her soft, brown hair; and Emmeline then wondered at the beauty of her magnificent eyes, now soft with tears.

5 I.e., leaping about. This scene of Legree's neighbors coming to join the hunt is a bit surprising, since we have come to think of the plantation as almost totally isolated. But these men are clearly not the sort of neighbors that any of Legree's slaves could or would run to for help.

**6** It is unclear how exactly Tom knows where Cassy and Emmeline are hiding, but this knowledge heightens the drama of this scene. Tom pronounces Jesus' last words, "Thou hast redeemed me," and it should dawn on the reader that Tom will likely also suffer and die at the hands of his oppressors.

"O, Em!" said Cassy, "I've hungered for my children, and thirsted for them, and my eyes fail with longing for them! Here! here!" she said, striking her breast, "it's all desolate, all empty! If God would give me back my children, then I could pray."

"You must trust him, Cassy," said Emmeline; "he is our Father!"

"His wrath is upon us," said Cassy; "he has turned away in anger."

"No, Cassy! He will be good to us! Let us hope in Him," said Emmeline,—"I always have had hope."

The hunt was long, animated, and thorough, but unsuccessful; and, with grave, ironic exultation, Cassy looked down on Legree, as, weary and dispirited, he alighted from his horse.

"Now, Quimbo," said Legree, as he stretched himself down in the sitting-room, "you jest go and walk that Tom up here, right away! The old cuss is at the bottom of this yer whole matter; and I'll have it out of his old black hide, or I'll know the reason why!"

Sambo and Quimbo, both, though hating each other, were joined in one mind by a no less cordial hatred of Tom. Legree had told them, at first, that he had bought him for a general overseer, in his absence; and this had begun an ill will, on their part, which had increased, in their debased and servile natures, as they saw him becoming obnoxious to their master's displeasure. Quimbo, therefore, departed, with a will, to execute his orders.

Tom heard the message with a forewarning heart; for he knew all the plan of the fugitives' escape, and the place of their present concealment;—he knew the deadly character of the man he had to deal with, and his despotic power. But he felt strong in God to meet death, rather than betray the helpless.

He sat his basket down by the row, and, looking up, said, "Into thy hands I commend my spirit! Thou hast redeemed me, oh Lord God of truth!" and then quietly yielded himself to the rough, brutal grasp with which Quimbo seized him.**6**

"Ay, ay!" said the giant, as he dragged him along; "ye'll cotch it, now! I'll boun' Mas'r's back's up *high*! No sneaking out, now! Tell ye, ye'll get it, and no mistake! See how ye'll look, now, helpin' Mas'r's niggers to run away! See what ye'll get!"

The savage words none of them reached that ear!—a higher voice there was saying, "Fear not them that kill the body, and, after that, have no more that they can do."[7] Nerve and bone of that poor man's body vibrated to those words, as if touched by the finger of God; and he felt the strength of a thousand souls in one. As he passed along, the trees and bushes, the huts of his servitude, the whole scene of his degradation, seemed to whirl by him as the landscape by the rushing car. His soul throbbed,—his home was in sight,—and the hour of release seemed at hand.

"Well, Tom!" said Legree, walking up, and seizing him grimly by the collar of his coat, and speaking through his teeth, in a paroxysm of determined rage, "do you know I've made up my mind to KILL you?"

"It's very likely, Mas'r," said Tom, calmly.

"I *have*," said Legree, with grim, terrible calmness, "*done—just—that—thing*, Tom, unless you'll tell me what you know about these yer gals!"

Tom stood silent.

"D' ye hear?" said Legree, stamping, with a roar like that of an incensed lion. "Speak!"

"*I han't got nothing to tell, Mas'r,*" said Tom, with a slow, firm, deliberate utterance.

"Do you dare to tell me, ye old black Christian, ye don't *know*?" said Legree.

Tom was silent.

"Speak!" thundered Legree, striking him furiously. "Do you know anything?"

"I know, Mas'r; but I can't tell anything. *I can die!*"

Legree drew in a long breath; and, suppressing his rage, took Tom by the arm, and, approaching his face almost to his, said, in a terrible voice, "Hark'e, Tom!—ye think, 'cause I've let you off before, I don't mean what I say; but, this time, I've *made up my mind*, and counted the cost. You've always stood it out agin' me: now, I'll *conquer ye, or kill ye!*—one or t'other. I'll count every drop of blood there is in you, and take 'em, one by one, till ye give up!"

Tom looked up to his master, and answered, "Mas'r, if you was sick, or in trouble, or dying, and I could save ye, I'd *give* ye my heart's blood; and, if taking every drop of blood in this poor old body would save your precious soul, I'd give 'em freely, as the Lord gave his for me. O, Mas'r! don't bring this great sin on your soul! It will hurt you more than 't will me! Do the worst you can, my troubles'll be over soon; but, if ye don't repent, yours won't *never* end!"

Like a strange snatch of heavenly music, heard in the lull of a tempest, this burst of feeling made a moment's blank pause. Legree stood aghast, and looked at Tom; and

7 These words Tom hears are from Matt. 11:28. Again, we are to understand that Tom will suffer like Jesus.

A balding yet middle-aged Uncle Tom is threatened by a malicious Simon Legree. From *Uncle Tom's Cabin*, James Nisbet & Co., Ltd., London, n.d.

8 I.e., struck down (biblical term). This moment and the brutal scene following provoked an outcry among the pro-slavery press (see chapter 41, note 14).

9 I.e., Satan.

10 Stowe's relentless intermixing of "Master" and "Mas'r" reiterates her belief that the idea of an earthly master (of slaves) is a morally bankrupt concept. Thus at the beginning of the next chapter when we see the "Young Master," George Shelby, we are to question the moral worth of Tom's old friend.

there was such a silence, that the tick of the old clock could be heard, measuring, with silent touch, the last moments of mercy and probation to that hardened heart.

It was but a moment. There was one hesitating pause,—one irresolute, relenting thrill,—and the spirit of evil came back, with seven-fold vehemence; and Legree, foaming with rage, smote[8] his victim to the ground.

Scenes of blood and cruelty are shocking to our ear and heart. What man has nerve to do, man has not nerve to hear. What brother-man and brother-Christian must suffer, cannot be told us, even in our secret chamber, it so harrows up the soul! And yet, oh my country! these things are done under the shadow of thy laws! O, Christ! thy church sees them, almost in silence!

But, of old, there was One whose suffering changed an instrument of torture, degradation and shame, into a symbol of glory, honor, and immortal life; and, where His spirit is, neither degrading stripes, nor blood, nor insults, can make the Christian's last struggle less than glorious.

Was he alone, that long night, whose brave, loving spirit was bearing up, in that old shed, against buffeting and brutal stripes?

Nay! There stood by him ONE,—seen by him alone,—"like unto the Son of God."

The tempter[9] stood by him, too,—blinded by furious, despotic will,—every moment pressing him to shun that agony by the betrayal of the innocent. But the brave, true heart was firm on the Eternal Rock. Like his Master,[10] he knew that, if he saved others, himself he could not save; nor could utmost extremity wring from him words, save of prayer and holy trust.

"He's most gone, Mas'r," said Sambo, touched, in spite of himself, by the patience of his victim.

"Pay away, till he gives up! Give it to him!—give it to him!" shouted Legree. "I'll take every drop of blood he has, unless he confesses!"

Tom opened his eyes, and looked upon his master. "Ye poor miserable critter!" he said, "there an't no more ye can do! I forgive ye, with all my soul!" and he fainted entirely away.

"I b'lieve, my soul, he's done for, finally," said Legree, stepping forward, to look at him. "Yes, he is! Well, his mouth's shut up, at last,—that's one comfort!"

Yes, Legree; but who shall shut up that voice in thy soul? that soul, past repentance, past prayer, past hope, in whom the fire that never shall be quenched is already burning!

Yet Tom was not quite gone. His wondrous words and pious prayers had struck upon the hearts of the imbruted blacks, who had been the instruments of cruelty upon him; and, the instant Legree withdrew, they took him down, and, in their ignorance, sought to call him back to life,—as if *that* were any favor to him.

"Sartin, we's been doin' a drefful wicked thing!" said Sambo; "hopes Mas'r'll have to 'count for it, and not we."

They washed his wounds,—they provided a rude bed, of some refuse cotton, for him to lie down on; and one of them, stealing up to the house, begged a drink of brandy of Legree, pretending that he was tired, and wanted it for himself. He brought it back, and poured it down Tom's throat.

"O, Tom!" said Quimbo, "we's been awful wicked to ye!"

"I forgive ye, with all my heart!" said Tom, faintly.

"O, Tom! do tell us who is *Jesus,* anyhow?" said Sambo;—"Jesus, that's been a standin' by you so, all this night!—Who is he?"

The word roused the failing, fainting spirit. He poured forth a few energetic sentences of that wondrous One,—his life, his death, his ever-lasting presence, and power to save.

They wept,[11]—both the two savage men.

"Why didn't I never hear this before?" said Sambo; "but I do believe!—I can't help it! Lord Jesus, have mercy on us!"

"Poor critters!" said Tom, "I'd be willing to bar' all I have, if it'll only bring ye to Christ! O, Lord! give me these two more souls, I pray!"

That prayer was answered!

11 The allusion here is to one of the shortest verses in the Bible: "Jesus wept" (John 11:35). After Tom's prayer is answered—signaling their acceptance of Jesus Christ—Sambo and Quimbo disappear from the story.

## CHAPTER 41

### *The Young Master*[1]

Two days after, a young man drove a light wagon up through the avenue of china-trees, and, throwing the reins hastily on the horses' neck, sprang out and inquired for the owner of the place.

It was George Shelby; and, to show how he came to be there, we must go back in our story.

The letter of Miss Ophelia to Mrs. Shelby had, by some unfortunate accident, been detained, for a month or two, at some remote post-office, before it reached its destination;[2] and, of course, before it was received, Tom was already lost to view among the distant swamps of the Red river.

Mrs. Shelby read the intelligence with the deepest concern; but any immediate action upon it was an impossibility. She was then in attendance on the sick-bed of her husband, who lay delirious in the crisis of a fever. Master George Shelby, who, in the interval, had changed from a boy to a tall young man, was her constant and faithful assistant, and her only reliance in superintending his father's affairs. Miss Ophelia had taken the precaution to send them the name of the lawyer who did business for the St. Clares; and the most that, in the emergency, could be done, was to address a letter of inquiry to him. The sudden death of Mr. Shelby, a few days after, brought, of course, an absorbing pressure of other interests, for a season.

Mr. Shelby showed his confidence in his wife's ability, by appointing her sole executrix upon his estates; and

This chapter title brings us back to the world of the Shelby Plantation. As noted above (chapter 40, note 10), the appearance of the word "Master" is designed to make the reader a little uncomfortable. While we are happy to see young George, we are not happy to learn that he is still a "Master" of slaves.

2 Stowe's readers would be accustomed to such "unfortunate accidents," not only from Victorian novels but from their own experience with delayed mail. Southern mail delivery was notoriously unreliable as compared with Northern mail at midcentury, in large part because of the South's agricultural, rather than commercial, economy.

thus immediately a large and complicated amount of business was brought upon her hands.[3]

Mrs. Shelby, with characteristic energy, applied herself to the work of straightening the entangled web of affairs; and she and George were for some time occupied with collecting and examining accounts, selling property and settling debts; for Mrs. Shelby was determined that everything should be brought into tangible and recognizable shape, let the consequences to her prove what they might. In the mean time, they received a letter from the lawyer to whom Miss Ophelia had referred them, saying that he knew nothing of the matter; that the man was sold at a public auction, and that, beyond receiving the money, he knew nothing of the affair.

Neither George nor Mrs. Shelby could be easy at this result; and, accordingly, some six months after,[4] the latter, having business for his mother, down the river, resolved to visit New Orleans, in person, and push his inquiries, in hopes of discovering Tom's whereabouts, and restoring him.[5]

After some months of unsuccessful search, by the merest accident, George fell in with a man, in New Orleans, who happened to be possessed of the desired information; and with his money in his pocket, our hero took steamboat for Red river, resolving to find out and re-purchase his old friend.

He was soon introduced into the house, where he found Legree in the sitting-room.

Legree received the stranger with a kind of surly hospitality.

"I understand," said the young man, "that you bought, in New Orleans, a boy, named Tom. He used to be on my father's place, and I came to see if I couldn't buy him back."

Legree's brow grew dark, and he broke out, passionately: "Yes, I did buy such a fellow,—and a h—l of a bargain I had of it, too! The most rebellious, saucy, impudent dog! Set up my niggers to run away; got off two gals, worth eight hundred or a thousand dollars apiece. He owned to that, and, when I bid him tell me where they was, he up and said he knew, but he wouldn't tell; and stood to it, though I gave him the cussedest flogging I ever gave nigger yet. I b'lieve he's trying to die; but I don't know as he'll make it out."

"Where is he?" said George, impetuously.[6] "Let me see him." The cheeks of the young man were crimson, and his eyes flashed fire; but he prudently said nothing, as yet.

3 At some point Mr. Shelby must have had a change of heart about his wife's business acumen. Mrs. Shelby euphemistically began "straightening the entangled web of affairs," but she seems unconcerned with any slaves other than Tom.

4 We are left to imagine whether Chloe knew anything of these inquiries; if so, six months' time must have seemed not such a short interval.

5 I.e., buying him back for the Shelbys. George is described as now a man, not a boy, so we can probably assume that he has reached twenty-one.

6 I.e., vehemently. Both men are angry, but only George controls himself. Legree's speech has degraded further, offering a stark contrast to George's gentlemanly demeanor. When Legree swears and brags about his cruelty, we recognize sadly that Tom's short journey from cabin to shed represents his narrow and restricted existence under slavery.

7 We have been told from the very beginning that Tom is strong and powerfully built, so we understand that his body is too strong to die quickly. But more importantly, Stowe uses these days of suffering to reestablish the similarity with the suffering of Jesus on the Cross.

8 In other words, Tom had converted many of his fellow slaves.

9 I.e., dizzy.

10 This hymn by Isaac Watts was popular in the nineteenth century. Note that even while dying, Tom speaks perfectly when quoting words of scripture or hymns. George calls him by his old name, Uncle Tom.

"He's in dat ar shed," said a little fellow, who stood holding George's horse.

Legree kicked the boy, and swore at him; but George, without saying another word, turned and strode to the spot.

Tom had been lying two days since the fatal night; not suffering, for every nerve of suffering was blunted and destroyed. He lay, for the most part, in a quiet stupor; for the laws of a powerful and well-knit frame would not at once release the imprisoned spirit.[7] By stealth, there had been there, in the darkness of the night, poor desolated creatures, who stole from their scanty hours' rest, that they might repay to him some of those ministrations of love in which he had always been so abundant. Truly, those poor disciples had little to give,—only the cup of cold water; but it was given with full hearts.

Tears had fallen on that honest, insensible face,—tears of late repentance in the poor, ignorant heathen, whom his dying love and patience had awakened to repentance, and bitter prayers, breathed over him to a late-found Saviour, of whom they scarce knew more than the name, but whom the yearning ignorant heart of man never implores in vain.[8]

Cassy, who had glided out of her place of concealment, and, by over-hearing, learned the sacrifice that had been made for her and Emmeline, had been there, the night before, defying the danger of detection; and, moved by the few last words which the affectionate soul had yet strength to breathe, the long winter of despair, the ice of years, had given way, and the dark, despairing woman had wept and prayed.

When George entered the shed, he felt his head giddy[9] and his heart sick.

"Is it possible,—is it possible?" said he, kneeling down by him. "Uncle Tom, my poor, poor old friend!"

Something in the voice penetrated to the ear of the dying. He moved his head gently, smiled, and said,

> "*Jesus can make a dying-bed*
> *Feel soft as downy pillows are.*"[10]

Tears which did honor to his manly heart fell from the young man's eyes, as he bent over his poor friend.

"O, dear Uncle Tom! do wake,—do speak once more! Look up! Here's Mas'r George,—your own little Mas'r George. Don't you know me?"

"Mas'r George!" said Tom, opening his eyes, and speaking in a feeble voice; "Mas'r George!" He looked bewildered.

Slowly the idea seemed to fill his soul; and the vacant eye became fixed and brightened, the whole face lighted up, the hard hands clasped, and tears ran down the cheeks.

"Bless the Lord! it is,—it is,—it's all I wanted! They haven't forgot me. It warms my soul; it does my old heart good! Now I shall die content! Bless the Lord, oh my soul!"

"You shan't die! you *mustn't* die, nor think of it! I've come to buy you, and take you home," said George, with impetuous vehemence.

"O, Mas'r George, ye're too late. The Lord's bought me, and is going to take me home,—and I long to go. Heaven is better than Kintuck."

"O, don't die! It'll kill me!—it'll break my heart to think what you've suffered,—and lying in this old shed, here! Poor, poor fellow!"

"Don't call me poor fellow!" said Tom, solemnly. "I *have* been poor fellow; but that's all past and gone, now. I'm right in the door, going into glory! O, Mas'r George! *Heaven has come*! I've got the victory!—the Lord Jesus has given it to me! Glory be to His name!"

George was awe-struck at the force, the vehemence, the power, with which these broken sentences were uttered. He sat gazing in silence.

Tom grasped his hand, and continued,—"Ye mustn't, now, tell Chloe, poor soul! how ye found me;—'t would be so drefful[11] to her. Only tell her ye found me going into glory; and that I couldn't stay for no one. And tell her the Lord's stood by me everywhere and al'ays, and made everything light and easy. And oh, the poor chil'en, and the baby!—my old heart's been most broke for 'em, time and agin![12] Tell 'em all to follow me—follow me! Give my love to Mas'r, and dear good Missis, and everybody in the place! Ye don't know! 'Pears like I loves 'em all! I loves every creatur' everywhar!—it's nothing *but* love! O, Mas'r George! what a thing 't is to be a Christian!"

At this moment, Legree sauntered up to the door of the shed, looked in, with a dogged air of affected carelessness, and turned away.

"The old satan!" said George, in his indignation. "It's a comfort to think the devil will pay *him* for this, some of these days!"

"O, don't!—oh, ye mustn't!" said Tom, grasping his

11 I.e., dreadful. Tom has been speaking perfect English up to this word; at the mention of Chloe and his family, he reverts to slave dialect.

12 At the mention of his children, we realize that Tom has not mentioned them or dreamed about them for many, many months.

"Death of Uncle Tom." Lithograph by Thomas W. Strong. A distraught George Shelby laments Legree's treatment of Uncle Tom.

**13** Stowe reports Tom's death quietly with an adjective in the middle of a paragraph. "Asleep" at the end of the previous paragraph, his eyes are suddenly "lifeless." The exclamation "What a thing it is to be a Christian!" is from Tom. A few lines later, Legree's sullen refusal to "sell dead niggers" seems like an odd point of pride.

hand; "he's a poor mis'able critter! it's awful to think on't! O, if he only could repent, the Lord would forgive him now; but I'm 'feared he never will!"

"I hope he won't!" said George; "I never want to see *him* in heaven!"

"Hush, Mas'r George!—it worries me! Don't feel so! He an't done me no real harm,—only opened the gate of the kingdom for me; that's all!"

At this moment, the sudden flush of strength which the joy of meeting his young master had infused into the dying man gave way. A sudden sinking fell upon him; he closed his eyes; and that mysterious and sublime change passed over his face, that told the approach of other worlds.

He began to draw his breath with long, deep inspirations; and his broad chest rose and fell, heavily. The expression of his face was that of a conqueror.

"Who,—who,—who shall separate us from the love of Christ?" he said, in a voice that contended with mortal weakness; and, with a smile, he fell asleep.

George sat fixed with solemn awe. It seemed to him that the place was holy; and, as he closed the lifeless eyes, and rose up from the dead, only one thought possessed him,—that expressed by his simple old friend,—"What a thing it is to be a Christian!"**13**

He turned: Legree was standing, sullenly, behind him.

Something in that dying scene had checked the natural fierceness of youthful passion. The presence of the man was

The dramatic moment of Tom's death, as framed by the silhouettes of the other slaves in a tableau behind.

In this image by George Cruikshank, Tom is swaddled in blankets while George Shelby kneels at his side. Sambo and Quimbo watch from the doorway. A sulking Legree overhears their conversation just outside of the house.   From *Uncle Tom's Cabin*, John Cassell, London, 1852

simply loathsome to George; and he felt only an impulse to get away from him, with as few words as possible.

Fixing his keen dark eyes on Legree, he simply said, pointing to the dead, "You have got all you ever can of him. What shall I pay you for the body? I will take it away, and bury it decently."

"I don't sell dead niggers," said Legree, doggedly. "You are welcome to bury him where and when you like."

"Boys," said George, in an authoritative tone, to two or three negroes, who were looking at the body, "help me lift him up, and carry him to my wagon; and get me a spade."

One of them ran for a spade; the other two assisted George to carry the body to the wagon.

George neither spoke to nor looked at Legree, who did not countermand his orders, but stood, whistling, with an air of forced unconcern. He sulkily followed them to where the wagon stood at the door.

George spread his cloak in the wagon, and had the body carefully disposed of in it,—moving the seat, so as to give it room. Then he turned, fixed his eyes on Legree, and said, with forced composure,

"I have not, as yet, said to you what I think of this most atrocious affair;—this is not the time and place. But, sir, this innocent blood shall have justice. I will proclaim this murder.[14] I will go to the very first magistrate, and expose you."

"Do!" said Legree, snapping his fingers, scornfully. "I'd like to see you doing it. Where you going to get witnesses?—how you going to prove it?—Come, now!"

14  On November 5, 1852, the pro-slavery New York paper *Courier and Enquirer* published a long, unsigned piece accusing Stowe of slander. (There is some confusion about dates, since the *National Era* carried a story about the debate on October 21, 1852.) The article claimed the following:

[I]n the General Court of Virginia, last year, in the case of Southern vs. the Commonwealth, it was held that the killing of a slave by his master and owner, by willful and excessive whipping, is murder in the first degree, though it may not have been the purpose of the master and owner to kill the slave! And it is not six months since Governor Johnston of Virginia pardoned a slave who killed his master, who was beating him with brutal severity. And yet, in the face of such laws and decisions as these, Mrs. Stowe winds up a long series of cruelties upon her other black personages, by causing her faultless hero, Tom, to be literally whipped to death in Louisiana, by his master Legree; and these acts, which the laws make criminal, and punish as such, she sets forth in the most repulsive colors, to illustrate the institution of slavery! ("Slavery and its abuses—Mrs. Stowe and the N. York Courier and Enquirer")

Stowe wrote *A Key to Uncle Tom's Cabin* (see "Harriet Beecher Stowe and 'The Man That Was a Thing,'" p. xl) in response to this criticism and others.

15 Legend of St. George, Christian martyr and patron saint of England, who died about 303. The legend of St. George and the dragon claims that after St. George slayed the dragon that was killing the members of a town in Libya, the community became Christians. Although George Shelby may be a hero in the eyes of Stowe's readers, he has simply struck the dragon (Legree). The community has become Christian, but that is to Tom's, not George's, credit.

16 George's gesture is sentimental but empty. Stowe's point here is that no token action can compensate for the waste of a man's life under slavery.

17 This dramatic oath may call up for today's readers another Southern scene, that of Scarlett O'Hara's vow in the film *Gone with the Wind*: "As God is my witness, I shall never be hungry again!"

George saw, at once, the force of this defiance. There was not a white person on the place; and, in all southern courts, the testimony of colored blood is nothing. He felt, at that moment, as if he could have rent the heavens with his heart's indignant cry for justice; but in vain.

"After all, what a fuss, for a dead nigger!" said Legree.

The word was as a spark to a powder magazine. Prudence was never a cardinal virtue of the Kentucky boy. George turned, and, with one indignant blow, knocked Legree flat upon his face; and, as he stood over him, blazing with wrath and defiance, he would have formed no bad personification of his great namesake triumphing over the dragon.[15]

Some men, however, are decidedly bettered by being knocked down. If a man lays them fairly flat in the dust, they seem immediately to conceive a respect for him; and Legree was one of this sort. As he rose, therefore, and brushed the dust from his clothes, he eyed the slowly-retreating wagon with some evident consideration; nor did he open his mouth till it was out of sight.

Beyond the boundaries of the plantation, George had noticed a dry, sandy knoll, shaded by a few trees: there they made the grave.

"Shall we take off the cloak, Mas'r?" said the negroes, when the grave was ready.

"No, no,—bury it with him! It's all I can give you, now, poor Tom, and you shall have it."[16]

They laid him in; and the men shovelled away, silently. They banked it up, and laid green turf over it.

"You may go, boys," said George, slipping a quarter into the hand of each. They lingered about, however.

"If young Mas'r would please buy us—" said one.

"We'd serve him so faithful!" said the other.

"Hard times here, Mas'r!" said the first. "Do, Mas'r, buy us, please!"

"I can't!—I can't!" said George, with difficulty, motioning them off; "it's impossible!"

The poor fellows looked dejected, and walked off in silence.

"Witness, eternal God!" said George, kneeling on the grave of his poor friend; "oh, witness, that, from this hour, I will do *what one man can* to drive out this curse of slavery from my land!"[17]

There is no monument to mark the last resting-place of our friend. He needs none! His Lord knows where he lies, and will raise him up, immortal, to appear with him when he shall appear in his glory.

Pity him not! Such a life and death is not for pity! Not in the riches of omnipotence is the chief glory of God; but in self-denying, suffering love! And blessed are the men whom he calls to fellowship with him, bearing their cross after him with patience. Of such it is written, "Blessed are they that mourn, for they shall be comforted."[18]

18 Stowe closes the chapter by quoting Jesus' most uplifting words, from the Sermon on the Mount (Matt. 5:3–11).

## CHAPTER 42

## *An Authentic Ghost Story*[1]

1 Spirituality in the nineteenth century encompassed not only religious sentiment but also an interest in supernatural phenomena. Ghost stories and paranormal tales were very popular in Stowe's day; see Ann Radcliffe's *The Mysteries of Udolpho*, Samuel Coleridge's *Rime of the Ancient Mariner*, Mary Wollstonecraft Shelley's *Frankenstein*, and of course Edgar Allan Poe's stories.

2 Stowe's high-spirited assertion that the "authorities" don't quite know what occurred because covering one's eyes in fright in the presence of a spirit is "a custom quite prevalent among negroes" (and perhaps also among whites) becomes less funny when we are told that the spirit was wearing a *white sheet* (familiar to us as the garb of the Ku Klux Klan). Modern readers may also think that the scene is a bit too reminiscent of a "Scooby-Doo" episode.

For some remarkable reason, ghostly legends were uncommonly rife, about this time, among the servants on Legree's place.

It was whisperingly asserted that footsteps, in the dead of night, had been heard descending the garret stairs, and patrolling the house. In vain the doors of the upper entry had been locked; the ghost either carried a duplicate key in its pocket, or availed itself of a ghost's immemorial privilege of coming through the keyhole, and promenaded as before, with a freedom that was alarming.

Authorities were somewhat divided, as to the outward form of the spirit, owing to a custom quite prevalent among negroes,—and, for aught we know, among whites, too,[2]—of invariably shutting the eyes, and covering up heads under blankets, petticoats, or whatever else might come in use for a shelter, on these occasions. Of course, as everybody knows, when the bodily eyes are thus out of the lists, the spiritual eyes are uncommonly vivacious and perspicuous; and, therefore, there were abundance of full-length portraits of the ghost, abundantly sworn and testified to, which, as is often the case with portraits, agreed with each other in no particular, except the common family peculiarity of the ghost tribe,—the wearing of a *white sheet*. The poor souls were not versed in ancient history and did not know that Shakespeare had authenticated this costume, by telling how

> *"The* sheeted *dead*
> *Did squeak and gibber in the streets of Rome."*[3]

And, therefore, their all hitting upon this is a striking fact in pneumatology,[4] which we recommend to the attention of spiritual media generally.

Be it as it may, we have private reasons for knowing that a tall figure in a white sheet did walk, at the most approved ghostly hours, around the Legree premises,—pass out the doors, glide about the house,—disappear at intervals, and, reappearing, pass up the silent stair-way, into that fatal garret; and that, in the morning, the entry doors were all found shut and locked as firm as ever.

Legree could not help overhearing this whispering; and it was all the more exciting to him, from the pains that were taken to conceal it from him. He drank more brandy than usual; held up his head briskly, and swore louder than ever in the day-time; but he had bad dreams, and the visions of his head on his bed were anything but agreeable. The night after Tom's body had been carried away, he rode to the next town for a carouse, and had a high one. Got home late and tired; locked his door, took out the key, and went to bed.

After all, let a man take what pains he may to hush it down, a human soul is an awful ghostly, unquiet possession for a bad man to have. Who knows the metes and bounds of it? Who knows all its awful perhapes,—those shudderings and tremblings, which it can no more live down than it can outlive its own eternity! What a fool is he who locks his door to keep out spirits, who has in his own bosom a spirit he dares not meet alone,—whose voice, smothered far down, and piled over with mountains of earthliness, is yet like the forewarning trumpet of doom!

But Legree locked his door and set a chair against it; he set a night-lamp at the head of his bed; and he put his pistols there. He examined the catches and fastenings of the windows, and then swore he "didn't care for the devil and all his angels," and went to sleep.

Well, he slept, for he was tired,—slept soundly. But, finally, there came over his sleep a shadow, a horror, an apprehension of something dreadful hanging over him. It was his mother's shroud, he thought; but Cassy had it, holding it up, and showing it to him. He heard a confused noise of screams and groanings; and, with it all, he knew he was asleep, and he struggled to wake himself. He was half awake. He was sure something was coming into his

3 Stowe continues her mock-serious tone by quoting from *Hamlet*, act 1, scene 1. Horatio awaits the ghost of Hamlet's father; the question is whether the spirit is an omen:

> A mote it is to trouble the mind's eye.
> In the most high and palmy state of Rome,
> A little ere the mightiest Julius fell,
> The graves stood tenantless and the sheeted dead
> Did squeak and gibber in the Roman streets:
> As stars with trains of fire and dews of blood,
> Disasters in the sun; and the moist star
> Upon whose influence Neptune's empire stands
> Was sick almost to doomsday with eclipse:
> And even the like precurse of fierce events,
> As harbingers preceding still the fates
> And prologue to the omen coming on,
> Have heaven and earth together demonstrated
> Unto our climatures and countrymen.—
> But soft, behold! lo, where it comes again!

Stowe's point here is that the ghosts are not an omen of anything; they, as in a Shakespearean production, are merely actors in white sheets.

4 I.e., the study of spiritual beings. Stowe's writing becomes almost giddy in this chapter: Like Shakespeare, she knows the importance of comic relief.

room. He knew the door was opening, but he could not stir hand or foot. At last he turned, with a start; the door *was* open, and he saw a hand putting out his light.

It was a cloudy, misty moonlight, and there he saw it!—something white, gliding in! He heard the still rustle of its ghostly garments. It stood still by his bed;—a cold hand touched his; a voice said, three times, in a low, fearful whisper, "Come! come! come!" And, while he lay sweating with terror, he knew not when or how, the thing was gone. He sprang out of bed, and pulled at the door. It was shut and locked, and the man fell down in a swoon.

After this, Legree became a harder drinker than ever before. He no longer drank cautiously, prudently, but imprudently and recklessly.

There were reports around the country, soon after, that he was sick and dying. Excess had brought on that frightful disease that seems to throw the lurid shadows of a coming retribution back into the present life. None could bear the horrors of that sick room, when he raved and screamed, and spoke of sights which almost stopped the blood of those who heard him; and, at his dying bed, stood a stern, white, inexorable figure, saying, "Come! come! come!"

By a singular coincidence, on the very night that this vision appeared to Legree, the house-door was found open in the morning, and some of the negroes had seen two white figures gliding down the avenue towards the high-road.

It was near sunrise when Cassy and Emmeline paused, for a moment, in a little knot of trees near the town.

Cassy was dressed after the manner of the Creole Spanish ladies,—wholly in black. A small black bonnet on her head, covered by a veil thick with embroidery, concealed her face. It had been agreed that, in their escape, she was to personate the character of a Creole lady, and Emmeline that of her servant.

Brought up, from early life, in connection with the highest society, the language, movements and air of Cassy, were all in agreement with this idea; and she had still enough remaining with her, of a once splendid wardrobe, and sets of jewels, to enable her to personate the thing to advantage.

She stopped in the outskirts of the town, where she had noticed trunks for sale, and purchased a handsome one. This she requested the man to send along with her. And, accordingly, thus escorted by a boy wheeling her trunk, and Emmeline behind her, carrying her carpet-bag and sundry bundles, she made her appearance at the small tavern, like a lady of consideration.

The first person that struck[5] her, after her arrival, was George Shelby, who was staying there, awaiting the next boat.

Cassy had remarked the young man from her loop-hole in the garret, and seen him bear away the body of Tom, and observed, with secret exultation, his rencontre with Legree. Subsequently, she had gathered, from the conversations she had overheard among the negroes, as she glided about in her ghostly disguise, after nightfall, who he was, and in what relation he stood to Tom. She, therefore, felt an immediate accession of confidence, when she found that he was, like herself, awaiting the next boat.

Cassy's air and manner, address, and evident command of money, prevented any rising disposition to suspicion in the hotel. People never inquire too closely into those who are fair on the main point, of paying well,—a thing which Cassy had foreseen when she provided herself with money.

In the edge of the evening, a boat was heard coming along, and George Shelby handed Cassy aboard, with the politeness which comes naturally to every Kentuckian, and exerted himself to provide her with a good state-room.

Cassy kept her room and bed, on pretext of illness, during the whole time they were on Red river; and was waited on, with obsequious devotion, by her attendant.

When they arrived at the Mississippi river, George, having learned that the course of the strange lady was upward, like his own, proposed to take a state-room for her on the same boat with himself,—good-naturedly compassionating[6] her feeble health, and desirous to do what he could to assist her.

Behold, therefore, the whole party safely transferred to the good steamer Cincinnati, and sweeping up the river under a powerful head of steam.

Cassy's health was much better. She sat upon the guards,[7] came to the table, and was remarked upon in the boat as a lady that must have been very handsome.

From the moment that George got the first glimpse of her face, he was troubled with one of those fleeting and indefinite likenesses, which almost everybody can remember, and has been, at times, perplexed with. He could not keep himself from looking at her, and watching her perpetually. At table, or sitting at her state-room door, still she would encounter the young man's eyes fixed on her,

5 Stowe means that George was the first person Cassy met, but the word "struck" also refers to George's hitting Legree. This meeting of Cassy is not as unlikely as later chance reunions will be, particularly the upcoming meeting with Madame de Thoux.

6 Stowe takes pains to establish what one might call a kinship of good breeding between George and Cassy. Behaving well, especially toward others, is a precursor to spiritual redemption in Stowe's world.

7 *OED*: "lateral extension of the deck of a steamboat beyond the lines of the hull so as to overhang the water."

and politely withdrawn, when she showed, by her countenance, that she was sensible of the observation.

Cassy became uneasy. She began to think that he suspected something; and finally resolved to throw herself entirely on his generosity, and intrusted him with her whole history.

George was heartily disposed to sympathize with any one who had escaped from Legree's plantation,—a place that he could not remember or speak of with patience,—and, with the courageous disregard of consequences which is characteristic of his age and state, he assured her that he would do all in his power to protect and bring them through.

The next state-room to Cassy's was occupied by a French lady, named De Thoux, who was accompanied by a fine little daughter, a child of some twelve summers.

This lady, having gathered, from George's conversation, that he was from Kentucky, seemed evidently disposed to cultivate his acquaintance; in which design she was seconded by the graces of her little girl, who was about as pretty a plaything as ever diverted the weariness of a fortnight's trip on a steamboat.

George's chair was often placed at her state-room door; and Cassy, as she sat upon the guards, could hear their conversation.

Madame de Thoux was very minute in her inquiries as to Kentucky, where she said she had resided in a former period of her life. George discovered, to his surprise, that her former residence must have been in his own vicinity; and her inquiries showed a knowledge of people and things in his region, that was perfectly surprising to him.

"Do you know," said Madame de Thoux to him, one day, "of any man, in your neighborhood, of the name of Harris?"

"There is an old fellow, of that name, lives not far from my father's place," said George. "We never have had much intercourse with him, though."

"He is a large slave-owner, I believe," said Madame de Thoux, with a manner which seemed to betray more interest than she was exactly willing to show.

"He is," said George, looking rather surprised at her manner.

"Did you ever know of his having—perhaps, you may have heard of his having a mulatto boy, named George?"

"O, certainly,—George Harris,—I know him well; he married a servant of my mother's, but has escaped, now, to Canada."

"He has?" said Madame de Thoux, quickly. "Thank God!"

George looked a surprised inquiry, but said nothing.

Madame de Thoux leaned her head on her hand, and burst into tears.

"He is my brother," she said.

"Madame!" said George, with a strong accent of surprise.

"Yes," said Madame de Thoux, lifting her head, proudly, and wiping her tears; "Mr. Shelby, George Harris is my brother!"

"I am perfectly astonished," said George, pushing back his chair a pace or two, and looking at Madame de Thoux.

"I was sold to the South when he was a boy," said she. "I was bought by a good and generous man. He took me with him to the West Indies, set me free, and married me. It is but lately that he died; and I was coming up to Kentucky, to see if I could find and redeem my brother."

"I have heard him speak of a sister Emily, that was sold South," said George.

"Yes, indeed! I am the one," said Madame de Thoux;— "tell me what sort of a—"

"A very fine young man," said George, "notwithstanding the curse of slavery that lay on him. He sustained a first rate character, both for intelligence and principle. I know, you see," he said; "because he married in our family."

"What sort of a girl?" said Madame de Thoux, eagerly.

"A treasure," said George; "a beautiful, intelligent, amiable girl. Very pious. My mother had brought her up, and trained her as carefully, almost, as a daughter. She could read and write, embroider and sew, beautifully; and was a beautiful singer."[8]

"Was she born in your house?" said Madame de Thoux.

"No. Father bought her once, in one of his trips to New Orleans, and brought her up as a present to mother. She was about eight or nine years old, then. Father would never tell mother what he gave for her; but, the other day, in looking over his old papers, we came across the bill of sale. He paid an extravagant sum for her, to be sure. I suppose, on account of her extraordinary beauty."

George sat with his back to Cassy, and did not see the absorbed expression of her countenance, as he was giving these details.

At this point in the story, she touched his arm, and, with a face perfectly white with interest,[9] said, "Do you know the names of the people he bought her of?"

"A man of the name of Simmons, I think, was the prin-

8 In other words, Eliza was brought up in the manner of a Victorian heroine, as were, apparently, the "French lady" Madame de Thoux and her daughter.

9 Stowe's choice of terms to describe Cassy's emotional reaction seems a bit strange.

10 The narrator's strange, halting diction here is similar to Esther Summerson's in Charles Dickens's *Bleak House*, also serialized in 1852–1853, some months after *Uncle Tom's Cabin*. To wit, the final paragraph: "I did not know that; I am not certain that I know it now. But I know that my dearest little pets are very pretty, and that my darling is very beautiful, and that my husband is very handsome, and that my guardian has the brightest and most benevolent face that ever was seen, and that they can very well do without much beauty in me—even supposing—."

cipal in the transaction. At least, I think that was the name on the bill of sale."

"O, my God!" said Cassy, and fell insensible on the floor of the cabin.

George was wide awake now, and so was Madame de Thoux. Though neither of them could conjecture what was the cause of Cassy's fainting, still they made all the tumult which is proper in such cases;—George upsetting a wash-pitcher, and breaking two tumblers, in the warmth of his humanity; and various ladies in the cabin, hearing that somebody had fainted, crowded the state-room door, and kept out all the air they possibly could, so that, on the whole, everything was done that could be expected.

Poor Cassy! when she recovered, turned her face to the wall, and wept and sobbed like a child,—perhaps, mother, you can tell what she was thinking of! Perhaps you cannot,—but she felt as sure, in that hour, that God had had mercy on her, and that she should see her daughter,—as she did, months afterwards,—when—but we anticipate.[10]

# CHAPTER 43

## Results

The rest of our story is soon told. George Shelby, interested, as any other young man might be, by the romance of the incident, no less than by feelings of humanity, was at the pains to send to Cassy the bill of sale of Eliza;[1] whose date and name all corresponded with her own knowledge of facts, and left no doubt upon her mind as to the identity of her child. It remained now only for her to trace out the path of the fugitives.

Madame de Thoux and she, thus drawn together by the singular coincidence of their fortunes, proceeded immediately to Canada, and began a tour of inquiry among the stations,[2] where the numerous fugitives from slavery are located. At Amherstberg they found the missionary with whom George and Eliza had taken shelter, on their first arrival in Canada; and through him were enabled to trace the family to Montreal.

George and Eliza had now been five years free.[3] George had found constant occupation in the shop of a worthy machinist, where he had been earning a competent support for his family, which, in the meantime, had been increased by the addition of another daughter.

Little Harry—a fine bright boy—had been put to a good school, and was making rapid proficiency in knowledge.

The worthy pastor of the station, in Amherstberg, where George had first landed, was so much interested in the statements of Madame de Thoux and Cassy, that he yielded to the solicitations of the former, to accompany

1 Stowe gives to George Shelby the assignment of tying up loose ends and establishing Eliza's provenance, as it were, in order to return the focus to Cassy and the mysterious Madame de Thoux.

2 I.e., stops on the Underground Railroad that shelter fugitive slaves. See chapter 7, note 25.

3 Stowe proceeds in this chapter to answer the question "What will become of the freed slaves?" After five years of freedom, she suggests, the answer is that they will look like a typical Christian Victorian family.

**4** Another example of Stowe's awkward but dramatic plotting. Any quiet scene of dinner at home must be interrupted by the arrival of an unexpected guest.

**5** Not only is George Harris the perfect husband, as we recall from earlier chapters, but also he is the perfect father: attentive, supportive, and forward looking. He spends his moments of leisure, we have just been told, "making notes from a volume of the family library," of all things.

**6** I.e., a plan. It would be difficult to write this scene without a large dollop of melodrama; Stowe cleverly introduces a stage-managing pastor and puts the blame for the ensuing awkwardness on him. Thus the scene seems to unfold "naturally."

them to Montreal, in their search,—she bearing all the expense of the expedition.

The scene now changes[4] to a small, neat tenement, in the outskirts of Montreal; the time, evening. A cheerful fire blazes on the hearth; a tea-table, covered with a snowy cloth, stands prepared for the evening meal. In one corner of the room was a table covered with a green cloth, where was an open writing-desk, pens, paper, and over it a shelf of well-selected books.

This was George's study. The same zeal for self-improvement, which led him to steal the much coveted arts of reading and writing, amid all the toils and discouragements of his early life, still led him to devote all his leisure time to self-cultivation.

At this present time, he is seated at the table, making notes from a volume of the family library he has been reading.

"Come, George," says Eliza, "you've been gone all day. Do put down that book, and let's talk, while I'm getting tea,—do."

And little Eliza seconds the effort, by toddling up to her father, and trying to pull the book out of his hand, and install herself on his knee as a substitute.

"O, you little witch!" says George, yielding, as, in such circumstances, man always must.

"That's right," says Eliza, as she begins to cut a loaf of bread. A little older she looks; her form a little fuller; her air more matronly than of yore; but evidently contented and happy as woman need be.

"Harry, my boy, how did you come on in that sum, to-day?" says George, as he laid his hand on his son's head.

Harry has lost his long curls; but he can never lose those eyes and eyelashes, and that fine, bold brow, that flushes with triumph, as he answers, "I did it, every bit of it, *myself*, father; and *nobody* helped me!"

"That's right," says his father; "depend on yourself, my son. You have a better chance than ever your poor father had."[5]

At this moment, there is a rap at the door; and Eliza goes and opens it. The delighted—"Why!—this you?"—calls up her husband; and the good pastor of Amherstberg is welcomed. There are two more women with him, and Eliza asks them to sit down.

Now, if the truth must be told, the honest pastor had arranged a little programme,[6] according to which this affair was to develop itself; and, on the way up, all had very cautiously and prudently exhorted each other not to let things out, except according to previous arrangement.

What was the good man's consternation, therefore, just as he had motioned to the ladies to be seated, and was taking out his pocket-handkerchief to wipe his mouth, so as to proceed to his introductory speech in good order, when Madame de Thoux upset the whole plan, by throwing her arms around George's neck, and letting all out at once, by saying, "O, George! don't you know me? I'm your sister Emily."

Cassy had seated herself more composedly, and would have carried on her part very well, had not little Eliza suddenly appeared before her in exact shape and form, every outline and curl, just as her daughter was when she saw her last.[7] The little thing peered up in her face; and Cassy caught her up in her arms, pressed her to her bosom, saying, what at the moment she really believed, "Darling, I'm your mother!"

In fact, it was a troublesome matter to do up exactly in proper order; but the good pastor, at last, succeeded in getting everybody quiet, and delivering the speech with which he had intended to open the exercises; and in which, at last, he succeeded so well, that his whole audience were sobbing about him in a manner that ought to satisfy any orator, ancient or modern.

They knelt together, and the good man prayed,—for there are some feelings so agitated and tumultuous, that they can find rest only by being poured into the bosom of Almighty love,—and then, rising up, the newfound family embraced each other, with a holy trust in Him, who from such peril and dangers, and by such unknown ways, had brought them together.

The note-book of a missionary, among the Canadian fugitives, contains truth stranger than fiction. How can it be otherwise, when a system prevails which whirls families and scatters their members, as the wind whirls and scatters the leaves of autumn? These shores of refuge, like the eternal shore, often unite again, in glad communion, hearts that for long years have mourned each other as lost. And affecting beyond expression is the earnestness with which every new arrival among them is met, if, perchance, it may bring tidings of mother, sister, child or wife, still lost to view in the shadows of slavery.[8]

Deeds of heroism are wrought here more than those of romance,[9] when, defying torture, and braving death itself, the fugitive voluntarily threads his way back to the ter-

7 What might add to Cassy's confusion is the fact that her young granddaughter is also named Eliza. We can estimate that Cassy hasn't seen her daughter in some twenty or more years.

8 Stowe continues to use relational terms, here all female ("mother, sister, child or wife").

9 Stowe translates the courage of slaves into a more familiar and literary form, "deeds of heroism."

**10** A touching moment: Cassy has regained her daughter in little Eliza, but what of Eliza's regaining her mother, Cassy? This question will be revisited more than a century later by Toni Morrison in her novel *Beloved*.

**11** Stowe informs us that Emmeline—still separated from her mother, Susan—is now part of George and Eliza's extended family, for the time being. The family's continued dislocation serves to remind us that there are no happy endings for former slaves when laws such as the Fugitive Slave Act are in effect.

rors and perils of that dark land, that he may bring out his sister, or mother, or wife.

One young man, of whom a missionary has told us, twice re-captured, and suffering shameful stripes for his heroism, had escaped again; and, in a letter which we heard read, tells his friends that he is going back a third time, that he may, at last, bring away his sister. My good sir, is this man a hero, or a criminal? Would not you do as much for your sister? And can you blame him?

But, to return to our friends, whom we left wiping their eyes, and recovering themselves from too great and sudden a joy. They are now seated around the social board, and are getting decidedly companionable; only that Cassy, who keeps little Eliza on her lap, occasionally squeezes the little thing, in a manner that rather astonishes her, and obstinately refuses to have her mouth stuffed with cake to the extent the little one desires,—alleging, what the child rather wonders at, that she has got something better than cake, and doesn't want it.

And, indeed, in two or three days, such a change has passed over Cassy, that our readers would scarcely know her. The despairing, haggard expression of her face had given way to one of gentle trust. She seemed to sink, at once, into the bosom of the family, and take the little ones into her heart, as something for which it long had waited. Indeed, her love seemed to flow more naturally to the little Eliza than to her own daughter; for she was the exact image and body of the child whom she had lost.[10] The little one was a flowery bond between mother and daughter, through whom grew up acquaintanceship and affection. Eliza's steady, consistent piety, regulated by the constant reading of the sacred word, made her a proper guide for the shattered and wearied mind of her mother. Cassy yielded at once, and with her whole soul, to every good influence, and became a devout and tender Christian.

After a day or two, Madame de Thoux told her brother more particularly of her affairs. The death of her husband had left her an ample fortune, which she generously offered to share with the family. When she asked George what way she could best apply it for him, he answered, "Give me an education, Emily; that has always been my heart's desire. Then, I can do all the rest."

On mature deliberation, it was decided that the whole family should go, for some years, to France; whither they sailed, carrying Emmeline with them.[11]

The good looks of the latter won the affection of the

first mate of the vessel; and, shortly after entering the port, she became his wife.

George remained four years at a French university, and, applying himself with an unintermitted zeal, obtained a very thorough education.

Political troubles in France, at last, led the family again to seek an asylum in this country.

George's feelings and views, as an educated man, may be best expressed in a letter to one of his friends.[12]

"I feel somewhat at a loss, as to my future course. True, as you have said to me, I might mingle in the circles of the whites, in this country, my shade of color is so slight, and that of my wife and family scarce perceptible. Well, perhaps, on sufferance, I might. But, to tell you the truth, I have no wish to.

"My sympathies are not for my father's race, but for my mother's.[13] To him I was no more than a fine dog or horse: to my poor heart-broken mother I was a *child*; and, though I never saw her, after the cruel sale that separated us, till she died, yet I *know* she always loved me dearly. I know it by my own heart. When I think of all she suffered, of my own early sufferings, of the distresses and struggles of my heroic wife, of my sister, sold in the New Orleans slave-market,—though I hope to have no unchristian sentiments, yet I may be excused for saying, I have no wish to pass for an American, or to identify myself with them.[14]

"It is with the oppressed, enslaved African race that I cast in my lot; and, if I wished anything, I would wish myself two shades darker, rather than one lighter.

"The desire and yearning of my soul is for an African *nationality*. I want a people that shall have a tangible, separate existence of its own; and where am I to look for it? Not in Hayti; for in Hayti they had nothing to start with. A stream cannot rise above its fountain. The race that formed the character of the Haytiens was a worn-out, effeminate one; and, of course, the subject race will be centuries in rising to anything.

"Where, then, shall I look? On the shores of Africa I see a republic,[15]—a republic formed of picked men, who, by energy and self-educating force, have, in many cases, individually, raised themselves above a condition of slavery. Having gone through a preparatory stage of feebleness, this republic has, at last, become an acknowledged nation on the face of the earth,—acknowledged by both France and England. There it is my wish to go, and find myself a people.

12 Stowe employs one of the oldest novelistic devices, the letter, to allow George Harris to tell his own story. More importantly, the beautifully written letter is meant to demonstrate that George indeed profited from his university education.

13 The choice between races that confronts "mixed-race" people will continue to be a major theme in African-American literature—the "novel of passing."

14 Note that to George, passing for an American means passing as a white man.

15 Liberia, declared a republic in 1847 and viewed by many as a solution for a post-slavery United States. George's letter addresses the pros and cons of colonization. Frederick Douglass was actively opposed to colonization and spoke out against it often. He wrote the following, for example, in the *North Star* on June 27, 1850:

> [Colonization] has taught the nation that we are low, ignorant and besotted, that our elevation in this country is impossible—that Africa, and not America, is our country; and some of its members have gone the scandalous length of recommending the enactment of stringent laws against our rights and liberties, with a view to our coercion and final expatriation. It is not at all surprising that colored men should contemplate that society with other than feelings of complacency.
>
> For ourselves, we look with suspicion on any medium which proposes to free the nation from its unrighteous treatment of the colored people, that does not involve a deep and radical repentance. To remove the objects of American hatred, is not to remove that hatred itself. It is a climbing up some other way, and is therefore to be discarded. We beg and entreat our colonization friends to desist from their colonization scheme, and to allow its sufficient repose or resume that course of steady improvement which has marked and will continue to mark the progress of colored men, in this, the land of their nativity.
>
> For more than two hundred years, we have been the constant companions of

the white man, and the joint possessors, with him, of this country; and the readiness with which we adapt ourselves to the circumstances around us, induces the belief that we stand as good a chance of advancement, here in all things pertaining to human welfare as we should do, were we instantly transformed to the western coast of Africa. ("Letter of Benjamin Coates")

The debate about colonization, always simmering, reignited after the publication of *Uncle Tom's Cabin*. In a lengthy public debate with Martin Delany, the well-known black author and speaker who had recently published "The Condition, Elevation, Emigration, and Destiny of the Colored People of the United States, Politically Considered," Douglass wrote that while opposed to colonization, "We shall not . . . allow the sentiments put in the brief letter of GEORGE HARRIS, at the close of Uncle Tom's Cabin, to vitiate forever Mrs. Stowe's power to do us good" (May 6, 1853, *Frederick Douglass' Paper*). He continued:

We don't object to colonizationists because they express a lively interest in the civilization and Christianization of Africa; nor because they desire the prosperity of Liberia; but it is because, like brother Delany, they have not sufficient faith in the people of the United States to believe that the black man can ever get justice at their hands on American soil. It is because they have systematically, and almost universally, sought to spread their hopelessness among the free colored people themselves; and thereby rendered them, if not contented with, at least resigned to the degradation which they have been taught to believe must be perpetual and immutable, while they remain where they are. It is because, having denied the possibility of our elevation here, they have sought to make a good that denial by encouraging the enactment of laws subjecting us to the most flagrant outrages, and stripping us of all the safeguards necessary to the security of our liberty, persons and property—We say all this of the American Colonization Society; but we are far from saying this of many who speak and wish well to Liberia. ("The Letter of M. R. Delany")

"I am aware, now, that I shall have you all against me; but, before you strike, hear me. During my stay in France, I have followed up, with intense interest, the history of my people in America. I have noted the struggle between abolitionist and colonizationist, and have received some impressions, as a distant spectator, which could never have occurred to me as a participator.

"I grant that this Liberia may have subserved all sorts of purposes, by being played off, in the hands of our oppressors, against us. Doubtless the scheme may have been used, in unjustifiable ways, as a means of retarding our emancipation. But the question to me is, Is there not a God above all man's schemes? May He not have overruled their designs, and founded for us a nation by them?

"In these days, a nation is born in a day. A nation starts, now, with all the great problems of republican life and civilization wrought out to its hand;—it has not to discover, but only to apply. Let us, then, all take hold together, with all our might, and see what we can do with this new enterprise, and the whole splendid continent of Africa opens before us and our children. *Our nation* shall roll the tide of civilization and Christianity along its shores, and plant there mighty republics, that, growing with the rapidity of tropical vegetation, shall be for all coming ages.[16]

"Do you say that I am deserting my enslaved brethren? I think not. If I forget them one hour, one moment of my life, so may God forget me! But, what can I do for them, here? Can I break their chains? No, not as an individual; but, let me go and form part of a nation, which shall have a voice in the councils of nations, and then we can speak. A nation has a right to argue, remonstrate, implore, and present the cause of its race,—which an individual has not.[17]

"If Europe ever becomes a grand council of free nations,—as I trust in God it will,—if, there, serfdom, and all unjust and oppressive social inequalities, are done away; and if they, as France and England have done, acknowledge our position,—then, in the great congress of nations, we will make our appeal, and present the cause of our enslaved and suffering race; and it cannot be that free, enlightened America will not then desire to wipe from her escutcheon that bar sinister which disgraces her among nations,[18] and is as truly a curse to her as to the enslaved.

"But, you will tell me, our race have equal rights to mingle in the American republic as the Irishman, the German, the Swede. Granted, they have. We *ought* to be free to meet and mingle,—to rise by our individual worth, without any consideration of caste or color; and they who deny us this right are false to their own professed principles of human equality. We ought, in particular, to be allowed *here*. We have *more* than the rights of common men;—we have the claim of an injured race for reparation. But, then, *I do not want it*; I want a country, a nation, of my own. I think that the African race has peculiarities, yet to be unfolded in the light of civilization and Christianity, which, if not the same with those of the Anglo-Saxon, may prove to be, morally, of even a higher type.[19]

"To the Anglo-Saxon race has been intrusted the destinies of the world, during its pioneer period of struggle and conflict. To that mission its stern, inflexible, energetic elements, were well adapted; but, as a Christian, I look for another era to arise. On its borders I trust we stand; and the throes that now convulse the nations are, to my hope, but the birth-pangs of an hour of universal peace and brotherhood.

"I trust that the development of Africa is to be essentially a Christian one. If not a dominant and commanding race, they are, at least, an affectionate, magnanimous and forgiving one. Having been called in the furnace of injustice and oppression, they have need to bind closer to their hearts that sublime doctrine of love and forgiveness, through which alone they are to conquer, which it is to be their mission to spread over the continent of Africa.

"In myself, I confess, I am feeble for this,—full half the blood in my veins is the hot and hasty Saxon; but I have an eloquent preacher of the Gospel ever by my side, in the person of my beautiful wife. When I wander, her gentler spirit ever restores me, and keeps before my eyes the Christian calling and mission of our race. As a Christian patriot, as a teacher of Christianity, I go to *my country,*— my chosen,[20] my glorious Africa!—and to her, in my heart, I sometimes apply those splendid words of prophecy: 'Whereas thou hast been forsaken and hated, so that no man went through thee; *I* will make thee an eternal excellence, a joy of many generations!'[21]

"You will call me an enthusiast:[22] you will tell me that I have not well considered what I am undertaking. But I have considered, and counted the cost. I go to *Liberia,* not as to an Elysium[23] of romance, but as to *a field of work*. I expect to work with both hands,—to work *hard*; to work against all sorts of difficulties and discouragements; and to work till I die. This is what I go for; and in this I am quite sure I shall not be disappointed.

"Whatever you may think of my determination, do not

16 George plays with the image of the original colonists who saw the New World of America as a plantation where Christianity would grow and flourish. In his image, the tropical climate becomes a fertile ground for growth.

17 Stowe again sounds the note for community over individuality.

18 Stowe reminds her readers of the far-reaching changes on the international level in recent years. George's image of the escutcheon and bar sinister comes from heraldry. The escutcheon is the shield on which a coat of arms is displayed; the bar sinister is a horizontal line on the left ("sinister") side of the coat of arms.

19 The idea of particular qualities of a race is in keeping with the racialist thought of the time; it will resurface with explosive force in the opening decades of the twentieth century, fueling, for just two examples, Pan-Africanism and the Harlem Renaissance. In the following paragraphs, George's reading of the Anglo-Saxon race is pure nineteenth-century racialist thought.

20 While George is not choosing America, we understand that choosing one's country is in many ways an American concept.

21 Isa. 60:15. George, like Tom, finds comfort and guidance in the book of Isaiah.

22 I.e., an idealist.

23 Showing off his Classical education, George refers to the mythological paradise of Greek and Roman myth.

**24** One wonders whether Stowe's lapsing into these strange authorial moments is indicative of the difficulties in tying up her narrative after the death of the title character.

**25** French student.

**26** Stowe's postscript is odd but in keeping with the epistolary nature of this chapter. It is included for "some mother" who may wonder if Cassy ever found her son.

divorce me from your confidence; and think that, in whatever I do, I act with a heart wholly given to my people.

"GEORGE HARRIS."

George, with his wife, children, sister and mother, embarked for Africa, some few weeks after. If we are not mistaken, the world will yet hear from him there.

Of our other characters we have nothing very particular to write, except a word relating to Miss Ophelia and Topsy, and a farewell chapter, which we shall dedicate to George Shelby.[24]

Miss Ophelia took Topsy home to Vermont with her, much to the surprise of that grave deliberative body whom a New Englander recognizes under the term "*Our folks.*" "Our folks," at first, thought it an odd and unnecessary addition to their well-trained domestic establishment; but, so thoroughly efficient was Miss Ophelia in her conscientious endeavor to do her duty by her elève,[25] that the child rapidly grew in grace and in favor with the family and neighborhood. At the age of womanhood, she was, by her own request, baptized, and became a member of the Christian church in the place; and showed so much intelligence, activity and zeal, and desire to do good in the world, that she was at last recommended, and approved, as a missionary to one of the stations in Africa; and we have heard that the same activity and ingenuity which, when a child, made her so multiform and restless in her developments, is now employed, in a safer and wholesomer manner, in teaching the children of her own country.

P.S.[26]—It will be a satisfaction to some mother, also, to state, that some inquiries, which were set on foot by Madame de Thoux, have resulted recently in the discovery of Cassy's son. Being a young man of energy, he had escaped, some years before his mother, and been received and educated by friends of the oppressed in the north. He will soon follow his family to Africa.

# CHAPTER 44

## *The Liberator*¹

George Shelby had written to his mother merely a line, stating the day that she might expect him home. Of the death scene of his old friend he had not the heart to write. He had tried several times, and only succeeded in half choking himself; and invariably finished by tearing up the paper, wiping his eyes, and rushing somewhere to get quiet.²

There was a pleased bustle all through the Shelby mansion, that day, in expectation of the arrival of young Mas'r George.

Mrs. Shelby was seated in her comfortable parlor, where a cheerful hickory fire was dispelling the chill of the late autumn evening. A supper-table, glittering with plate and cut glass, was set out, on whose arrangements our former friend, old Chloe, was presiding.

Arrayed in a new calico dress, with clean, white apron, and high, well-starched turban, her black polished face glowing with satisfaction, she lingered, with needless punctiliousness, around the arrangements of the table, merely as an excuse for talking a little to her mistress.

"Laws, now! won't it look natural to him?" she said "Thar,—I set his plate just whar he likes it,—round by the fire. Mas'r George allers wants de warm seat. O, go way!—why, didn't Sally get out de *best* tea-pot,—de little new one, Mas'r George got for Missis, Christmas? I'll have it out! And Missis has heard from Mas'r George?" she said, inquiringly.

1 The chapter "which we shall dedicate to George" takes its title from the name of the famous abolitionist paper, William Lloyd Garrison's the *Liberator*, published from 1831 to 1865, closing at the end of the Civil War.

2 Readers must have cringed to anticipate the scene of homecoming. Not only Mrs. Shelby but, more importantly, Chloe will be hit hard by the news. We understand from the time marker given in the last chapter that some five years have passed since Eliza's escape and Tom's sale to Haley.

**3** Chloe uncharacteristically voices her anger at George for his selfishness. Mrs. Shelby's smile in response is more than a little patronizing.

**4** I.e., kind.

**5** In her anticipation of her husband's homecoming, Chloe is indiscreet enough to mention his leave-taking. This time, Mrs. Shelby sighs.

"Yes, Chloe; but only a line, just to say he would be home to-night, if he could,—that's all."

"Didn't say nothin' 'bout my old man, s'pose?" said Chloe, still fidgeting with the tea-cups.

"No, he didn't. He did not speak of anything, Chloe. He said he would tell all, when he got home."

"Jes like Mas'r George,—he's allers so ferce for tellin' everything hisself. I allers minded dat ar in Mas'r George.**3** Don't see, for my part, how white people gen'lly can bar to hev to write things much as they do, writin' 's such slow, oneasy kind o' work."

Mrs. Shelby smiled.

"I'm a thinkin' my old man won't know de boys and de baby. Lor'! she's de biggest gal, now,—good she is, too, and peart, Polly is. She's out to the house, now, watchin' de hoe-cake. I's got jist de very pattern**4** my old man liked so much, a bakin'. Jist sich as I gin him the mornin' he was took off. Lord bless us! how I felt, dat ar mornin'!"**5**

Mrs. Shelby sighed, and felt a heavy weight on her heart, at this allusion. She had felt uneasy, ever since she received her son's letter, lest something should prove to be hidden behind the veil of silence which he had drawn.

"Missis has got dem bills?" said Chloe, anxiously.

"Yes, Chloe."

" 'Cause I wants to show my old man dem very bills de *perfectioner* gave me. 'And,' says he, 'Chloe, I wish you'd stay longer.' 'Thank you, Mas'r,' says I, 'I would, only my old man's coming home, and Missis,—she can't do without me no longer.' There's jist what I told him. Berry nice man, dat Mas'r Jones was."

Chloe had pertinaciously insisted that the very bills in which her wages had been paid should be preserved, to show to her husband, in memorial of her capability. And Mrs. Shelby had readily consented to humor her in the request.

"He won't know Polly,—my old man won't. Laws, it's five year since they tuck him! She was a baby den,—couldn't but jist stand. Remember how tickled he used to be, cause she would keep a fallin' over, when she sot out to walk. Laws a me!"

The rattling of wheels now was heard.

"Mas'r George!" said Aunt Chloe, starting to the window.

Mrs. Shelby ran to the entry door, and was folded in the arms of her son. Aunt Chloe stood anxiously straining her eyes out into the darkness.

"O, *poor* Aunt Chloe!" said George, stopping compassionately, and taking her hard, black hand between both his; "I'd have given all my fortune to have brought him with me, but he's gone to a better country."[6]

There was a passionate exclamation from Mrs. Shelby, but Aunt Chloe said nothing.

The party entered the supper-room. The money, of which Chloe was so proud, was still lying on the table.

"Thar," said she, gathering it up, and holding it, with a trembling hand, to her mistress, "don't never want to see nor hear on't again. Jist as I knew 'twould be,—sold, and murdered on dem ar' old plantations!"

Chloe turned, and was walking proudly out of the room. Mrs. Shelby followed her softly, and took one of her hands, drew her down into a chair, and sat down by her.

"My poor, good Chloe!" said she.

Chloe leaned her head on her mistress' shoulder, and sobbed out, "O Missis! 'scuse me, my heart's broke,—dat's all!"

"I know it is," said Mrs. Shelby, as her tears fell fast; "and *I* cannot heal it, but Jesus can. He healeth the broken hearted, and bindeth up their wounds."[7]

There was a silence for some time, and all wept together. At last, George, sitting down beside the mourner, took her hand, and, with simple pathos, repeated the triumphant scene of her husband's death, and his last messages of love.

About a month after this,[8] one morning, all the servants of the Shelby estate were convened together in the great hall that ran through the house, to hear a few words from their young master.

To the surprise of all, he appeared among them with a bundle of papers in his hand, containing a certificate of freedom to every one on the place, which he read successively, and presented, amid the sobs and tears and shouts of all present.

Many, however, pressed around him, earnestly begging him not to send them away; and, with anxious faces, tendering back their free papers.

"We don't want to be no freer than we are. We's allers had all we wanted. We don't want to leave de ole place, and Mas'r and Missis, and de rest!"

"My good friends," said George, as soon as he could get a silence, "there'll be no need for you to leave me. The place wants as many hands to work it as it did before. We need the same about the house that we did before. But, you are now free men and free women. I shall pay you wages for your work, such as we shall agree on. The advantage is,

6 George's choice of words is bitterly appropriate: He means heaven, of course, but the implication is that America is not a particularly good country.

7 Coming out of Mrs. Shelby's mouth, this prayer is less consoling than if had come out of George's.

8 Readers might recall that St. Clare had only started to get Tom's papers when he died. George Shelby is proving to be a more efficient master.

9 However paternalistic George sounds, he has taken on himself the task of reeducating his former slaves.

10 An ancient Latin hymn of praise sung as thanksgiving: "Te deum laudamus," "We praise you, O God" (*Shorter Oxford*).

11 This hymn is entitled "Blow Ye the Trumpet."

12 George wants to assure himself that Chloe and her children will be part of the community, but readers have not been given a sense of the community already in place among the Shelby slaves, as evidenced by the late introduction of an unnamed "aged, patriarchal negro."

13 This is the final narrative chapter of the story (although it is followed by a chapter titled "Concluding Remarks"). Uncle Tom's cabin is thus made into a memorial. But we cannot help but ask: Where have Chloe and the children been staying? (When George wrote to Tom at the St. Clares, he had shut the cabin up but had great plans for renovations once Tom was home.) Will they live there now? Will anyone live in the Big House?

that in case of my getting in debt, or dying,—things that might happen,—you cannot now be taken up and sold. I expect to carry on the estate, and to teach you what, perhaps, it will take you some time to learn,—how to use the rights I give you as free men and women. I expect you to be good, and willing to learn; and I trust in God that I shall be faithful, and willing to teach. And now, my friends, look up, and thank God for the blessing of freedom."[9]

An aged, patriarchal negro, who had grown gray and blind on the estate, now rose, and, lifting his trembling hand said, "Let us give thanks unto the Lord!" As all kneeled by one consent, a more touching and hearty Te Deum[10] never ascended to heaven, though borne on the peal of organ, bell and cannon, than came from that honest old heart.

On rising, another struck up a Methodist hymn, of which the burden was,

*"The year of Jubilee is come,—*
*Return, ye ransomed sinners, home."*[11]

"One thing more," said George, as he stopped the congratulations of the throng; "you all remember our good old Uncle Tom?"

George here gave a short narration of the scene of his death, and of his loving farewell to all on the place, and added,

"It was on his grave, my friends, that I resolved, before God, that I would never own another slave, while it was possible to free him; that nobody, through me, should ever run the risk of being parted from home and friends, and dying on a lonely plantation, as he died. So, when you rejoice in your freedom, think that you owe it to that good old soul, and pay it back in kindness to his wife and children.[12] Think of your freedom, every time you see UNCLE TOM'S CABIN; and let it be a memorial to put you all in mind to follow in his steps, and be as honest and faithful and Christian as he was."[13]

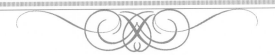

# CHAPTER 45

## *Concluding Remarks*

The writer has often been inquired of,[1] by correspondents from different parts of the country, whether this narrative is a true one; and to these inquiries she will give one general answer.[2]

The separate incidents that compose the narrative are, to a very great extent, authentic, occurring, many of them, either under her own observation, or that of her personal friends. She or her friends have observed characters the counterpart of almost all that are here introduced; and many of the sayings are word for word as heard herself, or reported to her.

The personal appearance of Eliza, the character ascribed to her, are sketches drawn from life. The incorruptible fidelity, piety and honesty, of Uncle Tom, had more than one development, to her personal knowledge. Some of the most deeply tragic and romantic, some of the most terrible incidents, have also their parallel in reality. The incident of the mother's crossing the Ohio river on the ice is a well-known fact. The story of "old Prue," in the second volume, was an incident that fell under the personal observation of a brother of the writer, then collecting-clerk to a large mercantile house, in New Orleans. From the same source was derived the character of the planter Legree. Of him her brother thus wrote, speaking of visiting his plantation, on a collecting tour: "He actually made me feel of his fist, which was like a blacksmith's hammer, or a nodule of iron, telling me that

1 The narrative voice here changes as Stowe begins to "own" the story she has just told.

2 The line between history (truth) and fiction was a sharp one in the nineteenth century, especially around the issue of slavery. Stowe must show that her story is true—i.e., that she has not simply made it up wholesale. Note throughout the chapter what Stowe claims as sources.

3 Stowe answers the charge that her portrayal is not representative of conditions under slavery in general. Recall Eva's shock at old Prue, beaten to death and left for the flies.

4 Horace Mann (1796–1859), known for his educational reforms.

it was 'calloused with knocking down niggers.' When I left the plantation, I drew a long breath, and felt as if I had escaped from an ogre's den."

That the tragical fate of Tom, also, has too many times had its parallel, there are living witnesses, all over our land, to testify. Let it be remembered that in all southern states it is a principle of jurisprudence that no person of colored lineage can testify in a suit against a white, and it will be easy to see that such a case may occur, wherever there is a man whose passions outweigh his interests, and a slave who has manhood or principle enough to resist his will. There is, actually, nothing to protect the slave's life, but the *character* of the master. Facts too shocking to be contemplated occasionally force their way to the public ear, and the comment that one often hears made on them is more shocking than the thing itself. It is said, "Very likely such cases may now and then occur, but they are no sample of general practice." If the laws of New England were so arranged that a master could *now and then* torture an apprentice to death, without a possibility of being brought to justice, would it be received with equal composure? Would it be said, "These cases are rare, and no samples of general practice"?[3] This injustice is an *inherent* one in the slave system,—it cannot exist without it.

The public and shameless sale of beautiful mulatto and quadroon girls has acquired a notoriety, from the incidents following the capture of the Pearl. We extract the following from the speech of Hon. Horace Mann,[4] one of the legal counsel for the defendants in that case. He says: "In that company of seventy-six persons, who attempted, in 1848, to escape from the District of Columbia in the schooner Pearl, and whose officers I assisted in defending, there were several young and healthy girls, who had those peculiar attractions of form and feature which connoisseurs prize so highly. Elizabeth Russel was one of them. She immediately fell into the slave-trader's fangs, and was doomed for the New Orleans market. The hearts of those that saw her were touched with pity for her fate. They offered eighteen hundred dollars to redeem her; and some there were who offered to give, that would not have much left after the gift; but the fiend of a slave-trader was inexorable. She was despatched to New Orleans; but, when about half way there, God had mercy on her, and smote her with death. There were two girls named Edmundson in the same company. When about to be sent to the same market, an older sister went to the shambles, to plead with the wretch who owned them, for the love of God, to spare his victims. He bantered her, telling what fine dresses and fine furniture they would have. 'Yes,' she said, 'that may do very well in this life, but what will become of them in the next?' They too were sent to New Orleans; but were afterwards redeemed, at an enormous ransom, and brought back." Is it not plain, from this, that the histories of Emmeline and Cassy may have many counterparts?

Justice, too, obliges the author to state that the fairness of mind and generosity attributed to St. Clare are not without a parallel, as the following anecdote will show. A few years since, a young southern gentleman was in Cincinnati, with a favorite servant, who had been his personal attendant from a boy. The young man took advantage of this opportunity to secure his own freedom, and fled to the protection of a Quaker, who was quite noted in affairs of this kind. The owner was exceedingly indignant. He had always treated the slave with such indulgence, and his confidence in his affection was such, that he believed he must have been practised upon to induce him to revolt from him. He visited the Quaker, in high anger; but, being possessed of uncommon candor and fairness, was soon quieted by his arguments and representations. It was a side of the subject which he never had heard,—never had thought on; and he immediately told the Quaker that, if his slave would, to his own face, say that it was his desire to be free, he would liberate him. An interview was forthwith procured, and Nathan was asked by his young master whether he had ever had any reason to complain of his treatment, in any respect.

"No, Mas'r," said Nathan; "you've always been good to me."

"Well, then, why do you want to leave me?"

"Mas'r may die, and then who get me?—I'd rather be a free man."

After some deliberation, the young master replied, "Nathan, in your place, I think I should feel very much so, myself. You are free."

He immediately made him out free papers; deposited a sum of money in the hands of the Quaker, to be judiciously used in assisting him to start in life, and left a very sensible and kind letter of advice to the young man. That letter was for some time in the writer's hands.

The author hopes she has done justice to that nobility, generosity, and humanity, which in many cases characterize individuals at the South. Such instances save us from utter despair of our kind. But, she asks any person, who knows the world, are such characters *common,* anywhere?

5 The Fugitive Slave Act, which strengthened Fugitive Slave Laws.

For many years of her life, the author avoided all reading upon or allusion to the subject of slavery, considering it as too painful to be inquired into, and one which advancing light and civilization would certainly live down. But, since the legislative act of 1850,[5] when she heard, with perfect surprise and consternation, Christian and humane people actually recommending the remanding escaped fugitives into slavery, as a duty binding on good citizens,—when she heard, on all hands, from kind, compassionate and estimable people, in the free states of the North, deliberations and discussions as to what Christian duty could be on this head,—she could only think, These men and Christians cannot know what slavery is; if they did, such a question could never be open for discussion. And from this arose a desire to exhibit it in a *living dramatic reality*. She has endeavored to show it fairly, in its best and its worst phases. In its *best* aspect, she has, perhaps, been successful; but, oh! who shall say what yet remains untold in that valley and shadow of death, that lies the other side?

To you, generous, noble-minded men and women, of the South,—you, whose virtue, and magnanimity, and purity of character, are the greater for the severer trial it has encountered,—to you is her appeal. Have you not, in your own secret souls, in your own private conversings, felt that there are woes and evils, in this accursed system, far beyond what are here shadowed, or can be shadowed? Can it be otherwise? Is *man* ever a creature to be trusted with wholly irresponsible power? And does not the slave system, by denying the slave all legal right of testimony, make every individual owner an irresponsible despot? Can anybody fail to make the inference what the practical result will be? If there is, as we admit, a public sentiment among you, men of honor, justice and humanity, is there not also another kind of public sentiment among the ruffian, the brutal and debased? And cannot the ruffian, the brutal, the debased, by slave law, own just as many slaves as the best and purest? Are the honorable, the just, the high-minded and compassionate, the majority anywhere in this world?

The slave-trade is now, by American law, considered as piracy. But a slave-trade, as systematic as ever was carried on on the coast of Africa, is an inevitable attendant and result of American slavery. And its heart-break and its horrors, *can* they be told?

The writer has given only a faint shadow, a dim picture, of the anguish and despair that are, at this very moment, riving thousands of hearts, shattering thousands of families, and driving a helpless and sensitive race to frenzy and despair. There are those living who know the mothers whom this accursed traffic has driven to the murder of their children; and themselves seeking in death a shelter from woes more dreaded than death. Nothing of tragedy can be written, can be spoken, can be conceived, that equals the frightful reality of scenes daily and hourly acting on our shores, beneath the shadow of American law, and the shadow of the cross of Christ.

And now, men and women of America, is this a thing to be trifled with, apologized for, and passed over in silence? Farmers of Massachusetts, of New Hampshire, of Vermont, of Connecticut, who read this book by the blaze of your winter-evening fire,—strong-hearted, generous sailors and ship-owners of Maine,—is this a thing for you to countenance and encourage? Brave and generous men of New York, farmers of rich and joyous Ohio, and ye of the wide prairie states,—answer, is this a thing for you to protect and countenance? And you, mothers of America,—you, who have learned, by the cradles of your own children, to love and feel for all mankind,—by the sacred love you bear your child; by your joy in his beautiful, spotless infancy; by the motherly pity and tenderness with which you guide his growing years; by the anxieties of his education; by the prayers you breathe for his soul's eternal good;—I beseech you, pity the mother who has all your affections, and not one legal right to protect, guide, or educate, the child of her bosom! By the sick hour of your child; by those dying eyes, which you can never forget; by those last cries, that wrung your heart when you could neither help nor save; by the desolation of that empty cradle, that silent nursery,—I beseech you, pity those mothers that are constantly made childless by the American slave-trade! And say, mothers of America, is this a thing to be defended, sympathized with, passed over in silence?

Do you say that the people of the free states have nothing to do with it, and can do nothing? Would to God this were true! But it is not true. The people of the free states have defended, encouraged, and participated; and are more guilty for it, before God, than the South, in that they have *not* the apology of education or custom.

If the mothers of the free states had all felt as they should, in times past, the sons of the free states would not have been the holders, and, proverbially, the hardest masters of slaves; the sons of the free states would not have connived at the extension of slavery, in our national body;

the sons of the free states would not, as they do, trade the souls and bodies of men as an equivalent to money, in their mercantile dealings. There are multitudes of slaves temporarily owned, and sold again, by merchants in northern cities; and shall the whole guilt or obloquy of slavery fall only on the South?

Northern men, northern mothers, northern Christians, have something more to do than denounce their brethren at the South; they have to look to the evil among themselves.

But, what can any individual do? Of that, every individual can judge. There is one thing that every individual can do,—they can see to it that *they feel right.* An atmosphere of sympathetic influence encircles every human being; and the man or woman who *feels* strongly, healthily and justly, on the great interests of humanity, is a constant benefactor to the human race. See, then, to your sympathies in this matter! Are they in harmony with the sympathies of Christ? or are they swayed and perverted by the sophistries of worldly policy?

Christian men and women of the North! still further,—you have another power; you can *pray*! Do you believe in prayer? or has it become an indistinct apostolic tradition? You pray for the heathen abroad; pray also for the heathen at home. And pray for those distressed Christians whose whole chance of religious improvement is an accident of trade and sale; from whom any adherence to the morals of Christianity is, in many cases, an impossibility, unless they have given them, from above, the courage and grace of martyrdom.

But, still more. On the shores of our free states are emerging the poor, shattered, broken remnants of families,—men and women, escaped, by miraculous providences, from the surges of slavery,—feeble in knowledge, and, in many cases, infirm in moral constitution, from a system which confounds and confuses every principle of Christianity and morality. They come to seek a refuge among you; they come to seek education, knowledge, Christianity.

What do you owe to these poor unfortunates, oh Christians? Does not every American Christian owe to the African race some effort at reparation for the wrongs that the American nation has brought upon them? Shall the doors of churches and school-houses be shut upon them? Shall states arise and shake them out? Shall the church of Christ hear in silence the taunt that is thrown at them, and shrink away from the helpless hand that they stretch out; and, by her silence, encourage the cruelty that would chase them from our borders? If it must be so, it will be a mournful spectacle. If it must be so, the country will have reason to tremble, when it remembers that the fate of nations is in the hands of One who is very pitiful, and of tender compassion.

Do you say, "We don't want them here; let them go to Africa"?

That the providence of God has provided a refuge in Africa, is, indeed, a great and noticeable fact; but that is no reason why the church of Christ should throw off that responsibility to this outcast race which her Profession demands of her.

To fill up Liberia with an ignorant, inexperienced, half-barbarized race, just escaped from the chains of slavery, would be only to prolong, for ages, the period of struggle and conflict which attends the inception of new enterprises. Let the church of the north receive these poor sufferers in the spirit of Christ; receive them to the educating advantages of Christian republican society and schools, until they have attained to somewhat of a moral and intellectual maturity, and then assist them in their passage to those shores, where they may put in practice the lessons they have learned in America.

There is a body of men at the north, comparatively small, who have been doing this; and, as the result, this country has already seen examples of men, formerly slaves, who have rapidly acquired property, reputation, and education. Talent has been developed, which, considering the circumstances, is certainly remarkable; and, for moral traits of honesty, kindness, tenderness of feeling,— for heroic efforts and self-denials, endured for the ransom of brethren and friends yet in slavery,—they have been remarkable to a degree that, considering the influence under which they were born, is surprising.

The writer has lived, for many years, on the frontier-line of slave states, and has had great opportunities of observation among those who formerly were slaves. They have been in her family as servants; and, in default of any other school to receive them, she has, in many cases, had them instructed in a family school, with her own children. She has also the testimony of missionaries, among the fugitives in Canada, in coincidence with her own experience; and her deductions, with regard to the capabilities of the race, are encouraging in the highest degree.

The first desire of the emancipated slave, generally, is for *education*. There is nothing that they are not willing to

6 Unintentionally ironic: The former slaves are listed as "worth ____ dollars"!

give or do to have their children instructed; and, so far as the writer has observed herself, or taken the testimony of teachers among them, they are remarkably intelligent and quick to learn. The results of schools, founded for them by benevolent individuals in Cincinnati, fully establish this.

The author gives the following statement of facts, on the authority of Professor C. E. Stowe, then of Lane Seminary, Ohio, with regard to emancipated slaves, now resident in Cincinnati; given to show the capability of the race, even without any very particular assistance or encouragement.

The initial letters alone are given. They are all residents of Cincinnati.[6]

"B——. Furniture maker; twenty years in the city; worth ten thousand dollars, all his own earnings; a Baptist.

"C——. Full black; stolen from Africa; sold in New Orleans; been free fifteen years; paid for himself six hundred dollars; a farmer; owns several farms in Indiana; Presbyterian; probably worth fifteen or twenty thousand dollars, all earned by himself.

"K——. Full black; dealer in real estate; worth thirty thousand dollars; about forty years old; free six years; paid eighteen hundred dollars for his family; member of the Baptist church; received a legacy from his master, which he has taken good care of, and increased.

"G——. Full black; coal dealer; about thirty years old; worth eighteen thousand dollars; paid for himself twice, being once defrauded to the amount of sixteen hundred dollars; made all his money by his own efforts—much of it while a slave, hiring his time of his master, and doing business for himself; a fine, gentlemanly fellow.

"W——. Three-fourths black; barber and waiter; from Kentucky; nineteen years free; paid for self and family over three thousand dollars; worth twenty thousand dollars, all his own earnings; deacon in the Baptist church.

"G. D——. Three-fourths black; white-washer; from Kentucky; nine years free; paid fifteen hundred dollars for self and family; recently died, aged sixty; worth six thousand dollars."

Professor Stowe says, "With all these, except G——, I have been, for some years, personally acquainted, and make my statements from my own knowledge."

The writer well remembers an aged colored woman, who was employed as a washerwoman in her father's family. The daughter of this woman married a slave. She was a remarkably active and capable young woman, and, by her industry and thrift, and the most persevering self-denial, raised nine hundred dollars for her husband's freedom, which she paid, as she raised it, into the hands of his master. She yet wanted a hundred dollars of the price, when he died. She never recovered any of the money.

These are but few facts, among multitudes which might be adduced, to show the self-denial, energy, patience, and honesty, which the slave has exhibited in a state of freedom.

And let it be remembered that these individuals have thus bravely succeeded in conquering for themselves comparative wealth and social position, in the face of every disadvantage and discouragement. The colored man, by the law of Ohio, cannot be a voter, and, till within a few years, was even denied the right of testimony in legal suits with the white. Nor are these instances confined to the State of Ohio. In all states of the Union we see men, but yesterday burst from the shackles of slavery, who, by a self-educating force, which cannot be too much admired, have risen to highly respectable stations in society. Pennington, among clergymen, Douglas and Ward,[7] among editors, are well known instances.

If this persecuted race, with every discouragement and disadvantage, have done thus much, how much more they might do, if the Christian church would act towards them in the spirit of her Lord!

This is an age of the world when nations are trembling and convulsed. A mighty influence is abroad, surging and heaving the world, as with an earthquake. And is America safe? Every nation that carries in its bosom great and unredressed injustice has in it the elements of this last convulsion.

For what is this mighty influence thus rousing in all nations and languages those groanings that cannot be uttered, for man's freedom and equality?

O, Church of Christ, read the signs of the times! Is not this power the spirit of HIM whose kingdom is yet to come, and whose will to be done on earth as it is in heaven?

But who may abide the day of his appearing? "for that day shall burn as an oven: and he shall appear as a swift witness against those that oppress the hireling in his wages, the widow and the fatherless, and that *turn aside the stranger in his right:* and he shall break in pieces the oppressor."[8]

Are not these dread words for a nation bearing in her bosom so mighty an injustice? Christians! every time that you pray that the kingdom of Christ may come, can you

7 J. W. C. Pennington, Frederick Douglass (misspelled by Stowe), and Samuel Ringgold Ward were slaves who became celebrated orators (or in the case of Pennington, a Presbyterian preacher).

8 See Mal. 3:19: "For lo, the day is coming, blazing like an oven, when all the proud and all evildoers will be stubble, and the day is coming that will set them on fire, leaving them neither root nor branch, says the Lord of hosts."

forget that prophecy associates, in dread fellowship, the *day of vengeance* with the year of his redeemed?

A day of grace is yet held out to us. Both North and South have been guilty before God; and the *Christian church* has a heavy account to answer. Not by combining together, to protect injustice and cruelty, and making a common capital of sin, is this Union to be saved,—but by repentance, justice and mercy; for, not surer is the eternal law by which the millstone sinks in the ocean, than that stronger law, by which injustice and cruelty shall bring on nations the wrath of Almighty God!

# BIBLIOGRAPHY

Adams, Henry Gardiner. *God's Image in Ebony: Being a Series of Biographical Sketches, Facts, Anecdotes, etc. Demonstrative of the Mental Powers and Intellectual Capacities of the Negro Race.* London: Partridge and Oakey, 1854.

Alexander, Robert. *I Ain't Yo' Uncle: The New Jack Revisionist "Uncle Tom's Cabin."* From the stage adaptation by George Aiken of the novel by Harriet Beecher Stowe. Woodstock, Ill.: Dramatic Publishing, 1996.

American Heritage Dictionaries, ed. *American Heritage Dictionary of the English Language.* 4th ed. Boston: Houghton Mifflin, 2000.

Ammons, Elizabeth. "Heroines in *Uncle Tom's Cabin.*" In *Critical Essays on Harriet Beecher Stowe,* edited by Elizabeth Ammons, pp. 152–65. Boston: G. K. Hall, 1980.

———. "Stowe's Dream of the Mother-Savior: *Uncle Tom's Cabin* and American Women Writers Before the 1920s." In *New Essays on* Uncle Tom's Cabin, American Novel Series, edited by Eric J. Sundquist, pp. 155–95. New York: Cambridge University Press, 1986.

Anonymous. [Review of *Uncle Tom's Cabin.*] In Harriet Beecher Stowe, *Uncle Tom's Cabin,* Norton Critical Edition, edited by Elizabeth Ammons, pp. 478–83. New York: W. W. Norton, 1994. First published in the *Times* (London), Sept. 3, 1852.

Anonymous. *Uncle Tom's Cabin Picture Book.* New York: Graham & Matlack, 1913.

Ashworth, John. *Slavery, Capitalism, and Politics in the Antebellum Republic.* New York: Cambridge University Press, 1995.

Baldwin, James. *James Baldwin: Collected Essays.* Edited by Toni Morrison. New York: Library of America, 1998.

———. *James Baldwin: Early Novels and Stories.* Edited by Toni Morrison. New York: Library of America, 1998.

Baym, Nina. *Feminism and American Literary History: Essays.* New Brunswick, N.J.: Rutgers University Press, 1992.

———. *Woman's Fiction: A Guide to Novels by and about Women in America 1820–70.* 2d ed. Champaign: University of Illinois Press, 1993.

Beecher, Catharine E. *Essay on Slavery and Abolitionism with Reference to the Duty of American Females.* Philadelphia: H. Perkins; Boston: Perkins & Marvin, 1837.

———. *A Treatise on Domestic Economy.* Boston: Thomas H. Webb & Co., 1842.

Beecher, Catharine E., and Harriet Beecher Stowe. *The American Woman's Home.* 1869. Reprint, New York: Arno Press, 1971.

Behn, Aphra. *Oroonoko, The Rover and Other Works.* Penguin Classics. Edited with an introduction by Janet Todd. New York: Penguin Books, 1992.

Berkson, Dorothy. "Millennial Politics and the Feminine Fiction of Harriet Beecher Stowe." In *Critical Essays on Harriet Beecher Stowe,* edited by Elizabeth Ammons, pp. 244–58. Boston: G. K. Hall, 1980.

Black, David. *Helen Macfarlane: A Feminist, Revolutionary Journalist, and Philosopher in Mid-Nineteenth-Century England.* Lanham, Md.: Lexington Books, 2004.

Bloch, Ruth H. "American Feminine Ideals in Transition: The Rise of the Moral Mother, 1785–1815." *Feminist Studies* 4 (1978): 101–26.

Bode, Carl, ed. *American Life in the 1840s.* New York: New York University Press, 1967.

Borgstrom, Michael. "Passing Over: Setting the Record Straight in *Uncle Tom's Cabin.*" *PMLA* 118 (2003): 1290–1304.

Boydston, Jeanne, Mary Kelley, and Anne Margolis. *The Limits of Sisterhood: The Beecher Sisters on Women's Rights and Women's Spheres*. Chapel Hill: University of North Carolina Press, 1988.

Briggs, Charles F. "Uncle Tomitudes." In *Critical Essays on Harriet Beecher Stowe*, edited by Elizabeth Ammons, pp. 35–42. Boston: G. K. Hall, 1980. First published in *Putnam's Monthly Magazine,* Jan. 1853: 97–102.

Brown, Gillian. "Getting in the Kitchen with Dinah: Domestic Politics in *Uncle Tom's Cabin.*" *American Quarterly* 36 (1984): 503–23.

Brown, Sterling A. *The Negro in American Fiction*. 1937. Reprint, New York: Arno Press, 1969.

———. "Negro Folk Expression: Spirituals, Seculars, Ballads, and Worksongs." *Phylon* 14.4 (1953): 45–61.

Brown, William Wells. *Narrative of William W. Brown, a Fugitive Slave. Written by Himself*. Boston: Anti-Slavery Office, 1847.

———. *The American Fugitive in Europe. Sketches of Places and People Abroad*. Boston: John P. Jewett & Co., 1855.

———. *Clotel; or The President's Daughter: A Narrative of Slave Life in the United States*. Edited by Robert S. Levine. New York: Bedford/St. Martin's, 2000.

Burke, Edmund. *A Philosophical Enquiry into the Origin of Our Ideas of the Sublime and Beautiful*. Edited by Adam Phillips. Oxford: Oxford University Press, 1990.

Chateaubriand, François-René, Vicomte de. *The Natchez: An Indian Tale*. London: H. Colburn, 1827.

Chesnut, Mary Boykin. *A Diary from Dixie*. Edited by Ben Ames Williams. Boston: Houghton Mifflin, 1949.

Child, Lydia Maria. "The Quadroons." In *The Liberty Bell*, pp. 115–41. Boston: Massachusetts Anti-Slavery Fair, 1842.

———. *A Romance of the Republic*. 1867. Reprint, with an introduction by Dana D. Nelson, Lexington: University Press of Kentucky, 1997.

Church of England. *The Book of Common Prayer*. Oxford: University Press, 1849.

Clark, Clifford Edward, Jr. *The American Family Home, 1800–1960*. Chapel Hill: University of North Carolina Press, 1986.

Clarkson, Thomas. *An Essay on the Impolicy of the African Slave Trade*. London: J. Phillips, 1788.

———. *An Essay on the Slavery and Commerce of the Human Species*. 2d ed. London: J. Phillips, 1788.

Classics Illustrated. *Uncle Tom's Cabin*. Classic Comic Books no. 15. New York: Gilberton Company, 1943.

Cleaver, Eldridge. *Soul on Ice*. New York: McGraw-Hill, 1967. Reprint, with a preface by Ishmael Reed, New York: Dell Publishing, 1999.

Crozier, Alice C. *The Novels of Harriet Beecher Stowe*. New York: Oxford University Press, 1969.

Denman, Thomas, Lord. *Uncle Tom's Cabin, Bleak House, Slavery and Slave Trade*. 2d ed. London: Longman, Brown, Green, and Longmans, 1853.

———. Letter from Thomas Denman to Harriet Beecher Stowe. In Harriet Beecher Stowe, *Sunny Memories of Foreign Lands*, 2 vols. Boston: Phillips, Sampson, and Company, 1854.

Dickens, Charles. "Letter to Harriet Beecher Stowe." In *Literary Sourcebook on Harriet Beecher Stowe's* Uncle Tom's Cabin, A Routledge Literary Sourcebook, edited by Debra Rosenthal, p. 33. London: Routledge, 2000.

———. *Bleak House*. Penguin Classics. Edited with an introduction and notes by Nicola Bradbury. New York: Penguin Books, 2003.

Douglas, Ann. "Heaven Our Home: Consolation Literature in the Northern United States, 1830–1880." *American Quarterly* 26 (1974): 496–515.

———. *The Feminization of American Culture*. New York: Alfred A. Knopf, 1977. Reprint, London: Papermac, 1996.

Douglass, Frederick. *Autobiographies: Narrative of the Life of Frederick Douglass, an American Slave; My Bondage and My Freedom; Life and Times of Frederick Douglass*. Edited by Henry Louis Gates Jr. New York: Library of America, 1994.

———. "What To the Slave Is the Fourth of July?" In *The Oxford Frederick Douglas Reader,* edited with an introduction by William L. Andrews, pp. 108–30. New York: Oxford University Press, 1996.

Downing, Andrew Jackson. *The Architecture of Country Houses*. New York: D. Appleton & Co., 1850.

Eastman, Mary Henderson. *Aunt Phillis's Cabin, or, Southern Life As It Is*. Philadelphia: Lippincott, Grambo & Co., 1852.

Eliot, George. "Review of *Dred: A Tale of the Great Dismal Swamp.*" In *Critical Essays on Harriet Beecher*

*Stowe*, edited by Elizabeth Ammons, pp. 43–44. Boston: G. K. Hall, 1980.

Fiedler, Leslie A. *The Inadvertent Epic: From* Uncle Tom's Cabin *to* Roots. New York: Simon & Schuster, 1979.

Fields, Annie, ed. *Life and Letters of Harriet Beecher Stowe*. Boston: Houghton Mifflin, 1898.

Finley, Ruth E. *The Lady of Godey's: Sarah Josepha Hale*. Philadelphia: J. B. Lippincott, 1931.

Foreman, P. Gabrielle. " 'This Promiscuous Housekeeping': Death, Transgression, and Homoeroticism in *Uncle Tom's Cabin*." *Representations* 43 (1993): 51–72.

Foster, Charles H. *The Rungless Ladder: Harriet Beecher Stowe and New England Puritanism*. Durham, N.C.: Duke University Press, 1954.

Fredrickson, George M. *The Black Image in the White Mind: The Debate on Afro-American Character and Destiny, 1817–1914*. New York: Harper & Row, 1971.

Garnet, Henry Highland. *Address to the Slaves of the United States of America*. In *Walker's Appeal, in Four Articles by David Walker and An Address to the Slaves of the United States of America by Henry Highland Garnet*. New York: Arno Press, 1969.

Gibbs, Laura. *Aesop's Fables*. Oxford World's Classics. New York: Oxford University Press, 2003.

Gleason, William. " 'I Dwell Now in a Neat Little Cottage': Architecture, Race, and Desire in *The Bondwoman's Narrative*." In *In Search of Hannah Crafts: Critical Essays on* The Bondwoman's Narrative, edited by Henry Louis Gates Jr. and Hollis Robbins, pp. 145–74. New York: Basic Civitas Books, 2004.

Goodell, William. *The American Slave Code in Theory and Practice: Its Distinctive Features Shown by Its Statutes, Judicial Decisions, and Illustrative Facts*. New York: American and Foreign Anti-Slavery Society, 1853.

Graves, Robert, ed. *New Larousse Encyclopedia of Mythology*. London: Hamlyn, 1968.

Hale, Sarah Josepha. *The New Household Receipt-Book*. New York: H. Long & Brother, 1853.

Hedrick, Joan D. *Harriet Beecher Stowe: A Life*. New York: Oxford University Press, 1994.

Hellerstein, Erna Olafson, Leslie Parker Hume, and Karen M. Offen, eds. *Victorian Women: A Documentary Account of Women's Lives in Nineteenth-Century England, France, and the United States*. Palo Alto, Calif.: Stanford University Press, 1981.

Henry, William Wirt. *Patrick Henry; Life, Correspondence and Speeches*. New York: B. Franklin, 1969.

Henson, Josiah. *Father Henson's Story of His Own Life*. Boston: John P. Jewett & Co.; Cleveland: Henry P. B. Jewett, 1858.

Herbert, George. *Jacula Prudentum*. London: Rivingtons, 1871.

Holmes, George F. [Review of *Uncle Tom's Cabin*.] In Harriet Beecher Stowe, *Uncle Tom's Cabin*, Norton Critical Edition, edited by Elizabeth Ammons, pp. 467–77. New York: W. W. Norton, 1994. First published in *Southern Literary Messenger*, Oct. 18, 1852.

James, Henry. *A Small Boy and Others*. New York: Charles Scribner's Sons, 1913.

Johnson, James Weldon. *The Autobiography of an Ex-Coloured Man*. Introduction by Carl Van Vechten. New York: Alfred A. Knopf, 1970.

Johnson, Paul David. "Harriet Beecher Stowe." *American Writers* supp. 1, vol. 2 (1979): 579–601.

Kazin, Alfred. *God and the American Writer*. New York: Alfred A. Knopf, 1997.

Kelley, Mary. *Private Woman, Public Stage: Literary Domesticity in Nineteenth-Century America*. New York: Oxford University Press, 1984.

Lawrence, D. H. *Studies in Classic American Literature*. Edited by Ezra Greenspan, Lindeth Vasey, and John Worthen. Cambridge, UK: Cambridge University Press, 2003.

Marx, Karl, and Friedrich Engels. *Manifesto of the Communist Party*. Authorized English translation. 3d ed. Edited and annotated by Frederick Engels. London: W. Reeves, 1888.

———. "The Communist Manifesto," translated by Helen Mcfarlane [Nov. 1850]. In *The Red Republican & the Friend of the People*, 2 vols., a reprint of the Chartist journal with introduction by John Saville. London: Merlin Press, 1966.

Milton, John. *Paradise Lost*. Edited by Alastair Fowler. 2d ed. New York: Longman, 1998.

Moore, Thomas. *The Complete Poetical Works of Thomas Moore*. New York: T. Y. Crowell Co., 1895.

Nagel, Paul C. *John Quincy Adams: A Public Life, A Private Life*. New York: Alfred A. Knopf, 1997.

New-York Historical Society. *Reading Uncle Tom's Image: A Reconsideration of Harriet Beecher Stowe's 150-Year-Old Character and His Legacy.* An exhibition curated by Kathleen Hulser. New York: New-York Historical Society, Oct. 1, 2002–Feb. 9, 2003.

Olney, James. " 'I Was Born': Slave Narratives, Their Status as Autobiography and as Literature." In *The Slave's Narrative,* edited by Charles T. Davis and Henry Louis Gates Jr., pp. 148–74. New York: Oxford University Press, 1985.

Orwell, George. "Good Bad Books." In *The Collected Essays, Journalism, and Letters of George Orwell,* vol. 4, edited by Sonia Orwell and Ian Angus, pp. 19–22. New York: Harcourt, Brace & World, 1968. First published in the *Tribune,* Nov. 2, 1945.

Page, John White. *Uncle Robin, In His Cabin in Virginia, and Tom without One in Boston.* Richmond, Va.: J. W. Randolph, 1853.

Pearson, Hesketh. *Oscar Wilde: His Life and Wit.* New York: Harper & Brothers, 1946.

Raboteau, Albert J. *Slave Religion: The "Invisible Institution" in the Antebellum South.* New York: Oxford University Press, 1978.

Railton, Stephen. "Mothers, Husbands, and Uncle Tom." *Georgia Review* 38 (1984): 129–44.

———. *Authorship and Audience: Literary Performance in the American Renaissance.* Princeton, N.J.: Princeton University Press, 1991.

———, director. *Uncle Tom's Cabin* & American Culture: A Multi-media Archive. www.iath.virginia.edu/utc.

Rugoff, Milton A. *The Beechers: An American Family in the Nineteenth Century.* New York: Harper & Row, 1981.

Rush, Caroline E. *The North and South, or Slavery and Its Contrasts.* Philadelphia: Crissy & Markley, 1852.

Sanchez-Eppler, Karen. "Raising Empires like Children: Race, Nation, and Religious Education." *American Literary History* 8 (1996): 399–425.

Sand, George. "Review of *Uncle Tom's Cabin.*" In *Critical Essays on Harriet Beecher Stowe,* edited by Elizabeth Ammons, pp. 3–6. Boston: G. K. Hall, 1980. First published in *La Presse,* Dec. 17, 1852.

Sewell, Anna. *Black Beauty, His Groom and Companions: The "Uncle Tom's Cabin" of the Horse.* New York: H. M. Caldwell Co., 1894.

Shakespeare, William. *The Arden Shakespeare Complete Works.* Edited by Richard Proudfoot, Ann Thompson, and David Scott Kastan. London: Thomas Learning EMEA, 1998.

Showalter, Elaine. "Responsibilities and Realities: A Curriculum for the Eighties." *ADE Bulletin* 070 (1981): 17–21.

Sklar, Kathryn Kish. *Catharine Beecher: A Study in American Domesicity.* New Haven, Conn.: Yale University Press, 1973.

Smith, W. L. G. *Uncle Tom's Cabin As It Is.* Chicago: D. B. Cooke and Co., 1852.

Southworth, Emma Dorothy Eliza Nevitte. *Retribution; or, The Vale of Shadows. A Tale of Passion.* New York: Harper & Brothers, 1849.

Stanley, Amy Dru. "Home Life and the Morality of the Market." In *The Market Revolution in America,* edited by Melvyn Stokes and Stephen Conway, pp. 74–96. Charlottesville: University of Virginia Press, 1996.

Stowe, Harriet Beecher. *The Mayflower; or Sketches of Scenes and Characters Among the Descendants of the Piligrims.* New York: Harper & Brothers, 1843.

———. *Uncle Tom's Cabin; or Life Among the Lowly.* Boston: John P. Jewett & Co., 1852.

———. *Uncle Tom's Cabin; A Tale of Life Among the Lowly.* With a preface by the Right Hon. the Earl of Carlisle [Oct. 8, 1852]. London: George Routledge & Co., n.d. [circa 1852–53].

———. *A Key to Uncle Tom's Cabin.* Boston: John P. Jewett & Co., 1853.

———. *Uncle Tom's Cabin, or, Life Among the Lowly.* Illustrated edition; original designs by Hammatt Billings, engraved by Baker and Smith. Boston: John P. Jewett & Co., 1853.

———. *Dred: A Tale of the Great Dismal Swamp.* 2 vols. Boston: Phillips, Sampson, 1856.

———. *The Minister's Wooing.* New York: Derby and Jackson, 1859. Reprint, Boston: Houghton Mifflin, 1896.

———. *The Pearl of Orr's Island: A Story of the Coast of Maine.* Boston: Ticknor and Fields, 1862. Reprint, Ridgewood, N.J.: Gregg Press, 1967.

———. *Lady Byron Vindicated: A History of the Byron Controversy, From its Beginning in 1816 to the Present Time.* Boston: Osgood, Fields, 1870.

———. *My Wife and I: or Henry Henderson's History.* New York: J. B. Ford, 1871.

———. *Uncle Tom's Cabin, or, Life Among the Lowly.* New edition with illustrations. Boston: Houghton Mifflin, 1888.

———. *Uncle Tom's Cabin: A Tale of Life Among the Lowly.* Philadelphia: International Publishing Co., 1897.

———. *Uncle Tom's Cabin; or, Life Among the Lowly.* Art Memorial Edition. Chicago: Monarch Book Company, 1897.

———. *Altemus' Young People's Library: Uncle Tom's Cabin; or, Life Among the Lowly.* Philadelphia: Henry Altemus, 1900.

———. *Uncle Tom's Cabin, Young Folks Edition.* Chicago: M. A. Donohue & Co., n.d. [circa 1900].

———. *Young Folks Uncle Tom's Cabin.* Adapted for children by Grace Duffie Boylan. New York: H. M. Caldwell Co., 1901.

———. *Uncle Tom's Cabin.* Classic Comics no. 15. New York: Classics Illustrated, Giberton Company, 1943.

———. *Uncle Tom's Cabin or, Life Among the Lowly.* Penguin Classics. Edited with an introduction by Ann Douglas. New York: Penguin Books, 1986.

———. *Uncle Tom's Cabin.* Norton Critical Edition. Edited by Elizabeth Ammons. New York: W. W. Norton, 1994.

———. *Uncle Tom's Cabin.* London and Melbourne: Ward, Lock & Co. Ltd., n.d.

———. *Uncle Tom's Cabin, or, Life Among the Lowly.* New York: Grosset and Dunlap, n.d.

Sumner, Charles. *Speech by the Hon. Charles Sumner, of Massachusetts, on His Motion to Repeal the Fugitive Slave Bill, in the Senate of the United States, August 26, 1852.* Boston: Ticknor, Reed and Fields, 1852. Reprinted in *Frederick Douglass' Paper*, Oct. 1, 1852.

Sundquist, Eric J., ed. *New Essays on* Uncle Tom's Cabin. American Novel Series. Cambridge, UK: Cambridge University Press, 1986.

Sweeting, Adam W. *Reading Houses and Building Books: Andrew Jackson Downing and the Architecture of Popular Antebellum Literature, 1835–1855.* Hanover, N.H.: University Press of New England, 1996.

Thomas, Emory M. *The Confederacy as a Revolutionary Experience.* Columbia: University of South Carolina Press, 1971.

Tompkins, Jane P. "Sentimental Power: *Uncle Tom's Cabin* and the Politics of Literary History." In *Sensational Designs: The Cultural Work of American Fiction, 1790–1860*, pp. 122–46. New York: Oxford University Press, 1985.

Twain, Mark. *Huckleberry Finn.* Everyman's Library Edition. New York: Alfred A. Knopf, 1991.

*The Uncle Tom's Cabin Almanack, or, Abolitionist Momento.* London: John Cassell, 1853.

Walker, David. *Appeal. In Four Articles, Together with a Preamble, to the Coloured Citizens of the World, but in Particular, and Very Expressly, to Those of the United States of America.* Revised edition, with an introduction by Sean Wilentz. New York: Farrar, Straus and Giroux, 1995.

Warner, Charles Dudley. "The Story of *Uncle Tom's Cabin*." In *Critical Essays on Harriet Beecher Stowe*, edited by Elizabeth Ammons, pp. 60–72. Boston: G. K. Hall, 1980. First published in *Atlantic Monthly*, Sept. 1896.

Washington, Booker T. *Up From Slavery.* Norton Critical Edition. Edited by William L. Andrews. New York: W. W. Norton, 1996.

Watts, Isaac. *Divine Songs Attempted in Easy Language for the Use of Children.* Boston: Printed for and sold by John Perkins in Union Street, 1771.

Weld, Theodore. *American Slavery As It Is*: *Testimony of a Thousand Witnesses.* New York: American Anti-Slavery Society, 1839.

Welter, Barbara. "The Cult of True Womanhood: 1820–1860." *American Quarterly* 18 (1966): 151–74.

Wilson, Edmund. "Harriet Beecher Stowe." In *Patriotic Gore: Studies in the Literature of the American Civil War*, pp. 3–58. New York: Oxford University Press, 1962.

Wilson, Forrest. *Crusader in Crinoline: The Life of Harriet Beecher Stowe.* Philadelphia: J. P. Lippincott, 1941.

Wilson, Harriet E. *Our Nig; or Sketches from the Life of a Free Black Slave.* With a new preface, introduction, and notes by Henry Louis Gates Jr. New York: Vintage Books, 2002.

Wright, Richard. *Uncle Tom's Children.* New York: Harper & Brothers, 1938.

———. *Native Son*. New York: Harper & Brothers, 1940.

Yellin, Jean Fagan. "Doing It Herself: *Uncle Tom's Cabin* and Woman's Role in the Slavery Crisis." In *New*

*Essays on* Uncle Tom's Cabin, American Novel Series, edited by Eric J. Sundquist, pp. 85–105. Cambridge, UK: Cambridge University Press, 1986.

# ILLUSTRATION CREDITS

Many thanks are due Karen C. C. Dalton and the Image of the Black in Western Art Research Project and Photo Archive at the W. E. B. Du Bois Institute for African and African American Research, who kindly supplied scans of many works in their collection, including, most notably, the first edition of *Uncle Tom's Cabin*, published by John P. Jewett & Co., 1852.

Other images in the book were generously provided to us by a number of sources, which are listed by page number below.

Page 74: Reprinted by kind permission of the Estate of Miguel Covarrubias

Page 114: Reprinted by kind permission of the Estate of Miguel Covarrubias

Page 127: From the copy in the Rare Book Collection, University of North Carolina at Chapel Hill. May not be reproduced without written permission

Page 129: © British Museum

Page 130: Chicago Historical Society

Page 155: National Museum of American History. Smithsonian Institution. Behring Center

Page 158: National Museum of American History. Smithsonian Institution. Behring Center

Page 165: © First Classics Inc. All rights reserved. By permission of Jack Lake Productions Inc.

Page 176: The Harriet Beecher Stowe Center, Hartford, CT

Page 206: From the copy in the Rare Book Collection, University of North Carolina at Chapel Hill. May not be reproduced without written permission

Page 209: © Bettman/Corbis

Page 244: The Harriet Beecher Stowe Center, Hartford, CT

Page 251: Reprinted by kind permission of the Estate of Miguel Covarrubias

Page 255: The Harriet Beecher Stowe Center, Hartford, CT

Page 257: © British Museum

Page 260: Reprinted by kind permission of the Estate of Miguel Covarrubias

Page 261: © British Museum

Page 263: Reproduced from the Collections of the Library of Congress

Page 264: © British Museum

Page 271: From the copy in the Rare Book Collection, University of North Carolina at Chapel Hill. May not be reproduced without written permission

Page 272 (bottom): Courtesy of Wyatt Houston Day

Page 273: National Museum of American History. Smithsonian Institution. Behring Center

Page 274 (top): Reprinted by kind permission of the Estate of Miguel Covarrubias

(bottom): © First Classics Inc. All rights reserved. By permission of Jack Lake Productions Inc.

Page 305: © British Museum

Page 311 (top): The Harriet Beecher Stowe Center, Hartford, CT

(bottom): Reproduced from the Collections of the Library of Congress

Page 312: Reprinted by kind permission of the Estate of Miguel Covarrubias

Page 313: © Bettman/Corbis

Page 334: © First Classics Inc. All rights reserved. By permission of Jack Lake Productions Inc.

Page 350: © First Classics Inc. All rights reserved. By permission of Jack Lake Productions Inc.

Page 351: Reprinted by kind permission of the Estate of Miguel Covarrubias

Page 352: © British Museum

Page 357: Courtesy of Larry Vincent Buster Collection, New Rochelle, NY

Page 368: Reprinted by kind permission of the Estate of Miguel Covarrubias

Page 373: Reprinted by kind permission of the Estate of Miguel Covarrubias

Page 374: © Bettman/Corbis

Page 376: Reprinted by kind permission of the Estate of Miguel Covarrubias

Page 377: From the copy in the Rare Book Collection, University of North Carolina at Chapel Hill. May not be reproduced without written permission

Page 380: © First Classics Inc. All rights reserved. By permission of Jack Lake Productions Inc.

Page 406: From the copy in the Rare Book Collection, University of North Carolina at Chapel Hill. May not be reproduced without written permission.

Page 407: © British Museum

Page 425: Reprinted by kind permission of the Estate of Miguel Covarrubias

Page 440 (top): National Museum of American History. Smithsonian Institution. Behring Center

(bottom): The Harriet Beecher Stowe Center, Hartford, CT